Jann Turner was born in France in 1964 and was raised on a South African fruit farm during the times chronicled by *Heartland*. She was educated in Oxford and New York and finally, in 1996, she returned to live in Johannesburg. She has written screenplays and produced and presented TV documentaries, winning an Emmy Award in 1995. *Heartland* is her first novel.

HEARTLAND

Jann Turner

ORIEL

An Oriel Paperback
First published in Great Britain in 1997 by Oriel,
a division of Orion Books Ltd,
Orion House, 5 Upper St Martin's Lane,
London WC2H 9EA

Second impression 1997

A CIP catalogue record for this book
is available from the British Library.

ISBN 0 75280 902 4

Typeset at The Spartan Press Ltd,
Lymington, Hants

Printed and bound in Great Britain by
Clays Ltd, St Ives plc.

for David

I did not write this book on my own. Many family members, friends, colleagues and experts supported, nurtured, cajoled and informed the process of its creation. I want to extend my profound gratitude to each one of them.

Thank you all.

ONE

However you looked at them, those mountains were the defining shape in everyone's lives. In the valley opinion was divided straightforwardly so that you saw them in one of two ways. They were either protection or barrier. A circle of wagons against hostile strangers or a merciless obstacle to the influx of friends. For Elise, when she was little, they were something more compelling: they were the wall between the known and the unknown world.

Elise was just ten years old when she conquered the known world. The day was a weekday in 1975. She was dressed in an orange T-shirt and neatly patched-at-the-knees maroon corduroys, carrying a stick easily as long as she was tall. She used the stick not so much for walking as for poking at and testing the bush while she kicked up dust along the path in her sturdy velskoene. Her straight hair was fine and pretty, bleached almost white by the sun and left to grow long and wild so that it flew behind her, catching the sun as she skipped lightly over stones and fynbos along the mountain ridge.

Sandile was, as always, one step ahead of her. He was the pathfinder. His face was as serious and inscrutable as hers appeared bright and open. He was wearing grown-up's cast-off jeans, cut up to fit his eleven-year-old frame. His T-shirt had as many holes as it had cotton and whatever colour it had once held was worn and washed away. He walked barefoot. He'd never worn shoes, but his bare feet were as nimble and sure on the stony terrain as hers were in their soft supportive boots. Sandile carried a stick almost exactly like the one Elise clutched, but his he planted surely in front of every step he took.

They were two tiny figures hiking sturdily across a vast landscape towards the great bulb-shaped summit of the mountain, the kop of Bosmanskop. It was not the highest in the range; on both sides of them other mountains raked higher. They had chosen this one thinking that the walk up and down would take only an afternoon.

Sandile reached the top first. For a moment he simply stood there, then he raised his arms and punched at the air, and from his mouth came a cry of triumph that slipped out into the sky and echoed only faintly in the great emptiness around them. Elise scrambled up on to the ridge next to him and grinned, beaming at the world spread out at their feet. It felt as if she was a giant straddling the ramparts of her castle. The bowl of the valley below them looked like the Tiny Town Elise had seen once, on holiday at a place by the seaside. The gleaming white matchboxes of farmhouses delighted her and the orchards with their neat lines of trees looked as if someone had measured them out with a ruler, except where they curved in against the dark gorges and out around the foothills of the mountains. There were little cars parked and trucks moving and there she could see her father's tractor crawling along the mud-red road near their dam. And far across the other side of the valley the new swimming pool at Ina's house looked like a precious stone, like an oval of turquoise standing out from the tiny emerald strip of garden.

It was one of those days in the Cape when the sky is so boundlessly blue and the light so pure that the luminance of colours is dizzying. One of those beautiful days that can stun you for life. So that no matter where you go nothing can ever compare with it and disappointment will be your companion until you pack that memory away in some attic of your mind. Neither Elise nor Sandile knew this then, and their exhilaration at slipping the boundaries of their world was as pure and powerful as only children can feel.

'Hey!' Both heads turned, eyes raking the mountainside immediately below them. Elise saw him first. Her hand shot up and pointed him out: 'There!' Scrambling out of the shadow cast by a giant split boulder was another boy, also eleven or twelve years old, dressed in tattered clothes and barefoot like Sandile.

'We're in big, big trouble if we don't go home now,' he bleated.

Sandile grinned at the way Xolile was struggling to keep up with them. 'Hey, Xolile, move your bum!'

At the use of the word 'bum' both Sandile and Elise burst into helpless giggling. The sound rolled round the mountains and the echo seemed to spring back at Xolile from all sides, making him start. He recovered fast, then sweated and huffed and puffed up the last few metres as if he was running away from something.

Both Sandile and Elise leaned forward, reaching out to pull Xolile up the final stretch of gravel to where they stood, but the boy wouldn't take Elise's arm, he shyly batted her white hand away and clutched instead at Sandile, berating him breathlessly and urgently in Xhosa. 'Why didn't you stop when you heard me shouting back there, man? It's late now, we must go down or we won't get back before night and I'm scared to be up here with . . . in the dark.'

Although Elise didn't understand all the words, she understood the frantic gesticulations and the fear in his tone well enough. Thoughts of all the stories they had ever been told about lions and wild dogs and snakes and scorpions flicked across her mind. She wasn't scared, but she declared it was time to go down.

They picked their way in a long curve down the side of the rugged koppie, the valley curving and stretching away below them. The sun was low, catching the tips of the hulking mountains opposite so that their shadows began to creep over the orchards and farms like an obliterating, inevitable tide. Xolile scrambled behind; he was quieter now and relieved to be going down, but anxious nevertheless. Neither spoke of it but Sandile and Elise were sure the light would stay with them long enough, that they would easily make it home before shadow covered everything.

The slope steepened and they picked up speed as together they moved down the mountain, skipping through dust, jumping from one rock to the next and down on to sandy earth again. They made quick progress this way and were halfway down the mountain and crossing the firebreak when Elise skipped ahead of Sandile, scrambled over a small pile of rocks and then suddenly sprang back. She leapt into reverse with a reflex like lightning, her feet skidding about a foot as she hit the path before stopping dead. Her little body teetered forward and then she nearly fell flat as Sandile smacked right into her from behind. He grabbed on to Elise a moment before Xolile slapped into the back of their pile-up. Both boys saw immediately what she'd seen. The massive Cape cobra slithered across the path ahead, just inches from Elise's feet. All three of them froze instinctively, but too late: their abrupt arrival had startled the snake, which coiled up with demonic speed. The sound of its hissing, the sight of its wide fangs, its reared, hooded head lurching, was all their most terrifying nightmares come true. Xolile couldn't contain his fear; his bladder let loose and he pissed himself. The stain spread across his pants. Sandile could feel the hot liquid trickle down the backs of his own legs, but he knew, like Elise did, not to move a muscle, not to flicker an eyelid.

The snake's spectacular hooded head swayed precariously, its glassy eyes scanning for the source of the tremor, the location of the threat. It had reared up to the height of the children, and to them it was monstrously huge. Somehow all three stayed dead still. Sandile's body was so close that Elise could feel both their hearts pounding and she was terrified at the thought that the snake must feel them too, pulsing fear through the hot afternoon air.

They seemed to stand like that for hours, gripping on to one another in the awkward position they had landed in. But only minutes had passed. Then the snake made the first move. Elise flinched, bracing herself, but it was already gone, moving with such speed and so vigorously that dead pine needles and dust flew up as it carried itself away into the bush like a long wave.

Instantly all three were breathing again, but still they couldn't move their feet. They gawped at the place where the snake had disappeared. Then they disentangled themselves from one another. Xolile looked away in shame. In spite of the stench of the piss and the puddle around his feet Sandile put his arm round the shoulder of his friend and squeezed it, but Xolile jerked away and fled, almost as fast as the cobra, but in the opposite direction. Sandile and Elise stared at each other for a moment, now with more curiosity than fear, their hearts still pounding. But Elise felt a growing sense of elation at surviving this encounter. They grinned at one another before they too turned and ran wildly down the mountainside, shrieking and whooping as they skidded through the bush.

He was faster than she and so he was ahead of her when she tripped, a branch catching her across the shin. Elise fell hard on to jagged rock. She was aware of a soft surprised groan as the breath flew out of her and then a dull thud as she hit the rock. She could hear the bush cracking as Sandile ran on, then nothing. He stopped and called out. She sat up shakily and waved to him. 'It's OK,' she said, but it wasn't. Blood oozed from her palm. She winced as the pain hit her. Sandile raced back up to her. They stared at her hand and the blood dripping on to the ground. Her already pale skin whitened as she slowly, helplessly raised her head and looked up at him.

Sandile knew what to do. He pulled off his T-shirt, yanking at it, trying to rip it in two. His scowl showed gritted white teeth as he strained. Finally the material gave. Squatting down in front of her, he took the fingers of her hurt hand very lightly in his and pressed the rag into the cut. Blood soaked into the cloth. For a moment he pulled it away and exposed the ghastly white flap of flesh. Then he let the bloody rag fall and wrapped the second strip round her wrist, then over the palm between her thumb and fingers and round and round again, pulling it tight to bind the cut. She flinched with every twist and pull of the cloth, but never once took her eyes from his face.

Once the bandage was finished he tucked its end neatly under the binding, then wiped his own bloody hands on his already filthy cut-off trousers and looked at her. Her eyes were dry, but wide with pain and concentration. Inspecting his work, they saw a small blot of blood oozing through the cloth, then no more. Her hand ached heavily, but the searing pain that came at first was gone. 'It's better,' she said. 'You fixed it.' He nodded. She gazed at him, so carefully and with such intensity that Sandile was forced to look away, squinting up into the sun. Then she said, very seriously and importantly, as if bestowing a gift, 'Thank you.'

'Come.' He took her other hand gently in his and pulled her to her feet. They set off down the mountain, moving purposefully and quickly now, but not running. Her clothes were covered in dirt and blood and there were twigs in her hair. She clutched Sandile's hand and together they went wordlessly all the way down the mountain.

At the sight of the dam below them at last Elise pulled away and skipped on ahead. Sandile began running too. This part of the track they knew well and their confidence grew as every step brought them closer to home. When they reached the road below the dam they were flushed and tired, but with their sense of adventure restored. They stopped to catch their breath. Sandile glanced over at the mountains and Elise followed his gaze. The sun had set, it was late and Xolile was nowhere to be seen.

'I hope he hasn't gone telling tales to Mama again.' Both of them knew there would be big trouble if he had. They set off again, racing towards the house, determined to get there ahead of him.

A bakkie lurched round the corner behind them, kicking up a trail of dust as it hurtled along the road towards the two children. At the sound of the hooter parp-parping Sandile and Elise spun round. The vehicle screeched to a halt, so sharply that the farm workers crowded on to the back were thrown violently forward. These men seemed neither young nor old; their bodies were thin but strong, their eyes dull and impassive as they lurched and straightened and settled to a sudden stop. Both Elise and Sandile saw at once that Xolile was also there on the back. The other men were pressed against one another, standing as far away from him as they could.

Elise's father was sitting up front in the bakkie and her brother, Dawie, was gloating in the driving seat. This was worse than Elise had imagined. Her heart sank and the throbbing in her hand seemed to intensify. Her father climbed down from the cabin of the bakkie, violently slamming the door behind him. 'Come here, my girl,' growled Van Rensburg. Elise whipped her bandaged hand behind her back, but the bloody T-shirt, dirtied knees and twigs in her hair made her quite a sight.

'I said come here, my girl!'

She didn't move, nor did her father. This was not their first stand-off.

'Look what a mess you are. How many times have I told you never ever to go up there on your own! Now get over here!'

He was bellowing now. She knew she was in the deepest trouble. She looked to Sandile who had shrunk, completely cowed by the presence of the massive, furious farmer. Elise looked again to her father and saw her way out.

She whipped around and pointed at Sandile with one finger of her bandaged hand. Her voice was loud and high as she said imperiously, 'He took me there. He said you said Bosmanskop was no problem!' The boy literally flinched, stinging from her words. Her father's eyes narrowed and he shifted his gaze from Elise to Sandile, shaking his head, though privately amused at her mendacity and impressed by her opportunism. At this she knew she had him and immediately she ran up to him, reaching coquettishly for his arm. 'I swear, I'll never do it again, Daddy. I promise. On the Bible!'

He looked down at her, then back at Sandile. 'Go home now, boy, go on!'

Sandile stared at them both in disbelief; the ground was shifting so violently that it made him feel sick. Elise's father snapped impatiently as he turned and opened the door of the bakkie. 'Get in, my girl, and you, I said . . . voertsek!'

Still Sandile simply stared so Elise screamed it out at him, 'Voertsek!' Instantly he turned and walked away, his feet scuffing the earth, his shoulders drooping and his head hanging low with terrible hurt.

Elise raised her little chin and looked her father straight in the eye as she walked with stubborn, regal slowness towards the bakkie and suddenly her father couldn't suppress a thunderous clap of laughter at the haughtiness of his filthy little princess. Hearing this Sandile stopped and looked back at the white man laughing and he burned with humiliation at Elise's treachery.

She didn't smile yet, though she knew she'd won. She knew that moments from now her father would pull her on to his lap, wrap his big arms around her and scold her in a voice full of laughter and amazement. She would put her arms as far round him as she could, pushing her face into his chest, and only then would she smile. She was as sure of this as the sureness of every step she took towards him.

Sandile had picked up the stone before he was even conscious of what he was going to do. His eyes narrowed as he took aim. His arm moved like a whip, his strength doubled by rage. He was already running when the stone cracked against the windscreen. The glass shattered, like a smooth sheet of ice cracks and splinters and yet coheres. Van Rensburg and Elise spun round at the sound and Dawie's startled face gazed back at them, oddly fragmented by the long jagged shards that had materialised in front of him. He was all right, no one was hurt, but the windscreen was finished. The farm workers on the back of the bakkie simply looked away. Sandile was already gone.

Later that day Van Rensburg came to his house and beat him. In front of his own silent father he pulled Sandile out of their hut, tore down his trousers and whipped him with so many cracks of a belt to his bare backside that Sandile lost count. The farmer beat him to the ground and even then he didn't stop until the belt slid on the blood from the cuts it had made. Sandile never forgot that. That night he thought he would never understand the cruelty white people had in them. He never forgot how his heart grew cold, like steel.

Two

It was the Sunday after the last of the winter rains ended. The morning was warm, the beginning of a spring day, but the light was as harsh as a bright winter morning. Everything appeared fragile and delicate and vivid. A strong wind agitated the trees, ruffling the new leaves of the usually implacable oaks, bending and pulling at the poplars so that they swayed crazily. Elise moved away from the window. The wind made her restless and filled her with a sense of anticipation for the coming day. She wanted to run outside on the lawn and spin in the wind like a child, with her hair whipping round her face. She smiled as she stood looking at her sleepy self in the mirror.

Elise knew that today would mark a turning point in her life and she savoured every minute of that auspicious morning, thrilled by a sense of the future. Everything seemed perfect. Everything seemed decided.

The night had been restless and edgy with anticipation. Something, some sound, had woken her in the hour just before dawn. Looking at the clock she'd seen that it was much too early for anyone to be up in the house. So she had slipped out of her bed to see what the noise was. She pulled one of Dawie's old rugby shirts over her head, opened the door that led from her bedroom on to the front stoep and down to the garden beyond that, and stepped outside. The black shoulders of the mountains huddled around. The sky was just getting light and the brightest stars shone brilliantly against the electric blue.

The stillness was shattered by the clatter of dogs barking, first startled, then joyful. Elise followed the stoep round to where she could look down the side of the house and she saw her father striding out across the back lawn. Van Rensburg was headed towards the mountain, the crowd of farm mongrels yelping and stretching and wagging their tails as they followed him in a pack. Watching him trudge across the grass leaving a dark track in the bright sheen of dew that covered it, she knew he had not slept at all that night. Lately he seemed hardly to sleep at all. She wasn't particularly concerned, though it must signify something. Elise assumed it was grief that kept him awake and he was entitled to that. If anything, her father's lack of sleep left him rather less prone to fly off the handle than usual. It was typically perverse of him that he should have an opposite reaction to the normal one, that he should buck even the consequences of sleep deprivation.

She watched his stooped frame, his heavy step, until he was engulfed by deep shadow at the far edge of the lawn. He must be going up on to the mountain, she thought. The wind fluttered lightly against her skin. The sky promised a clear, hot day, a perfect Cape day. Elise breathed in the morning air, then padded back to her room and climbed into the warmth of her bed, but she didn't sleep immediately. Today was a rare holiday for her, so she lay awake for a while, wrapped in the quiet of her house. Feeling luxuriantly idle, she slipped into fantasising about the future.

The future. How tantalising, how possible everything seemed that morning. Pictures of abundant harvests, of orchards extending up the mountain slopes, of a bigger dam, of Sunday braais with a family around her, of children, of growing older with the farm – images of herself in the midst of a full, rich life rolled deliciously round Elise's mind. And all this would come about through a single, simple act, a commitment she would make today to a man she loved, to the father she adored, to the community that was her family. Later today she would be engaged to marry. The thought pleased her in the quietest, deepest way. Bad times do pass, she thought, things do work out. Contentment wound round her and she slid from dreaming into delicious sleep.

When Elise woke again the day had started without her. She took a long, lazy bath and by the time she got round to thinking about dressing, people had already begun to arrive for the braai. Elise was amused by her neighbours' religious adherence to what she called the unofficial farm code. Farmers were more often too early than too late for everything, everything social that is, and today was no exception. It was quite another principle, no less religiously adhered to, that they should be the last to acknowledge and incorporate any sort of far-reaching moral or economic change into their tight society.

Elise knew she should dress quickly now. Her father was undoubtedly already stoking up a fire on the back lawn or else he was in the kitchen clucking to Mama Mashiya about the marinade for the meat. Elise had let the time get later and later so that she could avoid the agony of deliberation and the irritation of defeat at the hands of her wardrobe. She'd not had time to go and shop for the new dress her father wanted her to wear and she knew only too well what he'd say if he saw her appear in jeans again. 'Ag, no, Elise . . .' he'd sigh, shaking his head. 'Ag, Pa . . . ' she'd whine back, 'you know me, you know it's not me.' 'Ja, but princess, not today . . . please?' Today she had to wear something different, something for him.

There was a child in her that loved the way her father still called her princess. Deep down she loved to be his princess, though she found the name absurd, it made her laugh at times and sometimes it rankled. Elise was utterly unprincesslike, permanently rumpled and almost rudely informal when it came to even the simple social rituals of the dorp. She didn't remember the little girl's haughty arrogance which had made the nickname stick. She thought Ina was the true princess. Her friend Ina was truly the sleeping beauty, longing for some passing prince to lay siege to her ruined castle and wake her from the deep sleep of a lonely heart. Ina wasn't here yet, but Elise knew she soon would be, and that made her race to the cupboard. The last thing she wanted was a lengthy wardrobe consultation.

Pulling open the cupboard Elise sighed, staring at the familiar handful of best dresses, all of them reeking of times she wanted to forget. Static prickled on her fingers as she ran her hand over the textured crimplene of the Sunday-smart jacket she couldn't bring herself to give away, but certainly wouldn't wear again. Clicking the hangers along the rail she rejected the long, full floral monsters of a bad romance thankfully gone by, passed on the decade-old African print, then hovered over her mother's beautiful blue silk skirt. Elise was scared to wear the skirt, she knew she lacked her mother's delicate style, but she so wanted to wear something pretty today. Whenever she tried to dress in her mother's clothes, or to emulate her mother's style, she felt like a giraffe in gazelle's clothing. No, not the skirt, she thought irritably, and pushed that aside too. There were some of her brother Dawie's shirts hanging among her things and there was the black dress, the one she'd worn twice already and hoped she wouldn't wear again.

Elise sighed heavily and closed the cupboard. Today was a test, a day when she couldn't suit herself, the beginning of a life of considering and fulfilling the desires of another against her own. Elise stood staring into the solid old teak door, her arms folded, fingers of one hand resting lightly on her lips.

What would Daan want her to wear? It struck her suddenly as funny that she was more concerned about her father's reaction to her outfit than she was about that of her husband-to-be. Daan never seemed to mind much what she wore. In fact, now that she thought of it, he seldom commented on her looks. His mother was an entirely different matter, but, Elise mused, today wasn't about pleasing Daan's mother. Today was about her family's future and therefore the farm's future, and for once she was going to do it the way her father would like it.

In her drawer lay small heaps of folded T-shirts and jeans. She yanked a clean T-shirt from one pile and pulled it over her head. It was bright white and small, so it fitted comfortably the curve of her breasts and into her waist. Then she strode purposefully over to her cupboard, whisked her mother's skirt off its hanger, slipped it swiftly over her head and was standing there letting the silk fall over her hips and legs before reason could even think to intervene. She pushed her feet into soft leather sandals, with the thick soles that she so liked, then picked up the hairbrush lying on top of the dresser and began, with long hard strokes, to brush out her hair. Catching a glimpse of herself in the mirror, hair tumbling forward over her face, her eyes light with the relief of having chosen, Elise smiled. She wasn't yet thirty, but she knew she looked older, that time had changed and marked her face. What she didn't see was how this made her so much more beautiful than the pretty girl she once was.

Elise really did have cornflower-blue eyes and long sun-bleached, almost white blonde hair. She had strong laugh-lines, little crow's-feet at the corners of her eyes which made fine white creases in her sunburned skin. Her frame was small, like her mother's, but she had a strength in her posture, a confidence in the way she moved, an openness in her gestures, a largeness about her voice and her laughter that came from her father. Like his, her hands were big and grown coarse from their work. There was always an earth-dark line of dirt under her fingernails, always a scab or a graze along her arms and cuts around her knees.

Van Rensburg, her father, was a really big man, beautiful and rugged when he was young, like a John Wayne or a Spencer Tracy, as her mother used to say so wistfully. He didn't go to university; he learned everything he needed to know at his own father's side on the farm. His whole life was the farm. So much so that he didn't have time for the church socials and tea dances and Sunday braais where he might have met a companion to share his life with. His only friends were the neighbours he saw in the course of his work, the men from the co-op and his parents' friends. His mother was as tough as an old hippo and the unequivocal ruler of the farm. She never encouraged Van to bring girlfriends into her domain. When at last he did introduce Evelyn to her, the story went that Ounooi was hostile and utterly territorial. She almost scared the young woman off entirely, but though most people never guessed it from her manner or her frame, Evelyn was just as stubborn and as strong as the Ounooi. Nothing could deter her in her pursuit of the man she had chosen.

Evelyn was much younger than Van. He was already in his mid-thirties and she was only nineteen when they met. She was exquisitely pretty, slim and small with long black hair and light brown eyes. She modelled herself on a picture of Audrey Hepburn that she'd cut from a magazine and taped on her bedroom mirror. She first glimpsed Van in the dorp. Hot and sweaty in his work clothes, he was running an errand for his mother and he was in a hurry to get back to work. She saw him before he saw her and he did have an honest, steady, reliable, but untamed John Wayne look about him. She stared at the shop he'd disappeared into until at last he came out, and that was when she caught his eye. He was confused by her attention, but she kept smiling and so he smiled shyly back. From then on Evie made every effort to see him whenever and wherever she could contrive to. She took to walking on the mountain near his orchards, oblivious of the snakes and goggas she wouldn't go near before. It didn't take long to hook him. And once he was hooked it was simple. He adored her; he always had and always would. Elise knew he could never fully recover from losing his Evelyn.

Sitting in her mother's skirt Elise began to brood. Her own marriage would not be the cold war that her parents had unwittingly committed themselves to. Elise rarely looked back on that pain, but she'd slipped into a trance and was lost in remembering before she even knew she was drifting that way.

Ina's light, piercing voice drifted through to her from somewhere in the house, interrupting the bitter memory. Elise was glad; she put down the brush, scooped up her hair and pushed it behind her neck, then shook her head so that it cascaded down her back. Then she strode towards the door, but stopped just as she was about to open it – there was something she'd forgotten.

The ring seemed to wink at her from the dresser, tucked into its little satin cushion inside the box Daan had offered it in. It was pretty, unusually pretty, thought Elise, who never wore rings or earrings or any jewellery at all. Daan had taken a great deal of care over the design. Three bright white diamonds were set into a wide gold band. It was simple and bold enough to attract her, though there was something intimidating about the way it glinted at her. She was amused by this idea, of being intimidated by jewellery, and she smiled. She took the ring carefully from its perch and slowly slid it on to her finger. It felt strange as she pushed and stroked it with her thumb, something alien on her. She put her left hand out in front of her, frowning slightly as she studied the new look, but when she caught the stern expression reflected in the mirror she chuckled, pushed her hand behind her back and went to join her friend.

Elise found Ina in the kitchen where two extra helpers were steadily chopping and stirring under the busy command of Mama Mashiya. Ina had brought with her a tray of mouth-watering melkterts, freshly baked with a miraculous, doily-shaped snowflake pattern burned beautifully into their tops. Typically, she was giving Mama meticulous instructions for the storage of the tarts and just as typically Mama was smiling and nodding at Ina while her hands and her mind were busy with something else.

Though Ina was the older of the two by several years, Elise had lately taken the role of big sister and she jokingly scolded her friend as she entered the kitchen. 'Just leave those cakes on the side and let Mama get on with her work!'

Ina spun round with a smile that grew larger, like her eyes, at the sight of Elise in the fluid skirt. 'Wow!' Ina's voice was so full of surprise that Mama turned round to look too. 'My God,' Ina laughed, 'you finally ran out of jeans!'

Elise narrowed her eyes to slits and glared at both of them. 'No more, or I'm straight back into them.'

Mama Mashiya smiled broadly and said mildly, but with

emphasis, 'Very nice, Elise.' Her smile made Elise smile too and she knew she had chosen well.

'You – look – stunning!' Ina burst into giggles like a little girl and skipped across the room to hug her.

'Ina, enough.' Elise squeezed her friend hard.

As Ina pulled away there was still a smile on her face and she looked knowingly into Elise's eyes, her hands resting lightly on her shoulders. Then she said, breathlessly, 'Don't you love this wind, doesn't it feel so *exciting*?'

'Something very exciting is going to happen if you don't get out my way,' muttered Mama Mashiya, shooing them, literally pushing them, out of the back door.

Mama Mashiya was queen of the kitchen at Rustenvrede. There had been no one else in Elise's memory. She knew all the Van Rensburg family recipes and cooked them better than Elise ever would. She'd been well trained by the Ounooi. Elise's mother, the Jongnooi, as she was known when she first came to the farm, wasn't allowed anywhere near the kitchen while Ounooi was alive. If Ounooi had ever suspected how relieved Evelyn was to be barred from a place she so detested, she would have set her daughter-in-law to work in it daily. Evelyn was canny; she despised her mother-in-law for her serious and simple ways, but she knew exactly how to get what she wanted from her. When Evelyn became the Ounooi it was the natural thing for Mama Mashiya to take over in the kitchen.

Elise was often shocked by the thought that there was surprisingly little about her mother that she missed. She had never occupied much space in Elise's life, so there was no great void when she died. The house ran just as it had before, though perhaps a little more easily. The food was the same because Mama Mashiya still cooked it. Sitting down to eat with her father and whoever might join them from among their friends and neighbours in the dorp was in fact more pleasant than it had ever been when her mother sat at the head of the table. It was still to Mama Mashiya in her kitchen that Elise went at the end of every day to drink a cup of tea and chat, listen to farm gossip, or be silent for a while. When she was a child, and sometimes even now, it was Mama Mashiya who would console Elise when she needed it, wrapping her big arms round her and squashing her against the great softness of her breasts. Elise's tears had fallen often on the bright floral patterns of Mama's aprons, and Mama's smell of soap and woodsmoke was, for Elise, the scent of comfort. She even called her Mama, as did everyone else except Van Rensburg, who called her Betty. Elise once asked her if Betty was her real name and Mama roared with laughter in the way that she did that made her breasts and her fat arms jiggle. No, Betty was the name the old Ounooi gave her on her first day of work in the house. The name she was given at birth was Nomonde.

Ina skipped behind Elise as she strode out into the garden. Ina, like the rest of the Du Toits, was tall and willowy, with dirty blonde hair that she'd recently had cut fashionably short, wisps of it curling against the nape of her neck and around her cheeks. It was only since Elise's return to Fransmansvallei that the two women had become friends. They'd known each other for ever, but when they were children the gap in ages between them was too great for them to contemplate being close. They'd travelled on the same bus to school, but Ina was always at the back with Dawie and the older children, while Elise sat up front with the smaller kids. By the time Elise graduated to the back seats Ina had already finished school and was wrapped up in a world that was too grown-up, too remote from her own.

Ina barely noticed Elise at school, though she began to make an effort with the younger girl around the same time she set her sights on Dawie. Being nice to his cute little sister went down well. Elise had simply admired Ina from a distance, hoping that she too would find the easy way that Ina had with clothes and make-up and boys, but she knew she lacked Ina's innate grace and confidence. Even now Ina made Elise feel big and clumsy, but the old envy was long gone.

Ina was in her early thirties, still unmarried and still living at home, but that wasn't such an unusual thing in the dorp; after all, Elise lived at home. And Ina never complained about her life, although she longed to find a man to share it with and her quest seemed to have acquired a degree of urgency lately. Somehow, though, every potential suitor that came along was not quite right; they wanted to take her off to the city, or they couldn't get on with her brothers, or some other thing, and in the end they always fell short of her benchmark. None of them was a man like Dawie. Though Dawie was almost never mentioned Elise knew Ina was still not over him, even after all these years. Ina never talked much about the future or the past, she simply kept herself busy, filling up her days with the detail of her family and the farm. She had her Volkswagen Beetle which gave her a degree of independence that satisfied her and she worked hard running the farm stall.

The stall had thrived over the years that Ina had been in charge of it. Two years ago the local trade, combined with the tourists from Cape Town and even further afield, had justified a whole new building which now housed the produce stall and a teashop. Ina was intensely proud of the new place, which was a miniature Cape Dutch homestead, complete with green shutters and thatched roof. Over the entrance was an old oak board with newly carved letters picked out in green paint which read 'Hemel en Aarde'. In the central room there was a huge display of fruit and vegetables, all grown on the farm. Against one wall an old hutch was covered with jars of pickles and jams and preserves which came from the Du Toit kitchen. Opposite that was a glass case full of cakes: carrot, coffee, lemon and the peach cake that was Ina's speciality, decorated simply but irresistibly with buttery peaks of icing and fresh peach slices arranged around the top. The two side rooms opened out on to a broad, wraparound stoep where lunches and teas were served at the weekend. The teashop was always full on Saturdays and Sundays, especially during these summer months, and in her kitchen at the back Ina now employed four local women whom she'd trained up sufficiently to look after the place so that she could take off on a day like today.

Elise loved Ina for her chin-up, look-on-the-bright-side attitude to everything. She was never bowed by adversity, never prone to the moody depressions that gripped Elise from time to time. She was always there with a smile and some cheerful activity to pull Elise out of herself. Elise had come to depend on her for that and to rely on her almost daily visits. She loved to sit on her bed with Ina and chat about the day and the dorp, to pick over the elements of their universe. Yet Elise worried for Ina and longed for her to find her elusive husband.

Ina put her hand on Elise's arm as they strolled across the garden. Elise felt her friend's mood dip and knew that the familiar faces gathered in front of them made her despondent. 'Ag, no, everybody too young or too old or married,' Ina said chirpily.

'Or related.'

'Ja, or related . . . ' Ina let out an exaggerated sigh.

'Daan told me someone bought Die Uitkyk.'

'Daan never tells me anything!'

'A man. Single apparently.'

Ina gasped in mock excitement. 'A single man!'

Elise smiled a mischievous, knowing smile. 'But English.'

'Hm. Not great, but not necessarily bad. How old?'

'Old enough.'

'Ja! To be my father . . . '

Elise shook her head.

Ina stopped dead. 'Reeeeeally,' she said, but only after a moment, during which Elise observed this information travelling to every corner of Ina's anatomy. She tingled, visibly, at the news. 'What's his name?'

Elise shrugged; she didn't know. 'Pa, what's the name of the guy who bought Uitkyk?'

Her father turned to answer and his jaw half dropped, but he quickly shut his mouth, knowing she'd go straight back inside and put on her jeans if he made a fuss. Instead Van Rensburg's lip quivered and he didn't say anything for a moment.

Piet van Rensburg, Van to all who knew him, had invited his neighbours and friends over and was making a huge braai to mark the occasion of his only daughter's, his only child's, engagement. It was a day full of happiness and pain for him because he was opening the house for the first time since Evie's death.

Elise could read all the emotions there; they registered on his face the way the surface of the sea describes the shape of its depths, though it takes a trained and experienced observer to read it. Pleasure and sadness, excitement for the future and the sore reminders of the past. Things ought to have been another way. *They* should have been here. Elise saw all the feeling that her father couldn't ever utter.

The Dominee, who was helping himself to a beer, boomed that he'd heard the buyer for the Uitkyk was an Englishman. 'You look divine, my child,' he added, his eyes twinkling at Elise, as he strolled up to join them by the blazing fire. Van recovered and muttered that he didn't recall a name being mentioned. 'But yes, the buyer is an Englishman. That's what they're saying.'

THREE

It was night and Sandile was surrounded by darkness. He could have reached up and flicked the switch which would have circled him instantly in pale light, but he didn't. The darkness suited him, concealed him from himself, whipped away thoughts that would have taunted him in the confines of a spotlight.

Coming back was harder than leaving. Returning was like being suspended, trapped in a motion towards a present in which past and future would at last collide. The anticipation was unbearable. What had been, what might have been and what would be were gathering towards Sandile at a pace more dreadful and more exciting than he had ever imagined. And he had imagined it infinitely. This journey was the closing of a circle, but would it end where he'd started from? Would he find a beginning at the end?

Here he was in his own country at last, breathing the cool air of freedom, and it was strange to him. Nelson Mandela was President and the struggle, which was the only life Sandile had known as an adult, was finished. When it all ended it wasn't as he had expected it would be. His conquering army never marched victoriously through the streets of Pretoria. The revolution was negotiated. Old enemies made peace and in the course of doing so they became different creatures. Sandile didn't know what kind of creature he had become. If he wasn't a freedom fighter, who was he? He didn't know. He felt excitement, but also a vertiginous fear. He was on the edge of the unknown, of everything or nothing.

Sandile was sitting on the bed that had been made up for

him earlier by the conductor. He was on a train, travelling in a compartment within a carriage that bore marks on the paintwork from where the 'Whites Only' signs had not long ago been removed. The year was 1995. He was thirty years old, alone, and carrying with him little more than he took when he fled. Thinking back over the thirteen years of his exile Sandile knew it was a long journey that had brought him here and he was all too aware that he might still be very far from its end.

The slow clatter-clack of the train would not lull him into sleep as it had the other passengers on the long ride south. The night was warm and he had pushed down the window to let the cool air flow in and around him. The dusty, dry, sweet scent of the Karoo mingled with the acrid, steely smell of the railway, a strong metallic smell that he could taste. 'I am here,' he murmured to himself, 'I am almost home.' Just the thought of it made him breathless.

Sandile had stayed away longer than almost anyone else, long after all his comrades and co-workers in the struggle had gone home. It had been expected that he would go with them into government; he'd been told more than once that he would be needed, that there would be a job for him in some ministry. But Sandile had no taste for that kind of power; his appetite for politics was exhausted by all he'd seen and done of it. Sandile was returning with a different mission, one that burned in him with the fierceness and implacable power of the land itself. The only place Sandile wanted in the new South Africa was a farm. His farm.

As the train pulled him closer and closer, Sandile's stomach fluttered with anxiety. His throat was dry and tight. The hours flew by like the telegraph poles along the track. Panic gnawed at his excitement. He was humming to himself, muttering lines of poems he couldn't remember completely, childhood rhymes, anything to blot out thinking, because reality was racing too fast towards him.

He had never said goodbye to his family or his friends. His flight had been sudden and urgent. In the first year or so of his exile it had been impossible for him to get word to anyone inside. It was too dangerous to let his mother and father know where he was, more for their sake than his. Later, when he had moved to London, it would have been easier, but Sandile didn't know how to begin to explain after all that time. Worse, he was paralysed by fear of what news might come in return. He knew he couldn't handle it alone and so far away, so he had no idea if his mother and father and his brother and sisters were alive or dead, if they were still on the farm, if they had moved or been removed. He'd had no contact with them, heard no news of them at all in all his years away.

When the ANC was unbanned and everything went crazy and everything was possible again, he had tried to sit down and write something, but no words were adequate for the task, no paper large enough to fill in the years he'd been lost to them. And then there was the fear that the letter would come back, returned to sender, unopened and unread, and Sandile didn't want to learn of his family's fate that way. So he waited and decided that he would bring his story with him and explain himself there, when he arrived.

He tried to remember his mother's face, but the features he recalled were vague, though the memory of her voice, of her embrace, was stronger. His father was a figure in the orchards, a man who came home late, always very tired, and smoked his pipe quietly in the moonlit doorway when Sandile and his brother and sisters were in bed. On either side of him and his older brother were two sisters. Where would they be now? Would any of them even remember him? Would any of them still be there? For all he knew, the farm had existed only in his mind for the last thirteen years. What would he do if he found only shattered traces of the life he'd left? He knew it could break him. He had nothing else in the world, no one and nowhere else to go.

Sandile was sweating. He got down off the bunk and paced the short length of the compartment. The sky was lightening, doubling the fear that was loose in his brain. He'd put too much store by this homecoming. He'd allowed himself to feel things he'd long denied. He'd peeled himself open to feeling and the naked vulnerability frightened him. Sandile was flying towards a collision with his imagined future and his dreamlike past and he felt the shock might kill him.

He thought of turning back to the life he'd become accustomed to in Zambia. It was appealing, familiar. But he shook his head, so vehemently that he banged it on the edge of the bunk top. No, he thought, rubbing his sore scalp, he would never go back to Lusaka – that was ridiculous and impossible. Exile was over for him. He would do what he'd come here to do, even if he had to do it alone, without family, without friends. He was no stranger to solitude. It would be hard, but nothing could be harder than the journey he had made to return. In time he would make a new life for himself in this country, on this land, on *his* land, even if in the morning he found there was nothing left of his old life.

The decision calmed him, quietened the buzz in his brain. It was a decision he'd made a hundred times that night and he knew he'd be spun through the loop to make it again and again, until the moment he arrived.

As morning broke there was still no desire for sleep in him. He put his hands on the sill of the window and leaned out. The air whipping in his face thrilled him, and for a long time he watched the long curve of the train snaking ahead, straining towards his destination. He felt scared, but completely alive, every sense alert to the coming day.

Four

That Sunday morning was like almost every Sunday morning Johnny Kakana could remember. A telephone call came through to the station at dawn. This time it was from a farm on the other side of Bosmansberg – the panic-stricken farmer's wife screeching down the line about trouble in the labourers' compound and her husband out there on his own with only a shotgun. Johnny knew that if things worked out well he would arrive before the farmer blasted the hell out of some drunk worker wielding a half-blunt kitchen knife.

Johnny climbed into his van and drove out to Komweer, the farm of his boss, Daan du Toit. Daan, as usual, was asleep when Johnny arrived. He banged on the kitchen door and the maid – who was up and working already of course – answered it with a smile then went to rouse the young Master Danie.

Johnny Kakana was a policeman. *The* policeman as far as everyone in Fransmansvallei was concerned. He had entered the force years ago, when he wasn't yet twenty years old. Now, at nearly thirty, he had risen as far as a black man could in a rural police force in South Africa, even in the 1990s. He had hit the glass ceiling and was second-in-command at the station in Fransmanshoek. Everyone knew that if you wanted something done it was Johnny you should go to. If you wanted anything undone you'd go to Johnny's superior, Daan du Toit.

The area the Fransmanshoek station covered was huge. There was the valley itself and then the farms, which were scattered in a radius of twenty or so miles all round. Some of the farms were big and not always easy to get to because of the mountains. Fransmanshoek was only a short loop of shops and houses and one cottagey hotel at the base of a pass which wound steeply down the mountains that cut the dorp off from the Cape beyond. A series of farm roads, some tarred, some beaten earth, fanned out from the centre of the dorp across the wide, lush bowl of the valley. Fransmanshoek was once a significant stop on the drive from the north to Swellendam and Stellenbosch and then Cape Town. But the big roads had opened up easier ways to bypass the mountains, and now the dorp had become more of an out-of-the-way cul-de-sac than a watering hole on a long journey. The mountains all round were too steep and craggy for a wide multi-lane highway like the one that had blasted the drive between Cape Town and Paarl almost flat, linking many small communities to the city in a way that Fransmanshoek was not. Johnny's feelings were mixed on the subject of policing in such a remote area, yet he tended to shrug and say that it made for a quiet life.

Ten minutes went by before Daan came out to the van, still pulling his shirt on over his lanky frame. Mabel, the Du Toit family maid since anyone could remember, ran out of the house after him, a jacket and shoulder holster in the grip of one large hand and a mug of hot coffee in the other. First Daan took the gun in the holster and slung it on to the passenger seat next to Johnny. Then he pulled on the jacket and climbed into his seat, pushing the gun over with one effective wipe of his backside. Finally he wound down the window and reached out to take the hot coffee from Mabel. Daan barely glanced at Mabel as he took the coffee, but she always dipped her head respectfully before she turned and went back into the house.

Without a word having passed between them Johnny turned the key in the ignition and they set off. Daan spoke only after he'd downed all the coffee in his mug. Then he banged the cup into the holder on the dashboard, turned to Johnny with a huge grin and said loudly, 'Môre!' As usual his cheerfulness was infectious and even Johnny couldn't help smiling just a little.

'Middag.'

'Sunday special?'

'Yep.'

'How far?'

'Coetzee's.'

'Lekker! My favourite breakfast place. A big breakfast on a big day . . . ' Johnny actually chuckled. Daan was right: the Coetzees could be relied on for excellent food. That was Daan, always seeing the bright side. Life had never given him good enough reason not to. Johnny, on the other hand, tended to pull in the opposite direction.

By nature Daan was more gentleman farmer than police-man, but he was in the unlucky position of being the youngest of three sons in a family with only thirty cultivated hectares. While those happened to be thirty highly productive and immensely valuable hectares, they didn't need three people in charge of them. Since the death of their not-much-lamented father the older Du Toits had run the farm and they ran it well. Daan was a bit of a spare part. He went straight from school to army and from there he hung around for a while, unsure of what to do. He tried agricultural school, but the work was dull and without a farm to inherit what was the point? It was his oldest brother, Hennie, who suggested the police. After the training it was easy enough to arrange Daan's posting to the dorp, his rank, all of that. The Du Toits had friends in all the right places and where they didn't it was easy to make them. Their hospitality was legend.

Running the local police station was really a bit of fun for Daan, something that kept him busy, kept him at the heart of things and gave him a measure of the kind of power that the Du Toits liked, the power to do and undo things for people who mattered from time to time. That was how the Du Toits worked and they weren't unusual in that respect.

The Du Toits were the kind of people that most irritated Johnny, people for whom things are always easy. They breezed gracefully through everything, even the army. They avoided the worst that their already privileged lives dished up, charming everyone with their rangy good looks, their generosity and their confidence. Johnny had had years now in which to observe Daan at close range and he'd concluded that confidence was the key ingredient. Daan always knew the right thing to say, the appropriate tone, the perfect weight for the occasion. And the weight of most things in his life was slight.

Johnny knew that the reason Daan didn't take his job seriously was not only that nothing ever happened in Fransmansvallei. Daan understood as well as anyone that real position, real respect, real power attached to land. What Daan wanted was a farm of his own. Johnny also knew that Daan was very close now to getting it. The announcement of his engagement to Elise van Rensburg would all but finalise arrangements. Daan's marriage was Johnny's opportunity and so the day was auspicious for him too. My God, he'd waited for it long enough.

Johnny was a far better policeman than Daan. He knew it, everyone knew it, but being a good policeman wasn't what mattered, and that stuck in Johnny's throat. He didn't like the way Daan used his position to do favours for his friends and neighbours. To them Daan was a great guy. Nevertheless – and this made him bitter with frustration – Johnny realised that few other men would give him the free rein that Daan's lack of interest in the job allowed him. It was rare enough for a black man to come so far in this white heartland. In spite of President Mandela, in spite of the changes elsewhere, there was little that had changed in Fransmanshoek and Johnny wondered whether things ever would. There was a way of doing things here, a way of life that was as fixed and immutable as the mountains. In fact there had been almost no discernible change since the dreaded majority rule had come and apartheid had gone. The whites-only signs had been taken off the main entrance at the bottle store, but the blacks still bought their liquor round the back. It wasn't a black family who had bought Die Uitkyk and would soon be moving into the stately whitewashed homestead. No blacks owned houses or land here, no blacks ran shops or businesses. Blacks never tried on dresses in the boutique where the white women shopped. They were still never invited into the homes of white families, unless it was as cleaners or cooks or childminders. No black would be allowed to run the local police station, at least not for some time. Johnny didn't think he could wait that long.

Johnny wanted change more than anything, but he didn't know how to make it. He felt trapped both by his ambition and by the sleepy dorp where the changes that had rocked everyone and everywhere else right off the Richter scale had barely even rattled the centuries-old certainty that white and black were as different as, well, white and black, and no one was in any doubt as to which was superior.

When Daan and Johnny pulled up at the Coetzees' farm things had calmed down considerably. Most of the time it worked out that way, but their job was to come out when called and so they did.

There was uproar in the compound as Daan and Johnny went in to retrieve the farmer, but it was the bystanders who were shouting. The perpetrator was unconscious in a corner of the yard. He'd fallen asleep. By the time he woke he'd have a splitting headache, a burning gut and no memory of what he'd done. Meanwhile old Coetzee was berating a woman with a wound on her chest. 'This is my Sunday, my day of rest! You've shattered my peace! Why can't you control your husband!'

The woman didn't even wince as her daughter swabbed the cut and the farmer ranted. She just stared at him, her jaw slack and her eyes blank, while her eldest daughter, a girl with a face too thin and far too old for one so young, bandaged the cut. It was already an old story for her, a story as long as her life. The men come home from a long Saturday night at the shebeen and rage against the world and their families, and someone gets hurt. Always.

Both Johnny and Daan knew the story as well. After a long shift the evening before, the worker is treated to a heavy dop by a farmer eager to keep his overworked and underpaid men happy. He probably never even goes home; the dop of sherry will liven him up and send him bouncing down the road to the shebeen in the compound on the neighbour's farm. He staggers home at dawn, his head spinning with the cheap wine mixed with meths and God only knows what else he's swallowed in exchange for his hard-earned pay. Maybe his wife starts the fight, maybe he starts it. In the end he beats her up anyway. In this instance the offender had stabbed his wife with a kitchen knife that she obviously kept blunt enough to prevent serious injury after nights like this.

'Hey, give me a hand here!' Johnny pulled at the drunk's arm and three older women sprang to assist him. The other men hung back, observing sullenly from behind a gaggle of laughing children. Johnny and the three angry wives dragged the reeking, unconscious body to the van and loaded it into the back. Meanwhile Daan steered the farmer away, placating him with promises of action. 'Of course, of course we will. In the morning when he's slept this off.'

Sannie Coetzee was in her kitchen and already well into the routine of her Sunday morning. Her husband smiled at her; he seemed to have forgotten his rude awakening when he smelt the sputtering bacon and the fresh bread. Later, as old Coetzee sat down with Daan to a huge breakfast in the long dining room, he mellowed even further. 'Ag, what's the point in charging him? I'll dock his wages and that'll be the end of it!'

'Ja . . . till the next time,' laughed Daan, spearing a buttery mushroom with his fork. Sunlight streamed in through the tall windows and the farmer and his wife laughed too and they ate and talked of other, pleasanter things.

Sannie wanted to know if the rumour was true that an English family had bought Die Uitkyk. Daan shook his head, his mouth crammed with honey and bread. He swallowed. 'No, not a family, just the one guy.' He mopped the mushroom juice and egg yolk and bacon fat from his plate with a hunk of crust. 'Nobody's seen him yet and, believe me, every single eye in the valley has been trained on the place since we heard! But it's been dead quiet. He has to come soon, or he'll lose a fortune of fruit.'

Coetzee chewed thoughtfully. 'Hm, maybe he doesn't care about the fruit.'

Daan frowned and then said brightly, 'Maybe he doesn't. Coming from overseas with all his overseas money he probably doesn't have to.' Coetzee and his wife laughed, but it was a rueful sound.

Johnny ate his breakfast in the kitchen. He knew his place, he didn't need to be told. It was unthinkable that an African would ever eat in the dining room. The maid put a huge plate of food on the table before him. They didn't speak. She was a quiet, tired woman and Johnny, who was often and not unfairly described as dour, was in a particularly dour mood.

Daan's hearty laughter drifted through from the dining room. A gob of bacon fat jumped on to Johnny's uniform and in his irritation he rubbed at it, making the stain worse. The maid tried to help him, but Johnny swatted his hand at her, shooing her off as she approached. He left the grease mark as it was, ate quickly until he was full and then pushed the plate away. He got up from the table and stalked out of the kitchen without a word.

He waited outside in his van as the day grew older. It was nine thirty or so when Daan emerged, Coetzee shaking his hand vigorously and urging him to stop by again. 'Any time, any time.'

'Well, naturally, with cooking like Sannie's on offer I'd be a fool not to!'

'Ag, flatterer!' Sannie demurred, but she giggled girlishly and old Coetzee put his bearish arm round her shoulders. Daan jumped up into the van, Johnny started the engine and pulled away, Daan still waving to the Coetzees who waved back happily from their kitchen door.

Sandile walked out of the railway station feeling incredibly light, like an acrobat swinging out on a wild trapeze. He caught a bus that took him as far as the turn-off to Fransmanshoek.

32

There was no public transport from here – you either drove if you had a car, or hitched a ride on a farm truck, or you walked. Sandile walked. His hands were pushed deep into the pockets of his trousers, his leather jacket flapped open. It was spring here and it felt like spring. The colours were as vivid and dazzling as ice. The sun was strong and the shadows were cool. Sandile smiled into the wind, which filled him with a restless excitement. In the Cape all four seasons define themselves, unlike Zambia where it either rains or is dry and where the spring doesn't charge from the earth in a carnival of freshness and colour.

The road was wider and smoother than when he'd last travelled it, but the route was the same and the trees and the shapes of the rocks around him were familiar. Sandile had long ago forgotten, but now he recognised the last sharp bend in the road and instantly knew that around that bend was the point from which he would see the valley falling away below him. The memory hit him; the sensation was buried so deep in him that he actually felt it bubble up, and he quickened his step.

Johnny was driving fast. It was a road he knew so well he could spin the turns at 120 kilometres an hour. As they approached the last uphill bend he saw a black man walking at the side of the road. There was only one place that a man could be walking to on this stretch of road and Johnny was going that way, so he immediately pulled to a stop. The custom was to accept such an offer by jumping on the back of the van or truck and riding as far as it was going.

Daan didn't even glance round at the stranger when they stopped a few metres ahead of him and waited for the sound of feet running on gravel, the clank of him clambering on to the back and then the jerk of the van pulling away. Johnny watched in the side mirror as the man strolled up alongside the passenger door. His clothes looked new, unlike anything worn by a black man around here, and he walked with a suspicious ease, carrying himself with all the confidence of a white man. The thought crossed Johnny's mind that this could only mean trouble.

Sandile was smiling as he approached the van. He found it amusing that the police would stop for him and that he would accept their offer. Thirteen years ago it would not have been so. Nevertheless, he was grateful and pleased to have the opportunity to learn more about his destination on the way. The two cops up front looked round as he walked up to the passenger window. The smile froze on Sandile's face. He recognised both men, but only one of them recognised him.

Daan wasn't normally an observant man; in fact he prided himself on not being tuned in to the subtle undercurrents of interaction. He was a plain-spoken chap himself and he liked to encounter the world at face value. But he couldn't help noticing that Johnny flinched as the stranger's face appeared alongside the van. Daan wound down the window. This guy was certainly not from anywhere around here.

Johnny simply stared and there was fear in his eyes. Sandile recognised him immediately and dipped his chin, a terse nod of acknowledgement. 'Xolile.'

Sandile had used his real name. No one had spoken it in years. Johnny answered dryly, 'You have come back.'

Sandile made the same brief gesture with his chin. 'Yes. I have come back.'

Daan was growing impatient, and the hard stare and long silence between these men was stifling. He banged his hand on the side of the van. 'Come on, come on, let's go!'

It was hard for Johnny to say it, but he did. 'Climb on. I'll take you home.'

Sandile searched the familiar face. Xolile hadn't aged much, and he looked like a man who had slept soundly at night for all these years. Sandile shook his head and stepped back, away from the van.

'No. Thank you.'

A harsh, bitter snort of laughter burst from Johnny. It was a shocking sound, born of shock. Daan saw his colleague's face twist into an attempt at a smile.

34

'Nothing's changed?'

Sandile slowly shook his head. 'Everything's changed, Xolile. Haven't you noticed?'

Daan threw up his hands and let them fall, clapping them against his thighs in a gesture of hearty exasperation. 'If he doesn't want a lift then he doesn't want a lift. Let's go!'

Sandile watched as Johnny reached for the brake and released it with a shaking hand. He seemed to move in slow motion as he shifted the gear stick into first, released the clutch and pulled away. Then the van disappeared around the bend.

Daan was staring at Johnny. Things were strange between them this morning. Prickly with tension. He had no idea why, but he didn't like it. Daan liked things to be easy between himself and the world. He liked things light and smooth and he was usually able to charm his way through everything. But this edgy, dark mood of Johnny's ruffled him.

'Why did he call you Xolile?'

Johnny's face was twisted with a rage he could not express, yet could not contain. He spoke thickly. 'Because that is my name.'

'What? Why do we call you Johnny then?' Daan seemed to find this funny, like a silly riddle.

'I don't know. Why *do* you call me Johnny?'

Daan's features shifted with confusion. He was taken aback by the deliberate perversity that had replaced Johnny's usual polite servility. 'That's what everyone calls you.'

'That's what you people call me because you can't say my true name. Johnny is not my name. It has become my name because you people call me that.'

Johnny's mouth was tight with anger as he almost spat out the words. Daan was astonished; he simply didn't know what to say. He had never seen Johnny like this, had never been spoken to by him like this.

Johnny looked over at Daan's pale, amiable face and hated him. He couldn't resist this opportunity to chide him for not knowing who the stranger was. 'Didn't you know who that was?'

Daan raised his eyebrows; this kaffir was really getting too big for his boots, like all of them lately, and his good humour could only stretch so far. He responded tersely with an order in the thin guise of a question. 'Who was it?'

Johnny was sweating. He'd never pushed Daan before, but he was too angry to climb down now. 'You should know . . . It's no secret, look in the records. If you go back eight years plus – ' He paused, thinking, counting by pressing his fingers – one, two, three, four, five – on the steering wheel. 'Plus five years, that's thirteen years back. You'll find it all written up.'

'Hm . . . ' Daan was losing interest. Why should some black guy – even if he did wear smart clothes – be written up and where? Ag, it couldn't be that interesting. He sighed and gazed out of the window, eliminating Johnny from even the edge of his vision. But Johnny couldn't let it go. 'Under Mashiya.'

It worked. Daan swung round to look back over his shoulder, but the stranger had long ago disappeared from view. He turned back towards Johnny. 'Mashiya, huh? Mama Mashiya's . . . That's her boy, isn't it? The one the Security Police were always looking for. I thought he was dead.'

Johnny nodded, a little too vigorously. 'That was what we all thought. He was supposed to be dead.'

He swallowed hard. The inside of his mouth felt as if it was wadded with tissues. After a short while Daan laughed, a surprised laugh, as if delighted by the strange things this day was offering up. But the smile that broke on Johnny's face was frightening.

FIVE

Elise stood by the window looking out on to the garden as Ina put the finishing touches to her flower arrangements. Ina grimaced, noticing the dust that clung to the table she was working on. The main house at Rustenvrede had an air of uncared-for shabbiness about it now. Evelyn van Rensburg had furnished it carefully with antiques she'd bought over the years at criminal prices from local Coloured and African families who needed the money badly and couldn't believe the value that people like Evelyn attached to the old stuff built by their fathers and grandfathers and handed down. The homestead was big, far too big for Mama to clean on her own, Ina thought. Mama's domain was the kitchen, but once a day she cursorily vacuumed and wiped and dusted, mostly in Elise and Van's rooms. No one paid much attention to the rest any more and nor did Mama.

Outside, one of the Du Toit children ran across the grass, her long hair whipping round her head as she chased after an old lady's purple hat that was bowling along ahead of her, eluding her. Elise looked out across the lawn to where the little girl, with one great, final effort, pounced on the hat. The surprise on the child's face as she landed so abruptly and so effectively was so funny that Elise burst into laughter. Then the little girl reached underneath her and pulled out a disc of flattened purple felt. 'Ouma! I got it!' she yelled, picking herself up and racing across the grass, remains of the hat held triumphantly high.

Elise helped Ina carry the brimming vases out to the long table in the garden, near to where people were gathering. The Steyns, the Malans, the Van Der Walts, the Retiefs, the

37

Brands and the Jouberts were all there. All Fransmansvallei's old families, except the Lombaards of course. Elise was hugged and kissed and admired by everyone. Daan hadn't showed up yet, but the older Du Toits had arrived with their wives and their kids and were spread out among the crowd. Even the De Jagers were there, all except Madeleine. Elise hoped that Madeleine would come by. She wanted her to be here today and she had pointedly requested that Daan ask her, in the hope that there might be some sort of reconciliation. It was obvious what the source of the antagonism was, though Elise felt there was no need for it to persist and certainly hoped it wouldn't.

Madeleine was Daan's high-school sweetheart. They'd had a long and stormy on-off relationship which everyone joked would turn into marriage or murder. Of course everyone smiled and knew it would be marriage – it was one of the assumptions of life in the dorp. When Daan made his first play for Elise his relationship with Madeleine was mostly off. When Elise submitted, Daan and Madeleine were finally, once and for all, completely off. What had happened between them then was their business. But the tension around Madeleine now had become Elise's business.

The old tannies were sitting in a group, draped delicately over the wooden benches, chattering and fanning themselves. Van was holding his own among the men around the braai. Willem Slabbert, the Dominee, was nodding vigorously at the discussion, his face flushed from the several cans of cold beer he'd downed since his arrival. The Dominee was a big man, thicker now than the trim young rugby star he once was, but elegant and fit-looking. He was still regarded as a newcomer, having arrived in Fransmansvallei only thirty-odd years before, but was deeply embedded in the community nevertheless. In a way he was the heart of the community, being a friend to all and an enemy to none and having presided over all the important moments, every christening, marriage and burial that Elise could remember. Willem was also the local councillor for the Nationalist Party and had been since

Vorster's time and the days of grand apartheid. He was handsome and loud and as far as anyone knew, though no one really talked about it any more, he'd been single all his life. Since Elise's mother's death he'd become Van Rensburg's closest friend. The two of them often sat together at one end of Rustenvrede's dining table, drinking steadily and talking long into the night.

The flames had died down now and the fire was almost ready. Van wanted to start cooking the meat. He turned to his daughter who, with Ina, was putting the finishing touches to the table. 'Lise, where's Daan?'

'He'll be here just now. I'm sure he's waiting for his mother.'

'That's exactly what he's doing!' chimed Ina.

Van was poking at the charcoal on the braai, shaking up a shower of burning embers. 'Skat, go fetch the meat – this fire's going to be ready now, now.'

As Elise strolled back towards the kitchen she was arrested by the sight of a black man walking up the drive. The trees obscured her view of him as he approached, so she couldn't see who it was. She didn't know why she should notice such a thing – she didn't normally keep an eye on the traffic of farm labourers along that road. But this man looked different; perhaps that was why he'd caught her eye. He was dressed very well, very attractively, she thought, with some surprise at herself. Instead of turning off down the track to the farm workers' cottages, he came straight towards the house and towards her. She stopped and waited. The light was in front of him as he approached and he squinted a little into the sun. There was something familiar in his face, but Elise was sure she didn't know him and she couldn't imagine why he would be coming up to the house today. Looking for work or looking for trouble, she thought irritably, and she moved towards him to find out which it was.

'What are you looking for?' Her question was chilly and Sandile didn't immediately answer. As he walked up to her he thought he recognised her, but he couldn't see clearly. Could this woman in front of him be that little girl, his traitorous friend, the princess of the farm?

The man was staring at her with an odd intensity. Elise wondered if there was something wrong with him. Perhaps he hadn't understood. She stared back, trying vainly to place the familiar features. He moved with the self-assurance of a foreigner. Maybe he was an American? Her voice softened, as did her eyes. 'Can I help you with anything?' He blinked and she smiled, a little uneasily, but there was warmth in her smile. The stranger cleared his throat to speak.

Just as he opened his lips Mama Mashiya came out of the back door from the kitchen carrying the huge meat dish laden with steak and wors for the braai. Her voice was shrill and urgent. 'Elise! Go fetch the rest in the kitchen for me. Come, child, be quick!' Both faces turned towards her.

Sandile saw an old woman struggling with a wide, laden dish. Was this his mother? Why didn't he know? Panic rose in him. Elise looked back at the stranger, but he didn't take his eyes off Mama Mashiya. Mama stopped to rest a second. 'Come now, my girl, I need you to go fetch the other dish.'

Elise nodded, then turned to the stranger and pointed him towards a stool by the kitchen door. 'If you sit in the shade there, I'll be back just now.' But she didn't move; there was electricity all round her, the moment was charged and she didn't know why. She couldn't keep her eyes off this man. The stranger still said nothing. Mama looked at him, tutting irritably, another wanderer thrown up by the new road who would make trouble soon enough if they didn't put him on his way. Yet there was something in his face that stopped her and made her stare.

Mama shook her head, but the vision didn't go away, it just wobbled and blurred and stayed there. It wasn't possible. She walked on, clicking her tongue at the strangeness of old age and keeping her eyes on the meat dish. 'Aikona,' she sighed, still shaking her head. But the vision stepped into her path and simply stood there in front of her, refusing to go away.

40

'Mama?' he said. She didn't move. She was frozen to the spot and her eyes had grown so wide that Elise was frightened.

'Mama!' Elise's voice rose as she reached for Mama Mashiya's arm. The old woman was shaking. She saw quite clearly now that the man standing before her was her son. How had she not seen it before? She was looking into the face of her dead son. She felt the adrenalin pumping through her. She realised she must be dying and the terror of that was mixed with the joy of knowing that in dying she had her beloved son restored to her. Space seemed to distort around her, panic sucked all the sound out of everything.

Sandile said something to her. His mouth was moving around words. 'Mama, I am Sandile.' Her hands came up to her face, covering her mouth, and she didn't realise it until too late, but she'd let go of what she was holding and the meat-laden dish crashed to the ground, shattering like a clash of cymbals.

What does a person feel in such a moment? Is there any space left for feeling by the inrush of memory and hope and wild, reckless joy? Can there be any sense of reality in such a moment? A crescendo of pure joy thrilled through Mama, a cascade of elation fell on her in that moment of recognition. Her heart felt like church bells pealing out on a hot Christmas morning, and yet she was as incredulous as any mother would be at witnessing the resurrection of her long-dead son.

Looking down at the smashed china all three woke up from their daze. Elise dashed for the kitchen. The dogs sat up, sniffing the air, and trotted over, while Sandile gripped his mother's shoulders and pulled her away from the mess of meat and shattered porcelain. In the kitchen Elise grabbed a big saucepan out of Nolitha's hands and raced back outside, but two of the dogs already had their jaws round the ends of one long twist of wors, uncurling it as they pulled the unexpected treat away, while the other dogs yelped with excitement and fear. 'Quickly!' Elise shouted. Lettie and Nolitha followed her out of the kitchen, both shrieking at the sight of the meal the dogs were making of their morning's hard work.

At the sight of Mama the pitch of their squeals rose. Mama was as near to pale as she could be and frozen like a statue, her hands still covering her face. Sandile was trying to push the dogs away from the meat. Elise was picking up as much as she could and tossing it into the saucepan when Ina, followed by Van Rensburg, came round the corner of the house to find out why the food was taking so long to arrive.

Van Rensburg went purple. He tried to speak, but his throat constricted in an apoplexy of rage. Elise saw his spluttering and told him to go back to the fire, she would bring the meat in a moment. But Van Rensburg didn't go back. He pulled his arm away from Ina who was attempting to steer him back to the garden and exploded at Mama Mashiya, bellowing like a mad bull.

'You stupid old woman. I told you not to do more than you can. I told you not to carry things around and now look at this. Do you know how much that meat cost? And now? Tell me, what am I supposed to do now? What am I supposed to give these people to eat?'

Van Rensburg was shouting into Mama Mashiya's stunned face. Sandile moved to protect his mother and Elise grabbed her father's arm, jerking him away so hard that he was about to turn his rage on her. But she yelled, in a voice so full of uncharacteristic fury that he was stunned, 'Shut up, Pa!' Van Rensburg, everyone, even the dogs, fell silent.

Elise spoke very quietly, this time her voice audible only to her father. 'Can't you see what's happening here? She's in shock. Leave her alone and go inside.'

Van was silent, pushing his hand back through his thin white hair. He seemed old and not so strong any more. He strutted round the smashed plate, pretending not to have heard her.

'Listen, Pa, this is Betty's son. She thought he was dead. She's had a helluva shock.'

Van Rensburg glared over at mother and son and his anger

seemed to subside. Elise knew that for a moment he understood, for a moment he was moved, for a moment his mind flicked to the image of his own son. But then he spun away and went into the kitchen without another word.

Elise gave the pot of rescued dusty meat to Nolitha who was staring at Sandile with her mouth hanging open and huge, her eyes boggling out of her face. 'Nolitha! Take this and rinse it off. Lettie, go fetch the other meat and take it to my father.' Nolitha took the pan, still gawping at Sandile as if at a phantom. Elise looked over at him uncertainly, wiping her fingers on her hip and staining the silk of her skirt.

Sandile turned to his mother and put his hand gently on her arm. 'Mama . . . will you take me to my father now?' His voice was soft and hesitant. Elise saw that he wanted her to say yes, wanted to know that his father was somewhere near and not gone. Mama Mashiya put her hands together and her forehead against the steeple of her fingers and closed her eyes as if in prayer. She made a sound that was like sobbing, yet she didn't weep. Her mouth moved in a crooked smile.

Elise touched Mama on the shoulder and said softly to her, 'Go, Mama. Take him to the old man.'

Mama looked blankly at Elise, her eyes shining with tears unshed, but her mouth now downturned. She was concentrating so hard, grasping so wildly for the quiet sense of reality she never knew she owned till it had left her so abruptly just minutes ago, that she couldn't speak. She just nodded vigorously and the tears flew out from her eyes.

Elise cleared her throat and looked up at Sandile. 'You take her to your father. He's up by the compound. It's where it always was.'

Sandile put his arm around his mother and the sense of her was so powerful he had to close his eyes. The softness of Elise's voice was unbearable to him. He knew he would cry at any moment and he could not weep here, not in front of these people. 'Mama,' Elise said, 'go, take him home now and come back in the morning. If you need anything you just send Lucky to come and get it from me.' Sandile steered his mother away. She was silent, still shaking her head and wiping her eyes as they set off up the road.

Lettie and Nolitha were watching from the kitchen steps. Elise saw them and told them to go too. 'You go, help her . . .' They looked at one another, knowing they should stay but wanting so badly to see what would happen next. They couldn't bear to miss the reaction this incredible arrival would cause, so they whipped off their aprons and house-coats, threw them behind the door and raced after Mama Mashiya and the son who had come back from the dead.

Ina walked over to Elise and saw tears in her friend's eyes. As they watched the little procession Ina said wickedly, 'Shew! Looks like an American movie star, doesn't he?'

Elise was taken aback. 'You're a funny girl, Ina.'

Ina smiled. 'Come, let's go help your father.'

At this Elise breathed a deep, sharp breath, took Ina's arm and the two paused together, looked knowingly at one another and then stepped bravely towards the house.

In the kitchen Elise found her father slapping the rinsed meat through a fresh mixture of pepper and oil. He was tightlipped and angry. Elise pleaded silently with the stiff back of his neck and head. Please, let it go for once, just for today, just this once, she thought. She knew him – this mood might stay for days – but Elise felt light; she knew that she had witnessed something marvellous, something incredible, and she knew that in his heart he felt it too. Salvaging the meat was simple enough and they did it together, quickly and in silence.

Six

Mama Mashiya was breathing fast and hard, trying to keep up with her son. Her feet flew, following Sandile's long stride. Nolitha and Lettie skipped and skittered behind them. Though he wanted to prepare himself, Sandile didn't dare ask his mother how he might be received by his father. He needed to see and feel it all as it came at him, no expectations, no second-guessing.

As children, Sandile and his brother were terrified of their father, terrified of his rage if they ever did something wrong. Now, on his return, he imagined anger, indifference even. Once, when he was twelve, his older brother, Vuyani, came home in the middle of the night after a disappearance of several weeks. His father had stood barring the doorway and looking suspiciously over his thin, shivering boy. Sandile remembered thinking their father would send Vuyani away, but he didn't. He simply nodded and said mildly, 'Mama, it's time to open a tin of fatted calf.' Then he stood aside and let Vuyani in. Vuyani couldn't laugh at the joke until almost a week later.

Sandile's mother had always been as forgiving as his father was hard. Now they walked side by side and in silence, neither one touching the other. Sandile strained forward, his face grimly set. The train journey and then the last long night seemed vividly clear compared with this. His arrival at Rustenvrede, his mother, this rutted dusty road, the women running behind them, this moment approaching his father: it was all like a wipe of colours, a blur of faces, a clatter of sounds. Everything was coming at him so fast he could barely register, let alone react. He had that hyper-adrenalised sense of time fragmenting that comes with panic and he knew he had simply to fly with it, as if he were riding a rip tide.

The day had begun with almost unbearable anticipation. He was afraid of everything, afraid of finding that the beauty he remembered was merely fantasy, afraid he would still feel a stranger, afraid he would feel nothing at the sight of his longed-for home. But the Cape was beautiful, even more beautiful than he remembered. Seeing it again he knew why it had stunned him for life. As he crested the last rise on the last bend before the mountain fell away into the valley of his childhood, his heart leapt, danced with joy. Unbridled. Wild. Joy as he hadn't felt since he was a child. It lay before him, the valley of his dreams. The land he had spent half his life fighting for. The land his ancestors had worked and loved. The land he would claim for his people again. There was no fear in him then. He knew he could face whatever lay ahead.

Sandile had learned long ago to fight the excitement of anticipation. He hated the welling up of it in him because he feared the disappointment, the dashing of expectations that always followed so close on the heels of hope. Yet today he was brimming with it. Hope soared and carried him with it.

From the slip track where the farm workers' children played on the long-abandoned frame of a wrecked lorry, the sight of this tall stranger walking with Mama Mashiya in such a trance, Lettie and Nolitha jogging along behind in a state of high excitement, was like a magnet. Something was happening. The string of children in torn old clothes, whooping and waving their long sticks, came racing up to follow the little procession. But Mama and the stranger and even Nolitha and Lettie paid no attention to them. So as the children fell in step they too were silent, and it was a strangely solemn band that entered the compound and crossed the courtyard towards Mama Mashiya's house.

As Sandile walked into the compound he was disorientated for the first time. Everything had changed. The ramshackle sleeping huts and the single concrete shed that was kitchen, bathroom and living room shared by all the workers in the compound and that had formed the centre of his life as a child were gone. In place of them was a square of ten single cottages grouped round the main yard. The houses were identical cubes from the front. Raw breeze-block structures with a central wooden stable door and two square windows on either side of that, capped by a tin roof, and, Sandile noticed with particular amazement, electricity lines feeding into each one.

Men came out from the shadowy doorways or stood up from their chairs, the women left their washing half hung and children dropped their schoolbooks and their games and rushed towards them to find out what was happening. Mama Mashiya looked neither to the right nor the left of her and seemed not to hear the questions that rained on her from all sides. A curious hush fell over everyone, everything suspended in the expectant silence.

Sandile followed his mother into her house, and the crowd followed them inside; who couldn't fit flowed around outside. She led him down a narrow corridor, to a large living room and kitchen at the back. The kitchen door led to a small stoep and a garden. Through the kitchen window Sandile saw the slender frame of an old man. He was faced away from the house, towards the dam, and so engrossed in his task that he didn't notice the crowd approaching.

In spite of the heat Ben Mashiya wore what he always wore, navy-blue all-in-one overalls and a battered felt hat to protect his head against the sun or the cold. He was a creature of habit; he always worked in his garden on a Sunday. Last spring Elise had encouraged him to plant flowers as well as vegetables and she'd brought him two big old oil drums which he cut in half. He put two at the back and two at the front of the house, filled them with soil and planted sunflowers. He liked sunflowers because they were big and useful. The seeds his sunflowers produced were delicious; in fact he'd had to guard his crop well against his neighbours' children who had developed quite a taste for them. At the feet of the tall sunflowers there were clusters of nasturtiums; their flaming orange and scarlet flowers pleased him. The rest of his garden was taken up with mielies and potatoes and turnips, and in the late summer there would be squash and pumpkins, though at this time of year he grew some herbs and garlic too. Mielies never grew well in this soil, yet he managed to get a delicious crop of slightly undersized but very sweet cobs every year. This spring he had begun to experiment with tomatoes and on that Sunday afternoon he was tending the line of tomato seedlings when his wife called to him. He turned slowly to see all his neighbours standing silently before him on the stoep and in the yard.

For Sandile the shock of seeing this bent old man was far greater than the shock of seeing his mother again. She had aged, but softly, while the years had ravaged his old man. The whites of his eyes were milky and clotted and he had a beard now that was grey and thinning to a wispy point. Yet there he was, his father, alive and still working in his garden as he had been on the day Sandile fled, when there was no time and he had no words to explain. The old man looked around him as if dazed.

'Ben.' His wife's voice was squeezed; she sounded unlike herself. There was a stranger, a big city-slicker type standing next to her who was staring too much. Oupa Mashiya clicked his tongue in irritation, just as Mama had done. What on earth was going on? He squinted at them, puzzled by the interruption and slightly afraid of what it meant. Monotonous as his life was, any change in the rhythm of things here was brought on by bad news or else followed by bad news. Anxiety gripped him and Oupa Mashiya braced himself for whatever it might be. His wife spoke again and this time she explained breathlessly. 'It is Sandile. Sandile has come home.' Sandile stepped towards his father whose head shook from side to side.

Ben Mashiya gripped the gardening fork in his right hand. When he opened his mouth his pipe fell out. He didn't say anything. He simply tried to move, but the effect was a frantic scarecrow-like sawing of his arms in the air, the fork still waving about in his hand. Then somehow his foot lifted off the ground and he felt as he looked, like a puppet, all stiff in the limbs and loose at the joints, juddering forward towards Sandile. His mouth and his eyes were so large that he looked mad as he opened his arms wide and embraced his son.

Mama Mashiya was witnessing a miracle. Sandile and his father stood before her in the garden among the tubs of sunflowers and nasturtiums and the new green shoots of the mielie crop. One of the neighbours came forward, wanting Oupa Mashiya to come and sit in the shade of the stoep, but he wouldn't take his attention from his son, so they brought him a chair and they peeled his fingers from the gardening fork, and Oupa sat down right there, still holding on to Sandile's hand. He wouldn't let go.

The silence broke and the buzz around them grew to chatter and to a clamour of amazement and in the midst of all this Oupa Mashiya sighed terribly. His lips crumpled and he said bluntly, 'I had given up hope.' Those first words from his father hit Sandile like a gut-punch. He, above everyone, understood the weight of them and he simply hung his head because there was nothing to be said. Children are not replaceable, the pain of his parents' lives could not be unlived.

Mama couldn't stop shaking her head. 'My child, where have you come from?' Sandile knew he had to explain, or at least begin to explain, but later. For now he wanted their news, news of the farm, news of his sisters and his brother. So his mother began to tell him. The headlines of so many years began to tumble out and there was grief to mingle with all the joy.

Vuyani was murdered in a township gang fight nearly ten years ago. She told it bluntly, there was no way to couch it. He had fathered several children before he was killed. For a couple of years after they buried him Mama received visits and letters, several from women who said Vuyani was the father of their child and they wanted support. One of them brought her son to Rustenvrede and simply abandoned him here. 'Lucky? Come here!' A wiry, wary boy who looked about nine years old stepped hesitantly forward. Mama put her arm round the child's shoulders, swamping his skinny frame with her bulk as she drew him to her. 'His mother called him Lucky. He's twelve years now,' she said.

The boy stared at him through wild eyes and Sandile searched his face for traces of Vuyani, but there were none and he felt doubly bereft. Yet he went to the boy and put his arms round him and Mama said to him, 'Lucky, now you have an uncle.'

The childish faces of his brother and sisters, faces of innocent mischief and boundless curiosity, flickered in Sandile's mind and he tried to superimpose on them the images Mama conjured up of weariness and cynicism and gangster-ism and death. He found himself awash with pain as Mama went on. His older sister, Unathi, was living in the squatter-camp sprawl at Kayelitsha. She hadn't been back to the farm in eight years; she'd left swearing she would never come back. Unathi didn't stay in touch, but Mama Mashiya always managed to find her. The last time Mama had seen Unathi was after she'd been to one of the back-street butchers for an abortion. She was twenty-six and she already had five children; she couldn't cope with another. Unathi was terribly sick for a time, nearly died, but as far as Mama knew she was OK, had a job in a shop. They were always expecting bad news of Unathi, though his other sister, Nosipo, was doing well. She'd gone to Joburg a few years ago and she had a job as a maid, working in a very nice house in Melville. Accord-ing to Mama, the Madam there was very kind to her and let her live with her child and her boyfriend in the domestic's flat at the side of the house. The child was a little girl called Nomonde, after her grandmother, and now she went to school with the Madam's children, since the white schools had opened to everyone. 'She's a good child. You will like her, she's like her mother. Nosipo was always your pet, your favourite. Do you remember?'

Sandile was speechless. His mother fell silent too, for she

saw that she was talking to him from what was still another world.

The silence was complete, enveloping them all. Like a silence in church for those who are being remembered and acknowledged. It was fitting then that Oupa Mashiya should end it. He stood up and declared energetically that one of his animals should be slaughtered. 'Tonight we will feast, for my son has come home!' Great excitement ensued. Tradition would have had him kill a cow, but now the only animals the Mashiyas kept were chickens. So the fattest chicken was chosen for the pot and everyone rushed to their houses to bring more food for the celebration.

While the children raced and skipped madly in all directions, the women built a fire and sang in and out of their kitchens and the men grouped themselves round the square at the heart of the compound. Jacob, who was the Van Rensburgs' right-hand man, produced an unlabelled five-litre plastic container filled with red wine and passed it round. That was the way it was given out on some of the farms in the valley. The dop system had been dropped long ago at Rustenvrede, so Jacob had to buy his supply from a friend over at Joubert's where wine and wages were handed out together at the end of each week. As the questions and stories flew, Jacob shared his wine with those who wanted it, even offering some to Ben Mashiya who declined lightheartedly and for once skipped his usual temperance lecture. The wine passed from mouth to mouth, all round the circle, and Sandile took a swig when it came to him. He grimaced as the liquid burned down his throat. It was harsh and sweet and horrible. The men laughed. 'Have some more, have some more!' But Sandile declined, passing the bottle on.

The container quickly emptied and Jacob declared that someone would have to go to Joubert's compound to fetch another. Change was collected and thrown into a pot and, to Ben Mashiya's dismay, Lucky was chosen for the task of fetching the wine. The men shouted him down when Ben protested, so he laughed and waved Lucky away.

'Today I am so happy I can laugh while you corrupt my children! I see now that happiness can make a man stupid!' Laughter clapped the air.

Lucky set off, his pockets heavy with clinking change, on a big black bicycle with bullhorn handlebars and a flat basket holder at the back, a cardboard box lashed down to that with string. He would cycle all the way across the valley, and down its tapering end, up the hill to Joubert's compound, load up his box and then cycle all the way back again. On any other day he would have groaned at the thought of the long ride and dragged out the journey there and back, but today he leapt at the task, infected by the excitement that was everywhere, even in the sounds of laughter that drifted from the garden of the main house. Lucky flew down the hill, freewheeling at speed past the Van Rensburgs' party. Heads turned to watch him go by and he took his hands off the handlebars, grinning madly and waving at all the guests on the lawn.

SEVEN

Slabs of steak and fat boerewors popped and sizzled on the braai, their scent drifting tantalisingly across the garden, drawing the guests towards the tables where Ina and Elise were laying out the salads and bread and sauces for lunch. Elise was silently bent on her task. The sun was hot on her skin and she was basking in the pleasure of familiar voices all around her. She glanced over at her father who stood in his solid, still way, surrounded by the peaceful conversation of Willem Slabbert and the younger Joubert and the oldest Du Toit. Van Rensburg's expression gave little away, but his arms were loose and relaxed as he stoked his fire and watched carefully over the meat.

The sight of him like that was so touchingly familiar it aroused in Elise a deep inward flush of joy. The explosion of Mama Mashiya's son's sudden homecoming had threatened to spoil everything, but the mood on the lawn now was light and it seemed no one else was aware of what had happened. They hadn't noticed Van Rensburg's stiffness when he returned from the kitchen to put the meat on the fire. And he did loosen up again. For once there was an occasion sufficient to overshadow the pettiness of what had happened with Mama, the kind of incident that Elise knew could otherwise spin him into weeks of sulking.

It mattered a great deal to Van that this day should go well. These were the people he'd known and lived and fought and worked with all his life and he was inviting them back into his home and back into his life, indicating to them that the pain of losing his wife was a pain he could live with, that he wasn't ruined by it as he had once believed. He was showing them how life could and should and did continue, but he was also proving it to himself and so Elise felt protective of him, a little scared for him for she knew how vulnerable he was. Now that everyone was here and happy she could see that her father felt safe in his life, protected by this familiarity, by this gathering. She put the serving dishes down on the brick next to the fire and squeezed her father's arm. He turned and smiled comfortably before turning back to the Dominee and a critical dispute over the previous day's Western Province performance.

Van Rensburg was famous for his quick, foul temper. Because of it he had more enemies than friends. But his world was small, and white people stood by each other in the dorp virtually no matter what. It was as simple as that. If his relationships lacked intimacy or warmth they made up for it in their constancy. People here were, on the whole, as reliable as the seasons. Of course there were exceptions, but the exceptions were functional. There always needs to be something or someone people can define themselves against. The previous owners of Die Uitkyk, the Lombaards, had performed such a service in Fransmanshoek, with their explosive marriage and their disastrous farming practices. The example of the Lombaards was enough to bring anyone back from the brink of any norm-shattering idea or action.

The qualities that had earned Van Rensburg respect among his friends were his doggedness, the determination with which he pursued a goal or an idea, the stubbornness which made it so hard to convince him of a goal or an idea in the first place, and his unswerving loyalty to his few friends. He was a plain speaker. He was not known for his fairness to the workmen he called his 'boys': he was a hard taskmaster, his temper was bad and he had been known to beat his workers if they infuriated him, which they did all too easily. Yet there were those labourers, like Oupa Mashiya, like Jacob, who had stood up to him and had earned his respect over the years, grudging perhaps, but respect nonetheless.

Elise operated entirely differently and it was she who had

brought the changes to the farm. Van Rensburg's new compound had caused quite a stir, though the logic of it was clear and soon other farmers followed, were still following. There were farms in Fransmansvallei where the labourers had no electricity, where the latrine was a pit in the ground and the only water was cold and came from an outside tap. On those farms bathing was an event; it happened rarely and involved a great deal of boiling up of water before the tin bath was ready. In the summer it was almost a festive occasion on a Sunday; in the winter it was hell, and in those cold months the farm workers simply washed themselves down with a towel dipped in hot soapy water by the stove. They didn't care if the farmers called them unclean.

Elise had insisted on redoing the labourers' houses and Van Rensburg had finally acquiesced. She had her reasons for making the changes and he found his. He was compelled by the argument she made for increased efficiency, for riding ahead of an inevitable change. So far everything she said had only been confirmed and Van Rensburg could boast that his boys were among the happiest in the valley. He was proud of the fact that he paid them less than most of his neighbours paid their workers. That was important to Van Rensburg: there was always a shortage of skilled men, and he liked to keep the ones he got. Van Rensburg had been heard to say more than once that kaffirs were hard to teach and that you had to pick the right ones, the ones who didn't get too big for their boots.

Van Rensburg was seventy-five years old. He'd always been a loner, never joined anything willingly. He was the only Afrikaner in the valley who had never been a member of the Broederbond. He just preferred to do things on his own. Of course he belonged to the co-op, but that was an extension of his business; that was necessary. He was an old-fashioned, paternalistic, racist Afrikaner. In his bedroom he kept the signed photograph of apartheid's architect, H. F. Verwoerd, that had been given to his mother by Verwoerd himself. Van's heart still beat faster at the memory of the time when things were clear and orderly and idealistic, when strong-chinned, grave-faced politicians talked of fighting on the beaches, of fighting to the last man to defend their land and their privileges. Respect for the land and for one's duties towards it were fundamental to his value system. Those values had built this farm and only they would sustain it.

Standing by her father Elise gazed at the vista of their garden, which was a riot of vivid spring colour, of almond blossom and violets, huge poinsettias, brilliant tissuey poppies, sweet peas and nasturtiums, hibiscus, snapdragons and armfuls of lilies-of-the-valley clinging to the shade under the massive old trees. Their homestead wasn't large, not compared with some, but it was solid and pleasingly proportioned and more than comfortable. Single-storeyed, with a high gable curving up to a point at the centre of the front, Rustenvrede was a classic Cape Dutch house. Van Rensburg had, in his safe, the documents dating back to when the house was built, in the 1810s. It was in the style in which the wealthier Dutch settlers liked to build, the tall gables reminiscent of those on the high, narrow buildings in their cities at home. In the Cape then there was all the space in the world and it was unnecessary to build up, so they built out, which is why Cape Dutch houses are generally large and low, spreading out from the ornate gables at their centre. The roof had been rethatched only a year before and the walls were whitewashed at the end of every winter, so on a day like today the house was dazzling in the bright sun. Terracotta tubs lining the stoep overflowed with spindly scarlet geraniums, and the bougainvillaea and jasmine and honeysuckle draping the side wall of the house, by the kitchen yard, were all beginning to bloom. Elise savoured the juicy scent of the wors mingled with jasmine and lavender and the hot sweet smell of freshly cut grass.

This had been her mother's favourite time of year and the garden was Evelyn's single passion, next to daydreaming. Perhaps it had been her favourite place in which to daydream. Nothing in the garden had been moved or pruned or pared down since the weeks before Evelyn died, when she was completely bedridden and everyone was too caught up in her sickness even to look out at the garden. It was now over-grown and gone slightly wild and Elise found it all the more beautiful for that. In that moment, looking around her and seeing everything so vividly, she felt as though she was at the height of a surge in a symphony, surrounded by flowers bursting delicately out all over, the orchards stretching up the slopes to the rugged, majestic purple and amber and rust of the mountains themselves. The dusky pink blossoms of the apple orchards rained down like confetti, carpeting the dark earth. Elise smiled up into the perfect turquoise of the limitless sky arching over her world.

'Here's the man!' Ina squeezed Elise's arm, bringing an end to her springtime reverie. Smiling, she turned to see a gleaming, immaculate old Mercedes Benz gliding up the long drive. The big boat of a car came to a halt several hundred yards before the house. Instead of parking on the flattened dusty earth of the yard, it stopped in a narrow track, a short cut leading from the driveway into the garden. Ina and Elise walked across the lawn to meet the late arrivals, ducking under the heavily laden, powerfully scented boughs of the lilac trees overhanging the path.

Daan du Toit jumped out of the driver's seat of the Merc and strode round the car, his long loose legs taking long loose steps. He opened the passenger door and put out an arm for his mother, who emerged slowly from the vehicle. Delicate and imperious, she was a white-haired woman in her early seventies, immaculately coiffured and heavily made-up. Mrs Du Toit, or Madame as Elise had privately named her, was fully decked out for this rare Sunday outing. Mrs Du Toit was not so old, yet for the last five years illness had slowly and debilitatingly begun to claim her body. Her voice and manner had become exaggerated, growing grander and more important as her body shrivelled and faded.

Madame opened her arms and Elise came forward to kiss her, once on each cheek, but not too hard and not too close.

The old lady grasped both Elise's hands and looked her up and down. She held her little back ramrod-straight, her neck still long and haughty. She had a wonderful, powerful head and her eyes were sharp and searching. At last Madame pronounced simply, in a voice as clear as glass, 'Beautiful, my dear. You. Are. Beautiful!'

Elise almost curtseyed. Ina caught her eye and they both laughed with slightly wicked delight, though Elise was genuinely relieved to have passed Madame's high standard.

'Now, my dear, Ina and I saw your Jacob driving the Mercedes through the dorp this morning. Did you know about this?'

Elise nodded, smiling through her patient reply. 'Of course I do, *I* lent him the car, Mrs Du Toit.'

Madame shook her head delicately, the lined loose skin at her neck twisting like that of an old bird. 'Tut-tut, Elise. He's going to prang that car and you'll have only yourself to blame. I've told you before, but you won't listen to me. They've got no distance perception. It's a fact and that's why they're always crashing all those BMWs and Kombis they steal. Don't say I didn't warn you!'

Elise was struck dumb. This was rare but vintage Madame. She looked from Ina to Daan and back, but neither of their faces registered the horror that Elise felt. Fortunately, Madame didn't seem to require a response. 'Shall we go?' trilled the old lady. And so, with her arm safely tucked into the arm of her son, and Ina and Elise in attendance on either side, Mrs Du Toit processed regally towards the party in the garden.

She was so small that she marched straight under the wisteria, while Daan was forced to stoop deeply, but not in time for one branch which swatted him softly in the face and made him sneeze. He let his mother go on ahead. The other tannies came clucking across the grass towards them, gathered Madame up in a gaggle and carried her off towards the sherry and their circle of chairs under the wide cool branches of an oak tree. For a moment Daan watched them totter off across the garden, then he turned to Elise and Ina and let out a loud, sharp 'Shew!' of relief. He squeezed his sister's arm and she tapped the face of her wristwatch. 'You made good time, boet. If it had been me we'd have been lucky to get here for the announcement.' Ina didn't have Daan's patience with their mother, but there was an easy understanding of that, as there can be between a brother and sister.

Daan chuckled and pulled Elise to him. She kissed him lightly. He squeezed her shoulders and kissed her harder on her mouth. She pulled away from him, laughing, and he slapped her backside proprietorially. 'Hey!' She glared at him in earnest, she didn't like that, though there was still a smile on her lips. Then she turned away because the Dominee had caught her arm, he wanted a word.

'She's such a lovely girl, Elise, but very *singular*. Don't you think?' Mrs Joubert was eighty-nine; she was already a grown woman when Mrs Du Toit was only a girl, and she'd been a hard-working farm wife all her life. Even now she hated to be idle. Though she spent long stretches of the day sleeping, when she woke she liked to sit up in bed with the snooker programme playing at full volume on her TV, a chopping board and bowl in her lap, and she'd happily shell peas or peel potatoes for her daughter-in-law while loudly offering up predictions and analysis of play to any of the grandchildren and great-grandchildren who happened to stray near the web of her rooms.

Mrs Joubert was something of a *grande dame* in the dorp and as the oldest in this group of old ladies she was accorded a particular respect and given the last word on most subjects. Mrs Du Toit, however, was a woman of strong opinions herself and a nimble sparring partner, who always made sure that her own views on matters of importance, like character, received the airing they deserved. She simply couldn't let a statement like that go by without comment, particularly when it referred to someone she could claim to know better than Mrs Joubert could. Mrs Du Toit was smoking now from her ivory cigarette holder and she exhaled disdainfully as she took issue with Tannie Joubert. 'What do you mean, *singular*?'

Mrs Joubert knew precisely what she'd meant and was eager to share her insight. 'I mean, for such an attractive young lady there is something so *unfeminine* about her, so . . . tough.'

'Well, really. After what the girl has been through! I think she has done admirably well.'

'Of course, there's no denying that. But her mother was *so* delicate – '

'Oh, her mother was all frills and bows! She's nothing like her mother.'

Mrs Joubert nodded sagely. 'There's no two ways about it, she and her mother never saw eye to eye. It must have been very difficult when Evie passed, knowing things hadn't been straightened out between them.'

Mrs Joubert pursed her lips and dipped her chin to puncutate this last thought, which hung in the air amid such a sucking in of breath that Mrs Du Toit had to tut loudly and rather sharply to stop the drift. Mrs Joubert raised an eyebrow at the gentle rebuke, but she wisely chose to remain silent. Heads bobbed on scrawny necks, craning together, waiting for the next lob. This was their favourite entertainment and had been all their lives. They were only just warming up, reviewing the story so far in the delicious soap opera of the lives around them, straightening out all the elements of the plot so as to heighten the suspense and drama of today's episode.

The women shifted round to look at the men talking by the fire, or gathering round the long table, the grandchildren running on the lawn. Ice clinked in tumblers of whisky. Sherry glowed in the sunlight. But the silence didn't last long. It was with these old women as it is everywhere: this was their time to talk. The men had talked and talked and talked when they were younger and their women had sat and nodded and given all the asurance that the talk needed, and now it was the men who were quiet and the women who spoke their minds. Mrs Joubert sighed heavily. A sigh of contentment, for the scene represented a perfect Sunday and she summed up for everyone.

'I haven't been here since the day we buried Evelyn. Before that, even after Dawie, we were here every two weeks. I suppose Evelyn was the last straw. Now everything seems almost as it was. Except for Dawie and Evelyn.'

'Mmmmmm,' they hummed.

'And the Lombaards of course,' Mrs Du Toit added.

'Of course.' At the mention of the Lombaards the flow of the conversation picked up again.

A year before, the Lombaards had caused a scandal in the valley that almost overshadowed the excitement of events in the country beyond the mountains. The Lombaards had owned and farmed Die Uitkyk for generations, until last year when the family fractured and the farm fell apart. Opinion was still divided over whose fault it had been. Mrs Joubert blamed Cathy Brookes, née Lombaard, for bringing the legacy of her family in Fransmansvallei to an end.

'She shouldn't have made such a fuss about it, but she couldn't leave him alone. Cathy brought her husband down and everything else with him. She has only herself to blame.'

'How ridiculous. That man pushed her too far. He brought it upon himself and dragged her down with him,' snapped Mrs Du Toit.

The rumours had started when a little boy was born to one of Cathy's black housemaids. Her light brown child was the spitting image of Stubb Brookes, Cathy's husband. The dorp was scandalised. Everyone whispered behind their closed front doors, though no one talked to Cathy Brookes about it; they just saw her in the dorp, growing thinner and more haggard with every week that passed. It wasn't long before the story filtered out that Cathy had thrown the girl off the farm and sent her back to the Transkei, baby and all. The atmosphere in the house was said to be poisonous. The housekeeper quit. Cathy sent her three daughters to boarding school and, after some weeks of speculation in the dorp, silence from the house and scandalous deterioration in the orchards, Stubb was thrown out and Cathy put the farm up for sale. She packed up everything and left not long after Stubb. Rumour had it she'd gone to Mauritius, but no one knew; she'd cut everyone off. Die Uitkyk had stood there like a ghost ever since.

'It's not the first time there's been goings-on in the packing sheds and it won't be the last. She should have turned a blind eye, like everyone else.' Mrs Joubert took a long sip from her glass. There was a distinct lull around her, as if everyone had agreed to a pause in the rhythm of their conversation and were now momentarily drawing breath. Mrs Du Toit pursed her lips and looked knowingly round the circle of her cronies.

Van Rensburg was very busy suddenly; the food was cooked and he was pulling the last of the meat off the braai, asking everyone to come to the table. Mrs Du Toit sniffed as she rose to her feet and the other tannies followed her example.

'Shame. Look at him now, he's gone so thin these last years. A man shouldn't have to live through what he's lived through. A farmer shouldn't have to lose a boy like that and then his wife too. That's losing everything – past, present, future . . . '

Her thin, liver-spotted hands flickered up and down for emphasis and the old ladies nodded and murmured their agreement. Mrs Joubert felt compelled to chip in with her summing-up. 'I suppose that's what's made Elise so, so . . . *mannish*.'

Hair-sprayed heads bobbed their agreement. 'Mmm.'

'Oh come, come, she's not so different from most young women nowadays. Young ladies aren't what they were in our day . . . '

This was, beyond doubt, an incontestable fact on which they could all agree. Mrs Du Toit had had the last word and that pleased her no end. 'Uhmmm,' the old ladies intoned and the sound rose up from them like the drone of bumble bees drifting up from the garden.

The table was a long one, set out so it ran parallel to the stoep, under the shade of the trellis of vines. Elise walked with Mrs Du Toit, supporting her a little.

'Now where shall I sit, my dear?'

Elise shrugged as she answered lightly, 'Oh, I don't mind. People can sit wherever they like.'

Madame tugged on Elise's arm, quite gently, but sufficiently to draw her future daughter-in-law's attention. The old lady's eyes twinkled and her mouth smiled as she delivered her quiet message. 'Now, as the matriarch of the family I think I deserve a certain place at table, don't you?'

Elise frowned, just slightly, but Mrs Du Toit was ready to enlighten her. With a barely perceptible dip of her chin and pointing of her eyebrows Madame indicated the head of the table.

'Of course! Of course, Mrs Du Toit. That's exactly where we'd like you to be.'

Elise steered the old lady towards the place she had chosen, pulled out the chair for her and offered her a serviette.

'Thank you, Elise.' She turned and smiled and Elise saw there was steel in Mrs Du Toit's twinkling old-lady eyes.

For the first time Elise suspected that Madame's charming, easy-going exterior hid a calculating, ruthless nature. Elise was, by nature and principle, plain-spoken. She believed that charm manipulates and conceals, no matter how appealing, and Daan was utterly charming. Elise had always thought the Du Toits' charm embodied something benign. She knew Madame was a racist, but that was beside the point; it made her no different from anyone else in the valley. Elise remembered her mother calling the older lady a social climber, selfish, an empire-builder, but coming from Evelyn this opinion seemed pretty rich and Elise had discounted it. On the day of her engagement she was suddenly no longer sure.

The wind caught the stiff white edges of the tablecloths, so they fluttered and flapped at the ends of the long table. Everyone had sat down to eat. There was wine and beer in their glasses and excellent food on their plates, and they all shared the unspoken knowledge that this was a good life they had. They were hard-working people, but once in a while there was a day on which they came together to rest and to enjoy the fruits of their work. Days like this were sacred.

Without Mama to help serve, Elise and Ina were doing the work of passing bowls of salad among the guests. When Elise caught sight of Madame craning her neck to scan the table, as if she was looking for something, she went over to help.

'Do you need anything?'

'No. Thank you, dear. I was just wondering where Betty and the other girls are.'

Elise set a plate of potato salad down in front of Madame. 'We had to send Betty home. The other girls went with her, to look after her.'

Madame pursed her lips. 'On this of all days? What on earth is the matter with her?'

She said this loudly, to attract the attention of the people sitting nearest to her, so they also heard Elise's reply: 'Shock. She's in shock because her son came home unexpectedly.'

Mrs Du Toit smiled haughtily, making an elaborate show of spreading her napkin across her lap. 'Well, I can't imagine what would become of us if I went into shock every time one of my sons came home unexpectedly.'

Even Elise laughed a little. She'd fed her the line – what could she expect? Mrs Du Toit loved to entertain.

'Well, he disappeared more than ten years ago. We all thought he was dead.'

Mrs Du Toit's expression changed. Now she was rapt. *'Really?'*

Daan, sitting on his mother's left, rested his hand in a proprietary way on Elise's waist and chipped in loudly. 'Oh my God! I forgot to tell you. Johnny and I saw this guy this morning. Up on the pass. He must have walked the whole way because he wouldn't take a lift from us. Cocky-looking oke.'

Tjaart Joubert broke off from a story he'd suddenly lost interest in telling. He leaned forward to grip his audience. 'Good Lord! Are you talking about the terrorist? The one who got away from that shoot-out just up the road – when was it? – seventy, no *eighty*-one – no?'

Daan nodded. 'That's the one.'

Most people remembered the story, and this new chapter in it sent a quiver of excitement along the table. Van Rensburg was shaking his head as he reached for the wine to top up his glass and those nearest to him. He declared coarsely, 'Bloody kaffir, almost ruined my braai. He better keep out of my way. We didn't want terrorists then and we don't want them here now!' That seemed to settle something and the conversation fragmented again.

Elise frowned, the bravado and the sentiment making her uncomfortable. She went inside to fetch more wine.

In Fransmansvallei the community was as small and entangled as the Platteland, like Karoo towns where everybody knows everybody and everybody's business. There was a sense too that they all had the right to know about this one's finances and that one's difficulties, this one's plans, that one's changes. Of course this information didn't flow freely; it was delivered through hearsay and gossip, but, as they say, 'Where there's smoke there's fire.' Towards Franschoek and Swellendam and Stellenbosch things had changed, the communities more fragmented, less claustrophobic. Not that there wasn't a great deal to fuss and gossip about. Everything the Cape farmers once held dear was endangered by the changes and many bitter words were spilled daily on the subject, but angry talk was inappropriate today. Elise certainly didn't want to hear any and she was glad that the conversation had moved on by the time she returned.

She poured wine into empty glasses. Somewhere along the table Ilsa Steyn could be heard making an acid comment about Stubb Brookes, who had been notoriously spendthrift as well as notoriously unfaithful to his wife.

'He was *so* big in the Broederbond and he took all the loans and tax breaks the government sent our way. The wife drove a Mercedes, the husband drove a Mercedes, even the oldest daughter had a brand-new Mercedes, for goodness' sake.

And now they say they've got one second-hand bakkie between the lot of them!' Ilsa Steyn was laughing so much she could hardly get the words out.

'But I heard they were living it up in Mauritius!' Mrs Joubert was shrill with indignation.

'Oh please, more like Mannenberg!'

This response caused much hilarity and Ilsa leaned back looking pleased with her contribution. Tjaart Joubert growled in agreement. 'They looked so rich but if you turned out their pockets only bus tickets would have fallen out.' This was another theory about the fall of the house of Lombaard. That they were bad farmers.

It was an old chestnut, a political game too, this subject of good farmers and bad. Piet van Rensburg was thought of as a good farmer, though almost no one ever said so. His harvests always rated top, or near to the top, in the co-op. He made money, but he didn't throw it around. He knew the land and he used caution and common sense in his business. He never borrowed for new cars or time shares in Knysna. He seemed like a good farmer should seem. And so he was allowed to opine on others. 'Whoever's taken Die Uitkyk will need to be one excellent farmer in order to make anything of the mess that family have left behind.' At this Tjaart Joubert stood up, his cheeks ruddy and his eyes merry from drinking, and bet a case of wine from his own estate that the new owner of Die Uitkyk would do the sensible thing – rip out his orchards and go over to vine.

Tjaart Joubert and his wife were generally a bit full of themselves. Tjaart's family seemed to have more money than anyone else and no one was sure if it was from loans or not. Most suspected it was not. They were the kind of people who would go on a trip into Cape Town and expect everyone to treat them like the big fish they were in the valley. They lived in the oldest and grandest Cape Dutch homestead in the valley. It was originally called, somewhat ironically it seemed now, Alles Verloren and had been built by Jacques van der Graaf near the tapering northern end of the valley, next to the Du Toit's farm. It was now called the Van der Graaf house, though its occupants were the Jouberts. Tjaart Joubert and his wife Etta made and sold an estate wine, also called Van der Graaf, that had lately been doing very well. Part of their success could be accounted for by increased overseas demand for South African wine. In fact lately things had been looking so good that Tjaart, who was famously loose-lipped, had even gone so far as to say on several occasions that if this was what the ANC could deliver then he'd be voting Mandela all the way next time round!

No one except Van Rensburg would take Tjaart up on his bet, because everyone suspected Joubert would win. Van Rensburg only bet him on principle. Die Uitkyk's orchards had once been some of the best and most fruitful in the valley and Van insisted it would be a sin to turn them over to vines, no matter how perfect the soil. Van persuaded Dominee Slabbert to give heavenly endorsement to his assertion and even the old tannies roared with laughter.

As usual the men dominated the conversation along the length of the table. The recent enormous hike in the value of land was a diamond mine for talk, if not for serious plunder. Everyone was wondering what the Lombaards' place had gone for. The Dominee said he'd heard a figure close to ten million and the women gasped in surprise.

'And it's such a small place!' declared Etta. 'There's hardly any point in farming it at all.'

Van Rensburg chuckled, though he disliked the Jouberts' boasting. He raised his glass towards Tjaart. 'Don't forget that I was offered nearly *six*. Million. We're not such small fry at this end of the valley . . . '

Tjaart lifted his glass in return salute. 'I'll drink to that!'

The laughter rolled down the table.

'Ag, but it's not about that, is it? This farm is priceless. I could never sell, you'd have to kill me first.'

Elise frowned slightly at the passion with which her father spoke. It was a frown not of disapproval, but of intense agreement. She was recalling the offer he'd referred to. It had come through a lawyer acting on behalf of an anonymous and evidently wealthy party and it had come quite out of the blue. Until that brief exchange of phone calls and letters with the lawyer the Van Rensburgs had never hinted at the possibility of a sale, nor had they received the slightest hint of interest from a potential purchaser. As far as they knew the prospective buyer had never even seen the place. Van Rensburg had taken the discussion a step or two further, but only out of an interest in the identity of the would-be purchaser. Negotiations ended with the lawyer insisting that he could not reveal his client's name and Van Rensburg explaining that Rustenvrede was not for sale, not at any price. It had been a curious episode in their lives and their fascination with the originator of the offer still lingered. He or she had become part of the legend of their farm. Most importantly for Elise that chapter had illuminated so much about her own and her father's values; different as they were in so many respects the bedrock was the same, literally.

'Another toast!' bellowed Tjaart.

While the men congratulated themselves the tannies were engaged in a quiet survey of the cast of characters around them. Elise turned to watch them, preferring to be amused by the sight of Mrs Joubert and Mrs Du Toit duelling than by the reruns among the men. From where she sat she couldn't hear what they were saying, which was fortunate since she wouldn't have liked it, though it would certainly have been of interest.

Mrs Joubert swallowed like an old crane and tapped a bony finger against Tannie de Jager's wine glass. Tannie de Jager was sitting opposite her, slugging back yet another sherry. She preferred the sweetness of it to wine.

'Where's your Madeleine today?'

Had she been sober Tannie de Jager would have been instantly alerted to trouble by Mrs Joubert's silky tone.

'Ag, Madeleine's busy with the hotel today.'

Mrs Joubert raised an eyebrow, a favourite and carefully practised trick of hers. 'But really, Tannie, everyone knows the hotel is so small it can look after itself!'

Madame Du Toit glared at Mrs Joubert, who went on regardless. 'It's a little *strange*, don't you think? Everyone else is here . . . I wonder what Madeleine is avoiding.'

'Or who!' blurted Tannie Steyn, whose complexion had turned from grey to florid since her arrival.

Mrs Du Toit's knife and fork landed in her half-empty plate with an ungraceful clank. 'Madeleine would *not* have been the right choice,' she said finally, and that seemed to close the subject, but Tannie de Jager looked confused.

'Choice for what?'

'For Daan, you silly woman!' Mrs Du Toit snapped. Mrs De Jager looked nonplussed. Tannie Steyn was getting out of hand, but Mrs Joubert was enjoying it. She turned a saccharine smile on Mrs Du Toit.

'Sophisticated Du Toit marries down-to-earth Van Rensburg. The rough with the smooth. I suppose I don't see why Madeleine would have been any better, or worse, in that respect.' The old lady paused and Mrs Du Toit waited with pursed lips.

'But there *is* something Madeleine lacks, isn't there?'

'Yes. Elise's beauty.' Madame smiled and raised her glass in a gesture of finality to Tannie Joubert.

Tannie Joubert raised hers in return as she intoned much too sweetly, 'And her land, my dear. To her land.'

Mrs Du Toit put her glass down and banged her hand on the table. She'd had enough. 'Really, Helmien! You are incorrigible!'

Tannie Joubert smiled naughtily and sipped her wine. From where she was sitting Elise saw this last part of their interaction and found the tableau sweetly amusing. Those old ladies are terrible, she thought, smiling.

When everyone had finished eating and the plates and the salad bowls and the baskets from the meal were put away, Ina carried out her fantastic melktert and Van Rensburg put a tiny liqueur glass down in front of every adult and poured each one a glass of sweet dessert wine. Murmurs of approval and pleasure at being treated to something so good from the farm cellar were hushed by Van who, after looking over at his daughter and receiving her small nod of approval, cleared his throat raspingly and, in a voice that felt suddenly reedy and dry and self-conscious, asked everyone to be quiet for a minute – there was something he wanted to say.

The children were hushed and the deafer of the tannies shushed and silence fell on the gathering. Elise looked at Daan, who was grinning at her from the other end of the table, and then around at the bright faces turned expectantly towards hers. She lowered her head and rubbed nervously at the ragged scar on her palm, a habit that was older than she could remember, because she couldn't remember the cut that had made that scar.

Standing next to his daughter, before all his friends and on such a happy day, Van Rensburg was suddenly at a loss for words. He looked round at all the expectant faces and then he laughed. 'You'll have to forgive me. I'm not good at this. If Evie had been here today she might have helped.'

His voice caught at the mention of her and he had to swallow hard to recover. Elise squeezed his hand and he flashed a smile down at her. Then he cleared his throat and went on. 'I've always believed that my daughter was the most beautiful girl in the Cape and it seems that I've finally found a man who agrees with me!'

This was met with a great deal of laughter. Mrs Du Toit put her hand over Daan's. She beamed approval.

'I'm sure you'll all agree when I say that Daan du Toit has always seemed like a man of fine judgement. Well, when he came to me and asked to marry my daughter, I began to wonder! I said to him, are you sure you know what you're taking on here?'

Another gale of laughter and Elise was caught up laughing too.

'Anyhow, he assured me he did and I said, in that case I'll be grateful if you would take her off my hands.'

Van Rensburg threw up his hands, grinning, then sat

70

down. The effect was an enormous rush of approval that swamped both Daan and Elise.

Daan took it all as if this was how he expected it should be, a lengthy surge of excitement that he rode with laughter and gurgles of pleasure. Elise spluttered with giggles and protests that only thinly veiled her defensiveness. A wedding in the valley was a big event and it belonged not to the bride and groom but to everyone. Everyone who mattered, that is. Elise knew she was handing herself over to the mob of a tiny farm society. That was part of the point: you surrendered to everyone else's excitement and traditions. But she'd harboured a vain hope that she might keep them at bay. 'No, we haven't set a date yet,' 'I'm sure it won't be for a while,' 'At least not till most of the picking is done,' 'Not till the end of the season,' 'No, it won't be a big wedding,' 'But of course it will be in the church' and 'Of course everyone is invited' and 'No, Tannie Joubert, before you say it, I am not pregnant!'

Elise lacked the grace that Daan and Ina wore instinctively. Daan saw her struggling with the moment and he stood up and strolled down the table to help her.

Daan was the youngest son and, as many youngest children are, he was the darling of all his brothers and sisters, in fact of the whole valley. He was Elise's junior by two and a half years. He had only just turned twenty-seven and in some ways was still working out his purpose in the world. This marriage was his first real opportunity to lay down the law about his own life and he intended to use it. Farming was in his blood, even if it didn't seem so compared with his brothers. It was all his family talked about and valued and knew. In marrying Elise he became a farmer and a land-owner. When he'd told his eldest brother of his plans to marry he felt his stature increase until his brother was almost looking straight, not down, at him.

Daan had been around at most of the celebrated occasions in the lives of the Van Rensburgs. He was there at Dawie's twenty-first, the night Ina and Dawie had announced their engagement, but then he was only a gawky adolescent and Elise was an unassailable young adult. She wouldn't even have looked at him then. Elise first noticed Daan only when she realised that he was so intent upon her and that was years later in Bloemfontein. There was an art to Daan's wooing, and a great deal of effort. It was the effort he made that had truly charmed her, that had finally won her over.

She had a passion that he lacked, while he had an easy-going nature that she envied. He'd been terrified she'd reject him, but he'd been willing to take the risk and he was almost floored by how she melted towards him.

For once, when he bent to kiss her in front of people, Elise didn't tense up and begin immediately to pull away. She let herself lean into his body as she did when they were alone. She felt completely sure of him at that moment and of her decision to join her life to a life as straightforward and as easy as Daan's. She, who always felt too complex, too burdened by past pain and struggle and grief, felt at last that she might unburden herself. She was casting off that old skin and stepping lightly forward into a new life with this charming man whose voice had become as familiar to her as her own, whose body was the greatest comfort she had known and whose expressed greatest wish was to spend his life with her. Elise saw marriage as a space into which she could retreat from the glare of neighbours' scrutiny and the tangle of other people's lives.

Willem Slabbert's deep and sonorous tone boomed through the hubbub. 'Words fail me!' They gave way and let him speak for all of them. 'Words fail me. Nevertheless . . . ' Laughter rolled round the table. 'Nevertheless, I cannot let such happy news go without remark. I think I speak for everyone when I say that your engagement is a signal of hope, of continuity here in Fransmanshoek. We have all come through a difficult time, but you in particular, Elise, you and your father have suffered so the pleasure this happy an-nouncement gives me is all the greater.' The Dominee paused here, looking up into the sky. Then he smiled broadly and lowered his gaze. 'I insist that I marry you and I insist that you all raise your glasses to toast Elise and Daan!'

Everyone did as they were ordered to and raised their glasses to drink to 'Elise and Daan and the future'. Elise bit on her lip, moved by the detail of the sun catching on crystal and the sweet wine glowing pale gold in each glass.

Elise turned towards her father, but his eyes were cast down at the tablecloth and as usual he betrayed little of what he felt beyond the benign smile he so often wore like a mask. She wanted very much to know what he was thinking.

Van Rensburg was thinking that the only true pleasure he took from life now came from the rhythm of the land he farmed. He knew the flow, the needs, the fruits of this piece of the earth as well as he knew the rhythms of his own body. He had renewed his relationship with Elise over this land. Through her love for it he had come to know her and to need her again. Elise's wish to live and work on this land restored to Van Rensburg the certainty and hope that his farm would survive and flourish in his family, even long after he was gone. Her engagement to Daan was like a certificate, a guarantee, an assurance of all that. On that Sunday afternoon he felt so full with renewed hope, so awash in this surging sense of continuing life that he couldn't look up; he didn't want his daughter or anyone else to see the tears standing in his eyes, so he looked down at the brilliant white of the tablecloth and smiled benignly.

EIGHT

Mama Mashiya was tiring of all the talking, of the press of people around them. She wanted to be left alone for a while and she persuaded her husband and Sandile to come inside from the sun and the chattering neighbours. The two men sat down in the big room which was kitchen and dining and sitting room and the heart of the house. Sandile felt calmer here inside the house. The quiet allowed the strangeness of everything to settle a little.

Everything in his parents' house was painstakingly scrubbed and literally shone. Mama had covered the sofa with a washable plastic slip in a mustard check pattern, with a little diamond-shaped flower inside each of the squares. The plastic was functional. This was, after all, a farm cottage and the great enemy of every farm household is the mud and dirt that treks in from the outside at the end of every day. The dust, the animal shit, the blood, the tractor grease, all were tireless enemies, but in Mama they had found an inexhaustible adversary.

Mama touched the soft, starchy collar of Sandile's shirt and said softly to him, 'My son . . . '

Sandile looked up at her. She was standing at his shoulder, the light streaming from behind her so that all he could see of her face was her eyes glistening darkly. When she spoke her tentative voice told everything, betraying a fear that had only now washed over her – the fear that she might lose him again.

'My son, are you married?'

It was the last thing he expected her to say and a snort of laughter escaped him as he shook his head. 'No, no, no. I am not married!' Mama didn't move. The silhouette of her head was absolutely still, but her words wobbled. 'Then . . . where are you living now?'

Sandile felt the enormous weight of her hopes ballooning outwards and pressing against him. The explanations he owed her were infinite. 'Mama, my home is here.'

She paused and her hand rested on his shoulder. 'But where are your things?'

'These are my things.' He pointed to the clothes he was wearing and to the small bag by the door. 'This is all I have. I have only ever gathered what I could carry. I've been . . . I've always been travelling back here, back home.' Sandile's voice nearly broke, it sank and cracked, grating over the dryness in his throat so that the words felt like gravel.

Mama withdrew her hand from his shoulder. Ben Mashiya shifted in his chair and the only sound in the room was the crack and whisper of a match igniting. His father's eyes were cast down and unreadable as he brought the match towards his face and lit his pipe. Sandile looked at both of them and realised they wouldn't ask the question, couldn't ask him to do what their hearts ached for him to do, to stay and never leave them again. They wouldn't force his hand in any decision, they wouldn't try to make him change the course of his life to run with the flow of theirs. This was how they survived, quietly, stoically. This was his mother and father's way. They let the heaviness, the pain, the burdens of their life sit between them and around them in the house. They didn't struggle any more to try to change the nature of things; they knew such struggle was in vain. They had nurtured so many dreams, only to watch them die in the nightmare of apartheid. They had learned that they could make no impression on the shape of things, so they knew not to tire themselves with trying, knew they had just enough strength, if they kept very still and very quiet, to bear the pain of it.

Mama shook her head. She was smiling, taking in the room that was transformed for ever by this day. Sandile smiled reassuringly back at her. 'I want to stay, Mama.'

75

She clapped her hands over her mouth, perhaps so as not to let out the cry that nearly escaped her. What she longed for would be. Her wonderful dream was not to end as quickly and as abruptly as it began. Oupa Mashiya sucked on his pipe, its cup glowing deep amber. His milky gaze caught Sandile's and then he looked away again. It seemed to Sandile that there was shame in that look, that his father felt ashamed.

Oupa took the pipe from his mouth. 'I had given up hope,' he murmured. 'I should not have given up hope.'

His father was so slight, so crumpled there in his chair. He was not at all as Sandile remembered him, no longer that tall terrifying man with a body as strong and hard as granite. He had carried himself then with a quiet, certain pride. He was the unbreakable one, the one Van Rensburg never dared to hit, the one Van Rensburg trusted with his life and the man that the other men came to for advice and help and leadership. Somewhere along the line he had become Oupa instead of Ben. Somewhere in those lost intervening years Ben Mashiya's pride had been broken, his dignity eroded.

An old wild anger burst inside Sandile, like a tree in smouldering veld can suddenly explode into flames. He stood up and almost flung out the words he'd meant to save for later. 'Father.'

Oupa Mashiya jerked his chin up to meet his son's gaze and Sandile caught himself. The atmosphere was already overloaded; how could he make it any heavier? But he was too angry to hold back completely, so he sat down again and part of what he'd almost said stumbled out. 'There *is* something I've come here to do.' Sandile shifted in his seat, looking first up at his mother and then at his father, who were visibly bracing themselves for his words. 'I've come to reclaim our land.'

His father shook his head warily. He didn't know precisely what Sandile had in mind, but he knew it wasn't good. He dared not ask this big, smartly dressed, well-spoken man, this stranger, this son of his, exactly what he meant. So Oupa

Mashiya decided that if he was quiet enough Sandile's meaning would emerge.

Mama Mashiya broke the silence, cutting through the questions that hung unspoken in the room. This was not the time for such conversation. 'Another time,' she said mildly, and after a few moments Sandile smiled. 'Yes, another time.'

He sat back in the chair. Silence intervened again, but this time it was too tense – Sandile had to break it. He asked brightly about the new cottages and his parents gladly stood up to show him.

From the back the new dwellings looked less regular than they did from the front. Each one had its own stoep; some were surrounded with plants, others were covered in dripping washing, one or two were stark and dusty and littered with junk. But there was something else: each house had a cube-shaped room that jutted out at the back and inside that cube was a bathroom. The fittings were absolutely basic landlord-quality fittings, but to Mama Mashiya they were a luxury she'd never believed she would enjoy in her own home. Most marvellous of all, better even than the electricity that ran through all the rooms, was the hot water that gushed from the taps. Mama explained to Sandile that when Elise came back from Bloemfontein she brought a lot of new ideas with her and it was she who'd had the old compound levelled and had personally supervised the building of these brand-new electrified hot-water houses.

Sandile was still a little shocked at how small and how poor the place was and yet there was no doubt that this house was better than the dwelling it had replaced. He understood his mother's pride in the place, but felt a stab of irritation, almost anger, at it too. This offering from the Van Rensburgs was a sweetened, but still harsh pill. It was comfort to cover up for the fact that this was stolen land, his mother and father's land. They should have had a house on it like the homestead just a short walk down the mountain, but he couldn't say that to her, not now – not yet.

Their tour was almost at an end when they were interrupted

by Lucky, who came racing up to announce that visitors had arrived. Mama tutted – she was getting tired of the circus – but Lucky blurted out that it was 'Missylees' and Mama suddenly brightened. She smoothed her apron and walked round to the front to greet Elise, but Oupa Mashiya simply sat down on the chair that had been put out for him earlier and sucked on his pipe while he stared at his garden.

Sandile stood looking around at the yard and the sun-flowers and his smiling father. Ben Mashiya could see his son was unhappy about this interruption. He waved his pipe, gesturing for him to follow Mama, but Sandile hovered uncomfortably.

'You should be nice to Elise.'

'Why?' Sandile meant this quite seriously.

His father was taken aback.

'She's never been nice to us,' Sandile continued flatly.

His father's eyes narrowed. 'She's been *very* good to us!' Ben insisted with a finality that told him to be wary on this subject. It was a moment that jarred, but only a moment. Sandile backed down, for now. Elise, after all, was a daughter of the family that had taken his land. It was her betrayal that had led to that beating he would never forget. It was her brutal father who had taken his parents' land and banished them and their offspring to poverty and hard work. He and Elise would be on opposite sides in the battle ahead. Thinking of that Sandile felt an oddly vengeful and manipulative interest in seeing her again. This was an opportunity to face his adversary while he was still very much in control.

Sandile followed his mother out of curiosity, wondering what had occasioned this visit and whether or not it was a new habit of the Van Rensburgs'. He rounded the corner just as Elise pulled up into the compound. With her was a tall slender woman whom Sandile didn't recognise.

Elise embraced Mama Mashiya, then held her at arm's length, regarding her with affectionate concern. 'Are you OK now, Mama?'

Mama laughed, as if to say that she'd never been more OK

in her life. Elise smiled and turned to Sandile. 'Hello.'

Sandile returned her look, but didn't say anything. He simply nodded and stared.

Her expression shifted; she seemed suddenly unsure of herself. 'I hope we're not interrupting . . . '

She looked from Sandile to Mama. She interpreted his silence as mild disdain. She hadn't meant to intrude, but perhaps, unwittingly, she had.

Elise said she didn't want to stop long, she just wanted to make sure that everything was all right, and she'd brought some food for them. Mama laughed again and put her arm through Elise's.

'Yes, everything is all right. Everything is *overflowing* with happiness! Now. You must come in for a cooldrink.' Elise glanced at Ina who looked distinctly underwhelmed by the idea, but Mama insisted and shooed them inside.

Ina went in reluctantly and hovered uncomfortably by the door, continuing to stand there even when invited to sit down. Mama pressed Elise into a chair at the table, opposite Sandile, who was watching the scene with bemused curiosity. He couldn't avoid noticing how uncomfortable Ina was, as if even the air was slightly soiled. The way she stood in this room reminded Sandile of what, as a child, he'd thought was intrinsically a white person's way. She had the stoical and patronising manner of one who will endure the disgusting and alien atmosphere of what she would call kitsch, of the smell of cheap soap, the clamour of uncoordinated colours, the smallness of the room, the rawness of naked breeze-block walls. Sandile's upper lip curled slightly. He wondered how she would stand up to the stench of true poverty as he watched her sip meekly from the plastic beaker of lemonade that Mama served. From the look on her face she was evidently surprised to find that it was extremely good and said so.

'Mmm, this is delicious, Mama. I should get you to make some of this for Hemel en Aarde.'

'Thank you, thank you, my child,' Mama muttered as she bustled off to fetch another jug.

'Mama, aren't you going to congratulate Elise?' Ina said teasingly.

Mama put her hands up to her face, remembering suddenly that there had been occasion to celebrate down at the main house as well as up here at her own.

'Ooh, congratulations, my child! I nearly forgot. Congratulations!' She bounced round the table to give Elise a smothering hug.

'What's the occasion?'

Both Ina and Elise started slightly. It was the first time Sandile had uttered a syllable.

He smiled suddenly back at them.

'Elise got engaged today.' Ina couldn't suppress a proud grin as she reported this. Elise actually blushed.

'Well, then. Congratulations,' he said quietly.

Elise looked away. His gaze was so intense that she blushed again. She was eager, like everyone else, to know where Sandile had been and where he was going now, but it didn't seem right to ask.

Sandile couldn't help being struck by her, by the warmth in her eyes, couldn't help noticing the tiny lines at her mouth when she laughed, the way she sat so comfortably in his house. As she talked to Mama about the party down at the house, Sandile watched, sizing her up. His eyes were wary, the eyes of a fighter measuring his opponent. He noticed how Elise moved, minimally yet with an innate grace. She had a statuesque quality, a stillness that he would never have expected of the child he'd known. Perhaps something, or someone has stilled her, he thought. Her quietness, her warmth could only make her more dangerous.

Mama was effervescent, proudly showing off her son. She recalled the moments of his arrival, her own shock at his homecoming, and rocked with laughter and amazement at it all. 'And you know we don't even know where he's been, we don't know anything except he says he's not married. Can you believe this beautiful big man isn't married?'

Elise laughed, amused by the question. But she looked hard

at Sandile and shook her head, agreeing with Mama. He was a beautiful man, if rather severe and a touch disapproving. Even Ina was drawn to him, though Elise could tell she was perplexed by her fascination.

He looked as if he'd done well for himself; he had a self-assurance that didn't just project from his solid, muscular frame. His face had the same strong lines and curves as his body. His light brown eyes were never still. He took note of everything with those eyes, but didn't comment much. Mysterious, she thought, but then he always was.

'Will you be staying long?' she asked, cupping her chin in one hand.

Sandile looked from Elise to his mother and back, then he shrugged and said ambiguously, 'Well, I don't have any plans to leave right now.'

Everyone drank their cooldrinks rather too quickly, but Sandile didn't touch his. He sat there, still and silent at the centre of their attention.

Ina finished her lemonade and put her beaker down on the table as a signal that she was ready to go.

Then Sandile said suddenly and rather bluntly to Elise, 'I suppose your brother is running things now.' He felt the chill instantly. The lightness in her eyes died. Everyone seemed to shift. Mama moved away from the table to rinse the tumblers under the tap in the sink. Elise blinked, her eyelids fluttering in the confusion of this sudden shift.

Ina spoke, tensely, with an edge to her voice that said Sandile should have known, but even if he hadn't known he shouldn't be asking such personal questions so bluntly. 'We lost Dawie years ago now.'

Elise was nodding in the pointless way that people do in moments of unselfconscious discomfort or pain. 'He's dead,' she said. 'Killed in Angola.' And she went on nodding. Typical Elise, stripping life of euphemism and laying it starkly before everyone.

Then she smiled abruptly, shone that bright, piercing gaze on him again. 'But where were *you*? We've all wondered . . .

imagined you in so many places . . . ' She didn't say they'd also imagined him dead, but she saw he knew that already.

Sandile looked down at the table in front of him, shrugging because he didn't know where to begin, then his gaze flicked back up to meet hers. 'Lusaka, London. Then Lusaka and London again.'

'Wow!' Elise bubbled, impressed. 'I've never even been overseas. What's London like? I'd love to see some of those old places, the Tower of London and Trafalgar Square and Buckingham Palace. Did you see those places?'

Sandile's eyes narrowed. All attention in the room was focused on him and he could feel their expectations. They saw friendly bobbies and picturesque palaces, none of which he'd ever seen. How could he explain to them the cold of exile? How could he make them feel the torpor of London in the 1980s, of passing time watching the planes crisscrossing the city's skies? Grey clouds scudding endlessly over the afternoons, skimming the chimneytops, squadrons of them; a blanket of drizzle clinging always to the tops of the tall brown houses. How could he describe the taste of the day when he stopped looking up at the sky and cast his gaze down instead on the forever water-washed, rain-soaked concrete and tar of those streets, forgetting how long ago it was that the chill first seeped through his jersey, under his shirt and into his blood? How could he convey to them the ever-dampness that turned his skin to tight, cold wax and deadened his heart?

He stared across the table at Elise. She leaned forward encouragingly, eagerly; she really wanted to know. She, who was one of those people who had sent him into exile, wanted to know what it was like.

Sandile shook his head then leaned forward. His voice rose suddenly. 'It was cold and harsh and the people were cold and harsh. Yes, I saw Trafalgar Square. I was standing there once, in the rain and this Brit said to me "Go 'ome wog!" It was the Brits, you know, who taught your people everything they ever needed to know about racism, you Afrikaners just gave it a name. "Go 'ome wog!" That's kaffir to *you*!' Sandile grinned provocatively, looking straight at Ina and then from Ina to Elise. Ina looked away, embarrassed, which was what he'd intended, but Elise held his gaze, as if she understood that exile was like being divorced from yourself. As if she was sizing him up, perhaps not as pointedly or purposefully as he was doing with her, but sizing him up nevertheless. Behind that beautiful surface, that easy smile, those smiling eyes, there was a depth Sandile realised he had yet to fathom.

A silence descended. Sandile watched for their reactions. His mother and father shook their heads, but there was no surprise there, not like the surprise on Ina's face, which was mixed with dislike. And Elise – Elise's expression had dulled, as if she'd frozen. Good, he thought, at least he'd flummoxed her. Never let an opponent think they know where you're coming from.

Elise's mind had one of those useful automatic trip switches that can flip thoughts away from the difficult to the dull in a microsecond, and it kicked in just then when she noticed that Mama Mashiya's house was furnished with things that had once lived down in the main house. Her eye fell on a misty mirror, tall and narrow, with a scrolled-gold-effect frame that had once been the centrepiece of her mother's dressing room. The floor was gold-flecked black and white linoleum squares, leftovers from a kitchen redecoration. And there was the marbled yellow Formica-topped table with its now battered chrome edging. The aged-effect leatherette mustard chairs, seats and backs all padded and puffed up with shiny plastic buttons in a pattern. Even the salt and pepper shakers, glass with chrome screw-on tops, were from the house and stood as they once did in the kitchen at Rustenvrede, grouped together with the plastic vinegar dispenser, dark yellow with a shiny metal top, and that fat little plastic red tomato with its plastic green leaves where the tomato sauce came out. Elise smiled when she saw that: she had coveted that tomato as a child. Suddenly she remembered the food. 'Oh my God, the meat! We've brought you meat – so you can celebrate tonight!' They all marched outside to fetch Elise's gift from the truck.

She had brought an apple crate filled with a packet of lamb chops, a bag of mielie meal and another of onions, and two fat multilitre bottles of Coke. Mama Mashiya positively beamed with gratitude when she saw it. Elise handed the crate to Mama, not to Sandile. In fact he noticed that she was careful to avoid his gaze. His anger had disquieted her. She squeezed Mama's arm and then glanced briefly at Sandile as she bid them goodbye.

'Thanks so much for the cooldrink. And welcome home, Sandile. I'm sure I don't have to tell you how happy this has made your mother and father.'

Sandile bit down on his lip as he dipped his chin in acknowledgement of her words. Her sincerity was plain and he suddenly regretted the way he'd behaved inside the house. Elise had come to his parents, and to him, in a spirit of celebration and generosity and he had answered her with suspicion and animosity. But there was nothing he could say now; an apology would have seemed odd.

Elise felt Sandile's eyes on her as she and Ina climbed into the bakkie and drove off, waving back to the children and scattering dogs and chickens right and left as they bounced down the track. What a strange day, she thought, what a strange man. Perhaps he would lighten up over time, perhaps not. The most important thing was the miracle that this was for Mama.

Sandile turned back towards his house and his neighbours. Night was falling. The meat was sizzling on the fire and nearly everyone had some more wine. Vuyo brought a radio from his house and turned it up to full volume, so that the music blasted over the laughter and chatter and spurred people to their feet to dance. It was a feast no one would forget in a long while.

Sandile sat and watched from an old red leather car seat which was propped up against the wall, and the youngest children stared at him and sometimes came shyly forward to touch him, then faded away, giggling and full of awe. He leaned his head back and the sunset colours of the Cape seemed even more vibrant than he remembered. And there was that sound, the soft cooing of the doves, which had been so faint and ungraspable, like a memory of music too faint to hear in those far-off cold winters.

He had come here from another world. One that was apart from, that might collide with, but that could never comfortably meet this world. That was clear to him after Elise and Ina's visit. Strange. That was what had been so unpleasant about exile, his apartness. He sighed. Being apart was exile and its legacy.

There was a man in Trafalgar Square who stood very straight and still under a pub umbrella encrusted with pigeon shit. Once every fifteen minutes or so he would jerk an arm out from under his awning and poke a stick at the crowd of pigeons that had grown since last he shooed them away. He was defending his livelihood, the little paper bags of birdseed he sold to the children and old men who came there, like Sandile, to while away the days. But on that day the rain dripped heavily all around him and nobody wanted to feed the birds, so the pigeons huddled round in damp disgruntlement. They didn't see him, though he'd been there for hours passing time with them in the rain. He'd escaped the mean square of grey brick that was the view from his window, the two thin orange bars of the heater, the meagreness of a half-dead card table and a purple Formica chair and no heart to read at it, write at it, even to sit at it. He'd come there to stare at that mirage of his country, that doorway into a parallel universe, that hulking advertisement of the truth, that building put here to tell Sandile his nightmare was not a dream.

He had never been inside South Africa House, and on bleak days like that one it seemed like he never would go nearer it. Not even to stand for a while with the pickets, that huddle of white Brits with their armour of anger and little tin badges and anti-apartheid banners. They looked as ruffled and damp and depressing and as pointless as the pigeons. When he'd looked enough Sandile turned to leave. As he walked away, he nodded sympathetically to the pigeon-seed man, but he didn't respond – and Sandile was increasingly persuaded by his theory that he was becoming invisible, that he was literally fading away, so the relief was enormous when he heard him speak, when the pigeon-seed man spat loudly at Sandile's back, 'Go 'ome, wog.'

Sandile turned round, smiling hugely at him. The fact of his existence had been confirmed and he was immensely grateful. But that thin-lipped, bitter, bile-filled pigeon-seed man was looking away. Staring stiffly at the rain from underneath his canopy of pigeon shit.

It hadn't started out that way. In the beginning London was an explosion of discoveries. He'd arrived at the start of a beautiful, mild autumn and taken up his place at University College, London. Sandile's scholarship was a big prize and he knew it meant that he was being groomed by the ANC for greater things. University conjured up for him images of swift-tongued, sharp-witted men and women bent on the great and important work of ideas. University was the place where you were given that most precious of all things, education – and education was power.

He began his studies with enormous excitement and pride, working harder than everyone else in his class, fitting into the immense bustle of the place without even a glimmer of doubt about his own significance in it. Sandile had felt himself growing larger as a person, settling into the cavernous university, forcing his teachers to engage with him. As far as he could tell his teachers only read and wrote books about politics; they never engaged in politicking. Their approach to the subject was remote and puzzling, as if they were looking for the traces of alien tyre tracks in a distant solar system and not rooting through the junk of their own back yard. Nevertheless, Sandile had never been so stretched intellectually and for that he was more than grateful.

His letters to Selina, the only woman he had ever called a girlfriend, were long, breathlessly scribbled lists of books and lectures and lecturers, streets, museums and monuments and movies. Selina wrote back from the ANC office in

Mozambique, describing the tedium and deprivation of her life in the midst of a war zone, saying she was deeply envious, that he'd better get hold of a camera and start sending her pictures so that she could share it all. But above all she wanted to know what the people were like: had he made any friends, were those Brits really as chilly as their reputation?

Sandile had quickly developed a quiet, ironic disdain for 'the Brits'. He laughed at the students who accosted him in corridors with their copies of *Socialist Worker* and *Socialist Organiser*. There could never be a revolution here, not in the muddy pudding of their politics, he argued. Yet, looking back, he realised that there had been a revolution occurring under his very nose. Thatcherism had transformed everything. He'd failed to recognise it because this change didn't come by AK47s and bombs and it didn't come overnight as the Socialist Workers insisted it would. They were revolutionaries, those Brits, but they conducted their revolutions according to the subtle codes of their impenetrable culture. Years later Sandile watched elections in Europe with more curiosity than disdain and found himself inexpressibly moved by the bloodless shifts of government after elections. It was this bloodlessness that he came to value more than he ever thought he would.

Sandile was older by a couple of years than the people in his classes, but their experience divided them by continents. They were boys and girls from all over, Guildford and Glasgow and Brixton and Blyth. Their parents were middle-class and working-class and a few were even enormously wealthy, but still they shared a cultural frame of reference that started with *The Magic Roundabout* and ended with *The Tube*, all the way from Harold Wilson to Margaret Thatcher. Their battles were those they'd fought with parents over the number of holes they pierced in their ears and how often and how late they could go out to the pub. Their nightmares were as real and as terrible as their parents divorcing, dogs being run over, beloved grandmothers dying quietly of old age. For a time, when he tried to share his own battles and his own nightmares, he seemed either to scare people, to literally strike them dumb with horror, or to excite some vicarious sense of danger in them. Either way he felt uncomfortable and he soon learned to soften his impact, to adjust towards others. It was a new way of being, a kind of translation of himself, that he described to Selina as chameleon.

Sandile was treated as an outsider by whites in his own country, but he had never felt truly 'foreign', a word he had never heard much before but which so often formed itself on the tight lips of the Brits, until he went to London. Sandile had expected to be stimulated, excited by crossing this gap into another culture and in time he was, but at first it stunned him, made him defensive about his own suddenly ill-defined identity. It was harder than he'd imagined it would be, but there was no limit to the energy with which he attacked life and so he rode through it until years had passed and he woke up one day to the sense that the worst was over: London was now more familiar to him than anywhere else; he'd made it his own.

He found strength, and sometimes a refuge from strangeness, in his work for the ANC. In the office there was a common frame of reference; there was no need to translate, for he shared with his comrades the same struggle, that bottom line to which he would come to cling as desperately as a man clings to a raft in rapids. At first he helped out with simple office duties over weekends, but in time he was given more and more responsibility until, politically, he was something of a rising star. So in the first few years Sandile's life was full. He was always busy, always meeting, always learning, but his solace and his greatest pleasure were his letters from Selina.

Selina was brought to the farm late one night, ferried straight from the President's office in Lusaka. She'd driven up from Gaberone with one of the staff and hadn't spoken a word in all the days they were on the road. Her silence continued after she arrived. She never averted her eyes – they blazed out of the grey paleness of her face, watching everyone – but she didn't move her lips or make any sound at all.

Sandile was assigned to keep an eye on her between debriefing sessions. Her debriefers quickly grew irritated and by the fourth day they would stay for only a few minutes of her silence. Sandile talked to her, telling her the story of his home, of his farm. After a time he too had become tired of the sound of his own voice droning on in lengthy monologues. Then the silence became too much, so one day he stood up and said he could take it no more, he was going for a walk. He set off along the track he knew well now, not looking back to see if she was there. He had begun not to care what had happened to silence her. The scuff of her footsteps on the path behind him told him she was following.

They had walked for nearly an hour. At the top of a small hill, the only hill for miles around, the track widened out on to a flat saddle between two low koppies. He stopped and she came up alongside him. This was where he liked to sit and rest and look out down across the plain and the river snaking through it in the far distance. The river was so far away that on most days it was invisible on the distant shimmer of the horizon. Today they could see it – a thin blue line below the crystal-clear sky. Selina was breathless, but she said quite suddenly and quite naturally, 'Wow!'

Sandile moved his head very slowly round to look at her. He was struck dumb by her speech, then he nodded and laughed and she laughed too, and for a while they couldn't stop giggling. The sound of their laughter bounced and echoed around the bowl of the saddle. Then at last she said her name was Selina and in a very formal way she extended her hand towards his and they shook hands on the hilltop with the wild sweep of savannah before them. 'Sandile,' he replied, but she knew that already. 'Your voice is so light,' he said, surprised.

Selina and Sandile became friends and then lovers. She told him that she came from a small township in Bophutatswana, near the border with Botswana. She had sometimes acted as a guide for people who were brought to her by a comrade whose name she did not know. She would walk with these people by night, over the border into Botswana and then back, alone, to her house and her sleeping family. It was a walk of several hours. One night Selina and the exhausted young white man she was guiding were stopped by a border patrol and arrested. They were taken to Kopfontein, to the South African border post. Selina never saw or heard of the young white man again. One of her debriefers in Zambia emitted a disgusted snort when she told him this and said bitterly that he was probably chugging Castle lager in a bar with his mates that very night, congratulating himself on the capture of another 'terr'.

Selina told her debriefers and Sandile that she was inter-rogated and badly beaten up at Kopfontein, but that she had managed to escape on the second night and walked all the way to Gaberone. She never told anyone the truth of what happened to her at the border post – it was a secret she took to her grave. She was chained up and raped by the four white men who had brought her there. Three of them were not yet twenty, but the fourth was as old as her father, with a thick wedding ring on his finger. He had screamed at her as he fucked her and sometimes the shape of his mouth and the word 'kaffir' that emerged from it were repeated over and over in her dreams. On the second night they were drinking hard and the older man, Steenkamp, made a braai. It was late and they were so drunk they could barely stand but one of them staggered into the cell and unchained her. She was led outside to the fire, where Steenkamp grabbed hold of her arm and tried to push her down on the ground. Somehow, because he was drunk and she was determined, Selina pulled away from him and ran blindly into the bush.

The night was pitch-black. Thorns scratched at her skin. She had no idea where she was going. There were angry shouts not far behind her, then shots. She struggled to breathe, her chest so tight she thought it would burst, but she told herself to keep running till they killed her. The shouts receded, the still night enveloped her and Selina ran on. She knew she was safe when she came to a familiar stream and realised she was in Botswana.

She had been given a name and address by the comrade who brought the 'clients' for her moonlit walks. She gave the address to the priest who saw her on the road, stopped his car and kindly insisted on taking her home, wherever that might be. At the house she gave the name, but the suspicious man who came to the door said there was no such person there. She insisted that this was the address and the name. He said he would make some enquiries and let her sit on a sofa on the stoep. When she woke up she was in the hands of the ANC.

It was only when Selina was posted for further training and an assignment in Mozambique that Sandile had realised the extent of his feelings for her. Selina had introduced him to the wonderful company of women. With her he could express what he felt, reveal his emotions, without her ever thinking him weak. He knew she valued him not for the feelings he could suppress, but for the feelings he could show. They never talked about the future – ties like marriage were unavailable, certainly untenable, in the lives they lived. When they parted it was without tears and with the certainty that distance would not change their feelings for one another. They wrote to each other all the time, though they never wrote of love or of other lovers. Sandile did have other lovers and he assumed it must be so for her. Selina was his one true friend, and the letters they exchanged were his greatest pleasure. In the last letter she wrote that she missed him, that he was 'the most disconcerting man' she'd ever met.

In London he had long ago formed the habit of going to the Students' Union every morning. The breakfast there was big and cheap and he read the newspapers while he ate. It was his favourite, the *Guardian*, which told him of Selina's death. The news merited only a short paragraph in the summary of international events. She'd been killed the day before in Maputo by a parcel bomb that exploded in her face while she was opening the morning mail.

Yesterday morning. A bomb exploded in her face. A bomb in her face in Mozambique. Sandile let his hand fall and scalding coffee slooshed over the table and over his lap and his legs. But he was completely numb; he felt nothing. His eyes flicked back and forth over the lines of the newsprint and there was a voice in his head screaming, no, this isn't possible. His grip on reality snapped. His lifeline was cut. He was adrift in the rapids with nothing left to hold on to. Sandile knew then that there wasn't even a shred of justice in the world. All sense and joy vanished from his life in the instant he read about the bomb that had blown her away. From that moment on, and for a long time after, it was all he could do to hold himself together.

London became a chapter of yearning. It was a desolate time in the struggle, too. Sandile felt imprisoned by cold, excluded from intimate contact by the impossible subtleties of the British and sapped slowly of any sense of purpose. Looking back, it seemed the years went by like days. But each day dragged on as long as a year. As he plodded the streets in ever-tightening circles of despair, a line from a poem kept spinning through his head: 'their branches dry like steel . . . dry like wire . . . like wire . . . ' He wondered why Serote had chosen that maddening word, for there was nothing dry here. It was a word for another exile.

The dream that kept Sandile going was a dream of returning. He imagined himself striding triumphantly into the valley where he grew up, back into the arms of his mother and father, brother and sisters. He dreamed of the day when his family's land in the Cape he so loved would be restored to them. He would take back the farm that had been stolen from them and build a homestead where his mother and father could grow old in comfort, where they could spend their final days side by side on the stoep looking out at the sun going down behind the mountains and at the fields of the valley where their children worked and the garden where their grandchildren played. Sandile dreamed of peace.

But peace didn't come. On the inside the network of police and legislation was indefatigable, seemed at times omnipresent, omniscient. On the outside there were infiltrators and spies and counter-spies. Bullets and bombs rained on ANC units in Botswana and Lesotho and Zambia. There were precious moments of hope, events that gave a sense that the monolith was cracking. In the townships a fire was raging that wouldn't die and there was a new name for a new kind of power, the necklace. But from where he was, with the ANC pushed back behind the front-line states, it seemed to Sandile that there was a river of terrorised girls and boys fleeing the brutal embrace of apartheid into the harsh arms of exile. Most news was of arrests and detentions and death.

Five years had passed and still he was stuck in London. Apartheid's total onslaught ground down his hopes and slowly shredded his fantasies. He stopped daydreaming and tried cheerfully to grit his teeth, to face the reality that the battle would be harder and longer than anyone knew. Still, the hopelessness he'd begun to feel then was nothing to the hopelessness that crippled him later.

Sandile finished his BA, graduating with Honours, so he registered for an MA and was almost finished with that when he decided it was time for him to move. He had joined the information department in the London office and he travelled throughout Britain and across Europe, speaking at meetings, liaising with members and organisations in the growing anti-apartheid movement, briefing workers from the European offices. He was at the centre of the widening sanctions campaign, working himself into the ground, filling his hours with activity in order to stave off the depression and loneliness that had crashed in on him on the day he read of Selina's death.

It was so long since he'd felt the stirring of it that Sandile had forgotten something precious to him, and that was his once insatiable old friend, curiosity. He lacked any curiosity about himself and what he was feeling, about what lay inside books beyond the arguments and ideas he needed to organise into essays. Curiosity that once would have led him to discover the sensation of his fingers on a pretty woman's hair, the texture of her skin, what made her eyes so locked on his. He took pleasure only in the beginning and end of each day, in the appearance and disappearance of light, and he measured that joy out in careful portions, as if too much sensation would knock him out.

His senses were so dulled he could barely even taste food. The past had poisoned his present. It had overwhelmed everything. Sex was as long forgotten as all the pleasure and astonishment and curiosity of feeling alive. Sandile had no idea how beautiful he was as he spoke evenly, undramatically, of the struggle and what people could do to help. He didn't realise how compelling was the taut purpose that quivered through his words, how exciting he was to those women who sometimes offered their beds and the comfort of their bodies. Sandile rationalised his celibacy, even told himself he was married to the struggle like a nun to God. Years later, recalling that rationalisation made him laugh uproariously. The whole notion, even his phrasing of it, seemed utterly absurd and it was shocking to him later that he hadn't even seen that.

There were days when he couldn't distinguish between the fog in his mind and the blanket of drizzle that clung to everything. Was he depressed or was it just grey? Where would he find the bridge back into his past, back into his strong self? When he spoke so stirringly at all those meetings he did in pubs and Labour Clubs and damp churches and echoing universities he always spoke of the struggle as if it were the bridge. A bridge that everyone must help to build, a bridge whose construction would always be besieged, but which cannot be stopped, it must reach the other side one day and it would carry them all, marching and singing, into the future. It would carry Sandile back home.

Home. The word made him irritable. To a nomad home is a point in the line of his journey, a resting place in the midst of motion. Sandile wasn't a nomad; he was a settler, a settler who'd been yanked from his roots. Home was only one place and now it was so distant that it might as well have been a place in a dream. In his home the line of the mountains, the colour of the light, the texture of earth between his fingers were all as familiar to him as the sound of his own voice, the shape of his arm, the sensation of his fingers on his hair. Home for Sandile had become a dream and every day it receded from him and every day the sense was receding from his life. He moved through the days, barely sensing the outline of moments. Everything had deteriorated, diminished, flattened out to the same plane. Plain grey.

It was hard for people to sustain an interest in reaching this unfathomably depressed, wildly intense South African with his terrifying stories of detention and torture and death and his longing for the coarseness of African soil and the emptiness of an African horizon. Sandile was so closed down that now even the invitations he often got from worthy, worried women in the anti-apartheid movement didn't move him at all. What did they want from him anyway? What could he have that they needed? He wished, in the worst, most uncharitable moments, that they'd get on with their own struggles and leave his alone. He felt their whispers and touches as pitying kindness and he couldn't take such charity. It was so humiliating. Once he turned viciously on a young woman who'd met him at the station, taken him to speak at a student meeting, fed him supper at her table and then suggested that, if he wanted, he was welcome to sleep with her. He'd stood up from the table, pushed away his plate and almost hit her in his fury. She was too shocked to respond and he'd slammed out of her house before she'd screamed back the rebuke he certainly deserved.

It was after this incident, as he sat shaking on the London-bound train, that Sandile realised he needed a change, a fresh start. He applied for a transfer to Lusaka. The day it came through Sandile was overwhelmed with relief. He took some of his comrades from the London office to celebrate with him. He looked at the beer-soaked, ash-drenched carpet with sudden new affection. He smiled at the ever-joyless bartender and drank pints of the hideous flat beer until he was so drunk he couldn't get up. He let himself be carried home by his comrades and there he embraced and kissed every inch of his vile exile room with delirious abandon.

The man who arrived in Lusaka one soft African morning was not the same man who had gone to London filled with hope and anger and certainty five and a half years before. Sandile was only twenty-four, but his was a serious, wise head on young shoulders.

He slept all night on the flight from London, exhausted from the anticipation of his departure. He was asleep even as the plane landed and so he missed the sight he'd fantasised about: the dawn splitting the night sky, the sun slipping over the horizon and the revelation of Africa. Sandile woke as the plane touched down. His head banged against the window and he shook it as they lurched along the runway. He was groggy, but he knew he wasn't dreaming the lush, scrubby flatlands that stretched away for ever. It was a clear morning, the sky blue and immense, and as he walked across the tarmac to the arrivals building he didn't laugh or dance as he'd thought he would; he only smiled a little at the calm that settled over him, the stillness that spread through him.

He'd been told that a representative from the ANC office would be there to meet him and he was delighted when he saw Ismail, his old friend and mentor, standing at the barrier. Ismail hustled him through immigration ahead of the long line of tourists and businessmen. He'd heard reports of Sandile's progress and successes in Europe, but he knew Sandile must be thrilled to be back in Africa. Ismail bubbled over with all the elation that Sandile still didn't feel, chatting and laughing as he drove him from the airport into town. Sandile smiled serenely and rolled his window down to let the air fly in and around him while he answered Ismail's questions, quietly supplying news of comrades and friends in Europe.

Ismail was particularly pleased with the parcel Sandile had brought him. He explained that it came from his brother's English girlfriend. Five years ago she had begged Ismail's brother not to go back to South Africa, but his longing was too great, England was too strange, and he'd volunteered to go back as part of an intelligence unit that would operate internally. She was sure that she would never see him again and she was right. He'd been arrested within weeks of his return and locked into the back of a Land-Rover with five other terrified men. They were given a bucket into which they had emptied their piss and vomit during the seven-hour journey from Durban, over bumpy roads, up and down steep passes and finally through the sounds of another city. When at last the doors of the Land-Rover were opened and they were allowed to get out they found themselves inside the vast complex of the most feared police station of all, John Vorster Square. Ismail's brother never knew freedom again until those last few seconds when the bastards let him go, when at last they took their hands off him and let him fly. He flew from a tenth-floor window of John Vorster Square with his eyes open, fingers spread wide, and for those last few seconds there was a wild liberation in the rush of the night air around him. And then there was nothing. His girlfriend never even saw the burial of the broken body of the man she'd loved.

Driving in a Landcruiser through Lusaka all those years later, Ismail was brimming with delight at the news that at last her wounds were healing. Sandile still smiled, but his heart was full of the knowledge that joy was a strange thing to men like Ismail and himself. He wept inwardly at the horror of this tale that was like so many he knew. He shook his head. What is this doing to us, what are we becoming?

Sandile arrived in the ANC President's office at the end of the 1980s. It wasn't long before he was asked to help manage it, which he did with enormous energy and much success. It was during those years in the Lusaka office that a kind of peace settled in him. He assumed the mantle of the power that was given to him and he wielded it fairly and well. It was clear to everyone around him, if not to Sandile himself, that he was destined for great things. It was also during that time that things in South Africa began at last to change, and once the change began events moved very fast.

On 2 February 1990 Sandile and all his colleagues from the office watched on CNN as Nelson Mandela, surrounded by his family and his old and new comrades, walked free from his prison in the Cape. In the cool of a garden in Lusaka the women were ululating and everyone toyi-toying and Sandile wept for the first time that he could remember, openly and joyfully. The tears welled up in him and washed him with relief. He knew the struggle was not yet over, but he fought on with new hope. And it was just then, when at last things were changing and they had all begun to talk again of going home, that Ismail was killed.

Sandile shook his head, pushing the memory away. All that was past now, finished, behind. He was home. Home at last, and the mountains were washed with lilac and indigo even more richly than he remembered. When the evening air was clear like this the Grootdrakensrug seemed to hang closer, seemed to advance. Sometimes in the winter there was snow on the highest peaks of that mountain and the ragged summits would shine with it.

As night fell and the firelight and food seeped contentment into his every limb, Sandile felt drunk with happiness. He noticed his father walk over to where the women were talking and put his hand on his wife's back. Such a small gesture expressing the deepest intimacy. She turned away from the fire and smiled at him. No words passed between them: there was no need. Sandile knew that talking was not their way. Suddenly Mama Mashiya began to dance, stamping her feet and swaying and jiggling her hips. She shouted to Nolitha and Lettie, who started dancing with her, 'Can you believe that this big handsome man is not yet married, that no woman has caught him and borne his children!' Nolitha and

Lettie were agreed that overseas women must be strange to have passed on such a man.

Sandile laughed at the sweet flirtatiousness of his mother's concern. He got up and walked back slowly through the empty house. Mama had prepared a bed for him in one of the front rooms. He stepped inside and looked around. It was completely strange to him, and yet it was home. The words formed on his lips and he whispered, 'Home . . . I am home.'

Later his mother came to look for him because he'd been gone such a long time. She found him on the bed, fully clothed and fast asleep. She sat down quietly and watched her son sleeping, watched the rise and fall of his chest and the flicker of his eyes under the delicate brown skin of his eyelids. Tears fell from her eyes and streamed down her cheeks, but Mama made no sound at all. She didn't want to wake him up.

NINE

As they drove away from the compound and back down to the house Elise felt a strange mixture of elation and disquiet. The intensity of everything that had happened that day, even Sandile's hostility, made her feel light-headed and a little drunk. Sandile's reaction to her had marred Elise's mood only somewhat. Nothing could overwhelm her happiness today. Nevertheless she wondered about the long journey that had brought him home at last. Had it made him as hard-bitten and bitter as he seemed? She was struck by the echo of childhood. Sandile was unpredictable and inscrutable even as a boy – that was what had drawn her to him then.

'What the hell was that story all about?' Ina blurted, as if she were wondering out loud to herself.

Ina glanced irritably at her. 'Your father would kill you if he ever found out about that meat.'

Elise raised her eyebrows, looking straight ahead, one arm dangling out of the window, fingers caressing the cool twilight air, and one hand resting lightly on the steering wheel. '*Would* he?'

Ina nodded vehemently. Elise simply shrugged and smiled. Ina shook her head at Elise's nonchalance and looked away, across the orchard, concealing whatever her eyes might have revealed.

They pulled up at the house after the sun had slipped behind the mountains and the dusk clung to everything, deepening the shadows, hushing the insects and the birds, cooling the earth. Daan and her father had been polishing off a bottle of wine on the stoep with Madame Du Toit. Elise and Ina were to have joined them, but now they were all leaving.

'That took you a while,' Daan said, pulling Elise to him.

'Ag, you know what a Good Samaritan Elise always has to be. We've been getting to know the wekkers.' Ina's tone was light but Elise couldn't help thinking that her sarcasm bordered on serious.

Madame Du Toit tutted disapprovingly. 'And we've been waiting for you.'

Elise started to apologise, but Madame quickly put her hand on Elise's arm and stopped her. 'Oh no, you are *too* sweet, dear! We didn't mind you being gone at all – it gave us a chance to gossip about you.' The old lady turned and winked at Van Rensburg, who looked nonplussed.

'Your father and my mother have been planning our future,' Daan explained.

'I haven't been planning anything. I haven't had a chance to get a word in edgeways!' Van Rensburg protested.

Madame laughed merrily. 'I must say, though, that the day has been a great success.'

Everyone murmured their agreement.

'Well, Ma,' said Daan, stifling a yawn. 'I think it's time to take you home.'

Elise helped Mrs Du Toit into the car, kissed Daan goodbye and watched, smiling, as they drove off down the road. Her father shouted a brief 'totsiens!' to Ina and disappeared back into the house. Elise put her arms round her friend and squeezed her tightly. 'Thanks for everything today, hey. Especially for that *incredible* melktert.'

As they pulled apart from one another Ina asked obliquely, 'You like him, don't you?'

It was a strange question. Elise's expression was open; she was genuinely unsure of Ina's meaning. 'Who? Your brother? Of cour – '

'No, no. I mean Sandile.' Ina cocked her head in the direction of the compound, an odd emphasis. Elise laughed. 'But of course, why shouldn't I?'

'He was fighting for the enemy. He's a *terrorist*.'

The word meant so many things, but it meant one very

particular thing to Ina. Elise understood her very clearly. 'That's in the past, Ina . . . It's from another time. We all have to put that time behind us. Everything's different now. Don't you think?'

Ina narrowed her eyes a little, her lips twitching with unstated emotion. She pulled Elise to her and they embraced again. Elise knew that Ina had expressed a feeling that would run deep in the valley. Elise had been struck only by Mama Mashiya's joy, but Ina's reaction was just as real. Sandile came from the other side, the enemy, from the ranks of the terrorists that had murdered Dawie and who had brought an earthquake of change in the country beyond their mountains. Elise knew that was how Ina saw it, though her own view of him was different. She squeezed Ina tightly, then her friend pulled away, smiling, and Elise saw that she had let it go for now.

Ina pinched Elise's cheek playfully. 'What a day, huh? Sister-in-law!'

Elise smiled and now emotion burned in her eyes. 'I suppose it was meant to be . . . some way or another . . . '

Ina nodded, then walked to her car, but just before she climbed in she twirled in a sprightly flamenco dancer's flounce. 'Don't expect me to behave myself on your wedding day – this maid does not intend to keep her honour!'

Van Rensburg was sitting in his chair in the darkening living room when Elise walked in. She wanted to talk to him, to tell him about the feast up at the compound and how delirious everyone was about Mama's son returning. But she saw that he was deep in thought and she knew, simply knew, what absorbed him. Nevertheless she plumped down on the big round cushion in front of him.

'It was a fantastic day, Pa.' He didn't say anything. 'And the meat was . . . ssssuperb!' He sort of laughed, but it was more like a sigh.

'Why are you sighing?'

He looked straight at her and after a while he said bluntly, 'I was thinking about your mother.'

Now Elise said nothing. Then, after a moment, she stood up and kissed him on the top of his head, whispering, 'Thanks, Pa, it was a lekker braai!' She turned away from his painfully hunched-over frame and walked out on to the stoep.

Elise didn't often think of her mother, certainly not as often as he did. She breathed in sharply, sucking in cool air and wincing away from the thought her mind had suddenly focused on. Elise had loved her mother. She must have loved her – she had forgiven her for so much, had let so much go by. But she didn't *like* her mother, really didn't like her, and she'd finally admitted that to herself on the day before Evelyn died.

She sat down on the cool tiles, her eyes open, apparently gazing up at the stars which were coming out thick and brilliant tonight. Yet it wasn't the stars she saw. She was looking on an inward darkness, a bellowing void, the huge space of the absence of her mother's love for her. An absence whose presence she now accepted.

There was nothing, Elise realised, nothing in her mother that she wanted to emulate. She had given no examples, had never shown her daughter the signs to find her way by, no map, no constellation to refer to.

She remembered all too well the irritable flick of her mother's hand, the dim glimmer of something malevolent in her eye, the tiny downward shift in the shape of her mouth. The always full and flimsy layers of nylon in her skirts would switch and swing as she disappeared into her room. To incur her wrath on such a day was easy and devastating. The laughter and shouts of a game too close to her window, a fall and the tears of a graze, a clinging childish melancholy that asked only for a cuddle: any of these might bring forth a clatter of smacks or terrorising screams to shred the afternoon. Elise supposed now that this was partly why she always played away from the house, why she had roamed so freely and so far over the farm. She was sure it was why she stayed so often at Ina's house and clung to Ina's mother. Ina wasn't frightened of her mother. For her there was never the anxious possibility of a sudden shift in mood, or the unpredictable and shocking clap of a thunderous rage. Elise's love for her friend's mother was as confident as the reliable warmth that she was given in return.

Elise always felt that her mother didn't want her around the house, not even in her kitchen. There were no secrets that passed from mother to daughter like the secrets of the land that were passed between father and son, between Van Rensburg and Dawie. Evelyn's good days were days when she was so sedated by daydreams, so numbed with yearning, that she could smile distantly and pull her children to her, her soft arms enfolding them, but not too tightly, not so tightly that she might crease her blouse. Her bad days were a bundle of frustrations as reality clung to her with its everyday smell and its ordinary emptiness. To run to her full of the delight of some child's thing was to run into the snare of her bitter disappointment.

It wasn't until she was much older and at an age so uncomfortable it had made the realisation worse, that Elise understood. Her mother felt she wasn't living the life she was meant to live. She had fallen in love with someone she thought Van Rensburg was and when she saw the reality of him and of her life, trapped in a small town in a valley cut off and encircled by huge mountains, she never forgave him. Van Rensburg was her rough diamond, her fantasy of the rugged primitive she would tame and transform. She knew he adored her, that he would do anything for her, but the essence of him could not change. Their wedding was the ecstatic denouement of her life, the climactic final scene that nothing else could match. Elise had resolved long ago that she would never make the same mistake.

As a little girl Elise had sat countless times with her mother, leafing through the gilded leather-bound photograph album of her parents' wedding. Her mother described the day to her over and over again, like a fairy story. Like a fairy story it ended with a kiss. Her father so proud and nervous, her mother in full command of the greatest day of her life. In the last picture her mother's long neck was exposed towards the camera as she leaned over the little heads of the bridesmaids, her eyes closed, her lips touching the lips of her man.

After that day her mother never looked so radiant again. She always had to struggle to get through the years of living happily ever after. She never fully accepted that life was not a series of episodes each ending in a golden, life-altering, rapturous embrace.

There was only one affair that Elise actually knew of. He was a man who ran the trucking company that carried their fruit from the packing sheds and the orchards on the farm to the cold store or to the co-op and then to Elgin where it became Cape Fruit. He was Italian. Elise would never forget him. His name was Mario. He started up the trucking company with almost nothing and he'd arrived at Rustenvrede one day to ask Van Rensburg for his business. Evelyn was evidently struck by Mario's potential, because she took an unusual interest and encouraged Van to try him out. Later, when the company was a success and Mario was running a huge fleet, he no longer needed to drive, but he always drove for the Van Rensburg's. Mario supervised their account with particular care and attention to detail. He would come by in the afternoons, with his shy smile and those vivid blue eyes under thick, dark curls. Elise couldn't remember her father ever being there. But she did remember her mother and how her mother went with Mario into the spare room and always locked the door behind them. It made Elise so angry she wanted to burn down the house, but she was too small to express her fury with anything but silence.

Once Dawie was there too and she asked him what they were doing. 'Why did Mommy lock the door? Why did she close the curtains?'

Dawie's face was tight and angry and he wouldn't look at his sister. She began to cry. Then, viciously, the words flew out of him, like spit: 'They are fucking.'

Elise understood from him that whatever her mother was

doing behind that door was terribly cruel. Dawie stormed away, pushing over the little table in the hall so the vase of flowers on it smashed and spilled all over the polished tiles. Her mother came flying out of the room, pulling her long soft cardigan down over her chest, her look so severe, so cold, that Elise shrank from her. 'What are you doing!' Elise said nothing. Instead she shuffled away.

She'd always thought that her parents would do everything she wanted; they'd made it seem that way. She wished then that she could make her mother stop going into that room with Mario. For a short while, after Dawie broke the table, it seemed as though her wishing worked. The visits to the house stopped. But then Mario came back. This time he took her mother for a drive in his car and they were gone all afternoon while her father was out working on the farm. The day that Mario returned marked the beginning of a sense of powerlessness, something new to Elise.

She and Dawie never said anything to their father. That would have been as terrible as the deed of which they wanted so badly to speak, and so each was mute – to each other, to their father, to their mother. A strange silence settled between and around them all.

Once, a long time after, her father had said something that made Elise think he knew. It was on a Sunday afternoon and the radio was playing very loudly, as Ma liked to have it. She loved to listen to a programme which played the pop charts and now it was playing a love song that made Ma close her eyes. Elise, who was watching her, thought she held her breath. Pa watched her too, for a moment, then he sprang across the room and switched the radio off, cutting abruptly across the climax of the music. He sat down quietly in a chair by the window. Evelyn's eyes opened and her face froze. The tension in the room was electric.

Finally her father said, softly, 'Those songs are lies. They are invented for people who don't want anything to do with reality.' Evelyn stood up and walked out of the room. She didn't come to the table for supper that night. Pa said she was sick.

It was around that time that her mother and father were supposed to go to Mario's wedding. Evelyn didn't want to go so she pretended to be sick again. There was an argument, but in the end her mother had her way as she always did and only Van drove off to go to the celebration. Mario never visited the house again, not in the afternoons, not in the evenings, not even for the Sunday gatherings of friends and family. After that the only other man in her mother's life was Dawie.

Elise remembered that time between being a child and becoming an adult only murkily. She never wanted to be a grown-up, and she certainly didn't want to be a woman. She really wanted to be a boy. In the world Elise inhabited only boys did the things she wanted to do. In every sense it was a confusing time, as if a glow had rubbed off the softness of her world and the starkness of everything was too hard.

Sandile was part of the starkness of things. Though Elise was barely aware of him throughout the years that they were teenagers, she was as aware as everyone else in the dorp of what happened that night at the old cold store in the early 1980s. The police had come to Rustenvrede in the middle of the night and woken the Van Rensburgs up with their banging on the back door. Elise remembered padding through to the kitchen where her mother and father were talking in hushed voices with two white men in safari suits and a uniformed cop. Evelyn had looked up, seen Elise standing in the doorway in her nightdress, smiled and gone over to tell her in a near whisper that everything was all right, there'd been some incident with the farm workers' kids, they'd get the whole story in the morning; meantime she should go back to bed. Elise yawned, pushing her hand through her mussed-up hair, and padded back to her room.

It wasn't the first time the police had been at Rustenvrede in the middle of the night. There was often trouble on the farm of one sort or another, usually something to do with the labourers drinking and beating each other up or beating up their wives or children. So Elise had thought nothing of it at the time. But the next day when she woke up there was a police car parked in the yard outside and a young cop asleep at the wheel.

She watched the cop through the kitchen window while she ate her breakfast. She pointed him out to Dawie when he strolled in yawning and slumped down in his place. It was their mother who explained the story, sitting at table in her frothy Woolworth's dressing gown, her hair perfectly pinned up, small soft hands weaving the air as she recounted it. 'There was a shooting up by the cold store. A boy died. The police didn't say much else.' Elise cupped both hands round her steaming mug of tea.

'Yusslike!' Dawie banged the table with his hand.

Evelyn van Rensburg lowered her voice, looking from Elise and then to Dawie as she spoke 'Anyway, the boy was a friend of Sunny Mashiya – you know – and apparently the two of them were involved with the terrorists. They were planning to hide guns or something here on the farm.' Evelyn shook her head in amazement and disgust and Elise moved hers in the same way.

Everyone knew there were terrorists at large, even in the heart of South Africa, bent on turning the place into a Communist dictatorship like in Russia, but Russia was a world away and the thought that they had come so close made Evelyn and her children shiver.

'The police got a tip-off about what the boys were doing and they were waiting when a group of blacks drove up in a lorry and started shooting. This boy, Baasie, was killed. Imagine that! They kill their *own* people.' Evelyn breathed out over the surface of the hot tea, trying to cool it.

Dawie leaned forward, his eyes bright with excitement. 'But did they get them?'

Evelyn shook her head. 'No, they didn't, the terrorists got away. The police stayed over because they're worried they might still be hiding somewhere in the valley.'

Dawie stood up suddenly as if he was going to go out and find the Commie bastards. Typical, thought Elise. For her it was the first time death had come so close and it had shaken her to the core.

Her father had walked quietly into the room and he put his hand on Dawie's shoulder. Van Rensburg spoke gruffly, importantly. 'I've just been out to the cold store. There was a major there, someone from the Security Police. He told me they've checked the whole area, but the terrs got away. He said they're probably over the border by now and there's no chance they'll be coming back, not after what happened.'

Elise put down her cup. 'What about Sunny?'

Her father shook his head gravely. 'He's disappeared, nowhere to be found.'

Sunny was what Sandile was called then by the Van Rensburg household. Elise's parents had never called him by the name his mother and father gave him. They renamed everyone who wasn't called something wholesomely Afrikaans, everyone except the English whose names were easy or silly and not worth changing. It was something Elise hated, but her rebellion hadn't started then and so in their company she did as they did.

Evelyn glanced nervously from her husband to her daughter. She put her hand on the girl's arm and said quietly, 'Elise, they arrested Betty and her husband, but your father's going down to the police in Paarl to find out where they are. We know *they* weren't caught up in all this.' What Evelyn didn't mention was that the Mashiyas' place had been turned upside-down during the night and the compound had been in uproar. Two of their workers had run away because their passes weren't in order and they were frightened for their own safety. Van Rensburg had a lot to do that day by way of sorting out the mess on his farm.

Elise was more shocked by the news of the Mashiyas' arrest than by any other part of the story. Her hands shook as she said quietly, 'Are they mad? How could they take Mama away? What are they going to do to her?'

Van Rensburg shot a cautionary glance in his wife's direction, then smiled, addressing his daughter in the lightest tone he could muster. 'The police have to be careful, but I'm sure it'll be straightened out very quickly. I'm going down to Paarl now, so if you two hurry up I'll give you a lift to the school bus.'

Elise stood up from the table. She pushed her two long plaits back over her shoulders and pulled her school blazer on over the short green checked dress that was her school uniform.

That morning she sat quietly in her usual place near the front of the bus and listened to her brother talking loudly and animatedly in the back with the other Standard Tens. Dawie spoke as if he knew everything about it, as if he had been there. Elise slipped down in her seat and stared silently out of the window. Later that day someone at school asked her about the incident and she looked at the boy and said blankly, 'Ugly, isn't it?' then she turned away. The story seemed too terrible for excited gossip, too terrible to make sense of, and she had pushed it from her mind.

Elise didn't see Mama Mashiya for nearly a week after that. She knew that her father was doing everything he could to get the Mashiyas out of jail, but for some days he couldn't even get the police to tell him where they were being held. In the end he got one of his friends on the municipal council to apply the necessary pressure and finally a phone call came through to say that the Mashiyas were being released.

When Mama came back to work she looked haggard and old. Her skin had a dull cast to it and she was very quiet. She never talked about what had happened to her when she was in jail, but sometimes, for months afterwards, Elise would come in from school and find her crying in the kitchen. She had had no word of Sandile and she was terrified that he was dead. Elise didn't know what to say, didn't know how to comfort the woman who for years had been her comforter. It had been so long since she'd really even spoken to Sandile, though she had seen him nearly every day for years and heard all about his progress at school from Mama Mashiya. He lived in a world apart from hers.

After a year or so Mama Mashiya stopped talking about her son. It was as if he was dead. Secretly Elise imagined him alive, having escaped to somewhere far away, somewhere exotic. Secretly she almost envied him escaping the bounds of their little world. Elise longed to escape, but she didn't know how to or where she would go. She didn't know what she was going to do with herself when she finished school. She knew what she *wanted* to do. She wanted to farm, but Dawie was being groomed for that – there was no question, no discussion about it.

Dawie was two years older than Elise. Her adored older brother. She never knew how much she adored him until his presence was transformed into a final, brutal absence. Naturally he had hated her and fought viciously with her, as adored older brothers do, through most of their childhood. It was only in the last few years, when Elise had finished school and Dawie was away doing his army service, that brother and sister leaned towards each other and found a bond, a special understanding that both of them knew, but neither consciously acknowledged, as love.

That was the time when every young white South African male went straight from school into the army. Elise never asked Dawie about what he did in the army and he never volunteered much about it: he wasn't supposed to. She knew he was fighting the war with the Communists in Southwest Africa, but no one mentioned Angola. The Van Rensburgs didn't ask about Angola until they were told that that was where Dawie died, though in his last visit he'd told Elise about the incredible landscapes of Namibia, its endless, arid ruggedness and how, when approaching Angola, he'd seen the Epupa Falls where the Cunene River thunders through narrow gorges overarched by clouds of spray and rainbows. It was near there that Dawie was killed and it was there that Elise imagined his spirit lived now, amid the spray and rainbows and the thunder of the falls.

Just before he'd gone back for his last stretch of duty Dawie celebrated his twenty-first birthday. They had a huge party for him in the garden. Evelyn rented the marquee, hired a band and had tens of local women cooking for days in preparation for the celebration of her darling son's coming-of-age. His schoolfriends and army friends and farm friends, dozens and dozens of them, came and danced and ate and drank and vomited into the flowerbeds. They all looked so young and so sure with their little moustaches and their uniforms and their cigarettes in their fingers.

Ina du Toit was Dawie's girlfriend. They'd been going steady since matric and that night they were secretly engaged, she in her pretty satin dress and her carefully curled hair and her blue eyeliner. She was so happy. Elise had envied them, their plans for the future, the life they would have together on the farm; she had felt a deep, bitter pang of resentment as she watched her brother that night.

Ina was giddy with excitement about everything. She sat with Elise on the low wall by the stoep while the marquee pulsed with dancing, mapping out her whole life: what she'd do when they moved into the main house, how many children she wanted, what changes she'd make in the decorating, in the garden. There was no place in this fantasy for Elise, and Ina, realising this, had turned to her younger friend and taken her hands and said, 'And of course there'll be a guesthouse where you will stay when you visit with your *husband*. Isn't it *so* exciting? Don't you dream about it? It'll be so amazing!'

There was something obnoxious, offensive about Ina's certainty that night. It would have satisfied Elise if the balloon had burst and the plans collapsed had it not been that Elise's own life was shattered by the same event that shattered Ina's.

Elise was nineteen then. In the two years since she'd finished school, since Dawie had been away doing army, she'd been kicking around, working for her father on the farm mostly. He didn't take her interest in the land seriously: she was a girl, a very pretty girl at that, and she would find a job or a man soon enough. Even when she didn't find another job or a man to distract her and her father came to rely on her increasingly, she knew that when Dawie returned he'd take the place she was holding for him. It was his place. Still, once he finished army she would have a grace period of several more years. Dawie had some scholarship money to study agriculture at the university in Bloemfontein. That was his plan for when he finished military service. Then one day he'd come back to Fransmanshoek, a grown man with a degree and the army behind him, and he'd marry Ina; they'd settle down and he'd work with his father on the land he would one day inherit.

Elise was too honest to lie to herself about how jealous she'd been of her brother on that night of his twenty-first birthday party. Still, she regretted their final parting, which for her was full of frustrated rage at the perfect symmetry of his life and the ragged open-endedness, the uncontrolled disorder of her own. Now that regret was part of the pain.

She would never forget the day the telegram came. She remembered every detail: what she was wearing, the colours of the flowers in the hall near to where it lay, waiting for her mother or her father to come home and open it. Innocent manila enveloping a single poisonous page.

The Van Rensburgs never buried Dawie: his body never came home. At the time they were told nothing about the circumstances of their loss, except that it was top-secret. The South African Defence Force refused blankly to disclose what had happened. But Van Rensburg had wanted to know, he burned to know. Knowing was the only way he could begin to make sense of his loss, so he pursued the case in his dogged way, pulling every string available until he got to the truth. The truth was a terrible secret; no one in South Africa knew then and no one was supposed to know. The Van Rensburgs stuck to their word and kept the painful story to themselves, even long after the whole world knew that South Africa was at war with Angola.

For her father the final disclosure of what had happened was a source of strange pride and Elise supposed that he needed to feel that, needed to think of Dawie dying heroically in South Africa's misunderstood but vital war against Communism. For her the news was drenched in shame and senselessness. The harsh forensics made her brother's death more painful and, though her mother never said so, Elise was sure that she felt the same: in her heart Evelyn could never understand or forgive the generals who saw fit to sacrifice her son in some pointless, distant desert war.

Dawie was killed somewhere along the Cunene River, along with three other young – much too young – men. They were ambushed. According to the survivors of the ambush the body of Elise's brother was taken by the terrorists and tied to the front of his captured vehicle, then driven away to be paraded in triumph before the enemy. There were units in the South African Defence Force that liked to do that with the corpses of the 'terrorists' they killed. Hook them to the front fenders of their vehicles and drive through the local villages, ghoulish emissaries of the death that would certainly come to anyone who harboured the terrs. It was a searing irony, lost in a million other terrible ironies of that war, that Dawie should meet the fate he had meted out on others.

Elise had never talked about Dawie's death with either of her parents. Whenever she had tried to the response from them was the same. Her father fell silent, absently silent, and her mother mumbled, rambling on and on about her fallen hero.

Elise wondered often if, in her last days when death clung to her, Evelyn's daydreams had fallen away. Did she have just one moment of cleansing regret, one moment when she realised that she had slept away her life? Did she see at last that her fantasies were all poisons she'd administered herself? Did she see just for a minute that her frustrations, her bitterness, her anger at the simpletons around her, the idiots who trapped her in this life and never understood her, that all this came from a mind bent on concealing from itself the richness and reality of the life all around her? Even amid the fluff and froth of her deathbed, covered in crocheted lambswool bedjackets and supported by her lace-edged satiny pillows, that niggardly voice remained. The soft nagging, the little needle-sharp rebukes issued forth until the end and her father's hangdog face hardened Elise's heart so that when at last she stood by him and watched the overblown coffin lowered into the grave, her heart was as empty, cold and impermeable as a steel box.

Elise was so exhausted after her mother died that no one noticed that she didn't cry. They noticed how thin and haggard she was and they mistook that for mourning and left her alone.

It was Dawie's death that her mother blamed for her own. She'd said so one morning, for the benefit of her doctors of course: such high-flown emotion would never have been wasted merely on those closest to her. She said Dawie's death was the blow that brought on the cancer. Elise remembered how her father appeared not to flinch at her remark, but a sound had escaped him, like the violent sigh of someone who has been winded. The sound had made Elise turn and look at him, but there was nothing in his expression that gave anything away. The doctor had nodded sagely, sadly, and her mother had dabbed delicately at the moisture in her eyes.

Sounds of the celebration up at the compound drifted down the mountainside on the cool night air. Van Rensburg stood by the window, crippled by the agony of all that love lost, watching his daughter and projecting on to her small back all his own desolation. Elise didn't see him watching her; she was caught up with her own remembering. He felt for her and he was half right: she felt alone and she felt pain, but hers was the pain of lack, not loss. Her mother's resurrection might have healed her father, but for Elise it would have been the return of an inadequate presence, a reminder of the terrible loneliness of having to grow yourself up. Elise shook her head, suddenly, violently shooing out the ghosts.

She'd wanted this day to be perfect, and it had been. Her engagement to Daan was a fulfilment of something, the last piece falling into place of a dream of coming home. She could hardly believe it was true, that she should be given such a happy day. Nothing could shake her mood, her sense of the richness of the lives around her and the fullness given them by continuity. Even these dark thoughts about her mother couldn't cast a shadow – she simply shook them off, all that disappointment, all that dark old anger. This flash of memory was her caution to herself on a day when her life lurched forward into a new and happy unknown.

Van Rensburg stepped back into the darkness of the house and climbed quietly into his side of the bed that he and Evie shared for so long, so long that he barely remembered the time before her. The bed was the worst place now, the most cruel, for it was full of the shadows of kisses, of her breath against his neck, her arms flung wide in sleep. It was full of the everydayness of her that was now for ever beyond his grasp. Van Rensburg lay awake as the hours of sleep dragged by.

TEN

In the days after his return Sandile unpacked his life into the small room at the front of his parents' house. They had settled into a new rhythm together, mother and father and son. There was so much to learn about one another, about all that time in between. Sandile spent his time working around the house while the evenings were taken up with hours of talking and listening. Slowly their stories unfolded and familiarity replaced surprise.

It was evening, almost ten days since his arrival. Sandile was sitting out front, staring up into the cloudless night sky. There was not even a hint of rain. The air was hot and sticky and pulsing with cricket song. The night was so clear the trees seemed almost too sharp and vividly patterned to be real. This was lovely, he thought, but he couldn't hang out this way indefinitely. Sandile wanted to work, to learn about the land; there was so much he would need to know if the land claim came through. Preoccupied though he was, Sandile noticed a brightness in the sky to the east. He watched curiously as the mysterious brightness grew and then suddenly he understood. A silver crescent popped over the ridge and within minutes the moon had risen, brilliant and full, casting its ghostly, beautiful light over the valley.

Inside the cottage Mama Mashiya was finishing the preparations for their evening meal. Ben Mashiya had washed and changed some time before Sandile and was sitting, as was his habit at this time of the day, in his chair on the back stoep, gazing out on his garden and the dark hulks of the mountains beyond. From where he sat, on the other side of the house, Sandile could see Lucky, his brother's strange, unhappily named child, bent over some work in a corner of the front yard. Vuyo's oldest boy was teaching him to perfect a small catapult which he would use to hunt birds. They worked with a thick wire frame to which they attached strips of rubber cut from an inner tube. Sandile smiled as he took stock: each member of his family in the place he had learned to expect them to be. The certainty of their routine, the domestic detail of their lives, of what was *his* life now, gave Sandile endless pleasure. He loved this peace at the end of the day and this new sense of potential, of burgeoning possibilities. He sighed deeply, breathing in the warm air, savouring the fragrances and freshness of it. Tonight he must begin, he told himself. Tonight he would share his plans for the land with his mother and father.

Mama Mashiya called out from the kitchen: it was time to eat. Sandile strolled through the house and stood by the table he had set earlier. His father wandered in from the stoep and sat down in his place. Their eyes met and Sandile grinned. Ben Mashiya simply nodded – he was a man of few words and little apparent emotion – but Sandile could read in the brightness of his eyes the pleasure the old man took in his son's presence, in the new familiarity of him. Sandile called out to Lucky, and the boy shouted back from the yard that he was coming. Ben Mashiya set his pipe down by the knife and fork in front of him and waited quietly for supper to be served.

Mama dished up steaming piles of pap with a thin meat stew. Sandile took the plates from her and brought them to the table. She smiled girlishly at the way Sandile watched and helped her. It was not his place to do so, but she didn't protest now as she had done in the first few days. He insisted and his attentiveness touched her indescribably, so she let it be.

Lucky slunk into the room and slid on to his seat. He glanced round at Mama and Oupa and Sandile, then bent his head over the food and tucked in. He was a strange child, surly even, with the reactions of a skittish dog – reeling from contact as if always expecting to be kicked. He was painfully shy of Sandile, who often caught the boy staring at him with a serious, unfathomable expression. Mama knew that he saw in Sandile the features of his own father and he feared them. So Mama was gentle with Lucky; his road had been a difficult one and who knew what horrors he had witnessed when he was far too small to understand? In time he would learn to trust this family, to feel secure in his life here.

Mama watched with satisfaction as her men ate hungrily. Sandile glanced over to smile appreciatively and she blushed at the look from her beautiful son.

'So what's new down at the house?' he asked cheerfully. There was usually some small thing, some snippet from the dorp or from another farm.

Mama chuckled deep in her throat and shook her head. 'Nothing new,' she replied, then remembered and put down the forkful of food she'd been about to eat. 'Except Miss Ina was there today, all hysterical because Connie, one of her girls from the stall, one of the Kriel children, has run away. They think she got pregnant and was too scared to tell anyone. So she trekked.'

Sandile slowly shook his head and took another mouthful of food.

'Those Kriel girls,' Mama added, 'always in some kind of trouble. Except Lettie. Lettie's not like her sisters.'

Silence enveloped them again and for a while there was only the sound of the clink of cutlery on plates.

Sandile thought of Elise. He had seen her only occasionally since her visit but they had not spoken. 'And how is Miss Elise?' he enquired. Mama had noticed Sandile's curiosity, but took it to be the same as her own. She loved Elise, almost as if she were her own child, and paid careful attention to every detail of her life. A chuckle bubbled up from Mama's throat again. 'Ina was nagging her about the wedding today.'

Ben Mashiya smiled. 'Have they set a date yet?'

Mama shook her head. 'Elise says she can't think about such things when there is so much work to be done. She says there's no rush, that the wedding can wait until the end of the harvest.'

Ben nodded and Mama went on. 'That Daan is so impatient with her, he wants them to get married at Christmas, but you know how stubborn Elise gets, she says there's too many other things to worry about.'

Ben smiled again. 'Yes, she was a stubborn little girl.'

Mama shook her head. 'Aaai! You can say that again.'

Sandile listened with some interest, noting his parents' affection for Elise. He felt differently, but he wasn't going to mention it now, not tonight.

When they were finished Sandile stood up and cleared away the plates. Mama shifted in her chair: that work was hers, she didn't know how to be still, but Sandile refused to let her do it. Ben Mashiya lit up his pipe while Sandile quietly instructed Lucky to help him with the washing-up. The boy obeyed and sloped towards the sink, his shoulders hunched over. Mama stood up from the table and went out of the room. Sandile heard the bathroom door click shut. He glanced over at his father. The old man seemed deep in thought as he sucked gently on his pipe, but Sandile knew he was watching and listening. That was his way. Sandile strode across the room and sat down at the table. There were things of importance to discuss.

'Father,' he began.

Ben Mashiya moved his head round to meet his son's gaze.

'Father, tell me the story of our family in this valley.'

The old man's expression barely shifted, but Sandile could tell he was reluctant.

His father lit another match and held it to the bowl of the pipe: the sweet, strong smell of burning tobacco filled the room. Sandile kept coming back to this queston of the land and Ben Mashiya shook his head, wondering what was to come of this. 'Aaai . . . That's an old, sad story.' He sighed.

'Tell it, Father, I haven't heard it in so long.'

Sandile spoke gently, coaxingly, trying not to let his voice carry the pressure of his resolve. He had to get his father to help him build the argument.

'Tell me the story of how our family bought the land.'

His father sighed and again shook his head. Sandile waited, his knee jiggling with tension.

Ben Mashiya raised his chin and his eyes met Sandile's. He sensed the anticipation and he wanted to know where Sandile was leading, so he began.

'Well, in the beginning it was our land for the taking. There was no one else on it, no one else who wanted it. The Boers were our neighbours, and we lived as neighbours until one day they told us, those Lombaards told my great-grandfather – Gideon was his name – that the land was theirs. The Boers had guns and we had nothing. So your ancestors worked hard on the white men's farms and saved the money they earned. It took them more than ten years of saving, but they bought the land back from the Lombaards. The land was from the top of the peach orchard, across to where the Van Rensburgs' dam is now and beyond it up to the end of the second orchard by Die Uitkyk. Gideon was no fool, he knew the Boers' ways and he got a paper to prove it was his land.'

Ben Mashiya paused when Mama came back into the room and went to sit in her chair. She picked up some sewing from the basket next to her and worked while her husband talked. It was often like this, and Sandile couldn't tell if she was listening tonight. He wasn't looking at her, he was focused only on his father.

'It was just before the big war, the Boer War, when the Lombaards took our land the first time.' Sandile knew the history and knew that would have been around 1895 when Cecil John Rhodes and his cronies passed the Glenn Grey Act, designed to push blacks off the land and into wage labour, mostly in the mines. The Mashiyas became tenants on their own land, but they hoarded all their meagre wages and saved enough to buy the farm back from the Lombaards. Sandile calculated that Gideon must have made the purchase around 1910; it had to have been before the Natives Land Act of 1913.

'I will never forget the year when they took it again. Nineteen fifty-eight. Old Mrs Van Rensburg wanted the land for herself, then Lombaards said they wanted it too. In the end they each took half and the law supported them. It was their law, not ours, and it took away what we bought and paid for.' In 1958 rural and urban blacks and coloureds were being removed from land they'd owned and lived on all their lives, making way for whites. Sandile knew the Ounooi was not an exception. Far from it – she was one of the people this system was designed to benefit and she had made sure she did. 'We had the proof. We had the title!' Ben Mashiya declared with weary indignance.

'They took it anyway, not long before you were born. That paper means nothing now. When Verwoerd declared us a "black spot" I tried to fight them. I got a lawyer and went to the courts in Cape Town . . . But the law was their law. The judge told me the title meant nothing and so they took it, everything.'

Sandile's eyes were bright as he concentrated on his father's words. Ben Mashiya dragged on his pipe, avoiding his son's gaze. 'When we were here in the village, when I was a child, we ploughed the land and raised cattle and we lived well. But the whites stole and killed many of our cattle. Hee, they were cruel. Then they made us work for them on their farms, they made us pay taxes, and in the end they just took our land. They just took it and in return they gave us nothing.' Another pause . . . 'All we wanted was a place to make a home for our families and leave something for our children. Shew! Sometimes I don't know . . . '

Sandile shook his head. His father spoke so seldom, almost never revealed bitterness or anger, or the disappointment that was more familiar to him than hope.

'There was no school then on the farms, I never went to school like you. But my father taught me to read and he taught me to stand up for myself. I was different then. Once the old Ounooi came to me and said I was getting too big for my boots. She was the Miesies . . . They sucked our strength, just wore us down. But *you*, you were lucky. You got education. There were many things the whites gave to you and you didn't want them. My children don't care about school just like they don't care about the land. They think they're so clever, trekking to the white mines and cities, chasing after money. But what kind of clever is it when they kill and get killed and leave behind women with children who have no fathers?'

Mama moved in her seat. She had put down her work and was leaning her head on her hand. Sandile leaned forward; this was exactly as he wanted it.

Ben Mashiya lit another match and held it to the bowl of his pipe. The tobacco ignited, crinkling up in a flame that shot out and quickly died. Then he clicked his tongue, shook his head and continued.

'Those white people never tired of saying that they were our friends and that they would see to it that we had justice. But their law is only for them. They ploughed up our ancestors' graves, there in that orchard.' Oupa Mashiya pointed with his pipe towards the back garden. He shook his head and a rueful chuckle escaped his lips. 'And we tried to talk to them. Ja, there was so much talk. Too much talk. We talked ourselves up our own arses and meanwhile they just took everything.' He banged his pipe on the side of the chair, still shaking his head.

The noise made Lucky start; he'd been standing stock-still in the shadows. Now he moved towards the door, but Sandile put his hand on the boy's shoulder as Lucky slipped by. 'Stay,' he said. 'You must listen.' The boy froze again.

The old man looked over at Sandile again. The story had come out in bitter, abbreviated fragments, but it was finished now. Ben Mashiya was waiting for his son, waiting to hear what Sandile meant to propose.

Sandile cleared his throat. His hands, which had been lying closed and motionless on the table before him, opened. His fingers stretched out as he turned the words over in his mind, preparing to speak. When he did his tone was measured and quiet, but urgent.

'Father, that paper, it meant nothing for many, many years, but not any more. Now the law is *our* law and that paper is our title to the land. It's proof of our *right* to the land.' He looked at his father, watched the words sink in. But Ben Mashiya didn't move; he dreaded what was coming. Sandile sketched out a curve on the table with his finger. 'There's a Land Claims Court now. Well, it's just starting up, but it's there to help us take back what was stolen from us.' He paused, then he tapped his finger on the table top, emphasising each word. 'I want to take our case to the court. I'm going to get our land back.'

Sandile looked from his father to his mother and then to Lucky. Lucky's eyes were cast down to the ground. Mama was staring back with an expression of abject horror, her eyes huge and welling with tears. Sandile couldn't tell if she was moved or terrified – perhaps it was both. She had started to get up, but froze there on the edge of her chair. His father simply sat very still. The silence was oppressive, like the silence that must fall in anticipation of an execution. Sandile realised he hadn't given much thought to their reactions; he had expected excitement and possibly fear, but he hadn't expected this.

'Ma?' Sandile wanted her to speak, for someone to say something. The shocked silence was too much.

Mama gathered herself together, wiping the tears from her cheeks. 'But how?' Her words came out in a hoarse whisper.

Sandile replied steadily. 'We make a claim for the land that Gideon and his family bought, the land that straddles the border of Rustenvrede and Die Uitkyk. If all goes well, and it should, then the Land Claims Court will return the land to us. It will belong to our family, its rightful owners, again.'

'But what will happen to the Van Rensburgs?'

Sandile had thought his meaning was obvious. He looked to his father for help, but the old man's eyes were blank. Sandile unfolded his hands, opening them towards his mother in a gesture that was partly an appeal and partly an indication of complete openness.

'They will lose the land with the dam on it and all the way up to the pear orchards, including this compound.'

His mother's hand flew up to her mouth. More tears fell, though she didn't make a sound.

His father broke the silence. 'This is suicide,' he muttered.

'How can we do that to the Van Rensburgs?' Mama interjected loudly.

Sandile looked from one to the other. He was now as shocked as they were. 'What do you mean? It was the Van Rensburgs who stole our land in the first place!' His words smashed their silence.

His mother simply shook her head. 'Sandile, you want to gamble everything your father and I have. We are old people now. We depend on this house and on our jobs here. If we are kicked off this land we have *nothing*.'

Sandile realised he had gone too far, way beyond anything imaginable, let alone possible in their view. He knew he was asking them to walk down a road beset with the greatest risks, but he was sure that it was worth it. He was absolutely sure they would win.

'Ma, we won't get kicked off the land. This is *our* land. *Your* land. Our case is very strong. I believe it is stronger than most.'

Neither of his parents would look at him. Sandile felt his resolve flagging. 'I would be lying to you if I said it won't be a struggle. Look, I'm asking for your help in taking back what is ours. I don't want to travel this road alone, but I must tell you that, if I have to, I will.'

Ben Mashiya was slowly shaking his head. 'Sandile, why do you do this to us?'

Sandile closed his eyes, bringing his hands up to his face to make a steeple of his fingers. He searched his mind for another approach and, finding one, expressed it vehemently.

'Pa, you told me the story about when you went to vote last year. You said to me that you were *shaking* with excitement and pride when you walked in to cast your vote. You were scared that your hands would be shaking too much for you to put your cross on the ballot, but when it came to it they didn't shake at all and you marked your cross clearly by Nelson Mandela's picture –'

Oupa Mashiya interrupted angrily. 'What does all this talk have to do with the Van Rensburgs' dam? President Mandela isn't going to come here and make them give us back our land!'

125

As he spoke he shook his head wearily and his left hand went up to his ear, as if to block out the words that Sandile would speak. Sandile leaned in towards his father, keeping his voice as low and level as he could.

'Father, when you voted for the ANC that day it wasn't the end of something, it was the beginning. It's *your* government that has set up the Land Claims Courts. The power is *ours* now. You don't think Mandela will let people like us be forgotten? He's *your* President, not Van Rensburg's!'

Oupa Mashiya put his hands over his face. The test was too great for him; President Mandela was too far away, a part of another reality of radio and newspapers, not this reality, not Fransmanshoek.

'But in *this* place, in *this* valley, it is the Van Rensburgs who have the power, not us, not the President. There are things we can't change.' He banged his hand on the table for emphasis.

Sandile was taken aback by the strength of his father's fear. It was utterly real and utterly irrational. As a parent can laugh at the fantastic fears of a child, laughter caught in the back of Sandile's throat, but his father's eyes were so full of terror, he believed so fervently in what he said, that Sandile stifled the laugh. Ben Mashiya staggered abruptly to his feet, scraping the chair back, almost knocking it over. His mouth moved, his elbow jerked up and he waved the pipe around in a gesture of confusion, spilling tobacco and sparks on to the linoleum.

'Why will the government help us? We are a small family, a small story in a small far-away place. The Van Rensburgs will throw us out and we won't have the money for lawyers to fight them. That will be the end of it!'

Mama wrung her hands, but she made no move to get up, and the sparks rolled and died on the floor. Ben Mashiya wouldn't look at Sandile. When he spoke he punched every word with a jerk of his elbow, his voice shivering with rage.

'They have taken everything, everything we ever had, everyone but you. And now when at last you have come back to us and brought to me – ' His voice faltered and broke, and he recovered himself with some difficulty. 'Since you came back I have been thinking that I could die with just a little peace of mind . . . But now you bring *this*!'

His eyes were bright as he pointed the stem of the pipe accusingly at Sandile. 'You, you who are so clever, don't you see that they will take away the little that we have left? Here we have food, we have work, we have this house. We know the people here, we belong here with them, like their family. And where will we go? I am old, your mother is old, there is nowhere else for us to go when they throw us out of here. Never! I will never let you do this.' His father shook his head and fell back into his chair.

Mama flew to his side, frightened by the suddenness of this collapse, but her husband wasn't ill – he was angry. Sandile leaned towards them again, but his father looked away; he didn't want to hear any more. Sandile had to be heard and he gripped his father's arm, insisting on attention. 'Father, this Land Claims Court is our chance. At last. We have the opportunity to get back what the Boers stole from us. I understand your fear, but let me tell you, you are wrong. You are so wrong to be ruled by fear.' His father shook his head, but Sandile continued: 'I promise you we will win and you will die peacefully. With dignity. On your own land.'

Ben Mashiya found a voice that thundered out. He slammed his fist against the table, breaking the pipe in two. 'I can hear no more of this!'

Sandile threw up his hands, stood up and walked out of the room. Mama started after him, but Sandile had stopped in the hallway, his face in his hands, subduing his temper. Lucky slipped out of the room, out the back way through the kitchen. Mama put her hand on her husband's shoulder, but he pushed her away. His pride was hurt and she was hurt for him. She began to cry again, huge sobs shuddering through her.

Sandile strode back into the room. 'Why do you give up like this, Father? All the wars that have been fought in this country have been wars over land. How can you give up, how can you submit when we are so close?'

127

His father wouldn't look him in the eye. 'Only God can help us now. If there is a God,' he said. Mama Mashiya glared at her husband. She still went to church every Sunday, but he had stopped going nearly twenty years ago.

Sandile paced round the room, trying to collect himself. 'God has nothing to do with this,' he shouted. 'Black people didn't become landless through an act of God. It was man-made politics aimed at enriching white farmers – at your expense, at my expense.' He was gesticulating wildly, dramatically, now. 'The wrongs of the past have to be righted. The landless must have land and that land has to come from somewhere. It has to come from the people who took it in the first place. And the white farmers will learn to share – they'll have to.'

Oupa Mashiya breathed in sharply. His response was terse and bitter. 'Piet van Rensburg will never share his land.'

Sandile clenched and unclenched his fists. 'He will have to. We will *teach* him to.'

Mama Mashiya was still crying, though soundlessly. Sandile put his arm round her to comfort her, but she shrugged him away angrily. 'The Van Rensburgs will never give up their land,' she said. 'They have money, they know powerful people, they will send us away from here and we will be left with nothing. Sandile, your father is too old, he has suffered too much. Don't make us suffer any more, I beg you.'

Sandile squeezed his arm round his mother's great soft shoulders. He spoke very quietly to her. 'Mama, Mama, please believe me when I tell you that I am not doing this to make you suffer. You will not suffer any more. We will win.'

Mama's tears began to subside. Sandile steered her back to her chair and knelt before her as she wiped her eyes with her apron. He'd not expected this kind of adversity and he hadn't intended to shatter the harmony of their house. For several minutes he said nothing more, letting the atmosphere subside. Then he stood up and addressed his parents very quietly.

'Let's not talk any more of this tonight. But please, think about what I've said and we will talk some more about it another day.' Mama nodded, but Ben was stony-faced. Sandile said good night, turned and went quietly to his room.

He slept very little that night. He had planted the seed of the idea and in the next few days he would work on them both. Recalling the fear and animosity that had burned in his father's eyes he knew it would be hard, but they would accustom themselves to the idea and, in time, he believed he would bring them round. If they didn't come around he would do it anyway, alone.

The next day when Sandile rose his father was already up and gone. Mama put breakfast in front of him and for the first time since his return she was cool with him. She said nothing, and shied away from his gaze. After the joy of rediscovering each other mother and son were separated by a painful sense of alienation. Sandile felt bowed by the weight of it. He stared down at the plate of food she had put in front of him and Mama bent over the sink, scrubbing the pots with more than her usual vigour. A terrible, unspoken hurt hung between them.

Sandile pushed the plate away and leaned back in his chair, staring at his mother's back, at the motion of her thick, strong arms.

'Mama?'

The rhythm of her arms working at the pot faltered, but she didn't look round.

'Mama, do you believe me when I say that I won't let you suffer any more?'

She stopped what she was doing, letting the pot fall with a clatter against stainless steel. 'Mama, I need you to trust me.'

She turned slowly round to face him, her eyes weary and bloodshot. He knew she had been crying. Soapsuds clung to her arms as she wiped her hands in the folds of her apron. She simply shook her head, leaning back against the sink. 'I have faith in you, my son, but you want me to stand against the Van Rensburgs, against Elise – who is like a child to me. How can I believe that your power is greater than theirs?'

Her hand went up to her face and she turned away. Sandile

stood up and went to her side, but didn't touch her. 'Mama, everything is different now. The power is no longer with them. It is with us. You may not be able to see that, especially not here where so little has changed, but it is true. You will see.'

Her gaze swung round to meet his. She wanted to believe him. After all, this was her son who had come back from the dead. She knew his strength and his will were immense and she wanted to believe that he could make things work out as he promised. But he had made her feel like a traitor.

'I promise you, Mama, I will not let either of you suffer any more than you have.'

'What about Elise?'

'Elise has never suffered, not like you. Why do you worry about *her* and not about yourselves? She's a grown woman with money and with land – she'll find her way without much trouble. Trust me.'

Mama nodded, though he could see she didn't believe him. Her eyes were sad and her body stooped with a weariness that she hadn't seen since his return.

Sandile parted from his mother that morning with a deep sense of disquiet. He watched her trudge slowly down the hill towards the house and his heart felt heavier with every heavy step she took. He felt uneasy throughout that day. He had no idea how to repair the trust that he'd broken.

As the day drew to a close and the sun sank lower towards the mountains Sandile was reluctant to be home for his parents' return. So he decided to take a walk instead, somewhere he knew he might sit for a while and clear his thoughts. It was magic hour when he approached the dam, the hour when the shadows are long and the light is soft and golden and there is a stillness about the earth. The surface of the dam swam with thousands of diamonds of sunlight so that it looked like a sheet of shimmering silver.

He sat down on the sunny edge of a wide flat rock, a place he knew well. As a child he came here to swim, along with all the others, Elise among them. They would play all afternoon in the water, diving and floating and splashing, and when they were tired they would stretch out to dry on the warm stone. That was until Elise was old enough to know not to play with the farm labourers' children and had gone her separate way. The memory was intense and vivid; it came to Sandile with all the sharpness and clarity of that uncomplicated time. He lay back, the rock still hot from the sun, and stared up at the sky which was deepening, darkening into sunset.

Until now his certainty about the land claim had been unwavering, but today his resolve had faltered. His parents were frightened by change. He understood that, and he wondered if he had the right to shake them up to this degree. Their questions nagged him. What if he lost? What if? What if he shattered the little security they had left in the world? He had taken many risks in his life, but they were all his own. Could he risk what was theirs? Sandile sat up and opened his eyes.

The sun had slipped behind the mountains and he shivered, suddenly aware of the coolness of the evening air. Still, he wasn't ready to go home and face them. He felt torn between loyalty towards his parents and a powerful sense of what was right. He'd known when he was seventeen that it was right to join the ANC. Later, even in the dark days of exile when it seemed the struggle would never end, he knew that what he was doing was right. But the price his parents had paid already was high and Sandile knew it. The peace that had settled in him after his return, his new sense of them, the new value he attached to their quiet life, made him think twice now about asking them to take this step. He wanted things to go right for them; he felt a gentleness towards them now that once he would have called indulgence. Yet the alternative was unthinkable. This was too important, an unmissable opportunity to right an historic wrong, a crime against his family which mirrored one committed against his people. Sandile had come too far, was too close to his dream to let it go now. It would be hard, but they would come round and he would have to exercise more patience than usual – though patience wasn't something Sandile had a ready supply of.

He shuddered, shaking his head as if that would rid him of doubt and fear, and as he did so he had the instant sense that he was being watched. He swung round and looked straight at Elise. She was standing fifty metres away, on the grassy track that led to this spot. There was a stretch of shimmering water between them, but he saw very clearly into her eyes and knew immediately that she'd been there for some time. What was she doing, watching him like that? Sandile felt a wave of irritation, as if he'd unwittingly revealed himself. He stood up, rather abruptly. Elise moved too, turning away with characteristically elegant sure-footedness, but then she hesitated and turned back. They moved warily towards one another.

A smile broke across Elise's face as she came up to meet him. She stretched her hands out at her sides, not really knowing what to say. 'I didn't mean to be rude. Sorry I interrupted you.'

Sandile smiled back. 'No, no. You weren't interrupting,' he countered quickly.

'But you look so . . . like you were lost in thought or something.'

He nodded, frowning slightly. 'Ja . . . '

'I was just checking the water level.' She spoke in a light singsong, covering her own discomfort. 'Its very low. But it's probably too early to worry about that. Plenty of other things to worry about in the meantime . . . ' She laughed slightly as her voice tailed off.

'Ja,' he said again.

They continued looking at each other like that, both lost for words, but neither wanting to move. Then Elise threw up her arms cheerfully and let them fall with a clap against her jeans. 'Well – bye . . . '

She spun away and was already several strides down the track when Sandile remembered something and started after her. 'Um, before you go!'

She whirled back round and came to an abrupt halt. Sandile almost walked into her. 'Er, there's something I wanted to talk to you about . . . I need a job. I thought you might have some work for me.'

Elise noticed that his face was as simple and as open as the request. All the shadows and mystery and anger of their last encounter were gone. Now he was blunt and businesslike. She looked away, thoughtfully. As it happened she did have work for him, but why on earth would he want a labouring job? she wondered. He didn't have that slow farm worker's lope. He walked with the cocky, confident strides of a man who had moved on. He looked like he'd done well for himself, like he'd achieved something. Surely this was a step back. Elise didn't feel it was her place to ask, so she didn't, but her reservations came through in the tone of her reply.

'Well, yes, I do . . . I *can* give you work – at least until the picking is over.'

Sandile grinned. 'Sharp!'

Elise frowned uncomfortably. 'But I can't pay you anything like you're used to.'

'How would you know what I'm used to?'

'Well . . . I suppose I don't. But the wages aren't fantastic.'

Sandile shrugged happily. 'Can't have everything.'

She scrunched up her mouth towards her nose, an expression of regret and discomfort. 'Ja, I suppose not . . . '

'So when can I start?'

'Tomorrow?'

'Great.'

'Come down in the morning with your father and we'll take it from there.'

'Sharp! Sharp!'

Elise raised her eyebrows and shook her head in amazement. She made no attempt to conceal her confusion at his obvious delight. They both turned to leave, ready to head off in opposite directions down the path, but Elise stopped. She hesitated, clearly unsure of what she was about to say. When she spoke she was utterly frank.

'Look, you probably know this already, but just in case you don't . . . Things might have changed everywhere else, but they haven't changed much here. People are . . . ' She stopped, shifting her weight from one foot to the other. Sandile waited and she started again.

'My father won't like the idea of having a terrorist working on his farm. It sounds awful, I know, and I'm sorry to even say it, it's so . . . petty. But it's just so you know where people are coming from.'

Sandile frowned. He rested his hands on his hips and stared over her shoulder into the distance, reflecting on what she had just said. After a few moments he shrugged. 'Thank you. I'm glad you've told me and I appreciate your being so straight with me. I know you don't have to be.'

Elise dipped her chin and her eyes lightened with the beginning of a smile. He noticed that her smiles always began in her eyes. 'OK,' she murmured before she turned and strode back along the track, disappearing as she took the path towards the road. Moments later her bakkie came into view, hurtling off in a cloud of dust towards the main house.

Sandile felt an immediate and surprising regret that she was gone. Perhaps she wasn't the person he'd assumed she was. He wanted to know more. He wanted to know what kind of adversary she would be in the battle that lay ahead. The encounter had been strangely blunt. At least he had gotten a job out of it. That thought pleased him, partly because he hated the aimlessness of not having one and partly because it would be a relief from the pressure of anxiety and argument at home. Sandile hugged his arms about himself and then he too turned and set off home. As he walked he wondered what Elise would think if she knew what he was planning to do. Would she stop him? Would she want to? Something told him that Elise would come round, that she would understand the history and adapt, even if her father couldn't.

ELEVEN

Elise told her father over dinner that same evening. 'Oh, Mama Mashiya's son asked me for work. I'm starting him tomorrow.' She would never have dropped this news so lightly had she predicted the strength of his reaction.

'*What* did you say?'

His incredulous hiss made her look up sharply. 'I said I'm starting Sandile Mashiya in the orchards tomorrow.'

He stared thunderously at his daughter who sat frozen in her seat, a forkful of food caught midway between her plate and her mouth.

'We don't give jobs to terrorists on this farm!' he growled.

'Ag, Pa, please . . . ' she tutted. This was ridiculous. Elise carried on eating.

'That boy will only be trouble. I'm telling you, he'll bring trouble,' he bellowed, stabbing his fork at the air between them.

'Oh please. He'll be less trouble than some of the drunks that you won't let go of.'

When it came to the running of their business Elise could be just as stubborn as him. The one who argued in the best interests of the farm would usually win. As far as Elise was concerned her father was simply giving vent to his worst prejudices.

It was hard to get good farm workers. She knew it and had heard her father say it adamantly and often enough, ranting on about how blacks didn't like to work, but when you did get one who would he was invariably stupid. 'Teaching a kaffir is as pointless as putting a handbrake on a canoe' was a favourite phrase.

Elise knew that the problem had more to do with the fact that there were better-paid jobs to be had elsewhere. In the old days, during apartheid, it was as much a problem as it was now, but the solutions then were simpler and much, much cheaper. Van Rensburg would set out with a farm truck and drive for a day, as far as the Transkei or Ciskei usually, and there he'd pick up a truckload of men and bring them all back to the Cape for the season. The men would leave their wives and children, taking the chance to provide their families with a bit of money. There was no lengthy discussion between a husband and wife, no consulting of glossy magazine articles about the pitfalls of long-distance relationships and commuter marriages. The job was there, the truck was leaving that night or the next morning and a man had to take the offer before his neighbour did.

Elise didn't mourn the death of the old system as her father did, but she did have to live with the fact that nothing better had replaced it.

'I think we should count ourselves lucky that he wants to work here. He's young, he's educated, the other men like him – he might even make a good foreman.'

'Your brother *died* fighting terrorists like him.' Van Rensburg was positively enraged. He half stood up from his chair, seething at her. 'Your mother's godfather – and half his family – were blown away by terrorist limpet mines up in the Free State. And now you treat this man as if he deserves something!'

Elise put her knife and fork down into the plateful of food in front of her. 'Pa, that war is finished, that time is finished. We also have to forgive and forget, just like they've forgiven – '

Her father slammed the flat of his hand down on the table – he didn't want to hear any more. Elise jumped, and when he saw the fear in her eyes he sank back into his chair, knowing that he'd gone too far.

'How can you talk about forgiving and forgetting? That stuff is a pile of kak.' He spat this out, not looking at her any more.

Elise knew that her father saw himself, saw all farmers, as being in the front line. He felt they'd borne a great deal for little reward. She sighed. 'Well, you won't ever have to see him. I'll make sure he works only with me.'

With that she got up from the table, leaving most of her supper uneaten. Her father shook his head and muttered bitterly at her retreating back. 'I wonder what Daan will think.'

'Excuse me?' Elise swung round angrily.

'Shouldn't you ask Daan what he thinks?'

'Maybe I should ask Daan if he thinks you're too old to be out on the farm every day. Maybe I should ask him if he doesn't think a retirement home would be the best idea for you!'

Elise threw up her hands in furious exasperation and stormed through the house to her bedroom. She would never relinquish the territory she'd fought so hard to gain in Bloemfontein and since her return to Rustenvrede. She knew he knew it and that was why he'd thrown such a low punch. 'Well, he should know by now that he gets as good as he gives,' she muttered darkly, locking her bedroom door behind her. Her father had grown older and frailer and the work was not as easy for him as it had been, though there was no sign, Elise reflected angrily, that his attitudes had mellowed with age.

During that night they kept their separate vigils. Van Rensburg, propped up against sagging pillows, under piles of blankets, read determinedly into the early hours until he was exhausted and could finally sleep. Elise lay back in the darkness and watched the sky through the window, listening to late-night radio and calculating how much of his Wilbur Smith collection her father would have reread by now until eventually she fell asleep to the DJ's sickly patter.

At breakfast the next morning neither of them spoke. Then, as Van Rensburg stood up to go to work, he said just one thing: 'The first *hint* of trouble and he's out. Off the farm.'

The kitchen door slammed behind him and Elise smiled – she couldn't help it.

Sandile arrived promptly for work with Jacob and the other men. Ben Mashiya had already ambled off to begin his day by the time they set out on the tractor. Elise had recently given him the gardens to look after; he was too old to take the heat and the hard work in the orchards, so now he worked at his own pace and in his own way and she almost never interfered.

It was a busy time on the farm, but Sandile fell quickly into the pattern of things. The first week was exhausting. He was no stranger to the stress of long hours and total concentration, but this was the most strenuous, the most physically demanding job he had ever done. He threw himself into it.

The routine was familiar, but remotely so because it was the routine he'd grown up with. The near-feudal, patriarchal order of life at Rustenvrede was one he recalled from childhood, but it was amazing how well and how pervasively it still functioned. The Mashiyas got everything from the land. Food, housing, water and electricity were all paid for by the farm; what they actually earned in cash bought next to nothing.

What Sandile had forgotten, viscerally, was the experience of living a routine that never varied. While in London and Lusaka his days had been long and he'd worked hard, but then his tasks had varied: he'd gone from one project to another, one city or country to another; the only thing he ever expected was the unexpected. There was an enemy to second-guess, to react to. The moment the enemy became predictable was the moment when the routine was about to change. Here at Rustenvrede the days followed a long-established pattern. Here the only enemies apart from the weather were the pests, and even those were largely predictable and somewhat controllable.

From the very first day Sandile noticed how the other men treated him differently. Jacob expected the respect due to an older man like himself, but the younger ones were slightly in awe of Sandile. He was their veteran, their soldier, the one who'd gone out to fight the battles while they'd stayed at home. At first, Sandile enjoyed the protection and patience they offered, but he didn't want special treatment and so he made it his business to fit in. This wasn't easy, not least because Xhosa no longer flew as easily from his tongue as English. He remembered even less of Afrikaans, which was what the men spoke with Elise. Sandile had spent nearly half his life forgetting those languages and learning to work and think in English. Now he spoke a mishmash of all three.

Elise seemed to enjoy showing him things the other men were too shy to teach him. She took him round the stem of a young tree, showing him how the bud he'd pruned was too exposed to make a really good fruit, but if he took this one and left that then the fruit would have just the right protection from sun and wind. She was never impatient with his mistakes and because of that Sandile found he was drawn to her. There was an ease, a natural openness about the way she worked which was appealing. She never scolded or shouted; she was always relaxed, too comfortable with herself and her men to behave any other way. He wasn't the only one drawn to her: she engaged and energised everyone with her bright, animated eyes, the way her hands fluttered up, moved constantly when she talked, the way she twisted her long hair and pushed it back behind her neck, the way she took such pleasure and pride in all their work.

During the first week Sandile found his mind often turned to thoughts of her. She was unlike anyone he'd ever met before. And yet she was most like that child who'd been his friend. There lay his caution, because when it came down to it, that child knew which side she was on, where her loyalties lay. People don't change that much, he told himself. She was the boss and he was the worker, no matter how sweet she made things seem.

Elise was pleased at the speed with which Sandile learned the work. He had an intuitive sense for it. He'd quickly picked up on the need for keeping all the detail – so many different orchards and fruits at all their stages and with all their needs – in his head at once. It was a busy time of year and a fragile one: the fruit was young and had to be watched, protected and encouraged. Sandile's greenness never got in the way.

Elise felt she'd slipped into an easy, pleasant rhythm with him. They didn't talk much, except about the work in hand, so she didn't learn any new details about him, but an incident from their childhood, a memory, surfaced suddenly one morning as they were working side by side. At the time Elise and Sandile couldn't have been more than nine years old. They had ridden their bicycles over to another farm, a big expedition for children of their age. When they arrived they'd gone into the kitchen as Elise always did and the farmer's wife had pulled bottles of Appletiser from the fridge and put out fruit for them. But the maid of the house was upset by Sandile sitting at the kitchen table and scolded him for his behaviour, yanking him off his chair against the expressed wishes of the white madam.

'No, child, don't sit there. That's white people's place. That's for people who eat with knives and forks!'

Sandile pulled away from the maid and got straight back on the chair. He scolded her sternly. 'Mama, don't you know that in our house we all eat with knives and forks?'

In Elise's house Sandile often did eat with the children in the kitchen. Looking back Elise realised this was unusual and she thought, uncharitably, that her mother had probably allowed it in defiance of her mother-in-law. It was another way of getting back at the old heffalump, another way of delighting in the thought of the Ounooi spinning in her grave. It was either that or because Mama Mashiya set the rules in the kitchen, a place where Evelyn rarely went.

The memory made Elise smile. She looked over at Sandile and watched him focus that same stern intensity on his work. That morning they were pruning the young trees at the mountain end of the Sungold orchard. 'The Sungolds,' she explained to him, 'are our best cultivar, our most important and valuable orchard.'

Jacob was working a few feet away from them, on the next tree, when he suddenly jumped vertically into the air and fell backwards on to Vuyo, who was behind him. Vuyo, shocked and irate at the accident, pushed Jacob away. 'Yusslike, man, what the hell are you doing?'

Jacob didn't say a word. Everyone stopped and looked at him as he stood up. His hand shook as he pointed in the direction of what had scared him and then he uttered the single word: 'Cobra.'

Elise immediately went to investigate and she too jumped away in fright. It was a moerse thing and now it was surrounded and upset. She wondered what could have chased it down there; snakes rarely came down this far off the berg, although they occasionally ventured into the garden, but the orchards were too well kept and too busy.

A quick assessment told her that she stood little chance of scaring it away, that she would have to kill it. Her father would have shot it, but Elise didn't carry a gun and she didn't like using them. She looked round at the anxious men, running through her options. She could call her father, but that would take time and the snake was ready to attack. Elise scanned the ground and caught sight of a stick that was long and thick enough to do the job. As she went to pick it up she thought to herself that the day was cool and they were still in shadow, so the snake would be slow. She approached the cobra and it reared up immediately, its hood extended and its fangs bared, ready to spit. It was too late to change her mind: she had to hit it as quickly and as hard as she could and then get away. If she didn't get it with one smack she'd be in trouble.

Elise brought the stick down with all the force she could muster. The blow was fatal. For a moment they all stared at the dying snake and then the men moved forward, beating it until it was surely dead. Even after death the cobra's long body jerked and writhed, its jaw opening and shutting, the hideous spasms of a nervous system shutting down.

Elise stood and stared, her hand still gripping the stick with which she'd delivered the lethal blow. Sandile touched her lightly on her shoulder. 'Are you OK?'

'Yes, yes thanks,' she answered quickly, a little taken aback by his touch.

He smiled and joked with her. 'I mean, I didn't mean that you might not be OK. I'm sure you do that all the time . . . hey, it's easy as falling off a bicycle.'

They both laughed, partly with relief.

That day his opinion of her changed. There was none of the haughty little princess left in her and he thought that perhaps she was also no longer the master's daughter who would betray him so easily just to save her own skin. He wondered about the journey she must have made from there to here and found he was curious to know about it.

Elise's eyes were drawn to him more and more that day. There was something so mysteriously familiar about him. Some inexplicable, deep communion existed between them and it made her nervous, as if she was standing on the edge of something dangerous and all her instincts were telling her to pull back, but she didn't.

He was an asset to the farm. She was pleased with her decision to hire him. Her father would come round, his sulks never lasted for ever. It just seemed like they would. That night she broke the silence at supper.

'Oh, I killed a snake today.'

'Where?' Van Rensburg was surprised out of his mood.

'Up by the Sungolds – cobra. Huge bloody thing – Jacob reckoned nearly five foot.'

'Shew!' Van Rensburg raised his eyebrows, looking at her with interest. She told the whole story and the chill between them thawed.

There was no change in his attitude towards Sandile, however. Sandile's first encounter with the farmer came the very next day and it was unpleasant, to say the least. Elise was not around to witness it or to defuse the explosion, which seemed, to Sandile, to have come out of nowhere.

The morning's work was almost finished and Sandile was

with some of the guys from Elise's team. She had asked them to go and help her father who needed extra muscle for the repair of a borehole. Just as they were approaching Van Rensburg, Jacob made some trivial joke which set the guys off laughing. Van Rensburg rose up from the group of bodies huddled over the water hole and roared at Sandile.

'What are you laughing at, kaffir?'

Sandile froze. The other men stopped too.

'I said – what the hell are you laughing at?'

'My name is Sandile, sir,' he said and his tone was respectful, but cautionary.

The farmer spat on the ground near Sandile's feet. 'Don't cheek me, boy. I'm watching you. If there's any trouble I don't need to tell you what the story is.' There was a dangerous edge to his voice.

Sandile said nothing; he just stared back at Van Rensburg. This was not the time for a showdown – he knew it, so he lost no pride in swallowing this behaviour. The other men turned towards the job in hand, reverting to the silent shadowy forms they assumed around the farmer. Sandile went to join them, but Van Rensburg took a step towards him, shoving his finger right into his face.

'I know what you are.'

The strange thing was that Sandile felt for him – there was something pathetic about this purple-faced anger. It was strange because he wasn't prone to such feelings, particularly when faced with someone as rude and aggressive as this, but then again Sandile had done his fair share of negotiating apparently unnegotiable situations. He needed to make this situation work, at least for a while. So he smiled, or at least tried to smile, and said as pleasantly as possible, 'Sir, I apologise if I have offended you in some way, but I was only laughing at a joke. I had no intention of making trouble.'

Van Rensburg was taken aback by Sandile's conciliatory tone. He'd been ready for, probably wanted, a flare-up. He narrowed his eyes and growled, 'I'm watching you . . . '

Then he turned and Sandile followed and they got down to work.

Sandile was shaken by the incident. He'd done nothing to cause it; it was simply a sign of the depth of feeling that already existed against him. He knew all too well that there would come a day when he *would* be making trouble, a day when he might not be able to defuse either Van Rensburg or his cobra-slaying daughter. For that day, he cautioned himself, he'd better be well prepared.

TWELVE

It was early in the season, but Hemel en Aarde was already busy. Ina was at work early, supervising the girls in the kitchen and keeping a particularly watchful eye on her nervous new trainee, when she received a surprise visit. Ina had been dimly aware of the sound of a car outside, but the stall wasn't open yet and she assumed the driver was just passing through. A minute or two later Madeleine de Jager appeared in the kitchen doorway. 'Well, this *is* a surprise!' Ina declared happily and rushed to give Madeleine a hug. Even if the connection with Daan was currently somewhat straining, Madeleine was an old family friend. Ina would always be pleased to see her.

Madeleine was all a-twitter with excitement and she blurted out the cause of it immediately. 'Alan Taylor.'

'Excuse me?'

'The new owner of Die Uitkyk is called Alan Taylor.'

Ina slowly narrowed her eyes; the effect was wickedly conspiratorial. Understanding dawned with excitement. She put her arm out to catch one of her girls who was bustling past in a stiff powder-blue uniform.

'Please, Violet, won't you bring us some tea?' Violet nodded and bustled right back into the kitchen.

'Now. Tell!' Ina slipped her hand through Madeleine's arm, guiding her towards an empty table on the stoep. She sat down and Madeleine followed suit.

'Well, it's unbelievable really, but apparently he took over the house earlier this week.'

'How do you know?' Ina leaned in towards Madeleine, her elbow on the table, chin cupped in her hand. Madeleine was a small, cute redhead. Sexy, but in a coarser, curvier way than Elise, who had that elegant thoroughbred look. Ina thought that Madeleine looked prettier than usual in this flustered state.

'Seven thirty this morning. I'm at work as usual when this lorry parks in front of the hotel. I'm not expecting any deliveries, so I go outside to find out what it's all about. It's quite a big truck, with a sort of – thing – ' Madeleine waved her hands in the air, describing an indecipherable 'thing'.

'Picture? Logo?' Ina prompted.

'Logo! Ja, a security-company logo painted over the side. Anyway, the driver gets out, Coloured, very strong accent – '

'And? Get to the point!' Ina was losing patience. Madeleine was like a younger sister to her and that was very much how Ina treated her.

'He asks for directions to Die Uitkyk.' Here Ina allowed Madeleine an effective and suspenseful pause before continuing. Both pairs of eyes were huge.

'So I ask him what his business is up there and he says he's got to put up a new fence around the farm. All the way around the farm? I say, and he says ja. So I say I'll take them to the place, but I happen to know there's nobody there and hasn't been in at least three months. So the truck driver shakes his head and says no, he knows the owner is waiting for him at the house.'

Ina stamped her foot with excited impatience and Madeleine laughed. 'Impossible, I say. So he waves his cellphone at me and he says I'm telling you he's there, I just talked to him on the phone. So I look him straight in the eye and I think I'm going to find out for myself if he's lying or not. So I thought to hell with the hotel, I grab my car keys, jump into the car and the truck driver follows me all the way out to the farm.'

Ina smiled at Madeleine's dedication – she made it her business to know everything first and she usually did.

'Imagine my shock and surprise when I arrive, press the bell and the gates open! I drive up to the house and there's this gleaming brand-new BMW several thousand series or whatever it is, parked right by the house. Then the front door opens and there he was!'

Ina knew, from Madeleine's rapturous expression, that 'he' was a sight to behold.

'Tall, good-looking, soft-spoken . . . He greeted me *very* nicely. I introduced myself and explained about the lorry and everything. He didn't ask me in, he said he had business to do with the security people, and so – I left.'

'And that was it?'

'That was it!' Madeleine slapped her hands down on to the table. It seemed she was already anxious to go.

'Wow!' Ina was astounded.

The tea arrived, but Madeleine didn't drink any. She was in too great a hurry to spread the news, she wanted to be sure everyone knew who'd got the scoop. Ina walked her to the door in a state of high amazement. Madeleine said a hurried goodbye, but from the way she hung back it was clear there was something she wanted to ask, and in the end she couldn't resist.

'How's Daan?'

Ina couldn't help noting the guilty, naughty, wide-eyed expression that flashed across Madeleine's face. Ina had super-sensitive social antennae, and her suspicions were immediately aroused. Ina frowned and Madeleine fiddled with her handbag.

'Madeleine, I know what my brother's like. And I wouldn't like to know that things were still . . . going on . . . between you.'

Madeleine's reaction was hasty and angry. 'Ina! How could you? Do you think I'd settle for *that*?'

'I don't know. But I hope not. I hope not for both your sakes.'

Madeleine tutted crossly, turned on her heel and took off.

Ina strode back into the kitchen, her head swirling with thoughts of this new arrival. How could no one have seen him? she wondered. In a dorp where nothing escaped anyone's notice this seemed impossible. Sooner or later a car would pass by the farms of at least half the residents in the valley and nothing, not even a trip over the mountains to shop at Pick 'n' Pay Hypermarket, failed to make the log. Yet somehow Alan Taylor had driven up to his place and was, at that very moment, moving in without a soul having caught sight of him until today.

Ina was on fire with curiosity. Madeleine's description of him had only fanned the flames. She rarely acted on impulse, particularly where men were concerned, but on that day she was gripped by boldness. She decided she would go over on her own and she would do it immediately. She put a cake and some flowers into her car, a neighbourly offering to the newcomer, told Lettie and Violet that she would be back later and set off for Die Uitkyk.

Ina smiled as she drove off – she couldn't believe herself. If anyone in the dorp got to hear of this they would agree in private that she was being amazingly forward and brazen. No doubt they would draw their own conclusions about her going alone to the home of a single man before even her mother had had a chance to stop by and introduce herself. Ina told herself that the dorp could go to hell. She didn't care what they said or thought; no wagging tongues were going to stop her.

Ina pulled up at the front gate of Die Uitkyk in her little old Beetle. The eye of a camera stared at her as she pressed on the square metal buzzer. After a minute or two a man's voice blurted out of the speaker. He spoke in English and his tone was imperious, even through the box.

'Who is it?'

Ina stammered into the gadget, her lips up close to the lens of the video camera. 'It's Ina du Toit, I'm a neighbour. If you – if it's a bad time I can come back another – '

'No. Please come in.'

The invitation was issued curtly. Ina began to regret her impulsiveness.

The huge gate slid open, disappearing into the thick plaster of the wall. Ina jumped back into her car and drove through. In the rear-view mirror she could see the gate sliding shut behind her. On her way up to the house she could see no one around; there wasn't even the customary clamour of farm dogs to greet her. The only signs of life were the BMW, the van and a long flatbed truck that must have arrived after Madeleine led the security people here.

Ina got out of her car and looked around anxiously; there was still no one in sight. She knocked tentatively on the front door. Nothing. She knocked again. Still no response. She walked round to the side and peered into a window. The house was dark inside and she could only dimly make out the shape of an empty room: no furniture and no movement.

'Hello?' The voice was level, strong and came from directly behind her. Ina swung round to see a man before her. He was smiling mildly, quizzically.

The stranger was much better-looking than Madeleine had described. He was tall, with close-cropped dark hair and strong features, though his skin was sallow, unusually pale. He was dressed in a well-cut suit, with tie and all. He extended his hand to her. 'I'm Alan Taylor.'

'Ina du Toit.' His grip was firm, but his hands were amazingly soft.

'I hope I haven't come at a bad time, but I heard you'd moved in and I wanted to make sure you felt welcome in your new home.'

He smiled slightly. There was a military fastidiousness about him, down to the clipped way that he spoke. 'Thank you. I do appreciate your kindness. Unfortunately I've really only just arrived, so I can't offer you anything.'

'Oh no, no, no, of course not,' Ina protested, then she remembered the cake. 'I've brought you something, just a little thing. I thought you mightn't have anything in the house yet.'

She went to the car and brought the cake and flowers out for him. Taylor was surprised and clearly didn't know what to do with the presents she put into his hands. He stared at her for a moment, then asked if she'd like to come in. Ina said she'd love to and followed him inside. She was still flustered, but Taylor's relaxed and coolly charming manner soothed her. He seemed like a man who wasn't easily ruffled.

The house was completely bare. Taylor put the cake into the empty fridge and set the flowers in the sink. He switched on the tap to pour water on to their stems. They were lilies-of-the-valley. Ina looked at his hands, checked his ring finger as he settled and spread the stems in the water. There was no wedding band, she noted with a small sense of triumph. His hands were unusual, unlike any man's hands she'd ever seen up close, and she continued to stare. They were soft and pale, with milky white webs between long slim fingers. The nails were perfectly clipped. He had manicured fingernails! Ina looked up at his face. Taylor was watching her, but his expression was blank and unreadable. She smiled, a little uncertainly. The silence persisted, too long for Ina's comfort, so she broke it with a question.

'Are you planning to farm here all by yourself?'

'What, alone? Oh no. I've never done a day's farming in my life, wouldn't know how to go about it, even if I wanted to . . . No. I'll be bringing someone in to manage the place.'

'Someone from around here?'

Ina was making small talk, but she had to – she didn't want the conversation to end before it had begun.

'Maybe. Yes, maybe from around here.'

'Everyone around here's been speculating on whether or not you'd keep the orchards, especially now that you'll miss this season.'

'Really? Have they really? It is a matter to which I've given a great deal of thought. I do rather like the idea of an estate wine.'

Taylor punctuated the end of his sentence and the end of that strand of the conversation with a slight, abrupt upward tilt of his chin. Nothing else. Ina realised she was staring at him and he at her and that they'd been silent again for an uncomfortably long time. Sizing each other up maybe. Yet he was so inscrutable. His eyes bored into her, blazing out of his forehead like ice. There was no fire in those eyes; they were cold and flat and frozen blue.

Ina giggled, a strange silly sound. She began to say something, but it came out as a kind of blather. He tilted his head to one side, listening. Ina was embarrassed because she didn't know how to put this, didn't know how to suggest that it was an extraordinary thing around here for a man to let his orchards lie for a season. She was thinking that he was either very rich or very stupid, but she was also convinced that he could read her mind with that seemingly frozen stare. Hence her fluster. Ina felt a lurch of desire. Did he know what she was thinking? Was he calculating everything for effect?

'Yes. I know it must seem . . . unusual,' he said mildly.

He looked away from her and stared beyond her out of the room. She was almost relieved, almost disappointed at the loss of his attention.

'But I'm not working entirely without advice.'

He *had* seen inside her head. Those hypnotic eyes came to rest on her again and Ina shivered and quickly, flirtatiously changed the subject. 'I noticed you're building a new fence. I hope you aren't going to try and shut us out?'

'Now why would I want to do that?'

'Well, I don't know. Our valley is very safe, you know. We've always taken pride in the fact that this is a quiet place where everyone looks after everyone else. There's been no trouble up to now. Not like everywhere else.'

While she spoke Ina's fingers played with the short hair that curled over the back of her neck. It was true that Fransmansvallei had been insulated from the turbulence and upheaval that had shaken the rest of South Africa in the past few years. While the rest of the country experienced the dismantling of apartheid and the coming to power of the ANC as a series of massive seismic shifts, small communities like this one had felt only the tremors of change. They took pride in that, liked to think that they still harboured the best of the old values, values of community, values of

Afrikanerdom. Ina didn't yet know whether Taylor under-stood that about Fransmansvallei.

'It is exactly the peace and quiet that I value so much about my new home,' Taylor murmured, looking round the bare room.

Ina looked round too, smiling. 'Well, good . . . Welcome to it.'

He fell silent again.

'If there is anything I can help you with, anything at all, please don't hesitate to phone or just drop by.'

'Thank you. I'm sure there is nothing I need, but thank you anyway for the offer.'

'Not at all, Mr Taylor, what are neigh – '

'Please, do call me Alan.' A smile twitched fleetingly at the corners of his mouth.

Ina halted her chattering tone at last and simply looked at him. She smiled back and finally said calmly, 'What are neighbours for, *Alan*?'

'Quite.' They stood without saying anything more for nearly a minute. Ina was starkly aware of the silence around her.

She rarely, if ever, went into a house where there was nobody moving, cleaning, cooking somewhere in another room, their presence distantly registered. Yet in this house there was only the sound of their breathing. Drifting in faintly from outside was the pulse of doves cooing and the intermittent sawing of the Christmas beetles. All the windows were closed. The stillness between them had become oppressive to her, yet Alan seemed not at all uncomfortble; in fact he leaned back against the table and cocked his head to one side, looking at her with his disarmingly candid stare. Ina didn't know if she was excited or afraid. She was powerfully aware of him, of his body just three steps across the room from her and of her own presence which seemed suddenly all too fragile. It was time to leave.

He walked her to her car. As she matched his stride Ina knew that she'd never met anyone quite like him. Outside, the fresh air washed over them. Ina welcomed it; it broke the stifling, inexplicable intimacy of that moment in the kitchen just now. She gulped in deep breaths of it. He held the door open for her as she got into the car and she smiled and said thank you and that he should drop in on the family any time. He thanked her in return and, with the engine already running and her hand on the door, he leaned in and looked at her a moment, then said unexpectedly, 'Where did you say you live?'

She realised her breathlessness betrayed her. 'I didn't . . . but I'm at Komweer. That means "come back" in Afrikaans. Ask anyone in the dorp and they will tell you.' Then she added, 'The best time is usually around sunset. That's when we're all at home . . . '

She kept talking because he kept staring, but suddenly he reached forward and touched something in her hair, his fingers running down the length of it, brushing her ear. It was almost a caress. Ina breathed in sharply. She couldn't see what it was.

'A spider . . . ' he whispered, throwing it on to the ground where it skittered away. Then he looked back at her. 'That's a sign of good luck.'

She nodded, stupidly she thought later, like that stupid nodding dog that used to sit on the back window ledge of her mother's Valiant. Then she said she'd better be going and goodbye.

'Goodbye, Ina, and thank you for coming.' He bowed slightly as he clicked shut her door and Ina drove off, felt as if she sailed off, down the road.

He had pronounced her name with a long 'uh' at the end, instead of the spiky, short 'ah' as in Afrikaans, so her name sounded languid the way he said it. She had spoken to him in English, which she spoke well but haltingly – it was clearly not her first language. His voice was not particularly deep or particularly thick – in fact it was rather soft – yet his words seemed to carry, they seemed to have weight. He was quietly sure of himself and that guarded self-assurance was the most compelling thing about him. Ina wanted to make those dulled eyes light up with real laughter or even anger; she wanted to discover the person beyond that smooth smile; she wanted to peel away the reticence that made his answers to all her questions so mysterious. That was the allure; there was mystery about him. Everything was held back yet seemed to lurk so promisingly close to the surface. Whether or not he had intended to, from that first moment she saw him Alan Taylor had her completely hooked.

Ina knew the feeling all too well. This didn't happen to her every day. In fact she couldn't remember the last time. As she drove home she was breathless, her heart banging furiously in her chest, her head tight with a new anxiety. The only time she had really fallen in love was with Dawie, nearly twenty years ago. That was when she met cute boys all the time and she was often flushed with the curiosity she felt now. But there was an element here that hadn't been there before and she woke up abruptly to it. It hit her like a bucket of ice tumbling over her head. She realised that this new element was fear.

THIRTEEN

The spring was slipping into summer and everyone knew, though no one wanted to say so, that it was unusually dry for this time of year. Elise feared that the lack of good rain didn't bode well, but it was still too early to cry drought, so – like everyone else – she kept her fears to herself.

Elise was working up on the high slopes of the farm. Her hair was tied back in a ponytail and the shorter strands around her face were stuck to her skin with sweat. She pushed a strand back from her eyes and squinted into the sun. From here she could clearly see the road and Ina's car barrelling along it from what could only be the direction of Die Uitkyk. Elise watched, expecting the car to turn in at Rustenvrede, but it didn't – Ina raced straight past and on towards the dorp. Very curious. What on earth could she be up to? Elise made a note to phone her friend when she got home later.

When she got back to the house it was just after sunset and the dusk was closing in. Daan's beautiful old Mercedes was parked in the yard and she stopped her bakkie next to it. It was Tuesday, one of the three nights each week that Daan visited and, since they'd made things official, stayed over. It was Elise who insisted on the routine. Daan preferred the spontaneity of dropping by if he felt like it, of doing things on impulse. But for Elise routine governed everything. Land never flourished spontaneously, fruit didn't grow on impulse and her days were marked out by its needs. Elise belonged, first and foremost, to the farm.

Since the engagement they no longer had to keep up the absurd pretence, insisted on by Van Rensburg, that they didn't sleep together. It was ridiculous, at their age, to have to slink out in the middle of the night, not to be able to go to sleep and wake up together. Nevertheless it was her father's house, 'a Christian house', he said, and Elise, instead of pointing out that her father's Christianity was usually more about convenience than conviction, had grudgingly abided by the rule. Now, at last, Daan could stay till morning, eat breakfast with them and then go off to his work.

Elise raced into the kitchen where Mama Mashiya was flicking through an already well-thumbed *Fair Lady* magazine, waiting to serve dinner.

'Mama, I won't be long. Let them start without me!' Mama looked up anxiously, dropping the magazine as she did so.

'Are you all right, Mama?' The old lady nodded, but she wouldn't look Elise in the eye as she stood up, raising her weight slowly from the chair.

Elise jumped into the shower and quickly rinsed off the dirt of the day. She realised there'd been something different about Mama these last few days: she'd been quiet and withdrawn, as if she was worried about something. Elise had no idea what it could be.

She found Daan and her father in the sitting room, as they always were. Van Rensburg was leaning back in his chair, a glass of beer on the table next to him. He looked tired out; the working day was increasingly a strain on him. She regretted flinging his age at him so angrily the week before. Van refused to acknowledge his growing frailty and resisted all Elise's attempts to help. The bruises left by their fight would make him even more difficult to deal with.

Van was listening to Daan with a faint upward curl at the sides of his mouth. Daan was telling the cattle-rustling story she'd heard a few days before. It was one of the thousands of 'can you believe what this country is coming to' stories that had so much currency lately and which Elise found so irritating. She slipped quietly on to the sofa next to Daan who put his hand on her thigh and gave it an affectionate squeeze, not pausing once in the tale.

'So these white farmers lose an *entire* herd of cattle. The police find out where the thieves have taken them, but they say they can do nothing about it. Nothing!'

Van Rensburg snorted with laughter.

'I mean it's not like it's easy to hide a thousand head of cattle! Anyway, the farmers got together in a posse and drove off in Land-Rovers one night and went and stole the cattle right back!'

Daan roared with laughter and Van Rensburg just shook his head.

'Unbelievable what things are coming to . . . and the police, they did nothing. They were all k's of course, they weren't going to do anything to help the Boers.'

'Ja, I tell you it's not funny what this country's coming to,' Van Rensburg agreed.

Mama Mashiya appeared in the doorway to say that supper was served. They got up and went through to the dining room, Daan with his arm round Elise's shoulder.

He beamed. 'How's everything going?'

'Good,' she said, smiling back at him. 'Busy, but pretty good . . .'

'I meant to ask you about how that Mashiya guy is working out.'

Elise glanced over at her father. He hadn't said a word about Sandile since their argument. Elise sat down, pulling her chair up to the table, and said cheerfully, 'Actually I'm really pleased with him. He learns fast, he's good with the other men. I'm thinking that he'd be a good foreman, someone to help Pa maybe.'

Her father looked up sharply, his eyes wary. 'If you want to consort with terrorists, that's your business. I don't want anything to do with them.'

'*Consort?* Ag, Pa!'

Van Rensburg continued to stare at her, fuming like an affronted buffalo. She wondered how he had the energy for these tempers.

Elise shook her head impatiently. 'It's not like good men

are queuing up outside the door. He could be a real help to you. You're not getting any younger, you've said it yourself. I'm asking you to give it a try. Please?'

Her father stared down at his food. 'Have I not been plain enough? I said no.' Van Rensburg took a big gulp of wine from his glass and then put it down. Elise shook her head and reached for the water jug.

Daan watched them both with interest. 'What I don't understand is why a guy like him would want to work on a farm. From what I gather he was pretty high up in the ANC – you'd've thought he'd take a fat salary and a cushy office in government, get on the gravytrain with the rest of them.'

Van Rensburg took another gulp of wine and muttered darkly, 'My thoughts exactly.'

Daan tapped his finger thoughtfully against his glass. 'But Elise does have a point here,' he said smoothly. 'Rustenvrede could be needing a couple of foremen soon.'

Elise put the jug down. 'What do you mean?'

'I mean after the wedding.' Daan smiled patiently. There was a smugness about his look that irritated Elise intensely.

'Oh really?' She laid on the sarcasm thickly. Daan looked puzzled.

Elise bent down to concentrate on her food and for a while there was no sound in the room but the clicking of cutlery against china. Then Van Rensburg chuckled, putting his knife and fork together and pushing his plate away. He had always derived a perverse pleasure from his daughter's stubbornness. He cocked his head to one side now, addressing her in his dry, teasing way.

'What a beautiful picture. One baby strapped to your back, one to the front and a flock of toddlers round your feet in the kitchen, while you stand over the stove waiting for your men to come home!'

Elise didn't laugh, but Daan did.

'What makes you think I'm going to have any children at all?' she snapped.

Van Rensburg threw up his hands in mock frustration.

Daan poured himself a glass of wine. The conspiratorial look he exchanged with her father as they clinked glasses made Elise bridle further. The silence was brittle.

Her father was old and she knew that in his heart he believed farming was man's work, that men were innately, instinctively and in every way better farmers than even the most determined woman could ever be. She'd also noticed that since the engagement Daan had seemed to fill out as a person, but until now it had struck her as the same expansiveness she'd felt about herself. This evening it occurred to her that Daan was developing an image of himself as a farmer, as a landowner. It suddenly felt to Elise as if the men in the room were bonded against her, part of that smiling, easy male conspiracy she thought she'd defeated in Bloemfontein.

Van Rensburg stood up from the table, stretched back his arms and rubbed the hard little pot of his stomach with satisfaction. 'Well, Daan, at least you know that when you're married you'll always have good food and wine, hey? Even if the company isn't always the best! Hey?'

He roared with laughter and clapped his hand down on his daughter's shoulder. Elise didn't smile. She felt strange and heavy.

Daan and Elise followed Van Rensburg through to the sitting room where he switched on the TV and sank down into his chair. The bearded, bespectacled presenter introduced himself as Max du Preez and then welcomed his guests, Archbishop Desmond Tutu and Deputy President F. W. de Klerk.

'So have you two decided on the date yet?' Van Rensburg kept his eyes on the screen.

Elise didn't respond. She wandered over to the window and stood with her back to them, staring out into the darkness. Daan was settled on the sofa, a glass of wine still in his hand. 'The week before Christmas,' he said, sounding very sure about this. Van Rensburg nodded, the sides of his mouth drawn downwards in a thoughtful frown. Daan glanced round at Elise, but she was still turned away from him and she seemed not to have heard.

The focus shifted to the television. The bearded presenter cut across, interrupting the Deputy President. 'But, with respect, you lied–'

'Let him finish!' ranted Van Rensburg. 'Blarry traitor to your people. I'm sick of this kak!' He banged the remote, changing to a channel with a documentary in Sotho about resistance theatre. 'Shit!' He pushed the remote again.

Elise was relieved to hear the sound of an approaching car. One of her father's favourite sports was railing against the rubbish on TV; he didn't seem to care that it was no fun for the spectators. Elise moved away from the window. The car sounded like Ina's, but it was unusual for Ina to come visiting at this time of night. Then she remembered seeing the volksie coming down the road from Die Uitkyk that afternoon and she wondered if this was connected in any way.

Elise opened the back door and saw Ina trotting towards her through the darkness, surrounded by barking, yelping dogs. 'Is everything OK?'

Ina skipped up the steps and into the kitchen. She looked flushed and agitated. 'Ja, ja, everything's fine,' came her singsong reply. Ina was grinning, literally radiating excitement. She tapped Elise on the nose, smiling wickedly.

'Have I got something to tell you – about your new neighbour,' Ina trilled, winking at Elise before she sailed into the lounge and stood right in front of the TV, showering greetings on the room. 'I *had* to come and tell you in person. About the Englishman. He's arrived!'

Three expectant faces stared up at her. But Ina wasn't ready to tell yet. She turned a cheeky smile on Daan. 'Aren't you going to offer me some wine, boet?'

'Of course!' Daan stood up obediently and fetched a glass for her. Ina sank down into his place and patted the sofa next to her for Elise to sit too. Van Rensburg switched off the television.

Having taken a fortifying gulp of wine Ina launched into her story. All three listened in growing amazement as she recounted the tale of her visit to Die Uitkyk. Daan was enthralled – he loved the gossip, was excited by the change. Elise enjoyed Ina's excitement. She knew that her friend was delirious about the possibilities represented by the arrival of a thoroughly eligible man in the valley.

Ina finished her wine, shivering at the memory of that moment when Taylor fished the little spider from her hair. She didn't mention that, nor did she explain the feeling she'd had as she drove away from Die Uitkyk. Watching her Elise sensed that something more than just a neighbourly encounter had occurred, but she knew she would have to catch Ina alone to get the full story.

'Now what does some soutpiel want with Die Uitkyk?' Van Rensburg said bitterly, squashing the excitement. He came from a people who had landed at this southern tip of Africa with a strong belief that there was a reason for their coming, with a sense of mission. Deep in his heart Van Rensburg believed that he had a calling, that he had inherited a sacred task. Land, translated from the Afrikaans into English, means country. The blacks had the same commitment to the land as Afrikaners, but the English just wanted to own it. They didn't belong. As far as Van Rensburg was concerned they were soutpiels, salt penises. They had one foot in England, the other in South Africa and their dicks hung in the sea.

Van Rensburg said good night and went off to his room. Daan and Elise walked Ina to her car. Elise hugged her warmly and told her with a wink that she would phone in the morning.

Elise and Daan were getting ready for bed when Daan made some comment about plum cultivars. He'd spoken as if it was a helpful and benign suggestion. To Elise it seemed like he'd dropped a bombshell. He said he'd been talking to his brothers and getting advice from them and they'd had one or two things to say about the plums on Rustenvrede. 'Perhaps the cultivars should be improved,' he mulled.

Elise stood by her dresser with her mouth open, not knowing what to say, wondering if he'd meant to step all over her territory and, if so, why, what was he trying to do? Her bad mood had been wiped out earlier by Ina's arrival and the tantalising Taylor story; now her disquiet resurfaced. It positively made her hackles rise to think of Daan discussing the quality of her fruit with his brothers. He ought to know how competitive farmers were, how the one thing you *never* did was share that kind of information.

Elise tried to sound mild. 'Why the sudden interest in plums?'

Daan sat down on the end of the bed and folded his hands together between his knees. 'Well, I've been toying with the idea of arranging some kind of retrenchment deal from the force.'

This was the first time Elise had heard of it. It simply hadn't occurred to her that Daan wouldn't keep his job. She felt a stab of panic. Rustenvrede was hers. After her father died she would inherit it and she behaved as its inheritor, in the way she knew Dawie would have done had he lived. She had struggled so hard to achieve the place she now had at her father's side. Suddenly Daan's plans and expectations for the farm reared, upsetting the balance of things.

'Daan, it's my farm. I can't explain it, it's – *mine*. I never thought that you'd want to be a part of it.'

'You don't think I want to settle for the police the rest of my life, do you?'

He was obviously offended. She moved towards him, wanting to close the gap between them, but he was all bunched up, too tense to touch.

'I suppose I hadn't thought.' Elise sat down on the bed next to him. She realised that she ought to have seen this coming. She was sorry he was hurt, but she was also angry with him. She'd assumed they shared a picture of their life together after the wedding and in that picture she was the farmer. Surely Daan knew her well enough to know that? Elise put her hand on his arm. She hated this tension.

'We'll have to take this slowly and do a lot of thinking about it.'

'Ja.' He echoed her words, but more pointedly. 'We'd better think about it.'

For Elise the engagement had been her act of commitment to Daan, her declaration of their coupling to her father and to their community. She hadn't given much thought to what lay beyond it, not to the detail of the wedding, nor to his moving in with her at Rustenvrede, nor indeed to any of the arrangements that needed to be made and the shift in her life that marriage would entail. She had never felt this before, this unpleasant resistance that his words had caused in her. She wondered if perhaps she was to blame, if she was simply being territorial and ungenerous. The love between them, their marriage, was supposed to mean that everything would move in perfect, automatic harmony. Elise hadn't expected such harsh dissonance and didn't know how to react. The memory of the day of their engagement still sent a flush of pleasure through her. Was this sudden tension her fault? Looking at Daan she felt a surge of love for him that made her feel guilty about all her apprehensions. She curled up against him.

Their lovemaking that night was mechanical, perfunctory. They had been together more than three years, and sex had cooled after the first year or so. It had never been a really grand passion. Sometimes Elise wondered why she wasn't overwhelmed by lust, wondered if she had sublimated desire like so many things she controlled about herself. The comfort of Daan's body at night was something she loved and yet that terrible melting of two souls, that lurch forward into another was something she had never fully allowed herself to feel. She didn't know if Daan felt it, but she knew subconsciously that if she had never let go of herself, how could he?

Elise didn't climax that night, but then she rarely did and Daan never asked, so she never knew if he noticed. Elise had decided long ago that not coming was OK because sex with Daan didn't so much arouse as comfort her. Not that she was cold, she loved the sense of their bodies together, the driving need of each other, the pulling towards each other. She clung to him as he came. There was a particular pleasure for her in that, and yet she often felt a tinge of disappointment, as if she hadn't got it quite right. But Elise never dwelt much on these feelings; she thought that too would change with practice and familiarity.

People often remarked to Elise that she was sexy. She didn't really understand what they meant. She very seldom actually *felt* sexy. Somewhere deep in her subconscious was perhaps the idea she wasn't 'that kind of woman'. Closer to the surface was her fear that feeling sexy was something like feeling out of control.

The first time Elise had sex was when she was seventeen. That was a story she had never told. Thinking back it occurred to Elise that she had always been more secretive than she admitted, even to herself. Perhaps this had something to do with her feelings and instincts being so out of kilter with everyone else's. And that episode certainly was not one that chimed with anyone's idea of a good thing.

Elise's best friend at high school was a girl called Tanya Bierman. Tanya went to secretarial school in Stellenbosch when she was eighteen and was married at twenty-one, to the rich farmer she'd been looking for. Soon she was the mother of two kids and caught up in a world of domesticity and narrow but particular social obligations – the highlight of which were her weekly ladies' lunches. So Tanya was lost to her after high school, but while there they were best friends and together they went through all the teenage initiations.

Elise's official boyfriend was at the Boys' High and he was called Piet, like her father. Piet was the star player on the rugby team, handsome and very shy. They made a good-looking couple and they went steady for about three years. The arrangement seemed to suit Piet as well as it suited Elise. High-school social life revolved around couples, and of course all the drama of encoupling and decoupling, but Piet and Elise stayed together. Once Elise had told Piet she loved him and Piet said he loved her back, but while there was passion in the necking and graunching that they did in discos and on the back seats of cars, they were not really friends. And it wasn't to Piet that Elise lost her virginity, or – as Elise preferred to think of it at a time when this was important – ended her virginity.

That role fell to her matric English teacher. It was a sweet secret she still cherished. His name was Paul Mitchell and he was an awe-inspiring twenty-eight. Paul was in South Africa on some year-long teaching exchange programme with an English boarding school. He wasn't particularly good-looking, not in the way that Piet was, but he was witty and knowing and had a wicked, winning smile. All the girls in the Standard Ten class were instantly in love with him.

Although the flirtation was a long one, Elise's affair with Paul was brief and beautiful. It happened at the very end of the year, when she was about to matriculate and he was about to go home. Paul was the perfect gentleman through-out and Elise knew that if she hadn't taken the initiative it might never have happened. The first time they made love was one afternoon, on a soft blanket at a wild beach, hidden in a tangle of milkwood. There were only three more times, each one totally secret, minutely planned and deliciously satisfying. Then high school was finished and Paul went back to England. Elise knew they wouldn't have done it had there not been such a perfect exit awaiting them. She did have sex with Piet after that and Piet would always believe that he'd 'stolen her cherry'. Elise knew for sure that she had stolen his.

The years in Bloemfontein were lean as far as romance was concerned and a virtual drought on the sexual front. Elise was sealed up, closed off from contact, she found any kind of intimacy was best avoided. She did date a few men, but they were mostly hopelessly unsuitable and the relationships never lasted very long. One romance, with a classmate, had bordered on serious. Elise knew she could have fallen for Marius had he been able to leave the girlfriend who was waiting for him back home, but he couldn't and so Elise ended it before anything had really begun. After that there was no one for a long time and then there was Daan.

Elise woke before sunrise, as the dawn chorus was beginning.

It was too early to get up, so she lay in bed, her eyes wide open, staring up at the ceiling. Daan was fast asleep next to her. Her stormy thoughts of the night before had cleared and now she saw him only in the light in which she so loved him. She loved Daan's charm, his humour, the way he seized a moment and made it fun. He was the romantic counterweight to her own straightforwardness and practicality.

Elise had always hated fantasy, always fought off the daydreaming that had numbed her mother's days. She wasn't one to be caught up in silly high hopes. She believed the world was brighter and more wonderful when the gloss was stripped away, the glow rubbed off and stark, solid reality was allowed to emerge. This hadn't taken the edge off her capacity to enjoy life, but it made her sure-footed in navigating her own way. She would never get knocked down or washed away in a flash flood of desire or false expectations or wild romanticism.

As a teenager and as a student in Bloemfontein Elise had a reputation for being 'difficult', for talking back, for questioning the judgement of people in authority who saw themselves as beyond question. Hers could have been the fate of so many little girls who get worn down and eventually give up. Evelyn had called her rebellious and insolent and washed her hands of her daughter at an early age, though her father never had any trouble with her. For him Elise would do almost anything. The only problem was that while he taught her so much about the farm and farming, simply by letting her watch him, he never expected her seriously to want to be a farmer. That wasn't at all unusual. There are dozens and dozens of farms, even now, where the older daughters have gone off to the city, escaped to universities, careers, marriages, while the baby brother, the pimply, irritating little boy becomes king of his little patch. His sisters will be ruled by him or they will not be welcome.

If there had been a nephew in the Van Rensburg family, or even a favourite farm manager to hand over to, Elise might have been in trouble. She was lucky: her father's taciturn, solitary, obstinate nature worked in her favour. After Dawie was killed, and given her proven and determined interest in and knowledge of the farm, she had struggled and won. After that only Elise could inherit Rustenvrede. For the first time it dawned on her now that marrying Daan implied a change that was more fundamental than she'd imagined.

Elise looked down at Daan's hands, running her fingers over his. They were so delicate and soft compared with her own; these were not farmer's hands. She leaned over and kissed him on the cheek, whispering that it was time to wake up. Daan mumbled something and turned over. Elise sat up and ripped the bedclothes off him, pulling them to the floor. Daan rolled over, disgruntled, but his eyes opened and when he saw her he smiled. She grinned back at him. 'Time to go!' He laughed groggily and reached for her, slipping his arms round her. They held on to each other like that until the day had started without them.

FOURTEEN

Elise telephoned Ina at lunchtime to catch up on the details her friend had omitted the night before. Ina let rip with the story of the pressure of Alan Taylor's presence, of the heavy silences in the kitchen and finally of the spider in her hair. She sounded as high as a kite. 'Madeleine tells me he's checked in to De Jager's. He's staying there till his furniture and things get delivered. So even if he doesn't drop by, chance meetings will be easy to contrive!'

Elise and Ina giggled together down the phone, thrilled by the scent of romance.

'I think *I'd* better go and meet this guy. I want to make sure his intentions are honourable.'

Ina giggled again. 'I can tell you that my intentions are anything but!'

It was only after they'd milked the meaning and thrill of every second of Ina and Taylor's meeting that they said their goodbyes. Elise was about to put the phone down when she heard Ina yelling down the line: 'Elise!'

Elise brought the handset back to her ear. 'What?'

'Listen, I've made the appointment at Baskin's, it's for next Saturday at nine thirty. You'd better keep that day free, I'm not going to Cape Town on my own.'

Elise's heart sank. Baskin's was a huge warehouse of wedding dresses. She was so busy that to take a whole day off would be difficult, but the trip had to be made and rather sooner than later.

'OK. I'll tell my father. We'll make a day of it.'

'Lekker!' exclaimed Ina and put the phone down.

*

It was near sunset when Elise drove up to the dam. She needed to check the water level and wanted to sit for a while and rest from the long day's work. The sky was clear and pale with just a few streaks of cloud, promising a beautiful sunset. She was filthy and hot, covered in dust and sweat and stinking of the fertilisers they'd been spraying all day. It would be nice to dunk herself in the cool water.

She left the bakkie on the road and walked up the steep path, crested the ridge and stopped, looking across the dam. Sandile was standing not twenty metres away, staring out over the shimmering sheet of water. Ruffled by a light evening breeze, it caught the sun from a million facets. Elise felt a stab of annoyance at the way he had taken over what she regarded as her private place and her private time. She almost left, but she couldn't – she had to check the water level. Sandile saw her only when she had come right up to him.

'What are you doing?'

She hadn't meant to say it crossly, but it came out that way.

He stared at her. His eyes were distant, as if he was still half caught up in whatever thoughts had preoccupied him. Elise dipped her head in a kind of nod, a prompt.

'Hi,' he said. There was a gentle reminder in his tone.

'Hello,' she murmured, chastened by his mild rebuke.

'I was on my way home, but it's so nice here. I thought I'd watch the sunset.'

Elise softened, looking up at the mountains. 'Yes, it is nice, isn't it?'

The shreds of cloud were edged now with red and the sky at the horizon was melting from pale blue to liquid gold as the fiery ball of the sun sank lower.

'Have you seen that?' Sandile stretched out his arm, pointing towards Die Uitkyk. Elise followed the line of his finger and noticed a fence. It was huge, taller than the trees, bristling with razors, stretching the entire length of the orchard. Beyond it was only mountain. It stopped just at the point where Die Uitkyk's orchards met Van Rensburg's. Elise let out an involuntary 'huh?' of surprise.

'I wonder why on earth he's done that.'

None of the other farms were fenced in like that, there was no need for it, everyone knew each other's boundaries.

'Well, he's either shutting something out or keeping it in,' Sandile said, a little obviously.

'Shew! I've never seen anything like it.' Elise shook her head in amazement.

They both stared at the steely gleam among the trees.

'Well, I should check the water.'

Elise took a step towards him, but Sandile didn't move. He smiled slightly as she stepped round him, her body almost brushing his. She strode on but within moments she heard his tread on the sandy path behind her.

Elise bent down to read off the water level, running her fingers over the notched post. It was dangerously low; that was obvious just from looking at the dam, but the reading confirmed the extent of the problem. She shook her head and frowned, then got up to leave. As she turned she met his gaze. Sandile was standing close behind her with his arms folded over his chest, his eyes dark and serious again. She sighed distractedly.

'We have such a struggle for water at the best of times. I don't know how we'll manage if we don't get some good rain soon. Last year was bad, but this is worse.'

Sandile looked up into the clear evening sky. Elise followed his gaze, folding her arms over her chest as she did so. The streaks of cloud had vanished. She looked back at Sandile and realised he'd been staring at her.

'You don't remember me, do you?'

Elise was startled by the shift in his tone and the way he was looking at her. The dam receded from her thoughts. 'I do. Of course I remember you.'

'What do you remember?'

'I remember . . . we played together when we were kids. I remember the cops coming to arrest you that night, when we discovered that you'd disappeared.'

He jerked his chin up, frowning slightly. 'Huh.'

Elise looked away from him, towards the point where the sun was sinking fast towards the ridge of the mountain. The colours were breathtaking.

'I remember you. You were the princess.'

He was mocking her, mildly but pointedly. Elise's laugh was tinged with embarrassment. She threw up her hands and let them slap down against her jeans, as if to say she would like to deny it but couldn't.

'Well, you do . . . you remember correctly.'

'I *know* you don't remember me.'

'You keep saying that. What are you talking about?'

Sandile reached out and took her fingers lightly in his, turning her hands palm upwards. Elise was shocked by the easy intimacy of what he'd done, of how coolly he'd invaded the space immediately around her. She wanted to pull her hands away, but she didn't, not immediately. She watched as he ran his thumb along the ragged scar curving across her left palm.

'Do you remember me now?'

Elise looked at her hands in his, at his thumb marking out the length of the scar, and the memory rushed suddenly in on her. She looked up at him and she knew where this feeling she had for him came from, knew why it was so familiar and so strange at the same time. She gazed into his face, as searchingly as he was staring down at her palm, and she remembered the contours of his childish face, bent in concentration as he'd wound a bandage round and round her palm. She shuddered. Elise had never spoken to anyone about what happened on the mountains that day. Now she recalled the adventure, their complicity and then her betrayal.

Sandile was looking at her very carefully now, as if he'd forgotten that he was holding her hands. 'How could you forget?'

'But I do . . . I remember now.' She shook her head violently, her hair shivering down her neck, and pulled her fingers gently away from his.

'You betrayed me that day.' He smiled provocatively as he

said this. Elise groped for words, but her mind was reeling from the shock of the memory and the flood of explanations and questions it brought. She said nothing.

'I decided then never to trust you.' He was still smiling. Elise felt he was laughing at her, but there was no anger in his eyes.

'Hey, we've almost missed the sunset!'

He sprang away from her, looking up, tracing the line of the mountains and the brilliant sky as he walked towards the swimming rock, the most comfortable vantage point for the show. Elise glanced at her watch then looked around. Why was she being so cagey? Was she worried that someone might see, had already seen? There was no one within sight or sound of them. She told herself she was being ridiculous and shook her head, shook out her hair and all her suspicions. Suddenly she tasted the cool evening air, felt it against her cheek. She felt free and light. Why not? She strolled towards the flat rock where he sat, watching her.

'Hey, don't look at me, look at the sky!' she said as she sat down next to him.

All around them the horizon seemed to catch fire. The whole sky was bathed in the luminance of the setting sun. Sandile chuckled, a pleasant, pleasurable gurgle in the back of his throat. The seriousness that she was accustomed to seeing in his face evaporated again in that brilliant smile. There was something else there, something mischievous, but his eyes were warm.

'So you're the boss round here now, are you?'

'Well, not really . . . Not officially. Officially my pa is the boss, but he's getting old. So in practice more and more falls to me. You know how it is.'

Sandile nodded, then he said, a little slyly, 'I never thought of you as a farmer.'

She looked him in the eye and smiled confidently. 'Oh, really? And why not?'

He laughed slightly. 'I thought you'd have been snapped up by some prince and gone off to live happily ever after in his little kingdom.'

Elise was watching him carefully, searching for signs of mockery. She didn't think she found any, but she wasn't sure.

'That's what my mother and father thought, maybe even Dawie too . . .'

Sandile nodded and then he said more seriously, 'But that didn't stop you.'

'No. That didn't stop me.'

Sandile stood, reached up and put both hands round the branch above them and his body hung loosely to the ground. He looked at her and for a second time she saw the guard drop, the wariness slip from his eyes as he regarded her. Then he looked back at the sky.

'Do you mind if I ask you . . . something personal?' She leaned towards him.

'Depends how personal.'

'Why did you come back here? I mean, there isn't much for you in a place like this. Why did you give up politics? There must be a better life for you than this.'

Putting the question made Elise squirm a little. It embarrassed her because it pointed to the gulf between them, the gap between mistress and servant. Sandile continued to gaze at the sky, but his expression didn't change. He didn't appear to have taken offence and she saw that and was relieved.

In fact Sandile did feel uncomfortable and dishonest about his response, but he didn't look at her, didn't let any of that show. 'I'm sick of politics. I've done my time in that game,' he said, shrugging off the question.

But Elise leaned towards him, curious to know more. 'Why *did* you leave? I only know what the police and the people in the valley said afterwards. Nobody seemed to know what really happened.'

Sandile laughed a small snort of a laugh. 'How much time have you got?'

Elise smiled and looked up at the darkening sky. 'Not much apparently,' she said.

Sandile let go of the tree and sat down again. He looked

puzzled and pained. 'It's so long ago now . . . Do you really want to know?'

'Yes.'

'Why?'

He shifted round to face her. Elise didn't have an answer. She shrugged, opening her palms as if waiting to catch something that might do for a response. He didn't wait for her to find one. He just took a deep breath and launched into it, looking down at the rock all the time he spoke, his hand sketching invisible, irregular patterns on the stone. 'It was crazy really. We were so young, we hardly knew what we were doing . . . It was me and Xolile and–'

Elise interrupted. 'Who?'

'Johnny Kakana.'

'Oh.' Elise nodded and Sandile continued.

'And another boy, Baasie. Did you know him?'

Elise frowned. 'No, I don't think so.'

He went on and was quickly lost, winding through a maze of memories.

Sandile was seventeen then. He had just finished his final year, the matric year, at school. Unlike most of the kids he'd started school with Sandile managed to finish. It was his own as well as his teacher's determination that pushed him through. Mrs Pretorius had taken a particular liking to him. She'd teased and cajoled and encouraged him all the way through to the end of his exams. When at last they were over Sandile had no idea of what to do. His future yawned like a chasm, a black hole. He didn't want to work on the farm, nor did he want to end up living on the edge of the city in a squatter camp, like his brother Vuyani. Vuyani worked occasionally for a pittance on building sites and in white people's gardens during the day and ripped off their houses at night. To continue with his studies was financially impossible for Sandile. For someone like him there was little choice, little opportunity, little to hope for without change.

In Fransmansvallei nobody talked about change. There, an end to apartheid seemed even less likely than the possibility of

P. W. Botha walking on water. But in Cape Town, in the townships and in the squatter camp where Sandile sometimes visited his brother, talk of change was everywhere. Change was happening. People were angry, were starting to organise themselves, just as they were doing around towns and cities all over South Africa. Organisation was loose and sometimes chaotic; nevertheless it was there, and the ANC were sneaking back from exile, catching the momentum of the time and directing it towards a future that was still unclear, but certainly brighter than the present.

The first contact Sandile had with the ANC was while he was visiting Vuyani near Cape Town, during the school holiday in the middle of the year. It was winter, a quiet time on the farm, so his mother had sent him to look out for his brother and try to persuade him to return to the relative safety of the valley. Vuyani clung to the edge of a seedy underworld of criminal gangs that thrived in the townships. He told Sandile he was never going back to that tiny, conservative, deathly quiet place where there was only one kind of work and one kind of baas. He didn't think much of the cardboard and corrugated-iron shack that he called home, but as far as he was concerned life in town was brimming with possibilities, with the chance of something better, and gang life at least offered a kind of respect. Farm life offered nothing. Sandile couldn't argue with that.

Sandile found something in activism. Hope is too strong a word for it; engagement, distraction, focus would all be better. It was something when previously there had been nothing. He was terribly young, but so were most of his comrades. They got involved in teaching, in consciousness-raising and civic organisation. It was illegal and dangerous. There were enough people sitting in detention and jail, enough people who had simply disappeared as a result of their activism to testify to the seriousness of what Sandile was doing.

Sandile had never been involved in military operations and he didn't know anyone who was. It was an older guy, a guy whose real name he never learned, who approached Sandile about a job that would spin everything round and flip his life into a new dimension.

This guy was different from any of the others that Sandile had met in the ANC. He was also terribly, painfully thin and he walked with an incredible swagger, staring out at the world from behind battered traffic-cop Ray-Bans. The skinny guy had heard that Sandile's family lived on a farm and he wanted to talk to him about that. It was only after several short, oblique conversations that Sandile understood the guy was looking for a safe place to hide something – it could even have been someone. Sandile certainly knew of such places, places where no one would ever think to look. The man seemed satisfied with this; he said no more and went away. Sandile didn't see him again for several days, until just before the time when he was due to go back home and start school again. He wanted to inspect a hiding place. Sandile said that would be fine and the guy let his Ray-Bans slip down his nose. For a moment he looked down at Sandile that way, staring inscrutably at him through tiny dark eyes. 'You can call me Skinny,' he said.

Sandile smiled, coughed back laughter at that and said, 'Fine. Thanks, Skinny.'

Skinny gave him a lift back to Fransmansvallei in an ancient powder-blue Zephyr. He drove as fast as the car would take them, in the slow lane all along the freeway and revving hard on the mountain passes. The ride was luxurious and fast compared with the trains and buses Sandile would have had to use otherwise. When Mama Mashiya saw her favourite son with the stranger her eyes narrowed suspiciously, but she offered Skinny food, which he accepted. Later, when it was dark, Sandile told his mother that he wanted to show his friend the way back towards town. Skinny went outside to the car and Sandile followed, but Mama intercepted him.

She stepped between her son and the door. Folding her arms over her wide breasts she gazed anxiously up at him. 'I don't like the look of your new friend. He seems like a gangster type to me. Are you running around with gangsters now?'

Sandile laughed, shaking his head as he did so. 'Ma, you've never even seen a gangster!'

She clicked her tongue, scolding him. 'You think you're so clever. How would you know what I've seen?'

Sandile squeezed her shoulders affectionately as he pushed past her, but she was unconvinced and hissed at him, 'Now you come back quickly. Promise me?' Sandile promised and went outside to where Skinny was smoking a little roll-up cigarette in the car.

He showed Skinny possible hiding places on Rustenvrede. He seemed to like the last place, which was near a small, dead-end road; he said he thought that could be suitable. The road was a short track off Skaduwee Lane, the main road from Fransmanshoek to three farms, the second last and last of which were Rustenvrede and Die Uitkyk. The track was never used now. It led up to Van Rensburg's old cold store that was invisible from the main road and had been abandoned a long time ago, when Sandile was a small child. The building was small and high and half ruined. Inside it was littered with twisted, rusting lumps of machinery. An excellent hiding place.

Skinny dropped Sandile off at the bottom of the drive that led up to Rustenvrede. I like this kid, Skinny thought to himself, he's like me, but still not spoiled. Sandile had the qualities of stillness and tension, calm and keenness that were the material for an ace operative. Just before he climbed out of the car Skinny clutched at Sandile's arm, digging long bony fingers into the soft flesh of the boy's forearm. He stared hard at him in the darkness and Sandile stared back. Finally, Skinny asked quietly, 'Sandile, do you have friends you can trust?'

Sandile thought for a moment, more about what this question might mean than about his friends – of course he had friends he could trust. After a minute or so he nodded.

Skinny's voice was a rasping whisper. 'We'll need two others to help us. Can you organise it?'

Skinny continued to stare and Sandile knew suddenly that he had fallen into something so deadly serious that he couldn't even begin to imagine its consequences. That excited him, more than anything ever had. Something was happening and he was in the middle of it, dead centre.

Sandile nodded again. Skinny grunted, let go of Sandile's arm and said, 'I'll be in touch.' Then Sandile got out of the car and Skinny drove away, the putter of the old engine fading quickly as it disappeared into the shadows.

It was a couple of months before Skinny made contact again. In the meantime Sandile got on with his studies, travelling for hours each day just to get to the crammed little rural school where absenteeism and strikes by the over-worked teachers were almost as rife as they were among the pupils. His matric exams had started and he'd almost given up hope of seeing Skinny again when the guy showed up unexpectedly one afternoon.

It was a warm summer day. Sandile was at the end of the long journey back from school, trudging up the road to the compound, when he saw the blue Zephyr. Skinny's long sticklike legs hung out of the door, his feet scuffing the ground. Sandile went straight up to him. Their conversation was brief and to the point. Skinny needed the hiding place in exactly sixteen days' time. He gave Sandile instructions for preparing the area and said that he should bring two other guys along to help with the preparation and with the stash, but they must be 150 per cent trustworthy. 'Are your friends a hundred and fifty per cent?'

Sandile nodded seriously, then Skinny's mouth cracked in a smile. 'I don't want them to know anything more than that this is important and that they will be rewarded. But' – and here Skinny paused for effect, dragging slowly on his slender cigarette – 'if they can't keep their own mouths shut we have ways of doing it for them. Understand?'

Sandile bit down on his lower lip and nodded. Skinny exhaled, smoke pouring from his nostrils and his mouth. 'Good. You handle them. OK?'

'OK.' Sandile was caught up in a rush of adrenalin. He wanted desperately to know what they were going to hide and, though he knew he shouldn't, he asked.

Skinny was edgy and excited and couldn't resist saying it. He leaned forward, right into Sandile's face. 'Guns,' he whispered. The word was so tantalising – Sandile could see that it made those tiny eyes shine behind the dark glasses.

Sandile's best friend at that time was a guy from his school, Baasie. Baasie was sixteen and, like Sandile, he lived on a farm, but in the next valley. Sandile and Baasie hung out together on the bus and at school. Baasie was the really good-looking one, the one all the girls went for. Sandile was the brains.

Then there was Xolile. There had always been Xolile. He was the straight man, the dupe, the dope, the vulnerable little brother. Baasie didn't have much time for him but he was part of the package that came with Sandile, so there was never any discussion about it: he was simply there. Sandile protected Xolile, they had known each other as long as either of them could remember, and being together was a habit that suited them both. Sandile had never feared the darkness or the mountains, nor even the farmer. Xolile feared everything. Sandile helped him, patiently, unerringly, to overcome his terrors. Like many friendships this one worked because Sandile derived strength from being the one that pushed forward, the teacher, the leader, and Xolile enjoyed the protection, enjoyed Sandile showing off for him.

Xolile was the one he told first. Xolile insisted he could keep a secret. Only then did Sandile reveal the plan, exactly as Skinny had instructed him, giving only the barest outlines of the operation. 'But,' and here Sandile paused for effect, just as Skinny had done, 'you can never, ever speak of this. Not to your mother, not to anyone. Ever.' Xolile was clearly excited, but also terribly unnerved. Sandile reassured him, telling him it would be a big opportunity, the beginning of something that might lead them out of the trapped tedium, the poverty of the valley.

Sandile said they shouldn't speak of it again until it was time to prepare the site. But the next morning Xolile said he was nervous about the impending adventure and he continued to speak of it every day after that, despite Sandile's urgings. Sandile grew anxious about him, yet he didn't make the phone call that Skinny had told him he should make if he was unhappy about anything. Then, five days before the operation, Xolile stopped talking about it. Sandile assumed this silence meant he was 150 per cent at last. Sandile knew that Xolile was a coward, but it never occurred to him that he could be a traitor.

Baasie was on board straight away and Sandile felt 150 per cent certain of him all the way. The appointed day was a Sunday. That weekend Baasie stayed over with Sandile and as the Sunday evening drew in they told Mama Mashiya that they were going over to Xolile's place for the night. Ben Mashiya was working in his vegetable plot at the back when the boys strolled away from the compound. Sandile raised his arm to return his father's wave as they set off across the orchards. His father stood for a while, sucking on his pipe, watching his son walk away.

There was no moon that night. Sandile supposed Skinny had planned for that. He and Baasie met Xolile at the old cold store. Xolile was a few minutes late and very jumpy, but they'd seen him like that before. Sandile hoped that Xolile's courage would return the minute they were in action. Their instructions were simple enough. They were to wait for the arrival of a vehicle around midnight, offload some parcels, hide them in the place they'd made ready and then clear out.

Sandile was to meet the vehicle at the crossroads where Skaduwee Lane intersected with Hoogtevreespas, the road that snaked up from Paarl and over and down the mountains and led eventually into Fransmanshoek. He hadn't told Baasie or Xolile about that part. At ten thirty he left them at the site and set off to walk across the orchards to the meeting place. If Sandile had made his way to the intersection along Skaduwee Lane things might have turned out differently because he would have noticed the three dark cars that slunk down the road in the direction of Rustenvrede as midnight approached. If he'd seen those strange cars he'd have known that something was wrong.

Xolile's nerviness had put Sandile on edge, had heightened his alertness. As he walked through the pitch dark with the trees above him, their leaves like black lace, like spider-webs between him and the sky, he tried to calm himself, told himself that the whole thing would be simple and straight-forward. It was a Sunday night in one of the sleepiest places in the world. There was one tiny little police station in the dorp and those dozy cops couldn't even catch a stray cow. Right now they would be snoring like motorbikes – they'd never know a thing. The whole exercise would take no more than half an hour and afterwards they would go back to Xolile's mother's house where they'd sip a little of her home-made beer together and savour the exhilaration of their secret.

Sandile waited at the intersection for nearly half an hour. Nobody, no vehicles, passed by him in either direction in all that time. A few minutes after midnight an old post office van pulled to a halt on the gravelly hard shoulder by the turn. A man stuck his head out of the passenger window at the side and looked around. Sandile stepped forward from under-neath the trees where he had been hidden by shadowy darkness. The crunch of his feet on the gravel alerted the occupants of the van to his presence. The passenger said the words that let Sandile know this was the vehicle he was waiting for. Then the side door slid open and Sandile climbed into the back.

Skinny was driving. He glanced back before turning the van down Skaduwee Lane. 'OK?' he asked quietly.

'OK,' Sandile replied, smiling broadly.

'Good,' grunted Skinny.

Sandile's heart was racing as they slid down the road towards the little cul-de-sac where Baasie and Xolile would be waiting. He knew that something was wrong the instant they turned into the slip track. In the dim headlights he saw Baasie burst out from behind the trees that concealed the cold store. He was running towards them, but he was still fifty metres away.

'Stop!' Sandile shouted. Skinny slammed his foot on the brake and both he and the passenger swung their faces round towards Sandile, who was staring at the road ahead like a frightened cat.

Baasie didn't stop running. Sandile said urgently, almost under his breath, 'Something's wrong. Turn round!'

At that moment all three of them saw the white man emerging from the trees behind Baasie. 'Shit!' Skinny swore as he jerked the gears down and spun the van round. They heard a car engine revving somewhere behind them, then there was a popping sound, then two more pops, like shots going off. Looking in the side mirror Sandile saw Baasie fall down in the road and that was how Sandile would always remember him, face down on the ground, bathed moment- arily in the red glow of the tail lights. Then they were round the corner and racing back down Skaduwee Lane.

'Fuck! What the fuck happened?' Skinny was incandescent with rage. Sandile didn't know, he couldn't absorb it. He snapped his eyes shut, screwed them tight. Skinny killed the lights on the van and screamed, 'Get me off this road. Is there another way?' Sandile opened his eyes: there was a way round the dorp, a way that would take them north, a way that only someone from the valley would know. He prayed then that those white men were not from the valley.

Sandile directed Skinny down a series of farm tracks, dirt roads that led out to the other side of town and to the old pass that would take them north over the mountains. If anyone was waiting for them, he calculated, they would be waiting on Hoogtevreespas, the pass that led south. Skinny swung the van round tight corners. Tree branches slapped and scraped the windscreen and the sides of the van; they crashed through potholes, pushing the engine as hard as it would go. Twice they skidded on the gravel and almost flipped over, but somehow Skinny managed to hold on. The passenger was intent on the road behind them, Skinny on the road ahead. Sandile swung his gaze between them. They passed no other cars and no other cars passed them.

When at last they cleared the top of the pass they knew they had slipped whoever it was who had lain in wait for them. Skinny flicked the headlights back on. Still, no one spoke until they had been driving for another hour and knew that the immediate danger had passed. It was Skinny who broke the silence. He was calmer than Sandile had ever seen him and that was reassuring, even if his words weren't.

'Great. Now we are in the deepest shit. The deepest shit, my broers. Did your friends get my name?'

Sandile shook his head.

'You sure?' he barked.

Sandile almost whispered his response: 'Hundred and fifty per cent.'

Skinny snorted bitterly at the irony, then pulled out his tobacco pouch and rolled up a cigarette on his lap with his left hand, his right hand clutching the steering wheel, his eyes fixed on the road ahead. 'But they know *you*, broer, they knew your name.'

It felt to Sandile like his mouth was full of sand. 'Ja, they know me.'

Skinny shoved the little roll-up into his mouth and lit it with the battered cylinder that he pulled from the dashboard. He was furious that his plan had fucked up, but his immediate concern was to get them all out of danger. As the road slipped by his irritation subsided and his sympathy for Sandile extended. He dragged deeply on another cigarette. 'You can't go back. We're gonna have to get you out.'

'Out?' Sandile panicked for a moment, imagining they were going to shove him out of the van, but that wasn't what Skinny meant.

'Out of the country. We're gonna have to get you out of South Africa.'

In the hours of driving that followed Sandile said nothing;

he simply allowed the weight of those words, the unknowable, massive vista of their meaning, to sink slowly into his consciousness.

Skinny pushed on through the night. Once they stopped to refuel from the tanks of petrol they were carrying in the back of the van. Then, just before morning, they came to a place that Skinny apparently knew. He took a dirt road that ended at a flooded quarry pit. They dumped the van there, pushed it over the side and watched it sink, along with its precious cargo, into the murky water.

Sandile shivered as it disappeared, mud-dark water bubbling up round the hulk of the thing before it was swallowed and the water was still again. Not a murmur on the surface to indicate the secret drowned there. Then they walked for an hour to a township adjacent to the small town nearby. Skinny and the passenger left him at a house which they said was safe. Skinny squeezed his arm and said, 'Stay cool, broer, you'll be all right. We'll see you again when the big day dawns.' Sandile smiled ruefully as he watched them walk away.

Sandile never forgot Skinny's words, nor did he forget a single detail of what happened to him in the thirty long days that followed that moonless night. The course of his life was altered irrevocably. There was no going back; everything, every ounce of energy, every single thought was directed forward, towards getting away. The people in the safe house in the Free State helped to arrange his escape. He was to skip through Lesotho. Alone.

Sandile made his way to the border on foot. It was a hard journey, in every sense. Sandile had never been further from home than Cape Town and now he was traversing South Africa, putting his life in the hands of strangers. He could have slipped out into the vastness of the country, he could have stopped and disappeared somewhere along the route, but he didn't. He had a destination now, he had a purpose.

Sandile didn't sleep in days. Fear kept him alert, outweighing the fatigue that pulled him down. He had to slip the border fence to get into Lesotho, but once he was over he felt light and dizzy, with renewed energy. It was night and late when he crossed the border, but he managed to hitch a couple of rides that got him to Maseru by morning. Once in the capital he found the High Commission on Refugees and there he knew he was safe at last. Sitting in the soft leatherette armchair in the front office of the High Commission, lulled by the distant sound of clacking typewriters, the soft English tones of the secretary who had brought him a cup of tea and was now making and taking phone calls at her desk in the reception area, Sandile fell asleep.

He was woken by the light touch on his shoulder of a beautiful, much older woman with almost completely white hair, cut so short that her tiny curls were tight against her scalp, like a silver cap. For a moment he was disoriented by the face, the dazzling smile and the light that flooded into the room behind and washed out all the colour around her to a bright, brilliant white. He didn't know where he was, or who she was, and he started, jumped straight up out of the chair and almost knocked the woman over. Then she spoke, telling him calmly where he was and that he was all right. She was from the ANC and she had arranged his passage to Zambia.

His destination was an ANC farm outside Lusaka. Zambia was where the ANC President's office was located, where the organisation was based in exile. The hustle of the President's office was breathtaking. Sandile was impressed that they were expecting him and knew what to do with him. In the office he was introduced to a man who was known to everyone simply as Ismail. Ismail was to take care of him, was to be his political adviser, the commissar who would act as Sandile's guide and mentor in the movement.

They set out together for the farm on the morning after Sandile's arrival at the office, following the main road south out of the capital for only an hour or so before the tarmac turned into dirt. There were tiny flowers in bloom all along the roadside. They drove for another hour, bouncing around in silence in the cab of the Land-Rover, till they turned off down an even narrower track. The winding road to the farm was bewilderingly long and the scrubby bushveld stretched as far as Sandile's eyes could see. At last the road took an abrupt turn and they halted sharply. Sandile's heart leapt at the sight of the men in military fatigues standing before them, AK47s hanging loosely at their hips. This was MK. The spear of the nation. The guerrilla army of the ANC. Ismail spoke briefly with one of the guards, then he saluted vaguely and pulled the Land-Rover away through the gates.

Beyond the gate stood a squat homestead with a red tin roof, small low windows and broad verandas. The paint was peeling off the crumbling plaster, but everything about the place was orderly, even the neat fields of rows of mielies stretching beyond it.

The farm was a sanctuary for Sandile and the men and women who worked and lived on it. During the day he joined them on the land and at night he was thrown into the work of the organisation. He learned to handle guns as well as politics. A whole new world was opening up to him and Sandile found the breadth of it exhilarating. Looking back on that time, at how he was then, he couldn't remember even a glimmer of the despair and hopelessness that came later. He was idealistic and angry. Rage made him completely, unshakeably sure that the day of freedom would come soon, sooner now he was there to join his strength to that of his comrades.

Those first few months were so exciting that Sandile gave little thought to what he had left behind, or to the future, so content was he in the moment. Then, three months after his arrival, Ismail came down from Lusaka one weekend and joined him at the braai he'd made on the stubbly lawn outside the homestead. He explained that while 'they' were delighted with his progress and with his work on the farm 'the movement' felt Sandile had potential for greater things and the time had come for him to make a choice. Both Sandile and Ismail were agreed that he should not be a soldier. The alternative was university. The ANC would organise a scholarship for him in Europe.

Sandile looked out across the sparse lawn towards the fields. Ismail was watching for a reaction, but he saw only the muscle working in Sandile's cheek. 'Of course you need a matric. Did you get your matric?'

Sandile realised that he didn't know. The exams he'd sweated so hard over were obliterated by the whirlwind of what had happened after. He looked round at Ismail and said bluntly, 'I don't know.'

The next day Ismail stood by Sandile in the post office as he dialled Mrs Pretorius's phone number. Sandile's hand was shaking from the prospect of contact with his old life, the fear of what he would hear of Baasie and Xolile and his mother and father.

'Hello!' Mrs Pretorius picked up almost immediately. Sandile felt his heart pounding at the sound of her sunny voice. He didn't know what to say.

'Hello, who's there? Who is this?' She sounded suspicious, worried now by the silence.

Sandile cleared his throat. 'Mrs Pretorius?' He said her name tentatively but he knew she knew it was him. He could hear her fear, could feel it slithering down the wire.

'Are you OK?' was all she said.

He stammered slightly, finding words. 'Mmm, I'm fine. How are my . . . friends?'

She was quiet again, then she said, 'We read in the paper that Baasie is dead.'

Sandile closed his eyes. 'What about Xolile?'

Mrs Pretorius said quickly, 'The article didn't mention anyone else.'

Sandile wanted to feel the relief of knowing that Xolile had escaped, that he'd slipped through the net that was waiting for them, but in his heart he suddenly knew it was Xolile who had betrayed them. If Xolile had been there next to him Sandile knew he could have killed him with his bare hands.

Sandile smashed his head against the wall in pain and frustration. Ismail pulled him back and angrily told him to pull himself together. 'You have a mission to accomplish!'

Sandile wanted to cry, but he found a voice that was level and calm. 'Mrs Pretorius... what happened about my exams?'

'My God, of course, you haven't heard. You got distinctions for everything! You came top in the region!' Her voice rang with delight.

Ismail was tapping the face of his watch. Sandile looked away. 'Listen, I have to go, but what ... Are my mother and father OK?' Sandile's lip quivered as he listened. She'd heard they'd been picked up by the police but that the farmer they worked for got them released in Paarl – they were OK now. He pictured his mother's fear, her incomprehension, her loss.

'But what about you? Are *you* OK?'

Sandile wasn't OK at all. He realised then the extent of the gulf between him and his parents, but he managed to say quietly, 'I'm fine. I'm with people who are looking after me.'

She heard the pain in his voice and spoke to him in that pull-yourself-together-you're-OK tone that he'd heard from her a thousand times before. 'Listen to me now. Wherever you are, find a way to carry on studying. That's what you must do, Sandile, go to university. Promise me that's what you will do.'

Sandile was nodding, his voice cracked as he replied, 'I will, I will, but ... thank you. Thank you for everything.'

Mrs Pretorius laughed. 'Thanks for nothing. Just do one thing for me?'

'Anything,' he said.

'Live. We need you back here one day. You hear?'

'That was how I went to London.' Sandile stopped making circles on the rock with his hand. He had finished. Elise breathed in sharply; her brow was creased by a frown but her eyes glittered. She was aware that he was breathing heavily, that he still felt the pain of what had happened. She wanted to touch him, to reach out and put her hand on the muscle at the top of his arm, but she didn't. She could have. There was an intimacy in the moment that would have made her touch completely natural. But her hand didn't move from her lap.

Sandile rubbed the flat of his hand over the stone, as if erasing the invisible marks he had made there with his finger. Then he looked up at her and smiled, his eyes bright but sad.

'Does Daan know this?' she asked.

'What?'

'About Johnny.'

Sandile shrugged. 'He may. But it's possible that no one from here knows. In time they will. The past doesn't go away. All the wishing in the world can never make it go away.'

Elise knew that. She looked down at her hands and rubbed them together, rubbing her thumb over the scar.

At that moment he wanted to confide in her, to share the weight of his secret about the land claim with her. Secrets corrode, they eat away at the soul. Secrets are toxic, he thought, looking away. Then he narrowed his eyes and looked back at her, quizzically. 'What do you want, I mean really want, from your life?'

Elise cocked her head slightly to one side, surprised. 'What a huge question.'

Sandile smiled, shrugging, and turned back to face the indigo arc of the mountains. Along the ridge the sky glowed a deep ember-red, the glow left by the sun after it sank below the crags of Groot Drakensrug. The sun was long gone and they hadn't noticed.

Elise almost whispered her answer. 'More than anything, more than love or friendship or money or anything . . . I want this land. I want to farm it as my father did and his father and his father's father before him. It's like it's a sacred mission or something, it's so powerful.'

Sandile shivered. Then he nodded his head, very slowly, very seriously. 'I know what you mean. I know exactly.'

The silence was full of meanings, hidden and revealed.

Darkness had closed in around them and night was falling fast. Elise stood up to leave and Sandile followed suit. They walked down to her bakkie in silence. Elise didn't ask him why he was walking with her, she was just glad that he was. As she climbed into the driver's seat he scuffed at the ground with his shoe, then looked up at her, all the seriousness gone.

'Thanks, that was nice.'

Elise agreed with a smile and a dip of her head. Then she pulled away. Sandile watched until the headlights of her car had disappeared into the darkness.

It was late. Van Rensburg and Daan had already sat down to eat when Elise raced into the house, quickly took a shower and pulled on some clean clothes. Her father looked up as she entered the room, his gruff voice cutting across a story of Daan's.

'What's kept you, my girl?' His voice was friendly and there was nothing unusual in his remark, but Elise felt suddenly flustered. She looked at them both and then down at her food and her hand flicked up agitatedly as she spoke. 'Sorry – I didn't realise how late it was getting.'

Her father was watching her, his eyes narrowed suspiciously. 'Everything all right?'

'Mmm. Been to check up on the apples,' she said hurriedly.

Her father grunted and went on eating. Daan offered some wine, but she put her hand over the glass without meeting his eye.

Elise attacked the plate of food in front of her. She couldn't believe she had lied so badly, so blatantly, and about something so small. Anyone might have seen her bakkie by the dam and she'd be caught out. Well, she could have gone down to check on the apples and then made a detour past the dam on the way back, she rationalised. And anyway, she hadn't lied, she'd simply omitted – it wasn't anything that really deserved a mention. Yet she knew it did. The encounter with Sandile had made a deep impression on her. Elise glanced over at Daan and felt a pang of guilt.

Before Daan found her in Bloemfontein Elise had lived a solitary life. By the time she came back to the Cape her sealed-off inner self had a life almost separate from her exterior. The outer Elise was the eccentric, attractive Van Rensburg girl who wanted to be a farmer and had managed it. Inside there was a person known only to Elise, one who differed from everyone else in more ways than just her desire to be a farmer.

'And how are they looking?'

Elise glanced up at her father. She clearly had no idea what he was talking about. 'What?'

'The apples,' he said.

Elise reddened, realising she'd been caught out. 'Oh yes, ja, the apples are coming on nicely.'

Van Rensburg seemed satisfied with her answer.

'What about you?' she countered. 'Everything OK your end?'

'Ja, fine. No problems, nothing to report,' he said and smiled stolidly.

Elise looked over at Daan. His eyes met hers and he smiled. She began to relax.

FIFTEEN

The next day was hot and hazy. The sky was a fine skein of high cloud. There was still no sign of rain. Just before lunchtime Elise took the bakkie with Sandile and two other men in the back and headed over to the orchards above the dam where she planned to run the final check on a new irrigation system. The success of the system depended on a good water supply from the dam, a supply Elise couldn't count on for long, unless the rain came soon. This problem and the problem of water generally weighed heavily on her mind as her bakkie rattled down the farm road.

The border between Rustenvrede and Die Uitkyk ran on the other side of a farm track which curved along the entire eastern edge of Van Rensburg's property. The track belonged to the Van Rensburgs, but the fence between the two farms was long gone and for many years now the Lombaards had used the road freely and helped to maintain it in return. The route from the main house at Rustenvrede intersected with the boundary track at a T-junction just beyond the dam.

Elise crested the hill above the dam and was descending towards the intersection when she saw, to her astonishment and disbelief, that her route was blocked by a dozen workmen standing in a massive trench, planting poles for Alan Taylor's fence. The trench was at least ten metres inside Rustenvrede, cutting across the road and right up against the peach trees. The crew had literally fenced in Van Rensburg's road all along the southern orchards and were moving rapidly north. In front of the trench, hopping up and down and screaming in apoplectic rage, was Van Rensburg himself.

Elise accelerated hard; the men on the back lurched forward, then back, almost falling off the vehicle. She screeched to a halt at what was now a dead end created by the fence and stalled the bakkie in her haste to get to her father.

The workmen were staring in dumb amazement at the huge old white man who was hopping around and waving and bellowing so hard it looked as if the veins in his face would burst.

'What the hell do you think you're doing? This my blarry road! Yussus. Get these goddamn poles off my farm! Get out of my orchards! Get off my land!'

One of the workers, distracted by the screaming, lost control of the pole he was placing and as it fell it knocked an entire fruit-laden branch off a mature peach tree. Van Rensburg reacted as if his own arm had been ripped out of his shoulder. He stormed up to the man, grabbed a long spade from the ground and raised it over his head, as if to beat him with it. The workman cowered, shielding his face from the imminent blow, but Elise reached the scene at that moment. She got hold of the spade just in time and held it long enough to let the terrified man scuttle away. Van Rensburg swung round angrily, but his anger gave way to surprise when he saw his daughter before him.

'Just let me handle this!' he hissed, yanking the spade from her grasp.

'Pa, I think we should take this up with Taylor himself – these guys are only doing their job.'

Her father fumed, momentarily caught by her logic, but only momentarily. His land was being defaced and vandalised; it was as if he was under attack himself, and Van Rensburg had to fight back. 'If you want to help me you can fetch my gun from the car. Otherwise shut up!'

The workmen, riled by his threats, moved forward, forming a circle round the farmer, who swung the spade at anyone who came near him. It was obvious to Elise that they were acting on instructions; they had no idea they were trespassing. Now they weren't defending the fence, they were defending themselves. It seemed there was nothing she could do – her father was hemmed in.

'Hey!' Sandile's voice boomed across Van Rensburg's yelling. Elise turned to see him jumping down from the back of the bakkie.

'Who's in charge here?' Sandile spoke in Xhosa. That and the authority in his tone commanded their attention instantly.

The crew seemed relieved, but kept an eye on the dangerous farmer while the foreman stepped forward to deal with Sandile. He made an irritable clicking sound, pointing towards Van Rensburg. 'What the hell is this old guy's problem?'

'There's been a mistake. This is his road,' Sandile retorted, looking anxiously from the foreman to Van Rensburg.

The foreman threw up his hands. 'Listen, man, this is where we were told to put it, but if there's going to be trouble we're out of here. This isn't my problem.' He turned to the crew. 'OK, guys, take a break!'

The men dropped their tools without hesitation. Elise rushed to her father's side and pulled the spade from his grasp. He walked away in disgust. The tension had instantly defused. Elise looked gratefully at Sandile.

Van Rensburg held on to the door of his bakkie to steady himself; he was shaking with rage. 'You boys are going to have to take out your poles and clean up the mess you've made.'

The foreman glared silently back at him.

'Go fetch your boss,' Sandile suggested quietly. 'Let him sort this out.'

Agreeing, the foreman strode away. Van Rensburg bellowed after him, 'You do that and meanwhile I'm calling the police! I'll have every bladdy one of you arrested for trespassing.'

The foreman replied by sticking two fingers up as he jumped on to the tractor that was nearby and drove off.

Van Rensburg turned and pointed his shaking finger at Elise. 'You! You stay right here while I get the police.'

Elise stared wearily after him as the bakkie hurtled away, kicking up a huge dust trail. Then he disappeared beyond the hill and she turned back towards Die Uitkyk and stood, hands on hips, contemplating the fence. Up close it was quite an awe-inspiring structure, more befitting an army base or a prison than a humble fruit farm. It was sunk several feet into the ground and stood at least eight feet above that with double razor wire rolled along the top.

Sandile came and stood next to her. 'This Alan Taylor character clearly believes he has something valuable to protect.'

'Ja. Surely it can't be the peaches,' Elise added, slowly nodding her head in agreement.

The crew, relieved to see the back of the crazy farmer, shuffled around and found places in the shade to sit down for the wait. Sandile asked the man nearest to him what the fence was for. The man shrugged – he didn't know. 'The boss paid for it, we're building it.'

For a long time nobody spoke. The day was still and hot. Sunlight glared off the clouds. The sawing of Christmas beetles filled the silence. After some time the chug of the tractor was heard again. They soon saw the foreman returning, followed closely by a large, sleek blue car. Elise watched their approach with interest. Tinted windows concealed the car's interior, so she had to wait until it stopped and the door opened to catch her first glimpse of Alan Taylor.

It struck her that Taylor wasn't a particularly big man, but nor was he slight. His size was elegant, unobtrusive. It seemed to Elise that his physical presence emanated tension, that his posture was stiff while his movements were loose and easy. Somehow he gave the *impression* of being a large man as he came striding towards her.

'You must be the person who's been making all the trouble!' he barked in English.

Elise was taken aback by the sneering tone, by the sheer arrogance of this approach. She responded almost mildly. 'No, in fact I think the troublemaker here is you. That road belongs to me.'

Taylor raised an eyebrow. His eyes glittered. 'And who, if it's not too much to ask, are you?'

Elise opened her mouth and then shut it again. It was clear that he had no idea, that he saw her as some interfering young

195

poppie. She stared at Taylor through narrowed eyes. She couldn't believe this was the same man whom Ina had described as Prince Charming. This man's rudeness made her blood boil. She took a step forward, so that she was standing with her feet slightly apart, and smiled slightly as she quietly delivered her response.

'I am the farmer whose land you are trespassing on. And given the fact that you are the one breaking the law here I have to admit I am amazed by your rudeness. In this valley we have laws of politeness and neighbourliness, Mr Taylor. I can see that you have a lot to learn.'

Elise punched his name, pointing out that she knew exactly who he was. The how-dare-you that had seemed to be dancing in his eyes and on his lips at the outset of her speech changed rapidly to a Good-Lord-if-only-you'd-told-me. Taylor put his hand on her arm, his mouth forming a smile. The adjustment to smarmy and conciliatory was virtually seamless.

'Ms Van Rensburg, I had no idea–'

Taylor was interrupted by the arrival of her father who charged up in his bakkie, almost skidding to a halt next to where Elise and Taylor were standing. Elise was relieved to have the unpleasant exchange cut short and relieved to see Johnny Kakana with two constables right behind her father in a police van. Sandile, who had been standing near Elise all this time, stepped back into the shadow under the trees.

Taylor appeared to relax. Elise found that odd, but it was as if, having made the adjustment from defensive aggressor, he was now prepared to go full-tilt as conciliator. He took the intiative and introduced himself, very cordially and in English, to Johnny Kakana. The sergeant was both flattered and flustered. Then Taylor turned and smiled tightly at Van Rensburg, while extending his hand.

'And you must be Piet van Rensburg. I'm very pleased to meet you.'

But Van Rensburg wasn't interested in being civil. He batted Taylor's hand away and bellowed at Johnny. 'I want this man arrested and charged with trespassing and malicious damage of property. Arrest the whole bladdy lot of them, those workmen too. Look what they've done to my road. And they've attacked my trees. In all my years on this farm I've never seen anything like this. If this isn't sabotage I don't know what is!'

Taylor stood motionless, waiting for Van Rensburg to run out of steam.

'Well, don't just stand there. Do something! Arrest him!'

Johnny was sweating. 'Before I arrest anyone, would you please explain to me what's happened here?' he said tersely, turning to Elise for help, but Alan Taylor jumped in first. Taylor glanced gratefully at Johnny and proceeded to explain.

'I think there's been a simple misunderstanding about boundaries. Both Mr van Rensburg and myself – and of course his lovely daughter here – believe that road belongs to us. Obviously it can't belong to both parties and there lies the problem.'

Van Rensburg listened, sizing the man up. He knew, just from looking at Taylor, that the man had no respect for the land and certainly no grasp of farming. Farming was hard, and harder now than it once was, though more profitable if you got it right. So he resented people like Taylor, deeply. They waltzed into an old community with no respect for its traditions and shook everyone up with too much money and no sense. No sense of the land.

Van Rensburg wasn't listening as Taylor went on in his clipped English. 'But I will tell my men to stop work on the fence until such time as we have established whose road this is. If in fact it turns out to belong to Mr van Rensburg I will be only too happy to instruct my men to repair any damage to his farm and re-erect the fence along the correct boundary.'

Johnny wiped the sweat from his forehead. 'Right. I see. Well, we can clear this up with one simple phone call, which I'm happy to make from the station, but I need to have an assurance from everyone here that you will go home and stay there calmly until we've sorted this out.' This last plea was directed at Van Rensburg.

Taylor smiled civilly. 'Naturally. But there's no need to go to the station. I have a cellphone in my car which you are more than welcome to use. And you, sir,' he added, turning to Van Rensburg, 'are welcome to accompany us.'

But Van Rensburg rounded on him. 'Why the hell do you need a fence in the first place? We never needed a fence before – everyone knows where their land begins and where it ends. There's not enough time in the day to work our own farms let alone go waltzing around on neighbours', so why the bloody Robben Island security?'

Alan Taylor took a handkerchief from the breast pocket of his jacket and dabbed at his upper lip. It was certainly very hot, but the gesture seemed excessive – he wasn't sweating. Elise noticed that even in the heat of the day Taylor's complexion was colourless, as if he absorbed light and reflected none. When he took the handkerchief away his mouth was smiling again.

'Mr van Rensburg, I am sure we are all entitled to our reasons, and mine are simple. South Africa is a violent place – I simply wish to ensure the safety of my property and myself. I can assure you that if this is a mistake it is a genuine one and I will set these men to rectifying things immediately.'

He put his hand out to shake on it, but Van Rensburg didn't make the slightest effort towards reconciliation; he had sunk to his most taciturn, his most dangerous. He'd usually have hit someone by this point, Elise reflected.

'Who's going to get rid of that trench and pay for the damage to my trees?' he sniped.

Taylor spread his arms expansively. 'As I've already said, if I am indeed in the wrong, I will do everything necessary to restore the road and the orchards to your satisfaction.'

He was smarmy, self-satisfied and arrogant, Elise thought, nothing like the dashing Don Juan Ina had described. She even wondered if this was the same man.

Van Rensburg glared contemptuously at Taylor, then turned and stomped away towards his truck. 'Some of these trees are as old as I am. They can't be replaced by the flash of a blarry credit card.'

Elise had had enough too. Johnny had the situation under control and she motioned to her men that it was time to go. 'Time for lunch,' she said. She thanked Johnny for his help, then jumped into her bakkie. Sandile and the other two men followed suit, climbing onto the back.

Taylor raised his eyebrows, observing their departure, then clicked his heels and walked over to the foreman who had been watching all this with half-closed eyes. The two of them stood in urgent conversation under a canopy of young peaches for a couple of minutes before Taylor turned and walked in the direction of his car. He motioned for Johnny to join him and the policeman obeyed.

Taylor produced a cellphone from inside his car. He held it out to Johnny, who reached for it, but then Taylor jerked it away. 'You see, trouble has come to us already, even here, in the unspoiled heartland.'

His tone was theatrical, overpompous. That and the sudden strange playfulness mystified Johnny, who said nothing at all. The remark didn't seem to require a response. When Taylor offered the phone again, Johnny reached over hesitantly and took it.

'So I gather that you're the man who runs things round here.'

'No, Daan du Toit is the station commander.' Johnny's eyes were blank, his demeanour suspicious and self-deprecating all at once. He felt himself shrinking with men like this, whites who decided to patronise him with their cleverness.

'I see. But you think you could do better?' Taylor twisted his gaze away from Johnny, who thought he saw the glimmer of amusement, of irony there. Taylor unnerved him. Johnny jerked his chin up, frowning as he punched numbers into the phone.

'That Mr van Rensburg strikes me as a bit of a hothead. Has he given you trouble before?'

Johnny put the phone to his ear. 'Mr Van Rensburg is an opinionated man.'

Taylor chuckled. He leaned back against his car, surveying the untended orchard around him, the abandoned poles and tools by the trench and Rustenvrede's neat rows of trees stretching beyond it and up the slopes of the mountain.

'He's certainly a very fortunate man.'

Johnny quickly got through to a Land Registry clerk at the Municipality and explained the situation. The clerk agreed to pull the records and said she would fax him at the police station within the hour. Johnny thanked her and handed the phone back to Taylor, repeating this information for his benefit. Taylor smiled distractedly, then said he would walk Johnny to his car.

As they strolled back towards the trench Taylor asked Johnny, quite casually, about his neighbours. 'Tell me about the Van Rensburgs.'

Johnny glanced slyly at Taylor. 'Around here people like to keep themselves to themselves – they don't ask too many questions about other people's business.' Johnny observed Taylor's reaction, his pause for thought then his jolly smile.

'Yes. Well, I didn't mean to be rude. I have to confess that I'm a bit nosy. It's an old habit.' Taylor said this with innocent charm.

They stopped at the trench. Johnny looked down at the red churned earth and couldn't help noticing Taylor's shoes. They were delicate, glossy, black leather slippers. Obviously expensive. Obviously not farmer's shoes.

'How do you *like* your job, Johnny?'

Taylor dropped the sentence like a velvet glove. Johnny was an opportunist, in the best sense. He knew how to turn any situation to his advantage. This was beginning to look like something useful, but he wasn't sure how. One never knew quite what was happening in negotiations like this, what precisely was being transacted, but Taylor reeked of power. *Why?*

'I like it well enough.'

Taylor paused again, glancing at Johnny. In his look was a question.

'But . . .' Johnny didn't know how to phrase it.

Taylor knew how to help him. 'But you feel you could be so much more? You feel squashed into a space that's grown too small for you, don't you, Johnny?'

Johnny's eyes narrowed. The two men stared at one another like that, sizing each other up. Then Johnny simply nodded.

'You can speak freely with me, Johnny. After all I'm a stranger here. Who am I to care?' He laughed gaily at this.

Yes, Johnny thought, who the hell are you?

'I don't know how much longer I'll stay here. I'm hoping some opportunities will open up, now things are changed . . .'

'Where there's a will there's always a way. Do you have the will, Johnny?'

Johnny nodded, a little too vehemently. Yes, he had the will. He waited for Taylor to explain, to give meaning to this exchange, but the subject veered abruptly.

'God, this place is lovely! I haven't walked enough on this farm. I think I must form the habit of walking on a new piece of it every day.'

Johnny was flummoxed. Sheer puzzlement was written all over his flabby features. He clasped his hands behind his back, looked at Taylor, then away, then back again. Taylor seemed not to notice him – he was so caught up in this sudden rapture about his farm.

At last Johnny spoke. Slowly and significantly. 'I must go. Thank you, Mr Taylor.'

'Please. Alan.' Taylor smiled suddenly and broadly and extended his hand.

Johnny eyed him, slightly wary, but then took his hand and shook it. 'Thank you, Alan.'

'Till next time.'

Johnny smiled as he leapt across the trench. He was flattered by Taylor's attention and he felt that something had been accomplished just now, even if he wasn't sure precisely what.

Taylor smiled too. He could feel Johnny's eyes on his back as he drove away.

Sixteen

Sandile knew dawn was approaching when he heard his mother moving around in the kitchen, preparing their breakfast. There was no sound of his father. Lately Ben Mashiya would either leave the house before his son was up, or would wait in his room in order to leave after Sandile. If by accident they saw one another in the course of the working day Sandile would greet him with a smile and say hello and his father would curtly acknowledge him with a dip of his chin, but he never spoke.

Sandile hadn't slept much; in fact he hadn't slept properly since he'd raised the land claim with his parents. It had been only weeks, but to Sandile it felt like months. The tension in the house was oppressive. His mother's anger simmered and his father's uncertainty hung like banners in the silence. It was as if things were building for a storm. It had to break. Out of respect he was waiting for them to speak, and they, out of fear, were waiting for him.

Sandile sighed, kicked back the sheets and swung his feet down to the floor. He couldn't wait any longer. Mama looked up sharply when he entered the living room. Her large dark eyes flicked anxiously from Sandile to the table and back. Ben Mashiya was sitting there, staring down at the tablecloth, his hands gripping a shallow tin box. He too jerked his head up when he saw Sandile standing in the doorway, then he nodded, indicating for Sandile to sit down. Mama dried her hands on a lappie in the kitchen and then went outside. Sandile hesitated, not sure what to expect but glad that something was happening. He sat down opposite his father.

Ben Mashiya looked hard at his son and Sandile's heart sank. It seemed to him that this stern face meant rejection.

'Father,' he blurted out, but was interrupted. Ben Mashiya's hand fluttered up, indicating a need for silence. When he spoke his voice was thick with weariness and significance.

'There are many things I cannot understand. Many, many things that are beyond my powers to understand. Our life has been hard. But I do understand the land. I understand your love for it, your wanting it back. You think I have given up, that I don't want to fight . . . I don't know . . . maybe it's true.' This was hard for him to say; his voice cracked with an emotion that Sandile understood to be the bitter pain of one who has experienced too much defeat.

'But I understand this thing you have about the land, more deeply than you know, than you want to think. I am old, my power has been drained, but you are young and strong and you are right to want to fight.'

At this he sighed and shook his head. 'I don't know where your land claim will take us, but you must do it.' Sandile clasped his hands together, quelling all his gratitude and emotion. His father had not finished. 'And if we lose, if we are sent away from here, we will go with you. We are in your hands now. You must do this thing, but I ask you to do it quickly. Remember that we are not strong like you.'

When he was finished speaking Ben Mashiya looked away, down at his hands gripping the box in his lap. Sandile said nothing. He was fighting to control the sadness and the joy that washed over him. Then his father put the box on the table and pushed it towards Sandile.

Inside the old biscuit tin were the papers his father had kept from the time their farm was declared a 'Black Spot'. There were letters from the Municipality, yellow newspaper clippings – stories about Verwoerd and his Black Spots – and correspondence between Ben Mashiya and a lawyer in Cape Town who said there was nothing he could do to help. Ben Mashiya's meek protest had been crushed so swiftly and so completely that the fight was knocked out of him before he'd even begun. The time of his forebears, of Gideon Mashiya, was a time when his people had fought back. There was no fight left in Oupa Mashiya now, just fear. Looking at those papers Sandile understood why and so he said, very simply and very quietly, 'Thank you. I won't let you down, Father.'

Mama Mashiya had come silently back into the room. She watched them with the box and the papers, her eyes ablaze with hurt and anger. Sandile glanced up at her as she put their breakfast plates down on the table. He put out his hand to touch her arm, but she jerked away from him. She looked guiltily at her husband, knowing it was not her place to object, but she couldn't contain herself. She stood at the end of the table and let her ballooning emotion burst.

'You know, I used to dream of a different, better life, but I am too old to dream any more. This is the life I have and I want to keep it! Now you make me a traitor to the people who have given us this life. Elise is like my child!' Mama didn't weep – she was too furious. Sandile had never seen her like this. From the stern shock on his father's face it seemed he hadn't either.

'Through all those years that you were gone you never sent me anything, you never gave me anything. It was Elise who fetched me to the doctor when I was sick, Elise who brought me little presents for my birthday. Even Master Dawie, before he died, he looked after me, took me shopping when I needed to go, helped me with small things. But none of my children have ever done anything . . .' She addressed this as much to her husband as to her son, clasping her hands over her breast, shaking her head, then she glared straight at Sandile. 'Where were you when those Van Rensburg children were doing everything for me?' Her voice shuddered with the strength of her feelings, but she spoke quietly.

Sandile was speechless. He couldn't deny what she said and that stung terribly. Now he was back he wanted to give her everything. Why couldn't she see that?

'I don't know how you can do this. How can you treat Elise and your parents like this?'

Ben Mashiya stood up from the table and walked stiffly from the room, without acknowledging her or what she'd just said. It was not her place to talk to him or Sandile that way. Mama knew it as well as he did, but she had finished her protest. She couldn't stop them, but she wouldn't let them forget how vehemently she disapproved. Mama picked up her husband's untouched plate, marched through to the kitchen and threw the food into the rubbish.

Sandile went up to her and put his arms round her, but she stiffened, resisting his attempt at reconciliation. He pulled away. Mama plunged her arms into the hot water in the sink, ignoring him.

'Mama, we'll work things out with Elise. I'm sure of that.'

'And her father? You better get a bigger gun than his if you want to work things out with Piet van Rensburg.'

'Mama, I promise you. Things will work out.'

She said nothing. In her heart she wished she could believe him, but she couldn't. Part of her winced from the pain of wishing he would go away again.

'Everything will be all right . . . everything will be all right!' Sandile broke into song. Mama shook her head. It was only when he was gone that she began to cry.

Stepping outside Sandile felt a rush of elation. The morning was brilliant, the mountains awash with colour. Under a perfect sky dogs barked, chickens scurried, flies hummed, beetles sawed. Everything was so beautiful and so alive it filled him with purpose and anticipation.

Sandile was totally wired, his mind flying through everything that must be done to set the claim in motion. Elise was away on farm business that day and he worked with Jacob, barely noticing the hours pass. At lunchtime he ran up to the compound where he ate standing out on the stoep – he couldn't sit down. Instead of sitting for fifteen minutes in the shade, resting like everyone else, as he usually did, Sandile looked around for something to do, something he could press his energy into. There was a pile of cut wood at the side of their cottage which needed to be stacked under the shed. That's what he would do.

In the kitchen Lucky was fiddling with his lunch, pushing a handful of pap round and round, making spirals through the gravy on his plate. Sandile came in to rinse his plate in the sink. He patted Lucky on the head, chiding him in a jocular tone. 'You're too thin, man. Stop playing with that food and get it down you! You need to get a bit of fat and muscle on that skinny body. Hey?'

Lucky looked up at him nervously, uncertainly. He didn't know whether Sandile was joking or whether the smile was the first sign of an explosion, so he obeyed, quickly shovelling food into his mouth.

Sandile bit his lip, hating to see this, the child's father's cruelty playing out in fear. So he softened his tone. 'When you're finished I want you to come and help me stack the wood.'

Lucky nodded, and seeing that Sandile was smiling warmly at him, he smiled meekly back.

They were already hard at work when they heard a vehicle approaching. Sandile looked round, his hands still working as he turned his head to see who it was. He never broke the rhythm of what he was doing, even when he saw the police van entering the compound. Sandile scowled, gritted his teeth and turned back to the woodpile. What on earth could the reason be for this visit? he wondered. He didn't doubt that it was a bad sign.

Sandile still had his back turned as Johnny climbed out of the van, stretched slightly to straighten out his crumpled jacket, then fixed a smile on his lips and slammed the door. A chicken, startled by the noise, squawked and scuttled away, but Sandile didn't miss a beat: he carried on with his task, taking the log handed to him by Lucky, swinging it over to his left hand and stacking it on to the growing pile while his right arm was already reaching for the next one. Johnny watched the two of them at work, waiting for them to say or do something to acknowledge his presence. Lucky did glance furtively over at him, but quickly looked away. Policemen, above all people, terrified Lucky.

After the incident over the fence up at Rustenvrede, Johnny Kakana had resolved to go and talk to Sandile. His motives were complicated. Johnny wanted Sandile to acknowledge him and his position in the dorp. He felt an old admiration for the man who'd been like his older brother. Yet he hadn't liked the way Sandile had refused to take a lift from him, nor did he like the way he'd withdrawn during the incident at the fence, but in a genuine, clumsy way he also wanted to make amends. He didn't like the fact that they had unfinished business. As far as he was concerned the bad blood was deep in the past. It belonged to another time and he hoped Sandile would feel the same way. Puffed up by Taylor's flattery, Johnny felt he could overcome anything this afternoon, even Sandile's hostile indifference.

Johnny stepped forward, coughing as he approached. Lucky backed away so that Sandile had to swing his arm further to take the logs from the boy's feed.

'Working hard, I see . . .' The tone Johnny tried to achieve was a casual, chatty one, but the words creaked out sounding dry and thin. 'I, er, was just down at the house . . . I thought I'd drop in . . . see how things are going.'

Sandile nodded. He wasn't pretending that Johnny didn't exist, he simply wasn't interested in wasting breath on the man. Johnny nodded too, then clapped his hands and rubbed them together as he looked around him. He spoke again in the strange staccato that had failed before, leaving long pauses between each non-sequitur.

'They've done this place up nicely . . . You must be glad . . . How are you settling in, Sandile?'

The sound of his own name on this man's lips jarred. Sandile looked warily over at him. He was clearly not going away. Johnny smiled at this, a triumphant, officious little smile.

'What do you want, Xolile?'

Johnny rubbed his hands again, trying to assume an air of nonchalance. 'Nothing. Like I said, I just thought I'd stop by.'

'What for?'

'Ag, I don't know. Just to, you know, chat. About what you're doing back here, what you plan to do . . . You know, I just wanted to catch up.'

Sandile shrugged, but said nothing. Johnny creaked on with his painful politeness.

'It's been . . . such a long time. I've been wondering how things are going for you, how long you intend to stay, you know, what you plan to do?'

'Why is that?'

Johnny's smile was replaced by a frown. He stopped babbling. 'Well, you seem to have done well for yourself out there, I mean you're educated, you know the right people. Surely there's nothing in this place for a man like you?'

The flattery was as rank and obvious as a cheap perfume. Sandile dropped a heavy chunk of wood on to the pile. It cracked against the other logs, shaking out dust and twigs. Still he didn't break the rhythm of his work as he squinted up at Johnny, searching his face for signs of mendacity. There was no way Johnny could have any inkling of his plans. Nevertheless, Sandile was wary.

'My home is here, so my life is here.' Sandile looked meaningfully at Johnny. Johnny didn't get it; he pursed his lips, thrust out his jaw and tapped his fingers against his chin in a pose that was supposed to indicate thoughtfulness.

'Of course I understand, family et cetera, but are you going to work as a farm labourer the rest of your life? I mean, look at me, even *my* position is frustrating . . . but I know you. I don't quite see–'

Sandile let go of the logs he had in each hand. They thudded and bounced to a rest around Johnny's feet as Sandile stood up, drawing himself up to his full height, which was not so great, but greater than Johnny's.

'Let me make it plain for you. I have nothing to say to you.

I do not want to see you or speak to you. So please leave me and my family alone.'

Johnny's lips were drawn back over his teeth in a confused but contemptuous smile. He stared at Sandile, blank from the shock that comes to one who has blundered on with absolutely no sense of the atmosphere around him and then is suddenly made aware of how poisonous it is.

Johnny felt foolish and angry and he wouldn't let Sandile get away with that. He cocked his head at an angle, narrowing his eyes. 'How did you get back into South Africa?'

Harsh laughter escaped Sandile's lips. But Johnny went on. 'I can check up on these things.'

'Please do.'

'You know what could happen if I find your paperwork is not in order–'

Sandile jerked his chin up, looking around for Lucky. The child was cowering by the side of the house. 'Lucky, go inside.'

Sandile was bigger than Johnny, and leaner. His body was taut with muscle, whereas Xolile, who was flabby as a child, had simply softened and filled out even more in adulthood. Sandile took a step forward, then another, as Johnny stepped back. Sandile had to control the desire to smack him. For a long time, when he was far away, he had fantasised about killing this man. That desire had subsided over the years just as his desire to destroy the lives of those who had shattered his had also dissipated. Sandile wouldn't hit him, wouldn't give him that satisfaction, but he certainly wanted Xolile out of his life.

Johnny took another step back and bumped up against his car. A bead of sweat rolled from his temple, down his cheek to his chin. 'Don't threaten me,' he bleated.

Sandile raised his eyebrows. He didn't move. 'I don't need to threaten you. You and your kind have had your day. You people are finished.'

Johnny chewed nervously on the inside of his cheek. He tried to meet Sandile's stare, but it was so intense that he kept on looking away, his gaze flicking back and forth from the stony look. He talked rapidly, trying to convey in a gentle sense some of the things he'd meant to say.

'A lot of things have changed, we've all changed. Even you, I'm sure . . . I only came to make peace with you. I don't want a fight. Don't make me.'

Sandile laughed, a harsh, sneering, bitter laugh. 'Tell that to Baasie's mother.'

Johnny's arms flapped at his sides. His eyes bulged with indignation and fear.

Sandile almost pitied him at that moment. He knew so many men like this, men who were burdened by knowledge of the terrible acts of violence they had committed or witnessed. They were all haunted. Sandile knew that he would never escape the things he'd done. In the struggle impossible options were chosen, sacrifices beyond measure were measured and made, unbearable responsibilities were borne. Sandile had borne them in the hope that the next generation would never know the violence that had scarred him. He could see that Johnny was one of those who hid from his demons.

Sandile knew and accepted all that he had done, knew he was damaged, knew that there was no scale to balance his acts of terror against Johnny's and weigh his as good, Johnny's as bad. There was no doubt in Sandile's mind that fighting against apartheid was a moral universe apart from fighting for apartheid, but tell that to the children of a politician killed by an ANC bomb, tell that to the mother of a farmer blasted to pieces by an ANC limpet mine. Loss was loss was loss. Sandile never shied away from the terrible responsibilities he bore. That was why he understood Johnny and that was why he pitied him, but pity is not compassion. Sandile was not going to let Johnny off the hook.

'Perhaps you should stop by her house for a chat. Give the old lady some peace before she dies.'

Johnny sputtered; his face reddened and the blotchiness of it made his bulging eyes seem all the more hideous. 'I don't know what you're talking about.'

'Maybe not. Maybe you'll go to the Truth Commission. I hope you're getting ready to file your application for amnesty? Or do you think you'll get away with what you did? Hey? That's what a lot of your kind seem to think, isn't it, Xolile?' Sandile's eyes burned with confidence and rage. He spoke slowly, punching every word to emphasise its significance. He didn't want the weight of what he was saying to be lost. Johnny stared back at him, surprised and frightened.

'Full disclosure. Straight from the horse's mouth is how those Commissioners want it. If they happen to hear the story from someone else you're going to find yourself in a sticky situation, aren't you?'

Johnny said nothing. He was dumbfounded by the speed with which the tables had been turned. He hated Sandile in that moment, as a bully detests the victim who finally turns and goes straight for the jugular. He fumbled for the handle of his car door. His hand shook, and knowing that Sandile could see his fear made him hate the man all the more. At last he found words and spat them out.

'I don't know what you're talking about, but I'm warning you to watch your mouth. I'll stay out of your business, but you stay out of mine!'

'Only too happy to oblige,' Sandile said dryly. He was glad to have made his point, but he didn't enjoy seeing Xolile like that and he turned away.

Johnny drove off, burning with humiliation and anger.

Seventeen

That evening Sandile knocked off work at the usual time. In the afternoon he had accomplished everything he needed, except the arrangements for travelling to Cape Town. He'd made a few phone calls from a tikkie box at the post office, having driven into town on the pretext of running an errand for Jacob. He was particularly pleased at having reached Simon Siluma, a comrade from Zambia who was now an ANC Member of Parliament. Simon had agreed to set up a meeting with a lawyer.

At knocking-off time Sandile peeled away from the other men who headed up towards the compound or down towards Skaduweelaan. He took a path that started between the tractor shed and the packing shed, following it all the way to the dam. This had become a habit since he'd broached the subject of the land claim with his mother and father and the atmosphere in the house had become so unpleasant. The stillness of the dam at this time of day not only gave him pleasure, it also promised to afford the occasional moment alone with Elise. Such moments were something he now looked forward to.

Sandile lay back on the rock, basking in the stillness of the late afternoon. Now that the land claim had lurched forward a step his parents were no longer the worry: it was the Van Rensburgs' reaction he had to focus on. Taylor was a stranger: he didn't care about him. Elise and her father were different – they were part of the tangle of his and his parents' lives. It would have been easier to have notified them from a great distance. Sandile thought of Elise and the passion that had quivered through her declaration that night, right there on the rock. More than anything she wanted this farm. More than anything he wanted it too. That was part of what drew him to her. He would have to tell her, but he was sure that would alienate her. Perhaps it would be easier, he rationalised, if he knew her a little better.

Sandile heard the bakkie on the road below. He stood up and watched Elise speed by, hoping she would stop. But she drove straight on towards the house. He sighed, looking down at the farm. From where he stood he could see that Taylor's fence had been pulled back about ten metres, leaving the road on the Rustenvrede side of the barrier. The trench had been filled in; the darkness of the freshly turned red earth was the only trace left of it. Everything else was as it had been, except of course for the huge wire-mesh construction itself, demarcating the end of Rustenvrede and the beginning of Die Uitkyk. The fence went straight through the middle of what had been his family's land, dividing it neatly in half. What a waste, he thought.

Sandile set off towards the house, hoping to find Elise there. He was eager not to prolong the anxiety he felt and that he knew his mother and father would endure until it was all settled. So he wanted to file the claim as soon as possible and he needed to go to Cape Town to do it.

Her car was parked out back, by the kitchen door, right next to Van Rensburg's bakkie and the family's old Mercedes. It was that time of evening when the sky is still light but has deepened to a vivid electric blue. Against the sky the house looked like a lantern, its windows open wide and all the rooms lit up invitingly. Sandile walked towards the back door, wondering if he would find her. He saw no movement from within the house. Perhaps they were already eating supper. If so there would be no chance of a proper conversation. She would certainly not invite him in.

Something at the edge of his vision distracted him. He looked up to the right. Someone was moving around inside the tractor shed. Looking closer he saw it was Elise. She stood with her back to him, bent over something on the hood of the tractor. A naked fluorescent strip flickered on the raw beam above her head. Sandile changed course and walked quietly towards her.

Elise was reading something, leaning on the engine cover with one elbow, her long legs slightly splayed, her other hand stretched out to smooth the paper that was spread before her. She was wearing a heavy cotton shirt, rolled up at the sleeves, and the faded, slightly baggy jeans that she always wore. Her hair was caught up in a band, the long ponytail twisted and pulled round to one side over her shoulder, leaving her pale neck exposed. She hadn't heard his approach and Sandile moved slowly forward, enjoying the pleasure of watching her unobserved. It would take an instant for everything about her to tighten and shift as she adjusted to his presence. Sandile wanted to prolong the moment.

She was too absorbed to notice him and he stood directly behind her for a moment, then reached out and touched the tiny hollow at the base of her skull with his index finger. She froze instantly, but didn't turn round. Sandile saw the goose pimples rise up on her neck as he traced the ridge of her spine, down her neck, over her shirt and into the curve of her back. She shivered, quivered all the way down her back when he took his hand away. A low gurgle of a laugh escaped her throat as she turned. When she saw it was Sandile her head jerked back in surprise and her hands flew up to her chest. He was about to apologise for giving her such a fright, but her head tipped forward and she put her hand on Sandile's arm to steady herself. Sandile smiled.

'Shew, you gave me such a skrik!' She shook her head as she withdrew her touch from his arm. Her hand went out to the leaflet that was unfolded over the tractor hood. She picked it up and folded it carefully while her eyes remained on Sandile.

'Sorry, I just couldn't resist – I didn't mean to give you a fright,' he murmured.

Sandile's sudden appearance, the tingling down her back, caused Elise's composure and her attention to wobble. She shook her head and laughed again. 'It's fine, it's fine. Actually it was quite nice.'

Sandile raised his eyebrows. His lips parted in a slight smile and his eyes emanated a gentle warmth that she hadn't seen before. It was as if the temperature heated up a degree or two every time she saw him and his initial frostiness, that suspicious chill, had completely thawed.

'You know, I think I was a bit in love with you when we were kids.' His eyes glittered wickedly as he went on. 'Well . . . maybe *love* is too strong a word, it was more like a big crush! I thought you were the prettiest girl in the world.'

Elise made a face, a scrunched-up smile. 'As if you knew!'

She laughed and then suddenly he was thoughtful again. 'You are now. You've grown beautiful.'

Those words can work a powerful magic and he said them so simply, so artlessly, they almost knocked her out.

Elise opened her mouth to say something, then closed her eyes and shook her head in mock disbelief, trying to undo the spell. When she opened her eyes he was looking away, towards the house. When he spoke his tone had reverted to normal. 'I see they've filled in the trench,' he said.

Elise looked puzzled.

'The trench,' he repeated.

'Oh, the fence. Ja, ja. All that seems to have been cleared up. Johnny was here talking to my father today and I spoke to Taylor on the phone about it just now. He was very courteous and apologetic about the whole thing, very apologetic . . . Not that my father will get over it in a hurry.' She laughed, a little ruefully, he thought.

Sandile nodded and looked around as if wondering what to say. Then he spoke with such nonchalance that, at the time, Elise thought nothing of it.

'I may need to go to Cape Town on personal business for a week or so some time soon. Do you think you can spare me for a week? It won't be next week, perhaps the week after.'

'Well, if you have to go then we'll spare you.' Elise shrugged amicably. 'Just let me know when – I'm sure it'll be fine.'

'Sharp!'

Elise's hand flew up to her hair. She'd just thought of something, but she hesitated a second before mentioning it.

'You know, Ina du Toit and I are driving to Cape Town the Saturday after next. You could come with us.'

Sandile's eyes brightened. 'Really? That would be great. That would really be great.'

'OK, that's that then.' Elise pushed the folded paper into her back pocket and smiled. Neither one of them moved, but Elise looked out towards the house, then back at Sandile. 'I'd better go in – your mother's waiting to leave.'

Sandile shifted slightly, pushing his hands into the pockets of his overalls. 'Ja, well . . .'

Now they both looked down at the house. Van Rensburg's hulking silhouette moved across the windows as he walked from one room to the next. Sandile took a step backwards. 'I'll check you tomorrow. And thanks, hey?'

'No problem.' Elise shook her head.

He grinned at her, then left, shouting over his shoulder as he jogged away, 'Sharp! Sharp!'

Elise watched him until he had disappeared into the shadows, then she strolled down to the house. She couldn't help smiling to herself.

Her father was waiting for her at the dining table. He didn't look up when she walked in but simply growled, 'You've got quite pally with that terrorist, I see.'

Elise faltered. Her hand went up to her neck and she wondered what, precisely, he had seen.

He looked up at her, her eyes dark, his body hunched over his soup, spoon poised to strike. 'What did he want with you?'

'He has to go to Cape Town next month so he wanted some time off. I said he could have it.'

'Huh.' Van Rensburg scowled. 'Let's hope he stays there.'

Elise sat down. She felt light, in spite of her father's dark mood. Her sharp, glancing encounters with Sandile had become a precious secret. She knew that in a way this was already a betrayal. But she told herself that she knew the boundaries; she could handle it, it wasn't that big a deal anyway. While she could lie to her father she would never lie to herself. She *was* attracted to Sandile. The fact of it was strange and quite unexpected, but not unwelcome. There were a number of men who had made her sit up and take notice since she'd been with Daan, but she never intended to take it further than looks and smiles and the fun of flirting.

Elise smiled broadly at her father as she poured herself some wine from the bottle he'd opened. 'So what's put *you* in such a good mood?' Her sarcasm was light, but it failed to brighten him.

Van Rensburg glared at her. 'Water,' he snarled.

He had this knack of souring any atmosphere – even the sweetest – in an instant.

Eighteen

It was Tuesday, still days before the planned trip to Cape Town. The Du Toits were at breakfast when the phone rang. Ina picked it up with a cheerful 'Hullooo.'

It was Elise. She launched straight into the conversation in her customary way. 'And?'

Ina giggled. 'And nothing. For the moment!'

'I tell you, if this is the same guy I met last week then I'm concerned.'

'Ag, Elise, I don't believe he was that awful. Anyway, your father could stir up a saint. Just you let me reintroduce you. You'll see – he's an absolute pussycat.'

Ina glanced over her shoulder, hoping none of her family had heard this. They hadn't – they were caught up in the usual mayhem of early morning.

'Maybe he turns it on for you. In my presence he's Darth Vader!' Elise teased.

'It's my maidenly charm . . .'

'Ja, right! Listen, I've cleared everything with my dad, so we're all set for next Saturday.'

'Cool!' Ina was very excited about it. Elise felt the opposite.

'Ja, better get it over with.'

'Elise!' Ina exclaimed. 'You make it sound like a trip to the dentist.'

'Ja, well . . . afterwards we'll treat ourselves to a nice lunch.'

'But I'll see you before, maybe tonight, hey?' Ina said lightly.

Elise responded knowingly. 'Well, if I don't see you then I'll know where you are!'

Ina giggled again as she put down the phone. She slid gaily into the seat next to Daan.

Her brother smiled at her. 'What's put you in such a disgustingly good mood?'

Ina tossed her head from side to side and smiled to herself. 'Oh . . . nothing. That was your fiancée on the phone. We're going to town on Saturday and we're going to splash out on the most gorgeous dresses ever seen at a wedding.'

Daan nodded, still smiling. 'I'm glad to know they have those in the discount section.'

Ina jabbed him with her elbow and they both laughed.

Daan headed out for work feeling dull and anxious. He was worried about the future generally, though he was sure that Elise's refusal to talk about his role on the farm was a temporary annoyance. Nevertheless he felt irritable with her, with her remoteness which he attributed to self-centredness. She didn't appear to even try to put herself in his shoes or to think of him at all. However there was no point in raising the subject: she would only clam up and slip defensively further away.

Wanting the land and being called to it are different. There is purpose in the calling that has nothing to do with wanting. Elise was called, like her father, like his brothers. Daan wanted. That was OK as far as he was concerned, just as long as she didn't expect him to have no role. Just as long as she didn't expect him to stay in the police.

A new strategy began to form in Daan's mind as he drove to work that morning. Perhaps it didn't really matter if they couldn't agree on everything right now. The discussion could wait until after the wedding, when he would be set up at Rustenvrede and in a better position to make the changes that suited him. His relationship with Van Rensburg was good; he believed that Van Rensburg was on his side about Elise. No need to mess things up ahead of time by arguing now. This thought cheered Daan up enormously. He even began to wonder if he'd been excessively pushy with her – all this angst was unnecessary.

So he decided that morning to put first things first and concentrate on clearing up his future in the force. He had to arrange a suitable departure. There were good retirement schemes available; hundreds of men were taking them on the grounds of stress, or they were going 'medically unfit'. The people higher up were doing everything they could to shuffle out the old and make space for new cops. But Daan would only leave under the right conditions – he didn't want to end up with nothing – so he had to plan. He knew how to make the best of a situation, but it seemed to him it was harder these days to swing things his way.

Daan parked at the side of the station and was sauntering round towards the entrance when he almost bumped straight into Madeleine de Jager. He grinned with evident pleasure at seeing her. She smiled back, more hesitantly.

'Hi.'

'You look great, gogga. It's great to see you.'

At this Madeleine laughed. 'You're unbelievable.'

Daan shrugged, clowning slightly as if to say, yup, that's me, nothing anyone can do about it!

'So, congratulations. You've got your farm at last.'

'Ouch.' He grinned.

Madeleine moved as if to go, but Daan reached for her elbow, his finger just grazing her skin before she could jerk her arm away. He frowned sadly, an exaggerated clown's frown. 'Don't you wanna make me lunch?'

Madeleine stared hard at him. Her expression was one of incredulity mixed with a deep affection. She shook her head and then smiled, a little sadly. 'Of course, don't I always?'

Daan grinned. 'Usual time, usual place,' he said. Madeleine didn't say anything. He was still grinning as he watched her cross the street and disappear into the hotel.

Johnny was already at his desk when Daan walked in. Daan noticed that Johnny's eyes went up to the clock on the wall – as usual he was late and as usual Johnny made a point of noting it. Daan sighed heavily as he sat down at his own desk. Lately Johnny was becoming a pain in the backside. To cap his pedantic ways he had adopted an irritatingly superior manner. There was nothing he could do about it; Johnny knew that Daan was on his way out and that had fuelled his rebellion.

Daan knew a lot of guys who were getting five years on their pension for stress. Lately the biggest certainty in the police was the uncertainty. Nobody was sure what was going to happen in six months' or a year's time. There were all those MK guys who had to be assimilated – one day they were a constable or a sergeant and the next day they'd become a major. The job wasn't what it used to be and the prospects weren't either. Johnny could have his precious police force.

Johnny was typing out a request for documentation and files relating to Sandile Mashiya. He felt furtive about what he was doing, but he knew it was unlikely Daan would notice. If he did, Johnny was perfectly within his rights: he was a cop with a community to look out for, he had every right to know. Johnny ripped the last page out of the old Olivetti, shuffled all the related papers and patted them into a neat stack. He glanced over at Daan as he fed the document, page by page, through the fax machine.

Daan had his feet up on the empty desk and the phone cradled between his shoulder and his chin. He was deep in jolly conversation with someone, no doubt one of their superiors because he was speaking in English and putting on that nauseating accent that he used for the regional bosses. Johnny's mouth twisted in a sneer as he tore the transmission report from the fax, then walked over to his desk, stapled the sheaf neatly together, yanked open a filing drawer and slipped the document into its correct place, slamming the drawer shut. Daan looked up, distracted by the noise, but then he roared down the line with laughter.

Johnny picked up his cap and strode out. De Jager's hotel was diagonally opposite the police station. It was easy to observe all the comings and goings to and from the little hotel through the window by Johnny's desk. Alan Taylor had been staying there for the past few days and Johnny had taken note of his movements. A few moments before he'd seen Taylor pull up, slide out of his car and stroll inside, but he'd left the engine running, so Johnny surmised he'd be out again shortly.

Johnny stopped alongside Taylor's humming vehicle just as the Englishman stepped on to the street from the hotel entrance. He had the *Cape Times* open in front of him and was scanning a page as he walked, so he almost bumped into Johnny, who smiled and greeted him. Taylor raised his eyes. Their expression shifted from absent concentration to seeming pleasure at recognising the man before him.

'Ah, Johnny. Glad to see you. Is all well?'

Johnny dipped his head slightly. 'Yes, thank you, Mr Taylor.'

Taylor smiled broadly. 'Good.' He swivelled round, still holding the paper open, and positioned himself so that Johnny could see what he was reading.

'Have you seen this?' He indicated the front page, which was illustrated with a garish colour picture of a bloodstained bed. The headline boomed: *Mother of Three Blasted to Death While Children Look On.* Johnny grimaced, shaking his head. Taylor became quite animated, apparently more excited than upset by the story. 'A farmer goes crazy because he's defaulted on his loans, so he shoots his wife to death and then goes for his children. The youngest child stares up at his father, who is coming for him with a shotgun, and something in that child's stare makes the farmer realise what he's done. He stops. Suddenly he's frightened and he runs away . . . They caught him in his car – he was sitting in a lay-by on the freeway, just sitting there, covered in his wife's blood.'

'Terrible.' Johnny stared at the picture. The caption said the murder had taken place the day before in De Aar. 'But that's over three hundred kilometres away, sir.'

Taylor blinked at Johnny. 'Yes,' he said, his tone suddenly clipped. He folded the paper neatly under his right arm and was about to step away when he looked over and remarked to Johnny, abruptly and somewhat cryptically, 'Killing is more easily done than anyone realises. The only danger for the killer is fear – without fear there is no danger. Fear eats the soul, Johnny. Even the great writers tell us that, mark Dostoyevsky, Shakespeare . . .' Taylor trailed off with a knowing smile.

Johnny looked mystified, astounded.

'Well, good day.' Johnny tipped his cap as Taylor marched round his car, climbed in and drove off.

Johnny had absolutely no idea what Dostoyevsky or Shakespeare might have had to say on the subject of killing, nor indeed did he know who this Dostoyevsky was. He was thoroughly disconcerted by the conversation. Why did Taylor talk about murder and look at Johnny in that pointed way? Did he know something about Baasie? Johnny had the distinct and eerie feeling that he might. Yet it was impossible. He tutted irritably as he walked back across the street, into the station.

Taylor drove in the direction of Komweer. He pulled up outside Hemel en Aarde where the only other car parked in the lot was the Beetle Ina du Toit had driven up in the other day. Inside, a young woman with a dull round face was leaning over the till. She stood up, brightening, when he walked in.

'Can I help you, sir?'

Taylor shook his head, murmuring a cool but not un-friendly 'No, thank you.'

The place was bright and pleasant. He wandered along the counter of bottled jams and preserves, noticing the tiny neat handwriting on each label. Ina's handwriting, he thought to himself, and smiled.

Ina was sitting at one of the tables on the stoep, sorting through a pile of receipts. Papers and notebooks were fanned out on the floral-print cloth in front of her. She saw him first. Her heart skipped a beat at the sight of his back, the line and perfect cut of his jacket. He was a sharp dresser, something else she liked about him. She put down her pen, quickly smoothed back her hair and stood up to greet him.

Taylor turned at the sound of her approach.

'You're giving those jars quite the thorough exam, Alan. Can I tell you anything about them?' She felt wonderfully brazen strolling up to him, in control, in her own place.

He was evidently pleased to see her. 'Well, I didn't really come to do any shopping. In fact I came in the hope of finding you here.'

Ina lifted her chin, stretching and exposing her neck, and gazed at him as she said softly, 'Well, here I am.'

'And here you are.' He dipped his head as he spoke, making a small bow.

Ina extended a long, pale arm, indicating the tables outside. 'Would you like a cup of tea? I know how much you English love your tea, but I think you'll find you like ours even better.'

'It seems that rule applies to most things about this valley,' he said. His eyes brightened and he held her gaze, but there was such distance in his look – What was he thinking? Ina couldn't tell. She turned, the skirt of her dress swinging beautifully as she moved. The top was sleeveless and fitted and the skirt clung prettily to her long, boyish body. Taylor followed her.

They sat down at a table overlooking the garden and Ina called out for Lettie, who came straight over. 'Bring us two cups of tea. Make it your special.'

Ina winked and Lettie smiled then hustled away. Ina looked after her. 'I've known that girl all my life. She's my best worker.'

Taylor didn't take his eyes off Ina, who leaned her elbows on the table and settled her chin in her hand, focusing entirely on him.

'What a beautiful garden,' he said, and she smiled.

'My mother's domain,' she answered lightly, thinking to herself that flirting is one of life's great pleasures – if only she had more opportunities to indulge in it. She felt high and brave and she wanted to tease him, to dent that ice-cool armour.

'I hear you met my friend Elise van Rensburg last week.'

Taylor raised an eyebrow. 'Yes, I expect she had rather a lot to say about that.'

Ina pursed her lips and nodded, but she already had a sense of his game and instead of launching into an answer she waited.

Taylor's mouth twitched. He laughed slightly, realising that she wasn't going to say any more. 'Yes, it wasn't the best of introductions.'

'I gather that's all been cleared up now.' Ina sucked in her lower lip, dropping her eyes as she traced the pattern of the tablecloth with her finger. He could see only the deep lids of her eyes and the short fair lashes on her cheeks. She was different today, the agitated girlishness gone and her voice silky smooth as she teased him. 'You've caused quite a stir in the valley, Alan. Everyone's talking about your fence and nothing else.'

Taylor shifted. Leaning his elbows on the table he cupped his chin in his hands, copying Ina's position. His face was very close to hers. 'Are they really?'

She looked up, straight into his eyes. 'So why the heavy security?'

Taylor leaned back again, still gazing at her. 'Why the heavy interrogation?'

Ina sat up, letting her arm fall across her lap. 'Well, I hope you didn't think that coming here you'd have extra privacy. We're so remote in this valley, all we have to feed on is each other. Sooner or later everybody knows everything . . . For instance, I can bet you that by the time you get back to the hotel Madeleine de Jager will already know that you've been here drinking tea with me. And I can also promise you that it won't be me who told her!'

Taylor was delighted. 'That's quite an information network!'

Ina widened her eyes. 'Don't underestimate it.'

'Well, thank you for warning me – I shan't.'

At that moment Lettie approached, carrying a full tray. Taylor watched Ina watching Lettie lay out the cups and tea service before them. When she was finished the girl withdrew quietly and Ina poured out two cups of tea.

'You haven't answered my question, Alan.'

Taylor tilted his head to one side.

'The fence?'

Taylor sipped his tea. Ina knew it was still too hot, but he didn't flinch at all. He began to speak as he settled the cup back into its saucer, launching into a gentle, teasing lecture.

'My explanation isn't as mysterious as I think you're hoping it will be. In fact it's pretty simple. As you know too well, I'm sure, South Africa is the most violent place – except for war zones – in the world. There are a lot of poor people here and very few rich. The poor seem to be becoming accustomed to taking what isn't theirs and doing so in the most aggressive way.'

Ina knew this was true. She closed her eyes and ears to everything – the television news that screeched into the living room, the newspaper stories that glared at her, the radio that muttered. There were dozens of violent crimes every day. Rapes and robberies and murder. The murder capital of the world wasn't a far-away American city any more. It was Johannesburg. Pangas, guns from the wars in Angola and Mozambique flooded into the country every minute. AK47s sold at fifty rand a pop near the border.

'Statistics show that there are about two hundred and sixty-two robberies nationwide every day, more than double the number five years ago. Last year fifteen thousand nine hundred and ninety-nine people were murdered and the number of rapes reported has trebled in the last six years, to nearly ninety-eight per day. Quite frankly, this new government leaves a lot to be desired as far as control of safety and security is concerned. Life is cheap for some, but not for me. And that's why I have my fence.'

He raised the cup in a brief salute, then put it to his lips and took a long sip.

Ina looked out at the tranquil garden. 'But that's Johannesburg. OK, some farms too. But not here. We've never had any trouble like that here.'

'Not yet.'

She nodded, still defensive, but without any argument left. The explanation was sound and perfectly reasonable. Simple, as he'd said.

'Well, let's hope never. But in case we do I've taken precautions. That's all. These are only precautions.' He smiled winningly.

They drank their tea and were silent for a time. Taylor sat perfectly still. Ina took it all in: the line of his jaw, the strong curve of mouth, straight nose, the ice-blue eyes. She couldn't believe that he'd just dropped into her world like this, couldn't believe her luck. She straightened her back, leaning in towards him again as she poured out another cup.

'Now, you haven't told me why you came looking for me.'

'No.'

Taylor helped himself to a teaspoonful of sugar, stirring it slowly with those milky, soft-looking hands. 'The other day you very kindly offered your help on anything I might need in the course of my move, and as a matter of fact there is something which you might be able to help me with. I need to employ a housekeeper. It occurred to me that you might know if there are any local women looking for that kind of work.'

Ina couldn't conceal her delight. 'Absolutely. You've come to exactly the right person. I'll find you what you're looking for and I can promise you the girls from around here are all trained in the best houses. Now, when will you need her to start?'

Taylor thought for a moment. His hand went up to his neck and he rubbed his fingers back and forth across his skin. 'As soon as possible. I have to go away for a few days – there are a number of arrangements I need to finalise as my things are going to be delivered to the house on Saturday, when I move in. So can we say Saturday?'

Ina blanched slightly. That was the day she was supposed to go to Cape Town with Elise.

'I hope that's sufficient notice, but as you can well imagine, there'll be a great deal to do and I'll need all the help I can get, so Saturday would be ideal.'

Ina looked up. The smile had returned to her face and there was a look of determination mixed in with it.

'No, Saturday is fine. There was something I was supposed to do, but I'm sure I can rearrange it. I'd like to bring the girl over myself and start her off, then if I can help in any way I will. I may even give you one of my girls from here – you won't get better, believe me.'

'Well, I'd hate to leave you without–'

'No, no, no. Don't even think about it for a minute. So, Saturday. What time?'

'Would nine be all right? I think my container is being delivered around nine.'

'Perfect.'

They had finished their tea and completed their arrangements, so Taylor got up to leave. Ina walked him to his car, deflecting his gratitude and protesting that it was only a pleasure to be able to help. She was already running furiously through lists of potential housekeepers. Privately she felt a guilty excitement at this opportunity. The housekeeper would be hers, her eye on Taylor. She giggled mischievously as she turned away from the departing car and told herself it was a perfectly innocent plan. It wouldn't be the first time a woman had done such a thing.

When Ina got home that afternoon she was so agitated she didn't know what to do with herself. Her mother was sitting at the table in the dining room. Everything was still laid out for tea, but the tea itself was cold. 'You missed tea.'

'Ja. Sorry, Ma.'

Mrs Du Toit was sitting in her place at the head of the table with her beautiful handpainted china tea service laid out fully as it was every day at exactly four. She was intent on doing what she had done every day at this time for as long as Ina could remember: pulling the ticks off her favourite old dog, Lulu, and dropping them to drown in the dregs of her teacup. The movement was precise, the focus absolute. Mrs Du Toit's soft old hands ran systematically along the length of the dog's body. The second she located the bump in Lulu's hair, her fingertips pushed back the coat to reveal the fat tick, blissfully ignorant of its imminent and ignominious fate. In one swift move she dug her nails into the dog's skin, picked out the tick and swung it round to the teacup, where she dropped it delicately to its death by drowning in Rooibos.

Mrs Du Toit's mouth was tense with concentration; her jaw moved back and forth as she slowly ground her teeth while she worked. Lulu looked mournfully at Ina. She was panting, her long tongue hanging right out of her mouth as she sat obediently and endured the procedure.

'Ma, I wish you wouldn't do that!' Ina exclaimed, standing up and walking away from the table. Mrs Du Toit said nothing, but she patted Lulu on the nose and kissed her.

'You don't mind me, do you, Lulu? No, of course you don't. Sugar, Sugar, come here, come to Mama!' She reached out for the little mongrel as it jumped up on to her lap and immediately the bony fingers were scanning the dog's coat for their next victim.

Ina should have gone round to see Elise, but she felt incredibly sheepish about having made a double arrangement for Saturday. She couldn't bear to tell Elise to her face and so she'd decided to telephone, but she didn't know what to say. Elise was a stickler about arrangements. Once committed, you had to go through with it – she detested careless changing of plans. Ina prayed that Elise would understand.

She sat down on her bed and picked up the telephone. She drew in a deep breath and dialled Rustenvrede. Mama Mashiya answered and was unusually brief – in fact Ina thought Mama sounded slightly depressed. Maybe she was in the middle of cooking or something. It was nearly a minute before Elise came to the phone. Ina sat on the edge of her bed, chewing on her nails.

'Where are you?' Elise exclaimed breathlessly.

Ina laughed. 'Ag, stop it, man, I'm home. But . . .' She dangled the *but*.

'. . . He did come to see me today.'

'No!'

'Yes!'

'Tell.'

'I was working and he just showed up at the stall. I went up, asked him if he was shopping or something, I can't remember, and he says, "Oh no, actually I came in the hope of finding you here."'

'Oh my God, what did you do?'

'I was very cool, very calm. I mean, for God's sake, I ought to be at my age! I asked if he'd like to have some tea and he sat down with me and . . . we talked.'

'And?'

'And nothing, except that he asked me if I would help him find a housekeeper.'

Elise was silent on the other end of the line. After a few seconds Ina realised that she was laughing.

'What? Elise?'

'I just expected something more – romantic. But it's a start.'

Ina could see the humour of it, but she didn't laugh. She realised it did sound pretty strange as a chat-up line, but then she remembered his eyes and the long silences between them and the pointed smiles.

'Listen, I know, I was there. This is just the beginning. You'll see.'

'Hey, I believe you, angels like you don't fall into a guy's lap every day!'

Ina grabbed her moment. 'Elise, there's a problem.'

'What! He's not married?'

'No, no, I told you that already – at least he doesn't wear a ring and why would he ask me to find him a housekeeper if he was married? No, the problem is much worse . . .' Ina twisted the curling wire of the phone cord round her neck. 'His movers are delivering all his stuff on Saturday. He wants me to bring the girl over on Saturday morning and he asked me to help as well.'

Elise was silent on the other end of the line. Ina pulled the phone cord tighter. 'Elise, I said I'd go. I thought you'd understand – you know I'd never do this to you unless the circumstances were exception–'

'Of course, of course I understand. But can we rearrange?'

'Of course we can. There's an appointment the following–'

'But I won't be able to get away. No, I'll have to go by myself.' Elise sounded quite determined.

Ina bit down on her lip. Elise had taken the news far better than she'd expected. She uncurled the phone cord from around her neck. 'I can always come with you for the fitting and choose my dress then, but will you be OK? I mean, can I *trust* you to come up with something suitable?'

Elise laughed. 'Probably not, but at least it'll be your fault if the dress is a disaster.'

'Ag, Elise, I cannot thank you enough for this. I'm telling you you'll be fine and you'll be glad not to have me fussing round you. Thank you for being so good about this – thank you, thank you, thank you!'

'Forget it! But who are you going to get for Mr Taylor's maid?'

'I don't know yet, but I'll tell you one thing for free – she's going to be the ugliest girl in the dorp.'

'Ina, you're terrible!'

They both cackled wildly down the line.

'I know. Listen, better go, but thanks, hey. I mean that.'

'It's only a pleasure. Let's hope that you have more fun than me on Saturday!'

'Well, remind me to brush my teeth!'

'Sis!'

'Till later.'

'Ja, till later.'

All guilt and anxiety stripped away, Ina felt pure elation as she dived backwards on to the soft covers of her bed. She stared up at the ceiling, playing back in her mind the conversation with Taylor. She sighed and closed her eyes. She was enjoying this game. Even the suspense of not knowing what he felt, not knowing anything about him at all really, felt exquisitely good.

Nineteen

One night Sandile came back from work to an unusually silent house. The quiet seemed to highlight an atmosphere of crisis. It wasn't until he'd showered and put on clean, cool clothes that Sandile realised what was missing. Mama always listened to her wireless while she cooked supper. First the news, then the evening church service. Before their argument over the land claim he'd often heard her quietly joining in with the hymns. Lately she wasn't so joyful. The radio was an old FM set that had once belonged to one of the Van Rensburg children and tonight it stood mute in its place on the windowsill.

'What happened to our evening service?'

She didn't answer, seemingly intent on peeling potatoes.

'Ma?'

Mama turned and glared at Sandile. The knife in her hand clattered against the sink. 'The noise was giving me a headache.'

'What's wrong, Mama?' Sandile said this with the utmost gentleness. He understood her anger and hated being the cause of it, but he couldn't change his mind and so she wouldn't change her mood. He expected another explosion, but she was too weary for that.

Mama dropped a cleaned white potato into the pot of water she'd stood on the draining board. She sighed, resting her knuckles against the edge of the sink. 'Lucky. He didn't come back at lunchtime and it's going to be dark soon. I don't know where he goes. I worry so much.' Tears welled up in her eyes. She jerked the edge of her apron up over her face, angrily wiping them away. Then she plunged her hand into the sink, fished out another potato and set about her task again.

Sandile stood watching her. She was completely sealed off from him. The anger was her defence against fear. Her anger festered; she'd buried it deep but it had infected every cell of her being. Now he couldn't reach her at all and every time he tried to he seemed to make things worse. So he left the silent house and went to sit outside.

The sun slipped behind the mountains and still there was no sign of Lucky. Ben Mashiya plodded up the hill and came to sit by his son. He'd been out looking for the child along Skaduwee Lane, asking after him among the evening traffic of people walking home. Ben Mashiya shook his head and covered his face with his hands. Sandile looked away. The tension and division he'd brought to his parents was too painful to watch. And now Lucky's disappearance came to top it all.

Lucky was furtive. Beyond his household tasks and the little bits of work he had on the farm, no one knew what he did with his time or where he spent his days. Sandile rarely saw him hanging out with the other farm children; he seemed to have no friends at all. So when he hadn't appeared by nightfall there was no one the Mashiyas could ask and nowhere obvious to begin looking for him again.

Mama was silently beside herself. Sandile could see it in the way she sat hunched in her chair, mercilessly punching her darning needle at a hopeless old sock. There was a direct relationship between Mama's anxiety and her output levels – the worse her worries, the harder she knitted, or sewed, or darned. It had always been so. These days she was working herself into the ground.

They ate supper in silence. Lucky's plate sat there, un-touched, the food going cold. Sandile had to do something, so after the meal he got up and went out to search for the boy. He took a high-beam torch from the tractor shed and traversed much of the farm, tracking back and forth in the darkness for nearly three hours. He was tired and his velskoene and jeans were wet from the dew in the long grass and the sprinkler systems he'd run the gauntlet of in the orchards. Searching in the dark was fruitless; he was irritated with himself for having tried and angry with Lucky for having got him out there.

Sandile trudged home. The beam of the torch had dimmed, but he scanned the track, left and right, left and right, as he walked. Dogs barked as he approached the compound and Mama appeared in the doorway, her arm raised to shield her eyes from the light. She squinted into the darkness.

'Is he back?'

Mama shook her head. Then she disappeared inside.

Sandile was frustrated and furious. It occurred to him that he'd looked everywhere but the compound, so he made a final attempt, a circuit of the cottages and their outbuildings. Light flashed over uneven ground, under the woodpile, into the lean-to garden shed – and there Sandile caught a glimpse of skin. He ducked under the roof of the shed, shone the light inside and there he was.

Lucky was fast asleep, hunched up, his head resting on his knees, next to Oupa Mashiya's gardening tools. Sandile fought to control his temper. The boy squealed with fright as Sandile yanked hold of him, dragging him by his arm out into the open. Lucky scrambled to his feet, shocked by the rude awakening and the glare of the torchlight in his eyes.

'What the hell are you doing?'

Lucky shrank back against the wall. He didn't say anything.

'Mama is worried sick and I've spent half the night trekking all over the place looking for you. Why didn't you come home?'

The child just cowered away from him. Sandile saw that down the outside of Lucky's left calf was a long and fleshy gash. The blood from the cut had dried and congealed in a long splash down what was left of the boy's pants leg.

Sandile picked the child up and carried him over his shoulder to the bathroom where Mama cleaned and dressed the wound. She pushed Sandile out of the way and went stoically about the task. Sandile leant against the shower and watched Lucky wince at her touch, clenching his teeth against the pain.

'Lucky, tell us what happened, tell Mama what happened, child.'

Gradually she coaxed the story out of him. He told it in a frightened whisper, not entirely truthfully at first. It turned out that he'd been stealing pieces of wire from Taylor's fence. He used it to make the catapults and toy cars that Sandile had seen him building and playing with.

'This morning I climbed up to get a long loose piece near one of the posts. But I lost my balance.'

Sandile was tired out and couldn't hide his exasperation. 'But why didn't you come and tell us? Look at your leg now, it's only got worse. I mean you should have a tetanus shot for that.'

Tears welled up in Lucky's eyes. For the first time he looked as if he might cry. He turned away from Sandile. 'I was frightened. I knew you'd be cross with me.'

Sandile sighed and put his arm round the boy's shoulder. 'We are cross with you now because you made us so frightened. We thought something had happened to you.'

When Mama had finished dressing the wound Sandile carried Lucky to his room and set him down on his bed. Ben Mashiya brought him a cup of boiled milk with honey stirred into it. The three of them sat around the bed as the child drank his milk and Sandile tried to explain that what he had done was not only dangerous, but wrong. 'Alan Taylor is a horrible man. I can tell you that if he ever caught you stealing his wire you would be in deep, deep trouble, worse than you can imagine.'

Sandile regretted the phrase immediately, realising that Lucky was probably capable of imagining the most terrible things. Mama, who was sitting next to the boy, put her arm round his shoulder and squeezed him tightly.

'If you want wire, you just ask me, OK?' Sandile changed to a kinder tone. 'We can go buy you some wire in the dorp on Saturday. Then you can make a whole fleet of lorries and catapults and whatever you need. OK?'

Lucky held tightly on to the warm, red-enamelled cup. His eyes flashed up and met Sandile's just for a moment, but Sandile saw that he had reached him, that the child was grateful for his offer, and he went to his bed feeling lighter for that.

TWENTY

It was with mixed feelings that Elise had accepted Ina's decision to cancel their outing and spend the day with Alan Taylor. She had been dreading this day trip to town to choose the dress. She knew precisely how it would play out, knew she would be completely overwhelmed and would end up letting Ina choose. Then she would hate the wedding-cake concoction that her friend was bound to decide on. Elise would lose her temper and want to give up; they would argue, and eventually Elise would choose something so simple that no one else in Fransmansvallei would be seen dead getting married in it, Ina would come up with some way to frou-frou it up a bit, and finally they'd agree that Elise looked beautiful and very Elise, which she would, and they'd be friends again.

Now part of her was relieved that she'd have the freedom to choose the dress quickly on her own, but on the other hand she was anxious that she'd be unable to make a decision without Ina there to bounce ideas off. Another part of her was nervous about driving alone with Sandile, though she was excited at the chance to spend several hours with him all to herself.

On Saturday Elise was up and out before the rest of the world. She loved that feeling. Sometimes, just occasionally, she liked to burst out of the bubble of the farm, and this morning felt like such a holiday. She pulled her handbag over her shoulder as she stepped out of the back door, then stopped a moment, arrested by the sight of the mountains all around her. The air was cool and the sky only half light. The sun would be up soon.

Sandile was waiting for her by the bakkie. He smiled at her as she approached. She smiled back and pointed to the old Merc. 'We're taking that one.'

He shrugged and fell into step alongside her. 'Sleep well?'

She frowned at him. No one except Daan and occasionally her father asked questions like that. But it would be rude not to answer.

'Yes, thanks. Did you?'

'Wonderfully, thank you!'

Sandile laughed. There was a flamboyance, a lightness about him at times which contrasted sharply with the serious, almost stern Sandile of their briefer encounters. Elise was glad to have the lighter version accompanying her this morning.

She climbed into the driver's seat and opened the passenger door for him to get in. He did, shutting the door quietly as she started up the engine. They set off down the oak- and poplar-lined drive. Sandile looked round at the interior of the car: the cracked leather back seat was littered with discarded bits and pieces of Elise's life. A sunhat, tatty old maps, a twisted-up beach towel and one or two lumps of metal that looked as if they might have fallen off the car itself. The Mercedes had been in the family for years – it had clearly been lived in and ridden hard all that time.

Elise glanced over at Sandile as she pulled out of the drive and on to Skaduwee Lane. 'What are you going to do in town?'

Sandile paused for a moment before replying. 'Just some . . . personal business.'

Elise didn't press the point; he clearly wanted to keep his business private and he had every right to, she thought.

There was another pause before he said, 'What are *you* going to do in town?'

She looked over at him again. He was spread out comfortably in the passenger seat, his right elbow resting on the back of his seat and his hand on the back of hers.

'Personal business,' she mimicked, smiling slightly. She

looked back to the road, then, shifting into a higher gear, she added, 'Well, some shopping really. I have to choose a wedding dress.'

'*A* wedding dress?'

'OK, *my* wedding dress.'

Sandile turned away from her, towards the road ahead.

The silence made her uncomfortable. Elise felt self-conscious. Oh dear, she wondered, how was she going to take hours of this? She silently cursed Ina for not coming with her as she reached across the dashboard and switched the radio on to SAFM, the early-morning news.

'Heightened drama in the race row which threatened to capsize the Truth Commission this week. Our correspondent Darren Taylor reports on the cold war–'

Sandile leaned forward to change channels. Music. Sheryl Crow singing 'Run, baby, run, baby, run, baby, run . . .' Elise's eyes flicked over to his hand which was almost touching her knee as he increased the volume; almost touching, but not quite.

The music relaxed her and she settled back into the soft old leather seat and concentrated on the road. It was almost five thirty when they drove up out of the valley, along the ridge of the mountains and into the incredible morning. The sun rose behind them and the countryside was aflame with summer colours. Falling away all round them were the gold and umber and moss-speckled mountains, rolling down to misty blue-green valleys where the sun glinted on silvery plates of water, glared brightly off roofs and glass. The sky was huge and pale and full of high-stacked Omo-white clouds. Elise wound down her window and over the music the sounds from outside were beautiful too, a constant ambient track of crickets and Christmas beetles and for a while the low drone of a Cessna flying along the ridge of the mountains. She loved the sound of those little planes. It reminded her of childhood days playing in the garden and up in the mountains, the tiny aircraft drifting along the craggy skyline like drunken bumble bees purring at the marvellous day.

Sandile broke the silence. 'How old are you now?'

Elise made a face. 'What a strange question.'

'You don't have to tell me – I can work it out.'

'Don't strain yourself. Twenty-nine. I'll be thirty next year.'

'Wow, the big three-oh.'

'Why does everyone make such a fuss about it? Is it very old or very young?' Elise turned towards him whenever she spoke, taking her eyes off the road momentarily to look at him.

'Young, definitely very young.'

'I used to think thirty sounded ancient. I mean by now I'm pretty far down the road, but I feel I should have done more, you know? I should have reached some calmer place.' She spoke the last sentence comically, as if she were narrating a commercial, her tone silky smooth and knowing. They laughed together.

Sandile's arm was stretched along the back of the seat. Elise was intensely conscious of his hand near her shoulder. Her hair swung on her back every time she looked round towards him.

'You know, I won't mind if you don't make eye contact with me while you drive.'

She swung her gaze back to the road. Laughter lurched from her throat. 'Sorry, it's a dangerous habit I have . . .'

'What other dangerous habits do you have?'

He had this disconcerting way of throwing things back at her, of shifting the drift of a conversation. Elise didn't mind. She felt wonderfully free and was happy to go wherever he led.

'Only that one.'

Sandile smiled broadly, at her laughter rather than her words. She felt his eyes on her, felt conscious of the exposed skin of her neck, her cheek.

'Mama said you went away for a long time, to Bloemfontein. Why there of all places?'

'Well, it was a bit of an accident really. Dawie was going to study agriculture at the university, but then he was killed. I took his place.'

'You ran away to Bloemfontein?'

Elise nodded, then she laughed again. 'It's true, there are better places to run to.'

'What did you do there?'

She sighed. Bloemfontein was something of a blur, a time that she enjoyed forgetting. 'I became a farmer.'

Bloemfontein was her exile. She almost never spoke of it because people rarely asked her and that suited Elise. But Sandile wanted to know. They had time and a long road ahead of them, so she told him the story.

No one had wanted her to go to Bloemfontein. Elise had managed to convince the registrar who couldn't, off the top of his head, see why there would be a problem with her taking her brother's place at the university. Nevertheless he was at pains to dissuade her. There were no other girls on the agriculture course; there never had been and perhaps there was a good reason for that. After all, how many women farmers were there in South Africa? Elise was undeterred; she had a response for everything and was finally accepted. Her grandmother had left her enough money to pay for the first year. After that she would make another plan.

She didn't tell her parents until the arrangements were already made. She wanted to surprise them with this fitting tribute to Dawie and to the family and the land. But neither her mother nor her father thought it was any such thing. She would never forget how her mother set down her knife and fork, pulled the linen napkin off her lap, dabbed her mouth, then demanded, with evident pain, 'How could you do that to your brother?'

Elise's face fell as she looked from her mother's frown to her father's grim stare. Anger was the first thing that surfaced and Elise blurted it out.

'What do you mean, to Dawie? Dawie's dead! Don't you think this is what he would have wanted? For me to go in his place. For you. For the farm!'

Evelyn stared back at her daughter, white with shock. Elise had mentioned the unmentionable. They never spoke of Dawie's death or even of his life. It was as if their lives had been rewritten, as if he had been completely excised not only from the future but also from the past.

Van Rensburg put his knife down with a clatter that silenced both women. 'That's enough, my girl! Have you lost your manners as well as your mind?'

Elise was stung by his gruff rage. She felt tears coming into her eyes and her mother, seeing them, started sobbing into her napkin.

'But Pa, I thought you'd be pleased. Why aren't you pleased?' Elise couldn't understand.

Her father stared back at her. After a while he shook his head and said, 'How dare you think that you have the right to step into your brother's shoes?'

Elise reeled from the vehemence, the viciousness of his words, but she couldn't let this go. 'So who's going to run the farm when you're gone – Dawie's ghost?'

Van Rensburg winced, then he stood up and walked out, flinging his parting words over his shoulder: 'You're a girl. A stupid, ill-mannered girl. You'll never make a farmer!'

Evelyn scraped back her chair and ran out after her husband.

Elise had tried to fathom her parents' displeasure, tried to win them over, but they were immovable. She got nothing but incredulous hostility. The atmosphere in the house was unendurable, as if all the poison from their wounds, from the loss of their son, was flowing out around Elise. What was the point of going to university when she was only going to marry and have kids? they snapped. Didn't she feel guilty about the waste? If she wanted to live on a farm so badly why didn't she clean herself up a bit, make herself look more like a woman and go out and marry a farmer? Jibes and barbed comments flew. From her mother they were coated in a bitchiness that shocked Elise, in her father they cloaked a deep sense of confusion and powerlessness. Elise guessed that he feared losing her, but he was too stubborn, too bloody-minded to climb down and say so. The last thing she'd said to him had been an angry retort. 'I'm going and don't you try to stop me.'

He had glared at her across the yard. 'What makes you think I'd want to stop you?'

Mama Mashiya had helped her to pack, clucking over her things, making sure she had all the basics, everything she might need. It was Mama who cried when Elise hugged and kissed her goodbye and Ina du Toit who took her to the station in Paarl and put her on the train to Bloemfontein. Elise recalled how, as the train drew in, the yawning sense of loss, the anxiety that had kept them both silent for most of the afternoon, was replaced with a sudden rush of excitement. Amid the screech of brakes and the gust of air from the train, Ina grabbed Elise's hand, her hair whipping round her face as she said suddenly, 'I wish I was coming with you!'

Elise smiled. The abrupt imminence of her departure filled her with a wild sense that everything was possible. 'Come then! Come with me!'

But Ina shook her head and pushed her hair away from her face so that Elise could see the sadness there. 'No, I can't. I'll never leave the valley.'

The conductor blasted his whistle. Ina helped her shove her suitcase into the carriage and then Elise turned to her. 'Why not? There's a whole world out there!'

Ina pushed Elise forward. 'Hurry up or you'll still be standing here when it's gone!'

Elise stepped into the carriage. The conductor whistled again, the train was hauling out of the station and Ina was running alongside, waving and laughing. Then she was gone. Elise found herself alone, standing at the window in an empty compartment, the familiar landscape racing away from her.

The university was not what she'd expected it to be. Elise felt shrunken, shadowy, like a cipher slipping and slapping around in a grown-up-sized identity. Other people saw a person there, but she didn't feel like she thought a person should feel. She felt like she was outside, looking in on all these purposeful, located lives. Going shopping on a Saturday morning she'd watch people with their lists: families and couples, their lives integrated, no broken circuits as far as she could tell, and she felt like a ghost hovering among them.

For Elise there was a terrible gulf between being lonely and being alone. Alone, she felt strong and sure. She found her eyes were open wider, that she encountered the world in stark shapes and vivid colour. Her responses were as sharp as a tack. Alone, she could read and work for hours on end, oblivious of time and hunger and the shifting slant of the light in her room. Alone, she could talk to strangers in a voice that was warm and level. Alone, she could sit in the cinema and lose herself in a movie, so much so that she'd be startled by self-consciousness coming out of the darkness into the dazzle of an afternoon or the brightness of street lights.

Elise couldn't predict when alone might flip into loneliness, but when it did the change was instant and awful. There were sounds and smells that might trigger it, or the trace of something familiar on a stranger's face, or the way the sun touched her skin on a hot day, or a gust of cold as she walked out on to the street on a winter morning. Loneliness was immense and belittling. When she was lonely Elise's vision narrowed to a tunnel, and she navigated her world like a mole. Spaces collided with her, crashed in on her, crumpling her. She couldn't bear to sit in her room – its walls confined her, pinned her down in the glare of her own inadequacy. She couldn't open a book without noticing the thinness of her fingers, without sensing acutely the shape of her body, the hardness of the chair beneath her and the empty, empty space around her head. She would get up abruptly, striding across the room to switch on the radio and twist up the volume to blast anything through the emptiness. And for a while the noise would push back the walls, but it would also shatter any concentration Elise had left and she would quickly escape her room for the streets.

She walked and walked and walked those days. Her encounters with the strangers all around her were full of frowns and bitter scowls and her voice was so thin and angry it made smiles retract and faces shrink from her. Loneliness made her want to climb out of her head and run away from its interminable monologues, half-remembered songs, snatches of replayed conversations which blared simultaneously like noise from a radio gone haywire. Loneliness sometimes made her drink wine until she fell asleep, or at least unconscious, for the sleep was never good. Loneliness could make her stand up and walk out of a cinema even in the middle of a movie she'd waited weeks to see. The pressure of other couples and families and friends became terrifying, the space they left around her, the empty seats on either side of her, were unendurable.

The only thing that was the same, lonely or alone, was the deep longing in her for connection, for rootedness. For Elise this was something to do with a jumble of a few familiar voices, the perfect taste of a plum just pulled from the tree, a quality in the light, the colour of a mountainside at sunset, the smell of turned earth, the wide scoop of a valley.

Once, on a horribly failed date, she tried explaining this to the man sitting opposite her, who was burgeoning with an altogether different kind of longing. He couldn't grasp this thing she was trying to describe about the land. After all, here they were in Bloemfontein – this was her land, wasn't it?

'Yes, yes,' she said, nodding vehemently, 'but in a different sense, I mean flat and scrubby. Don't you see?'

His eyes frowned, while his mouth smiled. 'Well, yes, we all feel strongly about the place we grew up in, but . . .'

The pause was long. She stared hard at him. He tilted his head in puzzlement; he didn't see. She pushed her chair back from the table, scraping it loudly on the restaurant's wooden floor. 'Maybe you're right, maybe that's all it is.' But she didn't mean it and her frustration was intense; she was furious that she couldn't explain.

Later that night, after some embarrassing head-ducking at

the door, Elise sat dumbly at her desk. She was, as she often did unconsciously, rubbing her left thumb back and forth over the scar on the palm of her right hand. She couldn't define this thing that ached in her – perhaps it wasn't as substantial as she believed it to be. Maybe she was fooling herself with sugary sentiment; maybe she was using it as an excuse not to get out and grab hold of the real life around her. Perhaps, she thought, she was dragging herself down with a past she could never recapture. But how to get rid of the longing? She became aware of the scar on her palm that she was rubbing over and over with her thumb, and she frowned as she traced the outline of the old cut. She couldn't remember how she'd got it.

In time, Rustenvrede, the dorp and the valley came to seem like the landscape of a recurring dream. It was pride, stubborn pride that made Elise stay away. Her father had missed her almost immediately and she him; there was no question of a serious rift, despite her ugly departure. Elise had telephoned as soon as she was installed in the women's residence on campus and her father's voice told her immediately that he was delighted to hear from her and to know that she was safe. They carefully skirted the soreness of what had happened and spoke and wrote of everything around it. As time went by the argument was forgotten, or at least buried, and Elise even sensed pride in the frequent letters that came from her father and the less regular missives from her mother. Ina's letters were the most newsy and she often confirmed the fact that the Van Rensburgs boasted around the dorp about their brave daughter's successes at the university.

Elise slowly settled into a small community of friends and a pattern of work. It was hard, but sheer determination got her through and her confidence grew with the knowledge she gained. She was never an insider, never a favourite in the department, but as the only girl she never would be. She always reacted politely and with charm to the jocular, sometimes offensive, usually patronising treatment she received from the men in her class. She understood, even if they didn't, that she had to take herself seriously if she was going to pull through.

Elise did more than pull through. When she graduated she was one of the top students in her class. The Van Rensburgs flew up for her graduation. It meant everything to her that they did and their pride in her achievement touched her more deeply than she could express. At the airport, moments before they were due to board to fly back home, it was her mother who at last put the question that had hovered around them all week. She wanted to know when to expect Elise back home. Evelyn was visibly shocked when Elise told her bluntly that she wasn't coming home. At least not yet. She saw her mother's pain that day at the airport, but she also saw in both her parents a kind of acceptance. They would let their daughter be the judge of what was best for her, in spite of the hole her absence created in their lives. And so their parting was full of sadness, but an important mutual regard had been born that brought tears flooding down Elise's face as she drove back into the lonely town.

What Elise hadn't said was that she couldn't come home until she had proved something. Elise wanted to prove herself as a farmer. She needed to prove her father wrong. Though he seemed to have long forgotten it, she would never forget the words he'd spat at her that day.

In the long vacation at the end of her first year Elise had taken a job on a farm not far from Bloemfontein. Terreblanche, the farmer, was an ugly man with a quiet, unhappy-seeming family. He was struggling with a thousand arid acres of mielies and grazing land. He hadn't wanted to take on a girl, but Elise was all he could get to fill in while his foreman went on annual leave. Elise had a rough ride. Looking back she often thought that if she'd known at the outset how hard it would be she would never have left Rustenvrede. Her innocence and determination got her through and she won over not only the farm labourers, who at first took to being bossed by a woman as either an insult or a joke or both, but also the farmer. The following year Terreblanche wanted her back and so, over time, Elise had become a steady part of that farm's life.

Just before her final exams Elise received a telephone call from the foreman at Kromdraai. Mr Terreblanche had suffered a massive heart attack the night before and he'd died that morning. The funeral was a sparse affair. Mrs Terreblanche was dry-eyed throughout, but at the end of the service she came to Elise and broke down over the fate of the farm. It was Elise, startling herself with her own opportunism, who suggested that Mrs Terreblanche hire her to manage the place. Mrs Terreblanche agreed on the spot and so it was to Kromdraai that Elise went after graduating from Bloemfontein.

The first two years were exhausting. Terreblanche's estate was a mess. Without Elise at the helm Kromdraai would certainly have met the fate of some of the neighbouring farms and gone under the auctioneer's gavel. At first she'd been terrified, thought she'd bitten off more than she could chew, and in fact she had. Nevertheless, failure was unthinkable and so she worked harder than ever before, mustering all her energy, all her knowledge, every resource at her disposal to pull the place through.

There was a part of the story that Elise didn't relate to Sandile on their long drive to Cape Town. During the second year on the farm, as the pressures were easing up, Daan du Toit came through Bloemfontein on his way back from a police training camp in the Transvaal. Elise had known him all her life, but she'd never paid him much attention – he'd always been the baby of the Du Toit family. When he telephoned her Elise had been only too delighted to see someone from home, even Ina's kid brother. Daan sounded different on the phone, but after all, Elise thought, she probably did too. When she saw him she almost didn't recognise him. He wasn't the gangly, skulking adolescent she'd known. Here instead was a tall, attractive man. She said so when she saw him.

He took her out for dinner. It was nice to talk the old talk with someone she didn't have to translate for, someone who didn't have to translate for her. It felt so easy, so comfortable, but there was something more for Elise, something heady: she was aware of a completely unexpected attraction.

Daan came through town again just a few months later and this time he asked if he could stay over with her at Kromdraai. Elise made up the sofa bed in her cottage for him, but at the end of a romantic evening he simply climbed into bed with her and that was that. It made perfect sense and it made Elise happy. She and Daan never discussed what was going on between them; the relationship grew with their encounters. Elise didn't feel a need to know where things were leading. Marriage and family were not in her sights then and Daan never pressed her, so she assumed it was the same for him. It was partly because of Daan that Elise was able to accept going back home when the time came that she was needed.

Van Rensburg's visit was a complete surprise. Elise was so startled, so delighted to see her father walking towards her with Mrs Terreblanche down the long aisle of the milking shed that at first it didn't occur to her that something was wrong. He looked tired and drawn, but so would anyone after a long day of travelling. Elise ran straight into his familiar bear hug. It was only hours later that Van Rensburg told her why he'd come.

They were sitting in the living room of her little cottage and Elise was bubbling over with excitement and pride at her achievements. Her father was sitting on the sofa, staring out at the slow slope of scrubland that stretched seemingly for ever. Elise brought him a glass of iced water and sat down next to him, talking all the while. He was subdued and smiled only faintly as he listened. After a while Elise fell silent. Her father sipped at the water in his glass. Looking at him, at how drawn and sad he seemed, she realised there was something on his mind and she kicked herself for not noticing before. Why else would he come all this way? It certainly wasn't just to see her showing off her work.

Elise stood up. She thought first of the farm, that something had happened to Rustenvrede. 'Pa. What is it? What's happened?'

Van Rensburg put his glass down. His movement was abrupt and clumsy and water slopped out and spilled over the table. Elise almost cried out – there was something sitting so heavily on his heart and she was suddenly terrified of what it could be.

'It's your mother.' Van Rensburg leaned forward with his head in his hands. 'She's got cancer. The doctor gave her six months.'

Tears fell from his covered eyes, ran down his fingers and dropped on to the floor, but he didn't make a sound. Elise couldn't move. She had never seen her father cry, not even after the news about Dawie. The sight of this huge, immovably strong man weeping shook her to the core.

Her father didn't say it but she knew that he wanted her to come home. The next day Elise drove him to the airport in his rented car and got a lift back with Mrs Terreblanche who had followed in her own car. Elise broke the news to her. Mrs Terreblanche was not as devastated as she might have been two years earlier. Kromdraai was in good shape and Elise had given her the confidence to know that she could now oversee it herself. It didn't take long for her to find a new manager and to finalise the arrangements for Elise's departure. And so, almost seven years after she'd left, Elise went home.

The homecoming was overwhelming. It seemed to give her mother a new lease of life too, for six months later Evelyn was still going strong. It would be nearly two more years before she died.

Elise didn't talk about her mother. 'You know what you said about London . . . In Bloemfontein I was so lonely, so isolated I actually felt sick. The beginning was the worst, but it got better. Once it was over I could see how bad it had been, but at the time I was walking around telling myself I was OK, even though I couldn't sit still or talk to anyone for longer than a few minutes. I had these – how shall I put it? – symptoms. The anxiety showed itself in symptoms which reflected a sense of chaos. Inside me and out. Does that make sense?'

Sandile nodded; it made perfect sense to him.

'Instead of experiencing myself in any moment as a definite cluster of memories, mannerisms, goals, moods, relationships, things that are all fluid but relatively solid and coherent, I experienced things as if the cluster was falling apart, had no glue to hold it together. As if I was standing on the road with the basket of my head dropped on the ground and all the things that I held in it, that were me in that moment, spilling out and rolling along the gutters. I didn't really know who I was.'

Elise talked with her eyes fixed on the road ahead, driving with one hand on the wheel, the other hand weaving and punching the air for emphasis. 'It's only since I've been back home that I feel I know myself again. In Bloem I tried to find a centre, something separate from people and places, something that represented "me". But I only truly found myself when I came back. It's strange how identity is tied up with place. Maybe not for everyone, but it's like that for me.'

Looking over at him she saw that Sandile had grown thoughtful, inscrutable again. 'But your farm may not be there for ever . . .'

'Why not?'

'Well, what if someone took it away?'

'No one would do that. I'd kill them if they tried!'

Elise had answered flippantly. It was like asking her how she'd feel if the sky fell in.

Sandile stiffened slightly, and she immediately felt embarrassed at her own insensitivity. He was landless, she was rich in it, always would be – at least that's what she thought she saw crossing his face. She blushed, gripping the steering wheel with both hands, tipping her head back slightly. Then his face broke into a smile, an unexpectedly impressed and mischievous one.

'I like that. I like that about you. I'd feel the same.'

His laughter was almost a guffaw. She thought she understood the irony in it. At the time it seemed plain. In her memory it would become murky.

'I suppose that's what any kind of struggle teaches you. The value of things that you previously took for granted,' she said.

'Ja . . .' His voice trailed off and he went back to contemplation of the countryside flying by. A while later he said he didn't know she talked so much. 'You're so still and so quiet usually, stalking round the orchards with that unshakeable purpose of yours.' She grinned.

They drove long stretches without speaking, letting the radio play while the road rolled away beneath them. In this way they drove over Sir Lowery's Pass, silent, but aware of what they were experiencing together as the incredible vista of the Cape peninsula was suddenly laid out before them. There was the sea, the unbelievable expanse of False Bay, the clutter of townships on the Cape Flats and beyond them the dazzling arcing beaches, and in the distance the majestic, massive Table Mountain.

They followed the snaking pass all the way down to Somerset West, sped past the acres of retirement homes that had sprung up there behind high white walls and raced along the freeway towards town. Once out on the Flats they couldn't avoid the sight of the ugly underside of Cape Town. Seemingly endless squatter camps lined the road; they would have spilled on to the freeway without the massive fences that hemmed them in. Sandile noticed a group of boys, black teenagers, covered from head to toe in white clay. They were initiates. Here, in this mess of corrugated iron, atop a rubbish dump, they were taking part in a ceremony as old as civilisation in Africa. The ritual of transition from boy to manhood. He pointed them out to Elise but she had already seen them.

'It's incredible, isn't it?' he said. 'I mean here, of all places. It's like a symbol for everything: the degradation, the insanity and the miracle of this place.'

Elise nodded, gazing at the boys in her rear-view mirror as they crossed the freeway, scuttling across the tarmac, dodging between the hurtling cars. Sandile's eyes darkened again as he went on, talking and staring out of the window, as if he were thinking out loud.

'What a terrible and incredible thing. Sometimes this country terrifies me.'

Elise smiled and Sandile swivelled round in his seat to face her. 'And yet, you know, apartheid was such a serious breakdown at the core of everything that I don't think things can ever be normal, at least not in our time. We've spent all our lives fighting a war or surrounded by war. We've been so distorted that normal life is impossible to achieve.'

'Surely not impossible?'

'Yes. I think some generations are irretrievable. I think ours is. The past is too overwhelming. I wish I could simply obliterate it, but I can't. I wish I could say that I have no past.'

'But there are lessons in the past. Lessons which can help to point the way forward.'

Sandile shrugged. 'Ja . . . I don't know. Part of me wishes, *hopes* you are right, but part of me cannot imagine any other way. For me it's all about survival. A battle for survival. It means making yourself invincible, knowing your enemy as well as you know yourself. It means–'

'But life isn't a war! All right, most of your life you've been fighting a war. But now it's over. And you won, nogal! Now we have peace at last and you've got to live in a new way . . . You have to *learn* to live normally.' She spoke quite gently, in contrast to Sandile who was caught up in the intensity of what he needed to express.

'There are always battles, even in peacetime. Wrongs to right. Rights to win. You know that. You've fought your own battles to get where you are.'

She glanced sideways at him. Sandile fell silent. He couldn't meet her eyes. He was thinking of the land claim, of everything he hadn't told her and everything she would soon know.

When he did speak again his tone had shifted back to a lighter note; he'd veered away from whatever dark thing he'd been alluding to. 'Have you ever thought it would be nice just to chuck it all up and live in a flat in a city and never even know your neighbours?'

She shook her head. 'Never have really. You?'

He nodded. 'But not any more.'

Elise smiled. 'There are some things I like about cities. I mean I love the neon signs, especially the red ones, just before dusk on a clear afternoon.'

A sound came from him, like a sigh, like a laugh.

They arrived in Cape Town just before nine. It was still early. Elise had time to kill before her appointment and Sandile didn't have to go anywhere in a hurry, so he suggested they get some breakfast in a café. She agreed without hesitation.

Elise parked in the Parade just as the square was coming to life and the vendors were opening up their stalls. They walked for a while and found a place to eat just off Greenmarket Square, the cobbled old square built long ago by Dutch settlers trying to reproduce the town life they had left so far behind.

They took their time over breakfast: a whole day stretched ahead of them. They talked, meandering through subjects sublime and ridiculous. They laughed a lot and were serious. Elise had grown up in a house dominated by men; she was used to their silences, being shut out of their world. Men in her experience never revealed their feelings, seemed not to have the endless post-mortems and analyses that were the domain of women. But talking with Sandile was like talking to a woman. He had a way of striking for the heart of things. There was nothing polite about him – at times he was blunt, almost aggressive, at others devastatingly charming. Either way he always cut to the point, never pussyfooted around. It was this that gave Elise the unnerving sense that he knew her and she him. She felt as if there was nothing they couldn't say to one another. What was the word that had come to her the other day to describe to herself the feeling she had with him? Communion. Theirs was an intense, a strange communion. She felt like someone else with him, someone she enjoyed being.

Elise ordered another cup of coffee. She had no desire to move and the thought of Baskin's rooted her even more firmly to the spot. 'So tell me about you? What are your plans?'

'Ag, my plans are a bit of a mess. They all depend.'

'Depend on what?'

'Oooh. Stuff.'

She laughed, he stirred the sugar into his cup, round and round and round with the little spoon. The two of them stared into the vortex of milky coffee, both of them smiling a little, like people do when they're flirting and can't stop themselves.

'What do you mean, stuff?'

He shrugged and stared over her shoulder as if distracted by something. 'I'll tell you when I get back.'

Then he looked her in the eye. 'I *want* to tell you about it. It's just it's all too complicated and boring right now – not like weddings!'

His tone had shifted abruptly from serious to mock light, almost evasively she thought. Elise was curious, but happy to wait for the explanation. 'Well, whatever it is, I hope it doesn't take you far away again. For your mother and father's sake,' she added hastily.

'Oh, not for your sake then?'

She shook her head, laughing again.

'Not even the teeniest, tiniest bit?'

'Well, perhaps the teeniest, tiniest bit . . .'

'Things are *soooo* clear for you, aren't they? Your family, your farm, your future. You must feel pretty heroic when you wake up in the mornings, with everything so perfectly worked out, so carefully managed.' Irony clung to his words.

Elise shrugged defensively. 'I don't feel at all heroic. What other way is there to live? I don't like drift or dishonesty, I don't like to feel there's a gap between appearance and reality, I don't like to hurt or be hurt. Rules for simple self-preservation, nothing to do with heroics.'

Sandile smiled at her, a little too knowing, then abruptly changed the subject. These wild lurches in the conversation were disorientating but exhilarating, like a fairground ride. He was provocative, demanded of her, challenged her, and she rose to it.

They had finished breakfast. Elise fixed her gaze vaguely on the other side of the street. The shops were all open now and she was going to be late for her appointment. She thought about the things he'd said.

'Maybe you're right about me managing everything. I like things to be neat and plain and visible. I don't like to get too stuck in the middle of anything.'

Sandile leaned forward, elbows either side of his coffee cup, his face cupped in his hands. 'Why?'

'Why? I don't know why! Don't even know why I'm telling you this.'

She laughed and swivelled her chair away, scraping the metal legs against the stones so that she was facing him sideways on.

'Maybe it's because the edge is the closest place to the escape route. Look at you, you're moving towards the exit already.'

Elise swung her chair back to face him directly.

'Don't run away, Elise.'

'What do you mean?'

Sandile laughed and leaned back, half exasperated, half exhilarated. Suddenly he was clowning, expansive again. 'I mean . . . I mean, I mean, I mean . . . I've had more fun with you this morning than I've had in a year, two, *ten* years!'

Elise blushed. He had this way of saying things directly that she would have died of embarrassment before admitting, but she held his gaze. 'Me too.'

Elise had enormous self-control. She hardly ever lost it, so there was little to remind her that the grip she kept on herself was iron. Until moments like this. By the time she knew it she had already lost control. She was out on the high wire with no safety net.

'But we can't hang around here all day! Things to do, people to see . . .' Elise knew she sounded reedy and unconvincing.

Sandile's expression changed again. It was as if a shadow had fallen across his face. 'Don't run away from things like this, Elise. Otherwise you'll spend your life drifting in a myopic daze of planned days and organised tasks and nothing spontaneous. You'll wake up one day and remember, but it won't be for years, and the regret will be so sharp it might even kill you. You will have sleepwalked through your own life.'

'How can you say that? You barely know me.'

Elise's guard shot up and animosity flared in her reaction. But was he right? In her heart she wasn't sure. She frowned at him. She had this feeling of falling towards him. She looked away, reaching for her bag. 'I should go.'

'Why? We have a whole day ahead of us. Nobody knows us here – what's there to run away from?'

Vertigo. She felt it wash over her and she gripped on to her bag. 'No, I really must go. I have an appointment to keep and you have your business to do.'

Sandile shrugged, sighing as he leaned back and threw up his hands. The gesture was small but heavy with disappointment. He was disappointed by her and he had no right to be. Elise hadn't meant to let things drift this far and he shouldn't have pushed it. She stood up and went to pay the bill. Sandile followed her and insisted on paying his half of it. He made light of it with the waitress and Elise was forced to laugh. She felt better laughing – she didn't want to part with any heaviness between them.

Sandile walked her to the end of the street, near to where she'd parked the car on the Parade. The square was bustling with life now; the day had begun for everyone else. He stopped at the corner of the street, shrugging his tote bag higher on to his shoulder. She stopped too. He looked at her expectantly and she didn't know what to say, so she laughed again, a silly pointless gurgle of a laugh.

'Well, I hope it all works out, whatever it is.'

He cleared his throat, his eyes too full of things unspoken, too intense. Elise stared over his shoulder – there was no denying what had happened.

She had thought of kissing him, imagined what it might be like, and the idea of being kissed by Sandile terrified her, though the sensation of his lips on hers was something her mind and body had flicked back to continually that morning. She was magnetised by his presence. The tension pulled her nerves so tight she felt her jaw might snap off and her eyes pop right out of her head. Then suddenly she wasn't scared at all, just overwhelmed by curiosity. In the end it was she who kissed him.

Standing there in front of him, the desire to touch his cheek with her cheek, to feel his lips on hers, overwhelmed all her controls and she didn't realise she'd done it until she had. She kissed him, gently, on his surprised mouth. His tongue touched hers, tasted hers, and the shock of that contact made her pull away as suddenly as she'd felt pushed forward. For a moment they stared at one another, startled, rapt.

Elise felt she was walking a tightrope, completely alone. The sensation was exhilarating; she couldn't believe how easy it was. There is a sense of freedom that flows from shattered certainties. Elise had tasted that freedom before, but it was never as rich as it seemed now, tasting him.

It was an instant before she realised what she'd done. She pulled away, stepped backwards, almost slipping off the kerb on to the street. She hurriedly said goodbye and turned away from Sandile, who was still staring at her, still shocked. He grabbed hold of her arm, not too hard, not hard enough to hold her if she didn't want to stay, and she turned back to him.

'You can't do that, you can't just kiss me like that and leave.'

Elise didn't know what to say or do, but all her instincts told her she'd jumped into the deep end before she was ready to swim. Sandile saw it in her eyes. The boldness was gone and sheer terror shone back at him.

'OK, OK . . .'

But he didn't let go of her until he had kissed her again.

Twenty One

That same Saturday morning just before nine – as arranged – Ina drove up to Die Uitkyk with Lettie Kriel in the passenger seat next to her. Lettie was Ina's choice to be Alan Taylor's housekeeper. It wasn't exactly the job Lettie would have chosen. She wasn't delighted at the prospect of working on her own in a bachelor's large house, but to be chosen was a sign of Ina's confidence in her, and above all it would mean a higher wage, so she had accepted with little hesitation.

Lettie was young, but no one would have called her pretty. She had a dumpy, pear-shaped body and a chubby, uneven face. Certainly not a head-turner.

'Have you got a boyfriend, Lettie?' Ina asked as they chugged up the leafy drive towards the main house.

Lettie scowled, as if the very idea were distasteful.

'Don't you want to get married?'

'Why would I want to get married, Miss Ina?'

She was suddenly positively animated, quite a surprise, thought Ina, from someone who was usually so blank and placid.

'I mean look at my mother and sister – they're always getting knocked up or beaten up. What's the point in being married? Men are all silver tongues and sweet nothings until they get you on the bed and then – it's over!'

Lettie illustrated her point with graphic gesticulation. Ina raised her eyebrows, nodding thoughtfully. 'I suppose I can't argue with that.'

'But I do go out. Me and Johnny Kakana go for a drive and a nice walk on Sundays, after church. My mother doesn't like me going round with a black, but he's a better man than any of the Coloureds I know round here. He's a decent man, he never drinks, he's quiet and he's serious and he has a proper career. And he doesn't ask for anything.' Lettie emphasised the importance of this last part with a wide-eyed dip of her head.

Ina couldn't conceal her surprise. 'What a dark horse you are, Lettie!'

Lettie shrugged and folded her hands in her lap. Her face settled and she was quite still again. Ina was doubly impressed. Lettie's family were of mixed race. Under apartheid that meant they were classified as Coloured as opposed to black. This made them second-class citizens, not third class. Coloureds spoke Afrikaans, not African languages, and Ina believed they were cannier and easier to teach than Africans. She'd trained Lettie straight out of school and the girl made an excellent, quiet worker. Given the chance, though, she loved to have a good chat. That was exactly what Ina wanted, someone reliable and efficient who was happy to have a gossip from time to time about how Mr Taylor was getting on.

They pulled up next to a monstrous removals van which was parked as close to the front stoep of the house as it could get. Half a dozen guys were hard at work to and from the house with boxes and furniture. As she walked up to the back door, Lettie trudging along behind her, Ina noticed that the van came from Pietermaritzburg. The name of the town was painted clearly on the side panel. She thought that was curious and made a mental note to ask Alan about it later, though she never did. She forgot the detail in the wash of events that day.

Taylor emerged from the house as crisp and as smart as Ina had expected him to be. She introduced him to Lettie and he led them into the kitchen. Ina chattered away in English as she followed him, with Lettie trailing behind.

'I think you're going to be very happy with this arrangement, Alan. Lettie is a sensible, nice, well-liked girl. You won't need to tell her what to do – she's got plenty of initiative and she knows what the job is.'

'As long as she's not a gossip.'

'Oh, no, quite the opposite. She's a quiet girl, likes to keep herself to herself. Well, you can see why . . .'

'I just don't like busybodies.'

'I know you're going to be thrilled with her.'

After a brief discussion about hours and wages, led mostly by Ina, the matter was settled. Taylor seemed perfectly satisfied and from the smile that appeared on Lettie's pudgy face Ina could tell that the arrangement suited her too. Ina was pleased and Lettie was immediately set to work.

Ina wandered alone through the empty house, stepping aside as furniture came through. She had never been particularly friendly with the Brookeses, so she didn't really know the place and she enjoyed the opportunity to explore. Die Uitkyk had been built in the Cape Dutch style, though more recently than Rustenvrede. It was a very large house for a single man, Ina thought, and from the speed at which the van was emptying it didn't look like the place was going to be overfull.

The removals company were extremely efficient. Every box was labelled with the name of the room to which its contents were to be delivered and soon there were boxes in almost every room. Ina offered to help with the unpacking. Taylor took some persuading before he accepted, then gave her very specific directions about what she should unpack and where. There were things he didn't want her to touch and so she didn't. Ina put this down to his fastidiousness. She was happy to be there and to be of use to him, so she did exactly as she was told.

She spent the morning unpacking books on to shelves in the room that Taylor had allocated for his study and office. It looked out on to the front lawn and was large and bright with shelves all the way up to the high ceilings. He had a great many books. In among them were a number of ornaments and a few framed photographs. Ina unwrapped them carefully, dusting them off before she set each one down on the mantelpiece. The first three were old black and white pictures of what looked like his mother and father at a family christening. Ina smiled as she set them down – they were charming portraits. The fourth was a colour picture of a woman. She was young and very beautiful with small dark features and a mass of dark curly hair. She was clearly not a relation. Ina felt a stab of jealousy, then doubt. Who was this woman to him? The next frame told her everything. It was a portrait from a wedding – Taylor's. And his bride was the beautiful brunette. So he *was* married! Ina's heart raced. She noticed that in the picture he wasn't wearing a ring. Was he *still* married? Where was the wife?

Ina's hand shook slightly as she put the frame down on the mantelpiece next to the others. She didn't dust it down, but left it dirty. She stepped backwards, moving away from the photograph and yet transfixed by it. She hadn't noticed Taylor coming into the room and she started when she heard his voice behind her. 'How is everything going?'

Ina swung round. He was standing in the doorway smiling at her. His eyes went up to the photographs on the fireplace behind her. Ina looked round to follow his gaze. She spoke apologetically, as if she'd intruded. 'I don't know where you want them in the end, but they look quite nice there for now.'

Taylor nodded stiffly and walked past her to look more closely at the line of frames. He said nothing as he scanned them. Ina couldn't see his face, so she had no idea what he was thinking. Then he reached up for the picture of him with his bride, took it down and dusted it off with the cloth that Ina had left on top of the packing case. Setting the picture down again he said quietly, 'That's me with my wife.'

He turned round to face Ina. There was a strange smile on his lips, but his eyes were frozen. Ina nodded, a little too vigorously, trying to make light, as if she hadn't paid particular attention to it. 'I had guessed that.'

Taylor seemed to laugh, but she couldn't tell. It was an odd sound; it might have been an expression of pain. He looked down at his feet. 'Yes. I suppose I was stating the obvious.'

Ina moved across the room, picked up the knife she'd been

using and cut into the tape on a fresh box of books. She tried to sound as nonchalant as possible, her attention focused on the box. 'Where is she now?'

'She's dead.'

Ina looked up sharply. It was the last thing she'd expected him to say and he'd said it in such a peculiar way – as if he'd been telling her that his wife had gone shopping. Ina put the knife down on the windowsill and straightened up. She was upset for him. At that moment all her acute self-consciousness fell away.

'I am so sorry, so terribly sorry.'

Taylor sighed heavily. He still didn't move. 'Yes, so am I.'

Ina felt she understood him, suddenly, very clearly. This explained so much about his manner, his remoteness, his desire for privacy and seclusion. Ina's hand reached forward involuntarily. She was nowhere near him, yet she wanted to touch him, to give him some comfort. 'How–'

Taylor cut across her question, his voice clipped, almost curt. 'More than a year ago. Breast cancer. Stupid, really, for someone to die of breast cancer in this day and age.'

'I can't tell you how sorry I am.'

Taylor's frosty glare seemed to thaw. A smile curled up the corners of his mouth and his face softened. 'You are very kind, Ina. Too kind.'

Ina shook her head, her eyes full of pity and understanding. Taylor walked over to the door, extending his arm to indicate that she should go before him. 'Actually, I came to call you to lunch and instead I'm telling you my life story. You must be hungry – won't you join me?'

'Well, you were hardly telling me your life story . . .' Ina's voice trailed off as she walked ahead of him towards the kitchen.

They ate lunch at the large scrubbed pine table that had been delivered earlier and recently wiped down by the more than capable Lettie. The removal men left shortly after they finished their own lunch break in the garden. In the afternoon Taylor set to work dusting and arranging furniture with

Lettie and Ina as his assistants and advisers. Ina was impressed by the furniture, though it wasn't to her taste. It was too new and heavy and ornate for her, very masculine, she thought. However, it was all very well made, all good quality, and quality counted a lot for Ina.

Neither of them mentioned his wife again that day, but she was very much on Ina's mind. In one respect she was relieved, not because it confirmed that Alan was available, rather because it explained so much about his manner. The man was still grieving; no wonder he was so private. As they worked she often felt his eyes on her and several times he brushed past her, or put his hand on her arm or in the small of her back. Ina knew she wanted him, but she also knew now not to push it.

Towards five in the afternoon they had finished most of the work of arranging the large furniture. The rooms still looked bare, but once there were pictures up on the walls and flowers in the place Ina felt it would seem more like a home. Lettie had made up Taylor's bed in the large room facing the mountains at the back. There was not much more they could do that day. Taylor paid Lettie in cash on the spot and told her he expected to see her on Monday morning. She was very happy. Ina said she'd give Lettie a lift home and quietly told her to go and wait outside in the car. Lettie obeyed.

Ina and Taylor stood facing each other in the kitchen. Ina was leaning against the pine table at the centre of the room. Taylor smiled at her. He seemed tired, and so was she. He was silent again and she didn't know what to say. She was hoping he would speak first, but he didn't. He took a step towards her so that he was almost next to her at the table, but he was looking away from her, as if she wasn't even in the room. In the end it was Ina who spoke.

'My mother asked me to invite you to have dinner with us this week. I hope you will come.'

He looked round at her, as if he'd just surfaced from some deep thought. He seemed genuinely pleased. Ina noticed that he was breathing thickly. She smiled – he must be feeling strange, alone in this new house.

'I'd love to, thank you.'

'Thursday night?'

'Thursday night.'

He looked at her with a penetrating gaze that was totally unreadable. She stared back, her eyes locked on his. The silence of the house enveloped them; the only sound she heard was his breathing. Ina was conscious of Lettie sitting in the car outside, but she made no move to go. Taylor slowly closed his eyes. Long dark lashes fell on the pale skin of his cheeks and the next moment she felt his smooth hand on her knee, pushing up her leg, underneath the skirt of her dress. He ran his fingers lightly up her thigh; his thumb slid into her crotch, over her panties. Still she stared at him and he opened those blue, blank eyes. His hand stroked light cotton between her legs, firmly but not hard, not at all uncomfortable, sliding back and forth over the mound of her vagina. She was suddenly, violently aroused. All this time his face was near to hers, but he didn't kiss her, nor she him. They stared at one another, her lips parting, shivering at the sensation. She pushed her hands under his jacket and pulled at his shirt, slipping open his belt, fingers trembling on the zip, opening his trousers and pushing them back over his hips, his buttocks, inside his underpants. All she wanted to do was pull him inside her, have him push inside her. The desire was so powerful it almost hurt. As her fingers moved around and cradled the silky sac of his balls, stroking the arc of his erection, he groaned. His eyelids flickered and closed again. He yanked down her panties exposing the soft mass of her pubic hair, the swollen lips of her vagina, then put both hands between her legs and pushed them apart as he lifted her on to the table. His hands round her buttocks, he buried his face in her pubic hair, kissing her. She felt his mouth, his tongue on her clitoris.

Ina gasped. The breath rushed from her body. She pushed his head into her crotch with a sudden violent desire. She had never done anything like this before. She came quickly and in shuddering bursts. Then he was on top of her and she pulled him into her. They fucked. She thought, as he moved on top of her, this is fucking, and for the first time she liked the sound of the word, knew what it meant. His mouth was on her neck; he was breathing in sudden short gasps, then she came again and now he did too. His body sagged, and for the first time she felt the weight of him on top of her. They were completely still. Ina stared up at the ceiling lights. She was smiling, she couldn't help it, though she was thinking that they hadn't even kissed.

They dressed in silence, side by side in the kitchen. Ina smoothed down her hair and pushed out the creases in her dress. It was almost as if nothing had happened, but everything had happened. She was flushed and smiling as Taylor walked her to her car. He didn't touch her again, nor she him, though Lettie barely looked at them as they approached. Ina smiled shyly at him as she started up the old Beetle and he raised his hand in farewell. Then she drove away and in her rear-view mirror she saw him watching her.

After Ina had dropped Lettie off at her family's cottage in the compound at Komweer she realised she didn't want to go home. Instead she drove back across the valley to Rustenvrede. She needed desperately to talk to Elise.

TWENTY TWO

Somehow Elise found her car. She clutched at the door handle and stood there, just holding on, for several minutes. She hardly knew where she was. When at last she recovered sufficient breath she looked round towards the corner where she had parted from Sandile. He was gone. Elise unlocked the door and sank on to the front seat. After a while her heart stopped beating so wildly, the dizzy, sickening feeling that had gripped her subsided and was replaced by a mad elation. She realised she was smiling; she couldn't wipe the grin off her face. She slammed the door shut, put the key in the ignition and started the car. She didn't immediately drive off; it was as if she could only act in short spurts between the waves of paralysis and amazement that crashed over her. At last she got herself on the road and pointed the car in the right direction.

After several wrong turns, Elise eventually found her way to Baskin's by sheer serendipity. She parked nearby and ran into the building, aware of the irritation that would greet her hopelessly late arrival. Once inside she found herself surrounded by white lace and bundles of creamy silk, satin, muslin and velvet. She panicked. Baskin's was vast, a cathedral-sized monument to the white wedding. Racks and racks of huge dresses were lined up along the walls, and down every aisle there were eager faces, fingers testing fabric, whispered consultations. Dozens of women swarmed all over the place. They all looked very much the same, either brides-to-be or mothers of the bride-to-be. The pervading atmosphere was one of anxious excitement. Elise was glad she'd come alone: if there'd been a friendly shoulder available just then she would have cried all over it.

At that moment a young woman stepped up to her. She smiled a huge pink-lipstick smile which perfectly matched the bridesmaid-bright-pink dress on which she wore a name tag that had 'Shereen' written on it in equally large pink letters. Shereen asked if Elise had a booking, then went off to check the appointments book. Elise stared at the bright patch of sunlight which was the door. She told herself to get a grip. This wasn't the time or the place to get hysterical. She must do what she'd come here to do and then she'd take herself off somewhere quiet where she could safely fall apart.

Shereen tottered back on her high heels. Fortunately someone had cancelled so they could accommodate Elise in spite of her lateness.

'Why did they cancel?' Elise wanted to know. The question came out shrill and startled-sounding.

Shereen smiled a knowing smile. 'It happens. Everyone gets the jitters before their wedding. It's perfectly normal. Just some people get it worse than others.'

'Right.'

Shereen indicated for Elise to follow her, which she did, all the way to a comfortable, enclosed lounge at the back of the shop. There Shereen sat her down and ran through the procedure. Elise heard nothing of what was said. She didn't know what had come over her. She went over the events of the morning with Sandile, wondered what he was thinking, wondered what the consequences could be of what she'd done. Did it mean she didn't want to marry Daan?

Shereen came to the end of her speech and handed something to Elise, who took it. Glancing down, she realised it was a brochure. Shereen looked at her quizzically. 'Did you hear what I said, miss?'

'Yes, yes, I did . . . I mean. What was the last part?' Elise knew she must seem like a total nut, but she was determined to try.

'Do we have an idea of the style we're looking for?' Shereen spoke very deliberately, making sure that Elise didn't miss a word.

'Yes, something very simple.'

'Classic?'

'Yes. Classic.' Elise had no idea what Shereen meant by 'classic', but it sounded like progress.

Shereen gently took the brochure from Elise's hands, opened it and flicked through the options. Elise pointed to the simplest, plainest dress she saw, a long one with an empire line, embroidered bodice and an elegant narrow skirt. Shereen nodded, then turned the page, suggesting that they try on at least one other for comparison. Elise pointed randomly at the least fussy, frilly things she saw.

'What about a veil?'

'No veil.'

'Oh, but I think we should try one.'

'Should we?' Elise asked meekly.

Shereen nodded again. 'I'll choose. You look like a size twelve – would that be right?' Elise nodded. 'Of course we'll do the final fitting just before the big day. You wouldn't believe how many times I've seen a bride come in here a few days before the wedding – and the shock they get when they see how much weight they've lost! Ag, it's always the same.' Elise tried to smile, but it turned out more like a grimace. At last Shereen closed the catalogue and went off to arrange everything in the fitting room.

Elise had no idea of how much time had passed when Shereen returned and found her client sitting frozen in exactly the position she had left her. She led Elise to the changing room where there were four massive dresses arranged on hangers in front of a three-sided mirror. Elise looked away from her wild-eyed, flustered reflection. She didn't want to see herself. She wanted to escape from herself, wanted to get right out of her head.

She stripped off under Shereen's watchful eye, down to her bra and panties as instructed. Shereen made some mention of underwear and tittered slightly. 'We'll get to that part later.'

Elise looked at herself in the mirror, realising that her plain white cotton bra and broekies from Woolworth's wouldn't do, at least not in Shereen's view, for the big day.

Shereen lugged the first dress over and helped Elise to climb into it. Elise felt sick. She didn't look at herself in the mirror, but watched Shereen's thick hands pulling out the folds, long painted nails carefully stroking out the creases in the silk. Once inside the dress she realised with absolute dread that she couldn't carry it off. She didn't want to be a bride or a wife. Anyone's wife. Slowly she raised her eyes to the image of herself in the mirror. She looked ludicrous. The wedding dress, like the whole idea of her marriage to Daan, was a construct which simply didn't fit her. She knew it wasn't her. She had tried to make it so, but she couldn't adapt to it, didn't want it. Perhaps everything she imagined she and Daan were and might be was a concept that had no location in reality. Perhaps no matter how much she desired the convention, no matter how much she longed to slip into the comfort of a role as wife with Daan as the husband at her side, she would always be squeezed into a space that she wasn't designed to fit.

The assistant was doing her utmost to help. From the tone of strained but determined patience she had adopted Elise realised that Shereen must have seen this kind of behaviour before. Was this 'the jitters', or was it something worse? She closed her eyes and tried to steady herself. Perhaps when she opened them everything would be all right. But it wasn't.

'I can't, I can't do it!' she blurted as she began yanking the dress off.

Shereen was stumped; she didn't have an answer for this one. She raised an eyebrow as she carefully took the dress out of Elise's hands, pursed her lips and said archly, 'Lady, why don't you go home and think about it? We'll make another appointment for you next week. Then come back, try on some more dresses and you'll feel different. Trust me. I know.'

Elise couldn't speak. She wanted to apologise, but couldn't get the words out. She hadn't meant to be so rude, to take out all this confusion on a woman who was simply trying to do her job, but she couldn't stop herself. She dressed, stormed out of the shop, found her car and got into it. She sat there for half an hour, until a parking warden came up and tapped on the window. 'It's funny, isn't it, how sometimes sitting in your car can be so much more exciting than driving it?' he said sarcastically. Elise mumbled that she was sorry, then started up the engine and drove off.

When she found herself on Signal Hill, she simply drove on, past Sea Point, Bantry Bay, Clifton. At Camps Bay she had to stop at a red robot and she looked to her right, to the sea. The water was a skein of the palest blues and greens, the wave tips translucent as they caught the sunlight before crashing down and rolling up on to the sand. She pulled over, left the car parked on a yellow line and crossed the road to the beach.

As evening approached, the sea turned to a dark velvet blue, crashing on to the rocks in a brilliant white foam. Elise sat on a huge flat rock which reached out from the beach and into the sea. Around her the fingers of other rocks jutting out from the beach were covered with people sleeping, talking, drinking in the soft light of evening.

The sunset sky was gorgeous, pink at the edges, seeping to tissuey soft purple clouds defined in pink and grey, and then suddenly the whole sky was on fire, as if the sun touching the horizon had ignited an inferno of scarlet and tangerine.

The slope of Lionshead was a deep moss green, clustered with lush trees and beautiful houses all the way down to the road and the broad sweep of cream to yellow sand curving round and reaching to where Elise sat. On the street behind Elise a restaurant spilled over with people coming and going, emptying and filling the tables. Loud music blasted from speakers, dozens of voices drifted above the clinking of glasses, but above all other noises was the sea.

Elise watched a couple walking hand in hand on the wet sand along the shoreline. The girl was black and the man was white. An 'interracial' coupling, in that bizarre old terminology. Still an unusual sight, though less rare than before – before it was impossible. These two were young. Talking and laughing together, they seemed to notice only each other, oblivious to the indiscreet stares of the mostly white beach-goers. It must be hard for them, Elise thought, but then maybe it wasn't. Maybe for them it was easy and hard only for everyone else.

As the sun sank below the horizon the air cooled. She felt a huge tension unwinding from her. She couldn't believe she'd been so self-deceiving. She knew now that she wanted to surrender herself to her feelings; she didn't want this to stop.

It was almost dark. Her father would be worried already and it was hours before she would reach Rustenvrede. Elise walked slowly to her car. She ignored the three parking tickets under the windscreen wiper and got in. She was hungry and her mouth was dry with thirst, but she started up the car, pulled out on to the road and didn't stop.

Occasionally she passed people walking along the side of the freeway, their faces looming in her headlights. Over Sir Lowery's Pass it was so dark that the cars in the opposite lane passed like ghosts; red lights chasing white lights and the black space in between as black as the night around. Elise forgot about Sandile, Daan, her father, the farm. She was lost in the music from the radio, the motion of the car, and the clean simple line of the road.

TWENTY THREE

When Ina got to Rustenvrede it was already early evening. She was startled to discover that Elise wasn't yet home. She found Van Rensburg in the lounge, watching the sports round-up on TV. He agreed that Elise ought to be back by now, but he didn't seem unduly worried. Nevertheless, he was particularly subdued, which suggested to Ina a degree of concern.

'But it's nearly dark,' she pointed out anxiously. 'Don't you think there's something funny about this?'

'Not really.' Highlights of the Western Province game abruptly gave way to commercials. Van Rensburg stood up, pulling his shirt down over his jeans. 'But I'll be happier when she's home.'

Van went into the kitchen and pulled a couple of beers from the fridge. He handed a bottle to Ina, kept one for himself and went back to watching the rugby.

Ina sank back into the sofa, feeling deflated. She was dying for Elise to come back so she could relive every delicious detail of her day. She stood up and went to the window. 'What time did she say she'd be back?'

'She didn't.' Van Rensburg didn't take his eyes off the television.

'Well, she must be planning to get here for supper. So if she's not back by then . . .'

'Ag, she'll be back by then,' he growled. 'I mean how long can it take to choose a wedding dress?'

Ina paced across the room, coming to a stop by Van Rensburg's chair. Now both of them were facing the TV screen.

'Brides get quite funny before weddings. Jittery. *Fair Lady* had a thing on it last week. Anyway, knowing Elise she's gone for a ride up Table Mountain or something and she'll come back all wide-eyed saying, I just *had* to see the view . . .' Ina said this more for her own benefit than his.

Van Rensburg took a long suck on his bottle of beer, swirled the liquid round inside his mouth, swallowed and then smacked his lips. He knew all about how mysterious and jumpy and unreliable women could be. But Elise wasn't like that. Elise wasn't like her mother: she was like him. He was suspicious.

He frowned. 'But it's not like her not to phone.'

Ina flopped down on the sofa again. Van Rensburg saw she was anxious. He hated anxiety and he didn't want to be infected by it. There was no point in getting worried about what might have happened, he thought – get upset when you've got reason to be. 'I'm sure she's fine. Like you say, she probably got distracted by the view from the mountain or something.'

The rugby distracted him. And Western Province had just scored. He leaned forward for the slow-motion replay of Chester Williams scoring a try of such breathtaking skill and elegance that Van Rensburg was cheering at the TV.

'Jusssusssss! Did you see that? I can't believe he did that!'

Ina wasn't interested in the rugby. She couldn't sit still, so she went to the kitchen and phoned her mother. Mabel answered. 'It's me, Mabel. Can I speak to my mother please?' Ina said brusquely. She felt tense and she didn't get any calmer waiting for her mother to come to the phone. Ina could hear her in the kitchen at Komweer, giving Mabel instructions for the table settings. It was more than a minute before the old lady's voice came trilling down the line.

'Where are you?'

Ina shook her head, rolling her eyes up to the ceiling. 'I'm at Rustenvrede, Ma. How am I? I'm fine, thanks. How are you?'

'Now don't get funny with me. Did everything go all right with Mr Taylor?'

'Ja, he's getting settled in. He was very pleased with Lettie.'

'He ought to be. God knows what we're going to do without her at the stall.'

'We'll manage, Ma. Listen, I just phoned to say that I'm going to stay over here tonight. I'll be home in the morning.'

'All right, dear. Did Elise find a dress?'

'Well, I don't know, she's not back yet.'

Ina could hear her mother sucking in her breath. 'That's a little worrying, isn't it? Lord knows, those roads are bad enough, but what with all the car-jack–'

Ina cut across her impatiently. 'I'm sure she's fine. I'm sure we'll see her soon.'

'Well, phone me when she's home, otherwise I'll worry. Promise me now, Ina.'

'I promise, Ma.'

When it got to suppertime and Elise still wasn't back Ina's anxiety shifted to a higher gear. They waited some more. By eight thirty there was still no sign of her. Ina wasn't hungry, though she knew Van Rensburg must be, so she dished up three plates of rice and bobotie from the casserole Mama Mashiya had left on the stove. She covered up the third plate and put it in the fridge. Elise could have it when she got back.

Van Rensburg ate in silence, while Ina picked at her food. The two of them sat in the lounge balancing their plates on their knees as they watched a movie on M-Net. The film was a tedious family drama about a troubled teenager and her tormented parents. Ina didn't give a damn. All she could focus on was the thought of Elise driving back alone in the dark. Everyone knew that the roads weren't safe, certainly not for a woman driving alone at night. The freeways near Cape Town were particularly dangerous. There were so many stories of car-jackings and hold-ups it didn't bear thinking about, and Elise was the sort of person who would pick up a hitch-hiker and then be amazed when they robbed and raped her. Ina got up and began pacing up and down by the window. Even if she'd got off the freeway safely the mountain passes were treacherous.

Van Rensburg finished his supper and put the empty plate down on the carpet. During a commercial break he got up and joined Ina by the window, looking for lights on the road. But there were none. He turned away and went back to his chair.

'I think we should phone Daan and get him to check with the traffic people and the hospitals,' Ina said.

Van Rensburg shook his head, glued again to the television, a beer in one hand and the remote control in the other. 'Not yet,' he said. 'If she's not back at ten I'll phone the police and the hospitals myself.'

Ten o'clock was when the movie finished. Ina sighed. Van clearly wasn't as beside himself as she was.

It was a quarter to ten when at last they heard the thrum of a car approaching. The dogs heard it first. They perked up suddenly and Van Rensburg switched off the TV and listened. Definitely the old Mercedes; it was definitely Elise.

Ina and Van Rensburg rushed out of the house to meet her. The dogs sensed the tension and ran ahead, barking and jumping all over Elise as she got out of the car. She looked a little dazed, but was clearly fine. Ina couldn't decide if she wanted to hug or throttle her.

Van Rensburg got there first and put his arm round his daughter without saying a word. Elise could feel him shaking as he pulled her to him and said gruffly into her hair, 'Please, don't do that again.'

Elise felt stricken with guilt. She put her arms round him, squeezing him tightly.

Ina didn't feel so tender. 'What happened?' she screeched. 'We've been going out of our minds here! Your father was about to call the police.'

Elise looked back at her like a startled deer caught in the glare of headlights. 'I'm so sorry,' she stammered. 'I wanted to take a walk on the beach and I just lost track of the time.'

'A walk? You must have walked round the whole bloody peninsula.'

'No, just Camps Bay. I sat down on the rocks to look at the sea and before I knew it the sun was setting . . .'

Ina looked at Van Rensburg, their eyes met and they both shook their heads. Van Rensburg shrugged and Ina let out a sigh of exasperation.

'I'm so, so sorry. I don't know what came over me. I just didn't think.'

'Next time don't think, just phone. OK?' Ina countered tartly.

'OK.' Elise said this so meekly it had the effect of defusing Ina's tirade. She slipped her arm round her father's waist and they walked that way up to the house.

Van Rensburg went straight to the fridge for another round of beer. Elise slumped into a chair at the kitchen table and Ina fussed around her, setting a place for her and heating up the plate of food.

'So?' Ina sat down opposite and smiled at her expectantly.

Elise wasn't really hungry any more, but she ate a few mouthfuls to placate Ina and to avoid the question. 'So what?' She was evasive.

'So what about the dress?'

Elise chewed another mouthful then put down her fork. She shook her head. She couldn't lie – Ina would know. So she told the stark, dreadful truth. 'It was terrible, just terrible. I was totally overwhelmed, I freaked out. I couldn't choose and I was rude to this poor girl who was trying to help me. The whole thing was a total fiasco.'

Ina's face fell. She shot a knowing look at Van who was leaning against the sink, the bottle of beer resting on his belly. Then she reached over and took Elise's hand, patting it comfortingly. 'Ag, Elise, I'm so sorry. It's my fault. I never should have let you go alone.'

'Don't be stupid. It's me – I think I'm just allergic to organza and lace and white dresses,' Elise said, shamefaced, trying her utmost to downplay the extent of her failure.

But to Ina it was nothing less than a disaster. 'We should have cancelled,' she berated herself. 'Why didn't we just rearrange? Now it's going to involve not one but at least two more trips.' She shook her head crossly.

'Forget it! I had a nice time at the beach. We can go to Baskin's another time. Anyway, I don't want to get married till the picking's over.' Elise smiled uneasily. 'And there was one dress I liked, it'll probably work. It was very simple, empire line with an embroidered top . . .'

'Ag, don't give me that.'

Ina wouldn't be consoled. Elise got up, took the plate and emptied everything on it into the rubbish bin, then set it down with her knife and fork in the sink. Ina watched thoughtfully as Elise rinsed the dishes. Van Rensburg sipped at his bottle of Windhoek lager.

'You know, I was just saying to your father, I read this thing in *Fair Lady* last week about how stressful weddings are and how so many women just freak out beforehand. *Especially* over the dress.' Ina stressed this quite vehemently and Elise turned round and looked at her.

'Do you think that's it? Do you think it's just jitters?'

'Absolutely.' She banged the flat of her hand on the table for emphasis. 'And I should have been there to support you.'

Elise slumped back into her chair and covered her face with her hands. She desperately wanted to talk about Sandile and what had happened, but she could never tell Ina, or anyone for that matter. Ina might in time be able to forgive her for a fleeting unfaithfulness to her beloved younger brother, but if she ever discovered it was Sandile that Elise was aching for their friendship would be irretrievable.

It was Ina who had taught Elise the word 'kaffir' in that childish rhyme, 'Green, green kaffir queen'. Although Ina, like many whites who'd previously been happy to know the man was safely incarcerated on Robben Island, thought now that President Mandela was the greatest statesman of the century and a real teddy bear to boot and was even fiercely, defensively proud of him, she could never contemplate, not in her wildest nightmares, the possibility of loving one of 'them'.

Elise's head was spinning with questions. She knew so little of Sandile. He seemed so singularly self-contained, so driven by things he had never revealed to her. She sensed in him a lack of barriers against her that was terrifying and exciting. Elise felt raw, as if all her nerve endings were exposed and her skin, her eyes, her fingers, her lips were violently alive to sensation. She felt as if she was just falling, falling, falling, and the feeling was wild and lost, but she didn't want it to stop.

Ina thought Elise's distractedness verged on evasive. She was in a really odd mood tonight. It wasn't like her to be so remote and agitated all because of an upset over a wedding dress. Elise was never fazed by anything.

Elise took her hands from her face and saw that Ina was watching her, suspicion beaming from her eyes. 'You're being very mysterious tonight, my girl,' she murmured.

'Maybe that's it!' Elise declared. 'Wedding jitters. Maybe that's exactly what it is. How boring – I'm behaving like someone in a magazine.'

'Why do you think so many people read them?' Ina snapped.

'Ja, ja. I suppose you're right,' Elise concurred, turning towards her father who was looking both thoughtful and sleepy. She smiled at him and he smiled back. 'Everything OK, Pa?'

'Ja, ja,' he said and yawned. 'OK, I'm gone. Let me know in the morning who's to blame for the lack of a dress. I'll have to report back to Daan.'

Both Ina and Elise smiled and bid Van Rensburg good night.

The second he was out of the room Ina leapt up and closed the kitchen door behind him. She had a wild conspiratorial look in her eyes. Elise felt panicky. She knew she wouldn't hold up under Ina's cross-examination and in her mind she started running through excuses that might get her out of it. But when Ina turned round her face was flushed with an excitement that Elise realised couldn't have anything to do with her.

Ina didn't sit down. She stood opposite Elise, her hands resting on the table, her eyes bright with excitement. She looked as if she might explode.

'What?'

Ina looked up towards the ceiling – she didn't know how to begin. Elise fetched two more beers out of the fridge. She put one down in front of Ina and twisted the top off her own as she sat down. She took a long gulp and then smiled a moist-lipped smile. 'You'd better tell me what's happened.'

'Oh my God, oh my God, oh my God!' Ina blushed deeply, then dissolved into laughter.

Elise was quickly infected by her giggles. 'What? Spit it out, girl!'

'Oh my God, Elise, you'll never believe it.' Ina was shaking her head, still laughing.

'*Tell* me!' Elise pulled her knees up to her chin, resting her feet on the edge of the seat.

Ina sat down and began. Elise listened, open-mouthed, her eyes growing wider and wider as Ina spilled the whole story: the photograph of Taylor's wife, the flirting at lunch, the discreet touches in the afternoon and finally the sudden, smouldering sex in Taylor's kitchen at the end of the day. Elise was speechless. Ina was transported – on cloud nine, in orbit.

'You wild woman!' Elise was breathless with admiration. 'I can't believe it. But this is fantastic!' Ina just grinned. 'And so, what now?'

'Who knows?' Ina raised her hands and let them slap down on the table top. 'I mean his wife just died. He's probably not ready for a big scene and it was so sudden . . . so *lekker*!'

She looked so wickedly gleeful that they both cracked up with laughter.

'Oh! But he's coming to dinner on Thursday. Why don't you come too?'

'Just you try and stop me!' Elise banged her beer down on the table and they both laughed again, but with less energy than before. Ina was yawning and Elise felt exhausted, leaden in her limbs and fuzzy in her head.

'Come, I need to get some sleep.'

Whenever Ina stayed over she slept with Elise in her bed, in Dawie's old room. Elise had taken down most of his pictures and replaced them with ones of her own, but she'd left up the two *Star Wars* posters: full-length pictures of Han Solo and Luke Skywalker that were now green with age. On the dresser below his heroes was a framed photograph of Dawie himself. He looked so young with his pale face, pale hair, thin moustache and his grown-up army uniform. The effect of the jumble of childhood and adult images, tragic and absurd, was incongruous, but Elise liked it.

Ina liked it too, though the memory of Dawie was still painful. Tonight she sighed as she glanced at the posters. 'I wonder what he'd have thought of Alan.'

Elise smiled sadly, then she said aloud, 'He would've hated him!'

Ina threw her jeans at Elise.

They climbed into bed. Elise switched off the light and lay back on the pillows staring at the ceiling. At first she'd been totally freaked out by the way Ina slipped into bed with her. She didn't much like sleeping next to a lover, let alone a friend. However, she'd got used to it over time and she thought to herself now that it was another thing she would miss when she married Daan. When she married Daan, she repeated to herself. Oh God. Being married to him. She still thought of it as an immutable part of a future landscape.

After a stretch of silence Ina's voice floated through the darkness. 'Elise?'

'Mmm?'

'Do you think there's a difference between making love and fucking?'

Elise let out a surprised laugh. Ina hadn't ceased to amaze her tonight.

'What do you think?' she insisted.

'Me?' Elise felt her stomach clench.

'Well, who else is in here?'

'Ja, well, I mean – I think so. But I've never really *fucked* anyone. Sometimes I wish I had, but I've never been able to have sex with someone who didn't arouse my curiosity as well as my . . . you know? You know what I mean?'

They both giggled. Ina and Elise had talked about most things, but this was closer to the edge than usual and the baldness, the frankness of it was liberating.

'It's so boring,' Elise continued. 'I've never had sex, pure *fucking* sex, with someone I didn't want to know, someone I didn't want to have some part of. That's very possessive, isn't it? I suppose that's why, or partly why, I always find it so extreme when I fancy someone. It has to be everything or nothing.'

Ina shifted round and the mattress springs creaked. 'It wasn't pure fucking with Taylor, but it was like nothing I've ever done before. It wasn't making love, you know? I couldn't believe myself, I felt so . . . reckless, so free.' Laughter gurgled up again.

Elise stared up at the shadows of the trees shifting on the ceiling and smiled. 'I think we should all do more fucking. I mean men do – why don't we?'

'Some women do,' Ina countered.

'But not as many as men. I've *thought* about it often enough, but I just can't face the idea of waking up next to someone whose mind I didn't want to know as intimately as his body. Boring, hey? I mean men don't worry about that, they just leave when they've done. One quick squirt and it's finished. Like pesticide,' she added darkly.

Ina was convulsed with laughter. 'Ja. It's easier to masturbate.'

'Exactly.' Elise twisted round on to her side and propped herself up on her elbow. 'No mess, no consequences, no explanations, no embarrassment.' Ina giggled.

Elise grew more animated. 'Why do we always make the mistake of confusing lust with love? I mean why do women always want to fall in love with anyone they want to sleep with?'

'All women?'

'Maybe not all, but how many do you know that don't?'

'Exactly none!'

'Right. It's a tragedy if you ask me,' declared Elise.

They both fell silent. After a while Ina asked quietly, 'When do you know that you're in love. I mean *how* do you know?'

'You're too far gone when you start asking questions like that,' Elise snorted.

Ina let out a gurgle of a laugh, then she sighed. 'It was so . . . hectic. I mean in terms of the mechanics. Very intense, very urgent. But smooth.' She drawled on the word 'smooth'. Then there was silence again. Some time later Elise could tell, from Ina's breathing, that she had fallen asleep.

Twenty Four

Sandile spent most of the morning drinking coffee at the table he'd shared with Elise earlier. It was a beautiful day, the sun baking down from a perfectly clear sky. Table Mountain was glorious. He could see only a corner of it from where he sat. Towering office blocks obscured the complete arc, but a corner was enough. He felt elated but confused. Angry with himself for creating the confusion. Things had veered out of control and it was very much his fault. What he felt for Elise was powerful, but massively inappropriate. Sandile winced at the recollection of all the opportunities she'd given him to talk about the land claim. He could have explained it right there, calmly and on neutral territory. It would have given her time to react and then to assimilate the idea, even to come to terms with it, and she could have broken the news to her father with the troublemaker safely out of the way in Cape Town. But he couldn't do it. He hadn't wanted to destroy that delicate, delicious bond between them and the result was that he'd slid deeper and deeper into trouble.

Sandile reflected that what he was about to do would explode not only his parents' lives, but also hers. Perhaps it wasn't too late. He could cancel his meeting with the lawyer, go back to the valley and talk it through with her on home ground before he took the next step. No, that was a stupid idea, and he discarded it almost immediately. He was confusing himself and the confusion arose from an entanglement he ought never to have allowed. And anyway, he rationalised, the processing of the claim would take months. He'd do what he'd come here to do and then explain it all to Elise as soon as he got back to the farm.

On the other hand, explaining it to her was ridiculous. She wouldn't accept it. Why should she? She would see things from her point of view, not his. And she'd told him point-blank that she would kill anyone who tried to take away her land. It was ridiculous to fantasise that they could work it out, that she would be happy about losing her dam and two of her orchards. Sandile berated himself first for not thinking of her and then for thinking of her too much. Then he told himself it was only a kiss and, while it had been a pretty spectacular one, no kiss could possibly deserve so much anguish. With that, Sandile decided that he'd had enough coffee, paid the bill and left.

He called Simon Siluma from a phone booth in the foyer of the Holiday Inn on Greenmarket Square. From the roar of excitement that greeted him Sandile gathered that Simon was glad to hear from him.

'Man, I've been waiting by the phone all morning!'

'But it's a cellphone.' Sandile laughed. The jocularity was a relief.

'So, you can imagine! Where are you, man? I'll pick you up.'

They arranged to meet in front of St George's Cathedral in a quarter of an hour. Sandile felt a stab of anxiety as he hung up the phone. The last time he'd seen Simon was in Lusaka, back in 1990. Their parting had been clouded by the murk of suspicion and doubt and grief that had surrounded Ismail's death. Sandile knew that Simon would also be feeling a degree of unease, still unsure of how things stood between them because that doubt had never really gone away. For Sandile that period had receded into the past, slipped into a new perspective. Simon's cheerful voice on the phone suggested that perhaps he, too, had put it all behind him. Nevertheless, it was with mixed feelings that Sandile set off for his meeting at the cathedral.

As it turned out there was no need for anxiety. Their reunion was coloured by recent events. They were here, in Cape Town, for a start, and no longer exiles in a hard and distant country. Simon was bursting with happiness at the sight of his old comrade, his long-lost drinking buddy, and Sandile felt a surge of joy and nostalgia too as they embraced and then stood grinning at one another on the steps of St George's. Simon looked trim and fit and successful. 'Wait till you see my place,' he joked. 'Then you'll know I'm one hundred per cent buppie.'

They picked up takeaway chicken and chips at Nando's along the Main Road in Seapoint and took it back to Simon's flat, where they spent the afternoon and evening joking and reminiscing and making steady progress towards the bottom of a litre of whisky.

Simon's place was in Bantry Bay, a wealthy, once whites-only suburb overlooking the churning, limitless Atlantic. The flat, luxurious as it was, came second to the view, which was spectacular.

Simon was a Member of Parliament, a fact which Sandile enjoyed immensely. He rented the flat for those months of the year when Parliament was in session, sharing it with another ANC MP from Natal. Sandile thought it was a great joke that they were together in Cape Town, in this elegant place overlooking the sea, and that Simon set off every morning to go to work in Parliament, inside that complex of old buildings where men of his colour would not too long ago have been lucky to work as gardeners or cleaners.

Without mentioning their parting they told each other where their lives had taken them since last they'd met. Sandile was happy to discover that the rawness and the pain of that last time had disappeared. And there were moments when he felt tender, like when Simon called him Sam.

'I haven't heard *that* name in a while!'

'Haven't you? I kept mine. Well, half of it anyway.' The name his parents gave him was Jabu. Simon Booi was the name he was given by the movement.

'I like Jabu.'

'It's the name of another person,' Simon said, and smiled a little ruefully. 'I grew into Simon, you know. And Simon grew into me . . .'

They both chuckled.

'And the farm?' Simon wanted to know. 'I can't believe that you of all people have opted for life on a farm.'

Sandile agreed that it took some getting used to. He shook his head and laughed as he thought about it. 'Ja, it's a tiny dorp and about as remote and verkrampte as it gets. But I like it. I'll like it even more when I get my land, but meanwhile – it's home.'

Simon cast him a doubtful stare.

'Ag, of course I miss the politics, the adrenalin . . . the power. There *was* something in it,' Sandile mused, taking a thoughtful slug of J&B. 'I *do* miss the power.' Then he looked straight at Simon. 'But that's finished. I need to break with all that, start over. The farm offers me something else, something . . . I dunno . . . *real*, you know?'

Simon smiled, pouring them each another thumb of whisky. 'What about the women? Don't you miss the women?' he said wickedly.

Sandile chuckled and stared into his glass. 'Don't even talk to me about women.'

His grin was obvious. Simon leaned forward, interested. 'Uh-uh, trouble already. You haven't been stupid and gone and seduced the farmer's daughter, have you?'

Sandile laughed. 'No, no, no.'

Simon took a long sip of whisky, waiting for the grin to be explained.

'Actually she seduced me.'

Simon spluttered into his drink. He laughed so hard he almost fell off his chair. Sandile laughed too. 'Well, sort of – I mean it hasn't gone quite that far.'

Simon flicked his wrist hard several times, snapping his fingers as he did so. 'You are in the deepest shit, my broer! I can see I'm going to have to send out a rescue mission sooner or later. If that farmer ever finds out, man, he'll lynch you!'

Sandile rubbed his fingers along his chin, nodding 'He'd enjoy that too. It'd be just like the good old days!'

'Ja, just like the good old days. Oh my God, you kissed the

farmer's daughter and now you're going to take his land – how did you say you want to be buried?'

It was a while before their laughter abated. When it did, Sandile wanted to know about Simon. 'I heard you left intelligence.'

'Ag, jaaaaa!' Simon threw up his hands as if pushing something away. 'Naah, I'm through with all that. I'm on the oversight committee, but that's as close as I want to get. We're a democracy now, we shouldn't even need an intelligence service. I see those guys even now – they can't shake old habits and those habits were designed for a different context. Ja, no, they offered me a job in the Deputy Minister's office, but I didn't want to be a bureaucrat any more than I wanted to be an operative. Of course there wasn't much else I was fit for, so they put me in Parliament and here I am.'

'And?'

'And now I'm tired. All I want to do is get married and get fat. Maybe go fishing at the weekends, read a bit, watch some movies. But I can't. There's too much to do, there's a huge job to be done in this country. We could use people like you.'

'You did use people like me.' Sandile emphasised the word 'use'.

'Yes. Yes, we did.'

Simon fell silent. He stared out at the sea, at the white crests of the waves emerging and disappearing in the inky blackness outside. Sandile hadn't meant to deflate the atmosphere. He changed the subject. 'Well, I'm not giving up on the world, you know. There have to be people like me at the coalface, not just up in management. So that's where I am and that's what suits me right now.'

'I'll drink to that.'

More whisky was poured and they did drink to it, clinking their glasses in salute to one another.

Simon shared his flat with another ANC MP, a guy called Sediq, but Sediq was almost never there. At the weekends he went home to his wife and kids in Durban and during the week he was usually out with one or other of the many women in his life. That night he showed up around midnight with an air hostess, still fully kitted out in her smart little South African Airways uniform. He'd been in Johannesburg for the day and must have walked straight off the plane with her. She tottered in on high heels and waited with a brassy lipsticked smile by the door while Sediq poured two vodka shots from the bottle in the freezer, winked at Sandile and Simon and disappeared after her into his room.

Simon chuckled and shook his head. 'For some people too much freedom turns out to be a bad thing.'

Sandile laughed too and turned up the music. The air hostess was already gone when Sediq emerged with his ear-to-ear grin intact the next morning.

Sandile had gone to bed in a pleasant whisky-induced haze. He thought about Elise and felt sure he could work with her on the land claim. He had to do this for his family as much as for himself, otherwise he could never live with himself. Somehow things would work out between him and her. Ja, I'll have my cake and eat it, he decided groggily. But he hadn't slept well. He was visited by too many memories. He tossed and turned and the unfamiliar, restless sound of the sea agitated rather than lulled him.

On Monday morning Simon dropped him off in the centre of town outside the Land Claims Commission offices. The offices were brand-new and clearly still in the midst of a design and construction phase. The receptionist was equipped with a large, elegant desk and a flashing phone system, but all round her were piles of boxes and lilac-coloured partition flats stacked against the walls. Sandile waited by the door as workmen milled round him. He had arrived without an appointment, but apart from the workmen the office was quiet, and it wasn't long before he was shown into the office of Fatima Mamdoo, head of research for the region.

Mrs Mamdoo had been practising as a lawyer in Cape Town for nearly forty years, including the years spent working despite two banning orders served on her by the previous regime. You wouldn't know it to look at her, but she'd given birth to five children and supported them single-handedly throughout the decade that she was left alone while her husband was on Robben Island, working tirelessly at her practice, shifting from political to domestic cases when she was banned. People often underestimated her because of her tiny size, her disarming smile and the mild, reasonable tone with which she fought back. And Fatima Mamdoo always fought back.

Their meeting was promising, but unexpectedly brief. Mrs Mamdoo offered Sandile a cup of tea; he took it and then got straight to the point. He sketched out his family history, the purchase of the land, how it was declared a black spot and taken over by their white neighbours, and finally his own return from exile and his family's desire to reclaim the land that was theirs.

Fatima Mamdoo listened carefully to Sandile's story and when it was finished she sat staring out of her office window for several minutes. Sandile was so tense he had to put his hand on his leg to stop it bouncing with agitation, because he'd started jiggling her desk. Finally she turned towards him, peering at him over her reading glasses.

'This is a very interesting case, Mr Mashiya.'

Sandile wasn't sure if this was a good or a bad sign. He said nothing, waiting for her to elaborate, but she just stared at him, so he spoke. 'How's that?'

'As you know, we are very much at the beginning of this process, we don't even have a functioning Land Claims Court as such yet. But nearly all the claims we've registered so far are group claims. That is, a village or a community. Not just one person.'

'Well, one family.'

'Yes, yes, one family. I shall have to discuss it with my colleagues, but I'd like to deal with this one myself. It's very important.'

Sandile smiled. Relief washed over him.

'Now, you're going to need a lawyer –'

'Yes, I'll be meeting a lawyer later on today.'

'Good. Good. Then he can help you get started on the paperwork. We'll need you to fill out these . . .' Some scrabbling around in a filing cabinet produced a wad of paper which Mrs Mamdoo slapped on to the table between them. 'And you'll need to provide us with certain records. The most important one, if you can get it, is the actual title, the deed that was sold to your great-great-grandfather. You'll have to go into the Archives for that, and you'll have to take a sackload of patience with you.'

It was clear from an initial scan of the forms that Sandile would have to do a lot of research and that it would take more than one week. He didn't get much chance to look over the detail as Mrs Mamdoo stood up and held out her hand to him. He shook it.

'A very interesting case, Mr Mashiya. I hope we'll be able to pursue it all the way.' She didn't give him time to ask her what she meant – she had already bustled over to the door and was holding it open for him. 'Don't you filthy our lovely new carpets!' she shouted at one of the workmen in the corridor and immediately became embroiled in an altercation with his supervisor, so Sandile didn't even manage to say a proper goodbye.

He sat poring over the paperwork in a Wimpy bar inside the Golden Acre. The place was crowded with office workers and schoolchildren and he found it hard to concentrate. It was plain that this whole process was going to take time. Three or four months at best. Sandile's heart sank at the thought of stretching out the anticipation all the way into the New Year. He dreaded breaking this news to his parents.

With a sense of anticlimax he went off to see Karel Smit, his prospective lawyer. Simon Siluma had arranged the appointment, explaining to Sandile that Karel was very young and an Afrikaner to boot, but 'shit-hot'. The best thing about Smit, as far as Sandile was concerned, was that he might be prepared to take on the case for free.

Sandile's first meeting with Karel Smit took place in his office in the plush suite of Booth, Case and Sands, one of the oldest Capetonian law firms – thoroughly white, proudly Anglo-Saxon and unashamedly Protestant. Their offices were high above the hustle of the city in a tall office block at the bottom of Plein Street.

The reception area was vast, with a knockout view of both the mountain and the harbour. After he'd cleared up a brief misunderstanding with the receptionist – she thought he was there to pick up a courier package – Sandile was given directions to Karel Smit's office. There was one other postal mishap on the way down a long, panelled corridor of offices. A sharp-suited bespectacled white man popped out of a doorway, looked up and down, then bore down on Sandile, officiously shoving a sheaf of envelopes into his face. Sandile smiled quizzically at the man, making no move to take the bundle of mail, whereupon the man in the suit, frowning over his glasses, barked, 'My post, boy!'

Sandile was completely taken aback. 'Is that how you address *all* your clients, or just the off-white ones?' he snapped back. The suited man tutted irritably and then walked off, unrepentant.

Karel Smit was on the phone when Sandile walked into his office. He stood up, grinned, shook Sandile's hand and motioned for him to sit down, talking at high speed into the receiver all the while. It was less than a minute before he slammed the phone down, dialled two digits on another phone, asked someone at the other end to hold all his calls and then turned the full force of his attention on Sandile.

Karel Smit was a medium-sized man with striking, aquiline features and wiry mouse-brown hair. He looked about sixteen years old; in fact he was twenty-six. It was immediately evident to Sandile why Simon Siluma had recommended him: the guy was high-octane, he travelled way beyond the speed limit and he was super keen to take on this type of case. The only thing that wasn't clear to Sandile was what the guy was doing at an uptight English place like Booth, Case and Sands.

'You're right. We're a little behind the times here, but I

represent the thin end of the wedge. I'm their token African!' Laughter didn't just trickle from Karel Smit, it erupted. 'Entrism!' he said gleefully. Then, the laughter dying down, he added, 'Ag, no, the money's lekker and they let me do all the pro bono work I can handle. Which brings me nicely to the point!'

Karel took Sandile's file and immediately dived in. After they'd been talking and flipping through the assembled papers for only fifteen minutes he looked up at Sandile, grinned and said, 'Piece of cake!'

He would give it his full attention if Sandile promised the same. And he would absolutely not discuss payment. This was about a principle. Sandile left the stuffy atmosphere of Booth, Case and Sands walking on air.

Twenty Five

In the middle of that week Johnny Kakana took a morning off work. He told Daan he had some personal business to deal with in Cape Town and asked to borrow one of the vans to get himself there. Daan shrugged – it was no problem as far as he was concerned. He remarked only that it seemed like everyone was trekking to Cape Town all of a sudden. 'Maybe I should do some "personal business" there too.'

Johnny left the valley just after dawn. He had a long drive ahead and wanted to get back to the station by the early afternoon. His destination was in fact not Cape Town, but Khayelitsha, one of the sprawling squatter camps on the outskirts of the city. Khayelitsha is a desolate, windswept place, a maze of shacks that is home to thousands. The apartheid government had kept the place under a state of siege; now it was a recognised community with an active economic life. It boasted not only schools and churches, but also spaza shops, shebeens, butchers, barbers and taxi kings. The official name for such places is 'informal settlement'. A euphemism if ever there was one, Johnny thought as he got out of the police van and the smell of rotting meat and raw sewage hit him.

After the failure of his peacemaking mission to Sandile, Johnny had realised that the job of putting the past behind him entailed some very hard work. After many sleepless nights and much soul-searching, he had decided he must face Baasie's mother. So he'd paid a visit to the farm where she'd always lived, in a neighbouring valley. He was so geared up for the confrontation that he'd omitted to prepare for the possibility that she was no longer there. Asking after Mrs

Gxoyiya he was met with blank stares. Finally one of the farm workers found a relative of hers who explained that Baasie's mother had left the farm after her husband died.

Johnny knew the all-too-bitter truth of it. Mrs Gxoyiya had been thrown off the land where she was born and had lived all her life because her husband and only son were dead. She and her daughters were no use to the farmer and so he'd evicted them to make room for new workers. It was a simple, blunt rule of farm life.

Mrs Gxoyiya's niece told him that she had gone to Khayelitsha. It was as useful as telling him which haystack the needle could be found in. After some prodding the niece took him to her house and there, after quite a search, she fished out an old letter with an address on it.

It was to this address that Johnny went and it was there that he found her. Mrs Gxoyiya lived in an extraordinary structure, a hut-sized post-modern sculpture woven out of corrugated iron and exhaust pipes, bed frames, tractor engine covers, driftwood and part of the flatbed of an old horse-drawn cart, all welded and wired together to form a dwelling. Johnny knocked on the front door, the only door, which had once served as the entrance to a South African Railways ladies' toilet. It still bore the inscription *Dames, slegs blankes* – Ladies, whites only. A young girl opened the door and shrank back as soon as she saw their visitor. Even in plain clothes Johnny was obviously a policeman.

Inside the place stank sickeningly of paraffin. Johnny held his breath as he gazed round at the mud floor and the single shelf that was made of part of an old marble-effect Formica cabinet. There was a kitchen, bathroom and cupboards all in one unit. The rest of the tiny space was taken up by a box bed, with storage underneath and a sheet of plastic under the roof just above. Johnny asked if Mrs Gxoyiya was at home. The girl said she was and pointed to the back of their plot.

Mrs Gxoyiya was tending a small patch of vegetables that she'd scratched miraculously out of the dried earth. She didn't recognise Johnny immediately, but she watched his tentative approach with interest, screwing up her face, straightening a bent body. The wind howled all around them, kicking up sand and dust.

Johnny took off his cap and stood before her. 'Mama, I want to tell you about Baasie.'

She tensed. Her eyes sank deeper into her lined, ancient face: she knew who he was. She wiped her hands on the front of her dress, her mouth tight as she nodded to him. 'I'm waiting for you to begin.'

'It is something that is very hard for me, Ma.'

She dipped her head again, very matter-of-fact, prompting him to get on with it. It was clear to Johnny that this would be harder for him than for her. There was nothing she could hear that would be harder than losing her first-born child, her only son, and then losing her husband and her home. There was nothing she could not endure.

Her simple serenity in the midst of this poverty and chaos and in the face of what he had to tell her disarmed Johnny. It upset him. He found himself choking back tears. For some time he couldn't speak. She sat down on the bench at the back of her plot and patted the seat next to her for him to sit down. Johnny sat, immediately covering his face with his hand, wanting to stop the tears. He squeezed the bridge of his nose so hard that when at last he took his hand away there was a purple mark between his eyes. She stared at that mark while he told his story.

Johnny began by explaining who he was and about his friendship with Sandile and Baasie, but Mrs Gxoyiya cut across him – she knew that part of the story already. 'What I don't know is how my son came to be shot dead.' She said this as quietly as someone remarking that she couldn't remember where she'd left her shopping list.

Johnny found her calm more shocking than anger would have been. 'I was very frightened. Sandile doesn't know it, but the police were watching him when he came here, to Guguletu, and started working for the ANC. They knew he was up to something, but they didn't know what, so they were waiting. They had people at school, on the bus, everywhere. It wasn't difficult to work out that Sandile and Baasie and me were a click.'

Johnny paused, his nostrils flaring as he tried once again to control the anger and hurt that welled up in him. 'I suppose it wasn't difficult to work out that I was the weak link.'

The old lady didn't say a word. Johnny pressed his cap into a tighter, smaller bundle between his knees, sighing before he continued. 'At first I didn't know who they were, I didn't even know they were policemen. They hung around the school and visited our farm once or twice, gave me cigarettes and were very friendly towards me. Once of them was a young guy. Dup they called him. Stephan du Plessis. Then Sandile told me about the hiding place. I don't know how they knew. Perhaps they didn't, but they *seemed* to know. They came to my father's house in the night, wanting to talk to me. Suddenly a lot of things were clear.'

Johnny swallowed hard, shaking his head. He had never told this story before and it was harder than anything he'd ever had to do. A tear escaped and rolled down his cheek. Mrs Gxoyiya turned her pitiless gaze away.

'They were Security Police. They wanted to know what Sandile was up to. They said they would hurt me and my family if I didn't co-operate. But if I did, they would pay me, put me through school, maybe even university. They made a lot of promises. I was terrified. It wasn't a choice then. Now I know I should have told them I knew nothing, I should have told Sandile what was going on. But they seemed so powerful, it seemed there was nothing I could do to stop them . . . So I told them everything and they kept their word. I got money, I got educated, I got my rank. Baasie got shot.'

Johnny frowned, concentrating on his words. 'I told them everything Sandile had told us. And that night they were waiting, hidden all round the old cold store where the ANC were going to make their stash, where I was waiting to betray my friends. The last thing he said to me, when the Branch people were all over us, the last thing Baasie said was – "Damn you. You will rot in hell for this."'

Johnny faltered again. Mrs Gxoyiya's hand flew up to her mouth.

'Dup shot Baasie because he was trying to warn Sandile.'

The sounds of neighbours, of hawkers calling, of bicycles and animals and the wind all around them seemed to Johnny to be pressing in on him.

'But it was me who killed him. If it wasn't for me, Baasie would be alive.' Johnny's voice rose dramatically, his pain ringing out. Mrs Gxoyiya said nothing. Her eyes were fixed on the horizon, on the misty bulk of Table Mountain in the distance.

His story finished, Johnny could no longer meet her eye. He stared down at the beaten earth, his hat in his hands, bowed by the incredible pressure of his terrible deed. He was ready now for that earth to swallow him, for whatever punishment was necessary to come. There was no future, nothing but him and his terrible betrayal and this mother.

Baasie's mother reached out to him. She was tiny, but she reached up and put her hand on his forehead. Her hand was as dry as paper. He flinched from her, but she did not move to strike him, merely to touch his head. 'Thank you,' she said. Her tone was blunt, unsentimental. The strangest expression of gratitude he had ever heard, because it contained a rejection. 'I will die in peace now, knowing my son's end.'

Johnny looked at the dry-eyed old woman in amazement. Surely she wanted more, surely she needed to express more, to hit him, to hurt him. This was something he would never understand – there was nothing in her face but calm indifference.

Johnny wanted more. He felt he had to pay. He reached into his pocket for an envelope he had prepared. 'Mama, you have no son to care for you now you are old. Please, allow me to care for you. I will send something every month.

She pushed the envelope back at him, shaking her head. 'No. I want nothing more of you.'

That was when Johnny felt shame, when he understood every colour of it, when he knew the full, terrible taste of it. That was when the earth swallowed him up. That was her revenge. Baasie's mother wanted nothing of him. He had ruined her life. He had murdered her son. Those deeds could never be undone.

He left without another word, staggering out of her yard and on to the sandy track that led him deeper and deeper into the squatter camp. He quickly realised that he was hopelessly disorientated and lost. His saviours were a group of children, no more than seven and eight years old but wily as young wolves. They had watched him lose his way and followed him for a while, then cannily offered to take him to his van – in exchange for five rand. Johnny accepted gladly and gave them ten.

Driving home he thought of Lettie. Johnny had never married; there had never been anyone he wanted to marry. Girls scared him. They were an encumbrance on his friends, they bore litters of children, made unfathomable demands. He avoided them. But Lettie was different. He wanted her comforting presence at that moment. She was so still and sure and undemanding. He longed for the silence of their Sunday afternoon walks and longed even to confess and to feel her forgiveness. But he knew he would never speak of this to her or anyone.

Sergeant Kakana wasn't missed at the station that morning, except perhaps a little by Constable Pelser, who had to remain awake in order to cover for his colleague. Nothing out of the ordinary happened, except for one thing, which seemed perfectly innocuous at the time.

The package arrived while Daan was joking on the phone at the front counter. The courier parked his van outside and strolled up to the charge desk, a smouldering Chesterfield locked between his lips, his eyes narrowed against the smoke curling up from the cigarette. Daan barely glanced at the parcel as he signed for it, not missing a beat in his chat on the phone. Paperwork complete, the courier strolled out just as he had strolled in. When Daan put the phone down he glanced at the address. It was marked for the attention of Sergeant Kakana, so he dumped the envelope on Johnny's desk without even a thought for what it might contain.

Johnny found it on his return. He slunk into the station after three, slumped down into his chair and his eye fell on it immediately. It was a perfectly ordinary-looking, padded, legal-sized manila envelope. He didn't open it until he had taken off his jacket, checked his file for the day and made himself a cup of coffee. He assumed it would be something mundane, a new set of rules, a new guidebook, a new workshop or training session on offer. That was all the new people in government and in the regional HQ ever seemed to produce: workshops and policy papers. No wonder crime was soaring. At best the package might be files requested so long ago that he'd forgotten the case, or no longer needed the information. Something like that, he thought. But as soon as he opened up the parcel Johnny knew it was nothing like that at all.

The envelope contained a single file. A plain brown regulation-size police-issue folder. A typed label in the top right-hand corner read *MASHIYA, Sandile*. There was no letter attached, which was irregular, but not surprising given the state of the force. Johnny opened the folder carefully, noticing that it had hardly been thumbed through at all: the paper was still stiff and clean. At the front was a series of uninteresting statements from ANC headquarters at Shell House, forms granting indemnity for Sandile's return, one or two details from immigration and then – forming the bulk of the document – something quite unusual. Johnny thumbed the corners of the Security Police intelligence reports. This was the story of Sandile's life since his exile had begun.

Flipping through the pages, Johnny came to the most interesting part of all, the end. 'Lusaka, 1993. Sandile Mashiya – detained by Mbokodo.' Mbokodo was a name sometimes given to ANC intelligence. It meant 'the stone that crushes', though from what Johnny had heard they never crushed very much. He smiled, reading on. 'Comrade Mashiya was detained on suspicion of murder and spying for Pretoria.' The smile widened over Johnny's lips as he read the clumsily written but devastating report. Sandile had been accused of not one but two murders. The Security Police were unable to conclude their report 'due to other operational factors'. The relevant agents were withdrawn before Sandile's case was closed. His guilt had not yet been established. At that stage the paper read: 'Mashiya detained in green house! His name is mud.' Sandile was believed by the ANC to be a double agent.

The agent who'd compiled this report hadn't commented on the veracity of this accusation. Johnny wondered about that, but guessed that was because those guys rarely knew what they didn't need to know. Either that or they were keeping quiet for other reasons. Johnny was stunned. Could Sandile have been a double agent, working not only for the ANC but also for their sworn enemy? It did happen. But could it have happened to someone as vehemently principled as Sandile? What had happened between the end of the agent's report and Sandile's return to Fransmansvallei? Johnny's hand shook with excitement as he closed the file. He slid it back into the envelope, looking cautiously around as he did so. Daan wasn't paying attention. No one else seemed to have noticed.

That night Johnny sat up late at the station, reading through the file with great care. When he was finished, he didn't know what to do with it. Confront Sandile? No: what would he gain from that except further enmity? No point in showing it to Daan. For now Johnny would simply hold on to it. Wait until its value went up. He would know that moment when it came.

TWENTY SIX

Government buildings, Cape Town, on a wet and windy morning. The cloth had fallen over Table Mountain. It swept over in minutes, a fine white mist of cloud that obliterated the mountain. Sandile had woken up later than he meant to, his head thick with dreams. Simon and Sediq had already left for work, so a taxi brought him here, to this place of endless waiting where he had already spent too many pointless days.

When he arrived there was already a queue outside which shuffled him forward, caught him up in a revolving door then pulled him into yet another line. The security guards processed each person too quickly for safety. 'Stop, go, wait, now! Next!' Men and women, bureaucrats with Security Clearance cards flapping, flew through the lobby, crisscrossing towards the lifts, sidestepping the clusters of people who were there to lodge claims or seek papers or hand in forms to those who were rushing past. A sign told Sandile he should keep left. His instructions were to go to the Deeds and Titles section of the Archives. He asked a guard where that was. She barely moved her lips to utter the word 'directory' then shifted her eyes vaguely towards the right. The directory was less helpful than the guard. He turned back towards the guard, but she had shifted across the lobby, lizard-like, her gaze flicking away from anyone contemplating an enquiry.

Eventually he found an arrowed sign and followed it to a tatty room, where dirty old orange ropes suggested a shape for the queue. People were stepping over the low dips in the ropes and the line shuffled quickly forward. Sandile dared to hope that it wouldn't take so long after all. 'Next!' Incredible. An officer was free. Sandile stepped up to the counter, but this woman had the same lizard eyes and barely moving dry mouth as the guard. She looked dully at Sandile and said she was leaving, he must wait for someone else.

A man across the room with a maroon jacket, collar dusted with dandruff, indicated with a lazy glance and a small upward jerk of the chin that Sandile should step over to his counter. He shuffled through Sandile's papers, then looked up to gaze at some distant horizon before pronouncing, 'Go to the booth near the exit to get a ticket.'

'But which room must I go to?'

'Just go to the booth and get a ticket.'

The man in the maroon and dandruff jacket clicked his tongue in irritation, dragging his body into motion when he saw that no one was in the booth to give out the ticket. He gestured limply for Sandile to follow him. Sandile obeyed, surrendering himself to the logic of people enveloped in the deepest shades of boredom. At the booth the official pulled a red ticket off a thick fairground roll and handed it to Sandile. The ticket said, 'Your number is 074.' On the back someone had written in ballpoint 'Room 3-112.'

Sandile looked up at the official quizzically. The man's eyes were once again fixed blankly on the distance. Then he raised his left arm and pointed with a signet-ringed finger to a door that led back into the lobby. 'Third floor.' The words drifted out of his mouth like burps.

It was like being caught in a time warp. The personnel were the same, the style was the same, only the whites-only signs were missing. It felt as if nothing had changed except, of course, his reason for being there.

Room 3-112 had a no-entry sign on the door. Sandile went in anyway. Rows of orange plastic seats on beige carpet tiles awaited him. Somebody pointed him towards a long beige room divider. A continuous buzz dipped and clicked from time to time, coming from a dirty beige speaker on the wall. About a third of the chairs were full, their occupants slack and quiet, staring forward at the beige partition. Sandile hesitated, then walked to the front. A black plaque dangled drunkenly from a single wire on the ceiling. Its message read sideways: 'Neem asseblief 'n sitplek tot jou afspraak ange-kondig word.' He translated word by word: Please be seated until your appointment is called. OK. He sat, then stood up again. As far as he was aware he didn't have an appointment.

Sandile ventured beyond the partition where two women sat side by side in putty-coloured booths. These were the Crimplene-clad hulks, the hair-spray-hardened old tannies that he needed to see. These were the suspicious Guardians of the Archives. One was busy, the other was not. With a by now familiar gesture, a flick of dull eyes and a loose raising and dropping of the wrist, the unoccupied woman said in Afrikaans, 'She'll call your number. Have a seat. She'll call your number.' So Sandile sat, on an orange chair in an empty row.

No numbers were called. An endless roll of numbers rapped out in another room echoed into Room 3-112 where the tannoy buzzed and crackled hollowly. Outside, the small patches of sky visible between the buildings were a glaring grey. The trees on the street were shaken and bent by the wind, which filled and pulled at the red and blue, green, black and gold ribbons of a huge flag. From time to time the aisle of Room 3-112 filled up with people who wandered towards the front, bunching up near the beige partition before they too were repelled. The flock would scatter and then regroup at the orange chairs.

Suddenly the tannoy sputtered into life. Sandile sat up, hardly daring to hope. A voice called out numbers at last: '051, 052, 053, 054, 055 . . . Please make your way to the counter.' Sandile sank back into his orange bucket chair. His number was a long, long string away.

Outside, the flag cracked and curled in the wind. It had been two hours, maybe three. There had still been no summons for 074. A woman came into the room, past the no-entry sign like everyone else. She rang a small bell and barked out, 'Ten minutes! Coffee, tea, doughnuts, koek-susters, sandwiches! I'm here ten minutes!' Then she ducked out again and danced off through the other long beige rooms with their attentive orange chairs to bring the same cheery news.

Sandile walked back out to the corridor. The doughnuts and sandwiches had the desultory look of their lizard-eyed creator. He ordered a coffee, his voice sounding languid and minimal. He realised he hadn't looked at the woman while he gave his order. Why expend the effort? She bristled with the same bell-ringing energy she brought to the beige room, her voice demanding brightly, 'Sugar?'

'No.'

'Seventy-five cents, please.'

Sandile looked up, looked her straight in the eye. This woman was no lizard; she was alive, with bright blue eyeshadow to prove it.

They're trying to wear me down, he thought as he shuffled back to his seat, trying not to spill the scalding coffee. The day was beginning to take on the rhythm of an interrogation. He was resigned to not understanding their system, had surrendered himself to them – all he did now was wait. Still no numbers. A mumble of conversation rolled forward from the back of the room. Somewhere a man kept on loudly sucking down his snot. Sandile felt sick. He searched his pockets for a tissue or a handkerchief to give him, but he had nothing.

At one point in the afternoon a woman walked by. She was tall with long, straight blonde hair that swung over her neck and down her back, reminding him of Elise. As far as he was concerned the world was divided into two kinds of people. Those who sapped energy and those who emitted it. The personnel department here knew which type they needed. The sappers. Sandile imagined special training programmes where they learned the lizard look, where they were taught to drain a person's energy to virtually nothing with a simple jerk of the chin. Elise was the opposite. She was a life force, literally radiating energy. Am I a sapper? he wondered.

He rubbed his eyes and leaned his head back against the

306

seat, trying to push her from his mind. He didn't know what to make of what he felt about her and what he was now trying to do to her and the land she loved. There was still time, he told himself. He would tell her in time. But she would never have kissed him had she known. And he wanted her to kiss him again.

The tannoy jerked into life again: '068, 069, 070, 071, 072, 073, 074.' That was his number. They were calling his number! It was as if he'd found himself in the midst of some bizarre game show. Sandile leapt out of his seat and raced towards the partition.

A lady in an emerald suit and emerald eyelids handed Sandile a slender bundle of papers which he took, as directed, to the Reading Room. The Reading Room was a windowless, neon-lit cave where other jackpot winners were bent over their paper prizes in various states of concentration.

He found himself a space at one of the long Formica-covered tables and opened his bundle. There wasn't much in there and it didn't take him long to sift through the papers and to find what he was looking for. Sandile froze when he saw it. His fingers shook as he checked through the names and dates. They were all correct. He almost shouted out in triumph. He had struck gold. Suddenly the hours of waiting, the torment of these putty-coloured walls and carpets and the bureaucrats' torpor dissolved. Sandile was exploding with excitement. There it was, the title deed. He gave a silent shout of thanks to his forebears, not just for their strength and determination, but also for their foresight.

Over the course of nine days, Sandile had collected a not insignificant pile of documents which together formed a detailed history of the land he intended to claim, as well as of land purchases and transfers in the whole of Fransmansvallei over the centuries that it had been settled. In many respects the story of the valley reflected that of the whole Cape.

In the 1900s the Xhosa cattle farmers who peopled the area were driven off their land first by the Dutch, then by the English and finally by the Afrikaners. Waves of expropriations and forced removals eventually overwhelmed even the most determined communities, so that by the time freedom came, on the day that black South Africans went to elect a government of their own, there were virtually no legal black landowners in South Africa.

Among those nineteenth-century Xhosa who had stood their ground longer than most was Gideon 'Goliath' Mashiya, Sandile's great-great-grandfather. Goliath was the son of a lesser chief of the Xhosa nation. He established a kraal in the verdant and remote valley called Fransmansvallei. It seemed safely situated right on the edge of the Cape Colony. The land they farmed had natural boundaries. It was a small bowl at the south end of the valley; the legs of a mountain sloped down on either side and the dip in between was a wide pastureland, secluded, safe and sustainable because of a spring that welled up at the foot of the mountain. Here their community prospered, while supporting communities in valleys to the south and north disappeared as white farms slowly encroached.

The first white farmers to settle in the valley were poor frontiersmen, French Huguenots fleeing persecution in their own country to become persecutors in another. Hence the name Fransmansvallei. Pieter Lombaard and his son built themselves two huts on the eastern side of the southern slope of the valley. They then claimed all of the southern part of the valley, including the Xhosa kraal, as theirs. The law of the Colony supported them. By then Cecil John Rhodes had brought in the Glenn Grey Act, designed to push blacks off the land and into wage labour. So they became tenants on their own land.

Eventually the elders of the small community, led by Goliath, organised themselves and saved – over decades – to buy back their land. They paid with money they earned by working on the white farms. At that time they interacted civilly with the neighbouring white farmers and some of their children went to lessons in the church with the white children. Goliath had been to this school and could read and write and do all the sums a farmer might need to do. He was no fool. And the Lombaards were poor and needed the money. When Goliath represented his family in the purchase of the land he insisted on proof of the exchange, an official paper showing his legal entitlement to it. The transfer was registered in 1910.

Until 1958 the Mashiyas farmed peacefully alongside their neighbours. The story of their final dispossession of the land involved the Van Rensburgs quite closely. The Van Rensburgs had an interesting history of their own and Sandile traced it carefully.

The first Dutch settler in the valley was a man called François van der Graaf. He and his wife produced two daughters. The younger daughter married a cousin, Jan Andries Joubert, who was the middle son of a successful family in Swellendam, and together they had a son, Tjaart. The older daughter, a taciturn girl by all accounts, married a farm hand of her father's, Willem van Rensburg. The two daughters were viciously competitive: they fought terribly over everything except the question at the heart of everything – who would inherit the farm? The problem was insoluble – they simply couldn't live together. So Van Der Graaf bought a thousand acres from Lombaard, on the southern slopes across the valley, where his elder daughter and her new husband built a homestead and a farm of their own.

In between Lombaard's land and the Van Rensburgs' new farm was the kraal. Goliath's family worked part time as labourers on the white farms and continued to raise cattle on their own land. This was how things continued for nearly a century. The land was so out of the way that for a long time it went unnoticed that it was owned and run by blacks. Then, in the 1950s, Prime Minister H. F. Verwoerd – 'visionary' architect of Separate Development – coined the catchy term 'Black Spot' for land like that owned by the Mashiyas. Verwoerd's government made sure that all remaining peasant and community farmers were moved off the land and into reserves where they formed a massive, controlled pool of cheap labour. Sometimes people were moved to land in the vicinity of their old lives, but more often they were dumped nowhere near it – in the bleakest, remotest, emptiest places in South Africa. Apartheid's designers called these massive self-service concentration camps Homelands. Home Lands.

When Van Rensburg's grandfather, Willem van Rensburg, and his bride built Rustenvrede and cleared the land to plant orchards, they befriended their new neighbours and gave many of the Xhosa villagers employment on their farm. It was Van Rensburg's mother, a grasping old hippo, who took and shared the black-spot land with the Lombaards two generations later.

Ben Mashiya's protest was squashed so swiftly and so completely that the fight was knocked out of him before he'd even begun. The time of Oupa Mashiya's forebears was a time when his people fought back. They had a chance of winning. By 1958 there was no chance at all. There was no fight left in Oupa Mashiya now, just fear. Sandile understood why more clearly than before. But the days of waiting for certificates and titles had yielded a potent prize. Now, at last, the final round had begun.

Sandile had been away from Rustenvrede for almost a fortnight. Together with Karel Smit he had put together and filled out all the required documentation and at last they had filed the claim with the Commission. Fatima Mamdoo was delighted. She assured both Sandile and his lawyer that she would do her utmost to move the case along. 'I might even stop by for a visit one of these days,' she'd said, smiling. 'A quick site inspection might do me some good. I hear that part of the world is close to heaven.'

Sandile agreed it was, but warned Mrs Mamdoo to give him advance notice of her arrival. 'Otherwise we'll all find out just how close to heaven it really is!'

They had all three laughed at this and parted on quite a high.

On his second to last night in Cape Town Simon took Sandile along to a dinner at the house of a wealthy white lawyer, a man called Anthony Wolfe. The news had leaked out to the press earlier in the week that Wolfe was to be made a judge. Sandile didn't doubt that the evening would be celebratory. He was in the mood to celebrate, so he was more than happy to go along.

The house was a sprawling concrete bunker, all glass and steel and water, with lit walkways and a carefully overgrown garden. It was situated in the elegant, leafy suburb of Constantia. Sandile smelt money the minute they pulled through the huge security gates. Anthony Wolfe was at the door to meet them, and the cut of his suit and the brilliance of his smile confirmed Sandile's suspicions. He shook Sandile's hand vigorously – 'Please – call me Tony' – then immediately pressed Simon into a hushed 'pow-wow' about some Cabinet Committee or another. Sandile hovered at a comfortable distance while they finished their business.

Minutes later they were shown into a vast living room. A woman on glossy red high heels stalked Sandile across the expanse of cream-coloured carpet. Tony introduced her with more patting of backs and squeezing of arms and pumping of hands. 'My wife Lara.' Lara's full, painted smile bore down on him. Sandile couldn't help staring – he wondered how much those beestung lips had cost to install. Her neck was leathery and lined, like that of a scrawny bird. She extended a wiry, overtanned, heavily ringed hand towards him. He shook it.

'*Lovely* to meet you, Sandeelay. You are *so* welcome.'

Sandile nodded mildly and took the drink that Tony offered. Lara kissed Simon showily on both cheeks, then the doorbell rang and she stalked after Tony to answer it.

Sandile stood in the middle of the immense carpet, gazing round the walls at a beautifully displayed collection of African sculpture and paintings. It wasn't long before Lara and Tony were back, this time with new faces and introductions.

'You have a lovely home,' Sandile murmured.

Mrs Wolfe couldn't stop those gorgeous lips from smiling. She insisted that Sandile sit down, so he found a place for himself in the deep cream sofa, between piles of kelim-covered scatter cushions. He slugged back the vodka and tonic and suddenly dreaded the evening to come.

Sandile knew too many families like the Wolfes. They were all ANC supporters now, but in the past they'd preferred the tag 'liberal', which meant they made a fortune using the privileges apartheid afforded them, but spent hours at dinner talking about the terrible racist policies of the Afrikaner government and gave their old clothes to the maid, maybe even paid for the maid's children's schooling. He knew the fleeting passion that would swell in them as they talked about the great days of the struggle and the enduring passion that gripped them on the subject of Zermatt versus Vail for the best powder skiing. Sandile tasted bitterness in his mouth and wished he could simply enjoy himself, stop being so unchart-able. Apartheid was dead, he told himself. At least these people understood which was the right side to be on. Still, it didn't mean he should have to stomach their company.

The dinnertime conversation was animated, even impas-sioned at times. Naturally – this was South Africa and these were passionate times. The debate centred on proceedings in Parliament that week. Sandile couldn't help smiling at the way the Wolfes talked so familiarly about 'Nelson' and 'Cyril'. Tony was for 'Thabo', but Mrs Wolfe insisted gaily that Cyril was 'such a very *charming* man'. To which her husband countered that 'Thabo should *not* be underestim-ated.' No one could disagree with that.

None of the guests sitting at that beautifully set, feast-laden glass dining table guessed that Sandile would have given almost anything to be somewhere else. He was utterly engaging, 'charming' even, as far as Mrs Wolfe was concer-ned. He struck up a conversation with Tony Wolfe, who was particularly interested in the land question. Tony shook his head in amazement at Sandile's story, told him he thought what he was doing was fascinating and brave. Sandile laughed at that and said it really wasn't terribly fascinating or brave, but that he was perfectly happy with things so far. Mrs

Wolfe was delighted with him as a guest and insisted that he come and visit them again. Sandile nodded and smiled and lied blandly, saying he hoped he would.

Among the guests was a young Englishwoman, Janet somebody, a film-maker who had come over from London to make a documentary about the Truth Commission. Sandile avoided her as much as he could, she was overanimated and chain-smoked throughout the evening, but she came and sat next to him over coffee and launched straight into conversation. After telling him about her film and the 'extraordinary' progress of the Truth Commission, she finally asked him what he was doing in Cape Town. As he explained her eyes lit up.

'How *inter-resting*, oh, how fascinating,' she gushed. 'What a great story, oh, there's a film in that! Would you mind terribly if I took your phone number?'

Sandile explained that he didn't have a phone number but he didn't mind if she got in touch with him through Simon – he'd be talking to him often. After she'd taken the number down in her filofax he excused himself and stood up, crossed the expanse of deep carpet and put his hand lightly on Simon's shoulder. 'Sorry, boet, I have to pack it in,' he mumured into Simon's ear.

Driving back towards town, away from the glittering fan of suburbs under the mountains, Sandile teased Simon about being a yuppie buppie sell-out. In response Simon ticked him off for being such a curmudgeon. But Sandile was on fire, he was on a roll. 'Ag, it's not the pool, it's not the car or the house that piss me off. I'd take the house and the BMW and the pool any day. It isn't that, it's just that they're so fucking *pleased* with themselves, as if they fought the revolution single-handed over the dinner table. You know?'

Simon shrugged: of course he knew.

'But how can you stomach them? It's not what they've done as much as what they've *not* done. Anthony and Lara Wolfe. Guilty – of sins of omission! Sentenced to a life of smugness and arrogance and deathly dinner parties. I'm sorry, I just can't stand it. They never fought for anything. They've kept their heads down, taken all the privileges they can get, tut-tutted about the violence. They give their clothes to the poor and hand out food parcels every Christmas while they build their walls higher so that the world they're creating with their silence, with their consent, can't see in or be seen. They are culpable as all hell. They've never paid the price of all that privilege and they never will!'

Sandile was breathless. Simon made a thoughtful clicking noise with his tongue against the inside of his cheek. 'Their daughter was in detention.'

But Simon's charitable suggestion only wound Sandile up further. 'Ja, once, for a whole night before Daddy found out where she was and got her out! Shame . . . you can bet she dines out on the story still.'

'Well, at least they chose the right side in the end.'

Sandile swung round towards his friend. They were sweeping round the wide curve of De Waal Drive, past Devil's Peak, on the freeway towards town. Beyond them, way below, was Cape Town and the inky black sea, and there, not so far from Table Bay, were the lights of Robben Island.

'Ag, come on, man! People like that are always on the right side in the end. The right side is the one that works best for them. You think the National Party can offer them anything now? Of course not, no way, but believe me, there was a time when it did. There was a time when it suited them nicely to keep quiet.'

Simon smiled. 'Ja, ja, that may be so, but the fact is we need them.'

'OK, we need them, fine, but let's not make them into heroes of the struggle, OK? Let's not get too cosy with them.'

Simon laughed at the way Sandile squirmed at the idea of cosying up to the Wolfes. 'Our plaasjaapie's got a bit of fire left in him still, hey?'

TWENTY SEVEN

Elise was sweating. Pushing her fingers lightly back through her hair she could feel the droplets of sweat clinging to the surface of her scalp. Squinting up into the sun she realised that the morning was almost over. It had slipped away while she daydreamed, picking through every look, phrase, smile, frown, squint, laugh that he'd ever looked, frowned, squinted or smiled in her direction. 'Ag!' She waved her hands back over both shoulders, as if that would unhook the fantasy that had lodged in her mind. Elise caught Jacob staring at her. No wonder – what on earth was she thinking?

'Let's take a break,' she said, laughing at herself. 'It's nearly time anyway. Too hot to keep going in this.' Jacob moved slowly, dropping his shears and wading through the heat to the shade by the tractor. Elise slumped down next to him.

They were silent for a full ten minutes, staring at the heat haze dancing on the mountains. Not many words had ever passed between them; their interaction had little to do with talk. Elise reached for a bottle of water and gulped most of it down. Jacob did the same from his own bottle.

'Has there been any word from Sandile?' Her voice sounded weak – she felt her intentions were obvious. Stupid question, she thought immediately. Why on earth would Jacob have word from Sandile?

Jacob's Adam's apple jumped and jumped again under the loose skin of his neck as he drank. Water spilled down his chin. Then the Adam's apple jiggled back into place as he pulled the plastic bottle from his lips and shook his head. He stood up, walked his slow-motion walk round the tractor and climbed up into the driver's seat. 'Lunchtime, Miss Elise,' he called out. The throttle snarled, the engine stammered and the silence between them was restored over the clatter of their slow drive back to the house. Miss Elise was what everyone called her. It sounded like Missylees.

The timetable at Rustenvrede never varied. Elise and her father always rose just before dawn. They went separately to work, returning only for lunch which was at the same time every day, and every day it was soup with a roll followed by meat and salad and a baked potato. Elise ate in silence while her father ate and read *Die Burger* if it was a weekday, *Rapport* if it was a Sunday. When Van Rensburg had finished he slid the newspaper across the table to Elise and she was forced to snatch her reading between his bouts of ranting commentary on the day's news.

Van Rensburg was unusually silent today. The heat was exhausting and the water shortage, which was slipping now towards a drought, was making them both anxious. Both father and daugher knew that they could end up deep in debt or disaster, like Lombaard's. The dam was their basic water supply. Land was too expensive to waste by covering it with huge dams. At Rustenvrede there were nine boreholes as well as the dam, but even with those they would be short if the rain didn't come soon. It made Van Rensburg sick to think about it. He'd wasted a fortune of breath cursing the Jouberts, who'd always had ample water because of their situation on the river.

Van Rensburg pushed the newspaper aside and let his soup go cold in front of him. Elise ate while she waited: he had something on his mind but he would explain when he was ready. Finally he did explain, in the most sombre tone. 'I've decided to drill another borehole.'

Elise put down her spoon and carefully wiped her mouth on her napkin.

'I arranged it with the company this morning.'

The problem, Elise knew, was the cost. The process itself was virtually infallible and it would almost certainly yield the water they needed. It was the money that was troubling her father.

Elise always enjoyed the process. The drilling company would bring their archaeologist to poke around with all his tests and meters. Van would hire a water wyser who'd bring a stockie or a bottle and at the end of the day they'd have a fresh borehole and a large dent of maybe 70–80,000 rand in their bank balance. But at least they'd be pumping water, for the time being.

Elise put her hand on her father's arm, wanting to comfort him. 'I'm glad, Pa. I think that's a good decision.' He glanced briefly over at her, then away, lost again in troubling thoughts. 'Aren't you going to eat your soup? It's really good today.' Van Rensburg picked up his spoon and began to eat.

After lunch Elise carried the dirty dishes into the kitchen and found Mama Mashiya cooking up a bobotie for the freezer. Elise had seen a lot of food stacked in the freezer and it puzzled her. Mama was driving herself too hard. She'd grown unaccountably remote and edgy lately. Although preoccupied with her own troubles, Elise couldn't help noticing the difference in her. She was tense and quiet and often, Elise thought, the older woman would hardly meet her eye. She padded across the floor. Mama was so engrossed in her thoughts that she hadn't realised there was someone else in the room with her. Elise plopped the dishes down on the draining board and Mama started, wheeling round with fright. Elise saw that her hands were shaking. Mama put her hands over her eyes.

'You gave me such a skrik.'

Elise put her hand on Mama's shoulder. 'Mama, why don't you sit down and take a break? You're working yourself into the ground.'

But Mama turned back to the chopping board, murmuring, 'I'm fine, Miss Elise.'

Elise watched the old woman for a moment, curious as to why she had called her that. Mama always called her Elise.

It was Thursday and Elise was due at the Du Toits for supper that night. Van Rensburg excused himself from the whole affair – he had no desire to see Alan Taylor again any time soon. So when Elise set out for Komweer her father was already settled comfortably in the living room with the Dominee and an excellent Chardonnay for company.

As she drove over to Du Toit's Elise gulped the cool evening air which rushed in through the open windows. Her growing obsession with Sandile had driven her half crazy; she wanted to feel like herself again. She thought about Daan and realised that she was thoroughly rattled at the thought of seeing him. She'd become paranoid around him and as a result was unusually attentive and loving. She read every look, every gesture of his with great care, searching for clues as to whether or not he suspected anything. He didn't seem to, but how could he not? Elise felt as if she had the word 'traitor' blazing out of her eyes. In fact she was so preoccupied with her own infidelity that she was completely unprepared for the sight that greeted her on arrival at Komweer.

Elise pulled into the yard at Du Toit's just as Madeleine de Jager was leaving. Daan was bent over her car, his lanky body almost bent double as he leaned his elbow on her wounddown window. In his free arm he was holding a cake tin. To Elise it looked as if they were joking about something. Madeleine stiffened the instant she saw Elise and broke off the conversation rather too quickly. Yet Elise had seen an intimacy beyond friendship between them in that brief, unguarded moment, and she didn't miss the venomous glance Madeleine shot her as she drove away. Her look was hurt and angry and gloating all at once. Elise realised she was shaking.

Daan opened the door of her car and bent down to kiss her. He was cheerful, almost too chipper, standing there like a drinks waiter with the cake tin held high. Elise's heart was pounding; she was fraught with tension.

'Why was Madeleine over?' She managed to make the question sound quite light and immaterial.

'Brought me some of her koeksusters.' Daan lowered the tin to show her.

Elise stared down at the beautiful arrangement of glistening twists of syrupy cakes. She was puzzled and irritated. 'I wonder why she did that.'

'Peace offering?' he suggested lightly and offered her one. Elise shook her head, so Daan slid the koeksuster into his own mouth. Elise looked up at him stuffing his face with cake in his clowning, winning way. He was so easy, always so relaxed and easy about everything. Maybe he just doesn't see it, she told herself, brushing away doubt. She was sure he wasn't lying. Daan smiled as he licked his lips, which still glistened with syrup from the cake.

She was irked by the scene she'd witnessed between them, which made it easier to raise a thorny issue. Daan was steering her towards the house, but Elise stopped dead and said it right there. 'You know, sweetie, before we go inside, there's something I've been meaning to talk to you about. It's been worrying me since that night, you know . . .'

Daan nodded, indicating that he hadn't forgotten.

'I've been thinking a lot about what you said, and to be frank I think it was unfair of you to jump me like that. You'd never mentioned any plan to leave the force before, so how was I supposed to know that's what was on your mind?'

It was clear that Elise was only just getting started. Daan put his hand on her shoulder to stop her, but she carried on and so he gently covered her mouth. Elise was about to explode with rage.

'Elise, sweetie, I know. I know!'

She pushed his hand away, her eyes blazing with anger, but he rushed on before she could speak, taking the wind right out of her sails. 'I've thought a lot about it too and I agree. I was quite wrong to get pushy with you like that about the farm and the future. What can I say? I panicked about stupid stuff. It was ridiculous and it was my fault. I'm so sorry, my baby.'

Elise was speechless, totally disarmed.

'We don't need to worry about all that stuff now,' Daan continued. 'We have our whole lives to work things out. I say we get married first and then just see where things take us.'

Elise melted towards him. He not only adored her, but he was utterly reasonable to boot. Now she felt doubly bad and doubly blessed as he leaned forward to kiss her.

Ina came flying out of the house and disrupted their embrace. She grabbed Elise and hugged her, whispering an agitated reminder as she did so. 'Don't forget, no one knows about me and Alan!'

Elise pinched Ina's arm playfully. 'Do you think I'd dream of telling on you? I won't breathe a word.'

'Not even to Daan?'

'Not even to Daan.' Elise pushed her wide eyes close to Ina's and tapped her on the tip of her nose to emphasise her pledge.

Ina grinned. She was pink with anticipation and looking beautiful. Daan had disappeared into the house. No doubt he's put his koeksusters safely away, Elise thought darkly. She wasn't prone to jealousy, but something like it had surfaced in her just now. She pushed it away and slipped her arm through Ina's as they walked inside.

All the Du Toits were there, littering the lounge with their long legs and their rangy children. The mood was as genial and welcoming as always. Komweer was stuffed with beautiful old family furniture and pictures and objects collected over generations. The place emanated as much elegance as it did warmth and comfort. That was Mrs Du Toit's talent. Daan appeared, put his arm round Elise and squeezed her hard. It felt good – she felt she'd been drawn back into their circle.

Alan Taylor arrived dead on seven o'clock, as invited. The Du Toits all stood up to greet him. This was the first sighting for most of them, so his visit occasioned a great deal of curiosity.

Mrs Du Toit showed him into the room, gesturing with a flourish towards her family as he entered. Everyone was momentarily silent as they sized up the very smart-looking gentleman who towered over their mother in the doorway.

Elise was struck by how different Alan seemed from the man she'd met at the fence. She found herself agreeing with Ina: there was something arresting about him. It might have been his stillness, or the way his gaze raked slowly round, resting unflinchingly on any eyes that met his. Madame led him across the length of the room, introducing her family one by one. Finally they came to Elise, who looked steadily and rather sternly into Alan Taylor's icy eyes as Mrs Du Toit told him her name. Taylor bowed slightly, murmuring a greeting as he did so.

'Ms Van Rensburg, I'm so glad to have the opportunity to be properly introduced, and under such pleasant – far pleasanter – circumstances.'

Elise strained to smile. In spite of the difference in his manner his initial rudeness still irked her. Fortunately Madame whisked him away, insisting that Hennie give their guest a glass of champagne.

Elise was the only one to greet Taylor coolly; everyone else was falling over themselves to be nice to the stranger. Here he was, not stand-offish at all, in fact more affable and charming than one could hope for. Mrs Du Toit decided instantly that he was a wonderful and very private man who simply needed some gentle tutoring in the ways of the dorp.

Elise caught Taylor's eye across the room and his lips seemed to tighten slightly, but so slightly she wasn't sure if she'd imagined it. His eyes were blank and his bearing did not betray the fact that he'd been caught staring at her. She stared back, noticing how stiffly he held himself. He was so straight and angular, yet moved with a surprising fluidity. He had an unobtrusive way of being in a room, even a room as curious about him as this one. His detached air made her wonder what his story was. The flatness of his accent betrayed a fairly comfortable past. It wasn't the choking ponciness of the royal family, nor the sonorous tones of BBC World Service radio announcers; it was something in between, something deceptive, deliberately quiet, yet it instantly quieted every other voice around it. Commanding, she decided. There was something powerful and commanding in his presence – perhaps that was why Elise found him a little frightening.

Taylor now seemed anxious to talk to her. He crossed the room at the first opportunity and came over to where she and

Daan were standing. 'I gather that congratulations are in order. Apparently I just missed the engagement.'

'Well, make sure you don't miss the wedding!' Daan chimed back puppy-doggishly.

Elise smiled and looked down at her hand. She realised with a little shock that she didn't have her ring on, that she hadn't worn it in days. She never wore it for work, but she ought to have remembered to put it on tonight. She glanced up at Daan and knew immediately that he'd noticed. He had a hurt, cool way of letting her know when he was not impressed about something and she felt him shrink from her.

Taylor was chatting to Daan over her head. 'Any idea of who might replace you?'

Daan shrugged, he didn't really care. 'Oh, I'm sure they'll bring someone in from the region, but that's all in the future. How are things going up at your farm?' he said, swiftly changing the subject.

'Quite busy, quite chaotic. As I'm sure you can imagine. I've hired a manager who will be coming in after Christmas. I must say I'll be relieved to have someone else taking care of things. I'm no farmer.'

Elise agreed. 'You know you ought to pick what you can of the fruit.'

'Well, I'll let the manager decide all that. It'll be the last time we do harvest any fruit. I'm turning the place over to vine, you know.'

Elise involuntarily raised her eyebrows. She didn't know, though they had all speculated as much.

'I've got a man flying in from California, a consultant who's going to give me the lowdown on starting my own estate.' Taylor was rather puffed up with pride at this idea. He must have tons of money, Elise thought, but she didn't say so.

'The only problem for you with vine is that you don't really have enough of a stretch to the east – you want to have more land coming down this way, to the north and west.' Elise drew out the shape she had in mind, indicating it with a sweep of her arm.

Taylor was clearly a little taken aback by her forwardness. 'Yes,' he said with terse finality.

Daan refilled Taylor's glass and Elise thought about Taylor's plan. He would have to make terraces higher up the slopes for instance, but vine would fare better than peaches and plums on that land. Wine grapes don't need the irrigation that fruit trees need for starters. Water was a particularly big problem on Die Uitkyk, which had a worse situation than Rustenvrede. Furthermore, most of Die Uitkyk's orchards needed replanting anyway. Vine would yield a modest harvest in only a year or two whereas pears, for instance, wouldn't yield anything saleable for eight to ten years at least. It made perfect sense to Elise that Taylor would grow grapes. What didn't make sense was the idea of starting his own label. A cellar alone would cost three or four million, then there was the problem of the size of Die Uitkyk itself – the farm just wasn't big enough to sustain such plans.

Taylor seemed to have read her thoughts. The glance they exchanged told Elise as much. Taylor stuck his chin out, an expression like a shrug on his face. When he spoke his tone was measured. He looked her straight in the eye and gave nothing away. 'We still have to work a lot out.'

Daan sensed Taylor's discomfort and changed the subject again. They fell quickly into comparing South Africa's sparkling wines with French champagne. Elise half listened and wondered how much Taylor really knew about his land. There is a game of dumb and dumber that farmers play with each other. Taylor was clever enough to recognise that, but she sensed from their stilted conversation that he didn't know much, if anything, about fruit or vine or farming. She wondered if he knew how bad the soil was on the top slopes. It looked almost like sand. Stubb Brookes had recently planted citrus there, with grasses in between to put nutrition back into the soil, but the Port Jackson, an invasive alien shrub which had been partly responsible for depleting the soil, was already coming back. She was surprised Taylor's workers hadn't mentioned it to him. She would mention it herself only when the Port Jackson threatened to spread over into her own land. That was sometimes how farmers were, and Elise was no exception.

Elise poured herself another sherry and walked over to the window. She sipped the sweet sharp drink and stared out across the valley towards her own farm. The sunset seemed to set fire to the mountains tonight. Her mind flicked back to Sandile and their unsettling exchange in Cape Town. She could barely remember the words, but she vividly recalled his eyes and the curve and twitch and tightening and relaxing of his lips. She shook her head – she couldn't understand how she'd been gripped by such madness. But she wasn't going to beat herself over it, she decided. After all, it was only a kiss. And yet her mind kept wandering back.

Elise jumped when a hand touched her arm. It was Daan. 'Time to eat,' he said, smiling. Madame and Alan led the procession in to dinner. The children and in-laws smiled and sighed as she made a show of fussing over the seating plan. They sat where they always sat. The only difference tonight was that Alan Taylor was put next to Ina. Elise smiled at Ina across the table, though she was frightened for her too. Ina seemed so vulnerable, so completely wide open. Ina beamed back, radiating excitement.

The dinner was going excellently and Mrs Du Toit was bubbling over with the success of it. She regaled Taylor with stories of her childhood in the valley, stories everyone else had heard before so they knew when to laugh and to chime in. Taylor positively lapped it up.

'There was a time, you know, when our tennis club was the centre of everything! Everybody played tennis and we played against Elgin and the navy, all sorts of towns and clubs. The matches were always big events, because we didn't travel very much in those days. If you went to Swellendam it was quite a trek. Our fruit used to go down with a mule cart – sometimes it took days. Oh, we had a jolly time with the tennis, and we even had fancy-dress matches when we'd dress up in the Victorian clothes and play.' Taylor was charmed.

'Now, I want to know all about *you*, Alan.' She insisted that Taylor explain how he had come to end up in their valley.

'Well,' he purred, pausing for a sip of wine, 'in my previous life I was – how should I put it? A cleaner.'

He smiled broadly. The Du Toits all stared at him and he seemed to enjoy their surprise and the furious readjustment that took place as they tried to picture this elegant man in a role that no white South African in their right mind would consider taking. No one dared to ask if he really meant what they thought he meant. Ina giggled to fill the silence.

Taylor looked round the table, a smile still dancing on his lips. He was in no hurry to end the suspense. Finally he said, 'I ran a company. A cleaning company. We did a lot of work for the government.'

Everyone laughed. Mrs Du Toit and Ina were particularly shrill in their relief, but Taylor went on. 'My late wife was originally from the Cape. She always had this dream of coming back. I suppose I couldn't give it up, even after she passed away. So here I am.'

Mrs Du Toit was touched by this and expressed her feelings in a toast. 'And we are delighted to have you with us. Here's to you, Alan!'

As everyone hastily filled and raised their glasses Taylor added happily, 'And here's to being too far and too small for anyone to come meddling in our lives!'

Everyone drank to that. Everyone except Elise, who half-heartedly tipped her glass and then put it down again.

Looking back on that evening, much later, Elise realised that Taylor never once lied outright. He had always alluded, darkly, obscurely, to the truth.

Twenty Eight

When Elise woke on Sunday morning it was still dark. The moon hung low, a thin crescent in a black sky. In the kitchen she made herself a cup of coffee. Standing at the sink in front of the window she was arrested by the sight of the dawn creeping up. The horizon burned ember-red, seeping into orange as the blackness was pushed back and everything lightened to blue, the blue now tinged with pink until the whole sky was covered in lucid, brilliant colour. The hush of the sunrise was all around her; time seemed to stop as the earth and Elise waited for the arrival of the sun. The first burst of light, a dazzling corona beyond the ridge of the mountains, released her from the stillness of that moment of awaiting the day. She walked out into the garden as the sun drove up the sky and breathed in the rich scent of the still dew-wet earth.

She felt the echo of a remembered sensation. Detachment. From herself, from everyone who came into contact with her. She didn't like it, didn't want it, but it had helped her to survive before and it might help her navigate the difficult waters she'd sailed herself into now.

Sandile returned that very afternoon. Elise was sitting with Daan and her father on the newspaper-strewn stoep at Rustenvrede. The dogs were sleeping or lolling at Van Rensburg's feet. Her father was dozing and Daan was staring out across the valley, a can of beer in one hand, the fingers of his other hand trailing on the slate-tiled floor. Elise went back to reading the *Sunday Times* magazine. She didn't notice when Daan turned to look at her. Flipping the page she glanced up and caught his eye. He winked, making her smile, then he went back to his contemplation of the garden. Elise felt a sudden terrible pang of loss. She didn't know what her life would be like without him, yet all she thought about was someone else. Elise closed her paper.

One of the dogs sat up, sniffing the air, and when he started to bark the others followed suit. Elise looked around, scanning for what it was that had stirred them. Her heart leapt when she saw him. She knew it was him, even though he was still some distance away. Sandile was walking up the long drive. Elise felt all her controls slipping again. Joy and terror seared through her. No one had had this effect on her before – she was shaken to the core by him.

Daan stood up to watch his approach. Elise got up too and they both walked towards him. They followed the snaking path through the garden, under the lilacs, and met him on the road. Elise wasn't sure what they would say to him, or why they were going out to meet him together like this.

Sandile slowed down as he approached. The dogs, recognising him, stopped yelping and sniffed happily around him. Sandile was looking only at Elise. He smiled, his arm reaching out to pat the muzzle of the old mongrel that was begging for his attention. Elise was paralysed by that smile. She tried to smile back. They were standing only metres apart and neither of them said a word.

It was Daan who broke the silence. 'How was your trip?'

It struck her suddenly as funny the way everyone spoke in English when they talked to Sandile. Elise had never asked him how much Afrikaans he knew, yet he must know some – several of the men he worked with spoke only Afrikaans.

Sandile tilted his head to one side, then to the other. 'Well. It went very well, thank you.'

'We didn't expect you to be gone so long. Thought you might have been tempted by the big city.' Elise's voice shook.

He laughed. 'Oh no. At least not yet,' he answered quietly.

Daan folded his arms casually across his chest. 'But you've done everything you needed to do, I hope.'

Daan was assuming a new role, asking these questions as if

he was already master of the place. Sandile noticed that Elise didn't seem to mind. Perhaps she had managed to wrest back control of her desires, he thought. Perhaps this coupled greeting was a signal. Sandile looked up at Daan, narrowing his eyes slightly, sizing him up. 'Oh yes, I got everything done.'

'Your mother will be pleased to see you,' Elise said quietly.

Sandile assented with a smile. There was nothing more to say. This triangular chat was making him uncomfortable.

Daan chipped in. 'Well . . . good!'

'See you in the morning?' Elise wondered.

'Yes, in the morning.'

She smiled and then he walked on up the road. Elise followed Daan back down the path to the front garden, her thoughts churning. She turned to look back and Sandile looked back in that same moment. He was still watching her as she swung round again and fell into step with Daan.

If Daan could have imagined for a moment that Elise might find a black man even slightly attractive he would certainly have noticed the electricity of the interaction between her and Sandile. But he couldn't imagine it and so he didn't suspect a thing. Nevertheless, as they strolled back towards the stoep Elise resolved not to talk to Sandile in anyone else's presence until she had regained some equilibrium around him. She knew she couldn't even mention his name because her feelings would slip out with the sound of it. It flooded her glances and shaped the dip and flow of her voice. It wasn't mild flirtation that filled the narrowing space between them any more – it was the tension of desire.

Elise went back into the house to prepare for supper, her mind a mess of fear and desire and guilt. That evening the rains came at last. A thunderstorm raced across the darkening sky, with its wonderful gift of rain.

There is soft rain and rain that comes clattering down so hard it's like a drummer on the roof, racing out of the gutters, flooding the drains. This rain fell in heavy sheets, almost obliterating the view, so that the orchards were visible only fuzzily and the mountains were cut off, reduced to quarter-sized stumps by the great clouds that engulfed their crags and peaks. After supper Elise sat in her room listening to the radio and the wind lashing the rain against the house, clattering at the windowpanes, while Daan and her father glued themselves to the TV in the lounge. Elise surrendered herself to thoughts of Sandile. The fact of him, so close, simply heightened her longing.

By morning the weather had eased up and Rustenvrede felt like a warm cocoon. Elise woke a few minutes before the radio switched on. Her body always did that, woke her up a fraction of a second before the alarm, yet she never relied on it, never listened to or trusted her body enough. The news burst through the stillness. For once nobody murdered or raped, just an excitable DJ talking about how beautiful the day would be, how the President's overseas trip was going and something more about the Land Act and the Land Claims Courts. Elise switched it off and went into the garden.

Outside, the ground was a mush of clay and mud. Fallen blossom and leaves were smashed into a paste along the bankies dividing the rows of trees in the orchards. The sky was a filthy wash of moving cloud, cut in places by ragged patches of pure cerulean blue. Raindrops, like translucent pearls, clung to the almost black branches of sodden trees. The bark on their trunks was dark chocolate brown on the side where the rain had slashed at them, their other, dry, sides were still a pale dusty grey. The earth underfoot was muddy and puddled, the puddles mottled with leaves pulled down by the wind. The colours of everything looked fresh, as if all the vibrancy the sun had drawn from them had been restored by moisture. It seemed to Elise there were hundreds of birds out that morning, all squawking and singing and chirruping as if they too had been reawakened by the rain.

Things in the house were chaotic. For the first time in living memory Mama Mashiya hadn't arrived for work. Lucky came down to the house just as Elise was setting off for the orchards with the news that Mama was sick. Van Rensburg looked anxiously at his daughter. He literally couldn't remember a time when Mama wasn't in the house all day, every day, except Sunday. She was never ill. Elise went straight up to the compound to find out what was going on.

The cottage was silent. Both Oupa Mashiya and Sandile had already set off for work. Elise found Mama lying in her bed. Mama didn't look very sick; in fact she looked more scared than anything. Elise put her hand on the old lady's shoulder. 'Mama, what happened? Shall we get you a doctor?'

Mama shook her head, pulling away from Elise's touch. 'I'm so sorry, Miss Elise. It's my nerves. The storm was very bad for my nerves. I'm just resting now. I'm coming back to work at lunchtime.' She sniffed. Her voice was muffled and though her head was turned away from Elise it seemed as if she was crying.

Elise had the powerful sensation that her presence was making matters worse. She was perplexed and terribly concerned. 'I'm going to fetch the doctor.'

Mama waved her away; in her hand was a sodden handkerchief. 'I'll be working this afternoon. Please, I don't need the doctor!' She was so insistent that Elise decided it was best to leave.

'I'm going now, Mama, she said gently. 'But please don't come back to work until you feel yourself again. OK? If not, then you send Lucky to find me and I'll call the doctor.'

Mama's shoulder heaved with a sigh or a sob – Elise couldn't tell which. She left the room feeling profoundly disturbed. She was certain that this strange behaviour was connected to her, but she couldn't fathom how.

As she reached the front door she noticed a room to the left that must be his. She stopped and looked inside. The bedclothes were tousled, sheets and blankets thrown aside and hanging down over the side of the narrow iron frame. There was a chair next to the bed with a pile of books and the stump of a candle in a chipped enamel holder. Underneath the window his desk was strewn with papers and more books. She wondered what they were.

She stepped into the room, but a sudden movement in the

doorway behind her made her turn. Sandile stood before her. His face was set and tense.

Elise realised at once how odd this must seem. She felt she was intruding and immediately stumbled out an inarticulate apology. 'I'm so sorry, this must look terrible. I came to see your mother. I didn't mean to intrude like –'

She was silenced by Sandile who put his hand on her arm. 'You're not intruding.' He tried to smile, but his eyes betrayed his anxiety.

'I came to see your mother. She says she doesn't want the doctor. Do *you* know what's wrong?'

Sandile seemed to freeze. He let go of her arm, saying nothing, just staring at her with that worried look on his face. Elise knew that something was wrong. Why wouldn't they tell her? Had she got her wires crossed that day in Cape Town? Did he think as she did about what had happened? His expression told her nothing. Elise wanted to leave. She stepped towards the door, but Sandile moved in front of her. He didn't touch her, just blocked her way, his face close to hers, eyes searching hers, and Elise gazed back at him with the same intensity. She'd been holding on so hard, teeth gritted, knuckles white, straining every part of herself to resist this. And why? She just wanted to let go. She dropped her forehead on to his shoulder. His arms slipped round her. One hand slid over the ridge of her hip, up over her stomach, lightly brushing past her breast, her neck. He cupped her chin in his fingers, tilted her face up towards his, and then his mouth touched hers. His breath was sweet, his tongue sweeter. He kissed her slowly, his mouth probing hers with the same hunger she'd seen in his eyes moments before. It felt as if her skin was on fire; every cell, every nerve ending was electrified. He leaned into her, pressing against her. She felt drunk and high and wildly aroused.

'Lucky!' Mama Mashiya's voice called out from the bedroom, exploding the fusion of bodies and mouths. They split apart, falling against the opposite walls of the narrow corridor, both still breathing hard.

'I'm late. We have to go to work,' Elise whispered, pushing back and smoothing her hair. She moved past him and opened the front door. The rush of morning air and the blinding sunshine felt ecstatic. They climbed into the cabin of her bakkie and nothing more was said. Sandile leaned against the passenger door, watching her. She drove with one hand on the wheel, the other held up to her face, the tips of her fingers resting lightly on her mouth.

Later that day Mama did go back to work, but it would be a while before Elise understood what had happened.

Elise had never experienced anything like this feeling. It was romantic, lusty, secretive and way out of control. Days flew by punctuated by dangerous, mad encounters when they came together and kissed and flew apart again. They almost never spoke.

A part of herself had come alive again when she returned to the farm from Bloem, and for Elise that had seemed enough. Now Sandile brought something else, something she didn't know she'd lacked, and the word seemed astonishing. She gave in to it. She surrendered completely to his desire and her own. Rustenvrede was building towards the start of the picking season and everyone was preoccupied with the work. The hours were as long as the days. There were not many opportunities for Elise and Sandile to be alone together, but they found as many as they could. Two weeks went by and the moments when they met were filled with a crazy, charged excitement that seemed only to intensify. Elise was caught up in the adventure. She couldn't stop it and didn't want to. She had boxed him into a secret compartment of her life, but somehow the fun of it overflowed into an appreciation of everything. Neither Elise nor Sandile gave a thought to where this was taking them. It was high summer and everything was brimming with life and light. Elise looked radiant and she felt reckless. Having sex with Daan she would close her eyes and imagine it was Sandile inside her – she ached to make love with him.

Sandile knew it was a crazy game they were playing, but he was caught up in the headiness of romance; he simply surrendered to it, and the closer they moved to one another the harder it was to tell her what he had to.

The game became riskier and the stakes rose as their desire increased. Elise didn't realise just how risky until one evening they were almost caught. It was around sunset and she was working in the office when she saw Sandile strolling down the road towards the house. He hadn't seen her yet, but it was as if he was aware of her somewhere – it seemed as if they were always waiting for each other. He slipped into the darkened packing shed and without thinking she put down her pencil, walked across the yard and slipped in after him, sliding the high door shut behind her.

Sandile was sitting on the loading platform by the packing belts. He looked up as she came in, then swung his legs to the floor and went to her. He picked her up, his mouth covering hers, lifted her on to the flat platform and laid her back against the warm tiles.

Sandile was shorter than Daan and stockier, thicker in the body. As a lover he was much more intense. When he put his arms round her and kissed her it was almost terrifying. He was strong, felt overpowering. His body wrapped itself round hers, clung to hers. He felt hungry, full of need, full of warmth and fun. His body burned against her. She felt half suffocated by the sensation and the pressure of him and she had to fight for breath, for space. Elise spun them both round, moving from underneath to on top of him, straddling him, pinning his arms back against the floor. His eyes blazed at her with a wildness that she wanted. He smiled and stopped wrestling with her, let his arms go slack over his head. Then a sound from outside intruded, but only distantly. Elise realised someone was knocking on the door. She ached to lean down and kiss him, but she couldn't, shouldn't, wouldn't, and she sprang away from him. She barely knew where she was. She felt as if she was swimming up to the surface, filled with a panic that she might not reach it in time to breathe.

The door opened a fraction, casting a slant of evening light across the floor. 'Elise?' It was Ina's voice.

Elise's heart almost leapt out of her mouth; she felt herself crashing out of a tunnel of madness. She spun around and the external world began to reappear. She pushed down her shirt, straightened her hair and dusted her jeans. Suddenly Ina was standing in the doorway, peering into the shadows, light streaming in from behind her. Sandile and Elise both looked startled and guilty, but Ina only saw them frozen apart, him on the platform and Elise metres away on the lower floor. Ina stared at her, then stepped forward, gaping at her dishevelled friend with a look of total confusion on her face. She hadn't seen anything at all, but Elise knew at once that she'd seen everything.

'I hope I'm not interrupting?' Ina's voice was chilly. It reeked of suspicion.

'No, no, no. Not at all.'

Sandile jumped up, flung a last glance at Elise and mumbled something about finishing their discussion tomorrow. Then he was gone.

Elise and Ina faced each other across the cavernous, darkening shed. Elise knew that this was all too serious. She had to put a stop to it immediately.

'Elise, are you OK?'

Elise nodded, but she didn't look OK: she was flustered and flushed. Ina smelt serious trouble, but she just couldn't believe her suspicions – it was too far-fetched, too outlandish, too awful.

Elise ran her hands through her hair, which was loose and wild. She caught it up in a band she fished out of her pocket and tied it back, and that seemed to calm her. Ina followed her out into the yard. Elise slammed the massive door shut and smiled. 'Sorry about that. It's just a stupid thing. Discipline stuff. I'll have to deal with it tomorrow.' Outside in the warm evening she seemed quite herself again. Ina wondered if she'd been mistaken just now.

'No, I shouldn't have interrupted like that.'

'How are things?' Elise folded her arms over her chest as she and Ina strolled towards the house.

'Ja, fine.' There was a trace of tension in her voice that suggested things weren't really so fine. 'I made a new appointment for us at Baskin's. This time there's no way I let you go alone!'

Elise didn't seem to hear her. She barely reacted.

'Don't you want to know when we're going?' Ina chided.

'Sure,' Elise murmured absently.

Ina stopped. They had almost reached the house. Her Beetle was parked right by the kitchen door. 'I won't come in. I can see you've got a lot on your mind. You sure you're OK?'

The way Ina was staring at her made Elise uncomfortable. She shied away from her gaze and stared off into the distance. 'Ag, it's always a bit tense at this time of year. Waiting for the picking. Dealing with the workers. Just a lot on my plate . . .' Elise let her voice trail off, almost wincing at the lie – it sounded so obvious.

But Ina apparently hadn't noticed, or else she didn't want to notice, because she put her hand affectionately on Elise's arm. Then she suddenly burst out laughing. 'You know just now – I can't tell you what it looked like! I thought –' She put her hand over her mouth and her eyes were huge. 'It looked so strange, you and that Mashiya boy . . .' Laughter tumbled out of her and Elise heard her own laughter mixing hollowly with Ina's.

'Ina, you have a crazy imagination!'

They parted warmly just moments later. Elise watched Ina drive away. It wasn't until the volksie had disappeared between the poplars that the shock of what had almost happened hit her. She dragged herself into the office and sat there, staring at a blur of lists and figures until her father called her in for supper.

Ina drove home filled with the same disquiet that had prompted her to drop in on Elise. She was feeling confused and a little upset about Taylor. The sex was incredible, like glossy pornography. She was hooked. She'd taken to wearing

335

slippery silk and satin underwear and sometimes none at all. They did it everywhere, everywhere except in bed. He loved to pull her aside and put his hands up her skirt in places where people might see them. She loved to splay her legs when she drove next to him in his car. She would unbutton her dress, from the bodice down, slowly revealing the shine of her panties. Ina was turned on by the sensation of the soft leather seat against her thighs and he loved to watch her touching herself, sliding her hand inside her panties, pushing them down to show the tight blonde curls of her pubic hair. He drove while she slowly masturbated, until she was panting and so lost in herself that he'd stop the car and pull her astride him, pushing hard inside her, pulling her in towards him until they were both finished, both exhausted.

That was how it had happened that very afternoon. Ina was achingly aroused just thinking about it. But the intensity of it had begun to scare her – there was no intimacy, only this urgency and graphic lust. She wanted to mean something to him, beyond the games they were playing, but he gave her no inkling of his feelings. In fact he gave her very little of himself at all. Ina couldn't shake her sense of unease.

As soon as she got home Ina threw herself into a cool bath and soaked until the water was too cold for her to bear any more. She climbed out shivering and wrapped herself in a long, cosy and not at all sexy terry-cloth bathrobe. Then she wandered through to the kitchen to make herself a cup of tea and found Lettie there, deep in conversation with Mabel. Ina was pleased to see the girl – Lettie might be able to shed some light on what was puzzling her so.

Ina slouched over to the stove and took a look at what Mabel had put on to boil. Then she picked a carrot from the pile the maid had cleaned and munched on it while she listened in on their conversation. They were discussing Johnny Kakana's blackness, a subject that was of no interest to Ina, although it apparently offended Lettie's mother who was horrified at the thought of her light-skinned daughter getting mixed up with a 'kaffir'. The Kriels were concerned to maintain their status one level above Africans. Lettie thought it was ludicrous snobbery and Mabel, whose skin was a deep poppy-seed black, agreed.

When Mrs Du Toit entered both girls fell silent. Ina pulled out a chair for herself and sat down at the table. 'So tell us about Die Uitkyk, Lettie.'

Lettie glanced over at Mrs Du Toit who was fussing over Mabel's stuffing. 'Ag, I've got no complaints, Miss Ina.'

'How's your new boss treating you?'

Lettie squirmed slightly, screwing up her face and showing her terrible teeth with the wide gap in the centre. 'He's different. But he's English. I don't understand the English. They're so secretive and fastidious, né? We've got a lot to learn about each other.' Lettie chuckled, happy to be making light of it.

'You must look after him properly,' Mrs Du Toit said rather imperiously. 'Don't let him boss you around. He must get used to our ways.'

Ina joined in. 'It's lucky there's no wife around to get under your feet.'

Mabel flashed Lettie a knowing look. Fortunately neither Ina nor her mother noticed.

'I'm working on it. But he's got lank rules, shew! I've never known a man be so fussy. He won't let me sort through his washing. He won't let me go into certain rooms, he hides the door of the cellar behind a big horrible picture of people riding down this poor meerkat –'

'Fox,' Ina corrected. 'It's a fox hunt.'

'Right, this fox hunt, and he goes behind it and thinks I don't notice.' Lettie started giggling. 'It's so weird. Like he's pretending to be James Bond.' Mabel joined in and the two of them were quickly helpless with laughter.

'Oh, come on, Lettie,' snapped Mrs Du Toit, although she too was amused. 'Stop exaggerating.'

Ina couldn't help smiling too. There was something weird about Alan Taylor, but perhaps it was only as harmless as Lettie's teasing made it seem.

Twenty Nine

The next morning when Elise sat down at the kitchen table for breakfast it was six thirty and the sun was already high. She'd overslept. Right through the radio news. She was furious with herself. The chaos of her feelings for Sandile had infected everything. Mama put some toast spread with butter and her special plum jam down on the table in front of her, but she couldn't eat it. She had no appetite whatsoever. Instead, she sipped at the steaming coffee.

While she was sitting there in the quiet kitchen she recalled a dream she'd had during the night. The taste of it now was terrible. In the dream Daan was having an affair with Madeleine. It was the second or third in a series of dreams where she and Daan were apart and trying frantically to communicate, yet were unable to locate one another. It was a dream full of hurt and anger and pointless pain in which she travelled round a maze of corridors and hallways and crowds. Madeleine was somewhere in the midst of it, like a gloating queen bee. What a peculiar thing to have dreamt, she thought, and at such a strange time.

Elise had twice had her fortune told, on both occasions by palm-readers. In Bloemfontein she'd met a strange woman at a strange dinner party. The woman said she was half-Indian and that she'd studied palmistry in India. Elise smiled and the woman had seemed to take her smile for disbelief. Elise said, 'No, I do believe you,' and then the woman took her hand. They sat like that for a long time. Elise was mesmerised by her and by the wine and by the voices all around them. Finally the palm-reader spoke and told her a lot of vague things, things that could have been true of anyone.

It was disappointing. Then she said something Elise had never forgotten. It struck some sad, strange place within her and struck hard. She said there would be two men in Elise's life. Two men of great importance. At that time there was only one man of any importance, her brother. And he was significant because he was dead. Elise was sure that he was one of those men the palm-reader meant. And that was all.

Some time later, when she was still in Bloemfontein, she was out at a restaurant for dinner with a couple who had befriended her and who were soon to be married – she didn't recall much more about them. At this restaurant a fortune-teller was doing the rounds of the tables. She was a plain, middle-aged, tired-looking woman, not in costume like a fairground fortuneteller, just an ordinary woman who was offering to tell fortunes in exchange for money. Elise imagined it was a gimmick to give people something to talk about, but for her the past and the future were so powerful, they had her pinned down, immobilised. Anyone who claimed a connection to past and future held a strange fascination for Elise. She didn't want the woman near her. But her friends insisted that she join in the fun. The palmist hadn't said much to the couple beyond the platitudes and promises that were obviously due to an engaged couple. But she seemed puzzled by Elise and for some time she said nothing, her eyes moving up and down the tracery of five lines on Elise's hand that would reveal all. Finally she muttered a few words about 'a long life' before she let go of Elise's fingers and appeared to have finished. But then, unexpectedly, she reached for her hand again and looked searchingly into Elise's face. 'There will be two important men in your life,' she'd said.

Elise breathed in sharply at the echo of what the half-Indian girl in that house had said. 'Who are they? Who do you see?' she asked.

The fortuneteller sighed and stared again at the lines on Elise's palm. 'One is obvious, a straightforward man who will love you straightforwardly. The other . . .' She shook her head, puzzled. 'The other is in darkness. I can't picture him, yet he is the greater man of the two.'

Elise had shuddered at the time, withdrawing her hand. It seemed to her that the darkness was death, that the man the fortuneteller meant was Dawie. The other must be her future, formless partner. Then the woman added cryptically, 'The darkness is distance. This man is very far from you, but there was a time when he was very close and there will come a time when he will be close again.'

That bland voice speaking those chilling words had made her shiver. The future closeness must be her own death, a reunion in death with her dead brother. Now it seemed that perhaps the fortuneteller meant something different. Now it seemed to Elise that the distant man she saw shrouded in darkness was Sandile.

Something serious had happened. She needed time and detachment in order to reflect seriously and calmly upon it. Elise avoided any contact with Sandile that day. Things between them had shifted from wild adventure to dangerous; they were threatening to spill over, to have consequences in the rest of her life. She was angry with herself for having allowed things to drift this far. She despised drift, she saw life as a series of choices to be made, sometimes serious, more often mundane, but every decision embodied the elimination of possibilities and the assignment of a principle, a value. You are your actions and never your words, she often said. If you fail to assign value and if you fail to choose then you are adrift. For the first time Elise didn't know what she wanted and yet her actions, her inaction even, were moving her inexorably towards Sandile. She had put herself on a collision course and she had to stop it.

When she went up to the dam in the evening Elise was full of resolve. The life she had and still valued was incompatible with where her heart was leading her. She intended to tell Sandile that what had happened was a crazy mistake, a brainstorm. They hadn't arranged to meet up there, but Elise knew she would find him at the swimming rock. And she was right. She was relieved to see that he was pensive, that his face was as stern as her feelings. They both started to talk at once and then stopped just as abruptly.

'Sorry. You go ahead,' she blurted.

'No, it's OK. You start.' He sat down.

Elise remained standing. She got straight to the point. 'Last night. It gave me a terrible fright. Things seem to have gotten a bit out of hand. We need to calm down.'

'You mean you *want* to calm things down.'

Elise hunched up her shoulders. She didn't think that was what she meant, but maybe it was. 'No. I – whatever. But these crazy encounters . . . It mustn't happen again.'

She hadn't meant it to sound so staccato, so blunt. It was so hard to express what she felt without getting into difficult territory. But Sandile didn't argue; instead he started laughing. Genuinely laughing.

'What are you laughing at? How can you find this funny? It's not funny,' she countered angrily.

'But it is, it's ludicrous.'

Sandile became abruptly serious again and his tone urgent. He moved towards her. 'Do you think you can just kill something like this? Just chop it off. Baf! Like that, and it's finished?' His arm chopped the air for emphasis. 'It doesn't work like that, Elise. You can't control this, it's too powerful, the effort will destroy you. Do you think this kind of thing comes along every day? You have to yield. Sometimes. You just have to yield!'

She was stumped. His argument was persuasive. 'But where's it going?' she said almost meekly.

'I don't know. That's the whole point. We have to go along with it, let it take us where it must.'

Elise caught herself – he sounded too vague, but also too pushy. 'That's a very romantic idea.'

'This has been a very romantic sort of happening,' he answered with that disarming simplicity which had melted her before.

341

Elise couldn't help smiling. 'Yes, it has. It's been a very romantic sort of happening,' she echoed.

Sandile smiled back at her.

'You know, you are so . . . fearless about this,' she began. 'But then you have nothing to fear, do you? And I have everything. There's no one for you to hurt, nothing for you to jeopardise.'

'How can you be so sure?' Sandile snapped. His tone was suddenly antagonistic. 'What is it you want from me, Elise?'

She breathed in sharply. The question was abrupt, a stab from an unexpected angle. She didn't have an answer.

'Do you want to have an affair? Do you want me to fall in love with you? Do you want us to live happily ever after?'

She shook her head.

'What? No everlasting love?' The words danced on his tongue. His lips curled in a slight smile. He was laughing at her, or so she thought.

'What do you want from *me*?' she parroted, throwing the question back at him.

Sandile cocked his head slightly. He liked the way she did this, liked her unpredictable strength, but it was exhausting too. Just when she seemed defeated she would get up and challenge him again. He sighed. 'I don't know.'

She shot straight back, 'And you expect *me* to know?'

In a way she did – she wanted him to know, to tell her what she wanted, what she should do, but she knew that he wouldn't. He nodded, a snort of laughter escaping him. He spun away, but she followed him and put her hand on his arm to stop him.

Sandile stared at her, his eyes pulling her in. Almost. Not quite. Some reserve in her kicked in and slammed on the brakes. She wished it wouldn't. She wished she could be free enough to listen only to her body, to his half of her heart, but she wasn't. Self-defence? She didn't know.

Sandile reached out and put his hand lightly on her cheek, running his fingers down the length of her neck, then gripped her shoulder lightly. Elise didn't pull away. 'I'm not sure of

342

anything,' he said quietly. 'And I *am* full of fear. But this – this feeling is so clear. Isn't it?' His hand slid down her arm and round her waist.

'Please don't.'

He let go.

'Oh my God. There I go again. Behaving like someone in a magazine.' She was near to laughing as she pushed her face into his shirt, her mouth open, eyes screwed tight, arms limp at her sides. She wanted this so much and she couldn't do it. She felt angry with him, but most of all with herself. 'I can't handle this. I wish I could. I wish I could feel so free, but I can't. I'm sorry.'

He kissed her hair and said nothing. The kiss was tender, bitter-sweet. Then he stepped away. 'Elise, there is something you must know.'

Tears had welled up in her eyes. She didn't want to hear any more of his persuasive talk. She wanted to be alone. She shook her head. Why couldn't they just part sweetly on the understanding that they needed to cool off, that this was all getting a bit heavy and confusing? Why did he have to keep pushing it?

Sandile was tongue-tied, paralysed. There was no right way, no right moment to tell her, but it might as well be now, he thought. But she didn't want to hear.

'I can't. Not now. Please, just give me some time to think, then we can talk some more.'

'No, it's too important.'

Elise was almost crying, and that she had to do alone. She hardly ever cried. When she did it was only to herself. She turned away from him and broke into a run.

'Elise!' he shouted after her, but she carried on running.

That night Elise felt more lonely, more desolate than she had in years. She was terribly, terribly tired. She sat in the lounge with her father while he watched TV, curled up in her chair, flipping through a magazine, though the lines on the page made no impact, no sense. The TV newsreader said that representatives of farmers in KwaZulu Natal would meet the President to put forward their grievances and farmers were refusing to pay taxes because the government would not back down on the issue of tenants' rights.

Van Rensburg stood up and slammed off the set. 'My God, what is going on in this country? They're going to force us to sell land to tenants! To labourers!'

She carried on staring down at her *Farmer's Weekly*. There was a picture of a huge tuber on the page in front of her. Elise had an old habit of counting her way through difficult situations. She found she was counting through this one. One potato two potato three potato four, five potato six potato seven potato more. One potato . . .

'What's the point?' he bellowed. 'What's the point of meeting the bloody President? They're going to lose anyway, blarry fools! Can't they see he's sweet-talked us out of everything we ever had. Now he wants us to give up our land.'

Elise looked up. 'Maybe he has a point,' she said and shrugged.

Her father swung round and gaped at her. His eyes bulged with disgust and incomprehension. When at last he spoke his voice shook with rage. 'May God forgive you for that! May God forgive you! You are too young to understand, but you *should* understand. You'd understand if it was *your* land.'

Elise put down her magazine. She stared back at her father as she rubbed her fingers along the scar on her palm. 'Maybe,' she said at last, 'maybe you're right.' Her father flopped back into his chair, his face in his hands. The silence was explosive. Elise stood up, said a quiet good night and went to the office.

She sat in the dark listening to the soft rain outside. The trees swayed slightly, making shifting shadows along the wall. Everything seemed soft and slow-moving under the coat of drizzle. Why did she let herself get into pointless fights with her father? Why was she jeopardising the future she had pictured with such excitement? All those images of her marriage to Daan, her farm, her family seemed flat and empty now. Yet these were the foundations of her life. She couldn't blame Sandile for this hollow feeling. She blamed only herself. How could she retrieve that clarity she had felt such a short time ago? Her head spun with recriminations and regret. Had she sabotaged everything, or was there still time to save herself?

THIRTY

On the following day Elise had a welcome break from the farm. She had to go to the Pick 'n' Pay hypermarket two hours' drive away to do a shop that was now several days overdue. Every week, every two weeks in a crunch, she bought basic supplies for her workers. The arrangement was as old as the farm itself and not unique to Rustenvrede. The shopping was one part of a near-feudal system whereby farmers acted as bank, creditor, shop, medic and even disciplinarian to the workers and their families. Farmers still keep envelopes of cash in their safes, each envelope labelled with the name of the worker to whom the stash belongs. At the end of every week a few rand are moved from pay packets to savings packets so that by Christmas time the bits of cash put slowly aside will have accumulated into a nice pile of savings.

There were far too many stories of farmers who abused this system and of farm workers who lost all the money they thought they'd saved. Of course the law was no recourse for them – the whole system worked on honour, or rather dishonour in Elise's view. The worst part of her semi-feudal matriarchal responsibilities, as Elise saw it, the one she resented most, was the shopping. Each one of the families living on Rustenvrede, by an agreement made with her father, was entitled to certain amounts of meat and chicken and bread and flour and mielie meal each week. So every week Elise took the bakkie out to the Pick 'n' Pay and filled out the lists given to her by the workers, who all knew their ration system perfectly and who required their ingredients in unique proportions.

Elise was on her way home and Van Rensburg was out on the farm when Fatima Mamdoo arrived at Rustenvrede just before lunchtime that Thursday. Mama Mashiya was the only person in the house. If she'd known who Mrs Mamdoo was she might not have stayed around to show the tiny woman into the living room where she sat and waited for the Van Rensburgs to come home for lunch.

Piet van Rensburg was not in a particularly good or bad mood that day as he stomped towards the house. The morning had been fine and he was looking forward to lunch. Elise would be there, like a shadow at the edge of his vision, but that wouldn't trouble him. He wasn't talking to her – it was as simple as that. Sometimes she just pushed him too far. He wasn't one to pay much attention to feelings, nor did he waste time examining the reasons for why he felt as he did. He wouldn't discuss the problem with her; he'd simply shut her out until it went away, or at least receded. Usually this worked. He would wear her down with his silence and eventually she would come round, apologise and adjust, and things would go on as he wanted them to. He didn't recognise that he was eaten up by his own anger, how his sulks wore everyone down, including himself.

Van Rensburg kicked off his boots at the kitchen door and noticed how Mama looked up nervously when he walked into the kitchen. He strode past her towards the dining room, Mama following him.

'There's someone here to see you.'

Van Rensburg had just sat down. He glared up at her. 'Who?'

'It's a woman. An Indian woman. I told her to wait in the lounge,' Mama stammered.

Van Rensburg sighed. He wasn't expecting anyone and he didn't like surprises. 'What does she want?'

Mama shook her head. She was nervously winding and unwinding her apron around her hand. 'I don't know. She said she came to talk to you.'

Van Rensburg sighed and looked down at his lunch – it

347

was going to go cold. 'Put this on the stove,' he said irritably, handing her the plate. Then he stood up and strode through to the lounge.

Mrs Mamdoo was standing at the window, looking out across the valley. She turned when Van Rensburg entered the room, smiled politely and walked towards him, her hand extended to shake his.

'What a beautiful home you have, Mr Van Rensburg.' Next to him Fatima Mamdoo was dwarfed, her shoulders literally at the height of his belt.

'What can I do for you?' Van Rensburg grunted, as he briefly shook her hand.

'Mr Van Rensburg, my name is Fatima Mamdoo. I'm from the Land Claims Commission.' She paused, allowing the words to sink in. He didn't react at all. So she went on. 'I wanted to have a preliminary chat – about the claim?'

Van Rensburg's eyes narrowed suspiciously. 'What claim?'

Fatima Mamdoo sat down and started scrabbling round in her enormous handbag. She seemed to be thinking of what to say. She was clearly surprised that he seemed not to have the faintest idea of what she was talking about.

'Perhaps you'd better sit down too, so I can explain.'

'I'm a busy man, Mrs Mamdoo. I have a farm to run. I don't have time to sit around.'

Mrs Mamdoo produced a manila folder from her bag. He was now towering so far above her that she decided to stand up again. 'I had no idea that you had not yet been informed of this, but a claim has been made against a portion of your land. It's my job to investigate the validity and viability of that claim.'

Van Rensburg said nothing. His breath came in short sharp bursts. He couldn't speak.

'So I wonder if I could trouble you to answer some questions. You see the claim is for land that currently falls on the border between your property and that of your neighbour, a Mr Tay–'

Van Rensburg exploded. 'That's impossible!' Fatima

Mamdoo smiled patiently. 'It's impossible!' he bellowed again.

'Well, I can see that it may come as a shock to you, but I do assure you that it is the case.' Mrs Mamdoo continued to smile as she spoke in the level tones of a specialist explaining her prognosis to a dangerously ill patient.

'Who?' he demanded. 'Who is doing this?'

Mrs Mamdoo paused for a moment, praying that the silence in which he awaited her answer might persist a little while longer. 'The family's name is Mashiya.'

Elise was late for lunch and worn out by the long drive. She kicked off her boots at the kitchen door and left them on the step next to her father's. Mama Mashiya was in the kitchen.

'Whose car is that, Mama?'

Mama stared at her with wide, frightened eyes. Van Rensburg's voice boomed angrily through the house.

'What's happened?' Elise demanded urgently.

Tears rolled down Mama's face. She pulled up her apron to stem the flow.

'*What?*' Elise swung her gaze from Mama to the doorway and back.

Mama simply shook her head – she didn't know, but if it was what she suspected then she couldn't say.

Elise ran through the house and found her father in the lounge roaring at a diminutive Indian woman who was wearing a beautiful sari, patterned in muted browns and golds. Mrs Mamdoo glanced over in her direction, but Van Rensburg paid no attention to his daughter's entrance. Elise cut in sharply. 'What is going on?'

Mrs Mamdoo introduced herself and began patiently to explain, but Van Rensburg was so enraged it was hard for Elise to understand. He drowned everything out with his bellowing. Her father looked terrible, flushed and sweaty. His life was unravelling.

'I can stand almost anything, but not this! How dare he? How *dare* he! I've given them everything and now they turn round and do this. These bastards are getting so big for their boots they think they know how to run a farm. *My* farm! If you let a kaffir run a farm it won't be a week before the whole place is falling apart! I mean look at what they've done to the government!'

Elise looked from her father's purple face to Mrs Mamdoo's tightly controlled brown one. 'Will somebody tell me what is going on?' she hissed.

Van Rensburg, who had been rooted to the spot until that moment, turned violently and swung his fist down on the delicate yellow-wood side table next to him. It crashed to the ground and splintered into three pieces. He paced up and down like a wounded animal, ignoring the destruction he'd caused and ignoring Mrs Mamdoo, who pulled Elise aside and said very plainly, 'A local family called Mashiya has filed a claim for land that straddles the border between Rusten-vrede and Die Uitkyk, that is, part of your neighbour's farm and part of yours.'

All the time she was speaking her eyes followed the rabid farmer back and forth across the room, as if she were at a lethal tennis match, she thought, where she had to keep her eye on the ball in case it came in her direction. She smiled, hoping that this time she'd been understood.

Elise understood all too clearly. She couldn't believe her ears. Her knees shook so much she felt as if the floor underneath her was tilting. 'Mashiya? Sandile? Are you sure?'

'I'm positive.' Mrs Mamdoo almost laughed. She felt slightly hysterical. The scene before her had degenerated to such a melodramatic state of disbelief she wondered if she'd got the right place.

'We'll fight this. We'll fight them,' Van Rensburg hissed. He was simmering by the window.

Mrs Mamdoo turned towards him. 'Well, that's one of the things I wanted to talk to you about. This case seems to be a very clear one. I'm simply trying to establish –'

'I'll fight it anyway!' Van Rensburg rounded on her. 'I'll appeal. They can give them someone else's land. What about all the Defence Force land? What bloody right has he anyway? The man is a terrorist, he belongs in jail!' Van Rensburg paced round Mrs Mamdoo, who stood very still.

'I don't want to press the point, Mr Van Rensburg, but as I've already said, Mr Mashiya has an extremely strong case. It seems to me you should be –'

Van Rensburg stopped in front of the little woman, towering over her. 'You think he's got a strong case?' His head shook violently, his hands trembling as he pointed his thick finger too close to Mrs Mamdoo's face. She was very still; she simply held his gaze while he spat out his venom.

'Well, let me tell *you* something. I too have a very strong case. I have a strong case that this will ruin my farm. Do you want to see that, Mrs Mamdoo? Is that what you and your . . . *government* want to do? You want to ruin all farmers and turn this country into a bladdy mess like the rest of Africa. You are not even an African –'

Mrs Mamdoo had had enough; she cut him short. 'I think you've made yourself very plain, Mr Van Rensburg. May I suggest you try to collect yourself? You need to calm down. I find that being calm always helps me to avoid saying the kind of stupid things you've just said. I'll make a note of your reaction for now. We can speak again when you've had some time to think.'

'I don't need to think about this!' he stormed back at her.

'Good day, Mr Van Rensburg.' She said this stiffly, through gritted teeth.

'No! Water!' he bellowed back, completely beside himself. Van Rensburg wasn't making much sense. She stared at him as if he'd lost his mind. '*Water* is my problem, you stupid woman, and this kaffir bastard wants to take what little I have of it in my, *my* dam!'

Mrs Mamdoo reached into her handbag and fished out a business card which she handed to Elise. 'Perhaps you could telephone me tomorrow? I'll be back in my office and more than happy to explain the position when your father has calmed down.' Then she headed for the door.

Elise followed, apologising profusely for her father's rudeness. Mrs Mamdoo turned to Elise and smiled kindly at her. 'No need for you to apologise, my dear, it's your father who needs a lesson in politeness. *You* have clearly mastered the art.' She sailed out of the room, her sari billowing elegantly behind her.

Van Rensburg stomped towards the door, but Elise jumped ahead of him, barring his way. 'Pa, wait! Just think for a minute. Please, don't do anything stupid.'

But she couldn't stop him.

Mama Mashiya was cowering in the kitchen. It had come – the terrible day had come. It was as awful as she had imagined it would be. Van Rensburg stormed at her, hissing into her face, 'Betty, get out. Don't ever set foot in my house again. Get out!'

Elise jumped between them. 'Mama, stay right there!' she shouted hysterically. 'How dare you speak to her like that, Pa! Calm yourself. You're going to do something stupid. You're making this worse and we will *all* regret it!'

Van Rensburg wasn't listening. He stumbled out of the kitchen and jumped into his bakkie, dust flying as the wheels spun. Elise ran after him, coughing in the dust thrown up by his skidding departure. But there was no point in chasing after him. She had no time now to regret anything – she had to act. There was going to be trouble. She went back into the house and picked up the phone. Johnny answered at the police station.

'Johnny! It's Elise van Rensburg. We've got trouble on the farm. I need Daan to come over, straight away.'

'I think Daan's gone home for lunch, but I will come over personally –'

'No! I don't need the police up here, Johnny, just Daan. If you see him before I speak to him, tell him to get over here.' She hung up immediately and dialled Komweer. Ina answered.

'Ina, where's Daan?'

'Isn't he at the station? I don't think we're expecting him for lunch.'

Elise didn't have time to explain – she wanted to get up to the compound and stop her father from hurting anyone. 'Ina, please find your brother and tell him to come over here straight away. It's extremely urgent.'

She slammed down the phone before Ina had a chance to respond.

All this time Mama Mashiya was standing by Elise, wringing her hands inconsolably. Elise dragged the old woman outside and bundled her into her bakkie. She drove much too fast, banging the underside of the car, hitting potholes at speed.

At the compound Elise stalled the vehicle, jumping out before she'd switched the engine off. Both she and Mama Mashiya stumbled towards the house. Jacob and a few other men appeared from their houses to see what all the noise was about, but they quickly shrank back into the shadows. Van Rensburg was already there, crashing his fist against the front door. In his other hand he was waving a gun. Elise recognised it as the .38 revolver he always kept in the glove compartment of his bakkie.

Elise felt a sudden, deep sense of calm. The scene before her appeared in slow motion, every colour, every motion heightened as she approached her father. All she knew was that she must get to him before someone else did, before he did something terrible. But the front door of the cottage opened and her father's fist flew into the air, just past Lucky's head. He skittered out and found a hiding place under Elise's bakkie where he crouched in terror.

Van Rensburg stormed into the Mashiyas' cottage just as Sandile, followed by his father, rounded the corner at the side of the building. Sandile saw his mother first, then Elise. Elise was moving purposefully towards the front door when Van Rensburg burst out of it, waving the pistol. Everyone, everything froze.

Van Rensburg levelled the gun at Sandile's head. Point-blank range. Mama Mashiya screamed and collapsed on the ground, her hands over her eyes. Sandile blinked and stared at Van Rensburg. Elise noticed how Sandile's body seemed to relax, as if with relief. He was very still.

For Sandile everything was out in the open. He was glad to be facing them at last. It was he who broke the silence. 'What do you think you're doing, Van Rensburg?'

Van Rensburg spat the words at him, a vicious, threatening growl. 'Get out! I want you and your family off my land. Right now.'

Sandile began moving towards him, advancing slowly with small steps. Elise felt as if her heart had stopped.

Van Rensburg's finger stroked the trigger of his revolver. 'If you don't get out of here I'll shoot. I'm perfectly within my rights. You are trespassing on my land. I'm telling you now, get out!'

Sandile held his gaze and didn't stop moving towards him. Suddenly, out of nowhere, there was a flash of motion. Ben Mashiya leapt forward and hurled himself at Van Rensburg. The farmer lashed out, swiping the old man up across the chin with the barrel of his gun. A shot went off and Ben Mashiya fell to the ground.

Mama screamed again and Sandile ducked. In the moment of shocked silence that followed the shot Sandile sprang forward and pulled the .38 out of Van Rensburg's hand. Elise rushed over and grabbed her father.

'Pa, stop this! You've got to stop this now!'

Van Rensburg pushed her away, but she hung on to his shirt. He turned and slapped her hard across the face. Elise was stunned. He barely seemed to notice what he'd done.

Sandile swung the gun round and levelled it at Van Rensburg. His eyes blazed with anger. 'I should kill you for that.'

The farmer laughed viciously, insane with rage. He advanced on Sandile, who took a step backwards towards Oupa Mashiya. 'Stay where you are,' he barked.

Van Rensburg stopped, his arms out at his sides. He was steaming like a mad bull, ready to charge. Sandile shook his head wearily. 'Don't be a fool, Van Rensburg. Go home and I'll put this thing down.'

At that moment they heard the sound of a vehicle approaching. Elise shuddered with relief as she saw the police van rounding the corner. But it was Johnny not Daan who was at the wheel. For a moment Johnny couldn't believe his eyes. He swerved sharply, then jerked to a halt. Then he jumped out of the van with his own pistol drawn. A standard police issue 9mm. Elise could see that he was shaking. With the 9mm wobbling in his hand like that he looked more dangerous than anyone else.

Sandile knew he was staring at serious calamity now. He moved fast. Slipping the revolver on to the flat of his hand he crouched slowly down and laid it in the dust on the ground. Having disarmed himself he immediately turned to help his father.

Elise was already there. She ran her hands over Oupa Mashiya's chest, looking for the wound. Oupa Mashiya batted her hands away – he didn't want her to touch him. Then Sandile knelt down beside his father. Ben was bleeding so profusely that at first it appeared he'd been shot, but it turned out that the blood came from the hit he'd taken on his chin, not from any bullet hole. The bullet had ricocheted off the wall of the compound and disappeared.

Sandile helped his father up and dusted him off while Jacob quietly pulled Mama Mashiya to her feet and brought her to her husband. The three of them shuffled into the cottage, leaving Sandile to face Johnny, Elise and her father.

Van Rensburg was shouting again, insisting that Johnny arrest the entire Mashiya family for trespassing. Johnny slid his pistol back into the holster strapped to his chest. He was shaking more violently than before. He stuffed his hands into his pockets and breathed deeply, trying to control himself.

Van Rensburg was heaving with emotion and exhaustion, but he hadn't lost his voice. 'What are you bloody cops for? I'm telling you, arrest this man. He's trespassing on my property!'

Elise squeezed Johnny's arm. 'Johnny, take my father and

his gun and get him back down to the house. I can sort this out with the Mashiyas.'

Johnny looked at her, then shook his head. 'I think you'd better let me handle this, miss.'

'Well, handle it then!' Van Rensburg bellowed. 'Stop standing there like a paralysed bloody monkey!'

Elise squeezed Johnny's arm tighter. She didn't want him to tip over the edge. 'My father has just received notice that a land claim was filed against our farm by Sandile and his parents,' she explained tersely, although she was looking at Sandile as she said this. 'It's the first we've heard of it. My father lost his temper, which I'm sure he'll regret once he calms down. In the meantime I think you should take him back to the house.'

Johnny wasn't ready to be told what to do, not yet, and Van Rensburg wasn't ready to go home. 'I'm not going anywhere,' he roared. 'I want these people off my land!'

Johnny bent down to pick up Van Rensburg's gun. He held it carefully as he looked around at Sandile and Elise, and Van himself. 'If you are trying to evict this family, I can advise you now that the eviction would be illegal and I would be forced to arrest *you*, Mr Van Rensburg.'

For the first time in her life Elise was glad to hear the tight, plain tones of officialese.

'In addition, there seems to be the matter of an assault on the old man.'

Sandile shook his head. 'The old man is fine, he'll be fine.' Sandile didn't want any involvement with the police.

Johnny saw that and pressed the point. 'Perhaps I should speak to your father in person. He may feel differently – he may *want* to press charges.'

Sandile stepped between Johnny and the door; he was in no mood to be argued with. Johnny dipped his chin and said curtly, 'Very well.'

Van Rensburg spat in disgust, a gob of phlegm landing on Johnny's boots, then he stormed past Elise, who caught hold of him. He pushed her away, glaring at her. His lips were thin and tight and he had trouble speaking. His heart pounded so hard inside his chest it hurt. At last he spoke dryly, curtly. 'I told you he was a troublemaker.' There was cruel disappointment in his eyes.

Elise reached out to him. 'Pa! Please let me –'

He smacked her hand away. 'There is *nothing* you can say to me.'

Whatever understanding had existed between father and daughter was dissolved in that afternoon. Elise felt utter loneliness. She'd stepped out on to a tightrope and now she was aware only of the appalling drop; all the excitement, the exhilaration were gone. There was no one to help her.

Van Rensburg stomped over to his bakkie, climbed in and raced away. Johnny glanced from Elise to Sandile then went over to his van, pulled out his handkerchief and wiped the spit off his boots. He followed Van Rensburg round the corner and down the mountain to the house.

Elise was trembling, stunned by the speed at which everything had come crashing down around her. She felt betrayed, foolish, humiliated, manipulated. For a while she couldn't move for shaking.

Sandile was staring at the ground by her feet. He knew there was nothing he could say. The anger welled up in Elise, but she didn't know how to begin expressing it. She glared at him, then spun round and walked away. Sandile chased after her, catching her hand in his. She yanked it away and wheeled on him.

'Don't touch me!' Her voice was low, spitting fury.

He stopped, putting his hands up. 'Elise, I tried –'

'No you didn't. You didn't try at all. You should have told me! I've been so, so stupid!' She was pointing at her head, her finger stabbing violently in the air. 'I hope you're happy that you've made such a fool of me. But don't underestimate me, my friend. Don't think that because you've made an idiot of me now that you will ever do it again.'

Sandile was very still, but he was angry too. 'You are wrong about me. So wrong!'

She snorted with contempt. 'I think I can live with that.'

She spun away again and again he grabbed her. This time she waited for him to speak.

Sandile took a deep breath before he began. 'Elise, listen to me. Please. I was going to tell you. I just didn't know how – it wasn't something I thought you'd be very understanding about – but I should have said, I know. I'm sorry. It's just that – so much happened between us. I didn't want to spoil that and it got harder and harder to say it.'

Elise was overwhelmed with rage. She whipped back her arm and flung her fist into his stomach. Sandile was instantly bent over in half, his hands clutching his gut, his mouth full with the air pushing out of him. Elise stood over him, hands on hips, glaring at him. He glared back angrily. Eventually he found the breath to speak.

'Now you show yourself. It's in your blood, Elise.'

'Don't even try to give me that shit, Sandile. You deserve worse and you know it!'

It was painful, but he stood up. 'I take it back. I'm not sorry at all.'

With that he turned and walked back to his house.

Elise watched him walk away. She was exhausted, but somewhere within her she found the strength to move and she turned away, her head hanging down because she was crying. The tears rolled down her cheeks; she was crying like a child. Elise began to run.

THIRTY ONE

In her rush to get away from the compound Elise had forgotten her bakkie. She only remembered it as she ran into the yard by the main house and saw it wasn't there. But Johnny Kakana was. From the way he stepped forward in that unctuous, oversolicitous way of his, it seemed he was waiting for her. She slowed down to a walk, wiping her face and pushing the hair out of her eyes, trying to pull herself together as she approached him. She didn't want to talk to Johnny. She didn't want to talk to anyone but her father at that moment, so she didn't break her stride as she called out to him on her way to the house, 'Thank you for coming out, but there's nothing more for you to do today. I hope you'll agree that there's no need for a report on this.'

Johnny half smiled. 'I wouldn't be so sure about that.'

'Well, I'm sure you'll do what you have to do. Thank you, Johnny,' she snapped.

But Johnny hadn't finished. 'Miss Elise, I have to keep your father's gun. I will return it in due course, naturally.'

Elise sighed heavily. 'It makes no difference – there are two more rifles inside anyway. He won't try anything like that again. I know him. Now – I think it would be best if you leave. Thank you again for everything.'

Johnny pursed his lips, wanting to say more, but then he thought better of it and clicked his heels and walked away.

Elise went through the house searching for her father. He was slumped on his chair in the lounge, his hands covering his face. At that moment she pitied him, loved him with a surge of feeling. He was all she had and she felt that she was to blame for the cataclysm. As if everything her father had done was her fault too. She had betrayed everyone with her reckless passion for Sandile and her reward was betrayal. There was justice in that. She'd thought she was so tough, thought she could box everything up and manage it all. Perhaps she had really met her match in Sandile, but not in the sense that she'd so stupidly, blindly believed.

Van Rensburg was glad of her presence near him and repelled by it at the same time. God alone knew what insanity Sandile had put into Elise's head. And God alone knew what they were going to do, if there was anything they *could* do, about this land claim. Van Rensburg had only his daughter and the farm. He thought he knew them, thought he could be sure of them above everything else in the world, but he'd just discovered he was wrong. The loss he felt was worse than any he'd ever felt in his life. It cut him to the core. He was desolate with shame for everything he'd done that afternoon, but too proud and too shattered to admit any fault.

Rustenvrede was deathly quiet. Elise sat waiting for her father to say something. She was his daughter after all – she knew how to wear a person down; she knew that if she didn't let him out of her sight he would relent. And he was tired now. The only sound in the room was that of his coarse breathing and the heavy ticking of the old grandfather clock. The ticking marked the minutes as she waited for him to tell her what they were going to do.

A little later they heard a car driving up. The engine cut out and a door slammed. Daan's voice, cautiously calling out their names, drifted in from the kitchen. Neither of them said a word. They heard his footsteps approaching, but neither one moved. Then Daan was standing in the doorway. Elise looked up at him and he read their silence as a reproach.

'Elise, Van. I'm so sorry I couldn't make it this afternoon.' Daan was decidedly sheepish about his apology, folding and unfolding his hands nervously as he explained. 'I stopped in at Joubert's on my way home and didn't hear a thing until it was all over. Johnny flagged me down on his way over to Die Uitkyk. He told me everything.'

Van Rensburg took his hands from his face and stared at the blank TV screen. Daan went over to Elise and put his arms round her. 'I'm so sorry I wasn't there, sweetie. Are you OK?'

Elise shook her head – she was very far from OK. Daan tried to comfort her and she let him hold her, but she felt worse with his arms around her and began to cry. Daan kept saying everything was going to be all right but she could only shake her head. 'Nothing is all right, it can never be all right.' She didn't have the courage or the strength at that moment to tell him why. She certainly couldn't say it with her father present, and she knew he was watching them from across the room.

Daan kissed her on the forehead. Then he turned to Van Rensburg. 'Van. If there's anything I can do –'

Van Rensburg answered coldly, sounding almost like himself again, Elise thought. 'So far the police have been no help at all, so I can't imagine what you think you can do.'

Daan cleared his throat rather too thoroughly. 'Well, the truth is that there isn't really anything . . . Obviously, if there is any more . . . trouble, you just call me and I'll be right over.' He looked round at Elise when he said this.

'There won't be any more trouble,' she murmured.

Daan stood like a spare part in the middle of the room. Elise could see that there was something else on his mind, something he was going to ask. She dreaded it, but was ready for anything. However, it was to Van Rensburg that he finally addressed himself.

'Sir, there is one other matter. I'm sorry to have to do this, but I'm going to have to confiscate your rifles. I know that you –'

Van Rensburg waved him away. 'Ag, take the bladdy things!'

Daan knew where the guns were kept and he quickly accomplished his mission. Elise listened to his footsteps on the tiled kitchen floor. He fetched the cabinet keys, then clomped into the hallway with its echoey wooden boards and removed the rifles from their rack. The Musgrave .303 that had been handed down to Van by his mother and the even older Martini Henri, another single-shot rifle. Daan took them out to his van and then returned. Neither Elise nor Van Rensburg had moved in the interim.

Daan almost tiptoed over to Elise. He knelt down in front of her, put his arms round her and his cheek against hers and whispered gently to her, 'If you need me to stay I will, OK?'

'No, you don't need to stay. We'll be all right.'

Elise's eyes were red from crying. He didn't know that she had been crying for him as much as for herself and for her father. She put her hand on his cheek. He kissed her and she closed her eyes, tears welling from the corners of her lids.

'Not even tonight?'

She shook her head again. 'No, I want to be with him tonight. I'll come and see you . . . tomorrow. I promise.'

He nodded, then stood up and walked as quietly as he could from the house.

Some time later, in a silence so solid it felt as if they were set in it, like brittle shells in Perspex, the telephone rang. Elise jumped. Then she settled back in her chair. Neither she nor her father went to pick it up. It rang and rang, then stopped. Half an hour later it rang again. This time Elise got up and answered it. The caller was Alan Taylor.

His tone was as polite and measured as usual, but Elise thought she detected something underneath it. Animation. As if this sudden news of the land claim excited him. He was enjoying the drama. 'I gather from Sergeant Kakana that you were visited this afternoon by Mrs Mamdoo from the Commission on Land Restitution.'

'Yes . . .' Elise didn't elaborate. There was a long pause while she waited for him to speak again.

'I assume you do intend to fight this?'

Elise wasn't sure. Was that what they should do? 'Well, we don't really know what our position is yet,' she stammered.

Taylor interrupted urgently. 'Look, I really am most eager to meet both you and your father to discuss the situation. We must join forces on this. Perhaps I could come round and talk it over this evening?'

'I'm sure that's fine. We'll be happy to listen to anything you suggest. We haven't made any decisions yet.'

'Good. I'll be round in a quarter of an hour.'

Elise stood in the living-room doorway. Her father looked up at her. 'That was Alan Taylor,' she reported. 'He said he's going to fight the claim. He's coming over to talk about it.'

Van Rensburg turned away. He pushed out his chin, nodding his head thoughtfully.

Elise was actually relieved by Taylor's eagerness to talk. Whatever else she thought of him, she felt his restrained, polite manner would contribute positively to the situation. It sounded as if he had a plan and she hoped he'd be able to convince her father to fall in with him. She'd rather he did that than thrash around vengefully, spending fortunes on lawyers and an ill-thought-out and probably pointless strategy to ruin the Mashiyas, which she assumed was his present intention.

Taylor arrived exactly fifteen minutes later, as promised. Both Elise and her father were surprised to see Johnny Kakana following Taylor's gleaming BMW in his dirty yellow police van. Father and daughter went to the back door to meet them, but Van Rensburg put his arm across the kitchen door, barring Elise's way. 'I'll talk to him alone.'

Elise baulked, but he made it clear there was no point in arguing. It was a combination of protectiveness and pride that made him behave like this. She understood. Nevertheless she felt hurt at being excluded and a little anxious about her father's intentions. She consoled herself with the thought that Taylor was no firebrand – he was an operator, definitely a manipulator. His plan – whatever it was – would be based on cold reason, not impulse. So she remained standing in the kitchen doorway while her father went out to meet him.

Circumstances had thrown up an opportunity for Van Rensburg and Taylor to put the disaster of the fence behind them. That incident now paled into insignificance in the face of the land claim. So Van Rensburg reluctantly shook the hand that Taylor offered, but threw a hostile glance at Johnny. 'What's he doing here?'

Elise saw Johnny's fat fists clench and unclench with anger. Taylor turned towards him and smiled calmly, addressing him with the utmost politeness. 'Sergeant, if you wouldn't mind, I'd be grateful if you would allow Mr Van Rensburg and me a moment alone.'

Johnny was grateful to Taylor for his considerate tone, but he didn't want to hang around for any more humiliation Van Rensburg might choose to dish out. He shifted his weight from one foot to the other, his shoes scuffing the ground. 'No problem. Unless you're in need of my further assistance today, Mr Taylor, I think I'll be on my way.'

Elise noticed the conspiratorial glance that he and Taylor exchanged and wondered what it meant. Her father hadn't seemed to catch it. What was Johnny Kakana doing here with Taylor anyway? she wondered.

'Thank you, no. You may as well be on your way,' Taylor said, and with that Johnny climbed into his van and left.

Johnny had encountered Taylor on Skaduwee Lane in the late afternoon. As it happened they were on their way to see each other. Taylor's gleaming car was unmistakable and it had slowed at Johnny's approach. Johnny pulled up along-side and Taylor's window hummed down. Johnny had en-quired if everything was all right up at Die Uitkyk in response to which Taylor had asked blankly if there was any reason it shouldn't be. Johnny mentioned the land claim and Taylor switched off his engine. Then Johnny did the same.

Taylor didn't seem too panicked by the events; in fact he seemed quite animated. When Johnny remarked on this Taylor had raised his eyebrows and said coolly, 'I try to see every problem as an opportunity, Johnny.' Then he went on to explain why he'd been on his way to the police station. He wanted to know all about Sandile Mashiya and he was sure that Johnny was the man who could help him.

Johnny decided that this was his moment. At that point in

the day he was already seriously steamed up. He didn't know who he was more angry with, the Van Rensburgs or the Mashiyas. He'd been in considerable danger up at the compound and they had all behaved as if he was some irritating intrusion. Everyone wanted him out of the way, no one wanted him involved and yet if he hadn't intervened then who knew what might have happened? Van Rensburg could have killed someone, Sandile might have killed someone – it was pretty heated up there. Johnny had defused the situation and received no thanks for it. So he told Alan Taylor all about Sandile's file and Taylor was more than just a little interested.

He'd called the Van Rensburgs on his cellular and arranged to come over. He didn't see why Johnny shouldn't go with him. That was why Johnny had followed Taylor up to the house at Rustenvrede. Now Johnny drove away smarting from his abrupt dismissal. If the people of this dorp weren't careful, he thought, one day he would really show them. He wanted to show them that he was not just worthy of their respect, but also better than them. With people like Piet van Rensburg he sometimes fantasised about mad, violent retribution for the countless ways the farmer had slighted and overlooked him. Johnny hated people like Van Rensburg, hated him with a bitter, wild passion. Van was the kind of man who had made him think of himself only as Johnny Kakana. Xolile was a name that belonged to another person.

Yet Alan Taylor was different. Taylor always looked him straight in the eye, he always gave Johnny the respect he felt he deserved. Strangely enough that was what made Johnny fear him. He wondered what it was that Taylor was going to discuss with Van Rensburg. He knew the proposal would be supported by the information Johnny had given him on Sandile, but he had no idea of what it would be.

Van Rensburg did not invite his neighbour inside. Instead he stood out in the yard, his legs firmly apart, arms akimbo, ready to listen. But apparently not to relent. Elise strained to hear, but she caught only Taylor's monotone murmur; she couldn't distinguish any words. But his tone and gestures confirmed her expectation that he was trying to persuade her father to take a reasonable approach to solving their common problem. Her father's aggressive stance and sullen expression confirmed her worst fears about his intentions.

Van Rensburg had been nodding all the while he listened, but now he stopped and shook his head. Elise heard Taylor's next words distinctly. 'I don't think you understand me.'

Van Rensburg shifted, uncrossing his arms. 'No. I don't think I do.'

Taylor went on in a hushed, urgent tone. Her father was staring at the ground now, shaking his head vehemently. Taylor paused for breath, evidently stumped. Elise's heart sank. Now both men raised their voices.

'If we leave it even a matter of days we stand to lose.'

'I don't see how a few days can make any difference.'

'Look, it seems to me that there are times when we have to act, when we have to help the law to work for us. Surely this is one of those times, don't you think, Mr Van Rensburg?' Taylor could see that he had struck a chord, but Van Rensburg still didn't say anything. 'Why don't you think about it overnight? In the morning we can talk some more.'

Van Rensburg looked down at his feet. He drew a line in the dust with the toe of his boot, then he looked up and answered very firmly. 'No. No, I'm sorry, Mr Taylor. From the little I know of you there is little to like. I'm not interested in anything you have to suggest. I'll deal with my problem my way – you can do whatever you want.'

Taylor looked away. Elise could see the muscle in his cheek flexing. What on earth could he have suggested that her father was so vehemently opposed to? Was her father just being pigheaded and refusing to co-operate with Taylor because of the fence? Elise moved towards the door, intending to intervene. But something in Taylor's tone stopped her. 'Your way you lose. Believe me, Van Rensburg, you lose.'

Van Rensburg shrugged – he had nothing more to say.

Taylor walked away to his car. He stood as tall and as

stiffly as before, but Elise could see from the extra-sharpness of his movements that he'd found the interaction galling, that he was leaving Rustenvrede defeated.

As he put his hand on the door Taylor turned back to Van Rensburg and offered him one last chance to reconsider. Van Rensburg was adamant, he would waste no more words, so he simply, slowly shook his head.

'Very well. But I'm disappointed in you, Van Rensburg, very disappointed. From what I've heard and seen of you I thought you were a man with some fight in him.'

Van Rensburg thrust out his chin, glaring back at Taylor defiantly.

Taylor made his little bow, clicked his heels and climbed into his car. Elise turned away from the doorway and sank into a chair by the kitchen table. When her father came inside she couldn't look him in the eye, but she noticed that his hands were shaking.

Thirty Two

Sandile found his mother and Jacob in the kitchen, dousing his father's chin with Dettol. The old man had taken off his bloodied shirt and was leaning against the sink, his chin tilted upwards and his eyes closed in surrender to the gentle ministrations of his wife. Sandile stood by his mother as she cleaned the wound. It wasn't as severe as it had first seemed. What was more dismaying to Sandile was the sight of his father's sunken rib cage and skinny torso, the way his father's shrunken body trembled. The old man was still in shock.

Ben Mashiya had been quietly numb for weeks now. Ever since Sandile's trip to Cape Town, he had shut down, anaesthetised himself in order to have some chance of surviving the impact of the bomb that was ticking under them. Now their lives had exploded. Their worst fears were confirmed. Sandile knew that he had let them down terribly. He was enraged not only by his failure to protect them, but also by his failure to reach Elise before the catastrophe occurred. If only he had told her, he thought, it might never have happened.

Once the wound was dressed Sandile and Mama put Ben Mashiya to bed. Together they helped him lie down, stretching his shaken, slender frame out on the mattress. Then Mama pulled a sheet and a thick blanket over him and propped his head up on plumped pillows. Ben smiled at his silent wife and she responded shyly, with her own sweet smile. The tenderness of their exchange made Sandile's heart lurch.

'I owe you both an apology. I am so sorry and it seems so inadequate to say so. But I shouldn't have let things happen the way they have.'

Sandile felt his father's hand gripping on to his. The touch was all the reassurance he needed and he fell silent. His father's eyes told him that an explanation was unnecessary. But Mama, who had been mute for weeks, couldn't accept their foolish optimism. To be hopeful was to fly in the face not only of experience, but reality.

She narrowed her eyes at Sandile, glaring at him from the other side of the bed as she leaned across her husband, her knuckles pushing into the blanket. 'You are right. Sorry is not enough. And now it's not just you who are living in cloud-cuckoo-land, but your father as well. Look at the two of you! We are fugitives in our own home. We could be thrown out any minute. If it wasn't for Xolile we would be out already. Don't fool yourselves into thinking Van Rensburg will leave it like this. He'll find some white policeman who will be more than happy to evict us. Mark my words, they'll be back. They don't give up, those people, and in the end they always win!'

Sandile was taken aback by her venom. He had nothing to counter it, so he looked to his father. Ben Mashiya had closed his eyes and listened to her tirade with evident pain. But instead of the rebuke that Mama expected from her husband, he answered her with a kindness born of understanding. 'This is a long war. You are strong, my wife. You are stronger than all of us. You must help us to wait it out. If we went your way you would keep us enslaved to this man who attacks our house and our child, is so callous that he even hits his own child. I beg you – support our son, because he wants to win back our land, he wants to win back our dignity. Remember that he is struggling too.'

Mama looked from her husband to her son. 'I do hear you, Ben. But it is hard. This is too hard.' She shook her head wearily. Her voice spoke of her exhaustion. She was at the end of her tether.

'It will not be long now, Mama, I promise you. It will not be long,' Sandile whispered.

Although Ben Mashiya had calmed his family and broken the suffocating tension, an atmosphere of crisis persisted.

People came and went from their house that night, wanting to know what was happening, what this land claim and Van Rensburg's reaction meant. Ben Mashiya was patient with every one of them and stalwart in his support for Sandile. Even Mama, seeing the awe and excitement that Sandile's land claim had generated, felt a strange pride in the fact that her son had stood up to Van Rensburg.

Later, at dinner, she spoke again. Sandile was watching Lucky as he quietly demolished everything on his plate. Mama looked shattered. She hadn't eaten a thing.

'Mama, take some food. It will give you strength.' Sandile smiled at her.

She didn't smile back, but she said plainly to him, in a direct tone that he hadn't heard for weeks, 'What are you going to do with the land when you get it. Hey?'

Sandile was taken aback.

'Even if we had tractors and money to pay workers and everything else, which we don't, what are you going to do with it?' She was absolutely in earnest.

'It's good valuable land, Ma. We'll farm it. It's got water, it's got orchards. There are grants and loan programmes to help people in our situation. Maybe we'll even find a way to work with the Van Rensburgs.'

'Tcha!' His mother swatted the idea away. She didn't really want to know – she was making a point, not letting Sandile forget her anger at what he was putting her through.

Sandile lay back on the rumpled sheets of his bed and sighed heavily. 'So, at last it has begun,' he murmured. He had lately become accustomed to restless nights, sleeping for only a few hours at a time at best. Tonight it was Elise who plagued his dreams and his half-waking hours. Her face flew at him from all directions out of the darkness. It wasn't true what he'd said to her. He was more than sorry. He was wretched.

Sandile had once said rather flippantly, but challengingly, to a married woman he'd had an on-off affair with in Lusaka, that he'd never been in love. It wasn't quite true. There had been a lot of women in his life, but only Selina had lodged in his mind like this.

There was no doubt that Sandile was deeply disconcerted by Elise. He'd been pulled out of his depth by her. Until now there'd been only one thing he had wanted as badly: to come home and claim the land that had been stolen from his family. Now he wanted Elise. The irony was more than ridiculous, it was painful. Why did it have to be her?

The whole thing was impossible. There was too much standing in the way. Not least her father. Van Rensburg was a terrible man, the worst kind of a dying breed. His desperate behaviour that afternoon had bordered on the insane. Strange, Sandile reflected, that he should have produced a daughter like Elise. He couldn't be wholly evil if he had kept her love and loyalty.

THIRTY THREE

Evening came. The encroaching darkness seemed to still the madness of the day. Elise and Van Rensburg were alone at last in the quiet bubble of their house. The ruined lunch was a charred mess in the oven. Elise heated up some soup and coaxed her father to eat. He came to the table almost meekly, like a big injured child. They ate in the silence of the dining room and for a long time after they'd finished they sat there in the gathering darkness as the light faded and the sun set behind the mountains. They began to talk only once it was night when they could barely make out each other's faces in the shadowy room.

Elise had never seen her father the way he was that night. He was exposed and vulnerable and although there were things for which she could never forgive him, ways of his with which she could never agree, her heart went out to him. She reached deep into herself for an understanding which is only given by daughters to their fathers.

Within the stillness Elise felt free to talk to him as she never had, about Daan and the question that had troubled her so about her marriage.

'Pa, do you think Daan would make a good farmer?'

Van Rensburg frowned, deeply puzzled not only by her question, but why it had come at this moment.

'He's planning to leave the force. He wants to farm with me when we're married,' Elise explained quietly. It felt like a confession. Her father was clearly surprised.

He thought carefully about his answer. He had to express it carefully, because Van Rensburg had this intuition that Daan lacked true feeling for the land. It was something he had suspected about his own son, Dawie, a suspicion that would be beyond treacherous to give voice to. Nevertheless he felt that lack in Daan.

'He seems to show an interest . . .'

Elise could see the 'but' on her father's lips before he uttered it.

'But I think he's sort of lazy. I think Daan is never going to be a good farmer, just as he will never make a great policeman.' He said it as gently as he could, but Elise took it like a slap in the face. She was stunned. Van was shocked by the impact of his words on her.

'On the other hand he's as rooted in this valley as anyone, and he loves you. That's *more* than I could wish for in a son-in-law. And his family are good farmers. Daan is serious enough to know when to take his brothers' advice; they won't let him go wrong.'

Elise often noticed how her father never said anything about her own skills as a farmer, yet he was always talking about good farmers and bad farmers. He never complained about anything she did, so she had to assume he was happy, but she would have liked to know. She'd so long ago stopped expecting encouragement and good judgement from others, she knew how to rely on herself. In that way she was very much like him.

Tonight was different. Tonight the barriers were down and both Elise and Van Rensburg allowed everything to flow.

'There's a difference between wanting land and being called to it,' he said suddenly. 'You are called by the land. Daan merely wants it. You are a good farmer, Elise,' he added with his own gruff simplicity.

Elise was speechless. Her throat was dry and her eyes pricked with tears. She was indescribably touched. No words could express her gratitude – they would only have shattered the moment.

'You know,' her father went on, 'I should have seen this coming.' Elise didn't understand. Van Rensburg sighed. 'That land did belong to Ben Mashiya once.' He almost whispered it. His confession.

'What?' Elise felt as if she was taking punches from all sides. She couldn't believe her ears.

'The Verwoerd government declared it a "Black Spot" and they gave half to us and half to Lombaard's. It wasn't so long ago, not long before your brother was born.'

Elise pushed her plate away and leaned back in her chair. 'How come I never knew that?'

'Ja . . . it's a fact.' Her father tapped his spoon against the side of the plate so that it rang and echoed through the house like an alarm bell.

'So what are we going to do?'

Van Rensburg stared down at his empty plate, then put the spoon down. 'What can I do? We have to fight it. If we don't we may as well throw this farm away.'

Elise pushed a hand back through her hair and sighed. She didn't dare say that there might be an alternative: by working with the Mashiyas they might find a better way to survive. She wasn't sure she wanted to choose that way.

'Why won't you join forces with Taylor? Isn't that what he wants?'

Her father shook his head and was silent. Elise leaned forward to touch his arm and she was glad that when her fingers touched his skin he didn't pull away.

'I don't trust that man. It's better we do this our way.'

'I wish you'd let me come in on that discussion.'

'You would have agreed with me. In fact *you* wouldn't have been as patient as I was with his mumbo-jumbo. Mr Taylor wants to fight dirty. He wants to get rid of Sandile – says he's got evidence about a double murder or something, wants to crush the guy with it . . . But we're gonna take this to the court. I'll fight this straight and clean.'

Elise covered her mouth with her hand. Her father saw her shock.

'Your friend Sandile isn't what he seems.'

'Nothing is what it seems,' she murmured.

Van Rensburg pushed his plate away and leaned forward on his elbows, resting his chin on his folded hands. 'I'll ring the lawyers first thing tomorrow and we can start from there.'

Elise nodded. She agreed that consulting a lawyer should be the first step. 'OK, if that's what you want, but this time I'm coming with you.'

'Ja,' he said, 'that's what I want.'

Her father had taken such a blow that day there was little left to be kicked out of him. He said nothing more. The calm that had settled around them was the calm of exhaustion, like the stillness that follows an earthquake. Within it they could speak of things they'd never raised with each other before. It was like an ending. Elise was sad beyond description, sad beyond weeping.

The greatest pain for Elise she would from now on associate with Sandile. Desire was a terrible thing, she thought, so fierce, so obliterating. Desire took over, jumped into the driver's seat and revved you off at high speed, regardless of whether or not its object was worth all this heat. It should come as no surprise when a desired one could not stand up to the intensity of the desiring of them. Sandile had failed miserably. He had ambushed, completely sabotaged her life and shown her up for the fool she was. Perhaps that had been his game all along. Elise began to believe that he'd led her on simply to use her. His cleverness, all his insight – it wasn't for her. He hadn't delved into her soul for the pleasure and the intimacy of discovering the innermost workings of her; he'd done it for himelf. She felt violated, cheated, betrayed. She could convey none of this to her father. To him she'd been a co-conspirator, certainly foolish, but a traitor nevertheless. Her redemption lay in the battle they would begin tomorrow.

Elise raised her eyes and saw her father looking at her. She realised all at once how much he loved her and how poorly she had understood this, how fickle had been her will to understand. She'd always expected so much of him that he was unable, simply not equipped, to give. She had been coldly unforgiving about all the things he never said and didn't do, instead of accepting what was given as everything he had.

That thought made her ashamed. Elise stood up and went over to him, put her arms round him and held him. He buried his face in the crook of her arm like a child.

THIRTY FOUR

It was still early, only nine o'clock, when the Van Rensburgs retreated to their beds. Elise lay awake a long time and so did her father, the two of them restlessly sleepless in their respective rooms. Something, some sound, startled Elise some time around midnight. She slipped out of bed to go and see what the noise was. Pulling one of Dawie's old rugby shirts over her head she had opened the door that led from her bedroom into the garden and stepped outside. She looked up at the familiar, immovable black shoulders of the mountains huddled around the valley. The sky was pitch black and full of stars. The night was hot and bright, with a waxing moon.

The stillness was shattered by the clatter of dogs barking. Elise followed the stoep round to where she could look down the side of the house. There was no one there. Nothing to be seen. The dogs quietened down. Her father must have gone for one of his walks. Good, she thought, that would clear his head. The wind fluttered lightly against her skin. She took a deep breath of the scented night air, then padded back to her room and climbed into the warmth of her bed. She didn't sleep immediately but lay awake for a while, wrapped in the quiet of the house. After a time she must have dozed into sleep, for when she woke the sky was light.

Sandile had lain awake a long time too, listening to the night. He drifted in, but mostly out of sleep. He dreamed about losing the land, losing everything, and about Elise. He imagined her asleep in the arms of her husband-to-be. He thought of what that must be like – to fall asleep next to her – wondered what the scent of her naked was, longed to feel the

377

warm, still curve of her body sleeping next to him. After today it was unlikely he ever would, a fact which heightened his desire. And yet her own desire had been so strong. No, he thought bitterly, after today she would revert to the familiar, to the acceptable. He had only himself to blame.

Sandile opened his eyes and stared up at the hazy shadows of the rafters above him. There was something powerful between them, between him and Elise. She'd almost let herself go with it. Now she must be thinking that she was right not to have trusted him. He remembered the way she had first kissed him and then how she'd slammed the brakes on him. The way she looked at him sometimes, that distant smile. Sometimes she felt miles away even when she was there with him. He put his hands over his face and cursed himself for not having told her, cursed Fatima Mamdoo for having jumped the gun and cursed fate for Elise's spellbinding ways.

Sandile turned over, yanking the blankets so violently they fell right over him and off the bed. He swung his feet to the floor. 'Ugh! Get out of my head!' he muttered, then pulled the blankets over him again and lay back against the soft pillow.

Some time in the darkest hours he woke in a sweat and found himself sitting straight up in his bed. Outside, somewhere in the distance, dogs were barking. Sandile listened carefully, every sense alert. After a while the barks turned to growls, then stopped, and he sank down into his bed again. The dogs were as restless and anxious as everyone else. He slipped back into sleep.

Ina tossed and turned in her bed, tossing and turning the events of the day, of the week, over and over in her mind. She needed someone to help her through this marsh, this bog of her relationship with Taylor, but Elise was too preoccupied – she had no one to turn to except Taylor himself. Ina sat up. Suddenly she made a decision. She got out of bed, dressed and slipped quietly out of the house. The sound of her car starting seemed to her like the rattle of a gun going off. She waited, breathing hard, but no lights came on in the house. No one stirred.

It was well after midnight. Everything was dark; there were no lights on anywhere in the valley. Ina felt as if she was driving through the opening sequence of a horror movie. She decided not to think like that and drove faster. Leaves tumbled down like great snowflakes in the headlights. The narrow, single-track gravel road of her driveway climbed steeply into a tunnel of trees ahead of her. She could have driven this road with her eyes closed, but tonight it seemed frighteningly unfamiliar. She switched on the radio and hummed along to the music. Her heart was racing.

Ina wasn't sure she was doing the right thing. Everything she knew about him told her that this was wrong, but she badly wanted to see him and so she had to go. When she arrived at the entrance to Die Uitkyk she stood for a moment before she found the courage to press the buzzer at the gate. When at last she did, there was no reply. She buzzed again, this time for longer. Still no reply. Looking up through the trees she saw no lights shining from the house.

Suddenly Ina was angry, gripped by jealous thoughts. Then she clucked at how silly she was being. It was after one in the morning and she had begun to feel foolish. She opened the car door, ready to climb in. A light came on in the house. She ran back to press the button again and this time Taylor's voice barked back through the speaker.

'Who is it?'

She jumped. He sounded like a different person. Leaning forward she spoke tentatively into the microphone. 'It's me.'

Silence from the other end of the line. Ina panicked and started babbling. 'I hope you don't mind, I just wanted to see you.'

'This isn't . . . it's just a bad time. Why didn't you phone or something?'

Ina was alone outside in the pitch darkness, suddenly frightened. His tone was icy. 'Ag, it doesn't matter . . .'

'No. You're here. You must come in.' Suddenly he was gentler.

The gate began to slide soundlessly open. 'I was asleep, but come in. It will be nice to see you.'

Ina walked away from the speaker, cursing herself. This was a bad idea, stupid and impulsive, and it was having an effect that was not at all what she'd intended.

As the car rolled up the drive Ina noticed one of the outbuildings was streaming with light; the next second it was in darkness again. He was nowhere in sight as she approached. The mood that had driven her here was gone – she wished she was home in her own bed.

Alan met her on the step. His hair was combed back and he wore a long paisley silk dressing gown. Ina started blithering the second she saw him. 'I really just wanted to see you, I didn't meant to interrupt or anything, I'm so sorry, I just thought –'

Taylor gripped both her shoulders and looked at her sternly. 'Don't be silly. But you shouldn't be prowling around the roads at this hour. It could be dangerous. Next time, you phone me and I'll come to fetch you.'

Ina smiled. He kissed her and they went inside.

He was wide awake, a little hyper, but also more distant than ever. As they moved through the house he switched off all the lights. In the bedroom Ina slipped off her gown and stood by the bed, naked. Taylor looked at her for a moment, the sides of his mouth twitching, as if he was feeling some discomfort. The bed was fully made up, the covers untouched.

'I thought you said you were sleeping,' Ina remarked, a little peevishly.

'No, I was –' Taylor broke off to rub his delicate fingers against his forehead. 'I was working. Got a lot on my mind, what with this land claim and everything.'

He turned away, towards his dressing table. Ina felt like an idiot. She stood there watching him undress and then pulled back the sheets and climbed into bed.

Taylor was terribly careful and deliberate about the way he undressed, as if he was enacting a ritual. Everything had its place and its moment. First he took off his watch. It was a heavy, expensive-looking thing with a bright gold band. Sleek and solid and only slightly ostentatious. She'd noticed it before – it was impossible not to when his cuff slipped upwards on his arm. He laid the watch down on the dressing table, then took off the gown and hung it on the back of the door. Underneath he was wearing tartan flannel pyjamas.

When he got into bed his manner was formal. He kissed Ina on the cheek, but he didn't want to make love, and quietly but firmly rejected her advance. Ina felt terrible. 'You don't like surprises,' she said, pulling away.

'No, I don't like surprises.'

Ina curled up away from him. It was a long while before sleep obliterated her deep mortification.

Elise woke early. She couldn't remember falling asleep, but she could remember restless, terrible dreams. She pulled on some clothes and went to make coffee. It was nearly time to wake her father for his breakfast, but she didn't have the strength to prepare it. She needed a rest, a proper sleep, so badly. For some time she sat at the table drinking coffee. The hands of the clock shuddered round, the heavy tick-tock the only noise in the house. There was no sound from her father's room. Elise stood up and went to pour another cup of coffee – she would take it to him and wake him up.

She walked through the house towards his room. She knocked on the door but received no reply. Quickly she turned the handle. 'Pa . . .?'

His bed was dishevelled, but her father was not in it. Panic rose in her. He was up already, but what was he doing, where was he? The doors that led from his bedroom into the garden were open, the curtains billowing loosely inward. There was something lying on the grass outside. Elise pushed through the curtains and then she saw him.

The coffee cup flew from her hand, flinging hot brown liquid in a great arc along the wall. Elise ran to him. As she approached she slowed down – everything slowed down. Her father was lying on the ground, his skin a ghastly white, like wax, and spattered with blood. Blood soaked his pyjamas.

His neck had been gashed wide open by the long brutal slash of a blade. He had fallen helplessly, his body crumpled and twisted. Her first thought was to pick him up and she tried to. Putting her arms around him, she tried to lift him, to move him so that he could lie comfortably. But he was so heavy, she never imagined he could be so heavy, and she was shaking so much and the blood was so slippery she couldn't hold him. Blood had soaked into the rugby jersey she was wearing. It spattered her hair and covered her hands. The sweet, putrid smell of it was overwhelming.

All this time Elise was talking to him, quietly, urgently, pleading with him, begging him not to die, telling him everything would be all right. But it wasn't, couldn't ever be all right. He was dead. She knew he was dead. His head lolled hideously over her arm and she dropped him back on to the grass. Her hands went up to her own throat – the cut at his was horribly agape but she also saw that the back of his skull had been hacked wide open. His eyes were huge. Recorded there, in those eyes, was an image, a moment of realisation, of unimaginable horror. What had he seen, whose murderous face had he seen with those eyes?

Elise looked around frantically. She didn't know what to do with him or with herself. Everything was slowed down and speeded up all at once, like hallucination, like a nightmare, all sound and colour distorted. The buzz of flies was intolerable; they hovered round the slash in his skin, dancing at the edges of the drying and congealed blood that covered him. She tried to shoo them away, but they just came back. The smell was incredible. Elise would never be able to forget it, that smell of her father's blood drying on his skin.

She was acutely aware of being utterly alone. She felt absolutely vulnerable, totally exposed, but she didn't want to leave him either. She knelt down and straightened his head, pulled his arms down straight by his sides and untwisted his legs. Then she ran back into the house and found the phone. She was shaking so much that she dropped it as she dialled, but she picked it up again. The dial tone didn't come through immediately and she banged the thing, almost smashed it into the wall in her frustration. She dialled again. Then it rang and rang and rang.

The uniformed constable on duty at the station was sleeping deeply and snoring like a motorbike. It was a weekday morning, no trouble expected till Friday, pay day on the farms. Friday and Saturday nights there'd be several police-men on duty and more than several drunks in the cells by Sunday lunchtime. But the night Van Rensburg was murdered Officer Pelser was alone in the office at Fransmans-dorp. The telephone rang on and on with an ear-shattering warble. Pelser slept on, but eventually it began to penetrate his slumber and after a time the sound reached him. He sat bolt upright, his wide eyes clocking their surroundings and coming up blank for a moment. Then he went for the phone.

Pelser was no lightfoot: like most of the white guys from those parts he had a belly that boasted a history of steak and pap and sous in all-you-can-eat quantities with as much beer as was needed to wash it down. He moved sluggishly, as one might expect from a chubby chap still thick with sleep. Elise's terrified pleas cut through his grogginess like a blowtorch through lead.

'Please come! Quickly! My father's been attacked. He's . . . dead.'

To Elise the words fell like a stone, like the deep beat of a gong. The man's voice flew back at her down the wire. 'Miss, who – where are you?'

'Rustenvrede. Come! Quickly, please come quickly!'

The policeman was irritatingly dopey. 'Now calm down please, miss. Where are you calling from?'

'Rust-en-vrede! Get up here, now! I'm all alone!'

Pelser shook his head hard after he'd put the phone down. The morning air was chilly. Pale yellow light filtered through the shutters, and the charge office had a greenish cast from the fluorescent strips that buzzed dully on the ceiling. The clock over the door said it was just after five o'clock. I must be awake, Pelser thought to himself. Yet the phone call was unreal. There had never been a murder in Fransmansvallei, not in living memory at any rate. He shook his head a second time, trying to dislodge the last cobwebs of sleep from his brain.

He lifted the handset again and dialled Sergeant Kakana's number. Johnny picked up straight away.

'Sergeant, Pelser here, sir,' he panted. 'I just received an emergency call from Rustenvrede. I think it was Elise van Rensburg. She says her father's dead.'

Silence from the other end of the line.

'Sergeant?'

Johnny's voice came through clearly and calmly a beat later. 'Come and fetch me now. We'll radio out on the way over.'

Pelser was signing off when he heard the line go dead. He put the handset down thoughtfully, picked up his hat, pushed open the back door and let it slam behind him.

Johnny flipped from sleeping to awake in an instant. The truth was he never slept very well – he was always half anxious, half alert. This was the kind of moment he'd waited all his career for. Something big had really happened. Johnny checked his watch. The time was getting on for half past five. Normally he'd be up at six and in the office by seven, same as everyone else in the valley. Right now most people would still be asleep. Good, he thought, that meant a head start. Anyone they saw up and about would certainly be up to no good.

Johnny punched out Daan's cellphone number straight away. The recorded message answered: 'Hi, you've reached Daan –'

'Typical! What's the point in having the bloody thing?' Johnny muttered angrily as he dialled Komweer and then waited. They guy was supposed to be on call twenty-four hours a day. The telephone at Komweer rang and rang and rang.

Johnny tugged on his pants and then the shirt of his uniform as the ringing tone droned in his ear. He pictured the Du Toits, all of them fast asleep and oblivious; it summed up their snug lives. He sighed as he buttoned up his jacket. This was going to take a while, he thought, but he wasn't going to stick around. If Daan didn't pick up by the time Pelser arrived it was tough shit. Du Toit could find out about everything by watching the news.

It was Mrs Du Toit who finally picked up the phone. She'd lain awake a while, listening, waiting for Ina or Daan or perhaps Mabel to pick it up, but no one did. So the old lady swung her thin frail legs to the floor and slid her feet into the slippers she'd stepped out of the night before. Madame creaked shakily through the shadowy house to the kitchen. She moved as fast as she could, which was painfully, frustratingly slowly. The insistent ringing was giving her a headache and so her tone was distinctly irritable when at last she answered the phone with her customary 'Fransmansvallei 42235, good morning!'

It had been ten minutes, more, since Elise had called the police. Why wasn't anyone coming? She ran into the kitchen and redialled the number. This time someone picked up almost immediately. She didn't know if the voice was familiar or strange; she couldn't listen, only speak in a voice that didn't feel like her own. She felt as if she were suspended on the ceiling looking down from a nightmare at herself in a nightmare. The house was oppressive, the walls bent in towards her; everything familiar seemed dangerous. She dropped the handset.

For a long time Elise stood on the stoep, pacing up and down, not daring to go near him, starting at every noise, waiting for the sound of cars, but none came. The dogs gathered round her father, sniffing his body in bewilderment. She screamed at them to get away and they came whimpering to her feet. She couldn't stand the noise, she couldn't stand to be alone. Elise turned and ran.

She ran away from the house, away from the horror. She needed to be near someone, needed to know that she was safe.

She wanted to get into her car and drive to Komweer, but her bakkie was up at the compound and she couldn't bear to go back in the house, so she ran barefoot down the drive towards the road, all the dogs running with her. Like her, none of them made a sound. When she saw Sandile, Elise screamed, her voice shattering the early-morning quiet and echoing off the mountains.

Sandile had risen early. Surrendering to sleeplessness he'd dressed and gone out for a walk, knowing there would be no one around to see him for at least another hour or so. He'd walked for some time, absorbed in thoughts of this new and more difficult situation. The only solution, he decided, was to go to Cape Town and sit it out there until the Land Claims Court settled the matter. He was on his way back to the compound, cutting across the western orchard and walking up the road that led to the house, when Elise came running down the track towards him. She was barefoot and wearing only a rugby shirt that was covered in dirt – no, it looked like blood. Her scream inspired instant fear. Something was terribly wrong. She was covered in blood. Sandile broke into a run.

As he drew level with her Elise stretched out her arms and splayed her fingers, telling him to stop. There was blood on her clothes, on her face, sticking to her hair. She tried to push him away, but he grabbed her arm.

'Help us, oh God, my dad's . . .' Her hand flew to cover her mouth as if she couldn't let the words out.

'What? What happened?'

Elise couldn't speak. Her legs sagged and she fell to the ground, her knees hitting stones and dirt. Sandile pulled her up, trying to hold her, but her arms flailed against him. He was the one who had betrayed her.

'Don't! Don't touch me.'

Sandile didn't even hear her. He held on tightly, pushing his hand through her hair, pushing away blood to see if she was all right. Her body went slack, like a puppet. She was shaking so much that he had to hold her up.

'Pa, my pa, my pa . . .'

Sandile squeezed her to him. 'What's happened? What's happened?'

Elise began to cry. 'My father,' she said, 'my father is dead.'

As he raced over towards Rustenvrede, Daan had only two thoughts in his mind. Concern for Elise, a chill terror that something had happened to her, and the certainty that Van Rensburg's argument with the Mashiya boy had escalated out of control.

It was nearly half an hour after Elise's call came through before the police turned into the driveway of Rustenvrede. Daan hadn't bothered with his uniform; he'd just pulled on some shorts, grabbed a T-shirt and rushed out of the house. He took his brother's four-by-four and charged across the valley, steering dangerously with his right hand while with his left he dialled and redialled the number for Rustenvrede. But there was no response. Swinging into Skaduwee Lane Daan could see the dust trail from Johnny's van half a mile up ahead. He floored the accelerator and overtook Johnny just before the sharp bend. Daan waved the cellphone at him, but Johnny didn't wave back. Both his hands gripped the wheel and he drove as hard as the van would let him. Pelser was in the passenger seat, clutching on to the radio handset as if for dear life.

Daan skidded dangerously as he spun round into the driveway to Rustenvrede. Behind him Johnny had to swerve hard to avoid hitting him. In his rear-view mirror Daan saw a purple-faced Pelser yelling, probably begging Johnny to cut his speed. Daan told himself to calm down, to try to keep cool and get to the house in one piece.

When Johnny rang, he'd been half awake with a head full of cotton wool and the irritable sense that this so-called urgent call would turn out be yet another farmer wanting to teach yet another drunk worker a damn good lesson. But Johnny had said that Van was dead. It was like a bottle rocket going off in his face. His reaction was a whirlwind of panic and confusion and blind activity. His mother had almost fallen over trying to catch up to him, but he'd left her in a cloud of dust and stones in front of the house.

As Daan rattled up the dirt drive he was racking his brain to remember what Johnny had said about Elise. Was she all right? Why wasn't she picking up the phone now? But at that moment he caught sight of something on the road in the tunnel of poplars ahead of him. Two people in what looked like a struggle, or an embrace. Seconds later he realised it was her: Elise in the arms of Sandile Mashiya. He brought the Toyota to a skidding halt alongside them and leapt out on to the gravel. 'What the hell is going on here?'

Elise pulled away from Sandile and stood there, stunned, wild-looking. She had blood on her arms, on her hair; the shirt she was wearing was soaked with it. There was blood on Sandile too. Johnny Kakana took careful note of that, took careful note of everything from where he sat in the van with the engine idling. Sandile jerked his head up at Daan's thunderous approach. He put his hand out, palm down, fingers flat, indicating a need for calm.

Daan had no intention of calming down until someone explained to him what the hell was going on. He wrapped his arms round Elise and she pushed her face into his chest, her body brittle and taut and contorted. The mind has a vast capacity to absorb appalling pain, but it can't adjust instantly. It took Elise a while for her immediate surroundings to shift back into focus. It took a while for her to wake up again to the need for explanation and action.

Daan was peering at her, his face up close to hers, his eyes boring into hers, searching her face for a response. Elise finally registered the words.

'I was frantic. I've been calling and calling and there was no answer.'

Elise blinked. He looked hurt, as if he'd been overlooked. She pulled away, becoming shrill and angry. 'But you took so long. I waited in the house. I was all alone. I waited and waited, but no one came!'

The three of them were fixed with grief and anger and confusion. Daan, Elise and Sandile. Frozen in a bedraggled, bloody triangle. Johnny rolled down the window and listened to the voices carrying on the still morning air.

'Who could do such a thing, Daan? Why do such a thing?' She wasn't shrill any more, or hysterical. Her voice was bizarrely level and she stood in a strange stiff way, looking at him.

Daan just shook his head. 'Do you want someone to take you over to Komweer, or will you come with us?'

Elise shook her head – she didn't want to go anywhere now except home. 'I'll come with you.'

Daan nodded, then, jerking his chin in Sandile's direction, said, 'And you'd better come too.'

THIRTY FIVE

The dogs went into a frenzy of barking as they ran with the police vehicles, escorting them back up to the house. They jumped on Elise as she climbed down from the Du Toits' four-by-four, all of them yelping and whining with fear and confusion and awful agitation. Sandile hung back, trailing a short distance behind while Elise led Daan and the others through the house.

Elise didn't know how her feet put themselves one in front of the other. She felt as if she was sailing just above the ground. She was still barefoot and wearing only Dawie's ruined rugby shirt, the hem brushing her knees. For a moment, for one heart-piercing second, she imagined, she hoped, that she'd been wrong: that her father wasn't really dead, that he'd come striding across the lawn towards her, back from one of his dawn walks, smiling and with his arms reaching out for her.

But he was exactly as she'd left him, spread-eagled on the grass, his head thrown back covering the smashed bone and brains and his throat agape, a hideous flap of flesh, a mess of congealing blood. They all froze with shock at the sight. A strange, haunting calm settled on them as the weight of what had happened sank in. The only sounds were the grating hum of the flies and Elise's teeth chattering as she shivered. She didn't move from her father's side. Her eyes were locked on his deathly stare.

Daan was shaken to the core. This was his indomitable future father-in-law – a pathetic, stinking hulk of lifeless flesh. It was ghastly. Daan struggled to recover his senses. He looked up at Elise who was still staring down at her father's body, a strange distance in her eyes. He took hold of her arm. 'Elise, you should go inside.'

Elise pulled her elbow away from Daan's grip. 'I'm fine, Daan, I don't need looking after. But he does.'

All four men stared at her, wondering if they'd understood her correctly.

'We should cover him with something.'

'Sweetie, I want you to go inside. Mashiya, will you –'

Daan turned towards Sandile, about to ask him to fetch his mother so that she could look after Elise, but for the first time he saw the blood on Sandile's clothes. He stopped, thinking for a moment.

'Constable, you go and fetch Mama Mashiya. Johnny, take Elise inside and I want Mashiya to go with you. Don't let him out of your sight.'

Pelser trudged off obediently, only too happy to be sent away. He had never seen a dead body and the condition of this one had left him shaking with fright and nausea. Just before he reached the van he realised he could go no further. He leaned over and vomited into the flowerbeds.

Elise went inside, into her father's room, through the doors that he must have opened in the night. Johnny and Sandile followed silently. Johnny went straight to the phone and contacted the station. Sandile leaned against the wardrobe, his arms folded across his chest and his eyes on Elise as she yanked the bedcover off Van Rensburg's bed.

She strode out of the house with the coverlet bundled up in her arms. There was purpose about her now. Her body's emotional anaesthetic was working. Just being aware of that made her feel a little heroic. Everything had calmed down to manageable, even the unbearable sadness. She perceived everyone and every moment incredibly acutely and it seemed that there was infinite time in which to react and to deal with what had happened.

She knelt down beside her father on the grass. She put the index and middle fingers of her right hand on to the strangely cool skin of his eyelids. She almost recoiled at the sensation –

it felt like the skin on raw chicken meat. Elise stayed very still, collecting herself. His eyes were terrifying. She wanted not to see that stare and yet somehow closing his eyes was like the final acknowledgement of his death, a complicit admission. So she did it. That was her goodbye. Then she covered him with the duvet and walked back inside.

Daan was so shocked by the morning's events he could hardly figure out how to work his phone, let alone who to call. But he managed to pull himself together sufficiently to dial the regional SAPS headquarters in Paarl. The Area Commissioner was not around, but he was given the cell-phone number of Captain Kriek, the head of Murder and Robbery. Kriek said he'd get one of his men down as soon as possible.

Ina was woken by the sound of a telephone ringing. She sat up, pulling the covers over her as Taylor got out of bed to answer it. His footsteps echoed through the large house as he went to pick it up in the library. Ina leaned back against the pillows and looked out at the mountains in the early-morning sunshine. What a strange night it had been. They'd slept together for the first time and they hadn't even made love. Taylor had jumped her everywhere except in his own bed. Ina really didn't know what to make of him. Nevertheless she smiled. She was there, in his room; things were slowly working out. She felt better for the sleep.

When he came back into the bedroom a minute later Ina was up and dressing. He stood in the doorway, watching her. His expression was severe.

'I want to get back home before anyone notices I'm not there,' she said defensively, but she had misinterpreted his look.

'Your family are up already,' he said coolly.

Ina looked up sharply from buckling her shoes. Taylor frowned. 'That was your mother. It wasn't easy to under-stand – she's in a blind panic from the sound of her. Anyway, it seems something has happened at the Van Rensburgs'. Your brother was called out at the crack of dawn and rushed over there, but your mother doesn't seem to be able to raise anyone on the telephone. Of course, when she went to your room and found you not there, she almost passed out.'

Taylor's tone was as smooth as ice. Ina stood up, alarmed. 'It's all right, I told her you were here with me,' he added.

Ina bit her lip. 'I think we'd better go over there.'

Taylor put his hand on her arm as she walked towards the door. 'Let's telephone first.'

Ina paced the floorboards while Taylor dialled Rustenvrede. The phone was engaged. He tried several times – same thing. Ina's anxiety level was about to go through the roof. The awful prospect of explaining things to her mother combined with the growing strangeness of events around Rustenvrede were stirring her up like a food mixer in overdrive.

Taylor put the phone down. 'No luck. I think we ought to go over. I'll get dressed.'

Taylor emerged from the bedroom, immaculately dressed, five minutes later. By that time Ina had bitten nearly all her nails down to the quick. On their way down to the shed where the cars were parked, Taylor paused abruptly. Ina looked round at him quizzically.

'There's something I need to take care of, quickly. Why don't you go on ahead?'

Ina looked round, then shook her head vehemently. 'I won't go alone.'

Taylor stared at her, apparently frozen with indecision for a moment. Then he smiled understandingly, took Ina's arm and led her to his car. They set off down the drive, passing Lettie who was walking up to the house. Ina waved. Taylor clicked his tongue irritably.

'What's wrong?' Ina asked.

'Oh, it's nothing, just something I forgot to mention to the girl. Not to worry, I'll deal with it later.'

It wasn't long before Pelser reappeared at Rustenvrede. He brought Mama into Van Rensburg's room. Johnny had closed the curtains, so as to obscure the view of the scene outside. Mama was devastated. She went straight to Elise, who was sitting on the edge of the bed, hunched up and looking distractedly towards the billowing curtains. Mama sat down next to her and put her arms round her. Elise began to cry again, because Mama was crying. The two women held on to one another like that for some time.

Sandile hovered in the doorway, watching them. They barely noticed him in the shadowy room. Johnny was a few feet away on the other side of the curtains. After a while Mama stopped crying and pulled away from the embrace. She looked at Elise, at her wild hair and her eyes bright with tears. 'I must fetch you some clothes.' Mama stood up.

Sandile caught Elise's eye, just for a moment, while they were alone in the room. It was impossible to know what she felt and hopeless to try to reach her.

Mama came back a minute later, carrying jeans and a sweatshirt. Elise pulled the jeans over her goose-pimply legs. For some reason the goose-pimples struck her as fascinating – she stared at them as she slowly yanked up the legs of her trousers. Mama helped her to pull off the bloody rugby shirt. Elise felt like a little girl being undressed, her arms going floppy as the shirt was rolled off them.

For a moment, before she pulled the sweatshirt down over her head, Elise's naked back was exposed. She looked so slender, her shoulder blades angular and milky white. Sandile didn't look away. The extreme incivility of what had occurred stripped all politeness – there was no modesty or civility. Elise had been flayed down to the rawest, most vulnerable state. The awfulness and intensity of it were so sharp Sandile wanted to go to her, to be able to hold and protect her. His mother saw him staring. She clucked at him, tutting in disgust, and Sandile looked away.

Outside there were people everywhere. Panic, horror and confusion prevailed. All ten constables from the valley had arrived, bringing their dogs for good measure. They swarmed all over the place, fascinated and appalled. Daan clicked off his phone and turned to Johnny. 'It's gonna be a while before the Murder and Robbery guys get here.'

Johnny calculated about three hours. It would take about that long to get a team assembled, give orders and directions and then some time for the drive. They wouldn't dawdle. This was the kind of case that got the highest priority: killing a white farmer was second only to killing a white cop. All stops would be pulled out.

'Anyway, I think we can have this sorted out by the time they get here,' Daan muttered. He was tucking his phone into the pouch on his belt.

Johnny glanced away sharply, a touch irritated at Daan's cocky assumption that this mess had a neat solution. 'Have we even got a suspect?'

'Oh, please.'

Johnny nodded thoughtfully. He had already jumped to the same conclusion, but some instinct told him it was too easy. It wasn't the kind of solution Sandile went for. At least not the Sandile he'd known. Then again, the file told a different story. Johnny hadn't told anyone but Taylor about the file. Now he wondered if perhaps that was a mistake. Perhaps he should have told everyone. Perhaps exile had made Sandile a killer.

Daan pulled back the curtains. Sandile looked up at the policemen who were staring in at him. Daan jerked his head in the direction of the garden, indicating for Sandile to step outside, which he did. Sandile had a pretty good idea of what they were thinking – it had begun to dawn on him much earlier, when they were down on the road.

His boots had left a track of soft clay mud, leading all the way from the garden into the house. Daan pointed down at the footprints on the stoep. 'You been out in the orchards this morning?'

Sandile looked Daan coolly in the eye. 'Uh-huh.'

'Wasn't it early for a stroll?'

Sandile shrugged, responding quietly and matter-of-factly. 'I couldn't sleep, so I got up and went for a walk and it just happened to be this morning.'

'Do I recall seeing a panga up at your house yesterday?' Johnny asked.

Sandile raised an eyebrow. He said nothing, but turned to meet Xolile's gaze.

'Refresh my memory please,' Johnny insisted.

'There must be ten pangas up in the compound. Everybody has one. There are probably a couple in this house too.'

'Perhaps you could show me where *your* panga is.'

'You saw it yesterday – go look for yourself.'

Daan was tired of the to and fro. 'Show us. Now.'

Sandile shifted his gaze back to Daan, who was clearly overwrought. He understood their logic and he knew they had a job to do, but he didn't jump when told, he never had, especially not for policemen. However it was far simpler to show them the knife and get them off his back than it was to string this thing out as he knew he could.

He capitulated. 'All right. Come.'

All seven police vehicles from the local and the neighbouring stations were out by this time, jamming up the yard. The scene looked chaotic when Ina and Taylor pulled up at Rustenvrede. They caught sight of Daan in the Du Toits' four-by-four, taking off up the hill to the compound. Constable Pelser approached them, his hand out indicating they should stop. Taylor's window hummed down and he leaned out to talk to the cop. Ina was filled with dread. Whatever had happened it was terrible. She gripped on to the leather seat, bracing herself for the news.

Pelser stooped and stared into the car. 'I'm very sorry, sir, but I can't permit you to stop here. This area is a crime scene. We've got orders to seal it off.'

Taylor glanced at the pandemonium of dogs and cops in all directions. 'Doesn't look like you've done a very good job, does it?'

'Sir?'

'I'm a neighbour and Ina, as you know, is a very close friend of the Van Rensburgs. I hardly think we're going to get in the way.'

Ina couldn't stand the waiting. She leaned across Taylor and demanded to know what had happened.

Pelser swallowed hard. He looked back at the house and then into the car. 'It's Mr Van Rensburg, Ina. He's dead. Someone killed him.'

Ina jumped out of the car and ran towards the house. No one stopped her. No one even tried. She raced into the kitchen where Mama was making a huge pot of tea. Elise was sitting at the kitchen table. She looked up at her friend in the doorway. Ina's eyes welled up with tears. She shook her head, but Elise nodded back. It was true.

Sandile slammed the door of Daan's jeep and marched over to the side of the house where the panga always stood against the wall by the woodpile. But it was gone. All eyes followed his. There was nothing there.

Daan folded his arms and stood with his legs planted firmly apart. 'Well, where is it?'

Sandile sat down on the log stack. 'I don't know, do you?' He glared at Johnny accusingly.

Johnny cocked his head and responded angrily, 'Why would I know?'

'What's your story, Mashiya?' Daan demanded, sounding more pleased with himself by the minute.

'I haven't the faintest idea. It was there last night and now it's gone. What can I tell you? Do you want me to lie?' Sandile's heart sank. This was starting to look like very bad news.

Daan combed the compound while Johnny searched inside the house and Sandile sat with his head in his hands and his eyes closed. He longed to sleep, with total abandon, dreamlessly and peacefully for as long as it took to restore himself.

Daan and Johnny regrouped at the car. Both shook their heads – they had found nothing. By now Ben Mashiya, Jacob and Vuyo and their families were up and coming out to see what was happening. Daan was oblivious, counting off his thoughts against his fingers.

'Mashiya threatens to kill Van. Yesterday. In front of your very eyes. Last night Van Rensburg has a close encounter with a long blade. Today we're hauling the body out of here and Mashiya's panga is gone, unaccountably vanished! One plus one makes . . . a prime suspect.'

Johnny chewed his fingernail. He wasn't so sure. 'I – think it's a little hasty. Why don't we wait for the Murder and Robbery guys?'

Daan didn't take kindly to this advice. 'I know my job, Sergeant. Do I have to remind you of yours?'

'No, sir.'

Nevertheless Johnny had touched a nerve. Daan ran through the checklist again. 'Let's just think it through. The panga is missing. He has no explanation for its disappearance. It's pretty safe to presume the panga was used in the murder. Secondly, there's the circumstances – please, I don't have to explain that. Third, he's got blood all over his clothes. What are we waiting for?'

Johnny started to speak. He wanted to point out that Daan had blood on him too; it was obvious why – they'd both been all over Elise. But Daan was on a roll. He was convinced Sandile was the murderer.

'Why are you quibbling? He's obviously a suspect . . .'

Johnny couldn't argue with that. He finished the sentence for Daan, as he was expected to do. 'We *have* to arrest him.'

The words bounced off Sandile like hailstones bouncing off stone. 'I should warn you that anything you may say . . . ' He didn't move. He was immobilised by the speed and strangeness of events. It felt as if he was the static axis at the centre of a whirl of craziness.

Daan very deliberately took the handcuffs from his belt, clicking them open one by one. Sandile's eyes darkened, but he was icily calm. 'That won't be necessary.'

Daan smirked at him. 'I think necessity is for me to decide.'

Ben Mashiya was shaking his head. It was too much, too many blows in too rapid succession. 'No! It's not him. I'm telling you. He didn't do anything.'

He brought his hands down on Daan's arm, his fingers digging into skin. Daan clenched his jaw and tried to shake the old man off. It was Sandile's voice that reached Ben and calmed him.

'I *have* to go with them – we'll sort this out at the station. Please, Father, I promise you, I'll sort this out. OK?'

His father let go. The cuffs snapped closed on Sandile's wrists. Sandile raised his eyes to look at Johnny. 'So, things have gone your way at last, hey, Xolile?'

Johnny said nothing. He stared ahead, stony-faced.

THIRTY SIX

It wasn't long before dozens of people were crowded in and around Rustenvrede. Mrs Du Toit arrived not long after Ina and Alan Taylor, bringing a driver and help in the form of Mabel. Then Dominee Slabbert pitched up wearing a sports jacket over his flannel pyjamas, his massive frame shrunk with grief and shock. The Dominee murmured to Elise that he'd stopped off at De Jager's on his way and so it wasn't long before the whole of the dorp knew and the news fanned out over the valley. People milled round the house all day, shaken by their proximity to an event of such absolute horror, shocked by this reminder of their own mortality and stunned by loss.

The farm workers had arrived and, finding everything halted, were huddled in a solemn, silent group up by the sheds. Jacob went into the house and emerged a short while later with Elise at his side. Elise knew there'd been little love lost between Van Rensburg and his workers over the years, but she could see they were all upset. Even if Van was hated by most and tolerated by only a few, he was a large figure in this small community. The violence of his end was too much. It was Vuyo who encapsulated the general feeling when he said, 'We are so sorry, Miss Elise. No one deserves to go like that.'

Elise was grateful for their concern. She spoke quietly to the group. 'I think we've all had a terrible shock. You must all go home for the rest of today. We'll go back to work in the morning. If I am not with you then Jacob will be – he'll give the necessary instructions.'

Ina stayed close to Elise all morning, trying to make her

drink brandy, but the mere thought of it made Elise's stomach turn. Being even slightly drunk would be sickening. The sensation of it, the giddiness of it would make more of a mess of her head than it already was. So Ina downed every glass she poured for Elise and slowly subsided into a fuzzy incoherence as she sat by the phone fielding a stream of calls which didn't stop, didn't falter all morning. Alan Taylor, when he wasn't outside watching the police activity, sat quietly in a corner of the living room, his presence barely noticed by anyone.

The morning felt infinite. Elise tried to assemble the pattern of events of the night before, but moments came to her jumbled up. She sat in the living room, where Ina and Madame had moved her. People came and went from the room. Elise didn't seem to have to do anything. She was terribly conscious of her father's body on the lawn and the police milling around outside. Inside it was like a strange party with the Dominee and Madame Du Toit as acting host and hostess, receiving visitors at the back door, despatching gardeners, ordering tea and closing up rooms. Madame explained quietly to the Dominee, who explained to Elise, that they would leave Van Rensburg's room for her to clean.

Meanwhile Mama Mashiya commanded the kitchen with Nolitha at her side. They dealt with the food and flowers that people delivered in person or sent with their workers. Elise told Mama several times that she shouldn't, that she should go home and look after her husband and family. Mama just shook her head sadly and set the kettle on to boil again, or dumped a trayful of teacups into boiling soapy water in the sink, washed them up, dried them and set them on the wide tray with fresh tea and more plates of biscuits for all the people and the police who kept coming by. In spite of her weariness, Mama Mashiya seemed to function twice as smoothly. She was the life-support machine, the vital organ, the crucial pulse. Mama was the single functioning mechanism in the great machine of the farm that had otherwise ground to a halt.

The Dominee was distraught. He had insisted on seeing the body of his friend and afterwards came into the living room and slumped on the sofa by Elise. She could see that he was pushing all his sadness inside. When she tried to talk to him he sat up, not listening to her comforting words, and told her that she had to be brave now. 'At times like this I find the best thing is to keep busy.'

He was telling himself, not her. He got up and fetched a cellphone and his notepad, then sat down next to her again. 'Let's think about the funeral. There is always so much to arrange . . .' And with that he wrote the numeral one at the top of the page, with a firm full stop next to it, and turned to Elise.

Elise was willing to be drawn into his busy-therapy. Though her mind was slow, she would rather it was turned to lists than loss. 'The date,' she said.

'Yes. Now that will depend on the post-mortem, of course. So, number one, check with police re funeral date!' And he wrote it out as he spoke.

After the initial, numbing shock of the arrest Sandile had bounced around on the back bench of the speeding van, simmering with frustration. His eyes were fixed, reflecting the trees flashing past as the van raced down Skaduwee Lane towards the dorp. The ancient towering gum trees were in flower, lining the road where the dirt track curved away from the folded feet of the mountains and towards the dorp.

The morning had been so strange, so unreal, he had the feeling that he was half present in a dream gone out of control. He was furious with himself for having sunk so deep into this mire of tangled relationships on Rustenvrede, furious for not being more vigilant about the people around him, for not lying low until the land claim was settled. He'd relaxed, because he was happy. He'd begun to expand into his new life and his new identity in the valley. But it was too soon for a place like this. He'd known that all along, yet he'd blundered on anyway, lulled by comfort and energised by happiness.

He was too preoccupied to even feel the handcuffs chafing against his wrist. He knew he had to reach Simon Siluma. They had to let him phone as soon as they got to the station. Siluma and Karel Smit would help him sort through the mess – they'd run circles round clowns like Du Toit and Xolile.

There was a tongue-crinkling bitterness in Sandile's mouth. He was inured to setbacks; his life had vaccinated him against the shock of them. Until he came back to the Cape he had counted on them. But since he'd come home he wasn't expecting any serious trouble. He really was totally confident that everything was going to go his way. Maybe that was why he'd been so careless – about Elise, about losing his temper with Van Rensburg only yesterday. Once he'd found his family and settled back into the rhythm of the farm he'd been soothed into a sense that things were going to be all right, that this was the start of one long happy ending. Still, Sandile thought, gritting his teeth, he would come through, like so often before. It would work out in the end as long as he kept his cool. He felt numb, solid and numb.

When they got to the station Sandile immediately asked for the telephone. Johnny baulked; his shoulders and neck jerked slightly backwards as he considered the request. Daan glanced over at Johnny and shook his head.

'What for?' Johnny wanted to know.

'To call my lawyer. I think I'm entitled to that.'

Of course Sandile would have someone to represent him. Daan turned away and went to his desk. Johnny shrugged. 'Sure.' He pulled an old black dial phone from under the charge counter and put it down in front of Sandile with a clang.

Sandile dialled Simon's number. Christmas was approaching and Parliament was already in recess. Simon might be back in Durban, or Pretoria, or anywhere for all Sandile knew. The phone rang twice, then Simon picked up. Sandile actually laughed with relief. He sounded so happy that at first Simon wouldn't believe he was in custody.

'Howzit, broer! What's happening? Where are you?'

After Sandile had explained there was a long silence on the other end of the line, then a faint sound of chuckling which grew louder.

'What are you laughing at, broer?' Sandile asked, although he knew the answer. He even managed to smile at the absurdity of the situation. Both Daan and Johnny took note.

'Yusslike! I knew there was going to be trouble. What did I tell you, man! That whole scene was like a smouldering fuse –'

'Ja, ja, ha, ha! Now, how soon are you guys going to get me out of here?'

'I'll phone Karel Smit the second you put the phone down. Listen, have they charged you yet?'

'No, not yet.'

'OK. We'll handle this – just hang in there, hey? Now, lemme have a word with the cops.'

Sandile became deadly serious, his tone urgent. 'Listen, man, I really need your help. I have to get out of this place.'

'Yebo!'

'Yebo – gogo!'

Neither of them laughed. Sandile passed the phone to Du Toit, enjoying the change in Daan's expression as he realised he was talking to a Member of Parliament. Sandile saw Daan nodding, agreeing, assuring Simon that they were doing everything according to procedure and that they would inform him of any change in the status of the prisoner, wouldn't move him without telling them – yes, ja, ja, ja.

Daan collapsed into his chair, an old-fashioned beast upholstered in beige leatherette with four steel legs on wheels. He knew he could hold Sandile for forty-eight hours. After that he would have to release him or put him in front of a magistrate. Once the Murder and Robbery people assigned the docket to one of their investigators the matter would be out of Daan's hands. In the meantime there was procedure that he had to initiate and perhaps, in the course of that, he would elicit a confession. Shocked and strained as he was,

404

Daan knew that a confession would make Murder and Robbery's life easier and that had to look good on his file.

Johnny pulled out a chair for Sandile which looked as if it had started life in a school hall, then took a second one for himself, scraping its legs across the linoleum. Sandile looked round at the old fittings piled high with forms and files, at Daan's desk, which was a mess. He noticed how primly Johnny cleared a space for the charge sheet, flattening it out with the ball of his left palm before he clicked on his black Bic and started to write. The form began with all the usual particulars: name of accused, time and place and circumstances of arrrest, witnesses to the alleged crime, charge number, et cetera, et cetera. When at last they got to the statement section Daan got up and fetched himself a coffee. He didn't offer any to Johnny or Sandile and they both looked at the steaming mug with obvious longing. 'Right, then, let's get to it,' Daan snapped. Sandile told his story slowly and punchily in clear points that Xolile could keep up with.

He'd had trouble sleeping. He'd heard the dogs barking in the darkness some time before dawn. By the time the sky was lightening he decided to give up on sleep and go for a walk. He'd traversed the southeastern border of the farm, turned right to cut along the firebreak near the pass and was walking back through the pear orchards near the road when he met Elise, in obvious distress, her clothes soaked in blood, as she was running from the house. That was all.

They made him run three more times through the entire story of the land claim, Van Rensburg's threat to evict his family and finally the events of the previous night. Sandile kept his tone level, his head cool and his story honest and straight every time.

Daan pursed his lips. He kept running his fingers over his forehead. His agitation had been slowly, visibly increasing with each retelling. He didn't know how to take this further, didn't have much experience of interrogation at all, certainly not at this level. Sandile was unyielding – the story never changed – Daan was beginning to believe it. He sighed, stretching out his long body and stretching as far back as he could. He was tired out. He closed his eyes and banged the flat of his palm against the bridge of his nose.

'Look. You have to agree that, on the face of it, you *do* have a motive for the killing.'

Sandile leaned forward, furrowing his brow. Johnny remained bolt upright, not a crease in his uniform. Like a diligent student he scribbled every word Sandile spoke into his yellow CNA spiral-bound notebook – he had long ago used up the space allotted on the form. Sandile had noticed that, contrary to expectation, Xolile was the voice of caution, the voice of procedure, and Sandile appealed to that, planting seeds of doubt with which Johnny might later undermine Daan du Toit's apparent certainty.

'Yes. As you know, I even *threatened* to kill him,' he said very deliberately.

Daan sat up, too eagerly. His chair nearly overbalanced, but he managed to swing his weight back and the chair legs banged safely down against the linoleum.

Sandile looked him in the eye, continuing, 'But I *didn't* kill him. There is a difference.' He eyed Daan hard, his voice low as he punched out every word. 'What worries me is that you're so sure I did this. Meanwhile there's a murderer still out there. Doesn't that trouble you?'

Sandile was still sharp, still perfectly alert, by the mid-morning when both Johnny and Daan were flagging. The pauses between questions were getting longer and longer. They had no fancy tricks; they were ridiculously straightforward in their line of questioning. Sandile was comforted by that, knowing that the tenor of things would remain reasonable, that he had a lot of room in which to manoeuvre. He was sure that if he was simply polite and consistent they'd give up, either release him soon or at worst charge him, post bail and let him go. So he hung in. Daan's right leg was jumping, making the table shake. He held Sandile's gaze and Sandile could see the certainty wavering.

Johnny and Daan exchanged a knowing glance. Sandile was too clever for this to be over quickly. Johnny looked down at his watch. Daan understood it was time to get back to Rustenvrede to meet the Murder and Robbery people. Johnny closed his file and Daan stood up from his desk. 'Thank you, Mr Mashiya. We'll be back in a few hours to talk to you again.'

Then he signalled to Constable Reagon that the prisoner should be taken away.

Johnny could see that Daan scented opportunity. This was a chance for him to be noticed by the people who mattered. The people who could smooth his path to early retirement and get him out of the force on the terms he wanted. There was an opportunity here for Johnny as well, but he was wary of the direction things were taking. Nevertheless, he had to tell Daan about the file. If he didn't, he might be accused of withholding evidence. So Daan drove back to Rustenvrede listening to Johnny's story with rapt attention.

Neither Elise nor Mama registered Sandile's absence. No one told them of his arrest, until Daan got back to supervise the crime scene. It was around eleven when he and Johnny returned. Elise smiled as Daan entered the living room and Daan seemed pleased to see so many familiar faces. This was the perfect audience for the triumphant announcement he had to make.

'I expect you'll all be glad to know that I've arrested a suspect.'

It certainly got the attention he expected. All heads turned towards him and the ever-scowling Sergeant Kakana.

'Who?' prompted the Dominee.

'Sandile Mashiya.' Daan said this with a comfortable sigh and then sank down into Van Rensburg's chair, pushing his hair off his forehead with the air of one who deserves a good rest.

Elise stood up dazedly, her head shaking from side to side, eyes wide and full of distress. 'Why? Why have you arrested him?'

Daan was dismayed. Elise was insistent. 'He didn't do it. I'm telling you – he did not kill my father!' The atmosphere in the room switched from smug to horrified in a blink. No one said a word as Elise advanced hysterically on Daan.

Daan didn't know where this was coming from. He was tired and unable to conceal his irritation. 'Elise, what the hell are you talking about?'

'I *know* him. Sandile is not a murderer!'

She was so vehemently disbelieving, so distressed that everyone in the room had shut up and was staring at her, appalled and full of pity, but they were all astounded. Her face was already blotchy from crying, but fresh tears welled up in her eyes. She was muttering something, like a mantra, a prayer.

'No, no, no, no – it can't be, it can't be, please don't let it be, please don't let this be. It can't be!' Her voice rose to a shout as she ran from the room.

Madame Du Toit was speechless. After a moment of frozen shock Ina ran out after Elise. The Dominee closed his eyes and folded his hands, issuing a stern and heartfelt plea to his boss. 'What has this child done to deserve so much pain? Please, Lord, have mercy. She cannot bear any more.' The room echoed with nervous Amens.

Elise ran to her bedroom followed by Ina. She was so distraught she smashed her shoulder against the door post, then flung herself against the bed and curled up on the floor, like a frightened cat curling up beyond reach. Ina had never seen Elise break down like this – she was far, far gone. Raving and slapping the flat of her hand against her forehead. Ina shook with fear. She sat down on the duvet and took a numbing swig from the bottle of Klipdrift that she'd been trying to press on Elise.

Elise saw her through a haze of tears. 'I've been such a fool. I betrayed my father, I betrayed Daan, I betrayed everyone, and now look what's happened. Thank God, I just thank God he didn't know, he would never have forgiven me.'

Ina put down the bottle and tried to catch hold of Elise's hands, to stop her from slapping herself. 'Elise, you're just upset, you're talking nonsense . . . you're raving.'

Elise looked vaguely towards her. 'No, no, I'm not. Do you remember when we talked about pre-wedding jitters? I think that's what I've got, that's what I've got. I lost my head, Ina. I've done such a terrible, terrible thing.'

'No you haven't, sweetheart. You're just exhausted and emotional. You haven't done anything. Now why don't you get up, have some brandy and let us put you to bed? You're completely overwrought.' Ina knelt down on the floor in front of Elise and tried to grab hold of her flailing hands.

'I have, I have! How could he, how could I? I was so stupid.'

'Lise, what are you talking about?'

Elise looked up at her friend's kind, concerned, frightened face. She longed to unburden herself, longed to tell someone who might help her disentangle the mess of it all, might help her to come back to earth.

'Ina – I thought I was falling in love with him.'

Ina felt horribly drunk. She blinked slowly, trying to get a grip on what Elise was saying. 'Who?'

'With him. Sandile. It was mad. It was so – *lovely*. Like falling off a cliff and discovering I could fly. I just couldn't stop. I didn't *want* to fall to earth. And he led me on. He just led me on and on.'

Ina stared. Her lips were thin and her eyes dreadful. Elise reached out to touch her, to take hold of Ina's comforting arm and pull her back to her side, but Ina flinched as she stood up and stepped back, stepped away. Her mouth trembled and she was breathless with disgust when she spoke.

'How could you?'

Elise knew then that she was truly, awfully alone. If it was possible to drown in regret she would have done so in that moment – she was awash with it. She stood up, throwing up her hands. Harsh laughter caught in the back of her throat. 'You were the one who said he looked like an American movie star!'

'Shew! Do you know *no* shame?'

The words shot out of Ina like bullets. Elise couldn't believe this was happening. Ina turned sharply away. Elise levelled her voice, wanting to bring things back to normal, back into a manageable perspective. 'Ina, please –'

Ina swung round. Her long fingers flew, her palm slapped hard against Elise's face. 'Elise, this is South Africa. I mean it would be bad enough if this was a white, *any* white man, but . . . *him*. How could you?'

Elise was as furious now as Ina was disgusted and uncomprehending. 'What do you mean, *him*? You never had a problem with it when it was your brother screwing that black farm girl. You thought that was pretty funny, didn't you? That Wynand could be sweet on your maid. Don't pretend you've forgotten, Ina. It was you who told me and you were on his side when your mother sent the girl away!'

Ina brushed it off, her hand flicking up as if to push the memory away. But Elise wouldn't let it go. 'It's the same thing, Ina. You weren't disgusted then, but this is the same.'

Ina's eyes narrowed with scorn. Her tone was pure contempt. 'Of course it's not the same.'

Elise paused, fuming. She stared at this woman who was suddenly no longer a friend but a clawing, shrieking bigot. The monster that lurked in her had surfaced. 'You're right, Ina. It's not the same. That was about power. His power over her. He might as well have raped her!'

Ina's jaw swung up, as if she'd been struck. She spluttered as she fought to get words out. 'And you? Don't *you* think this is about power? Don't you realise that kaffir is getting back at you, at your dad? Don't you see that he's getting back at you, back at everyone, by . . . by . . . *fucking* you?'

The word seemed so strange, so terribly harsh on Ina's lips, not at all like it had sounded when they were half joking and half asleep that night a few weeks before. Something resonated in Elise. *Fear*. Part of her understood that buried deep in her was the same fear that had overwhelmed Ina. Part of her was scared that what Ina was saying was true, but she could hardly admit it to herself, let alone to Ina.

'He never *fucked* me.' Elise spat the word back.

Ina recoiled with disbelief, hissing with rage. 'Elise, you are right. You have betrayed your father – and everyone. I never would have thought you capable of this, of having an affair with the man who wants to take your land, who killed your own pa. I can only think you've lost your mind but I can't help you. I just pity you!'

She smiled cruelly, then spun on her heel and strode away, slamming the door so hard that it shook. Elise found that her legs no longer had the strength to hold her up. Her knees buckled and she sank slowly to the floor. Maybe she's right, Elise thought. Maybe they've all been right about him all along. After all, what reason has he really given me to trust him? He wants my land and he hated my father. He's always hated my father.

No one had heard them. Everyone outside that room was preoccupied with their own dramas. Johnny Kakana stood silently on the stoep, staring at the mound of blanket that covered Piet van Rensburg's body. He didn't realise that Alan Taylor had stepped out to join him. In fact he didn't notice Taylor at all until the man spoke.

'Death is the one great familiar in this land,' he intoned.

Johnny looked round sharply, wondering if this was another line from one of Taylor's poems. Taylor moved his mouth into the shape it so often assumed, the shape of a mirthless smile. 'This could be quite an opportunity for you, Kakana. Don't let it slip. It's amazing how opportunity falls into one's lap just like that, how one problem gets solved by another problem. The great danger is that you don't see it when it appears. Once you do, of course, the trick is not to balance too many balls in the air at once.'

Johnny looked as if he was thinking this over. In fact he was confused, as usual, by the riddles that Alan Taylor spoke.

Fortunately they were interrupted by Ina du Toit who burst out of the house and clung unhappily to Taylor, insisting that he take her home.

Madame Du Toit was in the kitchen, scolding Mabel, when Taylor brought Ina through. Ina couldn't speak. She leaned against him, stumbling as he steered her through.

'Oh!' cried Mrs Du Toit. 'What on earth is the matter here?'

'I'm going to take her home. She's completely over-exhausted, nothing a hot bath and a rest won't cure. But I don't think she should stay here any longer.'

Mrs Du Toit reached up to embrace her daughter, but jerked away when the stink of alcohol on Ina's breath hit her. Then the old lady leaned in again, her fingers digging into the flesh of her daughter's arms. 'You're drunk!' she hissed.

Ina pulled away from her mother and stumbled outside, almost tripping on the kitchen steps so that Taylor had to catch her. He seemed more amused than upset by her state. Mrs Du Toit couldn't look. She turned away, her hand covering her mouth as if to stop herself screaming.

Taylor had to pull his car over on Skaduwee Lane, giving way to a motorcade of police vehicles heading up towards Rusten-vrede. These were the guys from Paarl Murder and Robbery. And it was exactly as Johnny expected: Captain Kriek had put one of his best men on the case.

Inspector Stephan du Plessis, known to everyone as Dup, sprang out of his car and positively charged up to Daan, who was waiting to meet him. Dup was a big man, with a macho moustache and a manner to match. He was wearing neatly ironed khaki pants and a salmon-pink shirt tucked in at a tightly belted waist. Dup had clearly never spent much time in the slow lane. His eyes blazed manically out of a high forehead and he had reddish wavy hair which flew all over, suggesting that a part of him enjoyed flouting convention. He had brought a brace of detectives from his unit as well as a gaggle of forensics and logistics and photographic people.

Dup introduced himself and speedily explained every one of his guys to Daan, who in turn began politely introducing all his own men. But Dup wasn't interested in the Fransmansvallei constabulary. He had things to do.

'Ja, ja, ja. Time for that stuff later. Let's go. I want to see the body.'

Daan and Johnny jogged to keep up with Dup as he strode round the house. The sweet, sickening smell hit them as they reached the stoep.

Du Plessis swung away from the scene in disgust. 'Jeeesus Christ!' He shoved a cigarette in his mouth, lit up and dragged deeply.

Daan went up to him. 'I know. It's pretty upsetting,' he said kindly.

'Upsetting? It's a fucking *mess*! The place hasn't been properly sealed off, there are policemen all over . . . Look at them – touching everything, touching the doors and windows. My life! Just call your guys off. Call them all off!'

Daan did as he was told and Dup's men set to work immediately.

Dup smoked Texans. Healthwise that's probably the equivalent of spending your day sucking on the exhaust pipe of an old bus. He was big and macho and wired, always spoke with a cigarette locked in his mouth or trapped in the vicelike grip of powerful fingers. Dup pointed all the time with those fingers, stabbing at the air for emphasis.

Johnny Kakana needed no introductions. He'd recognised Du Plessis immediately as one of the Security policemen to whom he'd betrayed his friends all those years ago. It was Dup who'd shot Baasie Gxoyiya. Johnny knew it was only a matter of time before Dup made the connection.

Dup was ex-Koevoet and ex-Security Police. He came from the hard core of the bad old days. He'd got used to doing pretty much as he pleased and going anywhere he liked. Now he was chained to a desk and choked by rules. He was bored with Murder and Robbery and bored with the new South Africa – one of those guys who would never get over the trip of border duty, when the border was a war zone and anything went. It was unlikely he would ever really settle into civilian life. Every now and then he got a kick out of it, though, and now was one of those times.

Daan hovered at Du Plessis's shoulder, following him as he moved around the house barking instructions, occasionally flinging some question in Daan's direction. As they looked round the bedroom Dup couldn't believe that there was no sign of Van Rensburg reaching for a weapon of his own.

Daan cleared his throat and then confessed. 'Actually he didn't have any in the house.'

'What?' Dup was incredulous. A farmer without a gun was unheard of. 'This guy must have been a moffie – or mad.'

'No, I mean, I confiscated his guns.'

'You *what*?' Dup couldn't believe his ears.

'But he was threatening his workers,' Daan bleated.

'All the more reason for him to be armed. There was obviously trouble brewing.'

Daan was mortified, but Dup quickly forgave him as they went out to survey the garden. 'Ag, I wouldn't worry about it, Du Toit. A gun wouldn't have helped anyway. He didn't even see the killer. He was taken from behind. It would have been over in seconds. Look, see the way he's been hit? The guy never had a chance.'

Elise was slumped over her bed when Mama came into the room carrying a mug of warm milk sweetened with honey. She didn't react at all when Mama put a hand on her shoulder. 'Come, Elise. The doctor has arrived, and the ambulance.'

She raised her head wearily. 'Do you know they've arrested Sandile?'

Mama did know, but she showed no emotion. It was as if all feeling had been burned out of her. She just moved numbly from one moment to the next, one task to the next. 'Come, Elise. You must go outside.'

Elise walked out on to the stoep and saw how the ambulancemen came up at a jog, then stopped at the sight of the corpse, their habitual sense of urgency fading. There was clearly nothing that could be done. Dr De Klerk's knees shook and almost buckled when he saw Van Rensburg's body. He turned almost as white as the corpse. Dr De Klerk had known Van most of his life, knew the family perhaps more intimately than anyone after living through Evie's long illness with them. His voice shook as he stood over Van and quietly declared him dead.

Elise watched as they carried her father's body to the waiting ambulance. They had taken the bedcover off and draped a green-grey woollen blanket over him, covering his face. He was such a big man that when the blanket was over his head his feet and ankles were exposed. The young men struggling with the stretcher were strangers to Elise; they'd come from Paarl. There was no hospital and certainly no mortuary in Fransmansvallei.

For a wild moment she wanted to go with her father, wanted to say that she couldn't bear the idea of him travelling alone in the back of that ambulance. She felt that she ought to be with him on this final departure. But she didn't move, merely clutched harder at the warm mug that was cupped in her hands and watched as her father's body was loaded into the ambulance. All around were friends and farm workers, watching in stoical, respectful silence.

Later, when all the police were gone and there was no one left to make tea for, Mama began to prepare supper. She cooked what she always cooked that day of the week: roast chicken with roast potatoes and a can of mixed peas and carrots that she boiled up on the stove just before the bird came out of the oven. There was usually a fruit salad and cold custard to follow, but Mama didn't make that today.

Thirty Seven

The cell at the back of Fransmansdorp police station was a whitewashed, Dettol-soaked, pristine old place, the yard flooded with sunlight but cold behind the bars and inside the thick plaster walls. At least it was clean and he was reasonably well treated. Reagon brought him a bowl of stywe pap, which Sandile polished off hungrily.

He felt that now it was a matter of waiting the situation out. Having contacted Simon Siluma he was confident that he would be out soon, if not tomorrow then the next day. His view changed radically that very afternoon, with the arrival of Stephan du Plessis.

Dup was eager to get his hands on the suspect. He'd had a thorough briefing from Du Toit and Kakana and concluded they'd done well. He had been quick to work out the connection with Johnny Kakana. Nor did it take him long to realise that Sandile Mashiya was the one who got away all those years before. Mashiya was one of 'them'. He came from the other side and from the sound of it he'd been high up and in the heart of things. Dup was almost flexing his fists in anticipation.

On his arrival at the station he immediately asked whether the suspect had been fed. When Reagon said that he had, Dup rounded on the constable, clearly displeased.

'No more food. Nothing – not a morsel! Until I say so,' he bellowed. Then he swept through the yard and was let into the cell.

When Sandile stood up to greet his visitor his politeness was met with blunt antagonism. He was not a small man, but Dup was huge. Sandile knew that things were going to get ugly, fast.

'What have you got to tell me, kaffir?'

Sandile was more accustomed to hearing that word used ironically, in jest, than in earnest, as Dup used it. In the face of such hostility he had absolutely nothing to say.

Dup pulled a fresh packet of Texans from the breast pocket of his shirt, tapped it against his knee before opening it, then drew out a cigarette and lit up. 'I was just over at the farm you want to steal. Took a look at your work. Messy, I thought. Knives aren't really your style, are they?'

This man had 'danger' written all over him. All Sandile could do was try to keep the temperature from rising too suddenly and too fast. But Dup liked things hot. He overwhelmed Sandile with his sheer size and he used that, looming too close, stabbing too close with that always pointing index finger of his. 'You don't like me, do you, kaffir? Think you've seen me before, don't you? Well, you have – in your worst nightmares!'

Dup laughed, an ugly gurgle of a laugh that drew Sandile's eyes towards his gaping hole of a mouth. That was when he hit, his hand catching Sandile with a glancing smack across his face. Sandile reeled backwards, more from shock than pain. This was only a light tap with an open palm – Dup was just starting – but Sandile was in no mood to play the cowering kaffir. He straightened up, smiling a horrible smile, and then he slapped back. He hit hard and Dup was thrown. The cigarette was knocked out of his mouth and fell to the ground in a shower of sparks, rolled towards the gutter and was snuffed out by the water sluicing through. Dup hadn't expected that, but there was nothing Dup liked more than the unexpected.

'Nice one, Mashiya. Very nice.' He wasn't smiling any more.

Without warning his fist flew, smashing into Sandile's chest with the power of a sledgehammer. He felt the crack against his ribs and the dreadful sensation of air fleeing his lungs as he staggered forward, trying to keep his balance, but Du Plessis caught him with another blow, this one across his cheek. Sandile felt as if his face had crumpled inwards around

Dup's knuckles. He tasted blood in his mouth, then his hand flew up to his eye, where more blood streamed from the split across his left cheek.

Du Plessis stepped back, rubbing his fist. 'Game over, Mashiya. Tell me why you did it.'

'My lawyers will have you for this,' he spluttered and Du Plessis roared with laughter.

'That's if they ever find you!'

The cop folded his arms across his chest and casually leaned back, one foot up against the wall. He lit another cigarette and sucked on it as if it was the very essence of life. 'Now, there's something else. Something you haven't told us, isn't there?'

Sandile was clutching his chest, bent double. He tried to stand upright, but couldn't. It was hard even to speak, but he managed. 'I've told you everything. It's all in my statement. And you *will* have to kill me before I change that.'

'But that's just a fairy story to cover the truth, isn't it? Your little statement is pretty icing on a rotten cake. It's the tip of the iceberg.' Dup was enjoying his run of metaphors, enjoying the suspense he was creating, but Sandile had no idea what he was talking about.

'Let's just say – Ismail,' Dup explained, overenunciating every word.

Sandile lurched backwards as if he'd been hit again. How the hell did that story get out of ANC files into the hands of these bastards? He sank against the wall opposite Du Plessis. The pain in his chest was searing. Spies, he thought, the organisation had been riddled with spies. That was what it was all about then and now it had come back to haunt him. The tables had turned – both Sandile and Dup knew it. Aloud he said, 'How do you know about Ismail?'

'Doesn't matter how. The point is – we know.'

Sandile sat down on the bench. He had had enough; he was through. 'I didn't kill Van Rensburg,' he said as he turned his face and his body painfully away from Dup, then curled himself up against the wall.

Dup strolled out of the cell with a grin on his face. He beamed at Johnny, who stared back, not realising that he was scowling. Dup shrugged, lit a new cigarette off his dead one and tossed the smouldering butt into the yard.

Back inside the station he sank into a chair and swung his feet up on to the desk. 'Open-and-shut case,' he declared.

Daan was more than pleased. 'My view exactly!'

'I'm telling you, though, this guy is a hard nut. Cocky chap, thinks he can do as he likes now, thinks everything's his for the taking. That's what we have to teach these kaffirs. We have to hold on to what we've got. That's what it's all about now, Du Toit, holding on.'

Although Daan would never have put it like that himself, he liked the sentiment, he liked Dup's style.

'I tell you, Du Toit, it's all over. In a couple of years Cape Town will be downtown Lagos. Anarchy. For forty years we lived a dream and now it's over. Now the K's think they can have it all.'

Johnny Kakana watched from a distance as Daan grinned, nodding like an idiot, lapping it all up like a dog.

Sandile was devastated. He shrank back against the far wall of the cell. His ribs ached and there was blood all over his face and the shirt they had given him, but he didn't make a move towards the bucket of water that Reagon had placed near the gate for him to clean up with. He lay on the cold bench, trying to breathe in such a way that it didn't hurt and trying not to touch his face. And he thought of Ismail.

Ismail had been murdered, but not by him. Sandile was the one who found him, shot and bleeding to death in the flat they shared near the office in Lusaka. Sandile had broken his usual routine to go there during the day, and later the doubt that was cast on his actions would be exacerbated by this departure from the norm. But the truth was more mundane, more absurd than anyone believed.

Sandile had been out late the previous night and had arrived sleepy and only just on time for a 7 am meeting. During the meeting he'd looked down at his shoes and noticed that they were not a pair. He'd quickly pulled his feet under his chair, hoping nobody else would notice, but they did. Later in the day, with a few minutes free, he decided to go home and change before a scheduled meeting between the President and a high-ranking delegation of Swedish parliamentarians who were on a tour of the region. He could, of course, have sent someone from the office to pick up the shoe, but he felt a little foolish about the whole thing, so he went himself. Alone.

Almost everyone from the office either carried or kept a weapon. Sandile had two pistols – a Makarov 9mm and a Tokarev – as well as an AK that he kept by his bed. Lately there had been too many death threats and Sandile, at Ismail's urging, had taken to wearing one of the pistols in a small holster strapped to his chest. It was with that pistol that Sandile shot down the young white man he saw striding from Ismail's bleeding body.

He was standing at the door of the flat, keys in his hand, when he heard something inside that made him hesitate. Voices. Two men – one of them sounded like Ismail; the other, also a man's voice, was unfamiliar. The stranger spoke in English with a strong Afrikaans accent. The two men were arguing heatedly. Sandile caught only snatches of the discussion, but he could tell it meant trouble: something was up. So he drew his pistol before quietly unlocking the door and slipping inside. Neither Ismail nor the other guy heard him.

Inside, he could just make out the shapes of his flatmate and a tall white stranger at the end of the passageway. Sunlight flooded into the flat, bouncing off bare white walls and silhouetting the shapes of the two men and something, a briefcase or a box, on the floor between them. Ismail moved his hands in a categorical final gesture, his fingers cutting the air like wings.

'I'm finished. I won't tell you again. Now get out!'

The white man shook his head and the two men stared one another down for nearly a minute. Sandile didn't dare breathe. Then the white guy stooped, reaching for the object on the floor. It seemed as if he was going to leave. Sandile relaxed, lowering his gun. He'd find out now what the hell was going on. But suddenly the stranger's arm whipped out and Sandile saw too late that there was a gun in his hand. Three shots thudded into Ismail's chest, a silencer attached to the barrel making a sickening whine and a dull pop as each shot went off. Then the white guy grabbed the case and made for the door, straight towards Sandile. There was no time to ask for an explanation: the stranger was levelling his gun to shoot when Sandile fired. The man fell to the ground and the case landed on top of him, spilling its contents all over him. Bundles and bundles of sterling.

Ismail died in Sandile's arms. His eyes were full of terror and he said only one word before those eyes froze for ever. Struggling for breath, blood bubbling up out of his mouth, the word Ismail uttered was 'Sorry.' Sandile didn't understand what that meant until much later, when he was detained by ANC security and charged with two murders. The white guy had died instantly.

Sandile knew Simon Siluma well. They were drinking buddies. He worked in the same office, though Sandile didn't know precisely what he did – he simply knew that Simon was in intelligence, Mbokodo – the crushing stone. Simon was the first person to walk in on the scene. Sandile realised later that he must have been watching from somewhere, because he hadn't called anyone, yet they were already here, and he understood very quickly how suspicious this would look to a mind that turned on conspiracies. Two dead bodies and a pile of cash and Sandile was holding the gun.

Sandile's internment was bizarre and terrifying. His interrogators simply wouldn't believe that he was not involved in the transaction that had taken place in his flat and ended with two people dead.

It was Simon Siluma who revealed that Ismail was a spy working for Pretoria, but apparently he had wanted out. The stranger was a Security policeman who'd been sent to buy

Ismail back. If he wouldn't be bought, he was to be eliminated. At first Sandile wouldn't, couldn't believe it, but in the end he had to. The evidence was powerful, incontrovertible. Ismail had been turned years before and was working for the other side almost all the time Sandile had known him.

Simon had been on Ismail's trail for some time. As far as he could piece the story together it went like this: since February 1990 Ismail had been having doubts; he wanted out and had signalled this to his handlers. But they didn't want to lose him because of what he knew, because he was their contact with too many people. The South African cops had weighed up the options – they could go in hard, put a bunch of guys on the ground to take Ismail out, or they could use a low-key approach, send someone in to try to get him back. If Ismail didn't co-operate he would be eliminated. They chose the latter course.

Now a kind of justice had been done, but why was Sandile caught up in it? What, Simon wanted to know, was Sandile's connection with the deal?

Sandile told his story over and over again, yet he saw from day one that the interrogation team were never going to be satisfied with his answers. Why was he at the flat in the first place? Why did he wait until Ismail got killed before he did anything? Hadn't he been involved in the deal and then killed both men in a disagreement over cash? At first Sandile thought this was a joke, a trick. They were messing with his head. Sandile pointed at the mismatched shoes he was still wearing. Still they didn't believe him. They believed he was working for the fascists, and Sandile knew that whatever he said or did, even if he convinced them to let him go, that doubt would always be there, in everyone's minds.

Sandile pleaded with them, screamed at them, told them they were crazy and were making him crazy, but he was frightened. The organisation was leaking like a sieve and infiltrators and conspiracies were as rife as the mistrust and paranoia they engendered. Mistakes were made. He didn't want to be a mistake.

It was bitterly ironic that the only time he spent in jail his jailers were his comrades, the men and women with whom he'd fought, not the enemies of the struggle. The sense of betrayal was terrible to him, and the night they finally gave him a mattress to sleep on and left him alone, Sandile wept. It would be for the last time in many, many years. He thought of his friend. Ismail must have been a very poor spy; he was simply a kindly, stupid man, whose pain and confusion had been turned against him; they had used him. Sandile felt Ismail was as much a victim of the system as Selina. The only difference was that they never broke Selina before they killed her.

Sandile lost count of the days before his interrogators relented. It was Simon Siluma who eventually had him released from detention and officially cleared his name. All along Simon had been the soft touch, the nice guy. The boot boy was another comrade, Tusi, and Sandile could never look Tusi fully in the face again afterwards. But he knew Simon well, had sat up drinking with him countless times; they'd even slept with the same women and gossiped viciously about them later. Sandile understood that Simon was doing his job, and so in time he forgave him and they were able to resume a friendship that almost resembled the one they had had before.

After Sandile's release he went straight back to his job managing the office, but though nothing was said or done, the doubt was planted firmly in everyone's minds. Sandile sensed his comrades pulling away from him, saw that he was quietly neutralised, that responsibility swerved to avoid him. He knew through Simon that the cops in South Africa had picked up on the rift and were spreading disinformation about him that would only fan the flames, as it was supposed to.

While all around him there was growing excitement at the pace of the negotiations, the prospect of elections, the imminence of freedom, Sandile slipped into a numb disillusionment. While everyone else headed back to South Africa and sent news of the fantastic new headquarters at Shell House, of the incredible joy of being home, Sandile stayed behind in Lusaka to take care of the transition, shutting down the farms and scaling back the office, taking care of returnees, disposing of and shifting assets.

When his job was clearly done and it was time for him to leave too, Sandile realised he didn't want to. He didn't want to go back into the political arena wearing the stigma of doubt that would always attach to him. He wanted to escape the rumour and the mistrust, so he applied for and got another scholarship, again at London University, this time to do a Ph.D. With enormous relief and terrible sadness he flew north out of Zambia, away from the homeland to which everyone else was so joyfully returning, towards the familiar grey anonymity of London.

That was the worst time of his life. An initial burst of energy quickly tailed away. He made contact with a few old friends and comrades. He occasionally showed up at the London offices, but turned down offers of work, said he was taking some time out, concentrating on his studies. At the end of April 1994 he raced out each morning to buy the papers, left the TV and the radio on and basked in the sadness and joy of the news that came from home, the pictures of thousands and thousands of voters lining up at the polling stations, the incredulous faces of his compatriots as they voted for the first time in their lives.

Sandile cast his own vote at the embassy in Trafalgar Square. He had never been inside it before. Nearly two weeks later he was invited back, to join the hundreds of comrades and officials who had come there to celebrate the incredible. He stood in the panelled ballroom, surrounded by people who were laughing and crying and holding on to one another, embracing strangers and dancing with a joy that over-whelmed them all as they watched, on a huge screen over the stage, Nelson Mandela's inauguration as President of South Africa.

As he was leaving, blinking in the bright spring sunshine on the street outside, not knowing what to do with himself or where to go, Sandile bumped into a comrade from Lusaka.

Farouk smiled and opened his arms and the two men embraced warmly. Farouk was in the Foreign Office now, had just arrived for his first posting here in London. Sandile's was a rare familiar face. Farouk declared that there was no way he was going back to work while everyone down south would be partying through the night, so they hit a bar near Charing Cross and stayed to close the place.

It was Farouk who brought up the subject of Ismail and for the first time, fuelled by beer and elation, Sandile poured out his anger and frustration and disillusionment. He was grateful to Farouk, told him he felt better for talking, but he knew words could never wipe out the indelible stain on his reputation. Farouk threw up his hands, scoffing at the doubters, told Sandile that he should stand up and fight them, ignore them. In time they'd forget and, even if they didn't, why let them ruin a life like this? He looked hard at Sandile and through the haze of alcohol that blurred the rest of the night there was one thing that Sandile remembered with sobering clarity. He remembered Farouk saying to him, 'Go back, man. It's time to go home. I can see it in your eyes, it's all you really want. There are other things you can do – you don't need to be in government. Why deny yourself? Go home.' It would be a whole year, a whole summer and winter would pass, before Sandile mustered the strength to make that decision.

Spring arrived again. A weak sun appeared, veiled with a skein of cloud, frail and beautiful, like a ghost come to visit. Sandile never went to college that week. Instead he walked in the sun and his skin thrilled at its touch, its delicate caress. He felt strength stirring in him at the memory of another sun's hard grip and scorching smile. He walked in the parks which were burgeoning with new life, and he found beauty in London. Flowers were coming up in the grass and in the beds along the pathways and one day he sat down on the damp lawn of Green Park just to marvel at the return of colour to his world.

A man nearby seemed to feel as Sandile did. He laid his

briefcase on the ground and sat on it, then took off his shirt, shoes and socks, rolled up his trousers and leaned back to let the sunlight touch his skin. Sandile was so amazed that he stared. The paleness of the man's skin was incredible, so pale it was more translucent than white. Sandile was struck by an absurd fear that if he stayed here too long then his skin would become as sick-looking as this. At this image of himself baring his transparent skin among the crocuses and daffodils, he started to laugh. He couldn't stop it bubbling up and the sensation of it was like sudden movement in a long-forgotten, long-ago-immobilised limb.

The pale man turned towards Sandile. He was shaking a little, but with laughter, not anger. And the two of them sat there giggling on the damp grass in their own crazy celebration of spring. Sandile knew then that it was time to go home.

Home: it was a bitter, bitter irony now. A light burned in the station all through the night, but Sandile didn't see or hear anyone during the hours of darkness. The air was cold and the chill helped to clear his head. After a while he sat up on the painted plaster of the bench and stared at the Milky Way through the criss-crossing pattern of bars. Every half-hour or so he would pace the four corners of the room, trying to get warm. He didn't sleep at all. His mind kept flipping back to the previous night and Van Rensburg's murder. He couldn't see why anyone would really want to kill Van Rensburg. By morning he was beginning to believe that someone had set him up. Someone wanted him exactly where he was – but why? And why kill Van Rensburg into the bargain? It didn't make sense.

Sandile traced and retraced the hours of that restless night. The dogs had started yapping some time before dawn; they must have been roused by whoever had taken the panga from its place near the woodpile. It couldn't have been his father. There was no way his father would have had the strength to overwhelm Van Rensburg. Was it perhaps a horrible coincidence that the panga was missing? Perhaps Lucky had done something with it. But the thought nagged him that the knife had been taken deliberately, by someone who wanted the police to think *he* had killed Van Rensburg. But why? Who? Who could hate him that much? Who needed him out of the way? Sandile had no answers, only questions.

Thirty Eight

Daan returned to Rustenvrede at dusk, when the sun had sunk beneath the craggy line of the mountains and shadow engulfed the valley. Mama Mashiya's hope-filled face appeared at the kitchen window as his car rattled over the gravel in the yard. But Daan was alone and Mama's face quickly dropped.

Daan smiled at her as he stepped into the kitchen. He was sweaty and dishevelled, but he positively radiated triumph. 'Mama, I want to thank you for everything you've done today. I know Elise couldn't have managed without you. You should go home now, get some rest.'

Mama said nothing, but met Daan's gaze with a raging glare. She didn't know what to make of anything any more. Her son's return, the land claim, the awful scene at the compound. And now this murder, of a man she'd grown up with and who was as central to her life as the farm itself. And here was this boy she'd known since he was still pooping in his pants, standing there picking at her roast chicken while the keys to her own son's prison rattled in his pocket. Mama shook her head and turned her back on Daan, wearily pulling off her housecoat and dumping it on the dirty washing pile in the laundry. She trudged slowly home as the dusk faded and the deep red sky turned to black.

Daan was still dressed in the school rugby shorts he'd dragged on after Johnny's phone call that morning, days ago it felt like to Elise. The shirt was fresher; it was part of a spare uniform they kept at the station. He headed straight for the tall cabinet in the dining room where the drinks were kept, poured himself a large brandy and then one for Elise, who

428

took the glass, though she left it untouched. Daan sank into the sofa next to her and took a long, thirsty drink. He sighed when he'd drained the glass, wiping his mouth with the back of his hand, then he put it down carefully on the side table. They were both still stunned, still quietly numb. He put his hand on her shoulder. Elise mustered a smile; she squeezed his leg and then they both shook their heads, in perfect tandem, which made them laugh, though the laughter subsided as quickly as it had arisen.

Supper at every table in the valley that night was a sombre affair. Van Rensburg's murder had touched every household. Murder. The very word sent a chill through everyone. Every family, every household had told and retold the story and chewed on it over dinner. They tutted and clucked and shook their heads and said it was a terrible thing and they all hoped there would be no land claim, no dark stranger returning to shatter the peace of their own farms.

Daan had finished off half of the roast chicken, but Elise couldn't eat. Later her stomach growled as they lay in bed, side by side. Elise wasn't ready for sleep, but Daan was exhausted, dozing off already.

'What will happen to Sandile, Daan?'

His reply was muffled by the pillow. 'Mmm, dunno yet, we'll decide in the morning, see if Dup can get any more out of him.'

'What were you doing at the station?' she persisted.

'Taking statements. Working on the docket. Du Plessis and his guys have spoken to just about everyone: Ina, Taylor, the workers up at the compound. They'll need to take one from you, but I asked them to wait a bit. I didn't want them upsetting you.'

He put his hand over her tummy, cuddling up against her. Elise didn't move; she kept her hands folded behind her head as she stared at the ceiling. 'What did the workers say?'

'Not much of interest, except for Vuyo. He saw Sandile leaving the cottage around the time when the dogs were barking.'

Elise held her breath, her heart racing. She had to control her voice so as not to let her fear slip out. 'Did he see him take the panga?'

'Naah, he couldn't see that far, but apparently he lost sight of Sandile round the corner of the house where the panga would have been.'

Elise breathed again. 'I just can't believe he would do it,' she said quietly.

Daan turned away from her and murmured sleepily, 'Well, who did then?'

She didn't have an answer. After a few minutes the depth of his breathing told her that Daan was asleep, but his question lingered.

Who did do it? If not Sandile, then *who*? Mentally scanning the faces of each of the workers up at the compound, she knew it was none of them. They had no motive, and if they'd done it in a rage or a drunken outburst they would surely have run off or given themselves away by now. Nothing else made any sense. The story knitted together so neatly: everything pointed to Sandile. Doubt gnawed at her, corroding her certainty.

When she woke the next morning, as consciousness dawned, her mind was mercifully free for a few clear seconds. Then the terrible events of the previous day split through the soft surface of waking. She opened her eyes on the familiar sun-bright room and sat up with a jolt.

Daan had left before breakfast. He'd jumped out of bed with great alacrity and dashed off before Elise was awake. When she finally got up and wandered through into the kitchen she found Mama there, bent over the sink, weeping. Elise steered her towards a chair and sat her down at the table, where the old lady went on crying silently, huge tears rolling down her cheeks, her chest heaving with sobs. Elise didn't say anything, she had nothing left inside her.

'You know, sometimes I wish that he'd never come back to us.'

Mama heaved the poisonous words out between the spasmodic sobs that racked her whole body. Elise knew that for Mama this was tantamount to heresy – the most terrible thing she could imagine.

All her life Mama had let the laughter bubble out and kept back the sadness, biting down on it, holding it in. There was no point in succumbing, no point in expressing the awfulness and the pain of life. Nothing could be done about the terrible things that happened; nothing would change, so why let yourself wallow in it? However this thing was different; this had to come out. That she could feel so bitter about her adored son was an indication of the depth of her fear.

'Everything that's happened, all these terrible things that have happened since he came back! Why did he bring all this pain to us?'

Elise shook her head. She had no answers. Sandile was the only one who could provide them. And she felt she had the right to an explanation – they all did. 'Mama, you must go to the police station. Go and fetch Oupa and I'll take you to visit him.'

Mama looked at her gratefully. Elise felt a little stronger. She wasn't waiting any more: she was doing something.

An hour later Mama and Ben Mashiya were outside, waiting for Elise by her bakkie. In his hands Ben had a bag of clothes and some food for their son. Mama was wearing her air-force-blue belted raincoat, the one she wore every Sunday to church.

The station had been alive with movement and voices for two hours before Johnny Kakana came out carrying a tin cup filled with coffee for the prisoner. Sandile was surprised by the gesture, yet he accepted Johnny's kindness gratefully. Johnny hung around, as if there was something he wanted to say. So Sandile asked him, 'Why am I not being given food?'

Johnny looked shiftily away. Sandile blew on the surface of

431

the coffee, cooling it. 'I should be allowed to see a doctor,' he added. It was true, but he didn't elaborate on how badly Dup had hurt him. He didn't want to reveal just how much the cop had got the better of him.

Johnny stared down at his feet, scuffing at the dusty ground. 'Orders. You're not even supposed to be drinking that.'

Sandile raised his eyebrows involuntarily. He drank the coffee as quickly as he could, wondering what had prompted Johnny to this act of generosity. He handed back the mug with a warm 'Thank you.' Johnny merely grabbed the cup and disappeared.

Sandile wondered why the police were so nervous of him, all of them except Du Plessis who fortunately had not yet put in an appearance. They barely even pushed into his space. As the morning dragged by, this behaviour reinforced his sense that it was only a matter of manoeuvring by his lawyers, a matter of hours now, before he'd be out. But when at last Daan du Toit arrived, banging on the gate, Sandile knew immediately that it was not with the intention of letting him go. Not yet. His heart sank when he saw his parents shuffling across the yard towards him.

When she saw her son Mama Mashiya's mouth fell open in shock. Daan turned to her and put his hand on the bag she was carrying. 'I'm afraid I'll have to take that from you, Mama. We have orders not to give him any food for now.'

Mama let go of the bag. She took a swing at Daan and slapped him hard across the face. The crack resounded through the yard of stunned policemen. Daan's chin jerked up. His hand shot to his cheek, and for several seconds he stood there with his eyes closed. Then he turned round and walked quietly back to his office, stinging with humiliation.

Elise waited in her bakkie while Mama and Oupa Mashiya were inside. She turned the radio up to cover the silence and looked away from the station towards De Jager's. She knew what she had to do. When they were finished, she would go and face him. He must tell her what had happened.

Five minutes later Mama and Oupa Mashiya emerged from the station, their faces ashen. They climbed on to the back of the bakkie together, without a word or a glance in Elise's direction. She took a deep breath, jumped out of the car and strode into the station. She marched past Daan and his constables, outside to the yard and up to the barred gate of the cell.

'Elise!' He couldn't believe it was her. He came right up to the gate, holding on to the bars and pressing his face between them to get as close as he could. She didn't say any of the things she'd planned to. She just stood there staring at the mess of his face and listening to the awful sound of his breathing, as if there was something wrong in his chest or his throat. His left eye was a massive purple bruise, almost closed from the swelling of his cheek. There was dried blood all over his hair and shirt. When he smiled he looked monstrous.

'Listen, I'm so glad you're here. I want to say that I'm sorry I . . . what happened with the land claim. I should have told you and I'd been meaning to tell you. I just couldn't. You don't have to understand or say anything – I just want you to know that I didn't mean you to find out that way.'

Elise faced him, her chin tilted up and her eyes flickering with agitation as she scrutinised his bruised eye, his mouth. Words tumbled out of him. 'I mean, the land – we both feel so strongly and there's this . . . other thing. If you never speak to me again, if you never let me *look* at you again, I could bear it perhaps if I knew that you knew. That you *knew*' – Sandile emphasised that word again by putting his hand over his heart – 'it wasn't a game. Do you know that, Elise?'

Elise sighed heavily. She thought of her father, of their conversation two nights back, and her mouth crumpled slightly. She tasted bitter tears but she squashed them back when she spoke. 'You know, I promised my father that I'd fight you. It was the last thing that he and I . . . the first thing I have to deal with now.'

He nodded. 'I know, I know. It means as much to me as it

does to you. But just make sure you're strong enough, OK? make sure you look after yourself.'

For some reason his concern made her angry. What right did he have to express such feelings about her? 'I'm fine! I'm always fine. It's that farm that needs attention. That's what my pa cared about, that's what he . . .'

Her voice cut out, she couldn't say any more. Her eyes were huge and shining. She managed a smile as a tear rolled down her cheek and splashed and sank into the cotton of her shirt. 'Sorry, emotional overload, hard drive crashing, brain screen's frozen . . .' She banged the ball of her hand against her forehead. It was such an odd moment for a joke. They both laughed, though only a little, but it was a relief. He wanted so much to hold her.

She looked up at him and Sandile felt his vision tunnel down, his eyes only on hers, like they had been that first day, the day he came home. He saw the doubt that had fallen like a curtain between them.

'I don't understand how you could let things happen this way.' She was reaching for something else, but not daring to say it.

For that Sandile knew he had only excuses, nothing that was a good enough answer. His sigh was almost a sob. 'Do I have to tell you I didn't do it?'

'Well, if *you* didn't do it, then who did?'

'Elise –'

'Everything's just collapsed, it's all exploded since you came back. Everything. I don't think I can ever forgive you. And now they're charging you with murder . . . I just don't understand, Sandile. I can't understand.'

Sandile looked back at her blankly, not knowing what to say, not knowing either quite what she meant. She was pleading with him and pushing him away at once. Elise's words didn't add up to much sense and his own emotional and physical reserves were so depleted he didn't have much with which to help her. So he reached for her hand, but his fingers merely brushed hers before he swiftly retracted his arm. Daan du Toit and Dup du Plessis had appeared in the yard.

Daan put his arm round Elise as he introduced her to Dup, but Elise didn't even look at him. She was fuming with Daan for allowing Sandile to be knocked around. And with fate or circumstance or whatever it was for not allowing her more time with Sandile. Nothing had been resolved. 'Daan, I need to talk to him for a few more minutes. Please?'

'Nice to meet you too,' Dup butted in sarcastically. 'But I'm afraid that visiting time is over, Miss Van Rensburg.'

His patronising tone was too much. Anger overwhelmed her. 'And beating-up time begins,' she snarled. 'I don't think much of your style, Mr Du Plessis. I was under the impression we had laws against this kind of police hospitality.'

The corners of Dup's mouth twitched and his eyes sparkled with amusement. He made a slight bow and walked away, shaking his head. Daan was bright red with embarrassment. He grabbed her elbow and yanked her away from the cell, marching her all the way through the station and outside to her car.

Elise pulled away from him, breathless. 'What the hell do you guys think you're doing? It's barbaric to treat a man like that. How can you allow it?'

'Elise, this is not the time or the place.'

'Excuse me? This is both the time and the place.'

'Just shut up, OK? Before you embarrass me any further.' He grabbed hold of her arm again and dug his fingers into her flesh.

'Wha – Jesus! You're hurting me.'

'It's pretty clear to him who wears the trousers now,' Daan said bitterly, letting go of her arm.

'Daan! It's worse than cowardly to allow a man to be beaten like that. It's disgusting – that's old style. I thought you were better than that. I thought you had more principle than that.'

Daan was unused to things not going his way. The last couple of days had been hell – there was no way to charm a path through anything. That was probably what confounded him most. But he had to regain a measure of control. When he spoke again his tone had become measured and careful, as if he were consciously enacting a drama.

'Elise. He murdered your father. In my book a few slaps don't even compare to what he's done. And he's being charged,' Daan added irrelevantly. 'He gets transferred to Pollsmoor tomorrow.'

Elise's eyes widened. 'Sorry?'

'We're putting him in front of the magistrate tomorrow.'

'But he didn't *do* it, Daan.' She said this wearily, finally.

Daan shrugged. He looked shattered, confused and under unendurable strain. 'How do *you* know?' His tone was sneering.

Suddenly the silence was loaded. He spoke again and now his voice sounded dry and painfully thin. 'What is *with* you and this guy?'

'What?'

'Why do you care about Mashiya?'

Elise covered her face with her hands. It was a gesture of weariness, not drama. She pressed her forefingers against her temples. Her head was throbbing. She pulled her hands away, sliding her fingers down to the base of her neck. Her voice was tiny and terribly sad. 'I'm so sorry, Daan.'

Daan's eyes narrowed and his body tautened. The atmosphere around them had chilled abruptly. Elise shook her head, her eyes vaguely focused on the windows of the station from which Du Plessis and Johnny Kakana were staring at them shamelessly. 'I don't know why it happened, but it did –'

Daan was stunned. His incredulity told Elise that he'd been hoping there was some trivial reason to explain her interest in Sandile. He hadn't meant things to go this far; he just wanted her to acknowledge she was being difficult and say sorry, then they could return to their usual intimacy. But now she was unravelling everything.

'What? There *is* something with you and this guy?'

Elise nodded, the muscles in her cheek twitching, her jaw clenched so difficult it hurt. 'It's difficult to explain . . .'

She trailed off, not knowing how to articulate the shift in every perspective that Sandile's return had caused. She stared into Daan's eyes, which were enormous with disbelief. His whole body expressed a combination of puzzlement and disgust, amazement and sadness, and barely contained fury.

'But, he's . . . I mean he's a –'

'Kaffir?' She spoke the word for him.

Daan spun away and then back towards her, his voice thundering with rage. 'Are you off your head? I mean, have you completely lost your mind?'

Something sounding like laughter, though it was utterly mirthless, screeched from Elise's throat. Everything had become petty; everything was debased by Daan's crudely expressed amazement. There was nothing more to say. Now they both had heavy hearts and she knew she was responsible for his. She hung her head. Daan spluttered incoherently, not at all sure how to handle this; uncertain how much of the story he wanted to know and how much was best left unsaid.

'Just tell me what, *exactly*, has been going on.'

Elise tried to swallow, but her throat felt like sandpaper. She was raw, all her defences destroyed and flattened. Suddenly the idea of her unfaithfulness to Daan seemed so much less terrible to her than it had a few days ago. The importance of being honest, of seizing the moment, mattered more than anything else. So she said it quite baldly. 'Not much really. A few overheated kisses. Not much at all. I woke up pretty quickly once he showed his true colours. But that's not the point. The point is there's something wrong between you and me. And I don't think there's anything we can do about that, Daan.'

She put her hand on his arm, entreating him to understand, to agree, perhaps even to forgive. But he pulled sharply away from her. He was hurt and furious. 'What would your father say?'

He might as well have slapped her. Elise turned away. It

was cruel, desperate, to invoke Van Rensburg like that. It hurt her as deeply as he'd intended, though it also made it easier for her to be harsh. 'My father said you'd never make a good farmer. Just like you'll never be a good policeman.' Elise regretted it the minute she'd uttered the words, but by then it was too late.

Sadness surged up through her. It was a mixture of self-pity and genuine sorrow at the pain she was causing Daan. She put her arms out, reaching for him. 'Daan, I do love you.'

'That's not very helpful right now!' he shouted, shaking his head. He stepped back and away from her, not wanting her to touch him.

Elise began to cry. She was desperate to get through to him. 'It wasn't right, Daan. Forget about Sandile. It was wrong for us before he came along, – it wasn't going to be right.'

'What do you mean, it wasn't going to be right? It's been *perfect* – up to now!'

His voice rose with every syllable he punched out. He glared at her for a beat, then spun on his heel and strode away. Elise didn't move. She stood with her arms still out in front of her, her eyes closed, listening to the slam of the car door, the growl of the engine, and the roar of the van as Daan spun the wheels and revved away up the street. Johnny Kakana and Du Plessis turned away from the window.

Elise climbed into her bakkie and drove slowly off. She hadn't meant it to come out like this. At least she hadn't lied. Nevertheless the truth was a train smash. Part of her still wished that somehow it could have been avoided, that her inner life had remained her own. That way Sandile could have stayed her secret and Ina and Daan would never have been hurt.

She half hoped that Daan would come back, as he usually did after they fought. He'd go away and cool off for a few hours, then he'd be back and it would be good between them and neither one would mention the storm. But this storm had flattened everything in its path. There was no going back.

*

Daan drove round the farm roads for an hour or more, letting off steam. The very centre of his life had collapsed and he didn't know how to charm it back together. One thing was clear to him: he wanted Dup and the Mashiya boy and that whole circus out of his station and out of his life. He hoped that Sandile would rot in jail for the rest of his stinking filthy life.

He knew that it didn't matter how smooth a talker the suspect was, how well educated, how flimsy the evidence. It didn't matter that there was a President Mandela sitting in Pretoria or Cape Town or wherever. This was a small town and everyone knew the law here. If the suspect was black he didn't stand a snowball's chance in hell. Daan soothed himself with this thought. And the less he said the better. He didn't need to do anything at all: Dup and his buddies would throw the guy away for the rest of his life without any help from Daan.

It took no time at all. Sandile was bewildered by the speed of it. Du Plessis pulled him out of the cell, shouting that it was time to go. He slapped the handcuffs over Sandile's wrists and marched him outside, Johnny scurrying after them.

'Where are you taking me?'

'Shut the fuck up, your whining is starting to grate on me,' growled Dup.

'I demand to know where you're taking me. I want to see my lawyer!'

'Do you really?' He sounded almost reasonable and Sandile could feel the blow coming, like that skin-tingling moment a second before lightning strikes.

Du Plessis swiped him across the chin. Sandile thought he heard his jaw crack; his mouth felt like wads of cotton wool. He stumbled blindly the rest of the way, hardly aware of where he was. Then Dup shoved him towards Johnny, who helped him climb into the back of the old mellow yellow van. 'I think it's best to simmer down and do as you're told,' Johnny said calmly.

Sandile spat blood.

Watching him driven away Daan thought, with some satisfaction, that it could take as long as three months just to get the paperwork sorted out for a trial. Elise was potentially their only witness and she'd couldn't be spoken to until after the funeral at the very earliest – she'd be far too upset to talk sooner. Then there were forensics and background checks and who knew what the hell else. He could forget about informing Sandile's lawyers of his whereabouts. They would find him in the end if they really wanted to and meanwhile if anyone asked he'd lost Simon Siluma's number. The station had been a complete madhouse after all.

Sandile caught Daan's malevolent stare as he was slammed into the back of Johnny's van and wondered if that had anything to do with this sudden move. Oddly enough, Sandile felt no guilt about Daan. He didn't see him as cuckolded or diminished in any sense by what had happened between him and Elise. Sandile's philosophy was simple: if Elise loved the man, there had to be something to him, but if Elise was straying there must be something wrong in the relationship and that was something for them to sort out. Sandile felt their troubles had nothing to do with him. It was a rationalisation, sort of. He knew that too.

Johnny strained the van, trying to keep up with Dup's speeding car. Sandile stared out at the mountains and farms through the wire mesh that covered the windows, concentrating on the pain, focusing on willing it away. It wasn't long before he passed out.

In the early afternoon he found himself in the holding room at the magistràtes' court in Paarl. Sandile and a dozen or so other men, all of them in varying states of desperation, were herded like cattle into a long concrete cell underneath the courts. Most of them didn't have the faintest idea of what was going to happen to them; the few who did knew from experience. They were mostly black men, eyes blank and wide with fear, and a handful of white guys who seemed to be drunk or in some other state of intoxication. The stink of sweat was overwhelming, the press of bodies claustrophobic. Sandile stood against a corner of the low cell fighting off anxiety, employing every atom of stoicism he could find in him to endure this. At least they were fed: a thin soup with bread and margarine, and the bread was fresh. To Sandile it was manna from heaven. Shortly after the meal, a boy in a nurse's uniform arrived with a first-aid box and Sandile was called forward to be cleaned up.

The court orderlies hauled him up for his appearance before the magistrate in the late afternoon. The court was stuffy and smelt faintly mildewed. The magistrate, a narrow, grey-skinned man with a long thin nose, looked distinctly uninterested as he went through the motions of his job, his mind evidently somewhere else. Dup sat stroking his moustache and listening to a portly man in a suit who was apparently whispering a joke into his ear.

Sandile looked around at the dull wood veneer that covered or panelled everything. The rows of benches labelled 'Press' were empty except for one slouched reporter. In the public gallery a fat white woman in an ill-fitting salmon-coloured suit gripped hard on to a navy-blue handbag on her lap. Next to her was a scared-looking little girl, wearing what appeared to be her Sunday-school outfit, a floral dress with a starchy white bib of a collar. No sign of Simon or Karel. It was foolish to hope that there might be – they didn't even know he'd been moved. Nevertheless Sandile did hope. He barely understood the rules of this theatre. He desperately needed someone to navigate for him.

Sandile turned back to face the magistrate who had finished shuffling papers from the previous case and now stared down his nose and grindingly cleared his throat. He spoke very slowly and loudly, deliberately enunciating each word as if Sandile were deaf or stupid or both.

'Do you speak Afrikaans?'

Sandile dipped his chin, a terse nod. The magistrate grunted; the response had been adequate but apparently unsatisfactory to him. Next the charge was read out. The prosecutor might as well have been reading from last year's shipping news for the Bering Strait, for all the interest it elicited. The magistrate barked at Sandile to plead. Sandile did so, in English and with the utmost clarity, his voice resounding round the panelled room.

'Not guilty!'

The magistrate paused, studying him, dully surprised by Sandile's large, confident tone. Then he went on, still in Afrikaans. 'Mr Mashiya, do you understand what it means to enter a plea of not guilty?'

Sandile nodded again. He had the sense that this wasn't really happening, he didn't feel fully present, so he would sometimes pause before he answered, not clocking immediately that the term 'accused' referred to him.

The magistrate continued in his ponderous, patronising tone. 'To say you are not guilty means you are not guilty until proven so. If you plead not guilty then you will be tried. You understand?'

He eyed Sandile carefully. Sandile stared back blankly. The magistrate jerked his chin up, then shuffled some more papers and glared at the court recorder. 'Plea noted. The case is remanded to January the first,' he barked, 'pending further investigation.'

Sandile's heart was pounding. Surely that couldn't be it. Surely it couldn't be over so fast. It had hardly begun.

The local prosecutor nodded, making a note. Sandile noticed the look that he exchanged with Dup, who slouched in the public gallery. 'Anything else?' the magistrate enquired, sounding increasingly bored.

Sandile leaned forward against the stand, wanting to speak. The prosecutor reeled off his lines. 'I ask that the accused be kept indefinitely in custody without bail until such time as he is brought to trial.'

Then the magistrate turned to Sandile. It was like a dull tennis match. Heads turning this way, then that, then this again. 'What have you got to say about this, Mr, er, Mr Mashiya?'

'I want to talk to my lawyer. He isn't aware of this hearing and I should have a lawyer present.'

The magistrate glanced over at the prosecution, a glance loaded with irritating familiarity. Sandile could picture them discussing their golf handicaps in the tea break, all thoughts of him forgotten.

'The defendant does have a right to counsel.'

'Let him put his lawyer's name into the record.' The prosecutor shrugged, as if to say there was no point in holding things up by waiting for Sandile's lawyers to arrive in person. That wouldn't change anything.

The magistrate sighed and swung his gaze back to Sandile. 'Mr Mashiya, can you adduce reasons why you *should* get bail?'

'Yes, of course I can –' But he didn't know the rules and so he didn't know what the magic reasons were.

The minute he broke off the prosecutor cut in. 'Your worship, having perused the docket I can state that the accused is a person of no fixed abode – he may abscond. Furthermore, given his history, he may bring undue influence to bear on the state's witnesses.'

The magistrate nodded impatiently. He had heard enough and the prosecutor shut up. 'Having heard all the arguments I rule that the accused will be remanded in custody without bail until the case comes to trial. Pending further investigation, of course.'

Sandile interjected loudly and all eyes turned towards him. 'I'm sorry, sir, but I do have a lawyer whom I haven't been able to reach on the telephone. Surely you could –'

'You will have to represent your request to the prison authorities. They will permit you to contact counsel.' The magistrate banged his gavel and that was the end of Sandile's session in the court.

Court orderlies led Sandile back to the stinking holding room where he sat with the remaining prisoners and waited. He asked several times to be allowed to make a phone call, but the guards ignored or laughed at him. His mind was a blank. He sat very still, waiting for the hours to pass. Eventually he and the other prisoners were shuffled off and loaded into a van. The absence of windows in the van, in the holding room and in the court created, no doubt deliberately, a profound disorientation. Sandile closed his eyes, trying to quell the nausea that was rising in him.

When they were loaded out of the van inside the walls of Pollsmoor prison Sandile felt he was moving in a dream, but over the next few hours he woke up to the nightmare of his new reality.

The prison machine was sluggish but efficient. It processed Sandile with deadening thoroughness. He had a brief medical check, then police warders took away everything he had on him: his wallet, his watch, his clothes. They gave him a stack of khaki prison clothing and some sandals of hard thong which were too big and slopped around on his feet. He was told that he could receive visitors, who would be permitted to bring him food. The warders packaged up his stuff in a brown paper parcel, to be given to his parents or whoever came to see him first. If no one came, they barked, then the clothes would be disposed of after 'a certain period of time'. Sandile imagined the wallet would be stolen, but by then he didn't care, not about the cash in his wallet or the roughness of the ill-fitting prison clothes. He only cared about what he had to do next – get out of this place and get everything straightened out. This time he wouldn't let doubt defeat him.

THIRTY NINE

By now the news of Van Rensburg's murder and Sandile's incarceration had spread beyond Fransmansvallei. The story provoked a cascade, a veritable explosion of consternation among whites. It was like a new seam opened up in the face of the infinite mine of car-jacking, rape and murder-and-mayhem stories. Ladies who lunch all over South Africa could twitter happily for weeks on the details. The minutiae confirmed so much that they'd always asserted, in particular their opinion that no sense could be made of the actions of the blacks; 'they' would stop at nothing to get everything; 'they' had their democracy and now 'they' didn't only want 'our' BMWs and 'our' jobs, they also wanted 'our' farms. 'Heaven knows what they think they're going to do with them.' 'It's a known fact that an aff can't organise a you-know-what in a brewery.' Tones of clucking indignation rose from the elegantly set lunch tables of solidly barred and fully alarmed restaurants all over the Johannesburg suburbs. As if all the girdles and tight designer suits and the rocks glittering on those fingers had had no cost. In a charitable mood one might understand them for thinking so, for they had certainly never paid the price.

With Lettie gone Ina had to spend more time covering the till at Hemel en Aarde, especially since the valley had gained this sudden notoriety. Today, among the coach parties and the day trippers, Ina noticed a couple who seemed to have become regulars. When they reached the head of the queue she greeted them as old friends and they were delighted.

'We were so shocked to hear about the murder. Did you know him?' asked the wife.

Ina smiled tightly and nodded as she rang up their sale.

'Such a tragedy. We've been coming here for nearly two years, you know, and we've never heard anything like it,' said the husband.

'We used to go out to Franschoek every Sunday. It's so overrun now, tourists and foreigners buying up the farms. The place isn't the same,' she added.

'It just isn't the same. But *this* valley. So unspoiled. I can't believe such a thing could've happened here,' he concluded.

Ina nodded, first to her, then to him, then back to her. She felt nauseous. But the couple were happy – they'd said their sombre piece and they gaily waved goodbye, promising to be back next month.

Ina was more than relieved when Alan drove up to Hemel en Aarde in the middle of the afternoon. She pulled off her apron, handed it to Nolitha and told her to take over.

'But Miss Ina, I'm in the middle of baking.'

'To hell with the baking!' she shouted and ran outside.

They walked across the garden to the main house where tea would be waiting, Ina clutching on to Alan's arm as if for dear life. She felt so anxious it seemed that her head would explode, and the dizziness and intermittent nausea didn't help. Alan asked if there was something on her mind and she stopped in the middle of the lawn and blurted out everything that Elise had told her about Sandile.

Taylor showed no sign at all of shock. Ina wondered whether he understood the severity of the situation. Perhaps he didn't believe that it was unnatural for a black and a white to mix like that, that it just wasn't what the Good Lord intended.

She looked away from Taylor's impassive face and out across the garden. 'It's as if Elise has died as well.' A tear rolled down her cheek. Taylor nodded sternly, but still he said nothing.

'But the humiliation for Daan! And the betrayal – of her father. The dorp. Me –' Ina wiped the tears away, smudging mascara down her face. Taylor licked his thumb and carefully

446

wiped the brown streaks off her cheek. Then she smiled and leaned her head against his shoulder while he patted her head comfortingly.

'So what's happened with Daan and the De Jager girl then?' he enquired, as if it was something everyone knew about.

Ina pulled away from him, shocked by the question. How on earth did he know about Daan and Madeleine? *What* did he know? she wondered, but Taylor's eyes were as placid and unrevealing as ever. So she brushed the question off, downplaying her reaction. 'Ag, it's not the same. You know as well as I do that it's not the same for a man!'

'But does Elise know?'

'About what?'

'About Daan and Madeleine carrying on all this time?'

'No! Of course she doesn't, but that's not important, it's just fooling around. All that will stop when they get married.' Ina suddenly realised what she'd said and rephrased. 'I mean *if* they get married.'

They set off across the garden again. Alan took her arm as he said thoughtfully, 'Daan wants Rustenvrede, doesn't he?'

'Well, *and* her.' Ina bristled defensively.

Taylor shook his head, disagreeing with her. He had that strange half-smile on his face. 'He wants her land.'

Ina lost steam. 'Ja,' she said. And she suddenly felt the weight of it all.

'Well, don't we all?' Taylor added brightly, this time with a laugh.

Alan Taylor didn't stay for tea. He left Ina and her mother sipping Rooibos in the lounge. Ina laced hers with vodka and found that it had wonderful powers of anxiety reduction. They were still sitting there, Mama picking the ticks off her dogs and Ina staring vacantly into space, when Daan came home. He slumped into a chair and didn't touch the tea that Ina poured for him, in fact barely acknowledged either of them at all. When Ina fetched the vodka he brightened.

'Do you want some, Daantjie?'

447

Daan looked up at his sister. She saw it immediately in his eyes. He knew. Ina almost dropped the bottle. It slipped and she caught the bottom with her left hand, but the glass clanged against a china cup and the noise brought their mother out of her tick-picking trance.

'What was that, lovey?'

Ina paid no attention to her mother's interjection. 'Are you OK?'

Daan shook his head; he was both angry and resigned. 'This afternoon Elise very kindly told me, in front of half my men and within earshot of Inspector Du Plessis, that she and Sandile have been getting it together behind my back – from what I gathered, ever since he arrived in the valley.' Daan's tone remained eerily calm.

Mrs Du Toit looked confused. The delivery was so inappropriate for the content of the message she wondered if it was a joke. But Ina's expression told her it was rather more serious than that.

'I just don't know how she could do it. How could she do this to me? The bitch! If I could I'd . . .' A trace of menace slipped into his tone. Daan leaned forward, pushing his face into his hands.

His mother shoved the dog away and stood up to comfort her son. 'I don't understand, my darling. What are you saying about Elise?'

Ina put her cup down and took a swig of vodka straight from the bottle. 'He's saying that Elise has been screwing the farm worker, Ma. The one who's been arrested for Van's murder,' she snapped.

'Really, darling, there's no need to be so vulgar.' Mrs Du Toit's customary sweetness had turned suddenly to venom. She looked like a scrawny old owl as she reached for the bottle in Ina's hands, took it and poured some into a teacup for herself. Then she sat down hard and took a long sip. 'That little bitch. How could she do this to us? What humiliation! How awfully, awfully embarrassing. What are we going to do?'

Daan looked up. There were tears in his eyes and Ina was petrified that he would start crying – she couldn't stand the idea of a man crying.

'I just don't understand what happened to her. I thought I knew her . . . but I just don't get it,' he rambled.

'I think you are going to have to explain this again, my treasure,' Mrs Du Toit twittered. 'I mean what exactly did she say? Did she mention the marriage? The ring?' His mother wanted to know just how bad things were.

Daan shook his head numbly. 'She just said that we weren't right together.'

That was bad enough. Mrs Du Toit threw back her head and drained the rest of the vodka from her cup.

Then Ina had an idea. 'Daan, you mustn't give up. I think you should tell her you want to talk things over with the Dominee. If anyone can talk sense into her it's Willem.'

Daan nodded and looked gratefully at his older sister. Then he stood up. He looked terrible, his eyes red, his mouth crumpled. 'I never thought something like this could happen to me, Ina,' he mumbled.

She jumped up and gave him a hug. 'Maybe it hasn't happened, sweetheart. Maybe it hasn't happened yet,' she murmured as she stroked his hair.

The second that Daan left the room a shocked Mrs Du Toit reached for her phone. She dialled a number, waited and then launched. 'Etta? It's me, darling. I want you to know before you hear it second-hand. You are *never* going to believe this . . .'

Elise was conscious of the deafening silence around her. She couldn't eat so she drank coffee instead and sat alone in the office, jangled with caffeine and grief and fear. Being alone at Rustenvrede was eerie. Occasionally the house creaked or a tree moaned outside and Elise almost jumped out of her skin. She switched off all the lights, scared lest a killer standing invisible in the dark garden should see her illuminated from in-side. Her senses were both sharpened and dulled, the dullness

449

flooding her emotional responses, the sharpness heightening her physical reflexes.

Why me? she kept asking. Was it something she'd done, was this some cosmic, karmic retribution for the terrible thoughts she'd harboured about her dying mother, for her betrayal of Daan, for the sum of all the infinitesimal compromises and cheats and wrongs of her past?

Elise thought about her parents and how different their lives had been from hers. The pressures and challenges they had faced were so unlike the ones she was facing now. Her mother had complained about the stunning sameness of year after year of life on the farm. Her father had loved the infinite continuum of his unchanging routine. Breakfast at dawn, lunch at noon, supper at dusk. Work all week, shop on Saturday, rest on Sunday. The year marked off with planting, trimming, pruning, picking, packing, shipping, planting, and then everything all over again. Year after year went by. Van Rensburg had lived like that in perfect contentment. He'd never gone overseas, never gone further north than Maputo, or LM as he called it. He had no desire to see the world beyond the mountains; he only related to the rest of the world as the market for his fruit. The Europeans were simply the people that ate Cape apples and pears, often without realising it. During the sanctions years, when the British and the Scandinavians had eschewed and boycotted Cape fruit, they ate it anyway, though they never knew it.

Van loved that story; he always laughed about it, a deep belly laugh. It had been so easy to fool them, though it felt risky and courageous at the time. It was his small slap at the interfering, self-righteous Europeans. They'd manufactured the stickers and stamped the packing crates right there in Stellenbosch. He'd watched the labels go on the apples and pears and peaches himself – 'Produce of Botswana'. And there wasn't even a single fruit tree in Botswana. If the Swedes and the Brits didn't know that – he loved this punch line and his laughter always preceded its delivery – then what right had they to interfere in a complex and historically functional mechanism like apartheid?

And what right did Elise have to think she could fill his shoes? She had let herself be lulled into the sense that everything was OK, that they had ridden out the changes, faced down the worst that life could throw up and arrived in some safe New South African comfort zone. Elise sat in the dark office and felt anger rising in her. She was angry that no one had prepared her for how much junk life had to hurl at her; she was angry with herself for losing her grip. Out of the blue, life had smacked her right in the head just when she thought everything was all right.

FORTY

Elise woke up late, well after seven. She could hear someone in the kitchen, but she didn't move. Inside her room there was only the sound of her little plastic alarm clock ticking on the bedside table next to her. Then the occasional creak of the floor, a clank of pans knocked against one another, a rush of water flowing from a tap. Mama Mashiya was making breakfast. Elise felt incredibly heavy. So heavy she didn't know how she would get her body out of bed.

She should have been up and working by now, but she couldn't move a muscle. Around eight Mama came to her door. Elise heard the sound of her plastic heels clicking on the floorboards, getting louder and louder as they approached her room. The sound stopped right outside her door. There was a pause before the tentative knock. Elise made no response at all. Her hands and feet felt like air. She imagined that her body was dissolving, slowly disappearing, leaving only this leaden-weighted mind on the pillow. Her face cracked in a smile at her own silliness. Imagine if Mama came in and found no Elise, just this brain-shaped lead weight on the pillow.

Mama put her head round the door and caught Elise's sickly smile. Relieved, she stepped into the room. There was a mug of coffee in her hand and the aroma of it curled across, hitting Elise's nostrils, a reminder that she was alive. Mama looked tired, her movements a weary shuffle. The two women gazed at one another across the quilted expanse of bedspread. Mama had mustered a smile that was understanding and loving and sad all at once.

Lying there, immobilised on her bed, Elise realised suddenly that Mama Mashiya was the only person who'd stood by her. When everyone else had died or dumped her, here was Mama, ready – in spite of her own pain – to get her out of bed with a cup of coffee and the warmth of her smile. Elise sat up, swung her legs to the floor and took the steaming cup, murmuring, 'Thank you, Mama, thank you so much.'

Mama clicked her tongue as she folded her chubby hands over her stomach, in the dent underneath her breasts. 'Jacob came by the kitchen just now.'

Elise understood what Mama was saying, but she wasn't ready, not yet. She looked down into the cup, blew gently across the surface of the coffee to cool it, then took a sip as Mama watched her.

'Are you all right, my child?'

Elise felt her stomach lurch. The tenderness, the quietness of the words moved her. Tears welled up in her eyes, so she closed them as she shook her head. Once she'd swallowed back the tears and fought off the surge of sadness that had threatened to overwhelm her, she opened her eyes again and forced a smile. 'I'll be OK, Mama, I'll be OK.'

Mama nodded. 'It takes time. Just give yourself time.'

Her tired wise eyes glittered, but Elise saw no tears. The lines on Mama's face were like a landscape, the map of a life that had been relentlessly hard, but lived in hope. Elise thought she could see Mama's strength stretching out infinitely. Would there ever be a time when those unbowed shoulders, that straight back, could bear no more, when the load would be too great? Elise didn't think so.

She went back to work on the farm that day. It was the only way she knew how to move through the pain. She wasn't as fast or as clear as usual, but no one expected her to be; they hadn't expected her to be working at all. Jacob and the men were quiet and quick and hyper-attentive to everything that day. She knew they were watching her and watching out for her.

Elise was aware of herself as completely alone. She was too old to be an orphan, but that was the picture she had of herself now. Van had been an only child. Both sets of grandparents had died a long time ago. Now her father, her mother and her brother were dead. Daan was gone and Ina had disowned her. Elise didn't know how she was going to move forward, didn't know how she would manage so alone.

The beginning of the harvest season, the tensest season on any farm, was approaching fast. Jacob was doing his best, but Elise knew he couldn't do it all on his own. The nectarines would be ready within days and unlike her other cultivars they had to be packed on the farm. They were too soft, too easily bruised, to be put into the bins and sent off to the packing shed. The picking and packing operation was quite something to run. She would have to manage it alone while keeping up with the spraying that had to go on all through the picking season.

On a farm there is never one job to do at a time; everything runs concurrently throughout the year, but the pressure of the tasks to be done at harvest is the heaviest. The days were long and the work hard, but at least it was summer. Christmas was approaching and all the women and children and some piece workers joined the men in the orchards to pick. But they did so without their customary zeal at this time of year. Elise needed morale to be high among her workers, needed to have them pushing hard through the picking, but they too were anxious about the future of the farm.

Elise knew that if Rustenvrede was to survive she had to take on the responsibility which until now she'd sought. But what had once challenged and excited her suddenly appeared daunting. Could she carry the farm on her own? It was an immense burden to bear, the obstacles endless. A buzz of anxiety, a whining at the back of her brain, whispered doubt.

The obstacle to good judgement was her own fatigue and enervating grief, but she knew that time spent indulging her emotions was time wasted. She simply had to make decisions. And so she did.

Elise and Jacob worked late. At the end of the day, towards dusk, they took a detour to walk through the nectarines. The fruit looked excellent, their size and colour exceptional, much better than last year. The nectarines had been her project, and Elise knew her father would have been pleased to see the improvement, and that pleased her. She was thinking of him, strolling slowly back down to the house, when she heard a vehicle approaching up the drive. The car flashed between the trees and she knew her visitor was Daan. Jacob saw it too and rather too quickly took his leave of her.

Daan smiled broadly and bravely as he strode towards her. Elise squinted back at him, wondering at his confident demeanour. She watched the dogs go running up to him, jumping up to lick him, wheeling around him in circles of affection and excitement. He put his arms round her and for just a second she leaned into him, allowed herself to feel the relief of his warmth, though she didn't return his embrace. She felt her heart melting – she really would always love him. But there was something deeper going on that she had to work out for herself and on her own. She pulled away.

'It was difficult yesterday,' he said. 'I couldn't think straight. Can we talk now?' His tone was gentle, coaxing.

Elise smiled and dipped her head by way of a yes. She couldn't refuse him.

They sat down on opposite sides of the kitchen table, as if they were at a meeting. Daan shifted in his seat, struggling to find the right words. 'Elise, I don't know what happened between you and this Mashiya guy – and I don't want to know, to be honest – but there are things that have come to light about him which you should know about. The story is far murkier than we suspected. Johnny Kakana dug it all up in his files.'

Elise didn't flinch, she faced him fully and listened.

'The reports say that while he was in exile Sandile was involved in a double murder. One of the victims was his best friend.'

Daan had played his trump card. 'He's no good – you should know that, Elise. He lied to you as well, didn't he?'

Elise was frozen and for a moment incredulous, thinking it was a desperate ploy of Daan's. But she knew that he

455

wouldn't make something like that up, wouldn't lie about such a thing. Sandile was a murderer.

In the long silence that followed, Daan went to get himself a beer. He flipped off the bottle top and the cap bounced and clinked and rolled around the stone floor. Elise listened to him taking a long slow drink. Her eyes were closed, her hands over her face, the tips of her index fingers pressing against her eyeballs. She remembered Sandile's bruised and bloody face in the cell and while she believed Daan was telling the truth, she had to remind herself of his agenda. She wanted a beer too, but he hadn't offered and she didn't feel like getting up. Nor did she feel like saying anything. What *could* she say? She didn't know what was true about Sandile. He had thrown enough surprises at her already for her to know that she didn't have a handle on who he was. He didn't seem like a murderer. But wasn't that what people always said about con men? They made you believe in them. Elise had believed in Sandile and already felt once betrayed. She had to admit too – though only to herself – that, logically, he might have done it. The admission put her at the top of a slippery slope. She felt dizzy, profoundly shaken.

Elise finally got up and poured herself a beer. She was unreadably silent. Daan finished his drink, slugging back the last gulp before he put the bottle on the table and began to roll it thoughtfully back and forth under the palm of his right hand.

'He's a convincing liar, Elise. I understand it better now, after listening to the guy telling his alibi. Look, even *I* was mesmerised by his plausibility.'

Daan stopped rolling the bottle. He stood it up on its end and reached across the table to put his hands over hers. 'The point is, I want to forget about what happened, about all that shouting yesterday. It's been a helluva time, we're both emotionally overloaded. We shouldn't be taking this out on each other when we don't mean it.'

Elise gazed back at him, her expression unchanged. She didn't move her hands, though she felt the pressure of his fingers over hers. 'What are you saying, Daan?'

'Ag, little one, I'm saying I want to push things forward. Let's get married, quietly and quickly. Then I can move in here with you, help you out on the farm, and we can get on with our lives, get on with what really matters.'

Elise continued to stare at him. He leaned forward, bending across the table as far as he could, almost whispering, almost wheedling. 'We'll make it for as soon as possible after the funeral. I'll arrange everything – you won't have to do a single thing. No big fuss – my mother will do a small lunch, only family. Dominee Slabbert thinks it would be for the best, particularly for you, and the dorp will understand that a party and a big performance is inappropriate right now.'

Elise saw that he hadn't contemplated failure in this mission. Daan was treating her like a difficult patient who needed a gentle prod to be persuaded to take her medicine, to get better. She knew his frame of mind was going to make her answer all the more devastating. She was very sure of what she felt; she just wasn't certain she could handle Daan's pain on top of her own.

Daan mustered a smile. 'What do you say, sweetheart?'

Elise was shut down, but not that far. She did need Daan, she'd love to have him with her, love not to be alone on the farm. But she wouldn't fool him and she couldn't live a lie. She sighed, watching him. Her nostrils flared and she pursed her lips, as if she was swallowing. Then she spoke very softly, leaning into him, as if she was leaning against the opposing tilt of her words. 'Daan, I love you. I really mean that. But I will not go through with this.'

Daan pulled his hands away from her, palms down, backwards across the cool surface of the table. He brought his fingers up to his chin and rubbed them slowly over his parted lips. Then he shook his head, back and forth, back and forth, his eyes on hers all the time. Elise couldn't stand the pressure of it. She dropped her gaze.

Daan was prepared to swallow his pride, prepared to accept that whatever had happened with Sandile – he didn't

457

want to know specifically – was a blip, some crazy brain-storm of hers in the face of the infinity of marriage. He wanted to forgive and forget and move forward. There was self-interest in his plan, but also kindness. He was genuinely worried about her, feared for her being alone on the farm and wanted to help her get through. He knew how much strain she took, knew that his place should be at her side.

The chasm of loneliness and fear that faced Elise almost drew her to him. But there was a part of her that felt released, felt free, and that sense made her sure, confirmed to her that marriage to Daan would be the wrong thing.

'Daan, my decision has nothing to do with Sandile. I don't know what I feel about him, but I think my – infatuation, or whatever it was, might have had something to do with being jittery about the wedding. I don't know, but for some reason I was taken in by his flirting and fell into his trap. I know that now and I feel more stupid and terrible about it than you can imagine. The point is not my feelings about him, but my feelings about you. In the end I wouldn't have been happy.'

Tears welled up in Daan's eyes but he didn't shift his gaze from her and his voice was steady when he replied, '*I* would have been happy.'

Elise felt her heart would rip in two. She wobbled again in her resolve, though she was frustrated too at not being understood. She was certain that this was the right decision, that she and Daan were wrong for each other, that eventually they would have been tormented by pettiness, their affection shot through with cruelty, poisoned by mutual boredom and disgust, so that in time there would have been nothing left between them, and the air in their house would be stale and vile to both of them. Many people lived in houses like that, but Elise felt that both she and Daan deserved more.

She curled her fingers round his hands and now she too began to cry and every word she spoke seared her throat. 'Daan, I'll never regret the time we've been together.'

Daan recognised that he could no longer reach her, but he was so desperate that he made one last attempt. 'Elise, please?

Can't you see you're in no state to make decisions like this? At least come and talk this through with the Dominee. I could meet you there first thing tomorrow morning and we can think it all out. Hey?'

Elise said nothing. Daan jerked his hands away from hers, scraping his chair back as he staggered up. Elise knew then how badly she'd hurt him. He was loping round the kitchen like a great wounded animal. She stood up, barring the way to the outside door, and grabbed his arm, squeezing it as she whispered her answer to him. 'It won't change anything, but if you want it I'll come and talk to the Dominee.'

Daan's shoulders sank with relief. He didn't flinch from her, but nor did he touch her; instead he smiled a tight little I-think-I-know-better smile. Then he stepped round her, opened the back door and walked out.

'I really meant what I said, Daan,' she shouted after him.

He nodded curtly, his back to her. As he drove away he watched her in his rear-view mirror, watching him.

In the dull haze of grief and sadness and guilt there can be moments of lucidity, like sunbursts which are quickly obliterated by cloud. When Elise woke the morning after Daan had made his desperate proposal she had just such a moment.

She knew Daan was the wrong choice, the wrong man for her. The solution to their problem now was to convince him of that. She really believed they could work out a way to understand one another and to part amicably in the end. She would cancel the wedding and in the long run they would both look back and say that it was for the best. That was easy to conclude. The hard part of the equation was her own fear; it muddied the clarity she'd felt earlier.

Elise was part of Fransmansvallei as much as it was part of her. And if she turned away from Daan she would be turning her back on it. She would be connecting herself to that Mashiya 'boy', that 'kaffir'. This was at the heart of everything. It was the strongest taboo – biological, scriptural and moral. Elise knew it was foolish to think she could ride the storm of their disapproval. She felt nauseous even contemplating it. The fear made her hesitate, made her think that perhaps the Dominee might have something to say that would help to convince her to marry Daan. She feared being alone. She feared the deadly, silent punishment she had seen meted out on the Lombaards, a punishment that her own silence had helped to inflict on both of them, injured and injurer. She'd known loneliness before and the thought of it looming again terrified her.

FORTY ONE

Sandile didn't sleep at all that first night in Pollsmoor prison. He was dimly aware of people in the cells all round him. He was locked up with twenty-eight other men in a space that had been designed to cram in only eighteen. He tried to block the other men out, but the sounds of snoring, of muttering and once, for a short time, of weeping, floated up to his bunk in an eerily disembodied way. Cooped up in that pitch-black, claustrophobic space Sandile had to fight for shreds of sanity. He shivered from the cold. His tongue felt like layers of chalk dust and his stomach was tight and acid and angry. His mind was long loops of regret.

He knew that morning was approaching when grey light seeped in and dimly projected a square of brightness on the wall opposite the bars of the cell. The clatter and clanging of metal against metal roused him from where he'd lain all night on the splintered plank with its lumpy mattress that was his bed and bench. The smells and sounds of the other men waking almost choked him.

Sandile learned quickly how any approach was announced by a clatter of keys, the clanging of metal grilles and the slow, heavy tread of a warder. The noise brought a mixture of dread and relief. When at first he'd been shoved into the cramped concrete zoo of the cell he was relieved to have the Kafkaesque horror of the magistrates' court behind him. He'd hoped, vainly as it turned out, that he might get access to a telephone. But he soon realised that things had simply gotten worse, that he'd been dumped and would be forgotten here in his dark dungeon at the end of infinite corridors with their bitter chemical smells, raw concrete and rotting linoleum. Here he would stay until his trial. The thought was so unacceptable he feared he might lose his mind.

At the sound of the warder's approach Sandile got up, moving stiffly, and stretched out numbed limbs. His heavy shoes thudding on linoleum came closer and closer.

The trudging feet belonged to a white warder. The name embroidered on his uniform was 'Human'. The label was far from appropriate. Sandile had never seen a person resemble an ape quite so closely. This one was an orang-utan, but mousy blond, not a redhead. He had deep-set eyes which were surprisingly big and round, with long bleached white lashes. His uniform had to be a Large, to accommodate the spread around his belly, but that meant the shoulders didn't fit at all, because in Human's case the distance from the top of one arm to the other was at least half the diameter of his waist. The pants were ludicrous, extra-wide and too long for so short a body.

Sandile swallowed. This might be trickier than he expected. He could almost hear the sound of knuckles dragging on the floor as Human slowly approached and came to a halt, punctuated with a small, low grunt, in front of the bars where Sandile was standing. Uh-oh. Sandile moved his mouth so that its shape resembled the closest thing he could muster to a smile. Human squinted back at him. Sandile cleared his throat and said as patiently and politely as possible, 'Sir, can you help me, please? I need to use the telephone.'

Harsh laughter echoed round the cell behind him. Human's bushy eyebrows slid upwards on his low forehead before a sound erupted from him. It might have been a sneer, a yes, a no, a question – Sandile couldn't tell.

'Sorry?' Sandile pressed as far forward as the bars would allow.

The warder opened his mouth again. His upper lip was buried in the shaggy fringe of a moustache – presumably the cause of his strangulated speech. Human's voice was thick; he spoke as if there was a rag stuffed in his mouth and he could only use his tongue minimally and very close to the bottom of his mouth. 'What for?' he grunted.

462

Sandile almost staggered as the stench of foul breath hit his nostrils. Recovering, he peered at the creature before him, worried that it mightn't be possible for them to understand each other, ever. He spoke each word distinctly. 'I need to speak to my lawyer.'

Human shook his head very slowly. Then he turned and moved on, resuming the pace of his thudding trudge along the walkway. Sandile shouted after him pointlessly. His shouts only aroused yelling from the cells around him where people were either trying to sleep or were just happy to add to the noise. Sandile shouted until he was hoarse. Then he slumped against the bars and listened to the dying chorus of insults and pleas from his neighbours.

He had never in his life felt so powerless as he did that morning, not even during the time of his detention in Lusaka. He climbed back on to his bunk and closed his eyes. The raw wooden plank scratched his legs and he banged his skull against the rough cool concrete. Breathing deliberately, deeply and slowly, he tried to close his mind to the chaos around him. But his mind kept flicking from the hellish present to Lusaka. He recalled the building where they'd incarcerated him. He'd never been in the place before. It was clear that Simon Siluma and the intelligence people used it often; they knew its maze of empty storerooms, busted offices and windowless corridors only too well. The place had been empty. It must once have been an office or factory of some sort. It was certainly not purpose-built for prisoners.

Sandile remembered how frightening the emptiness of the place had been, especially as night fell and dragged on interminably. The fear was physical. There was no one and nothing that made his captors accountable. He was at their mercy, just as he imagined Selina must have been utterly at the mercy of her captors that night she'd been detained at Kopfontein. He'd always dreaded he might one day be at the mercy of the racist regime, but not of his own comrades.

Thinking back, he knew that in Lusaka it wouldn't have been so difficult to escape. He hadn't contemplated escape then – it only occurred to him now, where it was impossible. Then, there'd been no point. His only true release from that situation was to have his name cleared, at a minimum to survive the interrogation. He'd had no life outside the ANC and the struggle, so he couldn't run away from it. It would have been as impossible as escaping himself. So Sandile had sat it out, screamed it out, until they caved in and he caved in and they all walked away from the mess. Afterwards Simon went back to work as usual and Sandile was left to piece together the shards of a life that up till then had been his work. Afterwards he wasn't trusted with the work and he had to dream up something else. The something else was the land. His land. Until now the farm had been within his grasp.

Sandile opened his eyes and stared at the concrete beams of the ceiling. His life felt like one long, crashing descent on a helter-skelter. Was this the bottom of the ride at last? Would it all end here with a life sentence for killing Elise's father? He was all too aware that people had been hanged on less evidence. There was no death sentence now, but a life sentence was almost as bad, possibly worse. Decades drained of purpose and colour, an infinity in which to feel every shade of the deepest frustration, of thwarted desire. How could this have happened?

He tried to think of Elise. He pictured her in that warm light at the end of the day, her jeans and velskoene dusty from the orchards, her hair falling in feathers round her face, her mouth wide with a smile. She was a rare person, genuinely *nice*, genuinely thoughtful, quite something for a boere meisie. The quiet passion with which she worked was probably her failing as far as relating to other people went, but that single-mindedness, that simple, sincere conviction was the quality Sandile found so compelling. He had betrayed her over the land claim and lost his one potential ally. Strategically this whole thing was a disaster, but then strategically Elise was not supposed to feature at all.

Sandile got up and banged against the bars, straining his neck as far round as possible, scanning the walkway for the warder. He had to get out. He was panicking. He'd started to believe that no one would ever find him here. Nobody came, nobody listened and his cellmates turned away from him, locked in their own listless indifference.

Sandile realised, with horrible clarity, that certain things had not changed one iota. He knew that Dup and Du Toit had not told Simon Siluma when they sent him to Paarl and rushed him through the hearing. They wanted him put away and lost in the system for as long as possible. Sandile knew that Simon would find him in the end, but he was sure the cops would put as many obstacles as they could in his way.

By the evening of the following day, there was still not even a hint of contact from the world outside. The hours seemed interminable. Sandile was losing hope. He shuffled listlessly through the circuits of the exercise time the prisoners were forced to take. The walls of the yard they were taken to were so high the only view they got was a meagre hexagon of sky; nothing else, not even mountains. The air in the yard tasted stale, as if it had been trapped there for years, encased in the cold concrete. The aftertaste of the food they were served was bitter in his mouth. There was hopelessness and helplessness and a palpable latent violence all around him.

FORTY TWO

Elise arrived first. She pulled up into the gravel churchyard at eight and sat waiting in her car for Daan. She rarely looked around her in Fransmansvallei, knew everything too well to mark it every day she passed through. But this morning she was struck by the beauty of the church; she saw why so many tourists came to look at it, why so many brides draped themselves round its gardens for their wedding photographs. The church was typical solid Dutch Reformed design, all triangles and short spires; thick, squat arrows pointing to the heavens. The building was large, but simple and low and wide, with gleaming whitewashed walls, a dark slate roof and tall, narrow arched windows, their small-squared panes of glass so old they were almost opaque. Most of the flamboyance and decoration was in the garden, which was dominated by huge blooms of pale yellow and blood-red roses and the imposing bulk of two massive oaks which were probably planted not long after Simon van der Stel first brought acorns to the Cape at least 200 years ago. Beneath the spreading limbs of the larger tree stood the bright white arch of the church bell, once a slave bell and later the school bell. It had been there since before the church was rebuilt in 1841. In that church Elise, like her grandparents and parents before her, was christened, and her family had all been married there, just as she was expected to be.

The sun was still low in the sky, its light slanting over the mountains which were hazy and covered in fine tendrils of cloud that curled and clung to the jagged ridges. Elise sighed at the beauty of it all and at the stillness of the morning. She felt fine and strong while she was there alone, but the second she saw Daan, the minute he came up to her window with his easy grin and his pale blue eyes, she started to cry. Tears rolled down her cheeks as she strained to smile. Seeing her thus, Daan's grin faded.

He opened the door of the car for her to get out. They didn't say anything to each other as they walked together towards the Dominee's house, their feet crunching noisily on the gravel path. Elise slipped her hand in around Daan's arm, holding lightly on to him, and he squeezed his elbow against his side in faint acknowledgement of her gesture. The low iron gate opened with a terrible grinding creak and Daan said something falsely hearty and fatuous about the Dominee having so much money and failing to get the fundamentals, like the oil on his hinges, right. Elise made a sound like laughter and walked on, letting go of his arm as they went up the steps to the front door. Daan reached for the great question mark of the brass door knocker, pulling it to him and letting it thud back against the door.

Willem Slabbert took a while to answer. Standing on the long front stoep, Elise and Daan were silent. He sighed and shoved his hands into his pockets, staring out at the road and at the black mountains beyond. He had slumped visibly, as if he already knew what the outcome of this was to be, as if he was beginning to accept defeat. Finally the great panelled oak door opened and the Dominee smiled when he saw them waiting for him.

Elise noticed that Slabbert wasn't surprised to see the pair of them and didn't seem to need to be appraised of the situation. Daan must have confided in him already and she felt piqued at the idea. Elise hated people talking about her, even kindly, when she wasn't present. However she had to admit that, if he had to confide in anyone, Daan had chosen cautiously and well. If there was anyone who could be trusted completely, anyone who was utterly loyal to both her and to Daan, anyone in the dorp who came close to discreet, it was the Dominee. So Elise grudgingly accepted that Daan had done the right thing and quietened the irritation that was

467

rising in her. All the same, she already had the unpleasant sensation of being treated as a wayward child, which she was not.

The Dominee was dressed in a short-sleeved, bright-patterned plaid shirt with thin synthetic blue jogging shorts and flip-flops. He put his hand into the curve of Elise's back, gently steering her into his office at the front of the house, just off the main entrance hall. It had clearly been agreed beforehand, and without Elise's knowledge, that the Dominee would speak to her alone. Elise nodded, dipping her chin just slightly, when this was made plain to her. Then Daan left them, tiptoeing across the wide rug and closing the door very quietly behind him.

Elise sat down in one of the chairs arranged in front of Slabbert's enormous teak desk, a Cape Town Harbour Customs table. He had picked it up at an auction years before, considering it a bargain, not an antique. The table looked solid enough to withstand an earthquake, and in fact it had. Everyone in the valley knew the story of how the Dominee had taken shelter beneath it during the quake that threatened to flatten nearby Tulbagh and which had thoroughly rattled Fransmansvallei when Elise was a very little girl. The Dominee's house was filled with an odd mix of furniture – an expression of Slabbert's frugal nature and his carelessness over worldly things – which contrasted starkly with the elegance and grandeur of the old homestead's exterior. The rooms were dotted with junk-shop finds and giveaways from the valley farms. The chair Elise sat in, for instance, was a seventies monster covered in knubby-textured orange polyester and the curtains over the window behind Slabbert were gorgeous peacock-blue velvet drapes thrown out by Etta Joubert during her dramatic and much-publicised – in the valley at least – refurbishing ten years before.

The Dominee's study was perhaps the single most cluttered room in the house. Two walls were lined with bookshelves overflowing with alphabetically ordered books, in both English and Afrikaans, with titles like *Calvien Psalmen I, Faith on Trial* and *When Your Goals Seem Out of Reach*. Slabbert believed fervently that the Bible had an answer to everything and he studied it endlessly. For many years Elise had thought that he too had an answer for every problem, but that was a long, long time ago.

On top of both bookshelves were two neat rows of framed photographs, posed group shots of university sports and debating clubs with a young, always grave-looking Dominee somewhere in the centre of each. Pride of place was given to a large shot of Universiteit van Stellenbosch Skaakklub Eerstespan: four young white men in suits and ties with severe haircuts and scrubbed, clean-shaven faces grouped round a chessboard. Chess was the Dominee's passion. He had no equal in the valley, so every few months he travelled, occasionally even overseas, to a meeting organised by old chess club mates from his university days.

Behind Elise was a wall of putty-coloured metal filing cabinets on which were arranged some plastic toys: model tractors and tanks and Kaspirs for children to play with when their parents came in for a talk, or for Bible study. There was a collection of ammonites, found by the Dominee himself, and next to that a calendar with watercolours of the Cape peninsula.

The Dominee was silent for some time, leaning back in his chair, his hands together, fingers making a steeple. Light streamed in through the window behind him; from where Elise sat he was silhouetted against the glare. Elise had nothing to say; she was there to listen, to react, so she gazed around the room, sighing from time to time, her heart as heavy as lead.

Slabbert spoke at last, in a confidential near whisper, though the walls of the place were thick enough to withstand a battering ram and there was no chance his voice would penetrate them. Elise folded her hands in her lap and cocked her head slightly, listening, though her face wore a pained expression, as if she was having to concentrate hard, which she was, because for reasons of his own the Dominee was speaking in the third person.

'Elise, I want you to picture a situation. You get a call, late at night, from a person in the dorp and he tells you he is deeply troubled, that he needs to speak to you urgently. So you arrange to meet him and he pours his heart out about his fiancée who has just, out of the blue, told him that she has feelings for another man. Well, you've christened this girl, you're going to marry her, and now you hear that she's having second thoughts about her marriage. In such an event, don't you agree, you would want to talk to them about the, uh, the spiritual aspects of this . . . problem?'

Elise uncrossed her legs and folded her arms across her chest during the silence that followed this opening. She knew the Dominee's style all too well: the more complicated the situation the more ponderous and deliberate he became. Elise could hear her wristwatch ticking. Slabbert cleared his throat gruffly and ran his right hand over the shiny smooth skin of his scalp. Then, sensing her mood, he shifted gear.

'Now, when you and Daan first came to me and talked about marriage you each filled in the questionnaires for me and we went through them together and talked through the places where there were red lights and the places where things were good.'

He paused, as if expecting an answer. Elise shifted in her chair, crossing and recrossing her legs. Finally she nodded. The Dominee leaned forward, bunching his hands into fists which he put quietly on to the desk in front of him.

'When you came to me on your own afterwards I asked you – as I ask every young bride-to-be who comes in here – I asked you if there was anything troubling you, if you had any second thoughts. And you answered me, without hesitation. No, you said. And I was so happy for you both. On my life, I don't think I *ever* saw such excellent candidates for marriage in all the years I've been doing this. Elise, there are too many people in the world who are unhappily married, there is too much divorce. I'm not going to tell you to do something that will make you unhappy and therefore Daan as well. So let's talk about it. It's confidential, remains between us, but we must talk about it.'

So that was how their conversation began. It continued, sometimes fluid, sometimes staccato, but borne along always by the Dominee's strange mixture of occasional, startlingly progressive ideas peppering a mass of chokingly anachronistic assumptions.

'Look, I must be *dead* honest with you.' He emphasised the word 'dead' with a sharp downward bob of his head. 'Think of it like – like an Afrikaner marrying an English person! You have to admit there is a cultural difference. You have to face the problems and ask yourself if you really can, if you are *really* prepared to bridge them.' Elise had been correct in her expectations about this meeting and people's reactions to the cancellation of her engagement. Daan must have told the Dominee what she'd said about Sandile. He, presumably, like everyone else, assumed her rejection of Daan meant she was choosing Sandile. Elise didn't try to correct him.

He kept returning to this point about the incompatibilities of different 'cultures'. The euphemism infuriated Elise. He was talking about race, about pigment, about skin. As recently as ten years ago he would have felt perfectly comfortable bluntly using one of those terms. Suddenly the language had changed and now concealed the deep truth, which was that neither he, nor any white person in the valley, could conceive of a black man and a white woman living happily together. It was unnatural, almost disgusting; it was so deeply ingrained that even local black families were convinced of it as well.

Elise sat in increasingly frosty silence until the Dominee very quietly, and with evident pain, asked if he could trust her, said he wanted to confide in her. Elise looked up with interest, which had been Slabbert's intention – he had found no other way of reaching her. Then he said gravely that he too had once loved, or thought he loved, someone very, very deeply.

'I was consumed by it, infatuated. But the love was forbidden, it was not a love that I could speak of. I am surprised to find myself speaking of it now, but I think I can trust you, Elise. Mine was not a love that my community or my family could sanction. Now the community is your family, Elise. I can understand how you feel. I know what a terrible roller-coaster of emotion you're riding, but trust me. This isn't the time or the place. Such a . . .' He thought carefully. Elise could see his tongue rolling round inside his mouth as he searched for the word until at last he found it. 'Such a *connection* would be so difficult, perhaps impossible, to maintain here and now. You must think about this, think about reality, my dear, not fantasy. Romance is a narcotic – it distorts clarity and clouds judgement. Don't get hooked on it. Don't start making big decisions while you are under the influence.'

Dominee Slabbert paused, then shut his mouth and folded his hands in his lap, apparently pleased with his performance. He nodded, running back over his speech, agreeing with his own turn of phrase. It seemed to Elise that he liked the way he'd put it. He wore his pain like a personal trophy, his triumph over his own sinning flesh.

Elise swallowed. 'What did you do?'

He didn't understand.

'About your . . . the person you loved?'

Dominee Slabbert stood up and walked over to the window. He stared out at the garden, the perfectly arranged flowerbeds bursting with blossom and broom, at the ruby-coloured rosebuds against the brilliant whitewashed walls of the church. After a few minutes he turned and sighed and smiled. The smile was a shape on his lips. It didn't express anything; it wasn't rueful or sad or even happy.

'I cut it off.'

Elise was utterly taken aback, as much in terms of her own turmoil over Sandile as because of what the Dominee was revealing to her. She'd known him all her life. He'd never been seen with a girlfriend, never been known to have anyone in his life. No one had even thought to gossip about it. Suddenly she saw this as terrible. How lonely and isolated he must have been, because he had denied his love. This was the difference between his generation and hers, she thought, the difference between the mentality of the old order and the new. She could barely imagine putting her own feelings and future second to those of her community, even in the name of concepts like duty and obligation. Fundamentally, she had only herself to fall back on. The truth was that it wasn't duty or obligation that had driven Willem Slabbert's choice; he had made a coward's calculation. He knew that life would be easier if he didn't follow his heart, if he slunk back into everyday life and thereby avoided the sanction of his community. This way he had his job, his standing, this beautiful house, and he had the dorp. What a weak and lonely choice he had made, she thought. Aloud she said, 'You mean you never saw the person again?'

The Dominee continued to stare out of the window. He shook his head and said, almost inaudibly, 'Oh no, I saw. I just never spoke. Never acknowledged. It would have been wrong. Do you understand, Elise?'

He faced her now, trying to shift the focus back to her situation, but Elise needed to know the end of his story. 'Did my father know?'

'Know what?'

'About your . . . story?'

'No one knows.'

'But surely she didn't accept it?' she blurted, immediately regretting her choice of words because Slabbert blanched, the tip of his nose going white. Elise was stunned at the realisation – his lover was not a she.

'I mean, what did they do?'

Slabbert sat down in his chair. His large hands thudded, flat side down, in a cutting motion, on to the desk. He stared right at her when he answered, as if this was the line drawn under everything, the conclusive drumbeat, the trump card.

'Suicide.'

Elise's mouth dropped open. The Dominee's forbidden love had ended with one suicide and one lonely sham of a life. Clearly he didn't see it that way. He had no idea that his fable

473

was having the opposite effect to the one intended. She wanted to know more, but she didn't want to pry, and Slabbert was not going to say any more.

She tried to put herself in his shoes. She could see he was grappling with her problem, but the harder he tried the wider the chasm between them grew. Forty years ago things were so much simpler. Elise suddenly recalled a rhyme recited laughingly to her class by her history teacher in Standard Five: 'In days of old, when men were bold and pansy was the name of a flower.' He couldn't stand up to it, to stupid rhymes and lewd glances and bigoted gossip.

When at last she spoke, she did so very quietly, disarming the Dominee with her soft tone, while her meaning was hard. 'The simple fact, the thing that you're tiptoeing around, is that I felt an attraction for a black man. White girls from good families don't mess with kaffirs, right? The dorp can take me being a farmer, at a push, as long as I hang in long after they've all got tired of kicking the shit out of me. As long as I stick with it they'll pat me on the back in the end for that persistence. But this, *this* is too much. They'll never tolerate it, not until hell freezes over. Right? That's what you're saying, isn't it?'

She spoke wearily, like one tired to the core, as if she was much older than her years. Elise hated being the one who always fought. She hated being the angry, different, subversive one, the one who rocked the boat. She would have loved to be able to just roll over and die like most people, certainly like most of the women she knew. But that wasn't in her make-up. In some ways she resembled her father, who had had a kind of stubborn integrity, if that word could apply within the confines of a value system like his. She believed, adamantly, that it was a terrible betrayal of the self to hang back, half convinced, like the cowards who huddle in bleating herds and never make the leap for passion or belief, never stand up for anything. Their punishment, their reward, was a life in shadow, a life of drift and dull comfort and numbed pain.

Until now Elise had been scared too. Now she believed that fear had let her down. Her big rationalisation for the secrecy about Sandile was that she didn't really know what was happening and she didn't want to hurt Daan, but the truth was that she was afraid of incurring the wrath of the valley, she was unable to transgress the fundamental assumptions of life in the Fransmansvallei. She had valued the community and she'd allowed its rules to govern her choices. She knew how hard people could make life for her if she didn't conform. Slabbert knew that too, and he was cowed.

Elise was scared as hell of being an outcast, but she was about to become one anyway and now she wasn't sure that she cared. She had lost so much; she was isolated and vulnerable, but the world hadn't ended, at least not yet. She made a decision then and there. From now on she would do what pleased her, not what pleased other people. And that was how the conversation between Elise and the Dominee ended.

He saw that there was nothing more to be said. Elise got up from her chair and strode across the room, fuelled by determination that her life wouldn't sink to lies and drift. If she had to build high walls around her and live alone, she'd rather accept that than the company of people who'd turned out to be strangers.

Daan sat waiting for them, perched hopefully on the edge of the sofa directly outside the door to the Dominee's office. Elise emerged with Slabbert behind her. The Dominee was nearly as tall as her father; he loomed behind her, his face sombre. Daan looked hopefully from one to the other, but he knew immediately and was utterly crestfallen.

Elise put her hands together in front of her, as if in prayer. 'I'm sorry, Daan.'

'Yussuss, Elise.' He almost laughed. 'I thought I had you cornered at last, but you've slipped away again, haven't you?'

He had his arms folded across his chest and he shook his head, his eyes boring into hers. Elise thought then that she might have underestimated him. His defences were down, he was beyond sadness, and she saw just the pain, just the wide-open wound. At last there was something clear and pure in this communication; at last, glancingly, there was nothing but truth, no layers of anger or hurt or expectation.

'What the hell do I have to do? What do you want me to do? I've chased you halfway across the country and still I don't seem to be able to catch up with you. I still can't quite see you face to face. Whenever you stand still and I'm almost up to you, you disappear off round the next corner and I can't –'

Daan bit down on his lip and looked away from her, down at his feet scuffing the floor. 'I never could keep up with you. You never let me.'

Elise didn't know what to say. He was right, and that was like a stab to the heart. She'd always sensed herself as elusive, but she always hoped she wasn't, she'd always hoped she was plain-spoken, transparent Elise.

Something had snapped in Daan and that was it; that was the point after which all feeling he had for Elise showed itself in hostility. Now it would be a question of who was right and who was wrong. Elise knew that what she had done would only ever be judged wrong, but she no longer had any respect for the evaluation and that would only damn her further in everyone's eyes.

Daan hovered for a moment, as if there was something he wanted to add. He decided not to, and strode off down the hall. The heavy door slammed behind him and moments later they heard the rip of his bakkie on the gravel.

The Dominee's face was ashen when he turned to Elise. 'Will you be all right?' he asked.

Elise nodded. Then she put her hand on his arm and gave it a squeeze as she murmured, 'Thank you.'

The Dominee bowed very slightly by way of response. She made for the door. 'I take it then that the marriage is off.'

Elise turned back to look at him. 'Yes,' she said very clearly.

'And I take it the dorp will know of this soon enough?'

Elise swallowed. She raised her eyebrows, shrugging. 'They probably know already, Dominee!'

476

He laughed ruefully. 'As sure as God made little apples.'

Elise smiled slightly and then walked out of the house.

There is a sense of freedom that comes with shattered certainties. She'd read that somewhere once. The phrase had resonated, but she had never truly understood it before.

That night Alan Taylor telephoned through to Rusten-vrede. He was brief and kind-sounding, in his tight, chilly English way. He wanted to know if there was anything he could do to help out on the farm, anything she needed as far as the funeral arrangements were concerned. Elise said no, and thanked him for his thoughtfulness. Taylor said he might pop by later in the week and she said he would be most welcome. When she put the phone down she felt her legs buckle. His kind tone hit harder than any of the stern advice and angry words she'd heard that day.

At some point, not long after the hush of dark had fallen, she realised she was starving – she hadn't eaten or drunk anything at all that day. There was nothing in the fridge, but there were boxes of dishes in the freezer that Mama Mashiya had stacked recently. Elise couldn't face heating up the oven and dishing anything up, so she cut up some biltong for her supper and listened to music on the radio, filling the empty, lonely spaces of the house with it.

Later, much later, with all the lights in the house blazing to ward off the ghosts that lurked in the darkness, she went to the office and sat down to the work that needed to be done there. She knew it wouldn't be long before everyone in the dorp heard about the events of her life that day and she braced herself for the first evidence of her ostracisation. In the darkest hours, early in the morning, Elise put her head down on the desk and slept a little. She woke as the glow of dawn seeped into the office. Then she went to work again.

FORTY THREE

It was lunchtime a few days before the funeral when Elise received a surprise visitor. She was out on the farm when he arrived. Elise had no stomach for reminders of the routines she'd shared with her father, so she'd stopped by briefly in the kitchen, then gone out again, sandwich in one hand and an apple in the breast pocket of her overalls.

Elise was up in the middle section of the farm with Jacob and Vuyo when Alan Taylor's car bounced almost silently to a halt at the far end of the row they were inspecting. Elise glanced up irritably. She had nothing to say to anyone; she was relieved in fact that none of the people from the dorp had any desire to see her. What did *he* want? She'd assumed his promise to stop by had been courtesy rather than intention, but if she had to talk to anyone, she'd rather talk to an outsider.

Taylor smiled as he approached, waving his hand to indicate that she shouldn't stop what she was doing. Nevertheless Elise, jerking her chin up in brief acknowledgement, strolled downhill to meet him.

She was wearing the same overalls and boots she'd worn for the past three days; only her T-shirt was fresh. Her hair was unwashed, scraped back into a knot fastened with a scratched plastic tortoiseshell-look clip. Wisps of hair around her forehead and ears had escaped the severe bun and hung loose, a frowzy frame to her tired face. Her eyes were dully anxious; dark purple crescents curved outwards beneath them, emphasising her fatigue. She didn't feel tired, though. The shock-absorbers were still working. Elise seemed not to need any sleep; she was running on empty. There were still flashes of gnawing anxiety, a sense that something terrible was going to happen.

Taylor stopped, got out of his car, putting his hands on his hips, and stared up the row. Expensive matt black sunglasses masked his eyes. In his polished alligator slip-ons, his ironed shirt and sports jacket, he looked thoroughly out of place. However he seemed eager to connect himself to everything, even waving briefly and familiarly at Jacob and Vuyo. Jacob dipped his chin and reached up to touch the floppy brim of his hat. Vuyo turned away and went to wait in the shade, chewing on a blade of grass as he watched Elise with her visitor.

Taylor put his hand on Elise's shoulder and looked hard into her eyes. 'How *are* you?' His tone was thick with sincerity. Elise answered without hesitation, said she was fine and braced her arms over her chest, staring back at him as if to say she had no time for pleasantries, that he should get on and say whatever it was he had come here to say.

Taylor seemed to be sizing her up. He slipped his hands into the pockets of his trousers, tilting his head to one side. 'I was just passing. It occurred to me to pop in and see how things are. See if there's anything you need.'

Elise thanked him and reiterated politely that she was fine, she had everything she needed.

Taylor smiled rather too keenly again. 'Well, if there *is* anything I can do for tomorrow, anything, please don't hesitate – after all, what are neighbours for?'

Elise tried to smile back, but it looked more like a quiver of her lips, then her face set again. 'Thanks, but the Dominee has arranged everything. It will be very simple. We Van Rensburgs don't like fuss and frills.'

Taylor's eyes widened innocently. 'From what I've gathered, that's not how your mother would have described herself.'

Elise's eyes narrowed, wondering at his cheek, but her retort was quick. 'Ja, well, she didn't often describe herself as a Van Rensburg.'

Taylor looked up at the still young pears hanging on the trees all round them. He reached up and stroked the skin of a fruit, pulling the tips of his fingers down around the bulge of the pear. 'They look lovely,' he said.

Actually they looked weak. This was an old orchard, a poor cultivar to start with which had been producing an inferior fruit for too many years now. Elise was hoping to take out the trees and replant the orchard for the next season. Now, with her dad gone and the estate costs she would face, she wasn't sure she would be able to afford the time or the money, though all that remained to be seen. Taylor watched Elise tilt her chin upwards, scanning the tree. 'They look pretty bad to me,' she said.

Taylor shrugged and laughed, a small self-deprecating little laugh as if to say, well, what do I know? 'It's quite a trick to know when to pick, isn't it? I hear your father was a master.'

Elise raised her eyebrows, sighing as she did so. 'He didn't always get it right, but he was good, he had a – what's the English word again? A knack. Ja, he had a knack. But even without him I get a lot of help.'

Taylor looked back at her quizzically, so she continued wearily. 'Colour charts and balling tests . . . they give you a very accurate guide. Some years you have smaller fruit like this for some reason, like not enough sunlight, or the temperature has been wrong. One of the main factors here is that we didn't get enough cold last winter.' Elise reached up and pulled the pear out of the shade and into the sunlight. 'We need cold – especially for pears and apples. That's why Ceres does so well with them, because they have double the cold units we have. This is a better plum area . . .' Elise saw that Taylor's eyes had gone blank – either he wasn't interested or he didn't understand. Her voice trailed off.

She walked with Taylor towards his car, her head down, eyes on her boots and her arms folded across her chest. Out of earshot of Jacob and Vuyo, Taylor asked her if she was aware of what was happening to Sandile Mashiya. She shook her head and the knot of her hair fell out, uncurling down over her neck. She ignored it, staring at Taylor, her eyebrows knitted with concentration and questions.

'Well, you know he's been charged. Now they're holding him in Pollsmoor until the trial.'

Elise scuffed the toe of her boot against a clod of earth, then squashed her foot down on top of it. 'When's that?' she asked.

Taylor shook his head. He was also focused downwards, on the ground between them. He took his hands out of his pockets and rather delicately scratched his neatly combed hair with the index finger of his left hand, so that the gold band of his watch flashed in the sunlight. Elise was aware of the swelling and pulsing song of the Christmas beetle; it seemed deafening to her, as if the sound was pressing in against her. She didn't look at him as he replied.

'No date set. I gather you will be notified in due course, however. Anyhow the point is that I don't think we need worry about the land claim business. I spoke to Mrs Mamdoo again. She was extremely co-operative and informed me the claim will be put on hold pending their own investigation. They certainly won't take any action until the trial is over. And since Mashiya himself looks likely to spend the rest of his life in quiet contemplation of the inside of the South African prison system – unless another member of the Mashiya family comes forward, of course, but that seems unlikely at this stage – the claim will fall by the wayside.'

Elise bit her lip, not sure if she was depressed or delighted.

'Well, I just wanted to let you know. One less thing to worry about.'

'Mmm.' Elise was wary of confiding her thoughts to Taylor, but she wanted to sound him out, so she formulated the question carefully before she put it. 'What if they've got the wrong guy?'

Taylor nodded gravely, then gave her arm a sympathetic squeeze, which made her regret the question profoundly. 'Well, it's an interesting idea and logically, I suppose, it's possible. Logically, anything's possible. But you know, my dear, these people, Mashiya included, are so steeped in

481

conspiracy theory they'll bend themselves into a koeksuster to throw you off their track. They'll make you believe almost anything – anything except the truth.'

Elise looked hard at Taylor, but it was impossible to read his thoughts, impossible to tell if he meant what he'd said. The dark glasses reflected nothing back at her. When at last the silence grew uncomfortable Taylor made a move to go. 'Well, as I said, just thought I'd stop by in case, but delighted to see you coping.'

'Yes.' Elise dipped her chin and tried to smile. Was she coping? And why did he care? It occurred to her that maybe he just did and she shouldn't be so suspicious.

They parted somewhat stiffly at his car. Elise wondered if she had seemed rude. She didn't like the man, but part of her wished she had said something, even briefly, to express her gratitude for his concern.

As he drove away, she noticed that he took the right fork, the track that led to the compound and away from Skaduwee Lane. Elise sighed. No doubt someone there would quickly put him on the right road. He had so much to learn about the valley and about farming. She turned back to look up the row of trees. Jacob was squatting next to Vuyo in the shade, watching her. 'OK, guys, we're back!' Elise found her jaw was clenched tight as a vice.

The atmosphere in the dorp that week was strained and muted. There was no one who hadn't known Van Rensburg, no one who didn't feel the suddenness and violence of his death. Nor was there anyone who didn't know both Daan and Elise and wasn't lit up, one way or another, by the startling news that their engagement was off. Together these events sparked an unprecedented flurry of visiting. Life had become more interesting than TV. Now the dust on the roads was constantly churned with the trekking to and fro from one house to another as people spread commiseration and specu-lation and skinder in urgent, always hushed tones. The only house no one visited was Rustenvrede itself.

All week long only Dominee Slabbert had ventured up the long drive to Rustenvrede and his visits were joyless and dutiful. Elise didn't like them any more than he did. No one else from the valley came, though the Jouberts – because they were relatives – sent their driver over every day with food, a bobotie cooked by old Mrs Joubert one day, a chicken casserole the next, a tuna-cheese bake the next. Elise couldn't face food so she put the meals in the freezer or gave them to Mama Mashiya, who took them home with her and came back each night with the dishes empty and sparklingly clean. After the funeral, Elise thought, she'd send Jacob round to return the dishes with her thanks. She was never anything but polite, in spite of the fact that this gesture was a disguised affront, a gloved fist in Elise's face. The food was the Jouberts' way of pointing out that they were still good people, generous enough to feed her in a hard time like this, generous in spite of the fact that she was so undeserving.

Some of the offerings delivered to the house had a more straightforward message than that concealed by the dinners. A massive arrangement of pincushion Proteas came from the manager's office at the packing house and a basket arranged with dried fruit and shortbread biscuits and biltong was delivered from the co-op along with yet another 'In Sympathy' card. Cards arrived every day in the post. Elise was grateful, but also irritated by the syrupy euphemisms, the garish pictures of flower arrangements overlaid with heavy gold lettering. Inside there was always some drowningly shallow phrase or verse, intended to be inspirational, but having the opposite effect on her. She found them depressingly inadequate. She put all the cards back in their envelopes after she'd opened them and stuffed them into the hall drawer. All week the pile grew while the Proteas and the delicatessen basket wilted on the dining table.

After Taylor had taken his leave of her Elise went down to the packing sheds to check up on the nectarines. The last thing she needed was more interruptions, so when yet another expensive-looking car with tinted windows pulled into the yard she was positively hopping with frustration.

Two strangers got out of the car, one black, one white. Both men wore dark suits, colourfully striped ties and trendy mirrored shades. Elise left off what she was doing and stalked out to greet them. She was distracted and a touch irritable in her welcome.

The black guy made the introductions in flawless Afrikaans. 'My name is Simon Siluma and this is Karel Smit, who's an attorney.'

Elise shook Simon's hand. Karel, who was grinning from ear to ear and obviously pleased by the sight of her, took her hand, but instead of shaking it brought it up to his lips and kissed it rather showily. Simon chuckled. Elise was taken aback, but not unflattered. She pulled her hand away and stuffed it into her jeans pocket.

'Please accept our condolences – we heard about your father's tragic death.'

Elise smiled at Simon by way of a thank-you, though her eyes showed her puzzlement – she had no idea who these men were. 'I would invite you in, but I'm afraid I'm very busy,' she said hastily, trying to introduce a sense of urgency into her tone so that she could get on with her day.

'No problem,' Simon said. 'Actually we're here because we've been trying to trace Sandile Mashiya. Karel is his lawyer and I'm – well, an old friend.'

'Oh.' Elise was surprised. She'd assumed, like Mama Mashiya, that Sandile's lawyers had been working with him from the day of his arrest. Now it crossed her mind that Daan hadn't only turned a blind eye while Sandile was beaten up. Perhaps he'd omitted to contact Sandile's lawyers as well. If she'd known she would have tried to contact them herself.

'Perhaps you wouldn't mind walking with us for a moment or two?' Simon's glance indicated the packers, who were watching them; he clearly wanted to be out of earshot. Elise nodded and began strolling in the direction of the house. Simon and Karel followed.

'Actually this is quite a coincidence. I just got a visit from my neighbour, about half an hour ago. He said that Sandile has been charged, that he's being held at Pollsmoor until the trial.'

The look that the two men exchanged was loaded with meaning she didn't understand. Elise had no idea of the difficulties they'd had tracking Sandile down, or of the obstacles that had been thrown in their path by the police. They were grateful to Elise for her simple candour.

As they walked both Karel and Simon's necks swivelled constantly, like tourists, and they marvelled at the beauty of the place. Elise saw everything as monochrome and chaotic.

Simon said they wanted to speak to Sandile's parents and Elise decided to take them up to the compound herself. Karel said they'd follow her in their car, but Elise shook her head. 'Uh-uh. Your car's too low-slung to make it.'

'Are you sure you've got the time?'

'Nope, but what the hell! Come on, before I change my mind.'

They drove squashed up together on the front seat of the bakkie. Karel, who had jumped in next to her, teased her mischievously. 'So, if you don't mind my asking, what is it you see in him exactly?'

Elise blushed slightly. 'Who?' She smiled to herself, unable to avoid the knowing glance exchanged between the two men.

'It must be that *boy*-next-door syndrome,' Karel said to Simon and they all laughed, even Elise. It felt so good. She was surprised at how relaxed she felt, at how much she was enjoying the sheer niceness of frivolous conversation. Then Simon changed the pleasant tenor of things rather too quickly.

'Ms Van Rensburg, I hope you'll forgive my bluntness. But I need to ask you. Do you think Sandile killed your father?' Karel Smit grimaced, but he didn't intervene. Although Simon shouldn't have been asking, he too was interested in Elise's answer.

She was silent for a minute or so, thinking about it. 'I didn't at first, but I'm not sure any more. I don't know what to think. I mean, if he didn't – then who did?'

Simon sighed. 'Can you think of anyone else who might have had a motive?' he pressed on, ignoring Karel's pointed glare.

Elise shook her head. 'No, I've gone over it a million times. It doesn't make sense.'

'What about old grudges?'

Elise laughed, rounding on him. 'Old grudges! There's probably hundreds of those, if not thousands,' she exclaimed. She would have taken the point further had she not almost driven straight into Alan Taylor. 'Now what the hell is he still doing here?' she muttered irritably.

'Nice car,' Karel sang.

Taylor manoeuvred his car out of her way and then drew up alongside the bakkie and rolled down his window.

'Hello?' Elise said, frowning at him.

'I've just been up to have a chat with old Mashiya, wanted to clear a few things up about the claim. I hope you don't mind.' He was particularly smooth.

In fact she did mind. She was shocked by Taylor's audacity. He'd breached a fundamental rule, but as it had never happened before, she didn't really know how to deliver a rebuke.

Taylor's gaze settled on Karel Smit, then on Simon Siluma, and as it did so it seemed to turn to ice. As their eyes met both men froze – some instinct, some distant memory stirred. Alan Taylor looked away.

'Well, maybe let me know next time you want to talk to him,' Elise said irritably, then jerked her car into gear and pulled away from him.

Simon looked over his shoulder, peering through the glass for a longer view, but Taylor had retracted inside the car.

'That's the neighbour I was telling you about. Alan Taylor. He's new around here. English. That's probably why he hasn't realised that you never, ever go cruising round other people's farms without their permission. I cannot believe his nerve!' She was more than irked: she was furious.

Elise dropped them off at the Mashiya cottage and picked

them up half an hour later. Her goodbye was warmer than her welcome. She was glad that the Mashiyas had some support at this time, though she didn't mention Sandile's name again. Both Simon and Karel left their business cards with her and she promised to remain in touch.

They waved to her out of the open windows of their car and Elise waved back as they drove away. Once out of earshot Karel whistled. 'Shew! Babe-and-a-half!'

'Ja, and you better lay off her before your client gets his hands on you!'

Karel's laugh exploded out of him, ricocheting round the inside of the car. 'Well, well, well, isn't he just one lucky, lucky bastard!'

Simon laughed too. 'I knew this would get him into trouble and trouble doesn't come a whole lot deeper than this,' he murmured, slowly shaking his head.

'You're telling me.'

With one hand on the steering wheel Karel took a cigarette from the packet on the dashboard and shoved it between his lips. 'So how about we delay the trial a few months, I hang around, do some heavy casework with Ms Van Rensburg, take her out, cheer her up a little, *comfort* her. By the time he gets out she's forgotten him.'

Simon took out a plastic Bic and flipped it, holding the flame for Karel to light his cigarette. Their eyes met briefly and Simon shook his head and said, with heavy emphasis, 'I don't think so.'

Karel shrugged. 'Just a thought.'

They drove away from Fransmansdorp in the gathering dusk. It was near eleven when at last they crested the rise at the top of Sir Lowery's Pass and saw the spread of the Flats and Cape Town before them, the lights of the city and its suburbs glittering all around the curves of the peninsula. Karel and Simon turned to one another in the same spontaneous instant and smiled. Then Simon breathed a deep sigh. Karel kept his eye on the road while fumbling for another cigarette. 'What's on your mind?'

Simon sounded unusually grave when at last he replied. 'I don't know . . . I don't know if I'm starting to see things, but that guy – Taylor – I think I know him.'

Karel swung round to look at Simon who pointed his attention back at the road. 'Did you ever hear of a Branch guy who operated in Natal, went by the name of Stritch or Stitch. Martin Stitch?'

'Rings a bell. Businessman who turned out to be a cop, ran front companies, mixed up in third force violence or something, or that's what everyone thought, right?'

Simon nodded. 'Right, arms dealing, money laundering, murder, the whole boerewors roll. But nothing was proved. He got off and he got away, probably a golden handshake, no one knows, but by the time elections came he'd vanished.'

Karel still didn't know what Simon was getting at. 'And? So?'

'I'm sure that guy in the BMW was him.'

Karel whistled, a long low whistle. 'Holy shit! You don't say . . . What are we going to do now?'

Simon tapped his finger against the glass window. 'We're going to get the right people on it.'

Karel knew that Simon begrudged the time he'd spent on this case already. He wanted to be home in Durban, instead of on this wild-goose chase after Sandile. Karel on the other hand had nothing better to do; in fact traipsing around on a case like this was just his scene. And things were getting deeper and murkier by the minute.

After Simon and Karel left, Elise took Jacob up to check on the plums. It wouldn't be long before they were ready. Thousands of rand hinged on her decision about the start of picking. The longer she held out and the better their size and colour the higher the price they would fetch. On the other hand, if they picked soon she knew she'd get a reasonable price and she'd have them in the bag, as it were. Jacob was anxious not to wait; he didn't like the unpredictable weather that had characterised the season. So far, the nectarine harvest was proving excellent and the plums were looking good, but anything might happen before they were all picked and safely packed.

Jacob argued that it was less risky to pick as soon as all the nectarines were in. Elise just wasn't sure. The colour on her Sungolds was certainly close to good enough; they had yellowed perfectly and the balling tests suggested Jacob's instinct about sooner rather than later was right. But the size, colour and sugar content were still not quite at the levels recorded by her father before he started picking the previous year. Elise decided to hold.

By evening, having made that decision, she felt a little better. She'd made mistakes before – everyone did. But right now she couldn't afford any. She belonged on that land; it gave her a purpose, and that purpose was her identity. Divorced from her land Elise couldn't imagine who she would be. She feared she would not be.

Forty Four

Trouble is infectious and that week it seemed to spread across the valley. Ina was alone at the farm stall when Lettie paid her an unexpected visit. Dusk was falling and Hemel en Aarde was suffused with the golden light of that hour. Ina didn't have to be there; she was just hanging around, keeping herself occupied. Her real work was finished for the day, but she had no inclination to be home. Komweer felt like a storm had raged through it, everything shaken up and turned upside-down, the whole family rattled by Van Rensburg's horrible death and the sudden breaking-off of Daan's engagement. Ina needed to escape from the atmosphere, from the interminable post-mortems conducted by relays of relatives and neighbours around her mother's kitchen table. So she was finishing up an unnecessary inventory check when Lettie loomed suddenly out of the shadows at the back, startling Ina with the abruptness of her appearance.

Realising immediately that something was wrong, she dispensed with all chitchat. 'Lettie, tell me.'

Lettie bobbed her head, mumbling something about being fine. But the girl was unusually quiet, not looking Ina in the eye, focusing instead on her hands as she nervously laced and unlaced her fingers.

Ina was gripped by impatience. 'What is it, Lettie? Tell me what's the matter,' she snapped.

Lettie recoiled. Ina's hand fluttered up over her mouth. She regretted the flash of anger, but she was so frazzled and edgy it was hardly surprising. And the girl had such an unfortunate face. Big teeth pushed her upper lip higher than normal and forced her lower lip to lengthen and jut, simply to enable her mouth to close. The effect was a kind of permanent, pouting scowl. Not attractive, almost unforgivably unattractive, thought Ina. And still Lettie said nothing, so Ina moved away to carry on with the locking up, while Lettie trailed around after her. It was only when they were outside in the cool half-light that Lettie spoke at last.

'Miss Ina, I don't want to worry you, you know I hate to trouble you, but I want my old job back.'

Ina had been expecting something far more dramatic. This was almost silly. 'Ag, Lettie, reeeally!'

Then suddenly Lettie started to cry. 'I don't want to work there any more. I hate it. It's so quiet and creepy up there on my own. Please, please, Miss Ina, let me come back to work for you.'

Ina had heard this kind of speech before and sighed; it usually prefaced a rambling and involved complaint about low wages or long hours, whatever. 'Lettie, you know how much I hate excuses. You'll have to have a very good reason to leave Mr Taylor's house. I bent over backwards to arrange that job for you. He's not going to be very pleased with either of us if you just up and leave because it's too quiet. Haven't you got a radio or something to listen to?'

At this Lettie shook her head and sobbed even harder. So Ina crossed her arms, gathering patience until the real tale emerged. When the story did come out it was more chilling, more bizarre than anything she might have expected.

'You remember last week, when I came to work the morning they found Baas van Rensburg killed, and I saw you and Mr Taylor driving past?'

Ina responded with a single weary nod, dropping her eyelashes as she dipped her neck and tried to rub out the tension with her fingers. Lettie's tongue tripped on the words in her haste to get them out. 'Well, when I was doing my work, all the normal things, the kitchen, the washing, you know ... I ... I found some dirty clothes and gloves in a plastic bag in the rubbish. He didn't want them, he'd thrown them away, so I took them out because they were nearly new.

I couldn't see anything wrong with them and I knew they would fit our Alfred, my brother. So I put them in the washing machine and when Mr Taylor came back from Rustenvrede I was already hanging them out on the line to dry. But when he saw me, oh *my life*, Miss Ina, he was angry. I've never seen anything like it – I was petrified!'

Lettie covered her face with her hands, shaking her head as if trying to shake off the memory. Ina leaned towards the girl, putting a reassuring hand on her arm. 'What? Did he shout? Did he hit you?'

Lettie allowed her hands to drop. Her eyes were so fearful that Ina shivered. 'No, he – he stood over me and he just seemed like he would explode with – he looked like – like so furious – I've never seen anyone like that before. I got such a skrik I dropped the basket and ran inside the house. Then he went into that room, the one he always keeps locked by the shed. When I came out later the clothes and the gloves were gone.'

Night had enveloped everything. Ina felt uncomfortably exposed standing there with Lettie, their voices carrying through the darkness to who knew whose unseen ears. She dropped her voice to a whisper. 'What did he do with them?'

Lettie shook her head again and tears glittered in her eyes. 'I don't know, I think maybe he burned them. I smelt a fire, but I couldn't see him anywhere after –'

Ina was suddenly conscious of the melodrama they were spinning and she tutted irritably at herself and at Lettie. She was tired now and this scene was too over-the-top. 'But why, Lettie? What was on them?' she snapped.

A sound like a whimper escaped Lettie's mouth. Ina dug her fingers into the girl's arm, urging her through gritted teeth to finish her story. 'What? Lettie, tell me!'

Lettie spewed out the rest of it, the words tumbling out with the speed of a confession and in an order that made little sense.

'When I found them it was brown and all dried up, flaking – I thought it must be dirt. Then when I washed them it came out looking like blood. It was only the one glove and on the jersey.

But I wasn't sure and, anyway, once I cleaned them off they looked almost new. I didn't mean to steal from him, Miss Ina, but ever since that day he's been funny with me. It frightens me how he is. And now, today, when he gave me my wages there was double pay in the packet and he told me he hoped I knew how to keep my mouth shut, that the one thing he really hates is people talking about him behind his back. I'm scared to go back there, Miss Ina. Will you talk to him for me, please? Please?' Lettie's face was made uglier by the contortions of fear.

Ina didn't say anything for almost a minute. Her mouth moved, but she shut it without speaking, her right hand ruffling agitatedly back and forth through her hair. She had no idea what to make of this eruption, but it seemed too weird and far-fetched to take seriously. Blood is not so rare a sight on farms as it is in the city. And it may not have been blood. Ina wanted to believe that for some reason Lettie didn't want to work at Die Uitkyk any more and she was making up excuses to get out of the job.

Finally she shook her head and her impatience unfurled. 'Don't be ridiculous, Lettie. I'm sure that Mr Taylor had his reasons for getting rid of the clothes. It sounds to me like you were stealing something he didn't want you to have. He was bad-tempered because it was a terrible morning. Everyone was upset that morning. I've told you a thousand times before not to take it personally when people lose their temper like that. It's usually got nothing to do with you and everything to do with them. Just forget about it – you're only going to make things worse if you make a fuss. The bonus was Mr Taylor's own way of telling you that he was sorry and that he hoped you wouldn't go gossiping about how he lost his temper. Now, you go home and have a nice hot bath and a good sleep and tomorrow this will seem very silly and you'll be glad it was only me you mentioned it to. All right?'

Lettie didn't stop crying. 'Will you talk to him and explain?' she implored Ina. 'I wasn't stealing – I thought he didn't want the things. You know I never steal.'

'Don't worry. I'll sort it all out, but you must promise me that you'll stay there at least till the New Year. OK?'

'OK,' she mumbled.

It was patently not OK, but there was no chance, after Ina's outburst, that Lettie would confide any more of her disquiet. The girl looked as if she'd been slapped, and deep inside Ina derived a certain satisfaction from that, from having killed Lettie's histrionics.

'Sorry, Miss Ina. You're right. I'm sorry.' Lettie murmured these words like the serviceable mantra they were, the magic spell to calm the madam and put an end to misunderstandings.

That night Ina went home with a headache. Lettie's story had irked her, made her feel even more unsettled. She telephoned Alan, sounding perfectly chirpy on the phone, revealing none of the anxiety that her conversation with Lettie had stirred up, seeking reassurance in the increasingly familiar banter of their affair. Taylor's voice curled round her; his mood was coolly flirtatious, smoothing out her ruffled nerves. Ina particularly liked it when he took charge of her arrangements, and he insisted that he would pick her up and drive her to Van Rensburg's funeral. That was his way, she knew, of making public the connection between them, which pleased her enormously. Then he added silkily, 'If the village suspects my feelings for the young Miss Du Toit are of a powerful and unusual nature, then I will be only too happy to show them their suspicions are true.'

Sitting on her bed by the open window with the phone to her ear, Ina smiled and drank in the delicious evening air, swallowing every word Taylor spoke as if they were champagne bubbles.

Nevertheless, her gloomy and rather jumpy mood returned over supper. She thought of Elise then, but only for a moment. The stab of guilt was swamped by a wave of rage, on her own and her brother's behalf. Ina pushed it from her mind. She wished it wasn't so, that at a time when her own happiness seemed possible at last, there should be such a blot on the landscape.

The night before the funeral Taylor stopped by at Komweer and told Mrs Du Toit he was taking her daughter out to dinner. Madame had twigged the connection between them by now and while it pleased her enormously she was far too distracted to celebrate. Normally the revelation of such an affair would have elicited a tornado of gossip in the dorp, but Van Rensburg's murder had eclipsed everything.

Ina was thrilled. She ran into her bedroom to change and freshen up and emerged in a long, clingy black dress, emphasising her willowy frame and heightening the pretty paleness of her face. They drove over the pass to a farm restaurant, L'Auberge, in the neighbouring valley.

Ina was unusually quiet throughout supper. For some reason Lettie's strange story and frightened face kept coming back to her. Ina told herself that Alan must have caught Lettie stealing. But another scenario, one too dark to contemplate, lurked in her subconscious. She drank too much, trying to shake off her mood. She wanted this night to be pleasant; it was important to her.

That night she passed out fully dressed on her bed and next morning woke up feeling a mixture of nausea, shame and panic. She knew she had been very drunk and dimly remembered having sex in his car, but most of the evening was vague. In the shower she noticed there were small bruises on her thighs. 'Jesus,' she said aloud to herself, 'you need to get a grip, my girl.'

FORTY FIVE

Sunlight streamed into the corridor through the unseen windows, then moved and faded and darkness was there again. Inside, Sandile was always in shadow. Each day he looked forward to the single hour in the morning when he was taken out, along with hundreds of others, for compulsory exercise. That precious hour was the only time he could see the sky. It had quickly become his habit to move to the edge of the yard, which was in sunlight, lean back against the wall and stare up and out of the prison. He would lose himself in that hexagon of cerulean blue. In the first two days there were only thin shreds of cloud high in the atmosphere, but since yesterday they had been building up and cruising lazily lower and lower.

In the yard he would clear his mind and let go of any sense of his body, trying to lose himself in the sky. The rest of the time he spent in a loop of mental pacing, agonising about how to get out before he came to trial. He hadn't yet reached the stage where he was prepared to accept his confinement with its routines and its informal rules; he had no interest in knowing his fellow inmates and they shunned him for his stand-offishness. So, until the morning when the warders called him inside from exercise, Sandile had had virtually no contact with anyone but Human.

Human escorted him down long tunnels of unfamiliar corridors. When Sandile asked where they were going the warder grunted back the single word 'Visitor.'

The encounters with Human had become more interesting since the first morning. The man's vocabulary expanded with every meeting; to Sandile it was a daily miracle.

Eventually he led Sandile into a narrow hall. Chairs were lined up in front of a row of thick glass windows which looked into booths furnished with plastic bucket seats. There was nobody in any of the booths; this wasn't visiting time. Sandile noted that there was no possibility of contact in this terrible space.

But they weren't stopping here. Human pushed through a set of doors into another area where a notice read 'Lawyers' Consultation Room'. Waiting there were Simon Siluma, Karel Smit and an unctuous-looking white man Sandile didn't recognise. Relief crashed down on him. He felt as if someone was emptying a bucket of ice-cold water on his head after days of remorseless, stifling heat.

The nervous white man was introduced as Mr De Vries, the deputy assistant governor, or something like that – Sandile wasn't paying much attention. His presence had an interesting effect on Human who straightened himself up so as to look fully awake. Simon's position had apparently made an enormous impression on Mr De Vries, though he'd been at pains not to show quite how much. Once he was satisfied his visitors had found the man they were looking for the assistant deputy governor excused himself.

Sandile just grinned, shaking his head with relief and amazement. Both Karel and Simon were pretty pleased with themselves for having found him, but they were shocked by the state of him.

'What the hell's been going on? Did you get into a fight with a tractor?' Simon exclaimed.

'Mmm. Something like that.'

'At least you're here. Yusslike, I've never had such a performance locating a client!' Karel Smit guffawed and the crack of his laughter was the loveliest thing Sandile had heard in days.

They sat down round a little Formica-topped table and pieced together what had happened since Sandile's phone call to Simon from the Fransmansdorp police station. After some reflection Karel stated bluntly that things were not looking great. Both Simon and Sandile waited for him to explain.

'Look, it's my job to ask if you did it. Did you kill him?'

Sandile shot him a look of such incredulity that Karel didn't press the point. He went on, 'OK, so you didn't do it. Now, there are a number of factors working in our favour and a fair number working against us. Let's start with the problems. Our biggest problem is that so far everything in the docket points to you. We'll have to wait a while for the forensics report, but even that's going to look bad unless Elise van Rensburg comes up with a strong explanation for how you got that blood all over your clothes. Then there's the panga going missing, some pretty hot circumstantial stuff and of course the Security Report detailing your incarceration by Mbokodo on suspicion of murder and spying.'

Sandile looked away, pressing the tips of his fingers into his forehead. Simon Siluma stood up and made a slow circuit of the room.

'OK! In our favour —' Karel was manic, flipping through files with one hand and making notes with the other. 'Police cock-ups. We have a litany of violations. Probably wrongful arrest, certainly assault. The speed of the hearing is a travesty . . . Those guys have contravened just about every rule in the book. These charges just would not have been laid outside of Dorpsville RSA. They would *never* have gotten away with this in Cape Town or Joburg. To use the new jargon I am tempted to say that Inspector Du Plessis has been "perceptually influenced".' At which Karel grinned and closed his files with a flourish.

'Which translated into plain English means–?' Simon wasn't sounding so excited.

'It means he's a racist bastard who needs to be rooted out of the force!'

Simon chuckled, but Sandile slipped visibly deeper into despondency.

'Yes,' Karel went on more solemnly, 'as you've gathered, all this does not add up to an immediate release. And I've found out that the local prosecutor and this Du Plessis monster are tjoms. The speed with which all this was sewn up suggests they had a bit of a chat about you over the braai. The upshot is, they've tied us up into a pretty vicious knot and it'll take time for me to unravel it. Meanwhile, you're going to have to hang tight.'

Simon stopped pacing and sat down. Sandile sighed and mustered a smile. 'Well, thanks, guys. What can I say?' His tone was completely flat, though his gratitude was sincere.

Karel looked from Sandile's bruised, bleak face to Simon's tormented one and felt his energy fade.

'Sandile, what do you know about Alan Taylor?'

Sandile sat up. 'What made you ask that?'

Simon fiddled with the papers on the table. 'We bumped into him the other day, up at your farm. I dunno, something made me think he isn't who he says he is.' Sandile frowned, waiting for more. 'He reminded me of a guy who used to operate for the Branch out of Natal. Ever heard of Martin Stitch?'

Sandile shook his head. 'Naah. I was outside too long.'

'Ja, well, I could be wrong, but you never know. I've asked a pal in intelligence to run a check for me – maybe there's something in it, maybe not. At this stage we have to chase after everything that comes our way.'

Karel wasn't nearly as hopeful as Simon. 'Listen, I know these Murder and Robbery guys, they aren't looking any further. Far as they're concerned, he is it. Trouble-making kaffir, history of terrorist behaviour and violent activity, not even trusted by the ANC. Bingo. Conviction.'

Simon and Karel shook their heads in tandem, but Sandile was thoughtful still.

'Do you think it's possible that Taylor set me up?'

Simon jerked his chin up, interested. 'It's possible. But why?'

'To stop the land claim.'

'Ja. You know, I know I've seen that guy before . . .' Simon trailed off.

'The problem is going to be nailing him,' snapped Karel who kept trying to pull things down to practicalities, while Simon kept drifting back to this notion he had about Taylor. 'If he is who you think he is then we're going to have our work cut out for us. We all know guys like Taylor are out there. The problem is catching them.'

Sandile frowned. It made sense to him that Taylor had killed Van Rensburg. Elaborate sense, but sense nevertheless. If Taylor was indeed a murderer then his veneer of respectability was unusually good, so perfect it almost shone. Sandile had met killers like that. Men who were brilliant and charming and ruthless. Yet something kept nagging at him, the thought that he might be twisting the facts to suit his predicament. He sighed. 'Ag, the whole thing just seems so bloody far-fetched.'

'That's why you would never have made it in intelligence, comrade. It usually is far-fetched,' Simon put in grimly.

Simon was depressed and upset. He stood up restlessly for a second time and resumed pacing. 'This intelligence report. I can't believe it. I mean – I believe it, but I can't believe it! They were watching us all the time, those bastards, there was someone inside – and it wasn't you – someone handing over reports of everything we did, everything that went on in that room even.'

Human stirred over in his corner. Sandile shot a glance in his direction, but the warder quickly settled down again. He looked like he was asleep on his feet.

'It was bound to come out somehow. No point in kicking yourself about it, Simon. That's how it was.' It was a dull-sounding reassurance, but Simon was grateful for it nevertheless.

Karel shoved an unlit cigarette into his mouth and chewed thoughtfully on it. 'Listen, broer, about the land claim.'

Sandile's eyes flicked over to meet Karel's. He sensed worse news was on its way.

'Apparently Mrs Mamdoo of the land claims, blah, blah, has been informed about the charges against you. It looks like they'll put your case on hold, pending the trial.'

Sandile bit his lip. That meant months and months more waiting. It meant the first taste of the possibility of failure.

Simon picked up where Karel had left off. 'Your only chance is that your dad brings the case on behalf of the family, but apparently he's already communicated his intention to let it go.'

Sandile jerked his head back, letting his hands bang down on the table. This was unbelievable. 'What!'

Karel nodded wearily. 'This Taylor character told Mrs Mamdoo that your parents aren't going to pursue the claim without you. I think the words she used were, "They're not interested in making trouble." The Commission will check it out of course, but that's what they've heard.'

Sandile could hardly contain the frustration he felt at being so hopelessly powerless over his own fate.

Karel sighed, rubbing his chin thoughtfully. 'When we talked to your folks they made no mention of the land claim. It struck me that they didn't even know they *could* pursue it on your behalf. We should have thought about that, but we were a bit preoccupied with finding you.' Karel turned towards Simon as he said this.

Simon leaned back in his chair and stuffed his hands into his pockets. 'Meantime we pray that they find the real killer.'

Karel tapped his cigarette box against his files. There was nothing more to say, but for a while Karel and Simon made no move to go. They both wished there was more they could do, but there wasn't. Finally, when the silence had gone on too long for comfort, they stood up, straightened their jackets and collected papers and notes into their briefcases. They had said their goodbyes and were about to leave when Sandile put his hand on Simon's shoulder. He started to say something, hesitated, thinking better of it, then shook his head.

Simon frowned. 'What?'

'Listen, man, I'm desperate. You have no idea how shit this is.'

'We're doing everything we can, broer.' Karel patted him on the shoulder, but they both knew the awfulness of his position; they felt the same powerlessness.

'Sharp,' Sandile said fuzzily.

'Sharp, sharp,' Karel responded quietly. Then Simon and Karel turned in unison and walked out, keeping step with each other in a way that Sandile might have found comical had he not felt so desolate.

As soon as they were back in the car and on their way to Cape Town Karel Smit wound down the window and lit up a cigarette. Neither one of them had spoken since their parting words to Sandile in the grim visiting room. It was Karel who finally broke the silence. 'Things don't look so good, hey?'

Simon, who was driving with his wrists resting on top of the wheel and his big frame propped sloppily against the door, shook his head and said deliberately, 'No, things are not looking so good.'

Karel glanced across at Simon. 'You owe him, don't you?'

Simon stared straight ahead and nodded, just slightly, but enough to indicate assent. 'I spoke to a contact at National Intelligence about Stitch. They're checking it out for me.'

'Did you tell them why?'

Simon shook his head. 'Uh-uh. Not yet.'

'Shit, I hope something comes up, otherwise he's going to have one mean Christmas.'

Both men stared grimly at the road ahead.

Forty Six

On the morning of the funeral Elise's body felt like lead. She opened her wardrobe and ran her fingers across the fabrics; soft, slippery, synthetic – the mix of shapes and styles of her few neglected 'outfits', as her mother had called them. She pulled out the black dress. The shape of it was simple and plain enough, but to Elise it reeked of the pain of the two occasions on which she'd worn it before. Dawie. Mom. And now Pa.

She'd bought the outfit in Edgar's in Paarl nearly a decade ago. It occurred to her that the dress had never been washed or even dry-cleaned in all that time and as she laid it out on her bedcover she decided that after today she would burn it. Looking down at the fan of the gathered skirt and imagining the polyester melting and disappearing in bright flames, Elise was gripped by the desire to incinerate it immediately. It would have been satisfying, but too dramatic, bordering on nutty. Instead she swept the dress off her bed, almost ran through the house with it and shoved it into the kitchen rubbish bin. It lay there, scrunched up among discarded toast and potato peelings until Mama Mashiya emptied the bin on to the dump the next day.

She decided she would wear a plain black skirt, her navy silk shirt and a scarf to the funeral. The people of the dorp would be suited and hatted up to their chins and down to their eyebrows. Elise didn't care. This day was for her and for her father. She would wear what was comfortable, and he would either understand or he would never know. The rest of them could go to hell.

Mama Mashiya had set the kettle on to boil and was cutting bread on the counter.

'Morning, Ma.' Elise sighed.

The old lady turned and smiled at her.

'Mama, you mustn't come to work on your days off. You should be resting now. You're going to make yourself sick with all this work.'

Mama shrugged. 'Child, if I sit still then I'll get sick from all the terrible things that come into my head when I don't keep it busy.'

Elise smiled, only too glad of the old lady's presence, though they had barely spoken to each other these past few days. The silence was loaded with things still hanging between them: the land claim, the charges against Sandile, his incarceration and their feelings for him. Mama poured out two cups of strong coffee, put milk and heaped spoons of sugar in both. She gave a cup to Elise, held on to her hand, smiling slightly, and said, 'To give you strength, Miss Elise.'

Elise closed her eyes; her long pale lashes quivered. 'Mama, you are too good.'

Mama shook her head. 'You are like my own, Elise.'

Elise put her coffee down and slipped her arms round Mama, squeezing her so hard that the old lady had to flap her arms in order to loosen the tightness of the grip. Elise screwed her eyes shut, burying her face in Mama's chest, breathing in her sweet soapy scent as she'd done so often as a child. She didn't want to let go, didn't want to open her eyes on this awful day.

'Come, child, come now, you'll have the strength. You'll see,' Mama whispered, her hands patting and rubbing Elise's back.

Soon it was time to go. Elise pulled a dark silk scarf over her head, one that had belonged to her mother. It was very beautiful, but reeked of mothballs. Elise sprayed it with a squirt of lavender water, which made the smell worse, but it was too late to do anything about it, so she left the house stinking of mothballs and lavender.

Elise arrived at the church an hour before the service was due to begin. She parked the Mercedes in shade by the

Dominee's house and walked straight in to see him. The Dominee was waiting, along with her family's lawyer, in his living room. The curtains were drawn, so the room was dark, setting a sombre mood for a sombre occasion – the reading of her father's will.

Elise shook hands with Mr Hayman, who formally expressed his condolences and then got straight down to the business he'd driven all this way for. Basil Hayman, the Van Rensburgs' lawyer, was seventy-two years old. He'd dealt with Rustenvrede's business for more than forty years. He knew everything there was to know about the place. It was therefore curious that Elise hardly knew Hayman at all. His relationship with her father had involved complete trust, but no intimacy whatsoever.

Elise was sure of what to expect from the will. As far as she was concerned the reading was a pure formality, but her father had left very much less than Elise thought he would. She'd always known roughly how much was saved, how much invested. Van Rensburg had run his business on sound common-sense principles, suspicious of complexity in anything. He'd never borrowed much and at the end of most years he had managed to put something by. So it was a shock to Elise when she discovered that there was almost nothing left of their savings with which to pay the huge estate fees and taxes.

Both Hayman and the Dominee looked grave. Elise was stunned. 'Basil, I don't understand. What happened to all the savings?'

'I'm afraid that your mother's illness took quite a toll on the bank account.'

The Dominee was absolutely still throughout the meeting and Elise didn't say much more as her lawyer took her through the broad strokes of the will. He would go over the finer points at a later stage. Once it had been read and explained Hayman looked up at Elise apologetically. 'I'm so sorry,' he said. 'There's nothing more tragic – I hate to see a family business come to an end this way.'

Elise smiled at him quizzically. 'This isn't the end, Basil. What are you talking about?'

He didn't reply. Instead, he and the Dominee exchanged anxious glances. Was there something they knew and she didn't? she wondered.

As he was leaving Hayman took her aside at the door and spoke to her with great urgency and concern. 'Elise, are you really sure that you want to carry on? I don't have to remind you that you are a woman and alone. Do you have any idea of how hard this is going to be?'

Elise replied firmly, 'Both the farm and I will be fine, thank you.'

Hayman searched her face. 'I'll be blunt, Elise. If I were you I would sell immediately. Get rid of the place before it starts to run down.'

The date was 16 December. In the old days of apartheid that date had been a public holiday called the Day of the Covenant. It commemorated a vow made to God in 1838 by Andries Pretorius and a bunch of Voortrekkers travelling with him, escaping British rule. They promised to give thanks to Him on the same day every year if He would grant them victory over the Zulus. Whites, mostly Afrikaners, continued to give thanks until 1994 when the holiday became a Day of Reconciliation. In a crucial respect the date's meaning hadn't changed; it was still the day when the Christmas season gripped everyone and the holidays began.

In the shops in town the green and red, silver and gold tasselled tinsel twisted and bounced in the heat. The church too was decorated for the season, with pine branches and poinsettias and tissue-paper lanterns. Although the hall was packed, Elise sat quite alone in the front pew. She had entered with the Dominee, who was now before her, his voice booming over her head to the far corners of the congregation. Everyone had fallen silent when they saw her, their curiosity and their contempt palpable to her, though she met nobody's eye. As she'd sat down in the pew that had so obviously been left empty for her, Elise was only aware of a mass of bodies behind her.

Old Mrs Joubert, who had been so acid about Elise's 'singularity' in the past, couldn't help commenting again, in a voice loud enough to be heard by everyone, 'No hat. Who *does* she think she is?'

Elise almost stood up and shouted back. It would have been brave and brazen to give the cowardly old lady the telling-off she deserved. But she didn't have the energy for such a public stand-off and, besides, this was her father's funeral. Holding herself upright was enough. She made no sign that she had heard.

In the stunned silence that followed the Dominee glared at the old woman; Mrs Joubert sniffed and stuck her nose higher in the air. Her son and daughter-in-law, Tjaart and Etta Joubert, simply stared at their feet. Everyone agreed with the tannie, even if they all thought it was inappropriate to have made the comment aloud. They brought their ankles together and squared their shoulders and felt better about being people who never transgressed the code.

The service resumed. It was so strange and stark that none of it seemed real to Elise. The Dominee had outdone himself in the preparation of his sermon. He clearly didn't intend to stint on words for someone as important to him as Van Rensburg had been. Elise was semiconscious of his voice swelling and dipping and swelling, echoing through the church.

'Greater love hath no man than this, that a man lay down his life for his friends. Ye are my friends, if ye do whatsoever I command you . . . Ye have not chosen me, but I have chosen you, and ordained you, that ye should go and bring forth fruit and that your fruit should remain: that whatsoever ye shall ask of the Father in my name, he may give it to you. These things I command you, that ye love one another!'

The Dominee must have known every farming reference in the Bible, Elise thought. And there were hundreds, it seemed, one for every occasion, or sometimes, as on this occasion, several.

'I am the true vine, and my Father is the husbandman. Every branch in me that beareth not fruit he taketh away and every branch that beareth fruit, he purgeth it, that it may bring forth more fruit . . . As the branch cannot bear fruit of itself, except it abide in the vine, no more can ye, except ye abide in me. I am the vine, ye are the branches: he that abideth in me, and I in him, the same bringeth forth much fruit: for without me ye can do nothing. If a man abide not in me, he is cast forth as a branch, and is withered; and men gather them, and cast them into the fire, and they are burned. If ye abide in me, and my words abide in you, ye shall ask what ye will, and it shall be done unto you.'

Elise wasn't sure if it was the fogginess of her brain that made the sermon difficult to follow. Was the message about being cast into the fire a message destined for her ears? Fortunately the sound of his voice, its strength, his control over its timbre, was as soothing and pleasant on the ear as always. Van Rensburg had never shown much interest in religion or in the Sunday social. Elise wondered what he would have thought of all this. She imagined him nodding off next to her, as he had done within minutes of sitting down on the two or three occasions that she remembered him coming here. She wished for his counsel now, more than she ever had.

'Friends!' The Dominee's interjection broke through the surface of her thoughts. 'I'm not going to soak this service in praise of our departed friend – that is something I believe we must do while we live. We are heartsore today, but we can also be thankful that Van loved God and was loved by God. We must rejoice for what Van has done for his people, his farm, his family. We must also rejoice in and feel compassion for those who choose a different path. We all knew him, we all knew that Van Rensburg never took the easy road.' The Dominee's gaze came to rest on Elise, but his plea for compassion fell on deaf ears.

The service ended in a prayer. Everyone shuffled to their knees and closed their eyes, everyone except Elise who looked back, slowly scanning the hall and the muttering bent heads of those who had come to be there when she buried her father. She saw Jacob and his family, the Mashiyas and all her workers from Rustenvrede squeezed into the back rows. Mama was wearing a heavy black coat, buttoned up to her collar, and a severe black doek over her head. She saw Jacob's lips move, his mouth silently forming the words of the prayer. Without him rieither Elise nor the farm would have managed that week; she knew that just as surely as Jacob knew the orchards and the men who worked under him. The front rows were taken up by white families; the tannies had lined themselves up closest to the lectern and now Elise watched their heads wobble on scrawny old necks as they spoke the prayer.

At the end of the service everyone filed slowly out of the church and snaked in a long line to the cemetery next door. The Van Rensburgs owned a family plot there; Van would be buried next to his Evelyn. As they walked among the gravestones Alan Taylor made his way towards Elise. Behaving like the true gentleman he purported to be, he put his arm round her and for a moment she leaned into him. Then she smiled tightly and briefly, readjusting the scarf that she'd tied over her hair so as to keep him firmly at bay. Taylor dropped back, waiting for the crowd to shuffle past him and for the Du Toits to come abreast of him.

Johnny Kakana made a point of making eye contact with Taylor. Taylor nodded curtly, in that military way of his, but that was all. Johnny lingered a moment, hesitating to put the question he longed to ask, but he hesitated too long: the press of people pushing forward took him with it. Taylor turned back, waiting for Ina.

Elise stared down at the reddish earth of the empty grave as the casket was lowered solemnly into the ground. When it had come to rest at the bottom of the freshly dug hole, the Dominee read a passage from the Bible, something about living and dying and dust going to dust that she'd heard him read before. While the voice drifted up and around them Elise looked over to where the Du Toits were standing. Her eyes met Daan's, and it was like a shock, a minor electric buzz. She wondered how long he'd been watching her – perhaps they had both looked up in that instant. There was anger in his eyes and that hurt her, more than the sight of Madeleine and the De Jagers standing close by him. Elise looked across the family group and her eyes met Ina's. Ina was icy. With a brief, frozen glance she simply, silently let Elise know that the damage was irreparable. Elise bowed her head. The Dominee's reading came to an end and people began to shuffle away, back to their cars, their homes and their families. Elise had no one to grieve with. No one except Mama Mashiya.

Elise picked up a handful of earth and threw it down into the grave. The sound of it hitting his coffin was the hollowest, emptiest, most hopeless sound she had ever heard.

She had made arrangements in the customary way. Tea and cake were provided for everyone, as was usual at a funeral, on the stoep at the Dominee's residence. It was an important ritual, a time for people to talk and remember and cry. Tea and mountains of cakes had been beautifully and painstakingly laid out by the Dominee's housekeeper, but they stood untouched as the farmers and their families filed past, heading home.

Elise stood by the path, in the place where the family always stood to receive the sympathy and condolences of their community, but no one had addressed a single word in her direction, so she started when someone put their brittle fingers on her arm. She turned to find herself face to face with Mrs Du Toit. When Elise was a child Madame had felt sorry for the little girl; she'd never thought much of Evelyn and her frivolous, foolish ways. Now it seemed that Elise had inherited a dangerous dose of that lady's impulsiveness, though she couldn't be entirely to blame for that. Madame pressed her fingers against Elise's skin, just a light pressure, then a brief, pained look, and the old lady turned, more quickly than was probably safe for her, and tottered away. Elise almost shouted after her; she wanted to talk to Madame, to try to explain, but that was not what the old lady wanted. She watched the Du Toit family leaving together, huddled around Daan as if he was the wounded one, as if he was the one who had lost the most.

Mrs Du Toit took the Dominee's arm as she drew abreast with him at the gate. He stood clutching his hands with an expression of pain and embarrassment as the mourners filed silently and swiftly out of the churchyard, blatantly snubbing Elise. Mrs Du Toit whispered a thank-you for his beautiful sermon and invited him to lunch. Willem Slabbert put his hand over hers and squeezed it, whispering down into her ear, 'Thank *you*. I'll be by later. As soon as I can get away.'

Elise noticed that the Dominee was drawn aside again, by Alan Taylor. They had a brief urgent discussion, and from the anxious glances they cast in her direction she knew that their conversation concerned her and undoubtedly her farm.

The farm workers all hung back until Elise invited them to eat, then they attacked the food with relish.

Elise remained at the house long enough to fulfil the requirements of politeness, but no longer. She drove home down the shadow-striped track of Skaduwee Lane. So much for her idealised community, she thought, so much for her solid salt-of-the-earth extended family, the neighbours she'd believed would stick by her through thick and thin. That these people, her friends, and essentially her family now, could abandon her so cruelly at such a time was incredible. She had put so much store by them, by her place in their society, thinking it located her, gave her an identity. She hadn't seen the narrowness of the parameters within which they all lived until she stepped outside them. Then it was too late to go back.

FORTY SEVEN

Elise had given everyone the day off, so on her return to Rustenvrede after the funeral she found herself alone in the house. She thought of what Mama had said that morning – of the need to keep busy. She decided to clear her father's room. So Elise did not rest. She made herself a cup of coffee and charged purposefully, coffee slopping right and left, straight into his room, almost as she had done that morning nearly two weeks before. She tried to adopt the manner of a nurse she'd once watched dealing with her mother. Head down, eyes focused on only a portion of the disaster, not the daunting whole of it. If only she began she would surely finish, she thought. But Elise stopped almost as soon as she'd started.

The bed was still unmade, just as he had left it. The book he'd been rereading, one of the thicker Wilbur Smiths, was face down and open at the place he'd stopped. There was a long crack in the spine. His boots were in the corner by the door, as they would be if he were away in town or watching rugby in the living room on a Saturday afternoon. As they would be if he were here . . . but he wasn't here. Elise focused on the chest of drawers. The top drawer was empty except for a tiny leather jeweller's box. Inside was a ring, which she recognised immediately as her mother's engagement ring. A claw of platinum curled up round a huge multifaceted diamond. Elise had always found it ugly. It looked lethal, the diamond set so high you could have gouged someone's eye out with it. It had originally belonged to the old Ounooi, her grandmother, who probably had used it as a weapon, or at least threatened to.

Elise put the box away and made an effort towards the task she had set herself, but she couldn't face it. It was too lonely, too sad.

She sat down on the floor surrounded by all the drawers she'd pulled open, full of her mother's and father's belongings. She was living in a house full of dead people's things. Even Dawie's bits and pieces were still in cupboards all over the house. After his death Evelyn and her father didn't have the heart to get rid of anything. They gave his watch and some shirts and notebooks to Ina and the rest they left as it was. Elise had cleaned out the cupboards, boxed up most of the clothes and taken some of his pictures down only when she came back from Bloemfontein. Her father had said nothing, although he'd silently cleared a place in the attic for the boxes Elise filled. Van never went into Dawie's room, hadn't entered it since the day the telegram came and didn't go in even after Elise took it over. It was partly to dispel the ghost that Elise had moved in, but partly because it was the nicer·room.

She had tried to pack up her mother's clothes, but her father wanted them in the room with him, so he'd told Elise simply to leave everything. It was a strange habit of her family, she thought, one she had once condemned but now partly understood, even though it made her angry because she was the one who was left with it all. She didn't want to pack the stuff up; she wished it would simply pack itself or disappear. Yet she couldn't bear the idea of losing them – these clothes and books and hairbrushes that were all she had left of any of them.

Elise wished they would appear to her, wished that at least she'd have three ghosts to talk to. She wondered why she couldn't reach them, as so many did reach their loved ones, or said they did, in visions and in dreams. Neither her father nor her brother nor her mother came to Elise in dreams. She didn't even sense them in her house. They were all inaccessible to her. It occurred to her that this was the same in death as in life.

It occurred to her that they all, herself included, were unusually sealed off, unusually self-contained. Perhaps that was what Daan had meant when he said so unhappily that she was always just out of reach. Perhaps that was what had made the unexpected contact with Sandile so exhilarating, when he had caught her up in his wild tango, when it felt as if her soul had met its twin. And yet, she told herself bitterly, that moment, that contact, had been illusory. He was lying to her all the time.

She got up and walked out of the bedroom on to the stoep, just as her father had in those last few minutes of his life. She felt with her bare foot for some trace of him on the ground he had walked, but there was nothing. She lay down on the lawn, near the naked patch of earth where his blood had seeped out into the turf and where Ben Mashiya had later left a ragged puddle in his attempt to water out the stain, and stared up at the infinite sky.

As she watched the clouds form and dissolve, Elise slowly lost all sense of her body. She surrendered to the sensation, spread-eagled on the grass, gazing up at the shapes in the sky which formed and re-formed in infinitesimal variations. She was caught in their slow-motion transformations, sun glinting off their brilliant whiteness. She closed her eyes for a moment and it felt to her as if her limbs – her whole body – had dissolved – like cloud.

Some time later – she had no idea how long – Elise noticed that the clouds were gathering to bring some change in the weather. It didn't look like rain. A breeze had come up and was tugging at the oaks. She stood up too suddenly; her head spun slightly and tiny firefly stars made dizzy orbits of her head, then faded away.

She walked round the house to the office where she sat down to calculate her situation now she was the sole owner of Rustenvrede. Her father had relinquished his desk to Elise on her first day back from Bloemfontein; it had taken him longer to give her the same space out on the farm. She had always spent at least one night a week working late on accounts and planning for the following year, but now she spent almost all her free time there. A manager would have made all the difference, but Elise couldn't afford to hire anyone. Financially, fruit farmers are always at their low point just before they start harvesting. Elise was no exception and that increased the pressure on her.

A fax from Basil Hayman's office had arrived and yards of paper curled on the floor like rolls of starched ruff collar. Working with his numbers she calculated that as long as she could harvest as much as last year she would be able to pay off her debts and the taxes on her father's estate and be in reasonable shape for the next season. She had nothing to spare. She wouldn't be able to afford any of the clearing and replanting that she and her father had talked about, though she reckoned she might be able to give her workers half of the pay rise they were counting on for next year, but at least she would be surviving – and doing so without debt. Debt was the fatal trap, a slippery slope down which too many of her father's friends had disappeared. So if the numbers were good enough Elise would be all right. She'd had the highest rating in the district on her Delarosa plums last year; she secretly hoped she might do better this season.

That was the bottom line. If the plum harvest failed, if it came in under last year's numbers, then she'd be in trouble; then she really would have to think of selling. If she could just hang in and get through the season, with even an average crop at the end of it, she'd be OK. For the moment, she had to accept that she would be spread about as thin as she could go.

Elise felt as if she could sense those plums growing, sense how vulnerable they were – perhaps as defenceless as she was herself – waiting, like her, to fall. Anything, any shift in temperature or wind strength or rain, could jeopardise them. It seemed to be the same for her. Elise had a sense of heading towards cynicism and fatalism. If she could only hold out, only sleep a bit more, eat a bit more, stand in the sun a bit more, then the days would fly by, the danger would pass – she would survive.

FORTY EIGHT

Ina went straight from the car to the drinks cabinet in the lounge. She poured out two long gin and tonics, handed the weaker one to Taylor, then delicately took a long, strong sip from her own glass. They strolled out on to the stoep and wandered from there into the garden, which was cooling as a bank of cloud cover swept in overhead. Ina walked ahead of him, as if wanting to be alone, but Taylor followed regardless. She ducked under the wide canopy of the old chestnut tree at the far edge of the lawn. He sat down next to her on the bench that was nailed in a full circle round the tree's massive trunk. While everything was visible to them from under the chestnut's spreading umbrella, no one could see in through the dense foliage. Ina was vaguely focused on the ground in front of her, her lips still on her glass. Taylor stared back at the house and at the family sitting out on the stoep.

He sighed happily. 'A place like this could take the edge off everything, even off a man like me.'

Ina didn't move.

'Explain the family to me.'

This time Ina jerked her chin up to look at him. He literally shone with something that she wanted to call contentment. A few weeks ago this interest he was taking in her life would have made her heart soar; now it added to her confusion. Nevertheless she pointed out the newcomers and told their stories for him.

'The big balding guy, he's my father's brother, and that woman in the pink Crimplene, the one who hasn't stopped talking, she's his wife. They've got a fruit farm down in Ida's Valley, near Stellenbosch. Uncle Jan was the youngest – there was no way he'd have inherited a piece of Komweer – so he married a farm.'

'And I'm sure he wasn't the first to do so.' Taylor raised his glass in salute to Uncle; he was enjoying himself.

'Nor will he be the last. It was quite something at the time, though. Dorothy's family were English, you see. In those days Ida's Valley was all English, a tight little enclave of eccentrics and heavy drinkers who hated the Afrikaners. Loathed us almost as much as they loathed the blacks. Dorothy's father came out to fight the Boers during the English War and he liked it so much he bought himself a farm. Somehow Jan sweet-talked them and they let him marry their only daughter. It was a helluva scandal in those days.'

'Didn't they question his motives? I mean she isn't much to look at even now.'

'No.' Ina smiled at his observation. She enjoyed remarks like that; it was the kind of thing she would say. 'My mother says she was the plainest, mousiest girl you've ever seen! Anyway, it wasn't long before Jan got it all. His father-in-law died – drunk as a skunk, much as he'd lived – at one of their Sunday afternoon cricket matches about three years after Jan and Dorothy got married. The newlyweds moved straight into the farmhouse and Jan took over, even before my dad inherited here at Komweer.'

'Is Jan unfaithful?'

Ina shook her head. 'Never. Though Dot seems to have spent her whole marriage in the neurotic certainty that he must be.'

She threw back the dregs of her drink. Taylor looked at her, but she was staring down at the long, contorted half-exposed roots of the tree. She shivered. He took the empty glass from her hand and put it down next to his. Ina glanced at him, her eyes dull, lashes drooping.

Taylor put a hand on Ina's thigh and squeezed her leg. She stared at his fingers creasing the thin fabric of her dress. 'What's wrong?' he asked kindly.

Ina sighed. 'Ag, I'm just not feeling so good. It'll pass.'

Taylor moved round, crouching on the ground in front of Ina as he put his hands on her knees and gently pushed her legs apart. 'Well, I'm sure we can find a cure for that. Now open wide and say aaah . . .' He smiled impishly at his own joke, but somehow Ina couldn't muster the same cheerfulness.

'Don't. Please, Alan.' She pushed the skirt of her dress back over her knees and pulled away from him.

He paused a moment, evidently taken aback, then he sat down again on the bench. Looking at him Ina immediately felt bad about pushing him away. She felt bad about everything and had done so ever since Lettie's upsetting outburst the other night. She sobbed, covering her face with her hands, and suddenly the whole story poured out. She told Taylor all about Lettie's surprise visit, how the girl had wanted her old job back, how she didn't want to work at Die Uitkyk any more because he'd frightened her so over those dirty clothes and gloves she'd found in the rubbish.

Taylor listened stiffly. Ina put her hand on his thigh, pressing down with her fingers as she pressed her point. 'Lettie just thought you didn't want the clothes – you see she didn't see it as *stealing*!' Ina insisted.

Taylor put a pointed finger over his tightly pursed lips. 'Where is Lettie now?' she asked. He looked at her without anger, as if he'd already arrived at a solution. Ina was slumped over with relief.

'Working, I hope. At least that's what she's supposed to be doing.'

'You didn't let her go to the funeral?'

Taylor looked irritable and puzzled all at once. 'Why would she have wanted to go to the funeral?'

'Because everyone does. It's the way we do things here.'

'Oh. It's not the way I've ever done things. Perhaps I should have thought about that. Next time I'll remember to ask your advice.' This he said with absolute sincerity. It wrong-footed Ina. She couldn't be cross with him, he had made a genuine mistake, and yet she was upset. She just couldn't name it, put her finger on it. Everything was wrong. She had bottled up so much anxiety about Lettie and now she blamed the girl for the way she was feeling. She wanted Taylor to sort things out with Lettie, she didn't want anything more to do with their problems. Taylor seemed to take it on board.

'I'll have a word with the girl when I get back home tonight.' With that he stood up and Ina almost ran back across the lawn, back to the house. She poured herself another drink but it wasn't long before the tinkle of Mrs Du Toit's little silver bell announced that lunch was ready. The family drifted inside, all looking a little stiff in their dark suits. The dining room was furnished with heavy, gloomy furniture, the windows hung with dusky, scalloped velvet curtains. A flattening despondency settled quickly on the already sombre room.

Madeleine de Jager had stayed at Daan's side all that morning and she'd come back with him to Komweer after the funeral without invitation, as Madame had noted. Mrs Du Toit had quickly instructed Mabel to lay a place for her at table where she conveniently rounded numbers up from an uneven and unlucky thirteen. Madeleine pounced on the seat next to where Daan had sunk down. The haste with which she had staked her claim left everyone a little aghast.

Dorothy's high voice cut through the silence like glass scraping on glass. She was talking about her church with Mrs Du Toit, who was an equally active member of her own congregation, but Dorothy's apparently boasted a superior social life. 'Once a month we go to church and then we go to this one or that one's house, for a big tea with cakes and biscuits and melkterts. We have a bit of God and then a good bit of skinder. There are a lot of old folks who have marvellous stories, you know. Jan, you should hide in my kitchen one day and just listen.'

Jan seemed to wince at his inclusion in her outburst. 'This church tea thing is a bit of a racket, I can tell you,' he muttered darkly.

Dorothy's hands moved in her lap; she folded and refolded them distractedly. When no one else spoke she took the silence as her cue to continue. 'Well, of course, now that *everyone's* invited, it's an awful lot of work. Oh, but you should see the African ladies! Do *they* enjoy themselves! They never take just one thing – they always put about six things on their plate!'

'I can just imagine what they were like this morning,' Mrs Du Toit said tartly. Silence descended rather frostily again. It wasn't Mrs Du Toit's sentiment that put a stop to the conversation, it was the allusion to the events of that morning.

Wynand, the oldest of her sons, lifted his mother's little silver bell and rang for Mabel to bring more wine. He was quite clear about his formula for getting through the afternoon. His siblings all followed suit. Daan was almost catatonic and Mrs Du Toit didn't like the turn events had taken. She had never much cared for Madeleine – the girl had no style and no money – but on principle she never interfered with her sons' affairs. At least, she thought, Daan had someone to comfort him and she wasn't in any mood to be delicate about Elise's feelings. Elise had profoundly disappointed and upset Mrs Du Toit, who had always had a soft spot for her, but now she had gone and humiliated her son and her whole family through this mess over the engagement and rumours of a connection with the Mashiya boy.

'And *you* know how Jan is. On his birthday it was one female after the other – not the husbands but the wives – all phoning for him!' Dorothy's laugh rose like a bow being pulled and the invisible arrow was launched, but it was impossible to tell from Jan's look whether or not it had found its mark.

Mrs Du Toit didn't listen much, though she smiled a great deal, particularly at Alan, who was the one bright point in this dreadful scenario. Taylor had been given a position of honour at the head of the table, where Mrs Du Toit herself usually sat. 'Alan, I hope you took note of the floral arrangements this morning,' she said rather too sweetly.

An uncomfortable silence, broken only by the buzz of Mabel's electric carving knife, followed her question. Taylor coughed delicately into his napkin and then said carefully that he wasn't sure he did remember noticing them. Ina put in gently that her mother and some of the women from the garden club had done all the arranging the day before. They were a little upset that Elise hadn't said a word of thanks.

'But that's typical of Elise. She always has her head in the clouds . . . or buried in the earth.' Ina shut up, seeing that Daan was glaring palely at her. She was sitting next to her brother and côuldn't help noticing how Madeleine gripped Daan's knee and rubbed his thigh with her hand, a proprietorial gesture of comfort. Madeleine shot her a defiant glance. How long, Ina wondered, has this been going on?

'I wonder what she'll get for the farm,' Wynand chipped in.

'Elise will never sell,' Daan snapped, reaching for the wine.

'I don't see that she'll have any choice in the end.' Taylor's contribution seemed to settle the question, though he looked to the Dominee for support and it was given with a slightly sheepish nod.

'Don't be so sure. Elise doesn't give in without a helluva fight. Trust me, I know.' Daan's voice was shot through with bitterness and a thread of defiance.

'I think I agree with Daan. Elise doesn't give in. She's like a bloody Rottweiler,' Ina mumbled into her drink.

Her mother didn't like what she heard. 'Ina, language. Please!'

Taylor interjected again. From his position at the head of the table he had taken on the role of chairing this family conference. 'It may not be a question of her strength this time. I suspect that not even the strongest person could stand up to the forces threatening Rustenvrede.'

The Dominee nodded again and added his own grim prediction. 'There's no way Elise will be able to carry on by herself. She's bound to find it too much. Mark my words, she'll sell in the end. The sooner she does, the better the price she'll get, but she's stubborn – she'll hold out as long as she can and she'll only lose that way.'

'Oh please, I can't bear to think about it.' Mrs Du Toit's nose had turned quite red. The subject was a reminder of too much unpleasantness.

Taylor saw this and cruised neatly into a fresh topic, gently and expertly steering the conversation away from the impending disaster at Rustenvrede. 'I had no idea you belonged to a garden club, Mrs Du Toit.'

She smiled gratefully at him, thinking that Alan was really everything she could wish for in a son-in-law. She only hoped Ina didn't scare him off before he got round to popping the question. 'Oh, it's quite a recent thing,' she chirped. 'We've been going about twenty-two years now, but we have quite a nice tight group. We meet once a month at the church. In winter we have lectures on anything pertaining to nature or gardens.'

Mabel had by now put steaming slices of roast pork on everyone's plate and hands were reaching across the table, passing potatoes, dishing up peas. Mrs Du Toit spread her napkin over her lap, talking all the while to Alan Taylor, who was rapt.

'You must come one day. We visit some magnificent gardens in the summer, like the Knock Shaw garden, which has three *hundred* different types of roses.'

'Extraordinary,' he marvelled.

'Last Thursday we went to the Irma Stern home – that was quite fantastic. All I can say, Alan, and I hope you won't take this amiss, is that it beats Sissinghurst hands down!' She slapped her bony, liver-spotted hand down on to her thigh for emphasis.

For dessert there was a trifle with no fewer than nine perfect layers of different-coloured jelly. Not one of the layers had bled. Mrs Du Toit clapped at her first sight of it. 'Mabel, you've outdone yourself!' she exclaimed.

FORTY NINE

All that afternoon Karel Smit dialled Elise's number. But there was no answer at Rustenvrede until evening. Karel was at home by then, sitting with his feet up on the sofa, his sleeves rolled up, tie loosened at his neck. His flat was huge and virtually empty. No pictures on the walls, ashtrays full to the brim, stacks of books and papers piled all over the floor, a massive TV in the corner and one futon in an otherwise completely bare room. The TV was on and he was holding a remote control in one hand, the phone in the other, an ice-cold Castle balanced precariously between his thighs. When Elise finally answered he dropped the remote and reached for his cigarettes.

'Hi, Elise? It's Karel Smit here.'

'Oh, hi.' She sounded underwhelmed.

'Listen, I just called to say thanks for your help the other day. We tracked Sandile down at last. Saw him yesterday at Pollsmoor.'

There was a long silence at her end of the line, then a sound, as if she'd knocked something over. He wondered if she'd dropped the phone.

'How is he? Is he all right?'

Smit exhaled. 'Mmm. Well, not great – you can imagine. I mean, you know, it's prison. It's shit.'

'Mmm.' The tone was noncommittal. She *didn't* know. In fact she hadn't given it much thought.

Karel started to lean forward, not wanting to lose her attention, but pulled back just in time to avert a spillage from his beer can.

'Do you think you'll get him off?' She sounded hesitant.

There was a pause, then he sighed. 'We're doing everything we can.'

'That's what the doctors used to say to my father when my mother was dying.'

'Well, let's see, let's see.' It wasn't much of a conversation, Karel thought. 'Listen, what do you know about your neighbour – that Taylor guy?'

'Not much. He came over from England after his wife died, seems to have a lot of money. He had a cleaning company or something which he sold up.'

Karel sucked thoughtfully and deeply on his cigarette. 'Cleaning company. Huh. Did he say that?'

'Ja. At least I'm pretty sure that's what he said.' She didn't sound sure.

'Elise, Simon thinks Taylor is not who he says he is. He's got his spies looking into it.' Karel was speaking half in jest, then his tone shifted to serious. 'I shouldn't be saying this, not to you and not over the phone, but –'

'Come on. You don't seriously believe in all that stuff, do you?'

'What stuff?'

'Phone-tapping, big brother, that stuff.'

'You would be amazed, my girl, you would be amazed. But since you're so comfortable that no one's listening, I'll tell you.'

Elise listened as Karel told her that Simon Siluma thought he had recognised Taylor the other day at Rustenvrede. Simon believed that Taylor was an ex-Security policeman from Natal, a hard nut who'd run front companies for the cops and whose skills ranged from assassination to arms manufacturing to diamond smuggling. He'd disappeared just before the elections and people in the know thought he'd gone to ground in Ireland. Simon had asked a pal at National Intelligence to check it out. Karel sucked on his cigarette through the long pause after he'd finished his explanation.

'Too weird. Too James Bond,' she said at last.

'Let's wait and see.' Karel sounded a little flat. 'Anyway, how are *you*?'

'Fine.'

'Really?'

'Well, you know, considering . . . I buried my father today. That makes me the Last of the Van Rensburgs.' She laughed oddly.

'Are you sure you're all right?'

She didn't respond at all to this. Karel felt uncomfortable. 'Look, if you ever need anything, even just to offload a bit, then call me – OK?'

'OK.'

Elise's heart was pounding when she put the receiver down. Karel Smit had sounded both cocky and intense, not unlike his client. Elise liked that and she'd been glad of the conversation, but he was Sandile's lawyer. She was surprised at the strength of her reaction to news of Sandile, but she feared the flood of feeling he evoked in her. It was better not to think about him at all. She couldn't afford to be derailed; she was only just holding on as it was.

It was as if two men were involved; one was her secret friend and almost lover; the other was the character the dorp thought they knew. The angry exile who had returned, demanding his right to land appropriated by the family of an intransigent white farmer who was now dead, killed with a panga which just might have been taken from the back yard of the angry exile's house. The second version of Sandile kept intruding on what Elise felt was her own, private version. There was no way she could get past the latter to reach the former, not now, not while he was in prison and surrounded by people who would misinterpret and misconvey her actions and intentions. Besides – and she kept coming back to this, as if every avenue led to the same cul-de-sac – she didn't have the time. She had too much to do on the farm.

Outside a wind had come up. It felt like the advance gusts of a northwester, shivering through the trees and clattering at the loose windows and doors. Elise pulled the office door shut and locked up from the outside. As she went through the house fastening windows and pulling curtains across she

525

couldn't stop thinking about the scene in the church. No matter how low her respect for the people of the valley had fallen, she still felt terribly hurt.

Elise was so nearly exhausted that she couldn't focus properly on the fact that she needed desperately to rest. In the past week she'd got used to just moving from one vital task to the next; she'd forgotten how to come to a stop. That night she looked down into the huge old enamel bath, but the thought of running the water, of climbing in and out again, was too much. She went to her room, discarding clothing as she approached the bed. Finally she yanked off her shoes, peeled her jeans and socks off on to the rug and crawled under the covers.

She lay there with her eyes closed, begging for sleep to settle on her, her body rigid with relief at having come to a temporary halt but her mind still racing. She listened to the gale howling round the windows and rattling the glass. At one point she must have dozed off because she woke very suddenly when a huge gust of wind smashed open the doors that led into the garden. Turbulent air raced into the room, curling around her and knocking over the bedside table. Elise shot out of bed and dragged on the doors, trying to close them, but as she did so she got entangled in the billowing curtains. The cotton clung and tightened around her terrifyingly, fluttering in her face and covering her eyes. She tried to push it back, but the fabric had twisted round and restrained her arms. An image of her father with a murderous hand on his throat made her panic. She screamed, but there was no one to hear, and her cry was drowned out anyway by the howls of the raging wind. She yanked herself away from the doors and managed to rip the curtain down as she escaped. At that moment the doors clacked shut and the room was suddenly quiet.

Elise stood in the centre of the room. Every inch of her body shook. She was still trembling an hour later as she lay in bed and listened to the raging northwester.

The wind roared around the house throughout the night. Normally she and her father would have switched on the radio or dialled the weather centre for a report, but Elise didn't move. There was no point in knowing the strength of it or understanding precisely the danger it represented. Her knowing could make no difference to the damage that wind did that night. It would blow itself out by morning, tomorrow evening at the latest, gust its way through the valley and onward no matter how much she hoped it wouldn't, no matter how much she worried.

Elise always loved the sound of wind; it was the sound of motion, of things ruffled, stirred, moved, resisting, yielding to the force of the air. That was why it always made her so restless, why she loved the agitation of it, the freshness of it, the way it seemed to shove out all that was stale, the way it carried with it the breath of newness. But this wind roared destruction.

Elise did sleep, but sleep brought agitated dreams in which she was visited by her father. He was loving, he was angry, he was smiling, but always just beyond her reach. Whenever she tried to talk to him he seemed to spin away as if borne on a wind himself. In the last dream, or chapter of the dream, his restlessness had stilled and he put his arms round her, as he did when she was a child, and told her that he was fine where he was and that everything would be all right.

Elise got up as soon as the sky began to lighten. Through her window she could see the lines of poplar trees along the driveway bucking and writhing under the pressure. She dragged on some clothes, went into the kitchen and made herself a mug of coffee. Mama was nowhere to be seen; it was too early for her to be at the house yet. Elise cradled the mug in her hands and stared with dull resignation out of the window, surprised that things didn't look so bad. She would have to go up to the orchards and check for herself.

One of the things Elise liked about farming in this part of the Cape, as opposed to the Karoo, or even Natal, was that the elements rarely turned against you. The size and success of your harvest was largely in your own hands. Then, once every ten or fifteen years, a gale would blow through and

527

wreak havoc. She knew that all over the valley people would be out counting the cost of the gale.

The last really big wind had blown through when Elise was thirteen. That took about sixty per cent of the whole crop in just one night. She remembered waking up the next morning and finding her mother and father ashen-faced in the kitchen. Almost everything her father had worked for that year was gone. Van Rensburg walked to the shed where his workers were waiting, gave them instructions for what was to be done, then walked straight back down to the house. For the next three days he just sat in the office until his workers had picked all the fruit off the ground and disposed of it. None of the family ever spoke to him about it, not even Evelyn, but they all knew that he couldn't bear to actually witness the destruction of his hard work.

But until Dawie's death Elise's parents took such shocks in their stride. They might hesitate, reacting, like when her father stayed in the house after the wind, but life always went on. Their attitude was to forget about it, whatever the scale of the problem; it was past already, time to turn and face the future and get on with whatever came next. After Dawie was killed they learned that there are events which cannot be put behind you. Disasters which loom like deep shadows cast across the present.

Elise finished her coffee and put the mug in the sink. She went to the door where she pulled on her boots and a donkey jacket that always hung there on the hook. The sun wasn't quite up yet, the air would still have the night's chill, and she wanted to be warm. Then she stepped out into the morning, ready to face it, whatever the scale of the disaster. The wind whipped her hair and slapped the collar of her jacket against her cheek.

With Jacob beside her they drove the tractor along the lines of trees and as they drove their hearts lifted. Incredibly there was very little damage, not even five per cent in the worst-hit orchards, which were not the plums. Her Sungolds had come out almost unscathed. She and Jacob were more delirious with joy and amazement the further they went, as the orchards confirmed how little they'd lost. When he got down from the tractor Jacob toyi-toyied with happiness.

Everyone, even the women and children, came out to help that day, clearing the damage. At midday Elise gathered everyone at the packing sheds. She wanted to thank them all and explain that under no circumstances would Rustenvrede go up for sale, but that it wasn't going to be easy because she was already in financial trouble. Worst of all, she had to ask her workers to sacrifice their Christmas bonus, but if they would all pull together and if the weather held, there could be a bonus at the end of the season. It was not a rousing speech; it was plain and blunt for the listeners who counted on the extra money. Yet knowing that she would take the strain with them and that she was as good as her word pulled everyone on board. And so, in spite of the bad news, there was a sense of elation among the workers that afternoon. Not only had they been spared the brunt of the gale, but they would also – they believed – triumph over the adversity that faced them.

They heard the rattle of thunder all through the day, the whisper and rush of wind shaking the trees. There were patches of blue sky, but the cloud cover moved across as a storm rolled in, chasing the wind. Huge drops of rain slapped and sizzled against hot earth. They continued to work even as the thunder in the mountains grew louder.

It was nightfall when Elise returned home. She'd worked all day, sharing Jacob's food at lunchtime instead of wasting time going back to the house. Finally, when it was too dark to do any more, she trudged down towards the lights that were burning in the kitchen. Mama Mashiya was standing over the stove when Elise walked in. The old lady had her hands on her hips; she shook her head when she saw Elise's stooped frame and made her sit down and eat some of the soup she'd made. They didn't say a word to each other until Elise had finished methodically mopping out her bowl with the crust of buttered bread Mama had put out for her.

Elise had her elbows on the table top. She wiped her forehead with her right hand, smearing dirt across her face. Mama stood by the table with a lappie in one hand, the other hand planted on her ample hip. At last Elise looked up and met her questioning gaze.

'I don't know how, or why, but we were spared. We lost only about three per cent overall.'

Mama clicked her tongue. Relief and a kind of wistful pleasure spread across her face in a smile. 'It was your father who brought that wind. That was his last word. He spared you and sent trouble to the rest of the valley. He knows they need a dose of suffering right now.'

'Do you think so?' Elise sounded as if she wanted it to be so.

'I know because I saw him. I saw him on the wind.' She said this plainly, as if it were a fact without mystery.

Elise was a rationalist – she would never have believed Mama's vision had she not known that her father had also spoken to her during the wind, that he had visited her dreams. And she fell silent, wondering.

The silence was interrupted by the sound of an approaching car.

All that day not a single person had stopped by at Rustenvrede. So Elise had no clear idea how bad her situation was relative to everyone else in the valley. All she had to rely on were the tidbits Mama had picked up during the day. She hadn't the heart to go out and see how hard-hit the other farms were, as she would normally have done, as the other farmers would be doing now – getting on the phone to call up their friends, finding an excuse to stop by or drive past the land of someone they weren't such good friends with. Sometimes they would drive by anyway, just to double-check on their neighbour's word. If it was bad for everyone then prices would adjust to help out, to compensate for the loss. But if the damage was bad for only one farmer then it was their tough luck.

Mama Mashiya went to the window and watched as the Dominee pulled up, got out of his car, paused a moment to

530

cope with the onslaught of excited dogs, then moved towards the house. He greeted Mama with a familiar pat on the back, and the same for Elise, who didn't get up. He sat down at the table opposite her.

'Did you have any damage?'

Elise nodded, almost smiled. 'I feel like the local disaster machine.'

The Dominee rested his face in his hands; he looked shattered.

'But not much. Not more than three per cent, and the Sungolds survived. I've got no idea how.'

Willem Slabbert raised his eyebrows. 'That's incredible,' he muttered, shaking his head. 'Incredible.'

'What about the rest of the valley?' Elise asked hesitantly, afraid of the answer.

'Mixed, but nowhere less than ten. Du Toit's and Joubert's were worst hit. At Komweer it looks like they've lost nearly half.'

Elise caught Mama's eye and they both understood. It was a sweet revenge, but Elise wouldn't say so.

The Dominee's visit was no surprise: he visited everyone at times of crisis like this. It was his pastoral duty and he performed it diligently. The surprise came a few minutes later when Alan Taylor drove up, and Elise wondered if this was more than a coincidence.

She showed both her guests through to the living room. The room was dark and musty; it had been closed up for over a week. Both men took the sherry Elise offered, though only the Dominee drank any of it. After a brief, polite exchange Elise plumped herself down in her usual chair and said wearily, 'This looks like the Inquisition. I'm too tired for small talk. So let's get to the point, gentlemen.'

Taylor and the Dominee glanced at one another. The Dominee looked slightly sheepish, but Taylor's expression barely flickered. Taylor dipped his chin slightly at Willem Slabbert, prompting him to begin. The Dominee cleared his throat, fussing with the creases in his black trousers. Elise watched him as he hesitated, formulating the opening of his speech. What he did say was utterly blunt, even more so than Elise had expected.

'Elise, you know how worried I've been about you. I'm worried that you're not managing and I know all too well how stubborn you are and how *brave*.'

He emphasised that word; it was clearly supposed to flatter her, to sweeten the bitter taste of everything else he had to say. 'I understand that you are determined to hold on to the land, but I'm concerned that you may be setting yourself an impossible task. And I've been wondering if, in the best interests of the farm, you ought not to be looking for alternative solutions.'

Elise realised that she was rocking back and forth, balancing and driving her motion from the heel of her left foot. She stopped. This must have been what Taylor and Willem were so deep in conversation about after the funeral. She put her glass down on the little circular mahogany table that always stood by her chair. She hadn't touched her drink. She leaned forward, her eyes narrowed with fatigue and suspicion, her hands clasped in front of her in the 'ladylike' fashion she'd been taught in school. The Dominee could hardly meet her eye. Instead he threw his head back as he glugged down the entire contents of his glass.

Taylor was still standing, one hand calmly in his elegant trouser pocket, the other holding his untouched drink across his chest. He spoke next, in the velvet tone he so often employed and which began now to grate on Elise. 'Look, we know that financially, what with your father and everything, you were in a hard place anyway. After today it can't have improved . . .'

Elise didn't move; not a muscle flickered. She wanted the full extent of this plan unfolded before she said a word. To react immediately would be to stop them before their intentions were completely transparent.

Taylor went on, somewhat obliquely, 'Elise, I hope you'll forgive me for being presumptuous, but it seems to us that this can be no life for a woman. Not an attractive young woman like yourself.'

Now the Dominee chimed in – they had obviously re-
hearsed this duet. 'Elise, your whole life is ahead of you. Why
don't you think about doing something else, maybe going
away for a while, forgetting that all this has happened? The
farm is going to be a terrible drain on you, there's no
guarantee you'll get over this hurdle. In fact, you know better
than I do that there's every likelihood you're going to have
trouble making it to the end of the season.'

'Precisely what is it you're suggesting?' She was looking
directly at Taylor when she asked this, but it was the
Dominee who hastily answered.

'What Mr Taylor is *generously* offering, Elise, is to buy
Rustenvrede. But if you wanted to sell the orchards and stay
on in the house then he'd be happy to work with an
arrangement like that too. He'd be happy to talk through any
arrangement you suggest.'

Elise felt her throat constricting and her breath tightening
as the adrenalin burst through her. She was suddenly certain
there was something weird – no, something downright
sinister – about Taylor and his solicitousness. Karel Smit's
words from the night before echoed through to her. She
shuddered. Was Slabbert in on this? Elise frowned, searching
the Dominee's face for duplicitousness, for signs of conspiracy. But there were none. He seemed to really believe that he
was helping her, that he had her own interests and the
interests of Rustenvrede at heart. Elise realised that Slabbert
saw Taylor as the rest of the valley did. He was simply the
perfect gentleman, and just to prove it here he was coming to
the aid of a damsel in distress. Looking over at Taylor Elise
had to concede that his performance was virtually flawless.
She also had to acknowledge that, after all that had happened, it was tempting just to sell up and go away, tempting
to admit defeat. She leaned back in the chair and looked from
one man to the other, Taylor and Slabbert, standing before
her like captors – like champions.

'It's not what I thought I'd find myself doing and, God
knows, I really can't afford it, but I'm prepared to help you

out, to relieve you of your burden . . . Don't you think it's time to move on, Elise?'

Taylor spoke so softly his voice was like music, but Elise had a good ear and to her this music was carefully practised, competent scales that lacked sincerity, lacked any life in the playing.

'What exactly do you mean by "relieve", Mr Taylor?'

Taylor smiled. Without a pause he gave her the figure. It was a straight cash offer. Later she would gasp with shock, but for now she remained stony-faced. Elise was stunned – the sum would make her a millionaire several times over. She really could walk away from all this. He would be getting a good price and she'd be washing her hands of pain and suffering and endless struggle.

Taylor dipped his fingers into the inside breast pocket of his jacket and handed Elise a business card with the name and telephone number of his lawyer printed on it. 'If you would like to take this proposal further then do please call me directly, but if you prefer, you can talk to my solicitor.'

Elise put the card in her pocket without looking at it.

'I should add that I can't keep this offer open very long. Other . . . interests. Let's say it stands until the New Year.'

Incredible, she thought as he went on intoning that he understood perfectly this was a hard issue and that she would need time to think it through. Neither he nor the Dominee were under any illusion she would, or indeed should, make a decision quickly, although obviously the faster she moved the better it would be for the farm in the long run, et cetera, et cetera. When Taylor had finished he sat down, and the two men stared at her expectantly. Elise stared back, then, when the pause was bordering on intolerable, she cleared her throat to speak.

She gave her answer bluntly and briefly in Afrikaans, addressing them both, although she expected only the Dominee to understand. She didn't attempt to soften her tone. As far as she was concerned the Dominee had betrayed her; there was no reason to make any effort at concealing the offence she had taken.

'I'm not selling this farm. You might as well tell me to sell my arms and legs. Dominee, I thought you had come here to lend support, but it turns out you've come to deliver a vote of no-confidence. If I were you I'd be ashamed of myself.'

Willem Slabbert was completely taken aback. His arms wheeled as if he was floundering in treacherous water. On his face he wore an expression that was half smile, half grimace. 'Jussus! Jy's net soos jou Pa. Hardkoppig!'

They didn't stay long after that.

As the two men walked out to their cars Elise stood in the kitchen doorway and watched them leave. She couldn't help smiling when she overheard Taylor asking the Dominee what he'd called her. Slabbert explained in a rueful tone that he'd told her she was stubborn.

'Like her father, like most Afrikaners, she's obstinate and bladdy headstrong. They want to make their own decisions and their own cock-ups with no interference. That's why farming is so one hundred per cent suited to Afrikaners.'

With that the two men parted.

Elise felt the dying wind on her skin. She stood in the doorway until the sound of their receding vehicles had gone. She recalled, from the morning of her engagement party, the sight of a little girl chasing after her tannie's hat, how it had eluded her grasp, the wind tugging it, pushing it further, so that the child was always just a few steps behind. The whisper of leaves rustling and whipping like the swish of stiff silk filled Elise with an old, restless excitement. To hell with them all, she thought, as she turned to go inside, adding a mental note to get a quote on a high fence and a massive electronic gate for the entrance to Rustenvrede. She was sick of people just driving up to her house whenever they felt like it.

Back in the kitchen Elise knew, from the way Mama Mashiya was cleaning the table so vigorously, that the old lady wanted to talk. She was agitated about something. Elise asked her straight out what it was. Mama carried on,

535

energetically wiping down a shelf she had cleaned earlier.

'What did Baas Taylor want with you, Elise?'

Elise was chewing on an apple. She swallowed too soon and the hard skin scratched her throat. She coughed, her mouth as dry as paper, so she took a sip of water to lubricate her response. 'Baas Taylor and the Dominee don't think a woman can run a farm on her own. They said they were worried about me.' Elise spoke the word 'Baas' with heavy irony.

Mama threw her lappie into the sink and crossed her arms, squashing and flattening out her breasts. She was clearly vexed. 'Elise. You must not sell to him. There's something, something about that man . . .'

Elise threw the rest of her apple into the bin and waited.

'Last week he came up to our house. I was there with my husband. He knocked on the door and I opened it. He was all smiling and sweet, said he wanted to talk to Oupa, so I asked him to come in. Oupa was still sick, but he came out and Baas Taylor told us the news about Sandile going to jail.'

Mama glanced away when she mentioned her son.

'He told us that he was very sorry about the way everything had happened and he was worried about the farm, and then he wanted to know about the land claim. When he asked that, I knew what his purpose was. He wanted to know what we were going to do so my husband said we would decide in due course. Then he wanted to see Sandile's papers. That was when I got suspicious!'

Mama had grown more animated and at this point she raised one finger. 'Then I thought he takes us for complete fools. So my husband said, "Mr Taylor, those papers are safe in the bank. We don't keep papers in the house." This was a lie of course – all Sandile's papers were in the house. Well, not now because my husband has put them away –'

'Are you sure they're safe?'

'Yes, I'm sure. No one will find them where they are.'

'Good.'

'Taylor smiled when Oupa said that the papers were safe.

536

His teeth shone like knives. It was a strange time to smile. Then he carried on, his voice even quieter and sweeter than before. He said he understood our problems, he understood we wanted a house and security in our old age . . .' Mama Mashiya turned away from Elise as she recounted this part, hiding her face at the memory. 'He offered us money. Ten thousand rand. Cash! But he said we must forget about the land claim.'

Her words were like slivers of ice entering Elise's heart. She knew it was more money than they'd ever dreamed of having. It was a fortune. 'What did you say, Mama?' she asked quietly, trying not to betray the panic she felt.

'Oupa said he would think about it. But Taylor wanted to give us the money right there on the spot. When he finally understood that we didn't want it, he was all sweet again. Said that we must think about it, we must come and see him. His door is aways open for us.'

'What will you do?'

Mama shook her head crossly, dismissively. 'We must wait for Sandile. He must come home and he must deal with this mess. Baas Taylor can stick his money up his arse! He won't pay me to betray my own son.'

Elise chuckled with a mixture of amusement and admiration at Mama's brazen, angry words. Privately she gave thanks again for the old lady's strength and straightforwardness. But she wondered what all this was adding up to.

Dipping her hand into her jeans pocket Elise pulled out the card that Taylor had just given her. Someone had made an offer on Rustenvrede the previous year, but they'd put in their bid anonymously, through a lawyer. Both Elise and her father were aware of the increasing value of their land, but the amount tabled by the lawyer was monstrous, tempting almost, though in reality they were never tempted. The farm was their life; selling was unthinkable – it wasn't that kind of commodity. Nevertheless it had been exciting and wonderful to know that they could be millionaires if they chose to be and many jokes and jibes had spun from that knowledge.

Looking at the name on Taylor's card Elise realised what had irked her about it just now. It was the same lawyer who'd enquired after Rustenvrede the year before.

FIFTY

The next afternoon, while her brothers were out mopping up after the wind, Ina was at Hemel en Aarde when she received a phone call from Alan Taylor.

'How are things on your farm?'

'Terrible,' she said dully. 'Yours?'

'Not so bad. We seem to have had less damage on this side of the valley.'

'Huh.'

'To be quite honest I'm having more trouble in the house than the orchards. I'm afraid that today is the second day that Lettie has failed to show up for work. I'm struggling a little, as you can imagine.'

'Shame, Alan! But why didn't you tell me yesterday?' Ina paused, biting down on her knuckles. 'I'm so sorry. I've never had this kind of trouble with the girl before.'

'I gather then you haven't seen or heard anything that might explain her absence?'

'No, but I can tell you now, I'm going past her house on my way home to find out what the story is.'

Ina was furious. She felt let down and shown up in front of the man she wanted most to impress. Taylor on the other hand didn't sound angry at all, just eager to get his house-keeper back.

Before she had a chance to get away, Lettie's mother arrived at the stall in a state of utter hysteria. Ina was thankful that there were no customers and none of her neighbours present to witness the scene.

The Kriels had been on the farm almost as long as the Du Toits, so the Du Toits tolerated the occasional trouble the family caused. Lettie's father was a drinker, a wife-beater and a thorn in the Du Toits' side. Mrs Kriel was a heavyset woman, with a permanently sullen and disappointed expression. Life had not been good to Mrs Kriel.

In the late afternoon she stormed into Hemel en Aarde reeking of tobacco, her face smeared with the skin-lightening cream she always wore and which over the years had created unsightly pinkish blotches on her dark complexion. She had on an old dress of Ina's, with a tight felted cardigan pulled over the faded sunflower pattern. On her feet were a pair of tattered slippers thrown out by Ina's mother years before. She was beside herself with worry over Lettie, who she believed had disappeared.

'When she didn't come home again last night we thought maybe she had to work late, maybe she'd stayed over at Die Uitkyk. I mean he made her work the day of the funeral! Now this morning her bed was still made up an' so I went over there just now, to Taylor's place, to find her. Mr Taylor tells me that Lettie isn't there. He says to me that she left as usual the other night – you know – an' that was the last time he's seen her!' Mrs Kriel was wringing her hands, shifting her focus from Ina to Nolitha to Mabel and then back.

Ina found the woman's distress upsetting, but she couldn't stand to admit it and she poured all her feeling into anger. She told herself, Mrs Kriel and the girls that Lettie was an irresponsible ingrate. 'She's run off because Alan Taylor caught her stealing his things and she didn't want to face the music!'

Ina was furious. She felt that Lettie's disappearance reflected badly on her in Alan's eyes and it was also fresh confirmation of the fact that these people who whined and moaned about not getting the same responsibilities and wages as whites just weren't deserving; they just weren't up to it. Nor, Ina thought angrily, were they deserving of all the time and effort she put into training them.

Mrs Kriel hadn't come for a lecture; she just wanted her daughter back and she wailed loudly to that effect.

'Mrs Kriel, Lettie will be back. She's probably waiting for you at home already with some silly hard-luck tale!'

But Mrs Kriel could not be calmed. She insisted frantically that Taylor knew where her daughter was; she feared he was keeping her prisoner, that something dark and terrible was going on up there at Die Uitkyk and Lettie's life was in danger. Ina actually laughed at this. The hysteria infected her and she guffawed openly at the thought of Mrs Kriel's ugly daughter tied up and at the ruthless mercy of cool, urbane Alan Taylor.

Mrs Kriel's eyes darkened and she bore down on Ina and her giggles, speaking in a voice so shot through with fear it sent a chill through every one of the women in that room. 'Don't laugh, Miss Ina, or you'll be laughing the other side of your face tomorrow. I had a dream about him. The dream was full of blood and fire and he was there, that ice face staring through the flames. I told Lettie not to go back there, but she said she had to go, she said *you* told her she had to go back to work there! You would make everything OK.' Mrs Kriel pointed a stubby accusing finger into Ina's chest. 'She trusted you!'

Ina spun on her heels, ran into the toilet and slammed the door in Mrs Kriel's face. The screaming increased in pitch and intensity for a minute or so longer and then stopped altogether. Ina moved away from the door, took a tumbler down from the cabinet, turned on the cold tap and filled the glass with water. Then, very deliberately, because her hands were shaking so violently, she lifted the glass to her lips and drank.

She flew home, leaving the girls to lock up the stall. She poured herself a glass of neat vodka and took a packet of cigarettes out on to the stoep with her. The vodka and the garden soothed her. The cigarette tasted nasty and for some reason that felt good.

It was Daan who found her there. She looked wrecked. 'What's wrong?'

'Lettie's disappeared.'

Daan frowned, unclear why such a distant event could cause Ina to be so upset. 'When?'

'I dunno.' Ina shrugged and stubbed out her cigarette with a vigour that sent sparks and ash flying. Then her whole demeanour shifted and she became angry again. 'Ag, she'll probably turn up soon enough with some stupid bladdy story!'

Daan ran his fingers back through his hair. 'Well, I hope she's OK. I mean, I'm sorry to hear that.'

Ina shrugged. 'Ja, well, you know . . . Kaffirs – can't live with 'em, can't kill 'em!'

Ina let out a stuttering, half-apologetic laugh. Daan bit his lip. 'Ina, you're drunk.'

During the night of the wind Ina had woken up convinced there was someone in the room with her. All her hair had stood on end and she'd felt paralysed. By the time she was able to move again it was obvious she was alone. She got up and went through to the kitchen. The light in the fridge popped and died as she pulled open the door. The interior was suddenly, eerily dark. Ina reached for a bottle that felt like the peach juice, poured herself a glass of it, whacked some ice on top and put the bottle away. She took a sip and it tasted weird. It was tomato juice. Ina took it back to bed and drank it anyway.

The night was sultry and hot. She slept fitfully and woke the next morning with a vicious headache. She'd dragged herself out of bed and gone straight to her mother's room. She didn't want to be alone with her thoughts, didn't want to listen to the anxiety that irked her almost constantly now.

Mrs Du Toit was sitting up in bed with her breakfast tray on her lap and the radio playing. The wind was still blowing strongly outside. Ina didn't say anything to her mother. She sat on the edge of the bed staring vaguely at the picture on the cover of the new *Fair Lady*, sipping a cup of coffee Mabel had brought for her. Mrs Du Toit asked innocently if something was wrong and Ina looked up sharply.

'Ma, do you think there's anything, something . . . *strange* about Alan?'

Her mother's gaze flicked away; this was clearly not the response she'd expected. Mrs Du Toit reached forward and straightened the fold of her coverlet. She didn't seem to be enjoying the exchange; perhaps she didn't want to know too much about her daughter's private life. She spoke right over Ina who had begun to explain.

'Darling, you are not so old. Don't forget that I was married to your father when I was twenty-nine and that was a time when everyone else had been married ten years and was a mother four times over. Goodness, some of my friends were virtually grandmothers! It is never too late. You'll find happiness, my dear, and if it's not with Alan then someone else will come along and it will be a lovely surprise for us all. You'll see.'

Ina sighed, wishing it could be so. There was something so unreachable about Alan; beneath all the sexual heat he was stone cold.

Ina didn't know how long she'd been sitting out there on the stoep, but it must have been a while because the sky was deep blue and the smoky undersides of the ribboned clouds seemed to catch fire as they were caught by the rays of the sinking sun. She thought she heard the sound of a car pulling up, the low thrum of an engine piercing the ambient buzz and hum of insects. She turned her head away from the sunset to listen, but all she heard was the throb of crickets and the quiet pulsing coo of doves. All her brothers were at home and they weren't expecting visitors. Hopefully, whoever it was had gone away.

But he hadn't gone away. Alan Taylor found her sitting in the gathering darkness. Ina almost jumped out of her skin when his hand touched her shoulder; she hadn't heard his approach. She was clearly in a state and Alan was very good at unravelling such states. It wasn't long before she was sobbing out the story of her encounter with Mrs Kriel. Taylor merely frowned, said he was aware of her distress, that the lady had been at his gate that afternoon, ranting and wailing into the intercom.

Ina felt a chill shiver through her. 'Did you let her in?'

He shook his head, his mouth still turned down at the sides. It was hard to know if it was Mrs Kriel's histrionics that he was frowning at, or if his mind was really on something else. Until now that impenetrable, inscrutable air was what had excited Ina about Taylor, but suddenly she found it unnerving. She looked away. A sickly scent of cut grass mingled with lavender and honeysuckle drifted up from the garden.

Ina couldn't let it go. Part of her felt that Alan was to blame for the state she was in and she wanted to let him know. 'You know, Alan, Lettie is a particularly bright girl. She's been trained to use her initiative and that's what she does. You should just have let her get on with what she knows best and not concern herself with so much silliness, like that washing, for goodness' sake. Why did you have to make such a fuss about it?'

His response was delivered with a chill that was almost menacing. 'Unlike you, Ina, I do believe there are things one is entitled to keep private. I don't like other people interfering in my business.'

Ina couldn't imagine why anyone would have rooms that other people weren't allowed into. What on earth could he be keeping in there? She laughed, as if this was just a stupid man thing. 'Well, you shouldn't be so silly about it. They don't talk to us and they keep quiet – that's their job.'

Taylor didn't find any of this amusing at all. He was quite serious. 'Well, I'm afraid that I've had enough.'

He peeled twenty salmon-coloured fifty-rand notes from a silver note clip that he took from his jacket pocket. He handed them to Ina and suggested that she give them to Lettie's family as severance pay. Ina didn't know what to say. Taylor folded the notes delicately and pressed them into her palm. 'It's only fair, my dear.'

Ina wasn't concerned with the fairness of this gesture as much as with its strangeness, but she took the money and then hooked her arm through his as he escorted her inside.

'She may need it when she gets back. Next week we can look for someone to replace her, but for now let's concentrate on dinner, shall we?'

It was the first time they'd fought, if you could call it that. Ina had been frightened by the mixture of menace and entreaty in his eyes.

Later, as he pulled her hand through his arm, Ina noticed that Alan wasn't wearing his watch.

'What have you done with your watch?'

'Oh. The strap broke. I've had to send it off for repair.'

'That's terrible.'

Taylor shrugged. 'It's not so terrible. I have insurance.'

Fifty One

The weekly shop was now so long overdue it was unavoidable. Leaving Jacob in charge of the farm Elise set off early, vowing that next year she would get a mobile bank to come out to the farm, that wages would go up, these shopping trips would end and she'd set up more formal tenancy arrangements with all her workers. It was too much now, when she was running the farm by herself, to be doing this as well.

She drove in silence, without the radio, one hand on the gear stick, the other arm resting on the half-open window. Her shoulders were hunched with tension and she squinted into the glare because she'd forgotten her sunglasses.

She made a brief stop at the post office in the still empty dorp to pick up mail from the PO Box. Elise drove slowly, gazing out at the familiar homes and wondering if they would ever seem as welcoming and as warm to her as they had before. The dull calm with which she perceived everything lurched suddenly and violently when she saw Daan strolling out of De Jager's Hotel. Right beside him was Madeleine. It was too early for this to have been a courtesy call. They stopped in the doorway and Madeleine stood on tiptoe to kiss him. Daan kissed her back, not lightly, but hungrily. Then she faded back into the shadows of the lobby and he stepped out into the street. The whole scene was over in less than thirty seconds.

Daan was headed across the street towards the police station and didn't see her immediately, but Elise was driving straight for him. Their eyes met as her foot slipped off the accelerator and she stalled the bakkie, coming to a shuddering halt just a few feet from where he stood. Mixed with his surprise was a glimmer of satisfaction at her evident shock. But it was Daan who looked away first and walked on with studied nonchalance.

Elise restarted the bakkie and drove off as calmly as she could. She wasn't sure what she felt. Part of her was glad; this was so much easier than all the reasons she'd given him for breaking off their engagement, this was plain and unreasonable and final. She knew now, with blinding clarity, that Daan had never stopped seeing Madeleine.

Later, wandering through the aisles of the airport-sized Pick 'n' Pay, Elise succumbed to depression. After Dawie was killed, her strongest emotion had been anger. Anger had pulled her to her feet, restored her strength, burned through the grief. Fighting back had kept her from falling down. What she felt now, as she tossed loaves of white bread into her squeaking shopping cart, was nothing like that. This was an all-time low; there was no anger to ignite any feeling in her, nothing that might pull her up and out. It is hard to turn back from such a point, impossible to bounce back when morale has sunk so far. The weight of the task ahead of her, combined with the events of last week, was crushing. She wanted to weep, but there was no point, there was no one to comfort her; she'd just feel even more pathetic if she broke down over the chicken counter. Perhaps that was why her father never cried, because it would have been pointless. There was no choice, no giving up: he had to carry on and Elise knew she had to do the same.

She yearned for the intimacy of those first surprising and sweet conversations with Sandile; when she'd felt she could say anything, share anything. Her mind strayed to him and what he might be doing, what he might be thinking about her. That day in the police station he'd said he was sorry. Elise didn't know if that was another tactic in his game, or if he meant it. She still knew so little. What if she never had the opportunity to know him better? What if she was never able to challenge him again, to clear up the doubt that had pushed them apart? Reaching for another bag of flour she made a mental note to phone Karel Smit and report to him Mama's story about Taylor. He could fatten his conspiracy theory with it. Then it occurred to her that she could tell Sandile directly.

It was almost involuntary. She didn't debate the idea, just got in the car and took the turn that led her towards Pollsmoor. It was only when she reached the final intersection that anguished indecision hit. Approaching the junction she noticed that the sign shimmering in the heat haze up ahead bore the name that until now had meant nothing to her. Now its meaning was layered with dread and longing. She stopped at the crossroads and for a long time remained halted there, contemplating a U-turn instead of a left. The sun beat in on her. Elise knew she could so easily take that turn, drive up to the gate, ask anyone – no warder would refuse a brisk and purposeful white woman with an unstated urgent reason for seeing Mr Mashiya. If they did she could invent a reason, something medical, familial, anything – and she would be there, with him, in a matter of minutes.

The decision was made for Elise by the violent hooting of a car that was flying up behind her at a rate that jolted her into action. She banged her foot on the accelerator and jerked the bakkie round the left turn almost before she'd thought about it, the red Mercedes flashing by with its hooter blaring. She was relieved to find herself moving again, cool air flowing round her and the sign to Pollsmoor receding in the rear-view mirror.

When Human shuffled through in the late morning and told him he had a visitor, Sandile assumed it would be Karel bringing more bad news or, worse, no news. They were in the midst of the holiday season, which meant that getting anything done was like trying to drive quickly across London in the rush hour. Sandile tried to practise patience, but it didn't come easily to him. He strode ahead of Human towards the visiting bays.

But it wasn't Karel who was waiting for him there behind

548

the glass. Sandile stopped dead when he saw her. Elise smiled shyly. For a while they said nothing, just looked, taking everything in, waiting for the emotion to subside and for words to come. He was shocked to see her looking so thin and tired. Her illuminating presence, her grace, her vigour – all that had been dulled by grief. She was taken aback by how weak he looked; his skin was sallow and his normally brilliant eyes were lustreless.

Sandile moved towards the glass partition He asked her how she was, but she was staring so intently at him that she didn't respond. He smiled quizzically and sat down so that his mouth was nearer the holes of the speaker.

'Elise!'

'Hi.'

'I said, how are you?'

Elise shook her head, smiling back at him. 'Sorry – intermittent synaptic paralysis.'

They both laughed, an edgy sound.

She sat down and they stared at one another some more. Sandile knew he should say something, but his mind had gone blank. Eventually he murmured, 'You are the last person in the world I expected to see here.'

Laughter gurgled up in her throat. 'Ja . . . *I'm* not even quite sure how I got here . . . one minute I was sailing down the aisles at Pick 'n' Pay and the next I'm – here.'

Sandile pitched in again. 'How's the farm?'

'Shew! Ask me something else.'

'OK . . . um, how are you?' he asked a second time.

Elise stretched her arms out at her sides and they both laughed nervously, but gladly, again. She listed everything in a tone of light sarcasm, cocking her head and widening her eyes with an expression that was the converse of what was appropriate for the disasters she spoke of.

'Oh, pretty good, pretty good. Since my dad died and I've broken off my engagement, I'm doing everything on my own, which as you know means I'm working sixteen or eighteen hours a day with a bunch of guys who are overworked and underpaid. Then last week we had a gale come through that took about three per cent of my crop, and unless the rest of the fruit comes in safely it's not clear Rustenvrede will make it to the end of the season.' She laughed ironically. 'And then there's your land claim to look forward to when I'll only lose my dam and my best boreholes and a few top-rated orchards. Nothing that wouldn't bankrupt and destroy your average farmer.'

'Are *you* OK?' His eyes were ablaze. She looked away.

'I think so. I don't know really, don't think about it much, just push on. And you? What about you?'

Sandile responded with a sudden urgency. 'Listen, there are two things I have to say to you. The first is that I'm sorry. Really, from the bottom of my heart, sorry about the way I handled not telling you about the claim.'

Elise waved her hand in front of her face, as if she was pushing his apology away. 'Ag, next to everything else, forget it.' She was trying to remain light, trying to avoid being ambushed by the terrible weight of everything that had happened.

Sandile went on, still serious and urgent like before. 'But it would mean so much to me if you could put yourself in my shoes, try and imagine how I kind of divorced *you* – Elise – from my enemy – the Van Rensburgs. This wasn't supposed to be a fight between you and me. It was my mission to right a wrong, to retrieve my family's land from the thieves who stole it, and then you and I became embroiled and this whole thing and my feelings for you were – not at all what I expected.'

Elise raised an eyebrow, a teasing look in her eye. 'Oh. And what *were* your feelings for me?'

Sandile grinned suddenly, his face lighting up briefly with pleasure again. He looked round at Human who was pretending vainly not to listen by staring up at the ceiling. 'I don't think I could do that to Human. I don't think he can stand the excitement.'

Elise flashed a smile back at him. Then after a silence she

shifted from her light tone and said, 'Sandile, I've been a coward. I dressed it up as confusion, as moral crisis, but really it was just cowardice.'

Another gear change. He said to her in his laconic way, 'The Jongnooi and the kaffir boy never made it to the fairy-tale anthologies, did they?'

'No. No, they didn't.'

Sandile suddenly hugged his arms around his chest, as if he was cold, his eyes raking the space they were confined in and separated by. His gaze rested on her again with a look that was full of longing, wistful and worried at once. 'So you're OK?'

She shrugged and answered slowly, as if for the first time she was choosing words to fit her feelings. 'It's hard. You know? I wonder if the problem is that I was brought up to think that happiness was my right. Perhaps if I'd lower my expectations of everything I wouldn't feel so stunned when things go wrong.'

She sighed and shook her head and her long hair shivered, like a fan, like a long feather, on her shoulders. 'I dunno, with my father it's so much harder. At least with Dawie there were people, politics, to blame. With this, I just feel so *victimised*. It's terrible. I mean he was the victim, not me . . . But now I'm left all alone and I keep thinking why me, why has this happened to *me* again and again?'

Sandile tried to imagine the battering she had taken as she sat there with her eyes wide and vaguely focused, her fingers weaving in emphasis of the words she spoke so softly. It wasn't self-pity she was expressing. Her tone concealed a difficult truth. She was fighting for her survival and the outcome of this battle was by no means a foregone conclusion.

'You know, I have to ask you – I don't think you did. I don't know why, but I don't. But – did you do it?' It was the question that had brought her here and it came out as a cluster of confusion. Yet Elise looked at him with that level, sure gaze and he knew she could see everything. He shook his head. Of course not.

'And the killings in Zambia?'

Sandile shook his head again. It hurt, knowing how deeply she had doubted him. He told her the whole story of Ismail and her expression was solemn as she listened.

'I wish I knew something I could say or do that would make all this better. All I know, Elise, is you'll make it. Maybe because you strive for that happiness, or because you feel so much. Maybe because you *deserve* it.'

Elise looked down, bending her head so that he couldn't see her reaction as he spoke. The conversation had tapered from a focused, sharp exchange to one that was almost wistful, almost meditative in the way that thoughts were quietly expressed and mulled and developed.

'I've never anticipated justice, or fairness. In fact I generally anticipate the opposite. I regard it as my task in life to try and avoid the inevitable as long as possible and then, when the inevitable happens, to adjust and recover as fast as I can.'

Elise didn't say anything; she just looked up at him. It was true, what he said. And in a sense it was she, or her people at least, who were responsible for creating, or confirming, this sense that Sandile had of the world.

He went on. 'It's terrible to think how my parents have always lived in that way, expecting suffering and grateful for the slivers of happiness they were granted. I used to think that was part of their degradation, but perhaps it's really part of yours. Ja, maybe that's their strength. If you expect life to be the chain of suffering that it is, then pain won't be such a shock, won't be so devastating.'

Elise raised her eyes to meet his. She was quiet for a while as she thought about what he'd said. Then she spoke. 'Isn't that a little ironic?'

Sandile frowned slightly, not fully understanding. 'What do you mean?'

'I mean, I thought you spent all that time fighting so that everyone would have the opportunity for happiness that my people denied them.'

Sandile smiled, suddenly shifting his tone. 'You know, Elise, I like you.'

'You're avoiding my question.'

'Maybe all that lovely stuff is for the next generation. The little bastards who'll have it all with no idea of the price of getting it.'

'Maybe,' she said sadly. 'Maybe that's right.'

There was a long pause. Sandile found himself staring at her, unselfconsciously, quite without embarrassment, in just the way that she was staring at him. All the feeling that flowed in the slender exchange was conveyed through their eyes, as if a channel had been created between them. The moment was inarticulate and eloquent. It felt to Sandile as if his heart fluttered, as if there was a bird confined in his chest. For those few moments he transcended the putty-coloured claustrophobia of his surroundings in a flow of unfettered feeling.

The tension between them made Human uncomfortable. He started breathing hard: the sound of a furious attempt at ignition in the brain. He didn't like the silence, and the intimacy of their stares. He was sure they must be transgressing some subsection of a clause in the visiting rules, but he had no idea which. As if attempting to clear some plug of phlegm from his memory of the rules, Human snorted. The noise was a devastatingly mucoid rasping. Its effect was instant.

Sandile glanced irritably over at the warder. The rawness of his predicament had slammed suddenly back at him. They talked some more, about everything except their immediate circumstances, and in a way Sandile was glad of that.

'What are you going to do about the farm?'

'I'm just getting through this harvest first, then I can worry about the land claim and the rest. We'll cross that bridge when we come to it, as they say . . . but meantime, what are we going to do about you?'

'Elise, I did not kill your dad.'

She nodded, not hesitating for a moment. 'I know.'

553

'What makes you so different from the others?'

She smiled. 'I don't know. I just never thought you did it.'

'But *how* do you know?'

She shrugged, half laughing. 'Instinct! You don't even look like a murderer. I mean, really bad guys, you can tell them a mile off. Don't you remember Falconetti?'

He nodded, laughing too. '*Rich Man Poor Man*!'

Elise sighed happily. 'Right, you came to our house and watched it with us. You and Unathi and Vuyani and was it Nosipo?' He nodded. 'And your mother and me and Dawie. We were hooked. My mother and father watched it in the living room on the colour set; we sat and watched it in black and white in the kitchen!'

'Right . . .'

'Did Falconetti ever get caught? I don't remember.'

'Ja, he must have done. Bad guys always get it in the end . . .'

The memory was sweet and it washed over them soothingly.

'Elise, why did you come here?'

'I'm not sure. It's so unreal I'm not even sure if I am here.'

'But why?'

'Because you've got stuck in my head. Because I was so angry and hurt about – what you did. Because I wanted to know if you were the person I thought you were or the murderous tsotsi that everyone makes you out to be . . .'

'And?'

'And I'm glad you're not the murderous tsotsi.'

Sandile looked back at her, brown eyes locked on blue. She was frowning now, her hair falling all over the place because she kept pushing it back, her fingers running agitatedly over her head. Sandile reached out, slipping his fingers through the holes in the glass. Elise looked down at his hand and touched it with her own. Human took a step towards them, wondering if this meant trouble brewing – he didn't like the look of it all. Sandile pulled his fingers back and their hands mirrored one another's, trailing down the glass.

Human settled back against the wall. Elise looked down as she folded her hands into her lap. 'There's another reason I came. I think there's something that might help explain things, but it sounds a bit far-fetched, a bit crazy . . .'

Then she recounted the chronology: Taylor's visit to Rustenvrede the night before her father's death, then the proposal made to her by Taylor and the Dominee and finally the story that Mama told her about Taylor offering the Mashiyas money to let go of the land claim. Sandile was riveted.

'It just seems odd to me. He wants Rustenvrede. With you in jail he eliminates the land claim problem. And with my father gone he thinks he has a better chance of getting the farm.'

Sandile was on the edge of his seat. Elise warmed to her theory the more his excitement seemed to confirm it. The problem – and they agreed on this too – was nailing him. They both fell silent as they pondered this. 'Elise, you must be careful. OK?'

'I promise,' she smiled.

'Now do me a favour, will you? Call Karel Smit and tell him all this?'

'OK.'

It was time for Elise to go. They parted quickly; it was too painful to linger. No goodbyes were spoken, no hands reached out to touch the glass. She simply stood up and walked away. But as she reached the door Sandile called out to her.

'Elise?'

She stopped, looked back at him. The harshness of the moment seared his eyes. He was hugging his arms to his chest, his hands squeezed under his armpits.

'Thank you,' he said.

She bit on her lip, then tugged her bag higher up on her shoulder, turned and left. Walking away from the prison Elise's mood was lighter. The doubt that had so clouded her mind had begun to lift.

FIFTY TWO

Elise was lying in bed but she wasn't asleep. In that grey time between waking and rising she imagined he was there with her, his face near hers. She imagined him kissing her, holding her. Then she turned, shoving her face into the pillow, and struggled to swallow tears. Was she coping? She had no idea. She found it so hard to think clearly.

The work was hard and everyone was stretched to their limits, working Saturdays with no extra pay, pushing through all the daylight hours. Elise knew the picking was going well, but even with the extra workers she'd taken on the men were under strain, and she knew it.

The peaceful minutes she ritually spent in the kitchen with Mama first thing were shattered that morning by the distraught interruption of Nolitha, Jacob's youngest daughter. They heard her screaming moments before she appeared at the back door, bruised and bleeding. She looked as if she'd been badly beaten up, but a quick inspection by a brisk and unfazed Mama Mashiya revealed that the cuts were mostly superficial.

'It's OK, Nolitha. It's nothing serious. Just try to calm down, be still now. Mama will look after it for you.'

This reassurance had no effect on the volume and intensity of the siren-like wail that kept coming from Nolitha's mouth. It was ten minutes or so before she'd exhausted herself, the crying faded to a whimper and Elise was able to elicit the story.

Vuyo, Nolitha's boyfriend, had come home blind drunk in the early hours of the morning and started a fight over the paternity of the child she was expecting, which Nolitha knew could only be his. He slapped her and she slapped him back and then the kitchen knife had come out and things went crazy.

While Mama cleaned up and comforted the sobbing girl Elise noticed something going on up at the shed. She immediately assumed, correctly as it turned out, that whatever was going on up there also had something to do with Vuyo. It's OK, you can handle this, she told herself, and slammed out of the kitchen, banging the door behind her deliberately hard so that the men's attention would be caught by the noise. She was irritated and a little scared. This was the kind of scene only her father had dealt with up to now. And he had often depended on sheer physical strength. First he'd go up to the troublemaker and say, 'Listen, you drunk, go home.' Sometimes the guy would do as he was told, but more often than not he wouldn't. There'd be a group of thirty or forty people standing around, all looking at the boss and waiting to see what would happen. So Van would say, 'OK, you can go home now' and the drunk would say, 'No, I'm not going home.' He wanted a fight. Van would take a few steps forward, looming terrifyingly over the man, and that would be the end of it. He'd have thrown himself in there if necessary, but usually his physical bulk was enough. The worker would go home, sleep it off and have a day's wages deducted from his next pay packet. That was Van Rensburg's way, but Elise had no idea how she would cope. There was no way she was going to get into a fight.

Jacob stepped forward to meet her. He looked tired and smelt of beer. Jacob was taking a lot of strain and Elise wondered if this incident had something to do with him. Since Van Rensburg's death so much had fallen to him. It was possible he'd been obliterating his frustrations with Vuyo and things had gotten out of control.

'Jacob? *You're* not drunk, are you?'

He shook his head, speaking rather more deliberately than usual. 'No, missus, I *was* drinking, but it's not me, it's Vuyo.' He stretched out his arm to indicate the direction of the problem. The crowd of men parted and Elise saw Vuyo in the centre of the group – blind, roaring, shit-faced drunk, insisting that he be allowed to go to work.

'Why the fuck can't I drive? Hey, Jacob? Why you taking orders from that bloody woman like you a sissy? I won't take orders from a blarry woman. I want my orders from you! And I'm gonna drive!' And so it went on, in a stream of rage and contradictions.

Jacob was a man of very few words at the calmest of times, but this torrent of abuse had silenced him. Some of the other men were laughing and Vuyo was playing to the crowd. Elise walked straight up to him and grabbed him by the arm. 'Listen, you're drunk, so go home, all right?'

At first she thought he was going to co-operate. It must have been one helluva fight, Elise thought, though at least Nolitha had scored a few hits of her own from the look of things. It was probably fortunate for Vuyo that he was still so intoxicated. He wouldn't feel the pain from the gash on his forehead or the bruises on his arms. She grabbed his arm again and started to steer him away, towards the track that would take him home, but he jerked away from her, screaming.

'Don't touch me!' The stink of alcohol on his breath was powerful.

Elise let go of his arm and hissed at him through gritted teeth, 'Vuyo, you can go to your house now.'

He leered back at her, swaying slightly, his eyes narrowing as he concentrated on the words. 'No. I'm going to work!'

This was the moment she'd dreaded. Elise moved forward, right up into his face. Vuyo teetered on his heels, then swung his arm back and round, but Jacob pushed Elise away and took the punch full in his face. The crunch of Vuyo's fist making contact with Jacob's nose was horrible. Both men were momentarily startled, then a second later Jacob swayed and fell backwards. He was unconscious when he landed, ribbons of blood streaming from his nose. The other men looked on in silent horror, waiting for Vuyo's next move. He staggered towards Elise, but she'd had enough.

'To hell with you. I'm fetching the police.' She strode down to the kitchen, yanked the receiver off the hook and dialled the number for the police station. Her call was picked up almost straight away, by Johnny Kakana.

Hearing his voice she hesitated, catching her breath, then spoke as calmly and as matter-of-factly as she could manage. 'Johnny, listen, I've got a guy up here who's drunk and beaten up his wife and he just knocked Jacob down. I need your help.'

There was a pause, then a terse reply: 'I'll be there now.' The phone went dead.

'Hell!' Elise swore as she slammed the phone down. Calling the police was an admission of failure.

Nolitha was sniffling into a wad of tissues, repeating her story to Mama Mashiya. Mama rolled her eyes and tutted at Elise. It had been a while since they'd had a morning quite like this one. 'I'm not surprised that Vuyo is the one to cause trouble.'

Elise nodded in weary agreement. Vuyo had come to Rustenvrede only last year, from a farm where the dop system still functioned and the women bore the scars. When he first arrived he'd had huge problems taking orders from her, but she had deliberately, quietly taken time to work with him until she thought she'd won his trust. Now she'd have to start again. Elise watched from a distance as Vuyo threw punches at the air and the other guys dodged and provoked him.

Johnny arrived ten minutes later. He was accompanied by Constable Pelser, who was still wheezing after running halfway across the dorp in response to Daan's summons. Everyone, even Vuyo, fell silent as Johnny slammed the door of his van and strolled up to the gathering. Elise stood back and folded her arms across her chest, part defensive, part relieved. Johnny acknowledged her with a dip of his head, then he got down to work.

It didn't take long for them to chase Vuyo into the back of the van. Everyone knew the routine, even Vuyo, though this would be his first time in the cell. No one would bring

559

charges; he'd be kept there long enough to sober up and give him a fright. Then in a day or so he'd come home burning with contrition and a vicious hangover. He made a brief, half-hearted attempt at a protest, or perhaps an escape, by flinging himself against the doors of the van. But Johnny was already locking him in. The impact echoed metallically, then there was a final thud as Vuyo hit the floor and was quiet at last.

The rest of the workers began to disperse towards their tasks for the day, and Elise and Johnny were momentarily alone. She was glad of the opportunity to talk to him. 'Seems like you should just move the station up here. It'll save you all the driving.'

'Shew! You can say that again – hey?'

'Listen, Johnny, there's something I –' Elise bit her lip, uncertain how to put it, whether it was wise to put it at all, but nevertheless she did. 'It's about Alan Taylor. I wanted to talk to you about Alan Taylor.'

Johnny frowned, evidently taken aback. 'What about him?'

'That night my father was killed you came to the house with him. I've been wondering why.'

Johnny shifted, uncomfortable with the question and the directness of her gaze. 'I – it was –' Johnny stopped and cleared his throat very loudly. 'Taylor wanted to join forces with your father. He wanted to discredit Sandile. I told him about the file – the one with the report about the murders in Lusaka – and when I took it to him he thought it could be useful. He said he had a plan to frame Sandile, get him out of the picture. But he didn't tell me what the plan was. That's why I came with him. I just wanted to know what he was going to do.'

'And did he ever tell you?'

Johnny shook his head. 'Events . . . overtook.'

'Johnny, I don't know who else to tell about this, but something's been troubling me.'

Elise moved a step closer to him and in a quiet voice outlined each step in the ladder of suspicion that was building towards Taylor. Since she'd talked it through with Sandile she'd had time to find words and instances with which to articulate and clarify her intuition. She was surprised at the speed with which she captured Johnny's interest. He said nothing, but listened to her intently. She was acutely conscious of the delicacy of what she was doing. She ran the risk of confirming his belief in Sandile's guilt rather than arousing suspicion about Taylor.

'So, what are you saying?'

Elise swallowed hard, willing him to understand and to help. Her voice dropped almost to a whisper, yet every word she spoke was chillingly clear. 'What I'm saying is – I think Taylor is getting away with murder.'

'But you have nothing to prove it.' The way he put it was more like a question than a dismissal.

'But I have nothing to prove it,' she echoed.

From his expression Elise was sure that Johnny shared her suspicions. He seemed to be struggling to suppress signs of his growing agitation.

The end of their exchange was stilted and a little abrupt. Johnny thanked Elise for talking to him, said her thoughts were 'very interesting' and he would 'follow up'. She said she would appreciate that and if there was anything she could do to help he should let her know. He nodded and then began to move towards the van, glancing back at her while she held her gaze steadily on him. He was decidedly agitated.

'You haven't seen Lettie around, have you?'

'No, not for a while. Why?'

He shrugged. 'She's disappeared, run off, I think.'

'Oh. That doesn't sound like Lettie.'

'Ja. Well, if you do see her, perhaps you could let me know. I'm a little concerned.'

'Naturally.' Elise watched Johnny drive away. She was thinking about Lettie. Johnny's almost thrown-away news had sent a chill through her.

The next evening Vuyo came to see Elise, tapping on the kitchen door while she was having breakfast. She went to listen to what he had to say. His fingers played nervously with the floppy cotton hat in his hand. He shook his head a few times and then said vehemently, all his consonants pushed out and his r's rolled, 'Yussus! Sorry about yesterday, I wasn't myself, Miss Elise.'

'Yussus. That's for shaw.'

She imitated his vehemence and they both laughed.

FIFTY THREE

While Elise kept her insomniac night vigils, with only the whisper of papers shuffled and the sound of her bare feet pattering through silent rooms, on the side of the otherwise sleeping valley Johnny Kakana couldn't lose consciousness either. There was something going on, he sensed, but he was floundering for meaning and for a principle to guide him through.

Johnny had left Rustenvrede that day in a state of profound uncertainty. He'd always had the utmost respect for Elise's judgement and he didn't doubt that she'd thought deeply before deciding to speak to him. He knew that she never let emotion or sentiment cloud a decision or an opinion, even when her good judgement was at her own expense. But then there was the way she'd exploded her engagement to Daan du Toit. Did that show clarity of thought? Falling for a farm worker's son wasn't such a sin, except if he was black, then it was clearly insane. And this wasn't any old farm worker's son.

Johnny sighed. What bothered him most was that he'd already got his own questions about Alan Taylor. The problem was knowing what to do about them. Frankly the man unnerved him. There were questions he wanted to put to him, but it wasn't as if they had the kind of relationship that allowed for a quiet chat over drinks. The other options seemed too extreme. There were certainly no grounds for arrest, nor was it appropriate to haul him in for questioning. There was one possibility however. An informal but firmly couched request for Taylor to come by the station and talk over his statement. It would undoubtedly cause some discomfort, but that might work. By throwing Taylor slightly off guard Johnny thought he might get to the bottom of whatever it was the Englishman was up to.

Arriving at the charge office that morning Johnny was faced with a scene that would focus his thoughts about Taylor and provide him with a reason to put the questions that were bothering him.

Mrs Kriel was standing at the counter, surrounded by several of her daughters and they were demanding that Alan Taylor be charged with murder. Daan was at the centre of the mêlée, shouting to be heard over the hubbub. His expression was a mixture of amusement and exasperation. After some minutes Daan's request for silence was granted.

'Thank you! Now, could perhaps just one of you explain to me what it is that's happened?'

'I'm telling you, that Alan Taylor has murdered my Lettie!'

Daan's eyes widened. 'So you've found her body?'

Mrs Kriel sniffled, then blew her nose on the edge of her apron. 'No, I haven't found the body . . .'

Daan smiled patiently. 'Right, Mrs Kriel, I think that – since we lost Piet van Rensburg – everyone's getting a little too worked up. Don't you?'

Mrs Kriel nodded, stifling another sob. Then, more calmly, she explained her fears.

'My youngest daughter, Lettie – Johnny here knows Lettie – she's been missing three days now, since the wind. She was working up by Die Uitkyk for Master Taylor. Sir, I'm telling you – something happened at Die Uitkyk after Baas Van Rensburg's murder. Lettie was scared to go back. She was scared of him! So I told her she must go talk to Miss Ina and Miss Ina said she was being stupid –'

Mrs Kriel broke off, subsiding briefly into tears, before pulling herself together again. 'Miss Ina said she would talk to him and sort everything out. But now Lettie's gone. Something terrible's happened to her, re-ally, I'm so frightened for her. She's always been such a good girl –' Mrs Kriel's voice trailed off, then gathered momentum, rising like a siren to a terrible, hopeless wail.

Johnny told Daan that he could deal with this. Daan was patently relieved and went away to find some coffee and aspirin. Meanwhile Johnny gently explained that while he was not able to lay a charge of murder against Taylor, if Mrs Kriel would report her daughter missing, he would be able to initiate inquiries. Having established that, Mrs Kriel quietened down and Johnny sat her down in the interview room where she made a statement.

Later that day Johnny got himself a cup of coffee, pausing by Daan's desk to ask how everything was. Daan was curt. Everything was fine, he said, and that seemed to be the end of their exchange.

Then, as he was turning away, Johnny said, as if tossing out an aside about the low paper supply at the copy machine, 'Oh, I thought I might drive by Die Uitkyk. I want to have a chat with Alan Taylor about his statement.'

From the look on his face Daan didn't think it was such a great idea. 'Why?'

'I just want to clarify one or two things,' Johnny replied stubbornly.

Daan took a long sip of his coffee, keeping his eyes on Johnny all the time. Then he said slowly, 'Whatever . . .'

Johnny was sweating, his hands clammy on the steering wheel as he approached Die Uitkyk. Those few inexplicable exchanges in his encounters with Taylor up to now had been so opaque. He was not looking forward to this one.

Taylor met him at the back door, his expression indicating a certain wariness and surprise at this visit. Nevertheless he was as breezily calm and polite as ever. 'What can I do for you, Johnny?'

'Mr Taylor, um – Alan. I wonder if I could have a word. It's – it's about – Lettie.'

Taylor was clearly momentarily taken aback, but beyond that there was no sign that he was in the slightest bit ruffled. 'Right, fine, well – you'd better come in then.'

He showed Johnny into his study, where they sat down next to the elegant desk.

'This shouldn't take long. It's just a – a routine police thing. You see, Lettie's mother has reported her daughter missing. When she came to the station she was convinced that you'd be able to help us – um – locate her, I mean Lettie. In fact Mrs Kriel is quite sure you would know where she is.'

Alan Taylor raised an eyebrow. He sighed rather showily to indicate that he was already tired of this. 'Mrs Kriel is mistaken. If I knew Lettie's whereabouts I can assure you I would have notified someone. When and if she does reappear, she certainly won't be coming to work for me again. I've given a very generous severance payment to Ina du Toit. She'll pass it on.'

'You seem to have a lot of money to throw around.'

Taylor laughed. 'Yes, well, the rand is hardly money.'

'Well, if you would just bear with me, Alan, I'd like you to make a statement about this, if you don't mind.'

Johnny reached nervously for the briefcase he had brought with him. Taylor clearly did mind and he let it be known, in clipped tones, quite how distasteful and inconvenient he found it.

'Far be it from me not to co-operate with the constabulary of Fransmansvallei, but I do have a farm to run, so perhaps we could get this over with as soon as possible.'

His co-operation made Johnny squirm all the more. He was scrabbling through the papers in his folder, looking for Mrs Kriel's statement, when Taylor began suddenly to recite. The irony in his tone was rich.

'"What a piece of work is a man! How noble in reason! How infinite in faculty, in form, in moving!"'

His voice rose quickly, but he spoke ponderously, wallowing in the words. Johnny pulled out the statement and snapped his folder shut as Taylor continued to intone. ' "How express and admirable! in action how like an angel! in apprehension how like a god! the beauty of the world! the paragon of animals! And yet, to me, what is this quintessence of dust? Man delights not me." '

He paused and raised his eyebrows. '*Hamlet*. Do you know the play?'

Johnny blinked, jiggling the coins in his pocket in a manner that clearly grated on Taylor, but he took no notice. His pen was poised, he was ready to begin.

'Perhaps we could start with the last time you saw Lettie.'

Taylor leaned back slightly, his head turned to one side, his eyes narrowed thoughtfully. 'The last time I saw Lettie was on the evening of the day of Van Rensburg's funeral. She left at the usual time, possibly a little earlier than usual. She'd been rather jumpy, rather agitated for several days.'

'Did she say why?'

Taylor made a show of being taken aback. 'Good Lord, no. We hardly ever spoke to one another. Why should she tell me such things and why, for that matter, would I want to know?'

Johnny had stopped writing and was watching Taylor carefully. 'Well, don't you want to know now?'

'Needless to say, in retrospect, I'd have thought,' Taylor answered tightly.

'Did anyone else see her leaving that night?'

Taylor sighed, pushing his hands down between his knees. He looked up towards the ceiling while he thought about this. 'Possibly. It's possible the gardener would have seen her.'

'Can I talk to him?'

'Why, certainly.'

He went to call the gardener inside. Johannes, a man Johnny vaguely knew, stood uncomfortably in the doorway wearing ragged blue overalls, holding a multicoloured, multi-textured woollen cap in his hands.

'Johannes, Sergeant Kakana here wants to know when you last saw Lettie.'

'Ja, Master. I was in the back garden when I saw her leaving that night. It was after dark then. The night of the wind.'

'Was that the same time she always left?'

'Ja, she always leaves after dark, after putting out the Baas's supper.'

Johnny made a note. Johannes didn't seem to be lying, so he thanked him for his time and Taylor told him that would be all.

Johnny got out of his chair and made a circuit of the room before he sat down rather casually on the corner of the desk, a little too near Taylor for comfort. 'I can't put my finger on it, Alan, but I think you have a lot more to tell us about the Van Rensburg murder.'

An unmistakable smirk spread over Taylor's face. He answered immediately, in a tone intended to convey to Johnny his tiresome foolishness. 'I gave my statement to one of your policemen, I said everything I had to say then. Unless you want to know the brand of toothpaste I was using that night I fail to see what I could possibly add.'

Johnny nodded, but went on. 'How would you characterise the relationship between yourself and Van Rensburg?'

'Neighbourly.'

'That's not how Elise described your exchange the night before his murder.'

Taylor snorted with disgust. 'I hardly deem that worthy of comment!'

Johnny leaned back, folding his arms across his chest. 'It seems to me there was a lot you and Van Rensburg disagreed about.'

Taylor glared at Johnny, sizing him up. Then he made a decision and got to his feet, scraping his chair noisily against the floor as he did so. 'I have the distinct impression that you are wasting my time. I'm sure you have your reasons, but I have my life to attend to, so I'll say good day.'

Johnny didn't move. 'I understand that you've offered Mr and Mrs Mashiya quite a large amount of cash. Would you like to tell me why?'

Taylor snapped round. He'd had enough and he didn't conceal his indignation. 'I would say that's a private matter between me and the Mashiyas.'

'I wouldn't. Not in the circumstances,' Johnny snapped.

'Are you charging me? What offence have I committed?' Taylor was riled.

Johnny slowly shook his head, the sides of his mouth downturned. He said nothing.

Taylor laughed, a hollow, mocking sound. 'Am *I* a suspect now?'

'I just have a few more questions.'

'I understand that, Johnny. But I'd like to point out that I am under no obligation to answer them. Furthermore, I find your methods irrational and your manner discourteous –'

Johnny stood up. 'Please calm down, sir.'

Taylor was struggling to maintain his composure. He was practised at it – he didn't have to struggle very hard. 'I am *perfectly* calm.'

'Good, then let's finish our – conversation – and put this matter to rest.'

Taylor remained standing. After a long pause he said, levelly, 'I am not obliged to answer any of your questions.'

'How do you know that?'

'I know the law.'

Johnny opened his mouth to speak, but realised he didn't know what to say. He was stymied and he knew that Taylor sensed it. It was as if Taylor was prepared for this, as if he understood the psychology of this exchange better than Johnny himself. The balance of power had seesawed back in Taylor's favour. But how? Johnny had the growing, eerie sense that he had encountered Taylor's style before, but where?

'You might know English law, but this is South Africa.'

Taylor glanced over at him. The hesitation was barely perceptible, but Johnny was waiting for it and so he saw it, the briefest glimpse of a chink in the armour of self-assurance. Then Taylor was blank again.

'Same difference, I'm sure.'

They glared at each other. Johnny's spirits sank – he'd lost the heart for this. Taylor bit his lip. He turned, started towards the door and then swung back again. His composure was somewhat restored; his tone was level but not all the irritation was gone.

'Look, sonny, I gave my statement. I was at home and Ina du Toit was here with me so if you doubt my word, all you have to do is ask her. Neither of us heard anything about the murder until the next morning when Mrs Du Toit telephoned with the news. Since then I have done my utmost to be helpful to a neighbour who is clearly in difficulty. I understand that you must all have questions about me – I'm a stranger here in many ways, but that doesn't make me a criminal, even if you think it should. If it makes you feel better you can come and search my place and if I *can* be of any help to you I will. But you're going to have to explain what it is you're getting at. These veiled threats and vague accusations are simply insulting. I think you're intelligent enough to put yourself in my shoes and to conclude that you would feel the same way.'

When the speech was over Taylor showed Johnny the door. Johnny put his papers away and stood up to leave. Taylor bowed slightly, clicking his heels as he fired his parting shot. 'I suggest we never speak of this again.'

Johnny didn't say anything: he knew he'd lost this round. Taylor was devastatingly plausible – but Johnny was not about to give up. So far no one had taken a statement from Ina du Toit. That had to be his next step.

Daan had heard all about their 'conversation' before Johnny got back to the station. He was the recipient of an irate phone call from Taylor who said he took exception to the treatment he'd been given. Daan apologised profusely, but Taylor made it plain that although he saw Daan as blameless, nevertheless he did intend to take it further.

'That's your prerogative, Alan, and if there's anything I can do – You know I've heard that Johnny and the Kriel girl were sort of . . . going out. I wonder if that has anything to do with this.'

'Aah. He's a real dark horse, our sergeant, isn't he?' Taylor was suddenly purring again.

'Keeps himself to himself. Never been any trouble to me before.'

'Yes.'

Daan said nothing. He didn't really know how to talk to Taylor – the man stood on ceremony all the time, was so smooth, as if conversation was an art. Taylor was making a fuss over nothing, he thought. Johnny was certainly out of order, but there was no harm done, surely. Taylor, perhaps sensing that Daan had had enough, turned the subject to the cricket. A topic that could safely engage them for hours.

Daan was waiting when Johnny walked through the door. Typically his words were less than stringent. 'Look, Sergeant, we've got Van Rensburg's killer. It's not at all clear that Lettie's disappeared. We both know what these girls are like. Please, don't embarrass us any further with this sort of behaviour. OK?'

Johnny was unapologetic. 'This sort of behaviour, sir, is what I call thorough police work,' he hissed.

Daan sighed and rolled his eyes. Not this again, he thought. 'Let's just try and keep things quiet and controlled. OK, Johnny? This place is a bloody goldfish bowl – you can't just go questioning people without expecting consequences.'

Just then all heads turned as Madeleine de Jager walked into the station. She went straight up to Daan. 'I thought you might like to have lunch with me.' It was blatantly flirtatious, particularly as the hour was well past lunchtime.

'Ja, let's get the hell out of this place.'

Daan grabbed his jacket and strode out, steering her through the door ahead of him with his hand in the small of her back. Johnny heard his last comment, flung bitterly over his shoulder. 'I wish I could get the hell out of this dorp.'

Daan was right about the consequences. They came within the week and in a form that was quite unexpected. Johnny received a telephone call at home from his superior in Paarl, Captain Kriek. Kriek and his boys were in charge of the murder investigation. Kriek was also an acquaintance of Johnny's, from township duty days. The captain sounded worried; he asked Johnny to come in and see him on a matter of urgency. Johnny was puzzled, but not concerned. He even hoped it might have something to do with promotion, or at least a move. With that thought in mind he got into his van and set off alone for Paarl.

Kriek was a simple, plain-spoken man with a voice like gravel. He had a moon face, skin that was terminally flushed and sweaty, and the nose of a hard drinker. Johnny thought from the outset of their meeting that Kriek seemed unusually agitated. He quickly got to the point. The regional chief had received a couriered letter from one Alan Taylor, complaining about discourteous treatment by the Fransmansvallei police, naming Sergeant Johnny Kakana as the offender.

Johnny drooped, slipping further and further down in his chair as Kriek followed the form of reading him the riot act, concluding with a warning that would be noted for the record. He felt as if he'd been chewed up and spat out, and decided then and there that he'd had enough of policing and enough of Fransmansvallei.

When the dressing-down was over Kriek said he'd show Johnny out. He'd never done so before, but Johnny was in no mood to question him. In fact Kriek accompanied him all the way out of the building. Once outside, the captain was suddenly pally. The shift in tone was odd and there was an underlying note of anxiety in it too. Johnny couldn't work it out. He just listened as Kriek gabbled on.

'Ja, there's no respect for anything now. I don't think there's the discipline in the police that you had even ten years back. The whole world has changed, even the schools. Children don't get caned any more, they do what they like, there's no discipline in the world . . .'

Kriek actually looked over his shoulder as if someone might be following them. Arriving at the parking lot, the captain stopped. Something was clearly exercising him because he was breathing hard. 'Look, Johnny, there's something you should know about this guy Taylor. But you're going to have to keep it to yourself.'

Johnny froze. He turned slowly to face Kriek and waited for whatever was coming.

Kriek lowered his voice to a near whisper. 'It's a word of warning. I didn't want to talk about this in my office and I don't want to talk about it twice. Understood?'

Johnny nodded, understood.

'The guy was a policeman, a colonel in Natal. Special Branch.'

Kriek let the fact sink in. He didn't have to say more. Johnny felt vindicated and nauseous all at once.

'Why weren't we informed?'

'There's no reason you *should* have been informed. He's not there on police business. He's retired. And let's keep it that way. OK?'

Johnny was burning to know more and in one sense he had Kriek up against the wall. 'What if I don't?' He realised that he didn't have to let this go unless Kriek gave him good enough reason to.

'Then you'll only be making trouble for yourself.'

'If that's the case then why I am here?'

'Look, you can go ahead and stir things up if you want to, but you'll get nothing, not an inch of support from me. Take my advice – don't mess with those boys, Johnny.'

'And if I do? There'll be trouble for you anyway, won't there, Captain?'

Kriek understood. The sweat stood out on his forehead. He cleared his throat, at a loss for words.

This was Johnny's moment. 'I want to get out of that dorp, Kriek. I've been sitting in a poes job for ever. I deserve more.'

Kriek nodded nervously. Still stuck for a reply, he kept on nodding, like one of those little fake-fur dogs on the back shelves of old cars.

'I'm not going to lie down again, Kriek, not for nothing.'

Kriek hated him; Johnny had him in a vice. 'I'll see what I can do, Johnny.'

And with that Kriek turned and stormed back into the building.

FIFTY FOUR

Evening fell. A heavy, high summer evening. Mama and Ben Mashiya sat at the supper table in the brittle silence that embodied their anxiety over their son and all the problems he had brought into their lives. Ben ate his dinner slowly, his knife and fork scraping against his plate. Both were conscious of the empty chair between them – Lucky was still not home. Mama sighed. She couldn't blame him; the atmosphere in the house was so tense. Yet she was worried. There was evil loose in the valley. This could only mean more trouble.

A slight shadow filled the open doorway. Mama started. She stood up from the table and went to Lucky who was standing there shivering uncontrollably.

'Are you sick?' He shook his head. Mama put her wide arms round him, but he couldn't stop shaking. She tried to get him to eat, but he wouldn't. He simply clung to her. After a while Mama took him to bed. She and her husband fussed over the boy, pressing him to tell what had happened, but he didn't say a word. Worried, Mama tried to check him for snakebite, but he flinched and as he recoiled from her something dropped out of his pocket, clinking onto the floor. Mama Mashiya fished it up before Lucky could grab it. Opening her hand she frowned. There in her palm was a small glass disc. 'What is it?' Lucky shivered even harder and started to cry.

'Where did you get this, child? Did you steal it?'

Tears rolled down the boy's face and he wouldn't look Mama in the eye.

'You *should* be scared! But you are not scared enough. How many times have we told you not to steal?'

Mama was by now worked up and Ben Mashiya looked away as she raised her arm to strike him, but Lucky cried out sharply, with such horror and pain, that she stopped her hand in mid-air.

'I found it! I found it . . . I didn't steal it, Mama. I found it up there on the berg –'

He looked so terrified that a shiver of fear went through Mama. 'What?' she whispered.

'Lettie.' He stared with wide, wet eyes.

'Lettie?'

Ben Mashiya moved quickly from the window to Lucky's bedside. The boy covered his face, squashing himself up closer to the wall. 'Where is Lettie?' asked Oupa.

Lucky wiped the tears from his face; his mouth worked but no sound escaped it. He pointed up towards the mountain. Ben leaned in towards the boy, his hand on his arm now and his voice urgent. 'Where?'

'Up on the berg.' It was a hollow, terrible whisper.

'What was she doing?'

Lucky was petrified. Hoarsely he whispered the single, chilling word: 'Dead.'

In the stunned silence that followed the child started to whimper. 'It's not my fault, it's not my fault,' he repeated, over and over. Mama put her arms round him and held him close to her.

After more prodding and pleading, the boy told them how he'd been walking on the mountain, right up on the high, far boundary of the farm, near the corner of Taylor's fence. He'd gone there to fetch more wire.

'Why, child? Why do you steal from that fence? We *told* you there would be terrible trouble!' Mama wailed.

'But my uncle never bought the wire like he said he was going to,' Lucky snivelled.

Mama was about to scold him again, but Oupa shushed her: 'Let him finish.'

Lucky went on quietly. 'I heard someone coming – with a car – so I hid in the bush. It was Baas Taylor. He came

575

looking for something. He was walking up and down, up and down the fence, looking down all the time, then sometimes stopping and feeling around on the ground. There was one place where he stayed for a long time, kneeling down and searching, searching . . . That place looked . . . *funny*.' Lucky choked on a sob and Mama squeezed his shoulder.

'The pine needles there weren't right. Underneath them the ground was all turned up. Baas Taylor stood up again and he kept looking and looking, but he never found nothing, so he went away. I waited till he was driving down the mountain, then I waited some more. When it was quiet I went over to see if I could find what he was looking for and I found the glass under the fence by the place where the ground was all turned up. I dug around, thinking, like – maybe there's something there, something more. I was digging with my hand, the soil was all loose – and I touched some . . .'

Suddenly Lucky broke off, shaking his head. He covered his mouth with his hands. Then he went on, heaving his words out through terrible, dry sobs.

'I dug right down and it was her! She was just lying there, in the ground and she was staring at me!'

Lucky couldn't say any more. Mama gazed at the boy with eyes wider and more frightened than his own. She shivered violently, then crossed herself. 'Lord, help us,' she cried.

Ben went out into the compound to talk to the other men. When he returned Mama was sitting on the bed beside Lucky, who was drinking the hot sugary milk she'd brought him. She looked up at her husband. 'What will you do?'

'We will go there, first thing in the morning.'

They looked at one another, solemnly and tenderly. Then Ben turned and silently went away to his bed. Mama put the glass in the pocket of her dress and forgot about it in the business of getting Lucky off to sleep. When she joined her husband they sat up talking till late, but in the compound there was a hush around the place that persisted into the morning.

At first light Ben was up, ready, along with Jacob and Vuyo, to go up the mountain and look for Lettie.

It was a hazy morning, the sky chequered with a lattice of high cloud. The picking was going well, which meant morale had risen and that made things go more smoothly still. The harvest was by no means secure, but the pressure had eased up. Elise was sitting in the kitchen eating breakfast. She watched Mama Mashiya carrying a basket of wet laundry outside to the washing line. There wasn't much left for Mama to do now, with only Elise in the house, yet she maintained her usual routine. Mama moved slowly, pegging up the sheets so that the line sagged, dipping so low it looked as if it would break, but it held, and the sheets bounced up on the rope, the breeze making waves of the dripping white cotton. It struck Elise that Mama was as strong and as infinitely flexible as that washing line.

Finished with breakfast she took her plate to the sink. Looking through the window she noticed that Mama had stopped working and was standing with her hands on her hips listening to Nolitha, who was talking and gesticulating excitedly. Nolitha was still bruised and bandaged from her brush with Vuyo, but apparently her spirits were restored.

By the time Elise went outside both Mama and Nolitha were gone. The half-full laundry basket was abandoned, pegs on the ground, and there was no sign of either of them. There must be a problem up at the compound, she thought, and went off to work. Finding no sign of Jacob or any of the other workers, she headed up to Mama Mashiya's place.

Ben, Jacob and Vuyo were standing in front of the Mashiyas' cottage, surrounded by a restless crowd. Mama emerged from the centre of it; her hand covered her face and she was clearly distressed. Elise quickened her pace, fear gripping her as the conviction grew that something had happened to Sandile. She put her hands on the old lady's shoulders, holding on to steady her. There was horror in Mama's eyes. But it wasn't news of Sandile that had upset her so.

'It's Lettie. They've found Lettie. She was up on the mountain. Dead. Elise, someone killed her!'

Poor misnamed Lucky – nothing went right for him. Ben Mashiya explained that it was Lucky's obsession with his wire toys that led him to the grave where Lettie's body had been buried. They'd gone up at first light to find her.

Elise flew back down to the house and called the police. She asked to speak to Johnny Kakana, but he wasn't there; she would have to deal with Daan. He came to the phone and answered cheerily. 'Du Toit!'

'Daan, it's me. Look, my guys have found a body up on the mountain. They say it's Lettie Kriel.'

Daan and Johnny Kakana, accompanied by four constables, arrived less than fifteen minutes later. Elise didn't go with them to the site; she didn't have the stomach for it. They drove up in the four-by-four, Ben Mashiya and Jacob pointing the way. Everyone else went back to work.

As the day went on Elise watched more cars and policemen arrive. At lunchtime she went down to the house, where a group of vehicles were parked, among them Daan's. When he saw her he came over to where she was standing at the kitchen door. He looked haggard and nervous, and she enquired gently if he was OK.

His reply was unnecessarily sharp. 'I'm fine,' he snapped.

For some reason his tensed-up frame made Elise laugh. 'You look about as fine as someone with a barbed poker up his bum.'

She regretted the joke immediately, but then Daan laughed, so suddenly, so freely that it broke the ice. He'd created a gap for her to say something that might be heard as sincerely as it was meant. 'Daan, I'm sorry for all the pain I've caused you.'

He didn't reply, but the anger and defensiveness seemed to have gone from his eyes. There was a moment of simple, comfortable warmth between them. Elise smiled, a little ruefully, but warmly nevertheless. Her hand flickered up over her hair. 'Can I make you a cup of coffee or something?'

Daan glanced over her shoulder at the house, then shook

his head. But he made no move to go. 'How are you doing? Is everything all right?'

Elise sighed and looked down at her feet, at her velskoene kicking at the dirt. 'Ag, not really. There's a lot of problems, the money . . . the picking. But Jacob's been a great help. The picking's going well so far. I think we might make it.'

Daan smiled. 'Ja, I think you will. You always get what you want, don't you?' He said this with hint of bitterness. Elise didn't say anything.

He rubbed his finger back and forth across his chin. His parting words saddened her because they were so banal, and yet the ordinariness was touching too. He sort of smiled at her and said lightly, 'Well, so long for now and Happy Christmas, hey?'

Elise smiled back. 'Ja, to you too. Happy Christmas.'

She watched him drive away. Then she walked across the yard to a point where she could see up the slope of the mountain to where the police were busy with Lucky's grisly find. It was a fairly wooded area, but through the trees she saw sunlight shining off glass and metal. They had several vehicles up there now; she'd seen the traffic up and down her roads.

A trail of dust drifted up through the trees, the centre of it moving down the slope, so Elise knew that a car was coming down. Soon, the four-by-four emerged into view and she watched its slow progress over the rough ground, then saw it picking up speed once it was back on the track. Elise waited for the driver to come past her with some news.

Pelser was at the wheel, with Johnny Kakana beside him, both grim-faced. Elise walked round to Johnny's side of the van and he rolled down the window. 'Yussus, Johnny, are you all right? You look almost as white as me,' she exclaimed.

He shook his head. Johnny didn't beat around the bush. The body was definitely that of Lettie Kriel, he said, reporting it to her rather formally. She had been strangled. Johnny and Pelser were on their way to inform her family. They were all silent for a moment. A fly buzzed through the cab of the vehicle. The heat pressed in.

'Have you spoken to Taylor yet?'

Johnny hung his head. He was overwhelmed by grief and frustration. No one really knew of his relationship with Lettie and yet she was the girl he'd intended to marry. Now he wanted to nail Alan Taylor more than ever, but there was nothing he could do.

'Johnny, it's Taylor. I just know all this has got something to do with Taylor.' Elise put her hand on the door of the bakkie, but Johnny responded only by putting the vehicle into gear and impatiently revving the engine. Why was he suddenly so evasive? Elise couldn't make any of this out. 'Johnny, do you still believe that Sandile killed my father?' Elise leaned in at the window, speaking urgently.

Johnny shrugged and stayed mute. He clearly wanted to leave.

'Johnny, I know this is difficult, but – have you got something against Sandile?'

Johnny turned his face towards her again. 'No. But I believe Sandile has something against me.'

'Do you blame him?'

She thought she saw a glimpse of rare candour when he answered, 'No. No, I don't think I do. I –'

He was about to say something more, but hesitated. She held onto the van door. 'What?'

'Miss Elise, I can't explain. My hands are tied on this investigation. Just be careful, OK?'

With that he pulled away, in spite of Elise's hold on the car. She whipped her hand out, but the window caught her a glancing blow across the knuckles. 'Eina!' she screamed after them. What the hell is going on? she wondered. And where would all this end?

Back in the office Elise fumbled through the paper-strewn desk for the number. Karel Smit picked up almost immediately. It took her a couple of moments to recover enough breath to speak comprehensibly.

Karel laughed when he realised it was her. 'Howzit, Elise.

Shew, with all that heavy breathing I thought this was my lucky day!'

'Ja, well, maybe it is. Listen, something's happened. It might be important.'

'Uh-uh, you wanna meet up? I'm going over to Paarl this afternoon – shall we meet there?'

'No, look, I can't really leave. One of the farm kids found a dead body, up on the border of my land . . . It's Alan Taylor's maid.'

She could hear the whistle of him breathing sharply in. 'Wow.' There was a pause as he took it in. Then his voice flew back at her, this time concerned. 'Listen, isn't there someone who could come over and stay with you there, so you won't be alone?'

'Don't worry about me. I'm fine.'

'Ja, well – just make sure you lock yourself in and sit tight tonight, OK? One of us will phone you in the morning. Meanwhile, be careful.'

'Yeah, right,' she said and laughed, but when she put down the phone she did exactly what he had told her.

FIFTY FIVE

That afternoon, business at Hemel en Aarde was slow. Ina was in a weird mood. She felt crazy, like she couldn't handle anything, even routine things. On top of everything else work was gruelling. The holiday season was in full swing and the place was as busy on weekdays as it usually was at weekends. Alan telephoned for her just after lunch, but Ina told the girl to say she wasn't there. She didn't want to talk to him in the state she was in – she'd hardly slept since the night of Mrs Kriel's doom-laden visit.

Ina knew she was behaving hysterically and that made things worse. At last she had exactly what she'd longed for all these years: an attractive, single, wealthy man who seemed serious about her, yet she felt acutely depressed and lonely and scared. She was haunted by dreams about Lettie.

Around three o'clock Ina told Mabel she needed to fetch something from the house, got into her car and drove round to Komweer. Once there she headed straight for the drinks cabinet in the living room and poured herself a tumblerful of vodka. After several gulps she felt the tension uncoiling, slithering out of her. The obsessive buzz of anxiety and questions and doubt which all revolved around Alan began to fade.

The fountain in the garden filled the air with the tranquil sound of trickling water. The intermittent drone of a light aircraft and the sounds of the cricket test on TV wafting out from inside soothed her with their normality. Ina lit a cigarette. Lately she was smoking compulsively, like one possessed.

The day was hot. Ina sat in the sun until she was baking,

then slipped out of her dress and jumped into the chilly water of the pool. She felt her skin as a hot shell covering the inner coldness of her body. She wondered if she was sick. She climbed out of the water and pulled on her dress, becoming aware of where she was. For a few peaceful minutes in the pool she'd forgotten everything and now it all slammed back at her. She walked into the house, found her hand hovering over the phone – but she didn't know who to call. She wandered restlessly, fitfully, from room to empty room, not comfortable anywhere. Back at the drinks cabinet she poured out another glass of vodka and went outside to sit on the stoep.

After a while she heard the sound of a car arriving. Doors slammed and feet crunched on the gravel. From inside the house she heard her mother calling cheerily as she went to open the door. A few minutes later Mrs Du Toit came out on to the stoep accompanied by Johnny Kakana and two other policemen. Ina looked up blearily through a haze of alcohol. Their faces were grim.

Johnny walked towards her saying he had some bad news. Ina giggled. 'Oh, good, something's happened.'

Out of the corner of her eye she saw her mother pull a handkerchief over her mouth. Johnny frowned. 'We've found Lettie.'

Ina fumbled with the packet of cigarettes in front of her but couldn't get one out of the box. Johnny leaned over, took one and gave it to her, then he struck a match and held it out for her. He stepped back.

'I'm sorry to have to tell you this, but we found her up on the border of Die Uitkyk and Rustenvrede. She's been murdered.' Johnny spat out the words, upset and angry.

Ina stood up, but the movement made her head spin so she collapsed back into the chair. 'Does her mother know?'

Johnny dipped his head curtly. 'I'm going to need a statement from you. According to Mrs Kriel, Lettie had confided in you certain fears about her employer, Mr Taylor.'

Ina stared at him, too distraught to speak.

'Miss Du Toit? I said I'm going to need to take a statement.'

She continued to stare at him. Then her mother stepped forward, the old lady's movement a hazy, sickening motion on the edge of Ina's vision. 'I think, Sergeant, that my daughter is in no condition to speak to anyone right now. Perhaps later?' Johnny Kakana clearly preferred now to later, but Mrs Du Toit was digging her fingers into his arm insistently.

'There is one question you might be able to help with, Mrs Du Toit. On the night of Van Rensburg's murder – where was your daughter?'

Mrs Du Toit hesitated. 'It is not something we really want to talk about.' She sounded uncertain, but she got no help from Ina. Mrs Du Toit looked back at Johnny. 'Ina paid a visit to Die Uitkyk that night,' she whispered.

'What time?'

Mrs Du Toit simply shook her head. Then Ina chipped in, shouting very drunkenly: 'Tell him Ma! I slunk over there in the middle of the night looking for sex!'

Mrs Du Toit steered the policemen away. Ina heard her murmuring apologetically as she showed them out of the house.

Ina stood up and managed to get herself to her bedroom, where she collapsed on the floor. Reaching up for the phone, she pulled it down off the bedside table and punched out a number. Then she leaned back against the wall, waiting for someone to pick up on the other end. While she waited she fumbled for another cigarette and managed to get it lit. Finally the Dominee answered and she immediately started gabbling – about being haunted in her dreams, her fear of death – but her sentences were fashioned from a mind in chaos. After a few minutes she realised she was making no sense and abruptly fell silent. Stillness settled around her again and she hoped that, in a moment or two, clarity would follow.

'Ina, are you there? Ina, I'm worried about you. You feel terribly far away, like someone down a dark tunnel.'

Ina burst out laughing. 'Well, that I am, Dominee, in more ways than one!' She said it with bitter sarcasm.

'Ina, you must remember, in spite of everything you are in the midst of your life. You must grab hold of it, don't drift!' His exhortations were so vague they didn't help at all, only added to the fuzziness already clouding her mind. Ina laughed again, horribly, then started to cry. Through her sobs she said there was something weighing on her mind, weighing heavily.

'Tell me what it is, Ina. Share it. If you don't share your secret it will corrode your soul.'

Ina calmed down and stopped crying. She said she was ready to tell it. 'But I have to tell it to the right person, the person it means something to.'

'And do you know who that person is, Ina?'

'Yes. Yes, I think so.' Then she slammed down the receiver before he could say any more.

Ina sat for a long time with the phone in her lap, until well after sunset. She wanted to feel the life that she was in the midst of, wanted to catch hold of it. Somehow it had evaded her.

FIFTY SIX

Elise locked up carefully, closing the shutters on all the windows and shooting the bolts. There wasn't much in the way of security; the house had always been left open, or near enough to open. Tonight she closed the place up as tight as she could. She lingered in the doorway, drinking in the sounds of the wind ruffling the trees, the distant pulse of crickets, and music drifting from the radio in the kitchen. The crags of the mountains were pink in the evening light, the shadowy gorges midnight-blue. Long lines of fir trees clung like huge caterpillars to the distant slopes. As the sun sank the mountains stood black against the electric blue of the sky and the clouds were tissues of tangerine and pink. Wisteria blossoms, big lilac-blue bells of them, fell on the stoep and swallows played in the updraughts of the breeze, shooting up and sailing down like crazy dive bombers.

Elise could hear the insistent sound of a bullfrog barking somewhere nearby in the darkness. She went into the kitchen, made herself a cup of tea and turned up the volume on the radio. Music slipped out around her, filling the room.

The day had been so terrible she was filled with a new agitation. In the foreground of her mind was Sandile. She longed for the clarity and openness of those conversations with him, the way they meandered from subject to subject, serious to silly. She longed to talk this puzzle through with him. It seemed as if the pieces were coming together, but the partial picture still made no sense. How to find the missing pieces?

The night was humid and sultry. Elise closed her eyes as the music swelled around her. But something interrupted her thoughts, a sound outside, jarring her. She stood up, switched off the radio and listened. Nothing. Her heart was pounding. Then, through the throbbing of the crickets, she heard the sound of a car engine cutting out.

She raced through the house, switching off all the lights, grabbed a torch and then slipped into the garden through her bedroom door. She slunk round to the yard to investigate. A car had pulled up, but she couldn't see who was there. She called out urgently from the darkness. 'Who is it?'

No reply. Elise was shaking with fear, but she called out again. 'Who's *there*?'

Ina's frightened voice floated back to her. 'Elise?'

Elise switched on her torch and swung the beam until she found her. 'Ina! What the hell are you doing?'

Ina was standing on the back step holding a plastic Tupperware in her hands and blinking in the sudden brightness. 'I thought you might need some company . . . some food,' she said weakly pushing the box forward; the gesture seemed pathetic and bizarre.

'I've got lots of food.'

Ina looked down at the box, then back into the blinding torchbeam. 'Elise, I need to talk to you.'

'OK. Let's go inside.'

Elise switched on the light in the kitchen and they both stood there, blinking and shivering from the fright they'd given each other. Ina looked terrible. She dropped the Tupperware on to the table, reached into her bag and fished out a cigarette.

'Since when did you start smoking again?'

'Since about a week ago.' Ina found her lighter and lit up.

Staring at her old friend, Elise couldn't imagine how their lives had come to this point. Could she ever have foreseen this moment? Beyond the innocence of short skirts and Crimplene and plaits behind each ear, hair scraped to the sides from a perfect ruled line of a middle parting; beyond that sweet, expectant time, could either of them have predicted or prepared for the terrible journey ahead?

A glimmer of guilt flashed in Ina's eyes as she gazed at the woman who a month ago had been her most intimate friend. Smoke poured inelegantly from her mouth and nostrils when she spoke. 'So. Are you OK?'

Elise shrugged, something close to a smile stretching her lips. 'I don't know. What's OK? Are you OK?'

Ina shrugged too; the question was obviously rhetorical.

Elise ran her fingers back through her hair, then sighed. Ina stared down at her fingers fiddling with the burning cigarette, but she didn't say anything.

Elise looked out at the night which enclosed them. 'How are things with you and Taylor?'

Bluish smoke curled up from Ina's fingers. She kept her face down; her body was stiff with tension. Then she raised her head and her eyes flashed back, meeting Elise's gaze. It seemed to Elise that Ina wanted to say something important, but instead she dragged deeply on her cigarette.

'Do you think you'll marry him?' Elise really didn't care whether Ina would marry him or not; she just wanted her to talk.

Ina exhaled, shaking her head.

'I guess not?'

Ina shook her head. 'Uh-uh.'

With the index finger of her left hand Elise made a line on the table top. Ina's chest heaved. Finally she said, 'I think he killed Lettie.'

Elise breathed in sharply and Ina started to cry.

Elise helped her into a chair and sat down too. When Ina had recovered enough to talk she poured out the whole story. How Lettie had come to her, begging for help, how she'd turned her away, how Lettie had then disappeared and now she was dead. Ina was smoking like someone possessed, and her voice was gravelly and harsh. 'Alan killed her. He did, didn't he?'

Elise said nothing. Ina's weeping became uncontrollable. Elise stood up and pulled some paper towel from the roller that hung by the fridge, then handed it to Ina who pressed it to her face, muffling the sobs which punctuated their silence.

Elise paced several times round the kitchen. She checked the door, making sure it was locked. She still couldn't understand the picture that was forming, but a crucial piece of the puzzle had just fallen into place.

'What are we going to do?' Ina's words were muffled by the tissues.

'I don't know.'

'He's going to come looking for me. He's been phoning the whole day. I'm terrified of him, Elise.'

Elise nodded dumbly. To Ina she appeared vacant. 'Do you think I'm being hysterical?'

'I don't know, Ina, I just don't know.'

'Should we call the police?'

Elise shook her head. 'No – I don't think they want to get involved. I'm going to call a lawyer.'

'What's a lawyer gonna do?'

Elise didn't reply. She dialled Karel Smit's home number. There was no response. She tried him at work – still no luck. She dialled both numbers every few minutes for the next half-hour. Between calls she and Ina sat hopelessly on either side of the kitchen table. When she tried for the last time it was already ten thirty, but there was still no answer.

She slammed the receiver down angrily. 'Where the hell is he?'

Ina jumped, but it wasn't the noise of the phone that had frightened her. She rushed to the door and switched off the light. They stood in the pitch-dark kitchen, their eyes not yet accustomed to the lack of light, and listened.

'There it is!' Ina panicked. They both heard the sound of a car approaching. Then it stopped and someone got out, closing the door with barely a click. Ina didn't move. Elise padded over and stood next to her. They waited and heard footsteps on gravel, dogs barking.

'It's him! I'm telling you it's him,' Ina hissed.

Steps approached the kitchen door.

'Oh God, he knows I'm here, the car's right out there. What are we going to do?'

Elise put her finger over her lips. 'Sh . . .'

Her visitor knocked at the door, then waited. He tried again, several times, waiting silently between the knocks. Both Ina and Elise remained dead still.

Eventually the footsteps moved away. Elise tiptoed through to the dining room and peered out through a gap in the wooden shutters. It was so dark that she couldn't make out much more than the shape of someone moving round the house, towards the front door. Then she saw the car, which was unmistakably Alan Taylor's.

She went back to the kitchen. She didn't share what she'd seen with Ina in case Ina lost it. They waited for what seemed like an eternity while he banged at the front door and then walked back around the house to the yard. At last they heard the sound of the car driving away.

'Isn't that weird?' Elise remarked. 'He never said a word, never called out once.'

Ina was floundering for a cigarette. 'Elise, I have to get away from here!' She got up and darted over to the door.

'Wait! Let's just try and think about this.'

'If he killed her then he'll kill me.'

'Now you're hysterical!'

'But what are we going to do? What if he comes –'

'OK!' Elise banged her fist on to the steel draining board. Ina shut up instantly. 'We'll take my bakkie.'

'OK,' murmured Ina, a smile of relief spreading across her face.

Elise grabbed her keys and her donkey jacket. Moving swiftly and in silence now, they bundled themselves into the bakkie and crawled off down the drive. Elise drove without headlights; she knew they could be seen from Die Uitkyk and she could drive that lane blindfold anyway.

It was after eleven. They didn't pass any other cars on Skaduwee Lane. Once they reached the dorp road Elise put the headlights on and they flew into town, pulling up at the back of the police station. Johnny had a small box of a house on the plot behind it. Elise made sure that the bakkie couldn't be seen from the road, then she and Ina jumped out and made their way to Johnny's front door.

Elise was relieved to see a light still burning inside. Johnny was up. She rang the bell.

'Who's there?' he called out. Elise thought he sounded nervous.

'It's OK, it's Elise! Van Rensburg.'

Johnny opened the door just a crack, to check. When he saw Elise and Ina's harried faces he let them in. The three of them stood there, breathless and edgy, on Johnny's orange rag-weave rug. Elise was so tensely wound she didn't know where to begin. She wasn't even sure if Johnny could be trusted – but they were desperate.

'Johnny, it's about Lettie.'

Johnny had been at home all evening, pacing up and down the length of his small living room, his mind plagued by questions and possibilities. He had thought of confronting Taylor again, but discarded that idea almost immediately. In the unlikely event that he got as close as face to face with Taylor, Johnny knew the man would have a story and probably a good one. Even if he didn't, what then? Taylor was protected. His own force was concealing a killer.

Johnny was sure of that now. He had gone back over every encounter he'd ever had with Taylor. Then he mapped out the events leading up to Van Rensburg's murder. Taylor had gone over to Rustenvrede to propose something that would get rid of Sandile and his land claim. The information Johnny had given him must have been central to his plan, though what the plan was Johnny would probably never know. At that point Taylor could not have thought as far ahead as the murder. It must have been after Van Rensburg had declined to join forces with him that Taylor decided on the course that would get rid of both Sandile and Van Rensburg. And then he went on to kill Lettie. But why her? Johnny couldn't work it out. Elise had reached the same impasse – that was why Ina's story was so important.

When Ina had finished retelling her story both Elise and

Johnny remained silent. She looked from one to the other. 'I understand from Lettie that she was very fond of you, Johnny,' Ina murmured. Johnny grimaced with the pain of hearing that. He half turned away. When he turned back his face was no longer contorted, it was set against further hurt, he was angry.

'So what do we do now?' Elise demanded, clearly expecting Johnny to act, but he simply shook his head. 'I think I've got something. It's not much, but it's something.' He turned and went to fetch a small plastic bag that he'd left lying on the low table in front of his olive, velveteen sofa. It was just a plain, supermarket-bought, zip-lock bag.

'What is it?' Ina was the first to ask, though both she and Elise were flummoxed by the little glass disc that he held aloft.

'I think this was what Taylor was looking for up on the mountain. Lucky Mashiya saw him searching for something by the fence, but he didn't find it. When he gave up looking Lucky combed the area himself. That was when he found Lettie's body, this was lying near to her.'

A horrible dawning had spread over Ina's pale, drawn face. 'That's from his watch isn't it?'

'Is it?' Johnny asked.

Ina nodded. It had to be. Elise's eyes flashed with excitement. 'So what are we waiting for?'

Johnny shrugged. It was a gesture full of hopelessness. 'Like I said to you before. There's nothing I can do.'

'But you must arrest him,' Elise insisted.

'I can't.'

Elise tilted her head back, her brow furrowed with concentration, her eyes narrow and disbelieving.

Johnny sighed. 'I was called in by Kriek at Paarl Murder and Robbery. He told me to keep my nose out of this. He said Taylor was one of us – a high-ranking security policeman. He still has powerful friends and they want him left alone. Those people look after their own.'

'People are looking after him?' Ina repeated. She didn't understand.

Elise thought of her phone conversation with Karel and how she hadn't wanted to believe him. Now she understood. If Taylor really was who they said he was then they were messing around with dynamite.

Johnny turned away and flopped down on the couch, letting out a horrible laugh. He'd had enough. 'What can I do? Leave him alone – keep out of his way forever? Go over there now and shoot him down? I don't know, Miss Van Rensburg. I truly don't know. All I can tell you for sure is Daan's not going to side with me, the regional people won't side with me. If I try anything I'm going to look like a fool. Probably a dead fool or a jailed fool, or even worse a demoted fool. There's *nothing* we can do. He's sewn this up.'

Elise shook her head, not prepared to accept defeat. While Ina silently wept on one end of the sofa, Elise worked out a possible solution. It involved Simon Siluma and Karel Smit.

'We'll have to go to Cape Town. I know people there who can help us.'

Johnny looked up warily, but she could see the hunger in his eyes. He wanted any help they could get. He wanted to nail Taylor.

'It's Sandile's lawyer, Karel Smit. He also told me about Taylor, but he didn't have any proof and I thought it sounded – far fetched . . . Karel will help us.'

'Well, let's go get him!' Ina wailed. She was not going to stay in the valley. Taylor might be prowling around the dorp looking for them while they stood around chattering.

Elise felt Johnny's fear. As a child he had always lost his nerve at the faintest scent of danger. She feared he might lose his nerve now.

'You're frightened of Taylor, aren't you?' she said quietly.

Johnny's eyes flicked away, then back to her face and away again. A small dip of his chin indicated that yes, he was frightened of Taylor.

Elise shivered. 'Me too.'

He shot her a brief, grateful smile. This was Johnny's chance. They both knew it.

'Okay.' Elise said, 'we'll take my car.'

They drove together, squashed on to the seat of Elise's bakkie. They made it to the outskirts of the city in a little over three hours. Elise hardly said a word, her concentration glued to the road, but Ina talked virtually non-stop, spiralling round and round in a loop of anger and fear and hurt.

'The bastard! The bloody, lying, evil bastard! I mean, how could he? How could he do this to me!' She railed on and on against Taylor for drawing her in, toying with her, playing on her vulnerability. Elise couldn't help but feel sorry for her. Ina had so wanted her heart peeled open, but not this way.

Elise phoned Karel Smit from a coin box on the Main Road in Mowbray. It was three thirty in the morning. He was home now and very much asleep. He answered the phone by shouting gruffly into the receiver before she'd even had a chance to identify herself, 'This had better be good!'

'Hi, Karel. It's Elise.'

'Aaahh, Elise! Elise, Elise, Elise. Wake me up any time,' he purred.

'I've got something important.'

'What?'

'I don't want to talk on the phone.'

'Well, OK, I can be at your place by mid-morning . . .' It was the first time she'd heard him hesitant.

'No, I was hoping we could come over to *you*. I'm in Mowbray.'

'Now?'

'Ja.'

Following Karel's clear directions, it didn't take them long to find his flat in Newlands. He opened his door to them wearing a black and white striped Wits rugby jersey and the ultra-short, cheek-hugging shorts that seem to be regulation leisure wear for young Afrikaner males. Ina caught sight of a packet of cigarettes on the coffee table behind him and, without introduction, lunged straight past him and pounced on it.

Karel Smit's tousled head was spinning as he listened to the story tumbling out from Elise, Johnny Kakana and Ina, who took turns explaining. As soon as they'd finished he called Simon Siluma. After that, all they could do was wait. It was almost dawn. Elise had no desire for sleep; she sat bolt upright on Karel's futon, Ina's head lolling against her shoulder.

Simon showed up at six with two men who were introduced as Noah and Greg. They were both young and smooth-shaven; both sharp dressers, wearing suits and trendy mandarin-collared shirts, no ties. The New Guard. Simon explained they were from a Special Task Unit; their role was investigating the police. Karel whispered to Elise that they were spooks.

Outside it was a dull grey morning. The city was just waking up and the sound of it was a soft, enveloping hum. Elise felt sodden with melodrama. She longed for an ordinary day and for real, delicious sleep. Ina was too groggy to take things in, so Elise took her to the bathroom and splashed cold water on her face. Karel brought mugs of instant coffee and they got down to business.

They sat in a circle, on the futon and the floor, round the largest stack of books which doubled as a coffee table. Noah immediately took charge, asking each of them to recount their stories. Elise began, followed by an animated Johnny and ending with Ina. Karel Smit's left leg bounced manically all the time they spoke and Simon Siluma seemed jumpy too, but the Special Unit cops were impassive, nodding once in a while, when it was required, to confirm they were listening. It wasn't until the entire chronology of events, from Sandile's return to the present, was complete that Simon revealed the suspicion that his enquiries had confirmed.

He took a manila folder from his briefcase and opened it. Inside were a series of black and white photographs. They looked like mug shots or ID pictures and they were all different. Flipping slowly through them he asked Ina, Elise and Johnny if they recognised anyone. The third shot was of

Taylor; it was unmistakably him and they all said so. Simon and the two other men exchanged meaningful glances.

There was a double sense of urgency now. Noah explained why. Alan Taylor was no Brit: he was through and through South African. He came from Durban, though his parents had moved to Natal from Billericay, in Essex, at the start of the last war. Until two years before he'd been in the police force his entire working life, though for the last fifteen years that information had been concealed. Officially he'd retired and gone into business, but in fact he was recruited by the Security Police and had risen to the rank of colonel by the time the whole system was retired. He'd never had much of a profile beyond the clique of men with whom he worked. His job, or so it was believed, was to run front companies whose real raison d'être was to funnel weapons and anything else they chose to in and out of the country, wherever they were needed and wherever there was money to be made. His speciality was assassination. Murder was often how these guys in the Security Police solved their problems and they were masters at making the killings look like someone else's work.

Ina spluttered with disbelief and frustrated rage. Noah went on, ignoring her.

'His real name is Martin Stitch, but he's gone by quite a few others too. He comes from the hard core. Bit of a loner, always prepared to go the extra mile when no one else had the guts for it. His name has been linked to more killings and crimes than you would care to know. Just before the elections Stitch arranged a sweet deal for himself, retirement and a platinum handshake. He left the country and we lost track of him in Ireland. But apparently he couldn't stay away.'

'And apparently old habits die hard,' Karel added.

Noah explained that they would have to move fast and arrest Taylor that very morning, but they would have to send in a team and that required some arrangement. So Greg declared Simon would go back with them to the Unit and help set things up. The rest should wait in the flat.

'No. I want to be in on this.' Johnny hadn't said anything in so long they'd almost forgotten he was there.

'You positive about this?' Noah asked.

'I'm in till it's over,' he declared. Elise was surprised by such resolve. Looking over at Johnny she saw a determination in his eyes that had not been there before.

FIFTY SEVEN

It was raining. A huge mushroom of cloud had enveloped Table Mountain and was drizzling down onto the city. Karel took them to a coffee shop in Claremont, then he went to meet Simon and Elise and Ina drank more coffee while they waited for him and for news. Simon thought it would be safest for them to stay in Cape Town until it was clear what was happening in Fransmansvallei.

None of them said much. Elise was glad of the silence. Ina's endless loop of self-doubt and self-hatred and self-pity had burned out: now she just wept. She said she didn't see the point in anything, she felt unspeakably depressed. Elise listened to the clink of cups, the spurt and gurgle of a coffee machine, laughter and voices clinking like glass and an ambient track of music so low it was unidentifiable. Just noise. She worried about the farm, about Sandile and what would happen if they didn't find Taylor, but there was no point in going down that road. They had to get him. She hated not being able to do anything. She hated the waiting, but it was out of her hands now.

Taylor had wanted her land all along, she realised, even before his arrival in the valley. Then Sandile had come along and upset everyone's plans, not least Taylor's. By murdering her father Taylor must have thought he had killed two birds with one stone – framing Sandile and breaking Elise's grip on Rustenvrede. Elise thought with some satisfaction that he'd radically underestimated her.

A waitress brought some more coffees. 'Is Daan OK?' Elise burst the bubble of silence that had formed around them. Ina's glance flashed upwards, met Elise's questioning gaze for barely a second, then focused back down on the empty cup in her hand.

'He's fine . . . better than you might expect.'

She said this dully, with a hint of disapproval. Elise looked thoughtfully into her coffee, but didn't give voice to her thought, which was 'Madeleine'. She sighed, then raised her cup, as if making a toast. 'Guess we're going to end up old maids after all.'

'At least we've got each other,' Ina said, sounding gloomier than before.

'No matter what?' Elise countered.

Ina shook her head thoughtfully from side to side, hesitating for only a moment, then she too raised her cup. 'You mean no matter who.'

'Maybe. Maybe. It depends – on me, on him. Depends on today,' Elise replied.

'OK – no matter who,' Ina said, half grudgingly, then clinked her coffee cup against Elise's. It rang hollowly, like the bravado they'd mustered, the pretence that the gulf between them could be repaired.

Ina smoked almost an entire packet of cigarettes before Karel Smit returned with the news that the Special Unit was ready to go. They drove in a strange convoy back to Fransmansvallei. For Elise it was like an exhausting reprise of the journey out. Ina's fury had re-ignited. 'I mean, I thought I loved him. It's like a horror movie, it's so unreal. I shared the starkest intimacy with a man I *never* knew at all!' Round and round, like the circles of the passes that took them round and up into the mountains, then down again through valleys and across the Cape.

Ina didn't want to see what Johnny and the Specials were going to do, so while the rest of the convoy snaked off along the road to Die Uitkyk, Elise drove Ina back to Komweer. Mrs Du Toit and Mabel came out to meet them, but Elise didn't get out of the bakkie. She looked across at Ina, reached over and ruffled her friend's hair, smiling sadly. 'Thanks,' she whispered.

Ina nodded back, the briefest acknowledgement, but Elise saw her sadness too. They both knew that things would never be the same between them. Ina got out of the car and was caught up by the welcoming onrush of her family, while Elise drove away.

Pulling up at Rustenvrede Elise could see Mama Mashiya and Jacob waiting for her in the kitchen. Before going inside Elise stood for a moment, looking around. Mist covered the mountain opposite. Christmas beetles were sawing and there was the sound of people talking nearby. Elise noticed everything freshly and acutely, as if it had changed. Like her it had and it hadn't.

FIFTY EIGHT

The Special Unit guys insisted on speed. Noah explained to Johnny Kakana that they couldn't even trust their own; they had to make the arrest immediately and with absolute precision. They set out for Die Uitkyk armed with all the correct warrants. 'We can't miss a trick, not with this guy,' Greg explained. Johnny drove with them at the front of the convoy, followed by a posse of police vehicles. He was stiff with fatigue and anxiety.

Johnny had known all along that there was something powerful about Alan Taylor. He had good instincts even if he lacked good reflexes. His reactions were generally cowardly, always fearful. He never pushed anything too hard, lest it bite him. As they approached Die Uitkyk, Johnny was almost sick with terror at the thought of what lay ahead.

An anxious silence descended as they cruised up Skaduwee Lane. No one could predict what was to come. They all knew that Taylor was not the sort to go quietly.

Up to a point everything went as planned. The convoy stopped at a pre-arranged point on the lane, where they could wait, concealed from the entrance to Die Uitkyk by a sharp bend. There Greg and Noah climbed out of the van, leaving Johnny to go on alone. It had to appear to Taylor as though Johnny had come by himself, wanting to talk to him.

Johnny's hand shook as he pressed down on the buzzer. Taylor was surprised at the visit, that was evident from his tone. However, it didn't take much for Johnny to convince him that he needed to talk something over. The gate opened and Johnny felt his stomach lurch with relief. He pulled the van halfway inside, stopping it against the far wall, into which the gate had disappeared. Then he hit the hooter and the rest of the convoy came flying round the corner. Johnny could hear Taylor's dismay crackling through the intercom, then the gate crashed against the side of the van and stopped.

By the time Johnny got to the house the Specials were all over it already; a dozen guns drawn, walkie-talkies and weapons bristling from their flak jackets. He stood behind the line, wondering what Taylor could be thinking at that moment. There were very few options open to him. He could run – but there wasn't a chance of getting away.

Minutes passed. The house was absolutely silent and no movement was visible inside. Johnny walked quietly over to where Greg and Noah were standing, engaged in urgent discussion. They parted suddenly as he approached. Jogging forward Greg barked an order into his walkie and the scene burst into life. Cops smashed though windows and doors, shouting and running amidst the chaos of glass shattering and wood splintering. Within a minute they were all inside. Johnny followed, scanning nervously to his right and left all the time, not knowing quite where the centre of the action was. These guys were awe-inspiring, the way their cordon choked ever inwards.

They found Taylor in his study. Johnny entered behind Greg and saw him look up from something, as if his concentration had been rudely interrupted. He stood up, incredulous, absolutely furious as he slowly raised his arms above his head while the book he'd been holding bounced to the floor.

Greg smiled icily. 'Howzit, Mister Stitch?'

Before he could answer Noah jumped in with the obligatory speech: 'Martin Stitch, you are under arrest for the murder of Lettie Kriel. You have the right to remain silent.'

Taylor lowered his arms. 'Sir – be warned that you are making a serious mistake. It would be pathetic if it didn't carry such serious consequences.'

'As I was saying. You have the right to –' Noah was interrupted again.

'You have nothing to connect me to that!' Taylor snapped.

Greg stepped closer and held up the small square zip-lock bag that Johnny had handed over hours before. There was a flash of recognition, then Taylor fell silent. Johnny knew he was furious with himself. Van Rensburg was supposed to be found, but Lettie was meant to have disappeared. It was Lucky who had ruined Alan Taylor's scheme: Lucky and his fascination with the fence.

'She put up a fight, didn't she?' Greg sneered. 'Forensics tell some interesting tales, Mr Stitch.'

Taylor laughed harshly. 'You must think me very stupid. That bag hasn't been anywhere near forensics.'

Greg raised an eyebrow. 'Quite sure of that, are you?'

Johnny stepped forward, meeting no resistance as he slipped handcuffs onto Taylor's pale wrists.

Leading him out to the van Johnny couldn't resist a gloating stab at that frigid exterior. 'You said to me once that the only danger for the murderer is his own fear. What about carelessness, Alan?'

Taylor said nothing. He'd been meticulous enough, but in a different time, a time when such things weren't followed up, when the plodding little Sergeant Kakanas of the world knew their place or else were taught it. 'I was one of the best, Sergeant. In the old days even the best could be careless because then we did it for the people who mattered.'

'And now – who do you do it for now?'

'For myself. Now there's little else that matters.'

Taylor climbed into the car and Johnny slammed the door.

Taylor had presented Johnny with an opportunity after all, and when it came, he was ready. Yet it didn't bring with it the satisfaction he'd expected, just a sickening, hollow sense that too many things were not right in his world. Johnny watched as Alan Taylor was driven out of Die Uitkyk. He didn't give it even a backward glance.

But Alan Taylor had thrown one last obstacle in their way. Johnny realised it when he smelled burning and rushed in to see flames licking at the edges of the huge painting in the hallway. A moment later the picture disintegrated and flames burst through into the house. He had set fire to the cellar. Some hours later, as they sorted through the salvaged boxes of Security Police files and a small armoury of weapons, Johnny and the Special Unit understood why.

FIFTY NINE

.

When night fell Elise went inside and sat in the kitchen with
Mama and Jacob, who were bent over a teapot at the table,
waiting to hear her story. Mama described how that morning, she had almost jumped out of her skin when she found
the house empty and Elise gone. Now she was merry with
relief. They were interrupted continually by the telephone,
which had hardly rung for weeks and was now positively
clamouring for attention. When Elise answered the first call
of the evening she was greeted with straining chirpiness by
Etta Joubert.

'Elise, darling, I just wanted to make sure you're all right. I
heard the news – my life! I just can't believe it. Who would
have thought? On the face of it he was such a nice, nice, nice
man.

'Now, sweetheart, I know he's been arrested for killing
Lettie, but is it really true that he's also going to be charged
with murdering Van?'

'Yes, yes, that's true.'

'Well, I don't want to keep you with my chatter. I just
wanted to express my deepest shock and sympathy. If there's
anything I can do, *anything* you need, you just give me a
tinkle. OK?'

'OK, Etta – and thanks, hey?'

The other callers that evening were mostly neighbours who
hadn't spoken to her since her father's funeral. Elise wished
she were harsh enough to dismiss them all for their hypocrisy
and skindering, but she couldn't; she knew that their intentions
were partly genuine. They wanted to express their concern
and in so doing to admit, even if this wasn't articulated,

that if they'd been wrong about who had killed her dad, they might have been wrong about other things too.

Oupa Mashiya and Lucky came down to the house to fetch Mama, but Mama insisted they come in for some tea and to hear the news about Taylor. Ben Mashiya didn't sit down; he took out his pipe and smoked, standing against the sink. He was interested by events that day, but more concerned about their meaning.

'What will they do now with our son?' he wanted to know.

'They'll have to release him,' Elise said thoughtfully.

'Will it be soon?'

'I'm sure we'll hear from the lawyer tonight. He'll know.'

She watched Mama and Oupa Mashiya walk away from the house, their heads bent towards the ground, Mama talking all the while with her arm slipped through her husband's. Then they stepped out of the pool of light cast from the house and she couldn't see them any more. She was alone again. She sank into a hot bath and then slipped under her covers where deep, delicious sleep enveloped her.

She was woken near midnight by the telephone ringing. It was an overexcited Karel Smit and from the noise in the background, over which he was yelling, he was out celebrating somewhere. 'Thought you might like to know that they're releasing Sandile in the morning. Same time and same place that they charge Taylor. Ten o'clock at Paarl magistrates' court.'

'That's great, Karel, his folks will be thrilled.'

'You weren't asleep, were you?'

'No, I was only dead asleep.'

'Will we see you in court?' From his tone it was clear that he very much hoped so.

Elise paused, she was tempted. 'I can't. Too much to do. But maybe I'll see you after . . . here on the farm.'

'Lekker!'

Her alarm went off at five. She left the house forty minutes later as the sun was hitting the face of the mountains. The light was so dazzling and the shadows in the ravines so deep that the jagged face of the crags looked like the tall sails of a boat. Clouds clung to the mountaintops, the wind shaping them into peaks, like pure white banners atop the dark ridges. Bosmansrug and the mountains to the right were indigo-blue, massive still hulks against the sky, not even a hint of their contours beneath the shadow. It was the first day of plum-picking.

Elise felt joy creeping back into her, stretching its fingers into her limbs, filling out into every part of her. She simply let herself be. She felt calm and excited, afraid and assured. She would look back on that season as a part-willed, part-fated, but absolutely fundamental re-evaluation and reorientation of everything important to her. This was radical, absolute, a time which transformed her utterly.

Sandile did not look round when he entered the court, except to exchange glances with Karel Smit, who sat straight ahead of him. He was utterly focused on the moment. He had waited for this day for what seemed like an eternity. His now scrawny body was stiff with tension, he felt strained almost to breaking point. He held his chin up too high, his arms as stiff as planks at his sides and his hands spread against the khaki of his trousers.

Simon Siluma, having solved Sandile's problem, had flown off to Durban the previous night. He would be with his family for Christmas. Karel Smit was alone and rather more subdued than his normal fiery self. He was tense as well. But there was nothing to worry about. The magistrate shuffled papers impatiently, his mouth working while he chewed over the words he would utter, then he barked out the judgement and that was it. All charges against Sandile Mashiya were dropped and the prisoner was free to go. As the gavel clacked against the bench Sandile swung round and was met with a bear hug from Karel, who thumped him on the back.

Sandile was met with relief. There was none of the surprised elation of his previous homecoming, but there was a sweet celebration nevertheless. This time they were all there waiting for him and it was more like the homecoming he had pictured in his fantasy. The children ran out to see who was there, the dogs barked and those adults who were home stuck their heads out of windows or round doors. The ordinariness of the day was transformed. Mama and Ben Mashiya came out of their house, arms open to welcome their son. Karel Smit had brought a case of beer, which he lugged into the house, and the party began.

Elise gathered, from the cars up at the compound and from her excited workers, that Sandile must be home. She was exhausted and a little shy, but she wanted to welcome him, so she dropped by the Mashiyas' house at sunset. When the moment came and Elise and Sandile stood before each other, only an arm's length apart and without fear or doubt or bars intervening, they didn't touch. In fact they barely spoke at all – they just smiled and let themselves be drenched in the sight and proximity of one another.

'Don't they just make a lovely couple?' Karel teased.

Both Elise and Sandile frowned; Mama Mashiya clicked her tongue noisily. She didn't like that suggestion; she found it embarrassing. She had closed her ears to the rumours that had been circulating about a connection between her son and the woman who was almost her child. Such talk upset her – the very idea was unpleasant. There were sharp boundaries in her world, boundaries that one simply did not cross, and the line between masters and servants was one of those. Elise understood and so she had never spoken to Mama of her feelings for Sandile. Having welcomed him home, she left the cottage only minutes after she'd arrived. Karel tried to press her into staying on, but Elise stood her ground. She wasn't really part of the celebration.

The next day Sandile woke early and, having waved a rumpled Karel Smit goodbye, went off in search of Elise. She was standing in the doorway of the packing shed, a half-drunk cup of coffee in her hand, discussing plans for the day with Jacob. She seemed to sense his approach, because she turned, looking straight at him. He saw her stiffen.

'I came for my job,' he said as he came to a stop before her. Jacob left them alone.

Elise raised her eyebrows in mock surprise, replying with an affected Annie Oakley drawl, 'Well, we sure could use you!'

She was still struggling on several fronts and Sandile knew that some of the trouble was his doing – including, in a sense, her father's murder. Taylor had wanted their land, but Sandile had provided the catalyst, turning everything upside-down, providing Taylor with his opportunity. Sandile wondered whether Elise saw it this way, but in fact she didn't. What was most important to her now was getting through the harvest and securing her farm.

The picking went on for just over a fortnight, until after New Year. Christmas, with all its rituals, came and went with little fanfare. Everyone was still sore – it wasn't quite the usual holiday. Yet for Sandile it provided some important opportunities.

On Christmas Eve everyone in the valley went to church, as they always did, and Sandile was there – standing apart with Elise and his parents. It was a nice service, complete with candles and carols and a nativity enacted by all the local children whose bright faces shone with the heat. Afterwards Sandile looked around for Xolile, or Johnny Kakana as he had begun to think of his erstwhile friend. He scanned the crowd, but couldn't locate Johnny. What, Sandile wondered, could be keeping him away tonight?

He decided to drop in at Johnny's house and find out. In all the telling and retelling of the fantastic story of Alan Taylor's arrest, Johnny Kakana figured larger than anyone else. Sandile had known ever since the arrest that he would have to face Johnny, that he owed him some acknowledgement. So Sandile left the candle-lit church and the singing and went to find him.

Johnny froze on opening his door. Sandile found he didn't know what to say, then Johnny stood aside and gestured for him to come in. The door closed and the silence held while they looked at one another; Sandile still flushed from the service and a little sheepish at finding himself so tongue-tied, Johnny stern and sad.

'Would you like something to drink?' he offered.

Sandile nodded. Johnny crossed the room and pulled a quart bottle of brandy from the cabinet next to the TV. Sandile followed and stood by him as Johnny cracked the seal on the bottle, dusted out two glasses with his shirt and then poured two long drinks. The whisper of the liquid sluicing into the glass was the only sound in the room.

'I hear you're getting promoted,' he said at last.

Johnny nodded, handing Sandile a glass. He would soon be taking over as Station Commander at Fransmansvallei, the job he had wanted for all these years. Having got there he didn't know how much he cared for it. He didn't seem to care much for anything. He had shown them all and he had shown himself too. But so what? 'Ag, I don't know about the police . . . Not sure if I want it. Not sure about anything . . .' Johnny sat down on the sofa and Sandile followed suit.

'You should stay and do the job, you'll be setting an important example round here.'

Sandile meant this sincerely, but Johnny responded with an ugly snort.

'You've had a tough climb, haven't you, Xolile?' Sandile said.

Johnny took a sip of brandy, then he turned to face Sandile. 'It was always so easy for you, wasn't it? You were always charging ahead of everyone else, making everything look so simple.'

'Don't be bitter, my friend.'

Johnny shook his head, closing his eyes. He was struggling to push back the emotion that had suddenly welled up in him. He was pleased to be called friend and sad to find that he was bitter and even more sorry that Sandile knew it.

Looking away Sandile thought back to that time when Xolile was truly his friend. Then he'd protected him, never fearing anything, while Xolile feared everything. That was how they got to him, because he was so afraid.

'Why didn't you tell me?' Sandile asked suddenly.

Johnny frowned; he didn't understand.

'When the cops got to you. You should just have told me they were putting pressure on you. I would have called it all off.'

Johnny shook his head

'You know what they were like. You saw Du Plessis. They had hooks in me before I knew it. They would never have let go.'

'But you didn't know anything. I never told you anything. You didn't know what we were hiding, let alone who for.'

'*They* knew. They knew all about you.'

'Is there really nothing you regret?' Sandile wondered, staring at Johnny, who looked quickly away.

'I went to see her – Baasie's mother.' He took another hasty sip from his glass. 'I told her what happened. I told her what I did.'

Sandile looked down into the amber-covered bottom of the cheap glass he was holding. He didn't ask what she'd said, he wasn't sure he had a right to know. He had seen – from the pain in Xolile's eyes and in the twisted muscles of his face – how much that visit had cost him.

They parted quietly just a short while later, clasping each other's hands and holding them there for a minute at the door. Then Sandile walked back to the church and Johnny stood by the window staring out into the blank night.

With Elise Sandile was tender, but careful. She was preoccupied with the farm, as he was with the land claim. They worked together, but they didn't press each other with talk of anything but what had to be done on the land.

She had longed to be alone with him, but the moment had not yet come, and neither of them wanted to force it. The feeling between them was different from the giddy electricity of before. Something had changed, something had crystallised. They both seemed to intuit the pace at which they were moving towards one another, as if involved in a slow, precise dance.

611

On the day the picking was finished and the plums were safely in, Elise felt truly herself again. That day, when the world around her turned from monochrome to colour again, wasn't a day of exaltation, but simply one of quiet pleasure. And on the evening of that day she went up to the dam, where she found Sandile.

They said very little, simply sat near one another and watched the sun go down. It was he who raised the question, but she was glad he had. They had to face the reality of his claim. It was proceeding swiftly and the time would come soon when Sandile took back what had been stolen from his family. Both were agreed that there must be a way to work together. They would each end up with something the other needed. Sandile had the water she didn't and Elise had the equipment and the knowledge that he lacked.

'Well, we could farm it together,' he suggested rather vaguely.

'That's all a bit neat and tidy, isn't it?'

'Hey, I like happy endings and I've never had one before. Don't you think we deserve one?'

Elise laughed quietly. 'You should know by now – there are no happy endings. At least probably not till the big sleep at the end.'

Sandile laughed too. Then she was serious again.

'Let's wait and see what the court says. For now I've just got to get a good price for my fruit and hope to break even. If I don't it'll be someone else you'll be making that claim against! As far as the future goes, I don't have a picture of that.'

Sandile smiled, agreeing. 'OK, let's wait and see.'

And so they watched the sun go down.

SIXTY

Elise knew the farm would make it on the day she dropped off her last load of Sungolds at the co-op. She could see, though it would be weeks before she knew her rating relative to everyone else, that Rustenvrede had done better than any other farm in the valley.

It was only then that she could turn her mind to Sandile. His constant presence so close to her was intensely distracting. Elise found it harder to concentrate just knowing he was around. She knew, though they never spoke of it, that there was an inextinguishable feeling between them. And she longed for him. She had never known the ache that yearned in that word before. Longing. She longed for his lips, the sensation of his skin against hers, the taste of him, the softness of his tongue inside her mouth. The longing had become unbearable, an unslakable thirst. It slipped through into every moment, every conversation, every track she turned down, every second of every day. Were they meant to be? Could she deny fate? Elise had always thought that love and fate were only partners in some glowing retrospect. You choose. That's all. Somehow her heart had chosen him.

Elise knew now that she would never cave in under the pressure of universal disapproval and retreat, as Cathy Brookes had done. She would never be an exile again, stranded on her farm and cut off from the community to which it belonged. She wasn't going to quietly disappear. The dorp would have to face up to that and in the end it would, she was sure of it.

She was lying in bed on Sunday morning when she heard a knock at the back door and she knew it was him. She pulled on her clothes and went to meet him. They didn't fall on each other. It wasn't a sudden clashing of magnetised bodies which slam together having been held too long apart. If anyone had been observing they'd have witnessed two people gently circling each other through the shadowy rooms of an otherwise empty house. She went into the living room and he followed. At first he was obviously ill at ease, moving round the room as cautiously as if he was picking up pieces of broken glass. She switched on the radio and went to make some coffee. When she came back with the tray he was sitting on the sofa; he seemed to have relaxed.

Elise curled up on her chair opposite him. They talked, but not about each other. They spoke mostly about the farm, though they were both careful not to assume anything. Elise didn't try to keep herself from smiling and nor did he. This was exactly what she wanted. If she had pictured how it would be between them when at last they had time to themselves, this was how she'd have seen it. This was their time to explore one another, time just to let things be and see what happened. Elise already knew what she wanted to happen; she knew her instincts about him had been right all along.

After a while they were quiet, not for any particular reason, but somehow the flow of the conversation ceased and neither one of them made any effort towards starting another one. The music from the radio flowed round them, filling the silence, and that was enough. It felt to Elise as if they were suspended in a bubble; she had no sense of time, of how long they were there. The peace of the silence felt both infinite and momentary. Then he yawned. She murmured something about more coffee and he smiled.

Elise stood up and went over to him, holding her hand out for his empty cup, but he took her hand instead and drew her to him. She put her hands on his arms, her fingers gripping the skin above his elbows. She held him like that, at arm's length, then she leaned up and briefly kissed him. His mouth was slightly open; her lips closed softly round his top and then his lower lip. It was the strangest thing that happened that day: as if she was blind, hungry, thirsty, leaning into him the way she did. They made love there on the sofa and it was passionate and hungry and beautiful.

Later on, late that evening, they stood out on the stoep and looked up at the Milky Way. Sandile put his hand on her hair, cupping his palm round the back of her head as they stared up into the night. 'This is the place I want to be,' he said. 'This is where we belong.'

SIXTY ONE

Daan du Toit had his Christmas wedding after all. He and Madeleine were married by a justice of the peace in Stellenbosch, in the presence of two giggling witnesses who were a pair of art students they'd picked up at a bus stop fifteen minutes before. The ceremony was short and simple and private. Daan had the tact and kindness not to make an event of it in the valley. The result was that he drew fire from everyone in the dorp, because everyone was excluded from an event which was traditionally public property. Yet the secrecy preserved a modicum of dignity for Daan and his bride who were spared the humiliation of becoming a spectacle on a day when, they felt, spectacle was inappropriate.

Both Daan and Madeleine informed their families after the fact, announcing at the same time that Daan was taking a retirement package, buying a boat and heading out into the Indian Ocean for an unknown period of time. They would be back when they'd had enough, the implication being that that might be never. Daan desired the freedom of living somewhere he was not of; he wanted to be free of the responsibilities of rootedness, free of duty and obligation and expectation.

His marriage and departure were two more blows for Madame Du Toit, who had taken to her bed after Taylor's arrest and hadn't been up since. She held court there in her room, for selected friends, while rumours of her symptoms grew and varied among those who were not of her inner circle.

As autumn approached, the days grew blustery and colder. The orchards were the brilliant apple green of summer, though in the gullies and creeks that bordered them the trees were aflame with reds and russet and pale, pale gold.

Ina sat in her mother's rocking chair in the lounge, staring into the flames of the fire that sizzled and crackled softly in the grate. Sunshine streamed into the room in hard slants. Ina felt as if she was ill, poisoned by anger and pain, and she knew the only way through it was to endure, to wait for the minutes to pass.

Her mind was focused on the events taking place that day, far away in a Cape Town courtroom, where Alan Taylor would go on trial with a list of indictments longer than her arm. She was simmering with hatred, with incandescent rage, and she couldn't let go of it. She kept saying to herself, let go, just let go of it, but she couldn't. 'I hope you burn,' she hissed aloud, 'I hope you burn in hell!'

Elise was there in court, flanked by Sandile, Simon Siluma and Karel Smit. Taylor faced charges on more than a dozen counts of murder, her father's and Lettie's among others. As Karel had said to her, 'They'll get him on all of it, the other stuff included, thanks to us. What matters is they get him.'

Elise wasn't sure what mattered. She wasn't really sure what she was doing in the public gallery of a huge courtroom with people talking quietly all around her. There were bigger cases, but Taylor's had attracted considerable attention. The chatter around her was subdued; it felt like contained excitement. She sat silent in the middle of a mixed crowd squashed on to the long hard benches. Among the journalists there was a handful of white men who looked like cheap gangsters. Those guys, Karel pointed out to Elise, were Stitch's colleagues, guys from the old Security Police. They couldn't hide it – their identity screamed from their pinstriped suits with shiny lapels, their overpolished shoes and criminally out-of-date sideburns.

It was already an hour since proceedings were meant to have begun. The murmur of conversation was like a single sound at times, one that ebbed and flowed around her. Arrogant commentators, small-talkers, note-takers, sketchers. Every now and then there'd be the rattle of walkie- talkies and more people would move in and out again. No one could tell her what was going on, so she waited.

An old coat of arms hung on the wooden panelling above the judge's seat. It was an ugly plastercast thing with a mess of buck and leaves and little shields. An official 1996 calendar was sticky-taped to the wall next to an official whose eyes were fixed on the same vacant place they'd been fixed on for the last hour. He looked like he was stuffed.

Everyone fell silent when the court recorder walked in, watching as she put on a pair of glasses with lenses so thick they looked like goggles. She was a solid, squat woman with an iron perm tinted a bluish-grey. She wore a Crimplene floral-patterned scarf round a squarish tent of a dress and obligatory plastic pearl beads round her neck. She looked as clean and as fresh as Dettol.

Nothing more happened. The whispered conversations surged again. The man on the bench next to Elise sighed constantly and heavily. He had a notepad on his knee, a pencil in his fingers and his shirtsleeves rolled up. All round the room there were pens in mouths, pencils tapping knees, and still nothing happened.

Then at last, without warning, a long line of cops snaked through and positioned themselves between the public gallery and the court. They faced the crowd, positively bristling with weapons, scanning every face. It was like something out of a *Mad Max* movie. Elise felt her pulse quicken at the thought of Taylor approaching. What did she want from seeing him, what did she think she would get from the moment? Would she fly at him, wanting to kill him? The cops seemed to expect something like that, if not from her, then from one of the many others seated in the gallery. No, Elise didn't want to go near him. She certainly didn't want to talk to him. What words could possibly be adequate? What she wanted was to *know*. Perhaps, she thought, realising this, if I see him I'll know. And that was why she was there.

It was hard to accept that there could be such malevolence, that someone could do something so cruel, could want to hurt him as Taylor had. The picture of her father as she'd found him that morning kept coming back to her – that horror in his eyes would be reflected in her own forever. Of course he hadn't seen anything. He hadn't seen Taylor because he was attacked from behind. It was only the night that he'd stared into before slipping into fathomless darkness.

After the charges were read and the statutory murmurings of the rules of the court were dispensed with, the accused stood up. Elise couldn't take her eyes off him. She felt anger and sadness welling up in her and she know she would never understand. When she walked out of that courtroom free and Taylor was led back to his cell, her father would still be dead. The pointlessness of it hit her like a kick in the stomach.

The truth was plain and filthy and Taylor shared it all – as if he didn't care how bad it was, as if he relished the detail. He told the court how Van Rensburg had riled him that night. He was hot with rage and he decided to get rid of a handful of problems by just taking the old man out. It wasn't what he was best at, but he'd done it before. Lucky for him it was a moonless night.

He took a pistol and a panga and walked through the orchards to Van Rensburg's homestead. And it was so easy. A cool head, that was what he had. He never got scared. Fear had destroyed too many men he knew; fear and guilt had eroded their certainty, splintered their strength, crushed them into bundles of paranoia. Taylor never felt fear. It wasn't that he repressed it or kept it at bay; he simply couldn't locate it in himself. Like guilt. That was what he was thinking as he walked through the orchards that night and into the dew-soaked garden of Rustenvrede.

He'd padded silently across the stoep, seen Elise through her bedroom curtains, asleep. He wasn't interested in her. Van Rensburg was his target. After his great bulk toppled, the farm would fall easily into Taylor's hands, or so he'd thought. He had underestimated the daughter's determination. He easily found the room where Van Rensburg was restlessly awake. He had stood for a moment at the window, then stepped back, to wait, to think. At last he was decided. Not on whether or not he would do it, but how. He ran through his own actions and the possible reactions of Van Rensburg, then he simply tapped three times on the slate stoep with the blade of the panga, not loud, just very lightly. There was silence from within the house. He tapped again. Tap, tap, tap. Tap, tap. Tap. Tap. A musical touch. He smiled; he liked that. He thought again how lucky it was that this was so easy for him. There was adrenalin now, pumping through him.

Van Rensburg came out on to the stoep but he hadn't seen anyone and he said something, something like – Who is it? Who's there? Taylor's fist clenched, twisted the panga handle, gripped it, feeling the rough wood through the soft leather palm of his glove. It had been so easy to get and it was such a perfect foil. Taylor knew blacks and he knew the police. He knew the panga would point to Sandile. Van Rensburg didn't look behind him. He was standing on the edge of the stoep and Taylor was right there behind him. The farmer's hulking back appeared blank, a grey shape, a shadow-mass in the darkness. Taylor noticed how his shoulders heaved in a sigh, how his body relaxed and he folded his arms and stared out into the darkness.

At that moment Taylor moved, stepping up behind Van Rensburg, locking his arm then smashing the long blade down onto his head, hacking into skull and brains. Van Rensburg was finished but Taylor swung the blade round for one sharp, fatal pull across the all-too-soft skin of the old neck. The whole thing was almost soundless. Taylor stepped back to let the body fall and for a moment he met Van Rensburg's wild, wild stare as the farmer tried to breathe, to speak, to clutch at life. Then something unexpected happened. Van Rensburg lunged out for him. The man had so much rage and strength in him he tried to grab Taylor's leg, but it was too late – he was too hurt. Taylor had never seen anything like it though, not in any man wounded like that. It sent a shiver of horror through him. He turned and walked away. He brought his breathing quickly under control as he strode towards the road where his car was parked a safe distance away. He carried the panga as a trophy, as a warning lest he meet anyone along the way.

Listening to him Elise was numb with shock. *Nothing is as it seems.* That was what she'd said to her father the night before he was killed. Nothing in her world was as it had seemed. In a sense Alan Taylor was a monster of her father's creation. It was he and his generation who'd needed the Alan Taylors and who put them to work, enforcing and guarding their stolen privilege.

During one of the judge's breaks Karel and Sandile explained over coffee how many ex-Security policemen and their acolytes – the bizarre collection of people they handled for dirty tricks and whatever else the system required – had collected thousands of rand in kickbacks, protection fees and finally in golden handshakes when their services were no longer required. Some of the worst ones, mass murderers in the service of apartheid as Karel put it, got a million or more, as well as assurances of free legal aid, should they need it. As it turned out some of them did need it and that was costing taxpayers millions more. Karel was almost spitting with fury. 'Now those bastards have all got beach houses and farms and they're doing very well, thank you very much. All in the name of reconciliation.'

Weeks later Elise returned to the courtroom and felt an undeniable flush of elation as Taylor was sentenced to two life sentences for the murders of her father and Lettie. There was more, but she barely noticed the judge's sentencing for all the other crimes from which he had fled to Fransmansvallei. All she could think was that she wanted him to rot. She wanted him to sink into the worst of the stinking hellholes the prison system could offer and rot there for the rest of his days.

As he was led away Taylor looked round, his gaze scanning

the gallery. His eyes met Elise's. She smiled, with an expression of anger and triumph, but he returned only his icy stare. Then it was over.

Elise drove home alone through the gorgeous, melancholy autumn. The colours of the valley had turned to russet and gold, announcing the approach of winter.

There was one other legal proceeding Elise was obliged to attend during that mellow season, one she came to with a lighter heart. It was a special sitting of the Land Claims Court, held in the church in Fransmansdorp. The proceedings were merely formal, a ceremony for the transfer of deeds rather than an actual hearing. The decision on the Mashiyas' land claim had already been made.

Once the harvest was in, Elise had been able to turn her attention fully towards Sandile's claim and its repercussions for Rustenvrede. She'd spent a day with Fatima Mamdoo in Cape Town and took from that meeting a clear sense of the path she would follow. She did not oppose the claim, instead spending her energy negotiating a structure within which she and Sandile could work the land together, benefiting each other by doing so.

While Fatima Mamdoo's extreme interest in the case had proved a liability when she decided to swoop in unexpectedly on the affected farms, it now proved to be a great help. She was pushing to set a precedent and so the claim was processed with full speed and attention.

Elise was relieved by the pace at which things went ahead. She was eager to arrive at a settlement with minimum fuss. Although the loss of the dam and the land around it was devastating, the Department of Land Affairs did provide a hefty consolation prize. They bought the land at market value from Elise before handing it back to the Mashiyas.

Alan Taylor featured in the negotiations only in so far as no opposition was registered from his corner. His lawyers got a good price and that was all that mattered to them. The money mattered far less to Elise. As her father had so often said, the land itself was priceless.

The dorp experienced its first ever traffic jam when the Land Claims Court came to Fransmansvallei. Curious farmers and farmworkers alike flocked to witness the proceedings. They were joined by a sizeable contingent from the press. So it was a crowd that gathered to watch the Regional Land Claims Commissioner enter the church. He was followed by the judge and then delegations from the Department of Land Affairs and the Regional Commission itself. Sandile walked up flanked by Simon Siluma and Karel Smit while Elise came alone. Last to arrive were Mama and Ben Mashiya who processed slowly inside. Ben Mashiya smiled for the cameras, blinking into the glare. Mama's mouth was pinched tight from nerves, but her eyes told another story – they were brimming with joy.

The event began with a speech from the Regional Commissioner. He stood with his arms wide, hands grasping the edge of the lectern as his words rang out through the church. 'I would like to begin by quoting Sol Plaatjie who – as many of you will know – was a founder of the African National Congress. In 1913 Sol Plaatjie described with horror the consequences of the Natives Land Act of that same year. "Even criminals dropping straight from the gallows," he wrote, "have an undisputed claim to six feet of ground on which to rest their criminal remains, but under the cruel operation of the Natives Land Act, little children, whose only crime is that God did not make them white, are sometimes denied that right in their *ancestral* home." I am happy to be able to say to you today –' the Commissioner looked up and into the hundreds of listening faces, departing from his prepared script: 'I am so fiercely *proud* to be able to declare today – that it is no longer so.'

SIXTY TWO

It was a glorious Saturday. The kind of perfection, Elise thought, that you only see on a sun-drenched day in the Cape. Waking early and filled with excitement she recalled that Saturday had once been her favourite day of the week. She had loved the lack of routine, loved doing only what pleased her and never following the same steps she'd taken the Saturday before.

In the kitchen she made coffee and began to prepare breakfast. Standing at the sink in front of the window she couldn't suppress a smile at the sight of the sun rising over the great, solid, silent blue colossi of the mountains. The soft clamour of sounds was a chorus to her happiness; the cooing of doves, dogs barking in the distance, cocks crowing all over the valley, so many birds singing it was impossible to distinguish their different songs.

A pale golden glow spread from the cleft in the Grootdrakensrug. Already it was too bright to look over there and now the sun popped over the rim of the mountains like a ball of white fire. Suddenly it was up; the crags of the mountains emerged into the light and the whole valley was bathed in the glow. A long line of geese flew low over the treetops, dazzling white darts against the shadows and the glints of moisture, the facets of emerald in the mossy green face of the mountain.

Elise walked out into the garden and, as she had done so often before, drank in the rich smell of the still wet earth, the scent of woodsmoke drifting from the compound and of dew still clinging to the grass. The scents held a tangle of memories, but now the morning would always echo with the memory of her discovery of her dead father. Her mind returned involuntarily, as it would at unexpected moments for the rest of her life, to the image of his face, the gaping bloody flap of skin that was his neck and the terrible pity and pain that had pierced her heart.

Elise knew she would find ways of accepting the unacceptable. She would have to accept that Taylor, or Stitch, or whatever he called himself, was an embodiment of the logic and the psychosis of another time, a time now thankfully gone by, when men like him used and were used by an insane state bent on its own insane ends. It was a time Elise had never been able to explain, and now found harder than ever to understand. It was a reality she had to swallow – that there could never be an adequate explanation, that she might *never* understand. Elise wasn't sure she could swallow anything so unpalatable. Yet standing there on the edge of a new day she decided that, without forgetting, she had to find a place to put it all away. Today was for the present and for the future, not the past.

The weird, piercing cry of a startled guinea fowl echoed against the mountains and jolted Elise out of the daze of her thoughts. Vuyo shouted to her and waved as he walked by, headed down the drive in his green overalls and hat, a big yellow jersey tied round his waist. In one hand he was carrying a fistful of empty Pick 'n' Pay bags. He would return in a few hours weighed down, the carriers bulging with shopping. A line of men and women and children, some in pairs, most in groups, strolled from the compound towards the dorp at the start of their weekend.

Sandile was still asleep in her bedroom. Elise watched him for a while, still amazed by him and full of a strange gratitude for his presence in her life. Being with him felt so right, like coming home had felt after Bloemfontein. In all the ways they were together, she felt completely herself.

She made a breakfast of toast with fig jam and slices of ripe paw-paw, squeezing lemon juice on to its soft orange flesh. They sat and ate outside on the stoep, the dogs collapsed comfortably round their feet. Both were still tender from the pummelling of the previous months. They were gentle with each other and guarded their relationship carefully. They didn't hide the link between them, but nor did they advertise it. They wanted time together, needing the privacy to explore what they had come to mean to each other.

Elise still couldn't talk to Mama Mashiya about what had happened between Sandile and herself. She had been brought up by both Mama and her own mother to relate to him according to another code, one which the two of them had transgressed dramatically. She admitted to Sandile that she felt suddenly, sheepishly shy with Mama. Her hope was that he would do all the explaining, but in fact they both let things drift until the situation was unavoidably obvious. It made for some near-farcical moments, but Mama kept out of their way, sensing their vulnerability. It was strange and difficult for her, but she knew in her heart, as both Elise and Sandile did, that there was something profoundly right about their coming together.

Though it was hardly eventful, that Saturday afternoon was one Elise would always remember, as vividly even as she remembered Sandile's return. Near lunchtime everyone from Die Uitkyk and Rustenvrede gathered along Alan Taylor's fence. Once assembled they began digging and pulling together to dismantle it. Elise and Sandile worked opposite each other in the line, standing on either side of the massive panels of wire until they clattered down. They worked methodically, taking down one piece at a time, then wheeling round, moving towards each other until they were side by side, rolling up the stiff mesh. With Jacob and Vuyo helping in front and behind, they loaded each roll on to the flatbed attached to the tractor. Then, sweating and kicking up dust in the heat, and joking and laughing with everyone else, Elise and Sandile moved on to the next panel of wire. The day they took down the fence was so hot and so clear that if the mountains hadn't been in the way you could have seen for ever.

Glossary

aikôna	no
babbelas	hangover
bakkie	small pick-up truck
bankies	lanes in between rows of trees in an orchard
boet/broer	brother
braai	barbecue
broekies	undies/knickers
dames	ladies
dop	drink
doek	scarf
Dominee	Minister
dorp	village
Die Uitkyk	The Outlook
eina	ouch
ek sê	I say
fynbos	literally fine bush, but it is the name of wild scented herbal bushes
goggas	creepy crawlies
Hemel en Aarde	Heaven and Earth
Hoogtevrees Pas	Vertigo Pass
jongnooi	young mistress of the house
yusslike	gee!/wow!
Kaspirs	armoured personnel carriers widely used by police
koppie	hillock
kaffir	nigger

627

koeksuster	syrupy cake
Komweer	Come Again
lank	slang for 'very'
laatjies	lads
lappie	rag
lekker	great, or nice
melktert	milk tart
moerse	huge
môre	morning
middag	good day
nogal	as well/to cap it all
Slegs Blankes	Whites Only
oupa	grandpa
ouma	grandma
oke	guy
ounooi	mistress of the house
pap	porridge/limp
plaasjaapie	hick/farm boy
poes	shitty/cunt
poppie	doll
Rustenvrede	Rest and Peace
sis	yuk
Skaduwee	Shadow
skat	treasure
skrik	fright
skinder	gossip
spaza shop	a shop in a house or a private yard
stokkie	small stick
stywe pap	stiff porridge
tannies	aunts
tsotsi	hoodlum
totsiens	goodbye
toyi-toyi	victorious/celebratory dance
verkrampte	conservative – literally cramped
velskoene	simple leather shoes
volksie	abbreviation for Volkswagen
voertsek	stuff off

waterwyser	water diviner
wekkers	particular pronunciation of 'workers'
yebo	yes
yebo gogo	'yeah – cool' or 'yes, let's go!' – colloquial, literally 'yes granny'